A BOOK OF
MEMORIES

A BOOK OF MEMORIES

A NOVEL BY *PÉTER NÁDAS*

TRANSLATED FROM THE HUNGARIAN BY *IVAN SANDERS*

with Imre Goldstein

Farrar, Straus and Giroux
New York

Farrar, Straus and Giroux
19 Union Square West, New York 10003

Published simultaneously in Canada by HarperCollins*Canada* Ltd
Printed in the United States of America
Designed by Jonathan D. Lippincott
First edition, 1997

Library of Congress Cataloging-in-Publication Data
Nádas, Péter.
    [Emlékiratok könyve. English]
    A book of memories : a novel / Péter Nádas ; translated by Ivan Sanders with
Imre Goldstein.
        p.   cm.
    ISBN 0-374-11543-5 (alk. paper)
    I. Sanders, Ivan.   II. Goldshtain, Imri, 1938-   .   III. Title.
PH3291.N297E413   1997
894'.511334—dc21   96-50236

The English translation of this book was made possible in part by grants from the
Fulbright Program, the National Endowment for the Arts, and
the Soros Foundation.

Author's Note

It is my pleasant duty to state that what I have written is not my own memoirs. I have written a novel, the recollections of several people separated by time, somewhat in the manner of Plutarch's *Parallel Lives*. The memoirists might conceivably all be me, though none of them is. So the locations, names, events, and situations in the story aren't real but, rather, products of a novelist's imagination. Should anyone recognize someone, or—God forbid!—should any event, name, or situation match actual ones, that can only be a fatal coincidence, and in this respect, if in no other, I am compelled to disclaim responsibility.

Contents

"But he spoke of the temple of his body . . ."

—John 2:21

PART I

The Beauty of
My Anomalous Nature

The last place I lived in in Berlin was at the Kühnerts', out in Schöneweide, on the second floor of a villa covered in wild vines.

The leaves of the creeping vines were already turning red and birds
were pecking at the blackened berries; autumn had arrived.

No wonder this is all coming back to me now: three years have passed,
three autumns, and I know I'll never go back to Berlin, there'd be no
reason, no one to go to; that's also why I write that it was the last place
I lived in in Berlin, I just know it was.

I wanted it to be the last, and it worked out, just happened, that way
regardless of my wishes, no matter; and now, nursing an unpleasant head
cold I console myself—my mind being useless for anything else, though
even in its rheumy state hovering around essential things—by recalling
the autumns of Berlin.

Not that any of it could ever be forgotten.

That second-floor apartment, for instance, on Steffelbauerstrasse.

Naturally, I've no idea who but I might be interested in any of this.

Certainly I don't want to write a travel journal; I can describe only
what is mine, let's say the story of my loves, but maybe not even that,
since I don't think I could ever begin to talk about the larger significance
of mere personal experiences, and since I don't believe or, more precisely,
don't know, whether there is anything more significant than these otherwise trivial and uninteresting personal experiences (I assume there can't
be), I'm ready to compromise: let this writing be a kind of recollection or

reminder, something bound up with the pain and pleasure of reminiscence, something one is supposed to write in old age, a foretaste of what I may feel forty years from now, if I live to be seventy-three and can still reminisce.

My cold throws everything into sharp relief; it would be a shame to miss this opportunity.

For example, I could mention that it was Thea Sandstuhl who took me to the Kühnerts' on Steffelbauerstrasse, in the southern district of Berlin known as Schöneweide, "pretty pasture," which can be reached in thirty minutes from Alexanderplatz in the heart of the city, or, if one misses the always punctual connections and must wait in the rain, forty minutes to an hour.

Thea was the one who arranged or, more precisely, finagled this room for me, and naturally she, too, came to mind during these last cold-filled days, but strangely enough not with those conspicuous devices she used to draw attention to herself—her red sweater and soft red coat, the enormous amount of red she wore, nor the wrinkles on her girlish face, those pale quivering furrows she did not exactly try to cover up, yet one could sense she loathed by the stiff way she held her neck—somehow she always thrust her neck forward as if to say, Go ahead, look, this is my face, this is how old and ugly I've become, even though I, too, was once young and pretty, go ahead, have a good laugh; of course no one even thought of laughing, since she wasn't at all ugly, even if one guessed that it might have been her hangup about the wrinkles that gave rise to her unfortunate love affair—but none of that came to mind just now, or the way she used to sit in her red armchair in her room with the muslin curtains and red carpet; what came to mind was her crying and laughing, her big horse teeth yellowed by nicotine—not her stage cry and laughter, which hardly resembled genuine tears or laughter—and I could see her naughtiness when her eyes narrowed with scorn and her dry skin tautened over her jaw, also the tree in the courtyard of the synagogue on Rykestrasse, that withered acacia somehow connected to her, the sign nailed to its trunk saying it was forbidden to climb the tree, but who would want to climb a tree in the courtyard of an old East Berlin synagogue on a Friday night, nearly thirty years after the war? who would have the slightest inclination to do that? and as the long shadows of Jews streamed out of the lighted synagogue into the golden glow of the courtyard, I told her I had a fever, and with a motherly gesture she flattened her hand on my forehead, but I saw in her face, and my face felt it, too, that she was less interested in checking my temperature than in enjoying my skin, still young and wrinkle-free.

Hence the immediate and perhaps unreasonable apology that what is to follow cannot and should not be a travelogue, that Arno Sandstuhl, Thea's husband, who is some kind of travel writer, should not be compared to me or me to him: I realize of course that my open contempt for him, which may be attributable to jealousy, is not about his innocent passion for visiting faraway places and writing down his experiences, though this definitely aroused my suspicion, since very few people are permitted to travel from here and most of them know the satisfying feeling of travel only from hearsay, yet he, the privileged writer, had even been to Tibet and Africa if I remember correctly; I think my unjustifiable dislike for Arno was set off not by fleeting suspicion or contempt, not even by jealousy, but rather by the odd manner in which Thea had alluded, unwittingly of course, to a secret period of my life.

The first time we visited them, it was in their home, which was in yet another part of town, rather far away, somewhere around Lichtenberg, I believe, but I can't say for sure, because whenever we drove together I relied entirely on Melchior's knowledge of places, and from the moment I'd met him I looked at nothing but his face, absorbed his face in my face, and I couldn't be expected to pay attention to trifles such as where we were going; he looked at the road and I looked at him, that's how we traveled; and the last time I met Thea it was on the S-Bahn after Melchior had already disappeared from Berlin, and Thea was alone, too, because Arno had moved out of her place—we ran into each other at the Friedrichstrasse station, a few minutes before midnight, and she said, "My car's on the blink again," almost apologetically—I was coming from the theater and sat with her till we got to the Ostkreuz, where I had to change for Schöneweide (I was still living with the Kühnerts then), and she stayed on the train, continuing home, and from that I gathered she must have lived somewhere in the vicinity of Lichtenberg, where that Sunday afternoon when we first visited them I had had a talk with Arno that was very much like a conversation between two writers: cautious, serious, boring.

Actually, we had Thea's dubious little ploy to thank for that, for she was the one who made the encounter so stiff and formal: as soon as Arno entered the room, a bit late, and I rose to greet him, she took both our elbows and effectively prevented us from shaking hands, as if to indicate that only through her could we make contact, though we might also have something in common, independent of the connection she offered us—"Two writers in the throes of creative crisis," she said, alluding to one of my earlier remarks I had shared with her in confidence—which obviously she thought was more important than the thwarted handshake, since her words shamelessly betrayed Arno's torment to me, and mine to him; but it was Arno she had hoped to help with this double betrayal, helping him through me by using me to make the three of us totally interdependent, yet lumping Arno and me together in a separate unit; anyway, we did not look into each other's eyes, because one does not like to be seen through so completely—even by someone with the best of intentions—or be shown a likeness one does not or wishes not to resemble.

The situation was all too familiar to me, but of course the two of them couldn't be blamed for that.

Melchior was also laughing behind our backs—the spectacle of two bumbling writers must have seemed quite funny to him—and it was at that moment that I thought, in my discomfiture or perhaps out of spite, that Arno was allowed to roam the world because he was a military agent on the side, an informer, a spy, but it's entirely possible, I thought then, that he might just think it's all right, quite all right for me to believe that about him, since he knew something about me I would have preferred to keep secret: he had noticed that Melchior made no effort to control his glances in front of Thea, so what we had meant to keep secret, namely, that Melchior and I were not just good friends but lovers, was surely not hidden from Arno, either.

On top of that, I had to show the man some respect, partly because he was a good deal older than I, around fifty or so, and partly because I had no idea just what sort of things he wrote; all I knew was that they were travel books, published in editions of hundreds of thousands of copies, and for all I knew they may have been masterpieces, but in any event, I felt it would be wisest to couch my caution in respectful courtesy; this mutually considerate conversation, carried on while Thea, like some office girl on her day off, was setting the table for tea and listening to Melchior buzzing into her ear about me, made both of us feel awkward.

Arno did everything to do justice to the role assigned to him, and I sensed a kind of masculine charm in his questions about the nature of my drama studies and the kind of short stories I wrote, a charm born of male strength in a state of embarrassment; in fact, one of his remarks seemed gallantly designed to offer me a way out, suggesting that he did not wish to dig too deep, "just briefly, of course, it would be impossible otherwise; I'm not thinking in terms of content, only a hint," he said, and smiled, but the fine little lines running toward his mouth made plain that his more profound thinking rarely found release in a smile; he seemed more of a brooder, which is why he didn't look you straight in the eye right away, as if he were hiding something or had something to be ashamed of.

But as I was answering him he did suddenly look into my eyes, and although his interest settled not on what I was saying, it was a genuine look, and I should have appreciated it, because whenever a glance seeks what lies beyond our words—as in this case, for example, it sought to discover the relationship between my writing and the fact that, being a man, I was in love with another man, and I believe this was going through his mind as I spoke—when, in short, attention abandons the strands of meaning in the subject discussed and tries to grasp something of the speaker's emotional essence, then that moment must be cherished and taken very seriously.

But I knew full well that I had already stood like this once before in some room, facing and being completely at the mercy of another man.

Arno, who had apparently put up with all of Thea's quirks, was now trying with that very glance to get around the burdensome roles she had forced on us; it was impossible not to notice it in his beautiful dark-brown eyes, but I was too preoccupied with my own memories, and paid more attention to what Melchior was whispering about me to Thea than to what I was saying to Arno about my writing, which is why I didn't realize that his glance could have at last freed us both, for he was looking at me with a child's eyes, curious, open, and eager, and with some well-chosen words, or with none at all, we could have turned our conversation into not only a pleasant but also a meaningful one; yet I took no notice of this glance, I did not reciprocate, and having reached the end of my report, I managed to muddle up my own question; wanting to be polite, I settled for what was convenient, simply repeating the question he had addressed to me, and became aware of the rude indifference inherent in this repetition only when I suddenly lost his gaze, as in an odd self-mocking gesture he quickly tapped his temples with both hands, which he then turned palms forward and dropped resignedly.

This waving of the hands signaled no disparagement of his own avocation or work but was, rather, an expression of wonder, of being wounded and embarrassed, a renunciation of ever being understood— "Oh, I'm just a mountain climber," said the gesture, and indeed, it seemed to have come from a hiker being routinely asked what the hike was like and was the weather all right—but what is there ever to say about a hike or the weather?

Arno answered me, of course—after all, he too had had the benefit of a solid middle-class upbringing that teaches you to bridge moments of inattention, confusion, even hate, with innocuous chitchat—and he spoke as native Berliners do in general, producing words as if gargling with mouthwash; but even if I had managed to pay attention to him—Melchior was whispering to Thea about what I had cooked for lunch—even if I had understood what Arno was saying, his body language, his stooping posture told me that it was nothing interesting, mere talk, just keeping the conversation going, and at one point I lost even his voice, partly because I was fuming about Melchior's intimate disclosures and wanted to find a way to get him to stop, shut him up, but also because I realized or thought I realized why this neatly lined face talking at me looked so familiar: it could have been my grandfather's face, if my grandfather had been born a German, a face exuding seriousness, patience, humorless self-respect, a democratic face, if there is such a thing; and so I lost not only the gist of what he was saying but the sound of his voice, and he stood before me like an empty husk; the only thing I could grasp was that he was still wary of me, careful not to say anything that might be interesting, not to embarrass me by saying anything I really ought to listen to, and even before Thea had finished setting the table he gave up on me; I was left standing, leaning against an armchair, rocking back and forth, and Arno, excusing himself, quickly returned to his room.

How nicely these autumn images overlap.

Never more solitary experiences.

Experiences related to my past, but the past is itself but a distant allusion to my insignificant desolation, hovering as rootlessly as any lived moment in what I might call the present: only memories of tastes and smells of a world to which I no longer belong, one I might call my abandoned homeland, which I left to no purpose because nothing bound me to the one I found myself in, either; I was a stranger there, too, and not even Melchior, the only human being I loved, could make me belong; I was lost, I did not exist, my bones and solid flesh turned to jelly; and yet, despite the feeling of being torn from everything and belonging nowhere, I could still perceive myself to be something: a toad pressing heavily against the earth; a slimy-bodied snail unblinkingly observing my own nothingness; what was happening to me was nothing, even if this nothing contained my future and, because of the successive autumns, some of my past as well.

That autumn, in the back room of the flat on Steffelbauerstrasse, where two maple trees, still green and ripe, stood in front of my window, and where sparrows were nesting above the window frame, in the hollow left by a missing brick, there in that room, that autumn, I should have not only sensed but fully understood the nature of this situation, but I kept grasping at straws, hoping for an extraordinary insight meant only for me, for a new situation to arise, something, a change of mood, a tragedy even, that would at last define me within this indefinable nothingness; I kept hoping to find something worth saving, something that would lend meaning to things and save me as well, deliver me from this animal existence, not be something from my past—I was sick and tired of my past, the past was a reminder as unseemly as the aftertaste of a belch— and not anything from my future, either, since I had given up on the future long ago, always reluctant to plan ahead even for a moment; no, I wanted something in the here and now, a revelation, a redemption I was waiting for, I can confess this now, but back then I hadn't yet realized that precise knowledge of nothingness should have sufficed.

Thea gave me a lift to this flat, Frau Kühnert was her friend, and I spent a lot of time there by myself.

I might say that I was always by myself; never before had I experienced the solitude of a strange apartment the way I did then—the polished furniture, sunlight breaking through the slits in the drawn curtains, the patterns in the carpet, the shine on the floor, the floorboards' creaks, the heat of the stove anticipating evening, when people of the house came home and turned on the TV.

It was a quiet house, only slightly more elegant than the run-down buildings of Prenzlauerberg, those "gray birds, ancient Berlin back yards," as Melchior wrote in one of his haunting poems, and here, too, were the elaborately carved, dove-gray banisters like those in other places where I lived in Berlin, on Chausseestrasse and Wörther Platz, and the wooden stairs covered with dark linoleum, the disinfectant smell of the floor wax, and the colored stained glass in the windows at every landing, though here only half the panes still had the original intricate floral patterns from the turn of the century, the rest having been replaced by simple hammered glass, keeping the staircase in constant dimness, just like the staircase of the house on Stargarderstrasse where I had stayed the longest and where I had had time to adjust to staircases like this, though not even that house could become mine the way any apartment building in Budapest could have, since its past was missing for me; in various ways this past did signal to me, and I very much wanted to decipher the signals, knowing full well that these games of re-creating the past would not make Melchior more my own; nevertheless, coming home in the afternoon, going up the stairs, I would try to imagine another young man in my place who had come to Berlin one fine day long ago—the man was Melchior's grandfather, and he became the hero of my daily evolving fictional story, because he was the one who could have seen these stained-glass flowers when they were still new and whole, illuminated by light filtering in from the back yard, could have seen the totality of the patterns, if he had ever set foot in this house and while walking up the wooden stairs fully perceived his present, which is the past of my imagination.

Downstairs, in the dark entrance hall, even during the day you had to press a glowing red button that turned on the feeble lights just long enough to get you to the first landing, where a similar button had to be pressed again, but often I walked up the stairs in the dark, because the constantly glowing little button beckoned to me like a beacon in the night seen from the open sea, and I liked looking at the tiny source of light so much that I preferred not to press the button, so the stairwell remained in darkness, and while I did not know exactly how many steps there were, the creaks proved a reliable guide and the red glow helped me on the landings; I hardly ever missed a step.

I used to do the same thing in the house on Wörther Platz where Melchior lived, walking up the stairs almost every night, with good old Frau Hübner on the third floor looking through the peephole while sitting, I was told, on a high stool, but since I walked upstairs in the dark she couldn't see me, could only hear footsteps, and so she'd invariably open the door to peek out either too early or too late.

In the house on Steffelbauerstrasse the hallway lights didn't work properly, staying on only if one kept pushing the button, so if Frau Kühnert happened to be in the kitchen when I was ready to go out for the evening, she'd rush out to make sure I didn't walk downstairs in the dark; I tried hard to leave without being noticed, since I knew that Frau Kühnert faithfully reported my every move to Thea, who was anxious to know everything about Melchior, and after a while I imagined that even Frau Hübner was working for Thea and Frau Kühnert, but I almost never managed to move quietly enough for my landlady: "Hold it, my dear sir, I'm here to light your way," she'd say, and run out of the kitchen to hold her finger on the button until I reached the ground floor; "Thanks," I'd shout back, thinking that Frau Hübner must be waiting in her third-floor apartment, half-expecting me politely to say hello as I passed in the light emanating from her place; but if I happened to come home during the night and there was no light filtering in from the street, I had to feel out each step on my way up or use a match, because in this house on Steffelbauerstrasse even the tiny red filament of the button had burned out and could not guide me, and I was afraid of bumping into something live on the staircase.

Melchior had never been in this house.

Come to think of it, he never set foot in the house on Stargarderstrasse either; we were forever hiding or, more precisely, we were trying to be as inconspicuous as possible, which was something I was quite adept at, it came easily to me, a sort of behavior that also alluded, unpleasantly, to my past: once, on a Sunday afternoon in front of the building, when Stargarderstrasse was all but deserted, though anyone could have concealed himself behind drawn curtains, on a dull-gray November afternoon when everyone was sitting at home watching TV, drinking coffee, and we both felt we could not say goodbye, we didn't really have to, we could have stayed with each other, except that we'd been together for three days and our protective shell which kept everything and everyone out was getting thicker and thicker and we had to break out of it, we had to part, spend at least one night alone—I wanted to take a bath, and Melchior's flat had no bathroom, you had to use a washbowl or the kitchen sink, I felt dirty, wanted to be alone for the afternoon and evening at least, catch my breath, and then, before midnight, run downstairs and call him from a public phone, hear his voice while leaning against the cold glass of the booth, and perhaps go back to his place—and we agreed that he would walk me to the corner of Dimitroffstrasse, and then he'd buy cigarettes at the tobacco shop under the elevated that stayed open on Sunday, but we couldn't tear ourselves away from each other; first he said he'd walk me only one more block, then I asked him to walk another; we couldn't just shake hands, it would have been ridiculous, awkward, and cowardly, but we had to do something; we avoided looking at each other, and then he held out his hand, if only because we wanted to touch some part of each other, and so we kept holding hands; there was no one on the street, but this was not enough, it was his mouth that I wanted, there, in front of the house, that Sunday afternoon.

And the house on Chausseestrasse he also saw only from the outside.

It was a Sunday evening.

I pointed out the window from the streetcar taking us to the theater; on the empty platform he was telling me about the Berlin uprising, and I told him about the revolt in Budapest, our sentences dovetailing smoothly into one another.

He looked up at the window, but I could not tell whether he actually saw it; he kept on talking: to me it was very important then that he should at least know the house, if not the room, where I had first stayed and which, without his being aware of it, had become important in his life, too; but Melchior, though not indifferent to my past, distanced himself from it, he could not do otherwise.

I had been living in the flat on Steffelbauerstrasse for almost two months, was used to it, had even grown to like it, when one morning Frau Kühnert, lighting the fire in the stove, told me that electricians were coming that morning to fix the lights in the staircase, they'd be looking for her, but she couldn't stay home, and I'd be there anyway, wouldn't I? ... "Yes, of course," I replied, still lying in bed while Frau Kühnert knelt in front of the stove and, as she always did when working around the house, quietly hummed to herself; she was right, I spent most of my time at home, except for evenings, and since she was in charge of things concerning the building, she said, the electricians had to see her first, but I should tell them she couldn't stay home, "Who do they think they are, anyway?" and I should explain what the problem was, and whatever happened not let them leave, "the swine," until they fixed the lights.

I stayed home the whole morning, waiting for Melchior to call—we had only a few more days left—but he didn't call, and the repairmen didn't show up either.

If only he had called during that cloudless day of sunshine and complete silence; in the morning the Kühnerts heated only the living room and my room, and the nights were cold, occasionally there was even frost on the ground; from the dining room, which opened from the foyer, one could walk into the living room, but my room was at the far end of the apartment, approached like two small bedrooms from a long dark corridor connecting the kitchen and the bathroom; save for the living room and my own room, I left all the doors open to make sure I could run quickly to the phone if it rang, and if Melchior had called, I would have suggested we go to the Müggelsee if I could have talked to him from the Kühnerts' living room; the weather was perfect, I would have said, looking from the warm room into the cold sunlight, but I would have also told him that I wouldn't go with him to his mother's, because the only reason he wanted me along was to make this farewell easier for himself; he had to say goodbye to her, perhaps see her for the last time, without letting her suspect anything, and I could not imagine that he would never again share with me his boyhood bed in his unheated bedroom; it seemed too implausible that everything we had would now irrevocably come to an end.

"That bed? You really used to sleep in that? and it was standing in the same spot? and that stain on the ceiling, that was there, too?"

He laughed at my questions, as if he couldn't conceive of anything changing in his world or of anyone being surprised at the absence of change; he was right, things were not that changeable there, and his mother, Helene, named after her mother, who had died in childbirth, made certain that things no longer changed, so she could provide her son with the security of an ultimate haven, but aside from this home situation, Melchior had good reason to feel like that about changes: before he had met me, he told me, not without a small show of male pride, it had mattered very little whom he was with, he simply had no need to feel secure, was not very choosy; in fact, the most casual relationships were those that had often given him the greatest pleasure; and to have something assuredly constant in his desultory existence, he had rigorously developed his taste, honing and refining it, making it ascetically austere; in his inaccessibly hermetic poetry he had forced himself to be self-effacing and uncompromising; and no matter what happened, he could come back here to his mother's house every weekend, which he did, lugging his dirty laundry in a suitcase, because here everything stayed the same and his mother insisted on doing his laundry, nothing had changed "except for the stain, that got there later," and he laughed, but his laugh never meant very much; he laughed easily, lightheartedly, for no particular reason, and nothing could ever extinguish the cheer in his eyes, except when he thought no one was looking.

I couldn't imagine that come Sunday morning, when waking to the peal of church bells booming through the tiny windows of his mother's house, I'd be alone, no longer able to inhale in the cold room the fragrance of his skin mingled with the pungent scent of winter apples and the sweet smell of pastry baked to be eaten with freshly brewed Sunday coffee, the apples laid out in neat rows atop the closet, the sugar-coated coffee cake on the marble-topped sideboard waiting as the afternoon snack, and the tiny window always open; yet his face would cloud over and he'd look at my forehead, my mouth, when inadvertently I told him that I loved the smell of his sweat; my nose loved it, my palms, my tongue loved it, and as if my words had pained him, he hugged me; "I can taste and smell and feel you!" he said, emitting an odd sound, and I thought he was laughing, but it was a brief, tearless sob that later, on his creaky bed at Wörther Platz, erupted in whimpering, choking sounds of terror.

I also pictured the path around the Müggelsee, covered with multicolored leaves, and the tranquillity of the mirror-smooth lake itself, and the sound of our footsteps on the fallen leaves muffled by early-morning mist; actually, there was another reason I would have asked that we go to the Müggelsee: I felt that there I might still win him over, or commit myself unconditionally to him for good, but I knew it was impossible—oh, that incredible autumn!—or we could have gone to the zoo, of course, if he thought the stroll around the Müggelsee too troublesome or far away; if one could believe the colored posters on the S-Bahn—looking at them became my pastime while riding the trains—the zoo was also located in a forest, full of secluded shady paths, and we had never been there even though we often planned to go: but I also pictured myself taking a knife from the Kühnerts' kitchen and during our walk stabbing him to death.

In this last of my Berlin residences I used to get up late, or rather, I'd wake up two or three times before actually getting out of bed, sometimes close to noon.

First, it was always the waking with a start at dawn as Dr. Kühnert rattled down the hallway past my door toward the bathroom: I'd pull the pillow over my head so as not to hear what was to follow—his going into the bathroom and first urinating; I had to hear the precise sounds of the short, sharp splashes preceding the long steady stream that stopped abruptly and ended in a gradually weakening trickle, the wall was thin and I could tell he was aiming at the back of the bowl, the hollow that fills up with water even after flushing; as a child I had also tried to do the same, and in a way I found it amazing that someone at the age of fifty, a university professor, should still amuse himself this way—but if the only sounds I heard were a short tap followed by a muffled squirt of urine against the side of the bowl, I knew he was going to defecate, too.

Elimination was not necessarily indicated by breaking wind; farts sounded quite different when done while urinating, standing up, than when seated, in which position the bowl acted as an amplifier; there was no way to confuse the two noises, and the pillow didn't really help, for the groans, the gentle sighs of relief, the scraping and rustling of the toilet paper could be heard clearly through the wall; the pillow could not possibly help, because I was also listening, as if enjoying it all, as if tormenting myself with the knowledge that I couldn't and wouldn't want to close my ears—one can close one's eyes or mouth but ears can be stopped up only with fingers, ears can't close themselves—and Dr. Kühnert was still far from finished, the noisy flushing was only a brief pause, and if I hadn't known what else was still in store, I might have had enough time simply to roll over and fall back asleep, because during these startled awakenings, at night or early in the morning, one is hardly aware of the transition between sleep and wakefulness, and the fading characters in a dream sometimes aren't intimidated even by a suddenly switched-on light; they have faces and hands, and they recede just far enough to be out of reach, jumping on shelves, among the books, and sometimes the very opposite happened: the features of my room dissolved smoothly into a dream, I'd see the window, but it was already a dream window, and the tree in front of it and the hollow left by the missing brick where sparrows nested were also part of the dream, and suddenly my whole body would stiffen, because this was the moment when Dr. Kühnert would stand in front of the mirror, bend over the sink, right over my head, blow his nose into his hand, and, while the water was still running, begin to snort and hawk, spitting forced-up phlegm into the sink, directly at me.

At seven o'clock a knock on my door would wake me again, and "Yes, come in," I'd call out in what sounded like a completely strange voice, a sign that I first wanted to say in Hungarian what in the very next instant I had to say in German, whereupon Frau Kühnert would enter and, humming softly to herself, light the fire in the stove; in the evenings I'd walk to the theater over a soggy carpet of fallen leaves and the soles of my patent-leather shoes would always be soaked through.

But by that time Melchior was gone.

I was left with Berlin, slushy and gray.

After the show I went to the flat on Wörther Platz; it was cold, and the lamp's glare made the purple of the curtain look faded, but I didn't feel like lighting the candles.

It was raining.

The police could arrive any minute and break down the door.

The refrigerator was humming peacefully in the kitchen.

The next day I also left the city.

In Heiligendamm there was bright sunshine, though what happened to me there I still can't explain.

If I treated words lightly, I'd say I felt happy there: the sea, the journey, and the events directly preceding it must have contributed to this feeling, not to mention the pretty little place itself, which they call the "white city on the sea," a slight exaggeration, since the whole place consists of only a dozen or so two-story cottages facing the sea, on either side of the attractive spa, but white it was—the shutters, now closed, the benches on the smooth green lawn, the colonnade, the summer musicians' chairs stacked in neat piles, and the houses themselves surrounded by manicured deep-green shrubs and tall black pines—the most attractive feature of the place may have been its deceptively fair weather, and the silence.

Deceptive I say, because the wind howled here, and the embankment deflected enormous waves, crushed and cleaved them asunder, massive steel-blue waves booming thunderously into white foam; and silence I say, for between two booms one's sense of hearing fell into the trough of the waves, into a rapt anticipation, redeemed by the sounds of force turning into weight, though in the evening, when I set out for a walk, everything had calmed down, a full moon shone low over the open sea.

I began walking on the embankment toward Nienhagen, a neighboring town, with the rumbling sea and its glimmering crests on one side, silent marshland on the other, and I, the only living soul in the midst of the elements; I had run out of cigarettes earlier in the afternoon, and since Nienhagen, a town protected from the western winds by something called Gespensterwald, or Forest of Ghosts, did not seem that far away—I'd used a broken matchstick to measure the distance on the map and was sure I could reach it, because my eyes, though occasionally blinded by the wind, could pick out the flashes of its light tower—I planned to buy cigarettes there, maybe even have a cup of hot tea before returning; I pictured a friendly tavern with fishermen sitting around a table by can-dlelight and myself, not one of them, walking in; imagined their faces turning toward me, saw my own face looking at them.

I could see myself, clearly, transparently, walking in front of me; step-ping lightly yet gravely, I followed behind.

It was as if not I but my body was unable to endure the pain caused by our separation.

The wind got under my loose-fitting coat, pushing, shoving me for-ward, and although I had put on all my warm clothes I was cold now, without actually feeling cold, and that frightened me, because even if the usually merciful sensory delusion wasn't functioning perfectly, I knew that I ought to feel cold; at another time I might have turned back, let fear win out, and find no difficulty in explaining away my retreat by saying it was too nasty out, and catching a bad cold would have been too high a price to pay for such a nocturnal outing; but this time I could not delude myself, as if something had splintered the image we so painstakingly create of ourselves and wish to see accepted by others, until this distorted image seems real even to us; there was no room for deception: I was this person walking on the embankment, and though all my familiar conditioned responses were functioning, there was something amiss, a gap, more than one gap, distortions, cracks through which it was possible to glance at a strange creature, another someone.

Someone who long ago, yet on this very day, arrived in Heiligendamm and in the evening started out for Nienhagen.

As if what was about to happen took place fifty, seventy, a hundred years ago.

And this was so, even if nothing was about to happen.

It was a new, exciting sensation, rather unsettling, to experience my own disintegration, yet I accepted it with the serenity of a mature person, as if I were fifty, seventy, or a hundred years older, an affable elderly gentleman recalling his youth, but there was really nothing extraordinary or mystical about this, and though I couldn't imagine a more poetic setting for my death neither could I muster the courage to take the sleeping pills I had been carrying with me for years in a little round box; still, just to do something, I again called on my imagination to separate my two selves, liberating myself from my hopelessly muddled emotions, and saw that the future of my strange self was nothing more than the past and present of my familiar self, everything that had already or would still come to pass.

The situation was exceptional only in that I could not identify with either one of my selves, and in this overexcited state I felt like an actor moving about on a romantic stage set, my past being only a shallow impersonation of myself, just as my future would be, with all my sufferings, as if everything could be playfully projected into the past or the future, as if none of it had really happened or could still be altered and it was only my imagination that made sense of these entangled fragments from the various dimensions of my life, arranging them around a conventionally definable entity I could call my self, which I could show off as myself but which was really not me.

I am free, I thought to myself then.

I also thought then that out of this boundless freedom my imagination selected, quite haphazardly and not very adroitly, only potentially tiny possibilities from which to assemble a face that others might like and that I could then consider my own.

Today I no longer think this, but then the realization seemed so powerful and profound, I saw with such clarity that other being, the one who had remained free, untouched by any of my potential selves—he walked with me and I with him, he was cold and I feared for him—that I had to stop, but that wasn't enough, I had to kneel down and give thanks for this moment, though my knees did not like to bend in a show of humility, I would have liked to remain neutral as a stone—no, but even that wasn't enough—and I even closed my eyes: nothing, nothing but a tattered rag flapping in the wind!

The moon hung low, it was yellow and seemed only an arm's length away, but on the horizon its reflection grew pale, too feeble to outline the tremulous crests of the waves; the water seemed perfectly smooth but that, too, was an illusion, I thought to myself, the illusion of distance, just as on the other side of the embankment, in the marsh, where the light had no focus, there was no surface or edge in which it could be reflected and so the light ceased, vanished, and because the straining eye could find nothing to fix on, there was no darkness or blackness there, nothing but nothingness itself.

I had arrived in Heiligendamm in the late afternoon, just before sunset, and I set out for Nienhagen after dark, when the moon was already up.

I couldn't tell what was out there, the map indicated marshland, the guidebook mentioned a swamp, and whatever it was, it lay deep.

And silent.

As if the wind had halted and turned back over the embankment, stopped blowing there.

Was it covered with reeds or sedge, or, disguising itself as plain soil, did plain grass grow over it?

There was a time when the possibility of seeing ghosts gave me a thrill; now the thought that only nothingness was out there seemed far more terrifying.

Back then, years earlier—and much as I'd like to avoid it I shall speak about this at greater length later—if a shadow, a movement, or a noise unexpectedly materialized in something palpable and called me by name from behind my back, spoke to me or seemed to be listening to me, I knew it to be the very embodiment of my fears; now, whatever this was, it just lay over that moor, made no movement, emitted no sound, cast no shadow.

It merely kept watch.

Hung there over the marsh, an empty shell, an alien thing watching scornfully whoever strayed this way, and this scorn was disconcerting.

I wouldn't say it was frightening, more like chastening; its power lay in reining in my overwrought imagination, which wanted to gallop freely and invent its own story; it scorned all such ambition and gave me to understand that it was responsible for confounding my sense of time; it created the gaps through which I could peer into my soul, and in return for the playful doubling of my self, all it asked me was that I not forget it, which meant that I should not believe my own self-serving stories; and if I had neither the courage nor the good sense to do away with myself, I should at least be aware of *it*, as of a pain, and know that it was here, outside me but able any time to reach inside and touch my so-called vital organs, of which—no matter how cleverly I try to manipulate things, to become independent of *it*—I had no more than one or two; my existence could not be replaced by my imagination; I should not be too sure of myself, should not delude myself that a setting such as this, a moonlit night by the sea, could make me free, let alone happy.

I was standing up by then, and like one who has just completed his compulsory daily devotion, I reached down and with an involuntary movement dusted off my pants.

Much as I would have liked to excuse this little movement as a telltale sign of instilled orderliness, it made me feel again just how ridiculous I was, how fraudulent, and I quickly turned around and wondered if it might not be a good idea to go back, since after all, I could buy cigarettes in the restaurant, where I had had a pleasant meal earlier on, sitting in a comfortably furnished room set off by a glass door; I could even get a cup of tea there, the place stayed open until ten; the wind kept howling, and I would have loved to howl along with it and throw myself on the rocks, but by now I had got quite far from Heiligendamm, I hadn't even noticed how far, and seemed to be on higher ground, too, because some-where below, on the line dividing land and water, the twinkling of a few tiny stars suggested the presence of houses, and I would have been at least as ashamed of taking flight as I was disturbed by the vacuous stare of the marsh at my back.

I thought about how to continue.

I could not walk without part of my body, mostly my back, coming into contact with it, but what if I turned down to the beach?

When this idea occurred to me—quite uselessly, since by now I could clearly see the surf exploding in the yellow moonlight, pounding away at the foot of the embankment, and one part of my splintered self found it amusing that the other was seeking shelter at the embankment, hoping to avoid what inevitably he would have to accept—when this idea occurred, it was accompanied by a figure, not a ghost, but a simple notion of a young man walking through the glass door of that pleasant restaurant; he looked around, our eyes met, and the room was flooded with sunshine.

I made myself turn around once more and continued toward Nienhagen.

This is getting to be quite amusing, I thought to myself.

For there I was—and at the same time I imagined myself not there—and walking with me was this elderly gentleman whom I would one day become, and he brought along his own youth; the elderly gentleman at the seaside, reminiscing about his youth, perfectly suited my own purposes, now transformed into strictly literary ones, and so did that room with its comfortable chairs, the white damask tablecloth, the coffee cup he had just raised to his lips; and the young man who joined us, with his hand on the back of a chair bidding a courteous good morning to the group breakfasting at the table; to get a better look at him, for he was the one I was most interested in, I could send him back to the door where he had first appeared, because I felt that he was completely mine, since he did not exist; and there was someone else besides us, the one who was watching and who let me have this blond youth in exchange for allowing myself to become a helpless instrument of his power.

This had to be the moment when I finally concluded the silent pact that had been in preparation for years: for if today, much sadder and wiser, in full knowledge of all the consequences, I imagine the impossible and ponder what would have happened if, giving in to my fears, I had turned back and not pushed on toward Nienhagen, and like any sensible mortal in similar circumstances had taken cover in my boringly ordinary hotel room, then most probably my story would have remained within the bounds of the conventional, and those twists and deviations that have marked my life thus far would have indicated only which path not to follow, and with a good dose of sober and wholesome revulsion, I might have stifled the pleasure afforded by the beauty of my anomalous nature.

Our Afternoon Walk
of Long Ago

When I had arrived in Heiligendamm late in the afternoon of the day before, I'd been too tired to change and take part in the communal meal; I had my supper brought to my room, and putting off introducing myself until the morning, I retired early.

But I had trouble falling asleep.

It was as if I were curled up inside a large, dark, warm, soft cocoon besieged on all sides by the sea, and though I felt protected, water swept over the cocoon whenever I was about to unwind into my own softness, just above my head, the foam hitting me below the eyes.

The building was silent.

I thought I heard the wind blow, but the spiky crowns of the pine trees barely moved.

I closed my eyes and pressed my lids tight so as not to see at all, but when I didn't, I was there again, lying inside that dim cocoon where it would have been completely dark but for the images forming and dissolving before me, images of myself that would not let me rest, showing me scenes of myself that I thought I had forgotten because I had wanted to forget: on the bed where I lie now my father was sleeping, on his back, though I knew he slept not on this bed but on the narrow sofa in the living room; his shoes on the floor looked so forlorn without his feet; he spread his huge thighs shamelessly, and he was snoring; through the slats of the drawn shutters, sunlight fell into the room in stripes, intersecting those of the parquet floor, and in the depth of my sleep I felt my body convulse at the sight, I could not bear to look on, I wanted air and light; Father's breathing body made the past seem too near, too painfully present—but then I sank into darkness again and saw myself suddenly appear in the halo of a gas lamp, and then disappear again, and I was walking toward myself on a familiar wet street that may have been Schönhauser Allee, deserted on the night before my departure, a little after midnight, on my way home from my old friend Natalya Kasatkina; but on the corner of Senefelder Platz in front of the public lavatory I stopped to wait for myself, and while my footsteps were clattering toward me, the unlighted little structure at the center of the bare bushes on the square seemed to be making noises, as if panting, the wind was battering at its door, opening and closing it to the rhythm of my own breathing, and when it was open, I could see inside: a tall man was standing, facing the wall shining with tar, and when I finally got there he grinned at me and offered me a rose.

A purplish-blue rose.

But I didn't want to touch it, somehow I had to dismiss this image, too; how lovely it would be, I thought, to come to rest in some calm, luminous space—and then, quite gently, my bride floated into my cocoon. The moment she whipped off her hat and veil (rather roughly, I thought) and her massive red tresses fell to her shoulders, she breathed with bestial eagerness into my face, but instead of the aroma of her breath, I got a whiff of something unpleasant, foul almost.

Somewhere nearby a door was slammed shut.

I sat up in bed, awake and maybe a little alarmed.

The bedroom door was open, and I could see the bluish shine of the white furniture in the living room.

And there was no window through which to see the crowns of the pine trees, the curtains were drawn, there was no sound of wind, only the murmur of the sea coming from afar, because my room faced the park.

It was as if the door of the public lavatory that slammed shut became, in my wakeful state, the final chord of a dream that had just ended.

But I heard hurried, retreating footsteps out in the corridor, and in the adjacent room someone cried out, or screamed, sounding much too loud— or the walls were too thin—and then came a heavy thud, as if a large object or a body had fallen on the floor.

I listened for more, but heard nothing.

I was too frightened to move; the creaking of the bed, the swishing of the sheets might have obliterated the moment, a careless rustle made by moving the eiderdown might have covered up the noise of murder—but what followed was silence.

And I couldn't be sure I wasn't dreaming all of this, because we often dream of waking up, but it's not a real awakening, only a new phase of sleep, a slide downward, a descent to greater depths; and it's also true that the cry, the scream, and the thud of the falling body sounded familiar, reminding me again of Father; my eyes were open, I could still see him writhe in his sleep, start up, and then fall from the sofa onto the light-streaked floor; at the time, twenty years ago, he took his afternoon naps on the sofa that at night was my bed, and in those days we rented the very same place from which these peculiar noises were now coming, so it was quite possible that I wasn't actually experiencing these things but dreaming them anew, which was all the more likely, because the event that had put an end once and for all to the beautiful days at Heiligendamm had come to mind again just before I went to bed, as I was closing the terrace door.

Back then, on warm nights we would leave not only all the windows but the terrace door wide open, which made me especially glad, because it meant that shortly after my parents had finally closed their bedroom door, I could carefully get out of bed and, pretending to have overcome all my fears, steal out onto the terrace.

At times like that the terrace seemed menacingly empty, wide, enormous, reaching far into the park; on moonlit nights it was like a sharp wedge between the trees, on moonless nights it blended in more softly, almost as if it were afloat among the gently swimming shadows of the pointed pines, and if I kept watching this, this and nothing else, it would seem as if I were not here at all but aboard a ship quietly plowing the waves; but before stepping out on the terrace I always had to make sure I'd be alone, for it happened once that I hadn't noticed the lady who was our next-door neighbor standing in a corner of the terrace leaning on the balustrade, looking alternately like an apparition or a shadow depending on the moon, and if she was there I couldn't go out, for while we did have a secret nighttime understanding that never dared to test the light of day, I was afraid she might report me to my parents, and though her closeness at times felt wonderful and in a way I even longed for it, the nocturnal escapes were truly pleasurable only if I could be alone and picture the ship sailing away with me.

The first time I ventured out carelessly, in my stunned surprise I was rooted to a spot in the middle of the terrace, for she was there; the moon was out, thin and feeble behind a motionless cloud, and she was standing in the densely blue, glimmering night, her face turned toward the moon, and I believed her to be a ghost, a creature about whose peculiar nature I had been instructed by Hilde, our maid, who told me that ghosts had to be beautiful, "stunningly, stunningly beautiful"; and indeed, the sheer, flowing robe covering her graceful body, the silvery sheen of her waist-length hair seemed to bear this out; she was beautiful as she stood there— firm, yet also as if her feet were hardly touching the ground, as if her eyes were open but her eyeballs were missing from their sockets; when the cool night breeze touched my face I knew it was her breath, an exhalation that would be followed by an inhalation, and then with her next breath she would suck me in, draw me into her hollow body, and carry me off.

It wasn't fear that made me immobile or, if it was, it had to be fear of such a high degree that the senses are transported into the dimension of rapture, fear of such intensity that the body seems to break free of itself; I had no feeling in my hands or feet, thus had no means to move, yet without having to think about it I was aware of my entire life, all ten years of it, which I now would have to part with to slip into another form; only much later, when in love, did I experience anything resembling this feeling, but still, this extraordinary state of being seemed natural then, not only because Hilde's tale had warned me about its coming but because I myself had wished for it.

Of course, this mixture of sublime dread and vehement longing could last but for an instant; I realized quickly that it had been only an illusion, no matter how real it felt; "Why, this is Fräulein Wohlgast, our neighbor," and Fräulein Wohlgast, whose name came up often during our evening walks, was someone I myself frequently observed conversing with Mother at mealtimes; besides, this ghost business had begun to sound a little suspicious, even to me, ever since the time I thought I did see some sort of apparition and Father reacted by nodding somberly, almost gravely, but with the sardonic satisfaction of a man blessed with a sense of humor: of course, the ghost was most certainly there, in the sedge, where else would it be, hadn't I said I'd seen it? Father went on to say that he couldn't see a thing and he was straining his eyes to the limit, though now, just this instant, he thought he heard something, no, it was nothing, which didn't mean it wasn't there a moment ago; it was the very nature of ghosts to be here now and there the next minute, that was the way they were, sometimes they became visible, but mostly they stayed invisible; and I might be interested to know that it was also part of their nature not to appear for just anyone but only for very special persons, so I should be flattered and honored; and he, too, was happy that a ghost had favored his son with an appearance, for he, Father, was sorry to acknowledge that he hadn't experienced this sort of infernal pleasure for a long, long time, his ghosts had simply evaporated, vanished, which he regretted no end, and felt the poorer and emptier for it; in fact, he'd almost forgotten about their existence and eerie ways, but to see if there was any resemblance between his past experiences and my present ones, he asked me to describe, as accurately as possible, the outward appearance of my ghost.

That day we took a longer walk than usual, so the appearance of the ghost aside, it was itself out of the ordinary, because on our afternoon walks we never ventured beyond the immediate vicinity of the spa, and this area was no larger than the park itself, beyond which lay untouched landscape, the black-pebbled seashore, the craggy, precipitous rocks, and, in the opposite direction, the marsh, with a murky, opaque pond in the middle of it called the Snail Garden, and even farther, on dry land, the fabulously scarifying beechwood grove called the Great Wilderness.

True, the park, girded by slender whitewashed cottages facing the sea, was quite large and had wide driveways broadening into little plazas and radiating in every direction, with whimsical little footpaths crisscrossing the green lawns, but the solitary pines had more than enough space to display their solitude, just as the white birches with their meticulous nonchalance had room to arrange themselves in tidy clusters; the seafront promenade was also part of the park, protected by a tall stone wall adorned with elongated marble urns and running straight as an arrow, separating land from sea; in a sense, even the short first section of the embankment belonged to the park, too, being a direct extension of the promenade and different from the rest of the embankment because they had used fine gravel instead of crushed stones to make a rough surface suitable for walking—I could actually sink my feet ankle-deep into this gravel—but despite these efforts to turn this short section into a walkway by using soft, pleasantly crunching gravel, it remained bare as it rose between the sea and the marsh, a reminder of its convulsive origins, when in the course of a single night many centuries ago it had been flung here by a terrible tidal wave, thus cutting off water from water and letting a once lovely bay deteriorate into a marsh; properly speaking, then, only the tree-lined lane could be said to belong to the park, but that, too, if only in a mundane sense, led away from here, since it went from the rear entrance of the spa to the railroad station, where it ended for good; from the station there was nowhere to go, one had to turn back, for it was one thing to take a walk and quite another to go on an excursion.

It is also true that my parents never decided in advance which way we would walk, this was always determined by chance or simply by the dearth of choices; it seemed quite unnecessary to ponder which of the two routes to take—whether, coming from the spa, we should turn onto the seaside promenade or proceed farther on the embankment and on the way back, sweeping around the main building, walk as far as the station— or decide whether we should while away the time in the lobby's wicker chairs until so little time was left for the actual walk that on our return, instead of taking the sensible short route, we'd choose the impractical long one; but none of this really mattered; all these afternoon walks did was make us repeat the same diverting game of choices and possibilities, though only until the pearly hue of the sky began to deepen and we, back in our rooms or on the terrace, watched it turn completely dark.

On that day, however, nightfall caught us out-of-doors, for we had begun our afternoon walk, as usual, first going down to the shore for our fresh-air cure, which we took by leaning against the stone wall, no more than fifteen minutes, and simply relaxing our muscles as much as possible and silently inhaling and exhaling through our nostrils, taking advantage of the early evening air that, in Dr. Köhler's view, owing to the temporarily high degree of humidity and the presence of those natural substances the mucous membrane of the nose could experience as some sort of fragrance, was highly effective in clearing the respiratory passages and filling the lungs, stimulating the circulation and soothing one's nerves: as the much-respected doctor liked to emphasize, this worthy goal could be achieved only if the esteemed patients were willing to follow all his instructions and did not casually keep violating the rules, for example, not leaning against walls or trees while breathing, never mind simply sitting around the lobby or the terrace chattering away, and only with a lull in the conversation starting solemnly to wheeze and sigh, and only until one had something urgent to say again; no, such ladies and gentlemen were not even worth talking about, they were doomed, as good as in the morgue already; their thoughtlessness was understandable, but those who wished to extend their sojourn on earth, however slightly, should be able to stand on their own two feet for three five-minute periods, which is the time it took to complete all the repetitions of the breathing exercise, yes, stand up, loosely and without any support; excuses and objections should not even be acknowledged, for beauty and health were inseparable, and for this reason the doctor would be very pleased if he could convince people, especially the ladies, of course, that one's good looks were not in the least threatened but, on the contrary, enhanced, albeit in a more complex manner than with girdles and facials, if in the interest of good health we did not mind contorting our faces a little—anyway, grimacing was necessary only during the first five minutes of the exercise, until all that putrid air left one's lungs—and this was to be done not inside stuffy rooms polluted by tobacco and perfume, for there we only inhale the same foulness we blow out, but right here near the water, even if other people could see us; when it comes to health, there can be no room for false modesty, we must breathe through our noses—without puffing out our chests, though, as Catholics do, so arrogantly haughty in their humility; the air must be directed downward, into the belly—after all, we are Protestants, are we not?—and can safely fill our stomachs with air, if not our heads, because everything should be in its place and in its own good time: gray matter in our heads, air in our bellies, provided we don't tighten our girdles again beyond the reasonable limit, ladies, and provided, too, that we hold in the air, deep down, to the count of ten, and then slowly let out that horrid stench that was in us, yes, in all of us, for to keep it in would be not only unnecessary but downright indecent.

The sun was going down but darkness held off for quite a while, the sun's red reflection lingering in the graying sky; then suddenly the sea turned black, the whitening crests flashed as they rose and tumbled, and the evening mist which would slowly enwrap the park already hung over the water, seagulls were flying ever higher; as we stood there, hearing not only one another's breathing but also the relaxed, crunching footsteps of strollers behind us, I felt I was experiencing the sweetest silence there was: made of the triple rhythm of the seagulls' screeching, the sea's murmuring, crackling, and rumbling sounds, and my own breathing, which I realized I was trying to adjust to this rhythm; this was the silence in which all emotions subside, become motionless, in which state rising thoughts can only ruffle the surface of emotions before falling back, unformed and unformulated, to where they came from, until—prompted by a crunching footfall, a funny wheeze, the seagulls' choral screech and sudden silence, or by some physical sensation, like feeling the evening breeze, the buckling of a knee, perhaps an itch, or by a psychological impression of a fleeting, undirected anxiety, an overwhelming cheerfulness, or a fitful longing—something would be cast up again, something that needs to be expressed, that might be the object of consideration or of a plan of action, but the power of emotions will not allow it; the sway of emotions is the force that holds everything together, enjoying its own ephemeral wholeness, for it knows no greater pleasure than the realization of non-becoming, the calming pause provided by the state of inconsonance.

I have no way of knowing what effect these silences had on others, on Mother and Father, for example, but I know that during these silences I acquired experiences far more profound than my age entitled me to; in a peculiar way, I even surmised that this permanently transitional state of inconsonance would always be both benevolent and malevolent for me, and this frightened me, because I would much rather have resembled those who, landing on either side of this border region, managed to establish a firm foothold.

In short, I had a premonition of my woeful future, and I cannot decide even now whether this happened because, faithfully following Dr. Köhler's instructions, I had actually reached the state his cure had promised, or, conversely, because I was able to comprehend the old man's exercises since my fate had predisposed me to this more reflective state of being; the latter possibility seems more likely, though my predisposition may have been colored and strengthened by my sense of duty, which along with my pedantry stemmed not from diligence or interest in an active life—this I realized even before the Heiligendamm vacations—but much more from a desire somehow to conceal from the world my deliciously obscure conditions, brought on by my lascivious indolence, letting neither my face nor my movements betray my whereabouts (Please, do not disturb!), so that retreating behind the partition of compulsively performed duties I might be free to daydream about what really interested me.

I was born to lead two separate lives, or, I should say, the two halves of my divided life lacked harmonious congruity, or, to be still more precise, even if my public life had been the matching half of my secret existence, I would have felt an odd and jarring strain between them: it was the quagmire of a guilty conscience, something difficult to negotiate, because my self-imposed discipline in public resulted in a kind of dull and halting obtuseness for which I had to compensate myself by indulging in ever more fevered fantasies, and that, in turn, not only widened the gap between my two halves but made each of the two more isolated in its own sphere, rendering me less and less successful in rescuing anything from one and shifting it to the other, a process that in time became painful; the psyche would not tolerate my acts of self-denial, and the pain I experienced evoked a fervent desire to be like other people, who displayed no symptoms of a suppressed, tension-filled guardedness; I learned well how to read thoughts from facial expressions, how immediately to identify with these thoughts, but this mimetic ability to empathize, this desire for otherness, also led to bouts of mental anguish and brought no relief, for I realized I could not be another person, could only appear to be someone else, and total identification was as impossible as fusing my own two halves and making my secret life public, or, conversely, as impossible as freeing myself from my own illusions and compulsions and becoming like other people who are usually called hale and hearty.

I could not but consider my nearly uncontrollable inclinations to be a disease, a peculiar curse, a sinful aberration, although in hopeful moments I saw them as nothing more serious than an autumn cold which—even if I felt utterly lost when suffering from it—some hot tea, a cold compress, a few bitter, fever-reducing pills, and honey-sweet compotes could easily cure, and which I always knew, and could tell in advance, in the brief lulls between spells of fever, would ultimately, when I first got up and went to the window, make me feel light, cool, and clean, and also mildly disappointed, for though the swaying tree branches might seem to be lunging at me, their soft, leafy palms ready to snatch me away, I could see that nothing had changed on the street, nothing and no one had been disturbed by my illness, my room had not been transformed into a vast hall reverberating with the footfalls of giants; everything looked as it should—even friendlier and more familiar, actually, because the objects no longer evoked unpleasant memories associated with events thought to be long past—everything was safe and sound and exactly, almost indifferently, in place; it was some such release or cleansing I kept yearning for, though for those embarrassing and shameful reveries of mine I knew I'd have to find the remedy myself.

That day, having completed our fresh-air treatment, we first began to walk toward the station, and in this not even I, conditioned though I was by the very uneventfulness of our lives to notice the subtlest of changes, saw anything out of the ordinary, though Father, slightly out of breath, did stop the exercise a little before the prescribed time and, as if he had just gone through a terrible ordeal, leaned his pleasantly ample body against the stone parapet and with ironic self-satisfaction looked back at Mother; he meant to turn toward the sea, but could not resist looking back, which wasn't something unusual, either; he always did that, for the sea, which Mother invariably referred to as "enchanting," like the sights of nature in general, bored Father no less than these ludicrous breathing exercises; what was there to look at, anyway; "As far as I'm concerned, my dear, this is nothing but a large body of empty water," he would opine, unless a ship happened to move across the horizon, for then he could play at guessing its stupefyingly slow progress by picking a "reasonably fixed" point onshore, establishing its angle to the ship's original position, and then gauging the changes in the angle: "It has moved twelve degrees to the west," he might cry out unexpectedly, and on occasion he would also offer rhetorical remarks about the relativities observable in the trajectory of human existence; but just as he never expected us to follow the trends of his thoughts—"Human thoughts are for the most part the by-products of basic life functions," he claimed, "because the brain, like the stomach, needs always to be fed with stuff it likes to digest, and the mouth, let's not condemn it for this, merely brings up bits of this ill-chewed stuff"—Father was gracious enough, when his own temper didn't get the best of him, not to spoil other people's pleasures, and, indeed, made it clear that it was the plain sight of human pleasures and exertions that he found most interesting and entertaining, that were the very objects of his delight; and perhaps it was his lack of interest in natural phenomena that might explain why he was attracted to everything that was coarse, common, and lowly, experiencing the broadly and universally elemental through the raw, cruder forces of human nature and thus for him everything refined and sophisticated served only the purpose of concealing its own true essence and was therefore worthy only of anger and biting scorn—"Theodor, you are simply insufferable," Mother would say to him at times, clearly annoyed, though she must have been pleased if pained to know that her ingrained habits, to which she clung tenaciously, were being continuously exposed; but there was something alarmingly two-faced in Father's behavior, because he was reluctant to formulate a clear-cut, straightforward opinion about anything, though he did have opinions, very definite ones, about everything, but pretending to be indecisive and impressionable, he agreed with everyone about everything—oh no, he wasn't going to argue, he deeply respected everyone's right to an opinion, he merely weighed the pros and cons and, almost as if searching for evidence to support other people's assertions, put things in the conditional mood and posed his unwieldy questions so awkwardly that acquaintances, aware always of his ungainly, larger-than-average build, thought him charming;

"Pardon me, my dear Thoenissen," Privy Councillor Frick was wont to say, "but with such thighs and such a barrel chest, you cannot help being a democrat," or as Fräulein Wohlgast put it, "Our Thoenissen is playing the clumsy bear cub again"—counting on and enjoying this kind of reaction, Father kept on fussing until the whole edifice of the argument gently collapsed, without offending anyone, almost as if by itself; but at other times he wasn't so circumspect and would greet an assertion with such boisterous enthusiasm, such resounding astonishment (my ghost story was a case in point), and inundate it with such a fierce and exalted torrent of words which like all effusiveness had a certain childlike appeal, and go on to exaggerate, color, and embellish every little detail to such an extent that the statement completely lost its original dimensions, a riotous imagination inflated it into a monster of such absurd proportions that it lifted off, away from any notion of reality, no longer fitting into or connected to anything; Father showed no mercy in this game of his but kept embroidering and intensifying it until the original idea, the modest casing of reality, became so fatally distended that it burst from the pressure of its own emptiness; of course it wasn't these dubious if entertaining flights of fancy that so upset my mother—I think that words, insofar as they went beyond polite clichés and the vernacular of daily concerns, remained out of her grasp, so the subtleties of Father's verbal games were bound to elude her, by which I don't mean to imply that she was dull or limited, though alas the opposite wasn't true either, if only because her strict puritanical upbringing, or perhaps her inherently rigid and repressed nature, had made it impossible for her to realize her intellectual potential or to develop her other, emotional-physical sensibilities, so that everything about her was disturbingly unfinished, much like her life itself, and for that reason it probably would have been more appropriate if on her eternal resting place, instead of a winged angel tearing at her breast, Father had erected a statue of something more fitting, more dignified, for there was certainly nothing angelically feminine about Mother, and if we must dwell on this banal symbolism, picture a delicate pedestal supporting a densely fluted marble pillar that is brutally broken asunder, its ragged fissure exposing the stone's coarse inner texture, contrasting sharply with the finely polished exterior: this would have been a more apt representation, one that would have impressed me each time I visited her grave.

On my long walks back home (if I may still refer to the city of my birth as home), having had my fill of the narrow, chaotically bustling streets, I enjoyed cutting across the old city and resting my gaze on the fields stretching into the distance beyond the city gate, where I'd turn precisely and purposefully in the direction where, over the hills, I could make out Ludwigsdorf, the village that Hilde and I used to visit every Saturday afternoon; even though spending time in the cemetery was never part of my plans, I could not escape its attraction, and it also happened to be on the way, though I could have avoided it by not taking Finstertorstrasse, but it was so tempting to walk through the crumbling brick fence with little shrubs sprouting in the cracks and, like a frequent visitor, feeling at ease and glad to have returned, to roam about the moldering, weed-ridden crypts and bright, flower-covered mounds in this ancient cemetery until, finally, coming to our winged angel that was destined, rather tragically, to renew the appearance of our family vault—but perhaps that was the very reason I went there: to see it.

It had to be some self-tormenting impulse that led me there, because for one thing this work, irritatingly amateurish in its own right, offended my good taste and my aesthetic sense, and for another, here in front of this statue the anger I felt toward Father, the revulsion and hatred could finally surface and be intensified by the trite sentimentality and calculated falsity with which the stonecutter had tried to reconcile his client's express wishes with his own so-called artistic concepts, for while he hadn't modeled the angel's head directly after my mother's but had augmented his own memories of her with the artistic ingenuity of using the portrait of her hanging on the dining-room wall, a rose-tinted image of Mother as a young girl, he nevertheless managed to slip some of Mother's characteristic features into that sweetly virginal, little-girl face: the angel's abruptly protruding brow and close-set eyes were reminiscent of Mother's forehead and eyes; the thin, gently curved nose, somewhat impudent lips, and charmingly pointed chin did bring to mind Mother's mouth and chin; but to make the confusion utter and complete, the crudely articulated stone cloak—in itself completely alien to any human shape—revealed the outlines of such an ethereally fragile body—with high-set, small, barely budding, yet aggressive breasts, a round belly, softly bulging buttocks, and hips a little bonier than necessary—and the wind, blowing into the angel's face and dramatically sweeping back her hair, made the cloak cling to the deep groin of this slender, about-to-ascend figure with such intrusive shamelessness that a viewer, faced with this hodgepodge of coarse details, could not possibly contemplate death or the possibility of dying; oddly enough, the statue did not evoke anything lifelike or natural, unless one considered natural the pitiful imaginings of an all-too-accommodating, aging artisan; and the tomb was vulgar and tasteless, too vulgar and tasteless to waste words or feelings on it if its creation had been the result of an unfortunate accident—the stonecutter's inability to realize, with noble simplicity, what Father had asked him to do; but no, it was neither accident nor coincidence but, on the contrary, the secret nature of necessity—unmistakably signaling an imminent doom—revealed that this statue was more a monument to my father's depravity than a memorial to my mother's life.

But who could have foreseen then, in the mundane portents of our days, the future in its entirety?

"We'll be late for the train," Father said, still there on the seashore, and almost imperceptibly his expression changed, the ironic self-satisfied look he had worn while leaning on the parapet and looking at Mother now mingling with a kind of impatient embarrassment; Mother, however, appeared to ignore both the odd intonation and the unusual sentence— unusual in that it was uttered at all; she made no reply.

She couldn't, unless she was going to interrupt her breathing exercise, because at this moment she was busy keeping her mouth open, her tongue stuck out, and with rhythmical, panting breaths she was trying to expel from her stomach the gradually inhaled, forcibly held-in air—like many women, she found this abdominal breathing difficult; but there was also a sort of offended, provocatively didactic intent in Mother's silence, a suggestion of increased tension that chose silence as a means to indicate that what had just happened would not pass without consequences, because they had an agreement; they had an agreement, concluded sometime ago, in tones that for my benefit were meant to be jocular but turned out to be serious, fueled by heated emotions, for just such occasions, when Father could no longer endure this "bestial existence," as he liked to put it, and it came about during one of those fresh-air exercises when Father, totally unexpectedly and with his most unruly grin on his face, put an end to his sufferings, which he had tried to ease by much groaning, puffing, and wheezing, and glanced over at Mother: a transparently blatant curiosity appeared in his eyes, hovering like a cloud, a look neither amusing nor congruent with his otherwise laughing demeanor, a look I knew well even if at the time I did not understand it, and his face became frighteningly exposed, attractively vulnerable, as if every other facial expression of his, though perfected and deemed authentic for most social occasions, was a mere subterfuge, a mask to hide, guard, and protect him, and now he was revealed, the real he was freed at last, unable to hold himself back from himself any longer—and he was beautiful, he looked really beautiful then: his black hair curled over his gleaming forehead, dimples of silent laughter quivered on his round cheeks, his eyes turned a bluer blue, and his fleshy lips parted a little—and then, gliding with dreamlike swiftness up to Mother, he simply reached toward her mouth and, using three fingers with a sensitivity and daintiness that belied the abruptness of the move, seized the stuck-out tongue by its root, whereupon Mother, with the raw instinct of self-defense, first jerked her head back to keep from retching and then, probably surprising even herself, bit Father's fingers so violently that he cried out in pain; from then on it was agreed that during exercises Father was supposed to watch the sea "and not me, do you understand? not me, but the sea! you are unbearable, do you hear? your look is unbearable"—yet when the moment came and Father, bored with exercising, leaned on the parapet, I always sensed in the tension of Mother's body, along with fear and reticence, her wish that he not turn to the sea, that he do something to her, something startling and scandalous that would end those painful and pointless exertions which, because of her heavy menstruation that lasted for months, she had to continue if she wanted her health restored; she wanted to be free to follow Father to that secret region his dimpled smile and clouded glance so suggestively hinted at; yes, she wanted him to do with her as he pleased—yet she also may have suspected the situation was quite the opposite of what she wished for, because her fears and reticence were far stronger than her desires.

Since I was more inclined to comply with Dr. Köhler's instructions, Mother liked me to stand right next to her, quite close, I might say in the heat of her body's warmth, so close that the shoulder ruffles of her puffed-sleeve dress almost touched my face, but this certainly did not mean that in her frustration she sought solace in me or began to have impermissible and troubling feelings of tenderness for me—I don't think she harbored such feelings for anybody—no, there was a purely logical reason we ended up next to each other: this way she could hear and then follow the rhythm of my breathing, and by the same token, if she faltered or was out of breath or, letting her mind wander, got confused, I could wait for her and help her get back on track; I was able to hold my breath for a long time, wait for and enjoy the slight dizziness that would displace my feelings while things I could only see before but not feel grew sharper and pervaded my senses; I could lose myself at last and be anything I wanted—a distant sound, the crest of a wave, a seagull, a falling leaf landing atop the stone wall, or just vacant air—until in the redness of the blood rushing to my brain everything would slowly turn dark, yet the instinct to breathe would still force me to hear distinctly and sense how Mother, with a few interpolated exhalations and inhalations, was reverting to our previous rhythm and how, her own breath balancing at a precarious standstill, she'd wait for me to take the lead again; we did not look at and could not see each other, our bodies did not touch, yet only incaution and inexperience could explain and excuse the blindness with which she allowed us to stray into such emotionally dangerous territory; she should have known that we were doing something we shouldn't have, and that in this instance she was the seducer, because mutual sensation, when deprived of tactile and visual contact, will resort to more receptive, more primitive, one might even say more animal-like means, and then the other body's heat, odor, mysterious emanations and rhythms can convey much more than a glance, a kiss, or an embrace ever could; this is true in lovemaking as well: the various positions and techniques are never an end but merely the means of descent into the depths, while the end keeps concealing itself in deeper and deeper regions, beyond ever heavier curtains, and if it allows itself to be caught and exposed at all, it will do so only in the experience of unfulfillable pleasure and unattainable hope.

And now, twenty years later, and only a few days before my thirtieth birthday, which, on the strength of an intuition, a persistent though inexplicable premonition, I had come to consider—as it happened, correctly—to be a highly significant turning point in my life, I decided to forgo the pleasure of spending yet another pleasant afternoon with my fiancée and of being the guest of honor at my own birthday party, which her parents had arranged for me, and instead, seeking a refuge worthy of the supposed significance of the day, I turned to solitude, again to solitude, or rather to a more intimate tête-à-tête with my betrothed; delayed by some business engagement, my future father-in-law had not yet come home, and when the lovely Frau Itzenpiltz, using the excuse of having to see about supper, considerately withdrew, leaving the two of us alone in the room, I told Helene about my intention to travel; she had no objections at all—on the contrary, I felt she agreed and understood that it was imperative that the first chapters of the narrative I had been planning for years be committed to paper before our wedding day, to make certain that the expected change in our lifestyle would not divert me from my original ambitions or, worse, cause me to abandon them—"I feel, Helene, I really do, that you do not require a detailed explanation," I said

to her in a whisper, and the sincerity of my words was no doubt enhanced
by the fact that I clasped her hand gently, and our cheeks were so close
I could feel whiffs of my own breath mingled with hers on my face; the
red of dusk was playing with the patterns of the silk hangings on this
warm autumn day, the windows were open; "Still, I find it necessary,
Helene, to speak of something I can broach only with the utmost reluctance, for it is so dark and morally dubious . . . what I intend to tell you
increases the perils of your undertaking as much as it does my own responsibility, please realize that; you can still change your mind," I said,
and knowing full well she wouldn't, I laughed, teasingly; "What I intend
to say, then, is that happiness, though it ought to be at the very center of
my heart's desires, is not, for no amount of explaining and quibbling will
make it conducive to artistic creation, so if I leave now, I am deliberately
exchanging the happiness I know can be mine when I am with you for
the unhappiness I always feel when not in your company, the unhappiness
I knew before we met"—needless to say I was lying to her, while pleased
to be affecting an air of sincerity, or, I should say, my confession was
sincere inasmuch as it was a pretext only; and being able to deceive her,
seeing her fall under my spell so easily, made her even more attractive to
me, but at the same time, precisely because in her gullibility she laid
herself so open, precisely because she couldn't be anything but what she
was—tears of anguish were brightening her blue eyes—the real sentiment
I wanted to express grew ever heavier within me; "Away from here, I
don't ever want to see you again" is what I should have said to her,
because I could not resist the deep-seated urge to escape and, in a sense,
to disappear for good, as in fact once, while leaving their house, I did
catch myself mumbling, completely unawares and spitefully, "It's finished,
done with, I'm free"—and if now, having the luxury to fantasize, I try
to imagine what would have happened if that afternoon before my departure I had not merely looked for a pretext but spoken candidly to her,
what I see before me is the face of a young woman whose translucent
white skin and soft round features give her an uncertain, almost ethereal
look, though the pale freckles scattered around the delicate nose and the
thick bronze-red hair imbue it with a curious vitality, and this face shows
no surprise, on hearing my news, indeed breaks into a smile, as if it had
been waiting for these words; when Helene smiles like this, with full-
mouthed enjoyment, she looks older and more experienced, because in
her moistly gleaming teeth there is a touch of wanton willfulness; she
quickly wipes away the teardrop brought to her eyes by the moral supe-

riority of knowing she has acquiesced obligingly to my plan, and yet she makes a gesture that, in the heat of the moment, excited by each other's breath, we both long for: it would have to have been a very common gesture, but this is the point where my imagination comes to a respectful halt, given Helene's then still untouched sensuality; leaving, then, after a supper spent in a convivial family atmosphere and a farewell which in the circumstances seemed almost too lighthearted, I may have carried away with me Helene's earnestly given consent, yet I could not but feel our future to be ominous and threatening, since all signs indicated we would have to build it on insincerity, insincerity in the guise of mutual attentiveness and consideration, because, on the one hand, it seemed that my unavoidable physical attraction to her would be nourished not by the kind of raw and inexplicable force that, as far as I knew, one felt in real love, but only by an exquisite sense of beauty, a titillating vulnerability, and on the other hand, I didn't think she would ever admit that to endure living with her own fragile emotional sensibilities, she herself needed those coarser gestures, a secret lewdness which she could not possibly expect me to provide and the presumed lack of which would not be compensated either by the mysteriousness of my obscure silences or by the lies of my playful fits of sincerity.

Of course it wasn't coarse sensuality or an inclination to mutually shared lewdness that I was lacking, and in any case, I don't really believe in a refinement that can forgo physicality and still remain healthy; but beyond the simpleminded fear every young man must feel before leading his bride to the altar, I was fearful and anxious for another reason: our relationship, at least outwardly, reminded me very much of the unbalanced and unresolvable tensions between my parents; in every sign of physical coarseness I detected Father's gestures, and in the longing for them I saw Mother's needs; if I hadn't possessed the gift of self-knowledge that enables us to carefully separate the overlapping planes of cause and effect, thereby discovering the endless circular stairways of our emotions which, dissatisfied with mere form and appearance, lead us downward and inward to ultimate understanding—without this gift, even our engagement would have become unbearable by the knowledge that my malady was hereditary, that fate condemned me to the humiliating absurdity of having to repeat my parents' lives and misdeeds, of being the same as they, and even of dragging an innocent outsider into this fatal sameness.

The Soft Light of the Sun

The snow was already melting, and though I was afraid of the dogs I decided to walk home from school through the woods.

One had to step carefully here; the trail, beaten into the heavy, clayey soil, wound steeply around the gnarled trunks and coiling roots of ancient mistletoe-laden oaks and plunged through the underbrush, clumps of wild roses, elder, and hawthorn that looked impenetrable even in their barrenness; melting snow had turned the thick layers of leaves sodden and I kept losing my footing on the slippery surface; seeking an outlet, tiny rivulets had cut grooves right through the middle of the trail, creating a regular brook that ran sparkling and gushing in its rusty yellow bed, swelling up where the trail took a sudden turn, then rushing on, engulfing stones and pebbles; imagining dense forests and wild mountain rapids all around, I leaped from one bank of my stream to the other, zigzagging back and forth, trusting my body to the slope's pull, sensing that the more daring my leaps were—the harder I landed and the longer I stayed in the air, finding the site of my next takeoff with a single glance—the more confident I became and the less likely I was to slip or fall; I was racing downhill, I was flying.

At the bottom of the forest the trail reached flat ground, coming to rest in a clearing with patches of snow, at the opposite end of which I saw someone standing in the bushes.

I could not turn back, couldn't escape, but simply had to slow down my breathing, make sure I didn't pant or wheeze, so he wouldn't think he was making me so excited.

He stepped out from behind the bushes and started toward me.

I wanted to appear cool and calm, as if not the least bothered by this accidental encounter, but my back had got uncomfortably wet from all that running, my ears were burning and must have looked ridiculously red in the cold; my legs suddenly felt awkwardly short and stiff, and it was as if I were seeing myself with his eyes.

The sky above us was clear, a great blue expanse, distant and blank.

Behind the woods, caught in the tangled treetops, the soft light of the sun broke through, but the air remained piercing cold; crows cawed, magpies chattered in the eerie silence, and one could feel that as soon as the sun set everything would be silent and stiff again.

We walked toward each other very slowly.

On his long dark-blue overcoat gold buttons gleamed, and he slung his soft leather briefcase casually over his shoulder, as always, lugging it on his back, which made him twist his long neck and bend over a little; still, his gait was as loose and graceful as if he were swaying to and fro in some oblivious softness; he thrust his head high, he was watching.

It took a very long time to cover the distance between us, because from the moment I had spotted him behind the bushes I had to sort out, and also alert, my most contradictory and secret feelings: "Krisztián!" I would have loved to cry out in my surprise, if only because in his name, which I hadn't the courage to utter even during the abruptly cutoff budding stage of our friendship and kept muttering it only to myself, I sensed the same discriminating elegance I did in his whole being; his name had the same irresistible attraction for me I knew I mustn't yield to in any shape or form; saying his name out loud would be like touching his naked body, which is why I avoided him, always waiting until he began walking home with others so I wouldn't walk with him or his way; even in school I was careful not to wind up next to him, lest I'd have to talk to him or, in a sudden commotion, brush against his body; at the same time I kept watching him, tailed him like a shadow, mimicked his gestures in front of the mirror, and it was painfully pleasurable to know that he was completely unaware of my spying on him, secretly imitating him, trying to evoke in myself those hidden qualities and characteristics that would make me resemble him; he couldn't know, or feel, that I was always with him and he with me; in reality, he didn't even bother to look at me, I was like a neutral, useless object to him, completely superfluous and devoid of interest.

Of course my sober self cautioned me not to acknowledge these passionate feelings; it was as if two separate beings coexisted in me, totally independent of each other: at times the joys and sufferings his mere existence caused me seemed like nothing but little games, not worth thinking about, because one of my two selves hated and detested him as much as my other self loved and respected him; since I was eager to avoid giving any visible sign of either love or hate, I was the one who acted as though he were but an object—divulging my love, much too desirous and passionate to let him in on it, would have rendered me totally defenseless, while my hatred drove me to humiliating fantasies that I was too scared to act on—and it was I, not he, who acted as though I was unapproachable, impervious even to his accidental glances.

When he was no more than an arm's length from me and we both stopped, he said, "There's something I'd like to ask of you," calling me by my name, his tone cool and matter-of-fact, "and I'd appreciate it greatly if you could do it for me."

I felt the blood rushing to my face.

Which he, too, would immediately notice.

The affable artlessness with which he uttered my name, though I knew he did it only for the sake of good form, had a devastating effect: now not only were my legs too short but I felt like one large head hovering somewhere close to the ground, an ill-proportioned repulsive insect; and in my embarrassment I blurted out something I shouldn't have: "Krisztián!" I said, pronouncing his name aloud, and because it sounded too tender, frightened almost, anyway humble and out of tune with his own resolve to wait for me and even approach me with a request, he raised his eyebrows as if he had heard wrong or couldn't believe what he had heard, and obligingly leaned closer: "What's that? Come again?" he said, and I, finding some unexpected pleasure in his embarrassment, made myself sound even softer, even more amiable; "Oh nothing, nothing," I said quietly, "I just said it, just said your name, anything wrong with that?"

His thick lips parted, his eyelids flickered, his light brown complexion darkened slightly as if from repressed excitement, his black pupils contracted making the pale green irises seem dilated; but I don't think it was the shape of his face, the wide and easily knitted forehead, the lean cheeks, the dimpled chin and disproportionately small, almost pointed, perhaps still undeveloped nose, that made the most profound and most painfully beautiful impression on me; it was the coloring: in the green of his eyes, beaming out of the savagely sensual brown of his skin, there was something abstractly ethereal, clamoring for heights, while his chapped red lips and the unmanageably curly mass of his black hair were pulling me down into dark depths; the animal boldness of his glance made me recall our intimate moments together when, lost in each other's looks, which always suggested open hostility as well as hidden love, we could accurately sense that our mutual attraction was based simply on uncontrollable curiosity, which was only an illusion of something, though strong enough to draw us close, bind us together, deeper than any so-called dangerous inclination could ever be because it was undirected, insatiable; yet the synchronized narrowing of our pupils and harmoniously dilating irises surely disclosed something in our eyes that made palpably clear that our supposed intimacy had been a sham and that in reality we were irreconcilably different.

Looking into his eyes I seemed to see not another person but two terrifying magic balls.

This time, however, we couldn't hold each other's gaze for long; though neither of us tried to avoid the other or look away, I saw the change: his eyes lost their inherently brilliant openness, they filled with purpose and motive, and their surface became dimmer, glazed over; they took cover.

"I must ask you," he said quietly but sharply, and he stepped closer to keep me from interrupting him again and roughly gripped my arm, "I must ask you not to report me to the principal, or if you already have, go and try to take it back."

He kept biting his lips, pulling my arm, and blinking his eyes, and his voice lost its self-confident soft depth; he was thrusting out his words as if he wanted not even the air that carried them to touch his lips, wanted to expel these hated sounds, had to feel he had done all he could, although he must have had as little faith in the effectiveness of his own words as he did in my amenability, and for this reason alone I don't think he was very interested in my answer; besides, he didn't make it clear how he thought the report was to be taken back, so I think he knew all along he was treading on slippery ground; he was looking at me, but it may have been too much of an effort to make his voice sound so thin and humble, and it's very likely he didn't even see my face: in his eyes I must have been a mere blot, dissolving in its own vagueness.

But as far as I was concerned, a wonderful feeling of superiority made me more self-assured than ever.

A request had been put to me which I had the power to grant or refuse; the moment had arrived when I could prove my own importance, when at my own will and pleasure I could either reassure or destroy him, with a single word avenge all my secret injuries—injuries which ultimately were not even his doing, but which I had inflicted on myself because of him, the bitter pains of being ignored he induced in me, unwittingly and innocently, by simply being alive, by wearing nice clothes, by talking and playing with others, while with me he was unable or unwilling to establish the kind of contact I so yearned for and didn't even know what it should be like; he was almost a head taller than I, but at this moment, in the clearing, I was looking down at him; I found his forced smile distasteful, and as my body regained its normal dimensions, it assumed the lightness of that secure state in which our consciousness stops playing and struggling and, with a careless shrug, surrenders to all its contradictory emotions, rendering outward appearances and shows irrelevant; I didn't care anymore how I looked or whether he liked me or not, and while I felt the chill of cooling perspiration on my back, the dampness in my leaky shoes, the unpleasant prickles of my cheap trousers clinging to my thighs, as well as the burning in my ears, my smallness and my ugliness, there was nothing hurtful or humiliating in all this, because in spite of the unrelieved misery of bodily sensations, I was now free and powerful, felt free within and for myself; I knew I loved him, and no matter what he did I could not stop loving him; I was completely defenseless, and for that I could either take my revenge on him or forgive him, it was all the same; to be sure, he didn't seem just then as beautiful and attractive as he had been in my fantasies or when he'd overwhelm me with his sudden presence—his dark skin had turned sallow; he seemed to have eaten something with garlic in it and I didn't want to inhale the smell of his breath; to boot, the humility in his smile was so twisted, so exaggerated, that it betrayed his fear, which may have been genuine but which he was anxious not to show, preferring proudly to conceal it, to substitute mock humility; he was playing up to me and deceiving me at the same time.

I blushed and yanked away my arm.

But I did not, after all, have a choice; I couldn't simply tell him anything I felt like, since as far as my emotions were concerned every possible response led to a dead end: it hadn't occurred to me to report him, but if I were to, if now I really did, I might alienate him forever and they might even take him away; if, however, I pretended to be swayed by his plea, I'd be letting myself be misled by his clumsy show of humility, in which case his victory would be much too easy for him to love me for it; I wasn't ashamed of blushing—if anything, I wanted him to notice it, would have liked nothing more than for him to discover my feelings and then not mind them—but feeling myself blush made me realize all too clearly that nothing could help me now, that regardless of what I'd say or do, he'd slip through my fingers again and I'd be left with nothing but another unclarified moment, which he couldn't understand, and with my futile fantasies; but if that's the case, I suddenly thought, then I must be true to my convictions and act sensibly and cruelly, although this alternative would bring me close to my father and mother, even if I didn't actually think of them at the moment, because much as I would have liked to have my own convictions, I knew they weren't all mine; still, at the same time, the situation was much too unique and personal for my parents' faces or bodies to appear in my mind's eye and whisper in my ear specific words that I could then go on confidently repeating, like a parrot, but they were there all right, with the warm persistence of feeling at home, hiding out in my thoughts, ready to jump in; that's how I knew that there was a form of human behavior capable of eliminating emotional considerations and acting purely on the basis of principles known as convictions—except that I didn't have the strength to stifle my emotions.

"I'm not asking for myself!" he said even more sharply, and his hand, from which I'd just withdrawn my arm, was still in the air, hesitating; he had long fingers, a slender wrist, but I didn't let him finish, didn't want to, because I didn't want to see him like this, and I cut in: "First of all, it would be nice if you could tell the difference between denouncing and reporting."

But pretending not to have heard me, he continued the interrupted sentence: "I'd just like to spare my mother this latest unpleasantness."

We kept interrupting each other.

"If you think I'm a squealer, we've nothing further to discuss."

"I saw you go into the teachers' room after class, I did!"

"What makes you think I'm always busy with your affairs, especially yours?"

"You know my mother has a heart condition."

I burst out laughing. And there was strength in this laugh. "When you have to face the consequences of your words, then she has a heart condition."

His eyes regained their sparkle, they seemed to be illuminated from within by a cold flash of light, he was screaming, and the garlic-smelling thrusts of his words hit me in the face: "What d'you want, then? What? I'll kiss your ass, if that's what you want!"

Something stirred nearby and almost automatically we both turned our heads: a rabbit darted across the snowy clearing.

I wasn't looking at the rabbit, which having reached the edge of the clearing must have vanished in the thicket; I was watching him; in our anger, we unwittingly ended up so close to each other that if he'd paid attention he could have felt my breath, which I failed to control, pounding on his neck; the casually tied knot of his striped scarf was coming loose, the top button of his shirt was undone, and its collar must have slipped under his sweater, because his long neck appeared before me like a strange naked landscape: a vein embedded in tightening muscles and showing faintly through the smooth skin seemed to be pulsing evenly, and at slightly irregular intervals the tip of his gently protruding Adam's apple bobbed up and down; the blood that had rushed to his face while he was shouting was slowly subsiding; I could watch as his normal coloring gradually returned and his fleshy lips again parted slightly, the pale yellow light of the sun, sinking behind the woods, glimmered through the green of his eyes, his gaze following the rabbit's path, and when his eyes came to rest at a certain point, I knew the rabbit had disappeared; the persistent chatter of the magpies, the incessant cawing of crows, the smell of the air, even the tiny rustling noises of the woods seemed to have the same tangible certainty as his face, which was sharp, hard, mobile even in its immobility, with no emotions reflected in it, it simply existed, giving itself over easily and gracefully to whatever unfolded before it; for me, at this moment, it may have been not so much his loveliness, the harmony of his enviable, captivating features and coloring, though ostensibly that was what I longed for, but his inner ability to give himself over to the moment, totally, unreservedly; whenever I looked into the mirror and compared myself to him, I had to conclude that though I wasn't ugly, I really wanted to look like him, to be exactly like him; my eyes were blue, clear, and transparent, my blond hair fell on my forehead in soft waves, but I felt my sensitive, vulnerable, and fragile features were deceptively false because, though others found my face positively charming and liked to touch it, to caress it, I knew myself to be coarse, common, sinister, insidious; there was nothing nice about me, I could not love myself, I shielded my real self with a mask, and so as not to disappoint people too much, I made myself play roles that fit my outer appearance more than my inner self, trying to be pleasant, attentive, and understanding, lighthearted, cheerful, and ingratiatingly serene, though in reality I was sullen, irritable, all my senses hankered for raw pleasure, I was irascible, hateful, I would have preferred to keep my head bowed all the time, not to see or be seen by anyone, and I looked right into people's eyes only to check the effectiveness of my performance; I managed to deceive just about everyone, and yet felt comfortable only when I was alone, because the people I could easily fool I had to despise for their stupidity and blindness, while those who became suspicious, were not so gullible, or simply could not give themselves to anyone, I would cloy with such excessive attentiveness and solicitude—the effort taking up all my strength and energy—as to make myself absurdly, deliciously nauseated, and for this very reason I sensed most keenly my slyness, slipperiness, and urge to dominate when I succeeded in winning over people who were otherwise alien, even hateful or indifferent to me; I wanted everyone to love me and I couldn't love anyone; I felt beauty's seductive deception, knowing that anyone with such a fanatic craving for beauty, paying attention only to beauty, was incapable of loving and could not be loved; yet I couldn't give up this obsession, for I felt as if my allegedly handsome face were not mine, though it was useful in deceiving people; the deception was mine and gave me power; I steered clear of people who were crippled or ugly, and this was all too understandable, for even though they kept telling me I was good-looking, which I could see whenever I looked in the mirror, I still felt ugly and repulsive; I could not deceive myself, for my innermost feelings, more than the power lent me by my good looks, told me precisely what I was really like; therefore, I longed for the kind of beauty in which external and internal traits meshed, in which a harmonious exterior shielded strength and goodness, not the disarray of a twisted soul—in other words, I longed for perfection, or at least for a total identification with my true self, for the freedom to be imperfect, to be infinitely mean and wicked— but that far he would not let me go.

"I had no intention of denouncing you," I told him quietly, but he wouldn't even move his head, "and even if I wanted to, you could always deny it and say you were thinking of your dog; it would take some explaining, but you could have been thinking of your dog."

My whispered words were no heavier than the cloud of mist forming around my mouth in the cold light, and each one of them reached and touched his motionless face; I couldn't have been more cunning than this—holding out the possibility of doing something I had no intention of doing and, to counteract this mild threat, immediately offering a handy explanation with which to slip out of the net I might cast over him—but by doing this, I also betrayed my own supposed conviction: because I should have denounced him, yes, then and only then would I be strong and tough, and I just might, I just might—I couldn't possibly sink lower than this; by then I had lost all feeling of my body, I was hovering somewhere above myself yet way too low.

Words were of no consequence; nothing was more important than this mist, my exhaled breath touching his skin, but it seemed that even that wasn't enough, because his gaze became suspended; he must not have understood what I was getting at.

"It never occurred to me to do it, believe me!"

He finally turned his head to me and I could see in his eyes that his suspicions were gone.

"No?" he asked, also in a whisper, and his eyes again became open and penetrable, the way I liked. "No, it didn't," I whispered decisively, although I no longer knew what this denial was referring to; because I could finally penetrate that glance and no longer had to playact and, even more important, felt my own eyes opening up. "No?" he asked again, suspicious no longer but like one who wants to be sure of his own love, and the puff of mist accompanying the word touched my lips. "No, not at all," I whispered, and then suddenly there was silence between us, we were looking at each other, and we were close, so close that I hardly needed to move my head forward, with my mouth I touched his lips.

My mother, who had been brought home from the hospital three days earlier, was still bedridden, and when I was left alone after Krisztián disappeared behind the bushes, this was the first thing that came to my mind: Mother lying in her big bed and reaching out to me with her long, naked arm.

I could still feel his lips on my mouth, the chafing of that unknown skin, the softness and scent of the fleshy lips that stayed with me, on my mouth; I still felt the slight quiver of the two lips, their slow parting under my closed mouth, and then the slowly exhaled air that became mine, and the air he inhaled that was taken from me, and though I may seem to be contradicting myself, I don't think this could be called a kiss, not only because our lips had barely touched or because this touch was for both of us highly instinctive, and its purposeful, I might say erotic, application neither of us could have fully understood, but most of all because at that moment my mouth was but the ultimate means of persuasion, the final, wordless argument; with his last exhalation he breathed his fear on me, and when he inhaled, he drew in his newfound trust from me.

I don't even know how we finally separated, for there must have been an infinitesimal fraction of that moment in which I totally gave myself over to feeling his lips, sensing at the same time that with his breath he was also giving himself over to me. Being aware of this, I'm not about to claim (it would be ridiculous to do so) that our contact, our unique form of reasoning, lacked sensuality; no, it was very sensual but free—and this must be emphasized, it was purely free—of any ulterior motives with which adult love, in its own natural way, complements a kiss; our mouths, in the purest of possible ways, and regardless of what had gone before or what would follow, restricted themselves to what two mouths in the fraction of a second could give each other: fulfillment, comfort, and release; and that's when I must have closed my eyes, in that instant when no sight or circumstance could possibly have mattered anymore; when I think about that moment now, I still must ask myself whether a kiss can be anything else or anything more than that?

When I opened my eyes he was already talking.

"Do you know where rabbits stay in winter?"

And though his voice sounded deeper and perhaps even raspier than usual, there was no urgency in the question, asked with such self-evident ease, as if the rabbit had run across the field just then and not several minutes earlier, as if nothing had happened between those two points in time; as I watched his face, his eyes, his neck, the way he stood against a shimmering, opaline background laced with branches and treetops, as I took in this sight which seemed so very distant to me, I must have experienced momentarily the dread of a fatal, irreparable mistake: his question didn't mean that in his quite natural, almost obligatory embarrassment, he wanted to hide behind a neutral topic, for neither in his eyes nor in other features of his face nor in his posture could I discover the slightest trace of embarrassment, and he remained as poised, confident, cool as he had been on other occasions—or perhaps it would be more correct to say that after having been relieved of his fears by the kiss, he became his unreachable former self, which certainly did not mean he was unconcerned about or indifferent to what was happening to him; on the contrary, he was so open to each and every moment of his existence, always the very moment he was compelled to live in, that all past and possible future moments were forced out of him, so that he seemed to stand outside his own physical being, as if he were never really where one assumed him to be; but I forever remained a prisoner of what had already passed, and a single emphatic moment could arouse so much pain and passion in me that I had no time left in my being with which to create the next moment, and thus I, like him though in a different way, also remained somewhere outside; I could never keep up with him.

"I've no idea where," I mumbled listlessly, as if I'd just been awakened.

"Maybe they stay in the ground."

"In the ground?"

"I'd bet with some clever trap we could catch a whole brood."

Later, I must have opened the door calmly, without rushing, and most likely did not let my schoolbag drop as usual, hitting the floor with a thud, and the door didn't bang shut behind me, so people in the house had no way of knowing I was home; I didn't run up the polished oak stairs leading to the foyer, though I was not conscious of this alteration, of the skipped routine, and had absolutely no inkling that from now on I'd move about more quietly and cautiously, would slow down and become even more introspective, but of course that could not keep me from noticing everything going on around me, indeed from seeing everything even more keenly, only from the perspective of indifference; the dining room's glass double door was wide open, and from the faint clinking of dishes I could tell I was late, lunch was nearly over, though this didn't bother me at all, because it was nice and dark in the foyer, pleasantly warm, only a little afternoon light seeping through the opalescent panels of the front door, now and then the radiator giving out a scraping, bubbling sound, followed always by an echoing, metallic clang of the pipes; I must have stood there a long time, in the heavy smell of freshly fried beef patties, and could even see myself in the old full-length mirror, though at the moment the purple reflection of the rug was more important to me than that of my face or body, the black outlines of which faded gently into the mirror's silvery gleam.

I understood well—why wouldn't I—that by mentioning the trapping of rabbits he was raising the possibility of some joint undertaking, and I also sensed that, if he was expecting an answer, he was waiting for me to pull myself together, to revert to the customary norms of our relationship, to come up with a workable idea about what to do together—it could be anything at all, no need to insist on those stupid rabbits, any joint venture requiring strength and skill and therefore manly; but I found this possibility, offered to me with patient chivalry, much too simplistic and somewhat ludicrous, in view of what had just happened between us, not only because it no longer suited our age but also because its very childishness betrayed an idea born of defensive haste, aimed at ignoring what had just transpired; in short, it was a cover-up, an evasion, a diverting of emotions, though still a more sensible solution than anything I could have come up with in the circumstances; but at that moment, in that situation, the last thing I wanted was to be sensible; the joy of having been released, unbound, was pouring out of me like a stream of some tangible substance, something emanating from my body, rippling forward, seeking him out, and I had no other wish in the world than to remain in this state, the body yielding fully to everything that was instinctive, sensual, and emotional in it, losing as much of its weight and mass as was displaced by the liberated energies, indeed ceasing to be the body which we feel as a burden; I wanted to preserve this state and extend it to all my future moments; I wanted to break down all the barriers, the forces of habit, education, decorum, everything that robbed us of ordinary moments by preventing us from communicating the most profound truths of our being to others, until it is no longer we who existed in time but time that existed in our stead, vacuous, efficient; trying mulishly to preserve myself for this moment, unable to address him in anything resembling a normal, everyday voice, I had to feel that nothing I was going through could possibly reach him, though he had to marshal every bit of his apparently quite humane psychological skills to remain so calm and patient at the sight of such unbridled longing; he appeared to be a smooth, blank wall impassively deflecting and hurling back everything emanating from me in his direction, with the result that it was I, not he, who was surrounded by this emanation; I was encased in a shell, and I also felt that this shell and I were one; though I might quite pleasantly float around in it, I knew that one careless move and it would disintegrate, one emphatic word and everything that had erupted from the body would dissolve into thin air, as our breaths did; he was looking at me, straight into my eyes, and indeed we saw nothing but each other's eyes, yet he was becoming more and more distant, while I stayed where I was, because I wanted to stay where I was, and as I was, since only in this insanely defenseless state could I perceive my true self; I might say that there, and in this way, I felt for the first time the grandeur, beauty, and peril of the senses raging within me; this was the real me, not the uncertain outline the mirror may have shown as my face or body, but this; I could not help noticing his growing remoteness—first, the fleeting shock which, despite his good intentions and self-discipline, made its mark on his face, and then the tiny, childishly conceited smile with which, having overcome the gentle shock, he managed to move so far away that he could even afford to glance back at me curiously, and do it with a measure of compassion; but I said nothing, I made no move; for me, existence reached its perfect fulfillment in this wordless state, and I was so important to myself that nothing seemed to bother me, not even the disappearance of the last trace of smile, when silence once again became acutely perceptible and we could hear the woods, magpies, a creaking branch in the distance, a stream rushing over sharp stones, our own breathing.

"Come over later," he said, his voice a little higher and thinner, which meant a great many very contradictory things at once; the unnatural intonation seemed more important than the meaning of the words, suggesting that he was ill at ease, that nothing was as simple as he would have liked to believe, and that no matter how far he had managed to get away from me with his glance, I still had a hold on him, my very silence forcing him to make the kind of concession he otherwise wouldn't have dreamed of making, and also implying that our reconciliation could not be taken seriously, that therefore I shouldn't even think of accepting his vague invitation, in fact should consider it a polite warning that I had no more right to set foot in his house now than I had had before; but the words had been uttered, and they referred to an earlier afternoon when his mother had been shouting from the window and I was holding two walnuts in my hands.

"Krisztián! Krisztián, where are you? Krisztián, why must I keep screaming? Krisztián!"

It was autumn, we were standing under the walnut tree, the garden was glowing yellow and red in the twilight heavy with mist, and he was holding a large flat stone which a moment earlier he had used for cracking walnuts, but because he hadn't even left himself enough time to straighten up, I couldn't be sure if the next moment he wasn't going to bash my head in.

"You people haven't managed to steal our house yet, you got that? And as long as the house is ours, I will kindly ask you not to set foot in it ever again, you got that?"

There was nothing funny about what he said, yet I laughed.

"You were the ones who stole this precious house of yours, from the people you used to live off; it's no sin to steal back from a thief; and that's what you people are, you are the thieves!"

Some time had passed while we weighed the consequences of our words, but no matter how deliciously pleasurable it had been to say them, it was clear from his anger and my calm though abstract satisfaction that all this was nothing but revenge, a reprisal for barely noticeable injuries that had accumulated in us during our brief but all the more passionate and stormy friendship; for months we had spent just about every hour of the day in each other's company, and it was my curiosity that had helped me push past the glaring inequalities between us; so our quarrel was the inevitable reverse of our intimacy, but, plausible explanations notwithstanding, this unexpected outburst took both of us so far afield that turning back was impossible; and as improbable as it may have seemed, I had to drop the two walnuts I was holding and hear them plop down on the wet leaves while his mother went on shouting, calling him, and I started for the gate, quite pleased with myself, as if I had settled something once and for all.

He looked straight into my eyes and waited.

But that final attempt, that ambiguously phrased last sentence, also distanced me from the moment which otherwise I could not and would not want to leave; I had to sense the growing distance not only through his eyes but in myself as well, even if his evasive invitation had no stronger an impact than a fleeting memory does, a sudden flash, no more, a mercurial fish which, thrusting itself above the motionless surface of the moment, takes one breath in the strange environment and, leaving a few quickly subsiding ripples in its wake, sinks back into the world of silence; still, that sentence was a reminder, marked out a turning point, emphatic and compelling enough to be a warning that what was happening to us now was but the consequence of a previous occurrence and would have as much to do with events yet to happen as with those that had occurred earlier; no matter how much I yearned or insisted, it was absurd to think I could remain in the moment that gave me such joy, such pleasure, even happiness; the mere fact that I was forced to experience the quick passing and disappearance of my happiness indicated that, though I may have thought I was bound to it, in truth I was no longer there, had already stepped out of it, and am only now thinking about it; yet I could not answer him, though his posture still suggested a willingness to accept a reply, and at this point I would have liked to, since I thought I could not go on without replying; and he was standing there as if he were about to take the first step, but then, flinging his schoolbag over his shoulders, he suddenly turned around and started for the bushes, going back in the same direction, toward the same spot whence he had first appeared.

A Telegram Arrives

My progress was far from steady—each new gust of wind forced me to stop, and it was all I could do to stay upright while waiting for it to subside—so it must have taken me a good half hour of pressing forward on the embankment before I realized that something had changed ominously.

The wind wasn't blowing straight at me but at a slant off the sea, which I countered by moving sideways, head and shoulders thrust into the wind, at the same time using my upturned coat collar to shield as much of my face as I could from the spray sent up by waves crashing on the rocks, though I still had to keep wiping my forehead, where the spray collected into drops and the drops, heavy with salt, formed into rivulets that gushed into my eyes and down my nose into my mouth; I might as well have closed my eyes, for I couldn't see anything, yet I did want to see the dark, as if seeing this particular darkness gave some sense to the otherwise senseless act of keeping them open; at first, only translucent gray splotches and thin strips of wispy clouds rushed past the moon, coming offshore and racing over the open waters on their way to a destination hidden in infinity, their haste, for all the graceful grandeur of their movement, made positively laughable by the impassive calm of the moon; when more massive clouds appeared, denser and thicker but no less agile, it was as if a single projector on a giant stage had been blocked by scenery, and it grew dark, completely dark, the waters had nothing to reflect, and there were no more white streaks drawn in the distance by white foamy crests;

but then, just as quickly, it all turned light again, and then dark again, dark and light, always unexpectedly and unaccountably, dark and light and then darkening again; it's no accident that I've mentioned the stage— there was something theatrical, indeed dramatic, in the peculiar phenomenon of the wind above driving the clouds in exactly the opposite direction it was compelled to be blowing down here, a tension between the desires of heaven and earth—but the tension lasted only until some decisive turn occurred in the seemingly unalterable course of events on high—who knows what it was? perhaps the wind changing direction somewhere or, above the waters, getting entangled in the piled-up clouds, turning them into rain and dashing them into the ocean—and then the spells of light grew shorter, those of darkness grew longer, until, abandoning earth and water to their own darkness, the moon vanished altogether.

I could no longer see where I was going.

This way the game seemed even more exciting, for in the meantime, forgetting my fears, I had taken what is usually called the raging of the elements to be a game that embodied or substituted for the opposing forces struggling inside me, and with my own feelings thus projected into a living metaphor, I could pretend to feel secure, as if everything I witnessed were but a delightful spectacle of illusions put on solely for my amusement.

I admit, it was a pretty piece of self-deception on my part, but why shouldn't I have imagined myself to have the major role in this majestically grandiose hurricane when, in fact, for weeks I had been able to think of nothing but that I must put a violent end to my life; what could have been more reassuring now than to see this raging world locked into its own darkness, for all its destructive energies unable not only to extinguish itself but even to harm itself, with no real power over itself, just as I had none over my own self.

Recollecting the previous night, the night before my departure, the night of that certain yesterday—I hasten to emphasize this, because my encounter with the sea shifted the temporal dimension of all my previous experiences into such a soothing perspective that I would not have been at all surprised if someone had told me, "Oh no, you're quite wrong, you arrived not this afternoon but two weeks, nay, two years ago"—I must reassure myself that very little time had elapsed between my departure from Berlin and that stroll on the beach, and though this does not mean that the pleasant confusion about time could untangle my snarled emotions, the sight of the stormy sea in the night did provide a haven in which I could reflect on what had happened; so I thought of that previous night, now fading into a gentle distance, of arriving home at not too late an hour and in the dark stairway—they still hadn't repaired the lights—fumbling so long with my keys that of course Frau Kühnert, always in the kitchen at that hour, fixing her husband's sandwich for the next day, pricked up her ears; alarmed at hearing her hurrying down the long hallway, I still could not fit the key into the lock, and she stopped for a second, but then, beating me to it, threw the door wide-open and, holding a green envelope in her hand, smiled at me as if she had been long preparing to welcome me, as if she'd been waiting for this very moment, and before I had a chance to step inside, say good evening, and thank her for her trouble, she handed me the envelope, blushing as she did so; and at that instant, thanks to the ludicrous protection which the proximity of the sea raging in that starless night may have given me, I ceased to feel the faintness, bordering on loss of consciousness, which had gripped me while I was standing in the doorway and which had not left me until now; I was even amused, because the scene of my taking the envelope from a shouting Frau Kühnert registered as an overly sharp, totally unfamiliar picture.

"Telegram, my friend, you've got a telegram, a telegram!"

If at that moment I had not glanced at her rather than at the telegram—one automatically glances at anything thrust into one's hand—I might have failed to notice how strange and unusual her smile was, not that she hadn't smiled on other occasions, but with this smile she was trying to conceal her eagerness, an insatiable curiosity which despite all her theatrical experience she could not conceal; the moment the telegram reached my hand—suppressing my emotions I barely glanced at the name and address—I looked at her again, but the smile had vanished: from behind her thin, gold-rimmed glasses, her huge eyes, bulging morbidly from their sockets, seemed to be fixed on one point, my mouth, which she stared at intently and sternly, as if expecting to hear a long-delayed, thorough confession; an expression, maybe not of raw hatred, but of compassionless scrutiny, spread over her face; she wanted to see how I would react to what had to be shocking, though to her incomprehensible, news, and I had the feeling that she had already read the telegram, and felt myself growing pale, at that moment overcome by terrible faintness, though the very thought of giving myself away made me go on controlling myself, because I knew that whatever the telegram said, wherever it came from, this woman already knew or meant to find out too much about me for me to stay here; there was nothing I would more strenuously guard against than someone trying to pry into my life, so in other words, not only was I facing some sort of blow, which I had to endure with dignity, but I also had to find a new place to live.

Frau Kühnert was an astonishingly, fascinatingly ugly woman: tall and bony, with broad shoulders, from the back, especially when wearing pants, she looked very much like a man, because not only did she have long arms and big feet but her backside was as flat as an old clerk's; her hair, which she cut and bleached herself, was combed straight back, which became her but hardly made her look more feminine; her ugliness was so pronounced that it could not be mitigated even by the cunning placement of light sources in the old-fashioned, spacious apartment: during the day the sun was blocked out and heavy velvet drapes covering the lace curtains created a glimmering semidarkness; in the evening, light was provided by floor lamps with dark silk shades and wall fixtures whose glow was dimmed by little caps made of stiff waxed paper; because the chandeliers were never turned on, Professor Kühnert was forced to adopt rather peculiar work habits: he was a short man, at least a head shorter than his wife, and in build her total opposite, almost feature for feature: thin-boned, fragile, and delicate, his skin so translucently white that one could see pulsating purple blood vessels pressing against it on his temple, neck, and hands; his eyes were small, deep-set, and as insignificant and expressionless as his quietly unobtrusive way of doing his scholarly work in his poorly lit study—work that, by the way, many people judged quite significant—for there was no lamp on his huge black desk, either, and whenever Frau Kühnert called me to the telephone, I could see him rummaging with his long, thin fingers, like a blind man, among piles of newspapers, notes, and books until, by touch alone, he would identify the sought-after piece of paper, pick it out, take it across the room, past the bluish glare of the TV screen, stop under one of the small wall lamps, placed rather high up, and under its pale yellow light begin to read— sometimes leaning against the wall, which I could tell had become a habit with him, because during the day a spot, traces of regular contact left by his head and shoulders, was clearly visible on the yellow wallpaper—until, spurred on by an unexpected idea or simply by protracted brooding, he would interrupt his peaceful reading and return to his desk by the same route to jot something down; Frau Kühnert, enthroned in her comfortable armchair, seemed as unaware of the professor's repeated crossings before the television screen as the professor seemed undisturbed by the incoherent noises emanating from it or by the perpetual dimness of the apartment; I never heard them exchange a single word, though their silence did not seem to be the result of some petty, calculating revenge, and what had turned them mute to each other was not resentment—flaunted conspicuously yet indicating a very fervent attachment between man and wife, the kind of silence which rancorous couples often give as a present to each other in order to extort something—no, their silence had no express purpose, but it is possible that a slowly cooling mutual hatred had stiffened them into this neutral state, although nothing seemed to allude to its cause, since they appeared perfectly content and well-adjusted, behaving in each other's presence like two wild animals of different species, acknowledging each other's presence, but also acknowledging that the laws of the species were far stronger than the laws of the sexes, and since each could be neither a mate nor a prey, communication was also impossible.

There I was, watching Frau Kühnert's face with a certain resignation, in spite of my emotional state, for I knew from experience that I couldn't get rid of her easily, since the more I tried, the louder and more insistent she'd become; I kept on looking in her eyes and decided to suffer this one skirmish, since it would be the last; black-stemmed, bleached-blond hairs like brush bristles poked out of the fleshy welts of her low brow—my fingers were telling me the envelope was open—her nose was long and narrow, her lipstick cracked, and of course it was unavoidable that my glance would stray farther down to her breasts, the only part of her body that offered some compensation for so much ugliness: huge, disproportionately large breasts which, without a brassiere, might be somewhat disappointing, but the nipples pressing hard against the tight sweater were certainly no deception; as we were standing in the door of the almost totally dark hallway—at the same moment she began shouting again and Professor Kühnert emerged from the living room, with his white shirt opened to his waist (he always wore white shirts, and when reading or taking notes he would first yank off his tie, then slowly unbutton his shirt so he could stroke his youthfully hairless chest while pacing and ruminating) for he was going to bed.

At first, of course, the change did not appear to be very significant, even if there were some conspicuously unpleasant signs; if until now I had been able to proceed in the dark with total confidence because I felt the same, slightly slippery ground under my feet and, even without seeing anything, could hear the roar and crash of the waves from about the same distance, and feel about the same amount of salty spray on my skin, thus

being free to enjoy the tempest as well as give myself over to my fantasizing and recollecting, all I had to do now was to make sure I stayed on
course, not stray from the embankment, to accomplish which the sense of
direction possessed by my feet proved sufficient, with a little help from
the foamy waves; but then, while waiting for a fierce gust to subside, a
wave struck me in the face—which in itself wouldn't have been too serious, because I didn't get all that much water down my neck and, though
the water was certainly not warm, my coat wasn't soaked through either,
and actually, it was all rather amusing, and if the wind hadn't kept me
from opening my mouth, I probably would have laughed out loud—then
at that very same instant I was struck again, harder this time, and that
did make me lose confidence.

My guess was that until now I must have been walking in the middle
of the embankment, but now, having waited in vain for the wind to
subside, I edged toward its inner side, more protected from the sea, there
to attempt to proceed, but the attempt failed, not only because the wind
wouldn't let me and would have swept me away if I had given in to it,
but also because after taking just a few steps in that direction I thought
I had gotten to the edge of the embankment, with its sharp and extremely
large stones; nothing to be done here, I realized—the embankment was
narrower than I had thought, and it could not protect me from the
waves—but even so, I did not do what might have been sensible in the
circumstances: it didn't even occur to me to turn back, since I knew from
the guidebook that even at high tide the water here rose only twelve
centimeters, and that, I figured, could not be fatal, so I had simply reached
a dangerous stretch, I told myself, the embankment probably curved here,
that's why it was narrower, or for some reason dropped down, and if I
just got past this dangerous bit, I would soon see the unfamiliar lights of
Nienhagen and be safe again.

Suddenly the wind died down.

Still, I can't say I harbored any resentment toward Frau Kühnert; of
course she wasn't talking so unbearably loudly because she was angry:
even if our relationship had become unusually close over the last few
weeks, I was always careful to maintain a proper distance, which, I believe,
would have made it impossible for her to display so openly any feelings
or emotions, if indeed she had them; the truth was, she couldn't speak
quietly.

She seemed unaware of any intermediary tone between complete silence
and unrestrained shouting, a unique trait—what else could it be called—

that probably had as much to do with the tragic relationship between her and her husband, with whom she did not speak at all, as with the fact that she worked as a prompter in the Volkstheater, one of the most prestigious theaters in the city: in other words, she made her living by holding back an otherwise very pleasant, full-bodied, well-articulated voice, which nonetheless retained enough power to reach and be clearly understood in the farthest corners of the stage: no doubt about it, it was her voice that defined her life, and her ugliness was merely a rather comic addition, which I don't think she was fully aware of, since to her only her voice mattered, though she could seldom use it in its natural, normal range.

I myself had several occasions to witness how this voice could be the source of unpleasantness and how it could secure a very special place for its owner: we spent many a morning sitting next to each other on the raised platform built for the director in the theater's improbably vast rehearsal hall—it reminded one of a riding school or, better yet, an industrial assembly floor—and whenever a disagreement, a seemingly unresolvable situation, created tension and, trying to justify themselves, everyone began speaking at once, the noise level rose as rapidly as mercury in a thermometer when one has a high fever; adding to the noise, the bored stagehands, high-strung extras, wardrobe and lighting crew members were ready to use the chance to chat among themselves; at moments like these, Frau Kühnert was always the first to be admonished by some nervous actress: "Sieglinde, couldn't you say that louder?" or an overeager assistant director might tell her rudely to keep her mouth shut, this was not a kaffeeklatch, he had a good mind to throw her out . . . and only then would he add what really mattered to everybody, that he wanted quiet, and Frau Kühnert's face would betray such genuine surprise, like that of a little boy who in blissful innocence has been playing with his weenie under the bushes and suddenly discovers that grownups find this activity most objectionable, and she would act as if this was happening to her for the very first time, as if nothing even remotely similar had ever happened before: her bulging eyes could not open wider, her profound embarrassment was betrayed by a girlish flush that abruptly darkened her complexion from neck to forehead, beads of perspiration would form above her mouth, which she'd wipe off cautiously, looking abashed; let's admit it—no one can get used to being continually attacked for something so basic to their makeup, and these irritable admonitions, these undeserved, rude words implied not only that her voice could be heard above the loudest din, representing and symbolizing it, as it were, but also that it carried explosive passion of such elemental force that it offended the ear, a voice that was embarrassing in all its unintended shamelessness, in a certain sense, the way it exposed people; she managed to embarrass me, too, in fact, when in the doorway she handed me the envelope as her skin turned crimson, for in view of our relationship nothing could account for either her blushing or her shouting.

But that was precisely the difficult thing to do: to escape from the effects of this apparently shameless and inexplicable intrusion, to evade it somehow; her very first sentence was much more than a simple announcement—true, however great the volume of her voice (and it did resound throughout the house), all she said was that I had gotten a telegram, but that one declarative sentence was punctuated by intense loud panting, giving the sentence many rhythmic thrusts, and because I couldn't easily remain indifferent to so much excitement, I naturally assumed the very emotional state she meant to pass on to me; no matter how hard I tried to control myself, no matter how dark it was in the stairway and foyer, she had to sense and see my agitation; with her hand still on the door handle, and tilting her head slightly to the side, she even smiled a little, which she could afford to do, because with her second sentence her voice changed and, not without irony, she pounced on me:

"But where the devil have you been so long, my dear sir?"

"Excuse me . . . ?"

"It's been at least three hours since this telegram arrived. If you hadn't come home, I wouldn't have been able to sleep again."

"I was at the theater."

"In that case you should've been home an hour ago. Don't worry, I've figured it out."

"But what happened?"

"What happened? How should I know what's been happening with you. Will you come on in already!"

And when, wavering between indifference (how I yearned for it!), agitation, and fear, but determined to end the conversation, I could at last step into the hallway, Frau Kühnert closed the door behind me but, still staring at the envelope in my hand, wouldn't let me pass, and Professor Kühnert looked back before disappearing down the long corridor that led to their bedroom and nodded a greeting in my direction, which of course I couldn't return, partly because despite my effort to be demonstratively strong and aloof, I was preoccupied with the change taking place in Frau Kühnert's face and partly because he turned away, not really expecting me to return his greeting; I found nothing unusual in this, since he rarely acknowledged my presence; and not only did Frau Kühnert's facial expression go on changing with each passing moment but her entire bearing seemed to signal that she was preparing herself for a wholly new and to me unfamiliar outburst, not one from her usual repertory, and having breached all the old limits she now would not only reveal a new side of her character but also render me completely defenseless and, though I couldn't then have known it, would literally push me into a corner: with her lips trembling, she whipped off her glasses, which made her eyes look even more terrifying, then arched her back by pulling up her shoulders, as if she had sensed my straying glance of a moment ago and felt a need to protect her huge breasts; I made a last, desperate attempt to free myself, but it only made things worse: casting aside all pretense of politeness or good manners, I tried to slip away; I moved sideways, seeking the protection of the wall, but she simply stepped in front of me and pushed me up against it.

"Just what do you think you're doing, my dear sir? You think you can just come and go as you please and do your smutty little things, is that what you think? I haven't slept for days. I can't stand it anymore. And I don't want to! Who are you, anyway? What do you want here? And where do you get the nerve, after all these months, to pretend I'm nothing but air? Go on, tell me! It's not your fault I know everything about you; you can't help that, but nobody can expect me to keep my mouth shut forever. And I do know everything, everything, it's no use being so mysterious, I know all about you. But may I remind you, dear sir, that I'm a human being, too, and I want to hear it said, I want to hear it from your lips. I suffer because of you. I'm afraid to look at you. You had me fooled: I thought you were good and kind, but the truth is, you are cruel, horribly cruel, do you hear? I'd be most grateful if you people told me what you were up to. You want the police after me, is that it? Don't I have enough problems as it is, without you people? Yes, I want to know what's going on. You have some nerve to ask me what happened when it's I who want to know just what's going on, and what happened to him. The least you can do is tell me, so I can prepare myself for the worst. And don't act like I was your maid, who must take whatever you feel like dishing out. Did you have a mother? Do you still? Has anybody ever loved you? Do you really think we need the money you pay us? Your lousy money is just what I need. I thought I was taking in a good friend. But will you please tell me just what it is you do? What do you do besides ruin everybody, turn other people's lives upside down, is that what you occupy yourself with all day? Some occupation, I must say. But what is your occupation? When can I expect the police? Maybe you killed him. Well, did you? I wouldn't put it past you, so help me, you with your innocent blue eyes and polite little smile. Why, even now you act as if you didn't know anything and I was just a raving lunatic. Where did you bury him, huh? Now that I've found out about you, all I ask is that you get your things and get out. Go wherever you like. To a hotel. I am not running a criminals' hangout, you know. I don't want to get mixed up in anything. I've been scared long enough. When a telegram comes I get the shivers. When I hear the doorbell I get sick, do you understand? Haven't you noticed I'm an ill and tortured person who needs a little consideration? Didn't I confide in you, fool that I am, trust you enough, you of all people, to tell you my life story? And what about *my* goodness, *my* kindness, doesn't anybody want that? I'm asking you. Am I here only to be used by everybody? Why don't you answer me? As if I was some hole for everybody to toss their garbage in. Answer me, goddamn it! What's in that telegram?"

"But you've read it already! Haven't you?"

"Well, look at it."

"What do you want from me? That's what I'd like to know!"

We were standing quite close, and in the sudden silence, perhaps because of this closeness, her face seemed to relax, became almost translucently delicate, grew larger and even pretty in a sense, as if her irregular and ill-proportioned features had been held together only by the rigid frame of her glasses and her suppressed desires, and now that she had taken off her mask, her face was freed and regained its natural proportions; against her white skin the reddish freckles became more pronounced, decidedly charming, her thick lips seemed more expressive, her dense eyebrows more striking, and when she spoke again, much more softly than before, in her pleasantly penetrating prompter's voice, I surprised myself by thinking that, no matter how disheveled, distraught, and washed-out she might look, especially without her glasses, beauty might be nothing but the proximity of utter nakedness, the enthralling sensation of closeness; I wouldn't have been surprised if I had leaned over and unexpectedly kissed her on the lips, just so as not to see her eyes anymore.

"What could I possibly want from you, my dear sir? What do you think I would want? Could it be that I want to be loved, not a lot, just a very little? oh, not that way, don't get scared, though at first, yes, I was in love with you a little, you may have even felt it, and I can admit it now because it's over, but don't leave now, I don't want you to, you mustn't take seriously what I said before, it was silly, I take it back, you mustn't leave us; I do get scared, you see, please forgive me, but I am so very much alone and always fear that something unpredictable may happen, something dreadful, that some terrible disaster is approaching, so I don't want anything except that you read the telegram here, in front of me, because I'd like to know what happened, that's all I want you to tell me, nothing else. I didn't open it, you should know that. It came in an open envelope, that's how telegrams are delivered here. But please, look at it already, I beg of you!"

"But you did read it, didn't you?"

"Please look at it."

As if to emphasize her words, she placed her hand on my arm, a little above the wrist, so gently but at the same time so peremptorily that it seemed to mean that she would not only take back the envelope but also eliminate the tiny distance still remaining between us and in some way— the way itself being of no consequence in that millisecond—to possess me; she touched me, and I did not have the strength to resist, in fact was struggling with a little guilt of my own, knowing that the stray glance at her breast and the thought of possibly kissing her could not have left her unaffected, for there is no thought, however furtive, that in highly charged situations is not detected by the other person, and for a split second, therefore, it seemed entirely possible that our heated exchange might take an unexpected and dangerous turn, all the more so because not only could I not move or, by turning my head away, escape the gentle thrusts of her breath and her fixed stare, but also, against my will, I was becoming aware of the telltale signs of sexual excitement—so pleasurable but in the circumstances somewhat humiliating: mild tingling of the skin, dwindling lucidity of the mind, pressure in the groin, and faltering breath, all of which could have been the direct consequence of that one touch, occurring almost independently of me but in a very edifying way proving that seduction can completely bypass the conscious mind and need not even be physical or flattering, for most often physical desire is not the cause but the consequence of a relationship—just as ugliness from a certain distance may be seen as beauty—when tension has increased to a point where only sexual release can offer hope, and at such moments a single touch is enough to defuse the almost unbearable psychological tension or release it into sheer sensual pleasure.

"No, I won't look at it!"

Perhaps she did not exclude the possibility that I might strike her, because, hearing my somewhat delayed and rather hysterically shouted retort, she quickly withdrew her hand, as it was clear to her that my outburst, which must have seemed quite unusual, had less to do with the mysterious business of the telegram than with our immediate physical proximity, and not satisfied with removing her hand, she also stepped back a little, at the same time pushing her glasses up on her nose, and regarded me with a sudden look of blunt sobriety, as if nothing at all had happened between us.

"I see. There's no need to shout."

"Tomorrow I'll be going away for a few days."

"Where to, may I ask?"

"It would be helpful if I didn't have to take all my things with me. By next week I'll be gone for good."

"But where will you go?"

"Home."

"You'll be missed."

I started toward my room.

"You go ahead, I'll be here, waiting by your door; I can't sleep anyway, not if you won't tell me."

I closed my door behind me: raindrops were pattering on the windowsill, it was nice and warm in the room, and on the wall the feeble light from a streetlamp swayed in tune to the nodding, shiny branches of the maple trees, so I didn't turn on the light, I took off my coat and walked to the window, there to open the envelope: I could hear her, she was there all right, outside the door, waiting.

But here below, though the wind was less, the surging sea would not be tamed, and up above the wind kept howling and whistling; now and then the sky seemed to brighten just a little, as if the wind had ripped and dispersed the clouds covering the moon, but I imagine this was as much a sensory illusion as was my hope that I would soon be past the dangerous part of the embankment; I literally could not see a thing, a condition my eyes perceived as a state of emergency and rebelled against, conjuring up nonexistent lights to lull their disbelief, and, as if claiming their own independence, resented having to look, and also resented my forcing them to look, even though there was nothing for them to perceive, and so they not only devised rings of light and sparkling dots and rays but several times illuminated the entire seascape before me: as if through a large, narrow slit, I could see clouds rushing above the foamy, tempestuous sea and myself walking on the wave-pounded embankment, but in a moment everything would go dark again, and I had to realize that this vivid image had been sheer hallucination, since no natural light source could possibly account for it—it couldn't have been the moon, whose light was not present in these images; yet these dazzling internal visions, sources of a peculiar internal pleasure, made me believe that somehow I could still feel out the path ahead of me, though in fact there was no longer any trail, my feet kept getting caught on stones, I was stumbling and slipping.

I think by then I must have lost all sense of time and space, presumably because the capricious wind, the impenetrable darkness, and the rolling sea, lullingly rhythmical for all its stark grandeur, were like some narcotic numbing me. If I said I was all ears, I'd not be wholly wrong, since every other mode of sensory perception was now useless; like some odd nocturnal creature, I was dependent only on my hearing: I heard the rumble not of the waters or the earth but of the depths, and it was neither threatening nor impassive, and though it may sound much too romantic, I'd venture to claim it was the monotone murmur of infinity I heard issuing from the depths, a sound like no other, evoking nothing but the idea of the depths: where the depths lay, or the depths of what, was impossible to determine, since the sound was everywhere—on the surface of the water and in the air as much as at the bottom of the sea, seeming to fill out and dominate everything, so that everything became part of the deep until the sound itself became visible: a slowly rising boom, like the mighty effort of a vile mass rising up into motion somewhere at a great distance, ready to break free, to rebel against the fateful calm of this seemingly infinite rumbling, kept drawing closer and closer at a measured but forceful pace until suddenly it reached its own peak, sounding in a triumphantly thunderous blast that no longer allowed the depths to be heard; it rose above the depths, content, its goal achieved: it had defeated, for a brief moment obliterated, the depths; but in the very next moment all that apparent force, mass, surge, and victory crumbled away and with an unpleasant crackle disintegrated among the rocks on the beach, and the rumble of the deep could be heard once more as if nothing had ever challenged its rule; and the wind was there again, capricious and sinister, whispering, whistling, screeching; it would be hard for me to say when and how that subtle change came about; I perceived it not only inasmuch as the embankment was becoming narrower and the waves could therefore sweep right over it, but mostly in that I could acknowledge those rather striking environmental changes only long after they had occurred, and even then somewhat thoughtlessly, as if they had nothing to do with me, as if I were hardly concerned that my shoes and pants were sopping wet and my coat was less and less water-resistant; I yielded so readily to the sounds of darkness that even the fantasizing and recollecting, with which I had kept myself amused at the beginning of my walk, were now gradually dissolving into these sounds; what we might call self-preservation was thus functioning only in a limited capacity, as when someone waking from a nightmare keeps kicking and screaming and flailing his arms, instead of reminding himself of the moment just before he fell asleep and of the fact that what he is being forced to experience so painfully is real only in a dream, and he cannot remind himself, precisely because he is dreaming; similarly, I was trying to protect myself, but the means were dictated by the given situation: what was the use of hiding among the rocks, groping helplessly, stumbling and sliding, the water found me there too, and it never occurred to me that what had started out as a pleasant evening stroll had ceased to be that quite some time ago.

Then something touched my face.

It was just as dark as before and the silence came to an end, something I could not really account for came to an end, and when that something touched my face again, I realized it was water, cold but not unpleasant, and I knew this should remind me of something, but I couldn't, simply couldn't remember what it was, even though I heard, once again I was beginning to hear its sounds, so some time must have elapsed since I had last heard it, but despite this it was still dark, nighttime, and everything was wet; and indeed, it was dark.

And at last I understood that I was lying among the rocks.

Sitting in God's Hand

But then Helene's appearance solved everything, or at least for a few wonderful moments our future, thought to be so ominous, seemed to turn captivatingly bright again.

The next morning I was standing in front of my desk, unwashed, unshaven, undressed, lost in thought, absently scratching my stubbly chin, unable to begin what in the end would turn out to be a fateful day; also, I was filled with tension, because the night before, after the exhausting round of farewell visits, I had fallen into a deep, dull, dreamless sleep and slept so late one might have thought that all was well, but this coma-like sleep had been the direct consequence of my latest lies, my constrained acquiescence in the intractability of my life, and after awaking, my conscience, slightly more relaxed, rested, and tentative, was returning ever more forcefully and disquietingly to its familiar haunts, and by then I was also in the grip of wanderlust, of a thrilling anticipation that makes you believe that by merely changing locale you can put behind you all that is tiresome, unpleasant, depressing, or insoluble; my luggage had already been put out in the entrance hall, waiting to be picked up by a porter; all I had left to do was to gather the notes and books I'd need for my work and slip them into the black patent-leather case that lay open in the middle of the room, on the carpet, but since my train wasn't leaving until late that afternoon, I had plenty of time for this critical last-minute chore, which, for various reasons, caused me no little anxiety; and to avoid accumulating more unpleasant feelings, I tried not to concentrate on the task at hand and let my thoughts wander aimlessly; while waiting and dawdling, I heard the distinctive knock of my landlady, good old Frau Hübner, whose habit it was not to wait for permission to enter but to barge right in; I could consider it a great feat of education that she no longer burst in without knocking when she had something urgent to tell me, for I had been unable simply to make her understand that, even if she was my landlady, it was customary not only to knock but also to wait for a reply before entering. "But what could the gentleman be doing when I know for sure that you are alone?" she had said, rolling her eyes in exasperation and smoothing the apron on her distended belly, the first time I put this request to her, in my politest manner too; but she proved to be otherwise such a helpful and kind person that, though utterly incapable of learning something even this trifling, she amused rather than annoyed me with her habit, but now the noise she made could in no way be called knocking, for she was pounding with her fists, and the door was torn open as if by a blast of wind: "A young lady is here, wearing a veil, and she is asking for you, the young lady is," she whispered breathlessly, and spacious as the outside hallway may have been, the visitor must also have heard her, because needless to say Frau Hübner failed to close the door behind her; "A young lady is here, and I think she is the gentleman's fiancée."

"Please show her in, Frau Hübner," I said stiffly, a bit louder than necessary, trying to make amends for her rudeness and hoping that the guest waiting in the hallway would hear these more polite words, although my appearance and dress at the moment made me totally unfit to receive a guest, least of all a lady; I couldn't imagine who this inappropriately early visitor might be, but soon thought of several disturbing possibilities: for a moment it even occurred to me (maybe that is why I didn't rush out to see for myself) that it was an emissary of my dearest friend turned deadliest enemy, here to carry out the promise to annihilate me, hiding a pistol in her fine fur muff—"Even fashion is on our side," my friend had said to me laughingly when women began wearing muffs, which did indeed increase opportunities for criminal activity, and I knew for a fact he was surrounded by so many loose women that it could have been easy enough to find one who'd do anything for him; maybe my visitor wasn't even a woman but one of his assistants dressed as a woman—and none of these assumptions could be so fanciful as to be untrue, because, knowing as I did all the means at his disposal, I couldn't help taking seriously my friend Claus Diestenweg's carefully considered promise, couldn't simply shrug it off, if only because from his standpoint I was in possession of discomfiting, incriminating evidence and thus a potential traitor to his cause: "You must die. We'll bide our time and come for you when the moment is ripe," he wrote in a letter not penned by his own hand, but what should have surprised me more was why he hadn't yet acted on his threat, why he'd decided to do it now, though it did occur to me that this uncertain reprieve might have been part of the punishment, which he meant to impose only after he had first allayed my fears and suspicions and made me believe he had finally let me go; I was like a hunted animal, hoping to escape by darting from the open field into the forest, not noticing the gun barrels concealed in the foliage; no wonder, then, that the beast too is perplexed, why is this happening now, on this peaceful autumn morning; the lack of suspicion is what makes this death terrible, for in different circumstances the end may have been accepted with equanimity; for several months I had also felt shielded by foliage, no longer so defenseless, and by changing addresses several times I hoped that finally I was beyond his dreaded reach and that in due course he would forget about me; indeed, after a time, the messages and letters stopped coming, and getting engaged not only had afforded me emotional relief but also enabled me to return to that sensible and civilized way of life I had broken away from for a few years, mainly because of my passionate attachment to Diestenweg; at the moment I had to grasp the back of my armchair to support myself against the impact of a single, unexpected, and dizzying thought: words said out loud can never be taken back—but then, I had no real desire to take anything back, because I didn't feel like pretending my past didn't belong to me; if I must die, I must, so be it, let it come, but let it come now, quickly, I'm ready; but nothing happened, and Frau Hübner didn't make a move either, as if she'd not only sensed but was actually experiencing the fear that had suddenly seized me; she stood petrified under the gently curving arch separating my room from the always dim hallway.

"My dear Frau Hübner, let's not keep the lady waiting, please, do show her in"—I repeated my request, more softly but more emphatically, evincing a presence of mind that came as a surprise even to me, and in spite of that fleeting terror, I managed to remain cool and objective, my voice keeping the required dignity; I felt what I was going through was nobody's business: but I could see it was hopeless, and for some incomprehensible reason, the unusual situation so paralyzed Frau Hübner that, though she had had ample opportunity to learn it from me, she couldn't perform the simple ceremony of showing the guest in and behaved as if the gun was really pointed at her; quickly pulling my robe together and, like one resolved to face whatever awaited him, I turned without delay to welcome my guest, whoever she might be.

In spite of this resolve, stepping from the sunlit room into the hallway's pleasant dimness, whence I could see the entrance hall through the open door, I had to stop and cry out, "Is it really you, Helene?" for seeing her in this drab, almost wretched, though for me more or less natural setting, suddenly made my poor landlady's stupefaction not only understandable but almost palpable, as if I'd gone through the same experiences as this hapless widow, who had not had many opportunities to behold such visions—for that's how Helene appeared, standing in the hall, like a vision, and in these dreary surroundings it seemed that even I couldn't have had much to do with such an affluent, angelically pure, exquisite yet fallible human being; she was wearing a silver-gray dress trimmed with lace which I hadn't seen before and which, according to the fashion of the day, most artfully concealed and at the same time cunningly emphasized her body's slim and shapely features, carefully not highlighting one to the detriment of another, which would have made her indecently conspicuous—the effect was created by the totality, whose excessive artificiality was offset by the naturalness of the underplayed details. She was standing with her head slightly bowed, a posture that immediately brought to mind those afternoons when she'd sat at the piano or leaned over the embroidery hoop, and her neck, emerging in startling nakedness from the high, closed collar of her dress, was made to appear acceptably chaste and covered simply by stray curly ringlets escaping from a carefully combed bun of hair gathered up at the back; yet she appeared more exciting now, and not only because the deep crimson ringlets accentuated the bareness of her neck—what fires our imagination is never mere nakedness, which only evokes a feeling of vulnerability, painful defenselessness, but everything that is almost covered or barely concealed, urging us, by its very suggestiveness, to lay it bare, implying always that we and only we are entitled to view and touch such a vulnerable body, that only to us does it surrender its nakedness, for only a mutual thrill of discovery and possession makes it possible to tolerate, indeed enjoy, whatever is coarsely natural; although I could not see her face—the huge rim of her hat cast a shadow over it and she hadn't lifted her veil—I could sense her embarrassment, and I was thoroughly embarrassed myself, partly because the surprise was simply too great, and partly because I was overwhelmed by the unexpected joy that rapidly replaced my initial fright; I knew I should speak first, sparing her the further embarrassment of having to talk in front of strangers, for in the meantime two uncombed, pale-faced young girls, Frau Hübner's granddaughter and a friend, had stuck their heads through the slightly open kitchen door and with utter amazement were gaping at the tableau presented by Helene, a tableau in which they, too, were now involuntary participants, yet I could not bring myself to speak, for whatever I might have said would have been too obviously intimate and emotional for utterance in public, so I could only extend my arm toward her, whereupon she grasped her long-handled, pointed umbrella with one gloved hand, lifted her train with the other, and, gliding almost silently, began to move toward me; "What's come over you, my dear?" I said—it may have sounded like a stifled cry—after I finally managed to dislodge Frau Hübner from her spot, and having closed the door, we were left to ourselves under the arch between my room and the dim hallway, "or is there something wrong? What happened? Speak to me, Helene, I'm most anxious to hear!"

But she took her time answering; we were standing very close, facing each other, the silence was becoming too long, I felt like tearing the veil off her hat, just tearing it off, and tearing off the hat, too, that so annoyingly covered her face; I wanted to see her face, ascertain the reason for her unexpected visit, though I had a fairly good idea; or perhaps what I really wanted was to tear the clothes off her body, to stop her from being so ridiculously alien to me; but as my excitement was aroused further by seeing her whole body tremble, I simply couldn't make a move that might seem common or coarse, didn't dare touch that blasted hat, because I wanted to spare her; "I know, I know very well I shouldn't have done this," she whispered from behind her veil, and in our excitement we nearly brushed against each other, though both she and I made sure we didn't, "still, I couldn't make myself not come, it will take only a moment, my carriage is waiting downstairs, and I'd be so ashamed if I told you my true reason for coming! It's your eyes I wanted to see, Thomas, your eyes, and now that I've said it, I no longer feel ashamed; because last night, after you left, I couldn't remember your eyes; please don't turn away, and don't despise me for asking, do look at me; now I can see your eyes, good; all last night I couldn't remember them."

"But you seemed to understand what I tried to tell you."

"Oh, please, don't misunderstand me! I knew you would misunderstand. I don't want to hold you back. Go."

"But now how could I?"

"Now you will feel even better about going."

"Why are you being so cruel to me?"

"Let's not say anything, then."

"You are driving me insane. I am madly in love with you, Helene, now more than ever before, which makes me feel I haven't loved you enough, but now, by saying what you've said, by coming here, you are driving me out of my mind, and I can't express myself; I am being ridiculous, but you should know that you are saving my life, though that's not why I love you; and I'd really like to destroy all my notes, rip up all my books."

"Be quiet."

"I can't be quiet, but I can't find anything to say, either. With my teeth I'll rip apart all my writing, all my papers."

"All I wanted was to see your eyes and say your name, Thomas; I must always say your name; now that I have, I can go, and you should, too."

"Don't go."

"I must."

"My dearest."

"We must be reasonable."

"I'd like to see your hair. Your neck. I'm going to sink my fingers into your hair, grab you by your hair and pull so hard you'll scream."

"Do be quiet."

"I'm going to kill you." And this last sentence, uttered as she whipped off her hat and veil, came out with such conviction that my voice, hoarse with excitement, actually deepened, for those words, said in total ecstasy, seemed to hit upon the secret wish, the well-concealed desire, the very emotion that until then I'd been unaware of yet did not seem so new, after all; it was as if I had felt this wish all along, that and nothing else, as if all my endeavors had been fueled by the desire to kill her, and for this reason the sentence itself, and the emphasis I'd given it, sounded startlingly honest; though coming from me—especially since I who, let's not mince words, was the son of a murderer, a common ravisher—the sentence could not have sounded entirely innocuous, could not have been considered an empty phrase of love, at least not by me, for after a long and troublesome period of my life, I had experienced for the first time, in my own fingers, the urge that would explain to me Father's hitherto inexplicable and abhorrent deed; yes, it was like a new insight, unexpected and none too pleasant, felt for a mere fraction of a second, during which I could almost step outside myself and contemplate my own profoundest desires, which were similar to what Father in his time had acted on; this was like the shattering discovery that a tree's roots exposed to the light of day reflect the impressive shape of its leafy crown; at this moment I was very much in love with the creature standing before me and trembling helplessly; I felt I was quite beyond those carnal desires that entice our loftier sentiments with the promise of temporary gratification, or, I should say, I thought I was beyond them, if only because in the circumstances, until our wedding day, I knew I was not even to think about such things, I was to put them out of my mind, but just the same, I would have loved to wrap my fingers around her neck and tighten them until I squeezed every last breath out of this long-admired neck.

Except that in that sentence she could not discern her fate—just as Mother could not discern hers on that certain afternoon long ago—and therefore did not think she ought to take seriously what was in fact serious; if anything, the earnest resolve Helene may have sensed in my voice only served to intensify her fervor: "Here I am, take me," she whispered in reply, and laughed; and it was like seeing her for the first time, her lips were so full and moist and ripe; "You dirty little slut," I whispered back into her mouth, before touching it with my tongue; I was somewhat bothered by not having performed my morning toilette, I hadn't even rinsed my mouth, but I kept it up: "You little bitch, you whore, you dare talk like this before our wedding?" and I laughed with her, too, for these words, uttered not quite involuntarily, did not seem to surprise or scandalize her, and though my breath may have been unpleasant, it proved to be another source of pleasure, she now fully opened her mouth into mine, and I derived not just physical pleasure but a terrific mental satisfaction from hearing these coarse words, as if I were stepping over my father's body, daring to say out loud what he had so tragically suppressed.

It was such a joy, certainly one of the greatest joys I have ever experienced, for though I was grasping her neck with both hands (when and how they got there I couldn't tell), the fear, feeding on uncanny resemblances and echoes, as well as hate and anger implicit in our relationship, which induced so much shame and guilt and prevented me from enjoying the moment at hand, always reminding me of something old and familiar—all these feelings simply vanished, disappeared without a trace; I wanted simply to devour that lovely mouth and have that mouth engulf my body with its kisses. I did not dare hold her tight, because my light robe and silk pajamas would not keep down my powerful erection; my hands became an instrument of tenderness whose sole aim was to nestle her head in the gentlest, most comfortable position possible; her mouth transformed the force of my hatred into that of possession; fingers no longer wanted to squeeze and choke but to raise up, to make it easy for her to kiss and to explore with her tongue; though my consciousness tried to maintain control over itself, I couldn't say just when I closed my eyes or when she wrapped her arms around my neck, as if two dark orbs were flowing, sliding wetly into each other; still, a vestige of fear ran through me, attributable perhaps more to jealousy, since I didn't understand how she could kiss like an experienced lover, and at the same time I sensed that this was not experience at all but what she was giving me was the purest of instincts, and her purity affected me more than any experience possibly could; I was the one who, relying on my experience in love, wouldn't allow myself to yield to her fully; cunningly, and with a certain superiority, I merely tolerated her explorations and advances without really kissing her back; by unexpectedly and deliberately delaying my responses, by surprising her lips and her teeth with the tip of my tongue, or by actually obstructing the path of her tongue, I was enjoying her confusion and arousing further her desire for us to merge into one; what I really wanted was for her to abandon the last retreats of her modesty and shame and be totally at my mercy, which we both needed then—all the more so because the sober part of my consciousness had to realize that neither of us could stop or delay the chain of events without some risk; we would have to cope with the lengthy, intricate act of undressing, which would require all the reserves of skill and delicacy I still possessed, and the embarrassment of fumbling with buttons and strings and hooks would become a delicious new source of pleasure, a titillating memory only later, after the two naked bodies had already become one.

I may have planned out my every move, skillfully, sensibly, but there came a moment when I lost all my good sense, and now that I'm long past such matters and try to recall the events of that sunny morning with the detachment of an analyst observing his own activities, I realize that at this very juncture I run into the impassable barriers to free expression and have to crack that stone wall with my skull; and it's by no means modesty alone, obligatory and thus in many ways quite laughable, that makes my undertaking questionable: though it's not easy to call by their name the things that in daily life have their overused and hackneyed appellations, these words, denoting certain organs, functions, and motions, for all their spicy, down-to-earth vitality and expressiveness, cannot be used to describe my experiences, and not because I'd be afraid to transgress against bourgeois propriety—I couldn't care less about that; my task here is to give an account of my life, and middle-class decorum can be only the framework for such a life; if for this final reckoning I wish to chart as precisely as possible the map of my life's emotional events, then I should be able to spread out before me my own body, and no amount of squeamishness should hold me back from scrutinizing it in all its nakedness, just as it would be ludicrous to tell the coroner not to remove the sheet covering the body on his table; in other words, I should be able to remove my robe and pajamas and her fussily beautiful dress here and now, just as I did then and there, while naming every gesture and emotion in the process; but after some reflection, I must say that to use common words to describe the so-called immodest parts of the body—and, since we are talking about a living body and its quite natural functions—would be as ridiculous and false as it would be to change the subject politely; to demonstrate the true dimensions of the problem and the difficulty of finding a solution, if I were to ask myself the question as a kind of test: "So tell me, my dear, on that sunny morning, did you finally fuck your fiancée?" I could answer in the affirmative, but that would be no less a deceptive oversimplification or generalization as it would be to say nothing, because this word of affirmation would help to gloss over crucial details, just as silence would; yet narcissistic curiosity, interested only in details concealed and deemed unworthy of attention, finds it difficult to form a clear picture of its object, which is itself, because the body loses self-awareness precisely at those moments when it could be most revealing; consequently, memory cannot retain what the body had not been aware of, allowing crucial gestures to slip away, though it also endows them with a very special air, as the memory of a fainting spell can preserve only the curious sensations of losing and then regaining consciousness while the fainting itself, most intriguing to us, for it's a state like no other, remains inaccessible, unknowable.

Helene simply enclosed my lips with a bite, and this final decisive act, the only possible response to my little game of studied aloofness, luckily blurred the last sober bit of my consciousness, or so I believe now, after the fact, yes, I believe that the pain caused by this bite was the last sensation whose meaning and significance I could still register with some clarity, and which later enabled me to slip into a now barely remembered state of oblivion, for not only had her mouth abandoned all shyness and reticence by then, it also let me know in no uncertain terms that she wanted me, all of me, and would stand for no more delay or fuss, so it made no sense for me to play the seducer highly skilled in the techniques of love; she wanted me just as I was, she clung to me and would have me forget how I thought I should behave, all she wanted was to press her hips to mine, and not even the formidable layers of lace and silk undergarments could prevent us from feeling each other's body heat— although that, while making me very happy, strangely enough also aroused in me a feeling of humiliation, for by seeming to take control of our fate and by proving that my tongue's predictably unpredictable games were clumsy experiments compared to the eloquent testimony of her teeth, she may have cast doubt on my manhood or anyway deliberately offended my male vanity; as if exchanging roles, she became manfully aggressive, which of course I enjoyed very much, though in light of her decisiveness I appeared to myself as girlishly teasing and flirtatious and thus had to overpower her; my instincts, my conditioning refused to accept the exchange, and perhaps the deeply unconscious motive behind that bite was to arouse in me this wish to reassert myself; even my hatred returned, I felt like snatching her off me as one tears leeches off one's body; I grabbed her hair, the soft material of her dress, maybe even grazed her skin, and with a single jerk of my head I withdrew my mouth from hers; reaching lower with my hand, I grasped her buttocks and thrust her groin brutally against mine, letting her know in the most indelicate possible manner what I had been concealing in my pajama pants, under my robe; with lips and teeth, with bites of my own, I was now ready to take possession of her mouth, pushing in my tongue unimpeded, to which she responded, already on the floor, most tenderly, with even hand strokes and caresses of her tongue—I have no idea how we ended up on the floor, for by then I seemed to have lost the thread of our story, and perhaps this is the juncture after which only her gestures, features, the taste of her saliva, the smell of her perspiration, and the look of her fluttering eyelids allow me to surmise what might have happened to me.

She was lying on her back on the bare floor and I, propped on one elbow and bent over her, watched her closed eyelids, her almost motionless face, while my body was racked by deep, inexplicable, tearless sobs.

I sank my free hand into the red hair spread out before me, and almost as if the hand wanted to remind itself of that old, that very old promise, I began to pull her hair, actually pulling her closer to me by the hair; her face slid almost lifelessly on the floor.

This sobbing was like the memory of a childhood sickness, torrid, shivery, blurred, and it was as if we had been in the deepest of deep darkness and then stumbled upon a sunlit clearing, this room, where familiar yet strange-looking furniture stood silently about, and the heavy rug bunched up by our feet made a high mountain, and every wrinkle and pattern on the wallpaper remained unbearably still; this glaring, empty sight irritated me so much that I had to lay my head on her chest, carefully of course, it was the first time I'd touched her body; I had to close my eyes so that, feeling my own hot breath in the white ruffles of her dress already burning with her body heat, my tremulous sobs could take me back to the darkness from which I had been torn by this silence.

But she seemed to ignore my crying, made no attempt to console me—maybe I killed her, I thought then.

Among the ruffles and lace my lips eventually found her neck, and then I had to open my eyes again; I treasure even now the color of her skin and the smoothness that my mouth and tongue could also feel, for the silence in us might have been very deep, but my mouth, like a foreign body, like a slowly advancing snail, wanted to taste everything it had been forced to abstain from until then; that's why I had to open my eyes again, for though I could take in the sensation of her skin, it might be of some help if I could also see what I had so fervently desired and yet could not make my own, even if this would not compensate for the lost moments.

"I'd like to tell you something," I heard her whisper, and with my mouth I began to move toward her lips, to make her not say but breathe her words into me; I was in no hurry—with my teeth I first caught her sweet, pointed chin, so nice to hold, so firm I could easily bite into it and, like a dog offered a finer bone than the one already in its mouth, I was terribly confused by the choices before me, but her mouth was waiting, and that decided my course of action, though by then my eyes must have closed again, because all I remember is that I got a whiff of her breath along with her words: "Please undress me."

In the meantime, we had left my sobs somewhere behind; again something was lost forever.

Her voice must have brought me back to my senses, things began to clear, because I remember being amazed, not at what she had asked me to do but at her voice; she uttered those words so naturally—those words being the extent of her consolation—that I couldn't imagine her asking me to do anything else. Still, this voice wasn't the voice of a grown woman; it was as if unwittingly she had regressed to a time whose allure I'd also felt while sobbing just moments earlier, and by doing that she seemed to be making me a gift of that unknown time, wrenched from her own past, the same gift I had offered to her with my own, childlike tears. Thus, it wasn't amazement I felt at that moment, or not only amazement but wonderment, and admiration for her little-girl state, for the sublime quality inherent in our nature that enables one human being to bestow on another an experience rooted in times long gone.

And this odd, childlike, timelessly deep and lightsome state, unique perhaps because we had become vehicles of the tension between an indistinct past and an uncertain future, not only held us in its grace while we rather ceremoniously undressed each other but extended its spell—deepened by the gestures of mutual intimacy and trust—to the time when, half-lying, half-sitting among the ridiculous piles of our scattered clothes, we finally laid eyes on each other's naked body.

I was looking at her, but at the same time I also stole cautious, stealthy glances at myself, noting with some stupefaction what I had already felt quite clearly, namely that my member, so firm and rigid in its demand for a place of its own only moments before, was now shrunk to its smallest size and was lying on my thigh with infantine disinterest; though I tried hard to steal a glance at my body, she noticed the furtive look, for unlike me, she held her torso and head quite erect and stared at nothing but my eyes, as if trying consciously to avoid having to look at her body or at mine; we were holding each other's hand, and I had the feeling it wasn't her girlish modesty that made her so shy; she was trying, as I had done while undressing her, not to be distracted by details: when I undid the hooks concealed in the lace-trimmed folds in the back of her dress, loosened the strings of her corset, pulled off her pearl-studded, fine leather shoes and pink knickers decorated with tiny bows, and her cleverly fastened long silk stockings, when, in brief, concentrating on those little hooks and buttons and strings and knots, I purposely refrained from taking in piecemeal the hitherto unknown regions of her body unfolding before me, for I wanted it in its entirety, to contemplate her whole body undisturbed; yet now, when all her naked body was revealed to me, it seemed too much for my eyes to encompass, too beautiful to absorb; I had to look everywhere, everywhere at once, and at the same time I would have liked my eyes to rest on one particular part of her, to find a single place on her body that might be unique; and perhaps she was right (if one may speak in terms of right and wrong in such a case) in looking only at my eyes, for as sentimental as this may sound, there was more complete nakedness reflected in her beclouded blue eyes than her skin was able to offer; and that is as it should be, since the shapes and curves of the body, under the even coating of our skin, can communicate to us something of themselves only through the language of the eyes.

I am equally unable to explain just how we ended up in that peculiar position, for I cannot claim to have been conscious enough rationally to guide my movements; even the scraps of memory, the thought fragments flitting through my mind, annoyed rather than comforted me, as did the sudden realization that Frau Hübner might still be eavesdropping at the door and the coachman was still waiting on the street, at this moment giving feedbags to the horses; and I was troubled also by the fleeting reminder that Helene was so impossibly young, not yet nineteen, and if she yielded to me now, and if I likewise failed to restrain myself, then I, too, would have to give myself over to her; and at that moment I suddenly became conscious of all the difficulties of our possible life together were I to be the first to expose, if only for an instant, her dark and dormant senses to the light and that were to become the only bond between us; it was as if I was facing a helpless puppet with no existence of its own, whom I would have to bring to life so that it could ruin mine; and precisely because this act would be the only, albeit the deepest, bond between us, I should not do it; no, I mustn't lose my freedom, for if I did, I'd end up killing her; I also had to think of my exciting little adventure the night before, which, though inconclusive, hinted that my own senses might take me in directions she couldn't be expected to comprehend and where she certainly couldn't follow; thus I was liable to expose her, and myself, to the gravest of dangers, except that as we sat on the floor, naked, in need of each other, holding each other's hand, I did not feel rushed, I simply longed to pass over each and every part of her, see her in full, take in everything she had ever been and would become with me, and I knew she was mine; so those portentous thought fragments only served to strengthen my desire—there was still something between us, then, that needed to be conquered—and she must have felt the same way, that's why her glance did not stray to my body; like one who has just received a gift but is not yet sure it's really hers, she was very tense, though we seemed most relaxed there, on the floor, our positions somewhere between sitting and squatting. She pulled one leg under her, and with the other, which she bent at the knee so that it almost touched her nipple, she supported herself, laying her groin wide-open; locks of her massive hair fell on her little-girlish, fragile shoulders, and under the lighter red triangle of her pubic hair the lips of her vulva parted softly; and when I stole a glance at myself, catching sight of my own genitals resting softly on my thigh, I might as well have been Pan resting in the woods, on dewy grass; but more significant than this was that I was sitting in exactly the same position as she: one leg under me and supporting myself with the other; we were mirror images of each other; and her waist and breast were similar somehow, the sloping line of her breast bearing a striking resemblance to the curvature of her waist, as if the two curves were obeying creation's selfsame command.

Almost simultaneously, we began crawling toward each other on the floor, our hands proving to be of great help, she pulled me and I pulled her. However solemn and meaningful the moment may have appeared, the simultaneity of our desire to move could not but strike us as amusing; by then my eyes had located the reassuring focal points of her lovely body, though these were not isolated, single points, or some totality of what I was seeing; somehow I perceived her breasts, her waist, and her open vulva all at once, and I could afford to pick out these details from the whole because as I coolly surveyed the whole I could be certain I would not be disappointed, I was getting exactly what I had wished for, her dress had not deceived me: a perfect body came into my possession, and almost as if the attraction of those remaining, still distant points of her body had made me move, I began to laugh out loud, and heard as well as saw that she, too, had burst into laughter, so we actually began to laugh at the same time; and the fact that we both knew that we both had had the same thought, and found our simultaneous move and laugh comical, made this laughter so loud that it turned into an unrestrained roar, yes, we were roaring, I can still hear it, as if, with our gales of laughter, a huge wave of some irresistible force was crashing down on us. When my mouth was above her breasts I hesitated for an instant, catching a glimpse of her ripely glistening gums, because I couldn't decide which one I desired more, I may have wanted both, and the laughter shaking my whole body now reminded me somehow of my sobs of a moment ago; I placed my palm on her vagina, my fingers ready gently to penetrate the adored lips of her flesh, into softness, into wetness, into the depths; on my back and shoulders I felt her hair spreading over me like a tent; and perhaps the back of my neck was the spot she had been looking for, because as I carefully took her hardened nipple into my lips, she pressed her lips to my neck and also put her hand between my thighs; and now all at once it was quiet; as I recall this now, I cannot but think that then, there in that room, we must have been sitting in God's hand.

Slowly the Pain Returned

And now here I was again, standing in our hallway, perhaps at the very same time of the day, catching sight in the mirror of a coat hanging on the rack.

Looking at it like this, in the dim light, reflected in the mirror, I couldn't tell what color the coat was, only that it was made of a heavy, coarse material, the kind that repels water but attracts every bit of lint and fuzz.

Water was gushing and gurgling through the gutters on the eaves, on the steep rooftops snow was thawing, turning to slush, and there I was, schoolbag in hand, standing in front of the mirror.

Maybe it was navy blue, an old, mustered-out military overcoat with a single gold button under its wide collar, which mysteriously remained while all the other buttons had clearly been replaced.

And perhaps it was that gold button sparkling on the dark coat that made me think of him, again of him, as he was walking toward me across that snow-patched clearing, and the painful mood of that moment touched me once more; it was the same hour, and then, too, I'd been standing like this in our hallway and had not the slightest hope that the pain I felt for him and because of him would ever pass; I kept looking at myself in the mirror and believed that everything, everything, would forever stay the same, and indeed nothing really changed: the snow had been melting then, just as it was now, and to avoid having to walk home with him, I again took the route through the woods and, just as then, my shoes got soaking wet; I seemed to be hearing the very same sounds from the dining room, the sounds I heard then and always: against the background of clattering and clinking dishes, the annoying silly squeals of my little sister, my grandmother's voice, untiringly chiding and regularly interrupted by Grandfather's good-natured growls—sounds so familiar that one understands them without really hearing, without paying attention; it must have been this multitude of similar occurrences that made it seem that there was no difference between then and now; slowly the pain returned, but it was that strange and unfamiliar coat on the rack that suggested that I wasn't standing here then but now, after all, though it also evoked the futility of my struggle against the love I had for him, which I always hoped would pass, and if it wasn't then but now, perhaps this, too, would somehow also pass.

But Mother was still lying in her bed the way she always had, her head sunk into large white pillows, apparently asleep as always, opening her eyes only when someone entered the room.

And this time, too, I headed first for her room, just as I'd been doing ever since that day—where else could I have gone?

But back then, the first time, I had done so quite unintentionally—doltishly raw instincts led me there, I'd say; until then I'd always have my lunch before visiting Mother, and only from that day on did it become my habit to sit on the edge of her bed and hold her hand, waiting until my little sister was fed and the dishes cleared away before stepping into the dining room, so that I'd find only one setting on the table, mine, and I'd be alone, spared the sight of my sister, which was more and more burdensome, for what had seemed natural or nearly natural before was now turning repulsive: I hear myself saying "before" and "now," involuntarily dividing time into periods before and after the kiss, for that kiss, I now realize, caused fundamental changes in many aspects of my existence, ordering my affinities into a different sort of naturalness, but at the time whom else could I have turned to if not to my mother? the pain I felt over Krisztián stemmed not only from his inability or unwillingness to return my secret affections but mostly from the fact that these emotions and longings had inescapable physical manifestations—in my muscles, my mouth, fingertips, and, let's admit it, also the pressure in my groin, for is there an instinct stronger than the one to touch, to feel, to smell, and even to possess what can be touched, caressed, and smelled, possessed with one's mouth, devoured? but all these desires to touch I had to consider as unnatural, something peculiar to me, which separated me from others, isolated and branded me, even if nothing would have been more natural to my own body, which I alone could feel; I had to be ashamed of that kiss and of the desire to kiss; however subtly, he had managed to communicate this to me, once he could distance himself from me and, to a certain extent, from his own true impulses; because for a moment something did erupt from the deep, but it had to be suppressed, and he did suppress it; it had to be concealed, and he concealed it, even from himself, whereas I kept recalling it, relentlessly, obsessively; one might say I lived by it, but how could imagination satisfy the palpable desires of the body? and aside from Mother, who else was there around me whom I could touch and feel and kiss and smell as freely as I would have liked to kiss him?

At the same time, whenever I had to look at this hideous countenance, my little sister's face, I had to sense, especially after that kiss, that no amount of medication, administered in carefully measured doses, would ever alter it; the usual family explanation about hormonal imbalance could be nothing but a merciful deception, deceiving only ourselves, for what she had was not some cold, not even a sickness, just as I wasn't suffering from a sickness, we both were what we were; and she seemed unaware, luckily perhaps, of her abnormality—she was happy and carefree, yielding to every momentary stimulus, so to be able to love her, I should have accepted all this as most natural, but to do that would have been equal to holding up a mirror to my own nature, suspect of being somehow abnormal, confirming that it was indeed abnormal, deformed; I'd have to acknowledge it, and then there would be no turning back, all the more so since my little sister's face, for all its deformity, also carried our family features, she was a living caricature of us—impossible not to notice—and although I wasn't prepared to go on lying about it, neither could I any longer suppress my revulsion and fear.

If I looked at my little sister long enough—and I had ample opportunity to do so, for sometimes I was forced to spend endless hours with her—I sensed in her a kind of primeval patience coupled with an animal's docility: no matter what game I'd invent for her, no matter how simpleminded—it didn't have to be more than the repetition of a single gesture—she would, in Grandmother's words, "get on with it very nicely"; she had the capacity to enjoy the recurrent element in things repeated without being bored, she enclosed herself within the circle of repetitions, or to be more precise, she shut herself out of her own game, acting as if she were a windup doll, and nothing could then disturb her and I could observe her well: for example, we got under a couple of dining-room chairs and I would roll a colored marble across the floor so that she would have to catch it in the opening formed by the chair legs and then roll it back the same way; this became one of her favorite games and I also came to prefer it, partly because following the marble's path absorbed all her attention and, since it wasn't too hard to catch the marble, she could go on squealing to her heart's content, and also because all I had to do was repeat mechanically the same gesture: I was there, playing with her, doing what was expected of me, yet if I wanted to I could cut myself loose, pretend I wasn't there, retreat to more pleasant, imagined landscapes or events, possibly escape into coarser fantasies; or I could do just the re-verse—turn my full attention to her but observe only the phenomenon, not her, identify with her, drink her into myself, feel in her distorted features my own, recognize my own helplessness in her persistent, ob-durate clumsiness, and I could do this with cold detachment, from the outside, free of emotional involvement, yet also enjoy this cold scrutiny, toy with the thought of being a scientist observing a worm so as to be able, later, not only to recall the mechanics of the worm's locomotion but to experience the organism observed as if from within, to internalize its very soul, to feel the force that causes one movement to grow from an-other, creating a whole series of movements, so that by slipping under the protective membrane of this alien existence I could simultaneously live both it and my own existence; watching my little sister was like observing a translucent green caterpillar as it clings gently with its tiny feet to a white stone: at our touch it suddenly hunches up, shortening its body, the tip of its tail almost reaching its head, and sets itself in motion by means of this curled-up mass, inching its way slowly forward; as a form of locomotion this is no more odd or laughable than our own attempt at outwitting the pull of gravity and overcoming the impediment of our own weight as we carefully place one foot in front of the other; indeed, if we concentrate long enough and manage to relax into a wormlike state, we might easily imagine and can even feel such clinging little feet on our own bellies; our rigid spine might grow softer, more flexible, and if our concentration is powerful enough to discover these possibilities in our own bodies, then we are no longer merely observing the caterpillar but have ourselves become caterpillars.

At this point I may as well confess that there was a time when my sister's condition did not depress me too much, when I didn't think about why, following my parents' custom, I never called her by her name or talked about her simply as my sister, when I didn't question the nature of that peculiar game of hide-and-seek which compelled us to indicate, through an exaggerated show of affection, that no matter how much she might have appeared to be at the center of our family, in reality she was all but excluded from it—as our proper sense of maintaining family equilibrium required, when the tension, fear, and revulsion engendered by my own exclusion and strangeness had not yet alienated me from her and from myself; and at that time my experiments with my sister were certainly not confined to mere observation but took more practical, one might say, aggressively, physical forms, and even though they sometimes went beyond certain civilized limits and therefore had to be kept secret, more of a secret than the kiss—some of what happened I had to keep secret even from myself—I still don't believe I acted inhumanely toward her; I became far more inhumane later on, in my revulsion and by the air of indifference I forced myself to assume; I daresay that our earlier relationship was somewhat humane precisely because of my ruthlessly honest curiosity.

Our games took place in the afternoon, winter afternoons mostly, when the postprandial silence of the house melted into the deepest hour of swift-descending dusk, when the big rooms stood with their doors wide-open, when the muffled sounds of clanging, clattering, and soft thuds filtering in from the distant kitchen had slowly died away; it was quiet outside too—rain was falling, or snow, wind blowing, and I could not wander off in the neighborhood or disappear into the garden but lay on my bed or sat at my desk, glancing frequently out the window, my head propped in my hand over some unsolvable homework; the telephone didn't ring; Grandfather was napping in his armchair, his hands pressed between his legs, the kitchen floor was drying in patches; and Mother's head would be sinking deeper and deeper into her pillow, sleep making her head heavier, her mouth would open a crack, and the book she'd been reading would slip out of her hand; these were the unchecked hours of our house, when my little sister was put to bed in hopes that she'd sleep and let us have a bit of peace and quiet, but after dozing accommodatingly for a few minutes, she'd often wake with a start, climb out of her bed, and, leaving her carefully darkened room, come into mine. She stopped in the doorway and we looked silently at each other.

They made her wear her nightgown, because Grandmother wanted her to believe it was nighttime and she had to go to sleep, though whether the room was darkened or not, I doubt my sister could tell the difference between night and day; she was standing in the doorway, blinded by the light, her eyes completely sunken in her puffed-up face; reaching into the light as if she wanted to grasp it, she groped her way toward me, the blue-and-white cotton nightshirt almost completely covering her little body, but you could tell it wasn't just the arms sticking out of the loose-fitting sleeves or her large, almost grown-up feet, but every part of her, her whole body was thick and graceless, small yet heavy; her skin was an unusual white, a lifeless grayish-white, and for some strange reason it seemed to me to be thick and scabrous, as if the visible coarse surface was covering several other layers of finer skin, as if this hard shell, rather like an insect's armor, overlay the real, human skin that was more like mine: smooth, supple, and downy; this skin had such an effect on me that I used every opportunity to touch it, feel it, and the purpose of our games was often nothing more than for me to try to get close, quickly and with no preliminary fuss, to her skin; I could do it, too, without the slightest pretext—I could simply grab her or pinch her—and if a pretext was needed, it was only to elude my own moral vigilance and make what I wanted to do anyway seem more accidental; of course, the most conspicuously disproportionate part of her body was her head: round, full, insidiously large, like a pumpkin stuck on a broomstick, her eyes two gray dots set in narrow slits, her full, drooping lower lip glistening with abundant globs of saliva that, often mixed with snot, kept dripping from her chin onto her chest, leaving eternal wet stains on her dresses; taking a good look up close, one could see that the black of her pupils was tiny and motionless, which may have been the reason her eyes were so expressionless.

This expressionlessness was at least as exciting as her skin, however, and, insofar as it was intangible, even more exciting, for the lack of the usual signs of emotions differed from what could be observed in a normal pair of eyes which, when trying not to betray emotion, become their own mask, revealing to us that they do indeed have something to hide, suggesting the very thing they conceal; in her eyes nothing gained expression or, rather, it was nothing itself that her eyes were continually and relentlessly giving expression to, the way normal eyes express emotion, desire, or anger; her eyes were like objects one never gets used to; they appeared to be a pair of lenses used for seeing, an impassive outer covering, so when one looked into them and watched their mechanical flutter, one naturally assumed there must be another pair of eyes, more lively and feeling, behind these seeing lenses, just as we would want to see the eyes, the human glance, behind sparkling eyeglasses, convinced that without our seeing them a person's words cannot be properly understood.

When she'd stop at the door of an afternoon, she would say nothing, as though she knew that her shrill voice would only give her away, and rousing our grandmother would have meant depriving herself of the joys and agonies of possible games, the games of our secret complicity; she must have known this, though her memory did not seem to function or, if it did, worked most peculiarly, since there was no rational way to account for what she remembered or what she forgot; she could eat only with her hands, and though adults tried at every meal to train her to use utensils, she didn't catch on, forks and spoons simply fell from her hand, she didn't understand why she had to keep holding them; yet our names, for example, she did remember, she called everyone by their right name, and she was also toilet-trained, and if accidentally she wet or made in her pants, she would sit in a corner for hours, whimpering inconsolably, imposing on herself the punishment Grandmother had devised for her long ago, and there seemed to be an act of goodwill in this self-punishment, a great gesture of goodwill toward us all; although I could not make her learn numbers—we'd study them and she'd promptly forget them—and she had problems recognizing and distinguishing colors, she was always very cooperative, always willing to start afresh, and eager to please us; her strained exertions were quite touching to see, as when she looked for an oft-used everyday word and knit her brow in intense concentration, and would at first fail, because her language, after all, was not words, but then, when the sought-after word or expression did come to her lips in the form of a triumphant scream and she herself could hear it and then be able to identify it, her face lit up with her sweetest smile, her happiest laugh, a smile and laugh of utter bliss the likes of which we would probably never experience.

For while there was nothing in her eyes one could take for expressions of feeling or emotion, her smile and laugh may have been the language she used to communicate with us, the only language she spoke; it was hers, a language for the initiated, to be sure, but perhaps more beautiful and superior to our own because its single though endlessly modifiable word conveyed pure joy of being.

One day I noticed a pin on my desk, an ordinary pin; I had no idea how it got there, but there it was, at the bottom of the deep corridor formed by my scattered books and notebooks, gleaming just bright enough to be noticed on the brown wood; I couldn't really say why then I kept my eye on it for days or why I was so careful not to move it while turning pages in my books or while reading, writing, or just aimlessly shuffling my things, packing and unpacking my schoolbag; I may have also thought that it would disappear as unexpectedly as it had appeared, but no, it would be there again the next day; that afternoon the lamp with the red shade was turned on, though it wasn't quite dark yet, she was standing in the shadows and, looking out from the light cast by the lamp, I more or less sensed her presence in the pleasant warmth of the late afternoon, and she, blinded by the light and still groggy from sleep, could not have seen me very clearly; a few more soft tapping sounds were heard from the kitchen and then the silence was complete; I knew the silence would last for another half hour, so the game we had both been waiting for could begin, and we could start it with anything at all; the pin was still on my desk—all I had to do was to make the first move and the rest would follow by itself—so with my fingernails I picked up the pin by its head; I simply wanted to show it to her, to have her see it; she began to smile, most likely getting ready to laugh her most intimate laugh, reluctantly at first, because she was afraid of me and had to overcome this fear each time anew, and I was also afraid of her; but we didn't have much time and I knew I couldn't get out of it anymore, she wouldn't let me; if she didn't make the first move, I would, and if I didn't, then she would; in this we were at each other's mercy.

Later, discovering a true, deep, and therefore not easily explained attraction, I amassed a respectable collection of these pins, carefully storing them away, and not just those that turned up accidentally; after a while I began to look for them, track them down, hunt for them; strangely enough, once it became an obsession, I kept finding them everywhere, which was strange, since I'd never remembered them turning up before so conspicuously and persistently; now I'd come across them in the most unlikely places: in pillows, in cracks, in coat linings, on the street, in the upholstered armrest of an easy chair—with a flash and a prick, they would announce their presence; I began to classify them, having discovered the many different kinds, and as a test I would prick my finger and let it bleed a little; there were all sorts of pins: long and short, with round heads or flat, with heads of colored pearl; rusty pins, stainless-steel pins, straight pins and spear-shaped pins—and they all pricked differently; but that afternoon I had only that plain, long, round-headed one that had landed so mysteriously on my desk that I even had asked my father about it when he happened to stop in my room one evening, and he looked amazed, even baffled, as he bent over, not comprehending what I was showing him; pushing back his straight blond hair, which kept falling in his eyes, his gesture unconscious yet annoyed, he told me gruffly not to bother him with my silly games; this pin, then, the original piece of what later became my collection, I was just showing to her, with no special intention, as if I had to show it to everyone; I simply held it up to the light, and then my little sister took the crucial first step and approached the pin, and that made me move, though still with no specific purpose; I slid off my chair and slipped under the desk.

I may be trembling even more now, as this confession compels me to evoke a series of moves long completed and irrevocably ingrained in me.

Fear is primordial, immeasurable, and seems real only when put into words; it's what we hope is ephemeral but what proves to be permanently alive.

I was trembling quietly then, but not out of fear, and that makes all the difference—not this dark, faltering feeling I have now, but a simple excitement, light, clear, and pure, the kind we experience when placing our limbs beyond the influence of our will, letting insidious desires have free play; for a long while nothing happened; it was warm and dark under the desk, a little like sitting in an overturned cardboard box whose open end, like a mouth, was waiting for her arrival, waiting to swallow her up.

I was conscious of the smell of the wood, that raw smell furniture never loses completely, reminding one of origins, giving one a sense of security, protection, and permanence; I could even smell the characteristic dusty-paper smell of the prosecutor's office (my desk was a superannuated government issue which Father had brought home for me one day); she wasn't moving, but I knew she would come, because after the first move there was always a tension that demanded release and completion—that was our game; then I heard her heavy, clumsy footsteps, she was walking as if she not only had to bear the weight of her body but had to keep moving it forward.

I was sitting like a spider under the farthest corner of my crate-like desk, pinching the head of the pin between my nails, pointing its tiny tip in her direction, when her long white nightshirt appeared, she dropped to her knees, and on her face there was the broadest of grins; I can say that at that moment I was free of all emotion, though it might be argued that the opposite was true, that the moment distilled all my possible emotions; she began to crawl so fast toward me that I thought she wanted to pounce on me, but after a few hasty moves her nightshirt caught under her knees and wouldn't let her go on; suddenly losing her balance, she bumped her forehead into the edge of the desk and fell forward, her head hitting the floor with a thud; I did not stir; according to the secret rules of cruelty she had to reach me unaided.

Her resourcefulness was as unpredictable as her memory; she straightened out, grinned even more broadly and eagerly, if that was possible, as if nothing had happened at all, and with a very natural movement pulled her nightshirt from under her knees, quite casually; I said very natural movement, because this time she found a natural connection between the nightshirt and her fall, while in other, much simpler and more transparent situations, she had not made the connections—for example, wanting to have some fruit, she could quite easily climb up a tree but couldn't come down; she would sit on a swaying branch until somebody noticed her, hold on tight and whimper quietly, though it was no more difficult to come down than to climb up—at times she crept so high that we had to use a ladder to get her down; perhaps only joy, the desire for pleasure, made her resourceful, and as soon as she had satisfied her desire, the object of which may have been a red cherry, a shimmering peach, or even myself, her memory went dark, her resourcefulness expired, and she returned to a world in which objects existed in isolation: a chair was a chair only if someone sat on it, a table was a table only if her plate was placed on it; for her there was no connection between the events that happened around her, which simply happened if they happened, and at most may have blended into one another; it was her impossibly exaggerated grin and her eyes widening into unblinking immobility that suggested a desire to impose some order; now on her bare knees she was creeping closer and closer until she was completely under the desk, where she felt protected, where no one could find out what we were up to; in my own way, I must have been just as blinded by desires as she; she began to pant excitedly and I was breathing louder, too; my hearing sharpened by the straining senses: I could hear, like some strange music, the separate yet harmonious rhythms of our breathing, and if I hadn't raised my hand to point the pin straight at her eyes—her eyeball simply attracted the tip of the pin— she probably would have flung herself on me, for she liked to wrestle, and she didn't shrink back now, her grin didn't fade, either, but remained as it was; hoping for some resolution, she paused for a moment, catching her breath.

She did not flinch, her lids did not flutter, even though the pin point was only a few centimeters from the glistening curve of her eyeball. And my hand didn't move either, I only felt my mouth opening slowly, because I really didn't want to do anything to her, but there she was, wide-open, defenseless, and behind the visible part of her there may have been another being whose senses were more alive, who would have flinched, whose lids would have fluttered, who would have been afraid; if the slightest thing were to happen at that moment, like her hand accidentally swinging toward me or mine moving just a bit forward, who knows what would have been there to prevent the most dreadful end; but there was something, an invisible obstacle, a wall, a mere shade, something that seemed to be the manifestation of a force outside me and just as independent of my most mysterious and secret intentions as it was somehow bound up with them, even if I myself was unaware of them, of my curiosity, which had always triumphed over everything in me—except now!—but even if the thing were to have happened, I could not fault myself, because the insatiable desire to explore what lay behind the seemingly indifferent exterior of things and phenomena, to make the indifference speak and bleed, to conquer it, to make it my own, as I had done with Krisztián's lips and with so many lips after his—this desire made me the victim of that strange outside force; but the dreadful thing could not happen, although I am not sure that what happened instead did not turn out to be even more dreadful.

The frozen, unpromising moment passed, and her body plopped down, lightly, resting on her heels. The new distance between us had a sobering effect. The pin, still pressed tightly between my fingers, was nothing but the evidence of my absurd inanity, a bit of foolishness to be dismissed with a shrug, something that hadn't happened though it could have; I had to close my mouth again; once again I had to listen to the stupid excitement of my own breathing, and hers, too, which kindled in me a kind of simple and ordinary anger, therefore completely mine, mine alone; I failed to reach her; I was locked again in my own solitude; but I did reach after her, just as she was moving away, and with a single movement jabbed the pin into her naked thigh.

And once again nothing happened; she drew back, her body taut, no sound passed her lips; it was as if a moment ago we had been standing on the heights and now were sinking into the depths; she stopped breathing, but not from pain; her nightgown rode up to her belly and exposed the open slit between her outspread thighs, the darkened orifice between two firm, reddish mounds—my pin took aim; I couldn't not do it, but the pin did not prick or even touch the skin, it penetrated the opening. Then I stabbed her in the thigh again.

Not as lightly as before but hard and deep; she screamed; I could see her grin vanish, as if the physical pain had also ripped an invisible veil; and I could also see her look, seeking refuge, but by then she was upon me.

There was no doubt of it, the dark coat on the rack could mean only one thing: a guest had arrived, an unusual guest at that, because the coat was stern-looking, grim, quite unlike the coat that usually hung on that rack, so shabby and threadbare I didn't even feel like doing what I usually did when left alone with strange coats in the hallway and go through the pockets and, if I found some loose change, cling to the wall, listen for noises, wait for the right moment, and then steal a few fillers or forints.

This time I did not hear any strange noises or anyone talking, everything seemed normal, so I simply opened the door and, without fully comprehending my own surprise, took a few steps toward the bed.

A stranger was kneeling in front of the bed. He was holding Mother's hand as it lay on the coverlet, bending over it; he was crying, his back and shoulders shaking; while he kept kissing the hand, with her free hand Mother was holding the man's head; her fingers sank into the stranger's short-cropped, almost completely white hair, as if wanting to pull him closer by his hair, but gently, consolingly.

That's what I saw when I walked into the room, and as I took a few more steps toward the bed, the man lifted his head from Mother's hand, not too quickly, while Mother abruptly let go of his hair and, leaning slightly forward on her pillows, threw me a glance.

"Leave the room!"

"Come here."

They spoke simultaneously, Mother in a choked, faltering voice while her hand quickly rushed to her neck to pull together her soft white bedjacket; the stranger spoke kindly, however, as if he were really glad to see me come in so unexpectedly; in the end, embarrassed and confused by the conflicting signals, I stayed where I was.

Late-afternoon sunlight pierced through the window, outlining with wintry severity the intricate patterns of the drawn lace curtain on the lifeless shine of the floor; outside, the drainpipes were dripping, melted snow from the roof sloshed and gurgled along the eaves; the shaft of light left Mother and the stranger in shadow, reaching only as far as the foot of the bed, where a small, poorly tied package lay; the unfamiliar little bundle, wrapped in brown paper and clumsily secured with string, must have belonged to the stranger, who wiped off his tears, straightened, then smiled and stood up, showing as much impudence as strength in this quick transition; his suit also seemed strange, like his coat on the rack outside, a lightweight, faded summer suit; he was very tall, his face pale and handsome, and both his suit and white shirt were wrinkled.

"Don't you recognize me?"

There was a red spot on his forehead, and one eye still had tears in it.

"No."

"You don't recognize him? Forgot him so quickly? But you must remember him, you couldn't possibly have forgotten him so fast."

A hitherto unfamiliar excitement made Mother's voice dry and choked, though I could sense she was trying to control herself; still, her voice sounded unnatural, as if she felt she had to play the role of mother, addressing herself to me, her son, as if controlling not so much her emotions, the joy at seeing the unexpected guest, but rather some powerful inner trembling, and the cause of this inner fear and trembling was unfamiliar to me; her eyes remained dry, tearless, and her face changed, which surprised me much more than their intimacy had, or the fact that I didn't recognize the man; a strikingly beautiful, red-haired woman was sitting in that bed, her cheeks flushed, her slightly trembling, nervous fingers playing with the strings of her bedjacket—she seemed to be choking herself with them—a woman who had been intent on keeping a secret from me but whose lovely green eyes, narrowing and fluttering, had just betrayed that she was completely defenseless in this painful and embarrassing situation; I had caught her in the act, found her out.

"It's been five years, after all," the stranger said with a gentle laugh; his voice was pleasant, as was his way of laughing, as if he had a penchant for laughing at himself, for playing freely with his own feelings; he began walking toward me, and indeed became familiar; I recognized his easy, confident stride, his laugh, the candor of his blue eyes, and, most of all perhaps, the reassuring feeling of trust I could not help having in him.

"Five years, that's a long time," he said, and hugged me; he was still laughing, but the laugh was not meant for me.

"Maybe you remember that we told you he was abroad? Well, do you?"

My face touched his chest; his body was hard, bony, thin, and because I automatically closed my eyes I could feel a great deal of this body; still, I did not yield completely to his embrace, partly because some of Mother's nervousness rubbed off on me and partly because the trust evoked by his walk, his ease, and his body seemed to be too familiar and too powerful; the potential exposure of feelings made me more reserved.

"Why go on lying? I've been in jail."

"I told you that story only because we couldn't really explain."

"That's right, in jail."

"Don't worry, he didn't steal or rob or anything like that."

"I'll explain it all to you. Why can't I tell him about it?"

"If you feel you must."

He let this last remark pass unanswered and, as if slowly breaking away from Mother, and focusing entirely on me, he firmly grasped my shoulders, pushed me away a little, took a good look at me, fairly devouring me with his eyes; what he saw, the sight I must have presented to him, not only made his eyes brighter but turned his smile into a laugh, and this laugh was meant entirely for me, meant that he was pleased with me; he even shook me a little, slapped me on the back, planted loud, smacking kisses on both my cheeks, almost biting me; and then, as if he couldn't get enough of my sight and my touch, he kissed me once again, and this time I succumbed to this emotional outburst—I knew by now who he was, I knew it well, because his aggressive closeness pried open heavy locks within me, and suddenly, unexpectedly, I remembered everything, and of course he himself was right there, kissing me, holding me in a tight embrace; I'd never known that the locks were within me; after all, he had disappeared and we had stopped talking about him, he had ceased to exist, and I even forgot about that dark little corner of my memory that had been keeping alive the feeling of his closeness, his looks, his gait, the rhythms of his voice and touch; and now he was here, at once a memory and reality itself; so after that third kiss, with a clumsiness induced by my emotions, I also touched his face with my mouth, but he again pulled me over, almost roughly, once again pressed me against his body and held me there.

"Please turn around, I'm getting up."

Losing Consciousness and Regaining It

When I finally came to on the rocky embankment of Heiligendamm, I may have known where I was and in what condition, yet I'd have to say that this was nothing more than sensing existence in pure, disembodied form, because my consciousness was lacking all those inner flashes of instinct and habit that, relying on experience and desires, evoke images and sounds, ensure the unbroken flow of imagination and memory that renders our existence sensible and to an extent even purposeful, enables us to define our position in the world and establish contact with our surroundings, or to relinquish this connection, which in itself is a form of contact; during the first and probably very brief phase of my returning to consciousness I felt no lack of any kind, if only because experiencing that senseless and purposeless state filled the very void I should have perceived as a lack; the sharp, slippery rocks did make me sense my body, water on my face did make my skin tingle, therefore I had to be aware of rocks and water and body and skin, yet these points of awareness, so keen in and of themselves, did not relate to the real situation which, in my normal state, I would have considered very unpleasant, dangerous, even intolerable; precisely because these sensations were so acute, so intense, and because I now felt what a moment ago I couldn't yet have experienced, which meant that consciousness was returning to its customary track of remembering and comparing, I could not expect to absorb everything my consciousness had to offer, but on the contrary, what little I did perceive of water, stones, my skin and body, wrenched as it was from a context or relationship, alluded rather to that intangible whole, that deeper, primeval completeness for which we all keep yearning, awake or in our dreams but mostly in vain; in this sense, then, what had passed, the total insensibility of unconsciousness, proved to be a far stronger sensual pleasure than the sensation of real things, so if I had any purposeful desire at that point, it was not to recover but to relapse, not to regain consciousness but to faint again; this may have been the first so-called thought formed by a mind becoming once again partially conscious, comparing my state of "some things I can already feel" not with my state prior to losing consciousness but with unconsciousness itself, the longing for which was so profound that my returning memory wanted to sink back into oblivion, to recall what could no longer be recalled, to remember the void, the state in which pure sensation produces nothing tangible and the mind is in limbo with nothing to cling to; it seemed that by coming back to consciousness, by being able to think and to remember, I had to lose paradise, the state of bliss whose fragmentary effects might still be felt here and there but as a complete whole had gone into hiding, leaving behind only shreds of its receding self, its memory, and the thought that I had never been, and would never again be, as happy as I had been then and there.

I also knew that awareness of water, skin, body, and stones was not the first sign of this familiarly tangible world; a sound was.

That peculiar sound.

But as I lay among the rocks, once again blessed with the unpleasant ability to think and remember, I wasn't thinking at all about changing my dangerous situation or weighing my chances of escaping it, though that would have been the sensible and timely thing to do, since I could clearly feel waves washing over me, keeping me under icy water for long seconds; the possibility of drowning didn't even occur to me; what I wanted was to have that peculiar, strong, yet distant sound again within my reach, to luxuriate in the dim weightlessness of pure sensation where, banging, crashing, like some peremptory signal, that sound had first informed me I was still alive.

To this day I cannot decide how it all happened; later, it was quite a surprise to see my bruised and bloody face in the hotel-room mirror; I also have no idea how long I must have lain there, on the embankment, for hard as I tried, I couldn't recall the last moment before fainting, and the fact that I got back to the hotel at two-thirty in the morning meant hardly anything except that it was very late; the night porter, barely awake, opened the large glass door and didn't even notice my condition; there was only one small light in the lobby, I could see the clock on the wall: half past two, no doubt about it, but I had no way of relating the hour to anything that might have happened. I can't be sure, but in all probability a massive, very high wave picked me up—it's so pleasurable to imagine being carried along by it; maybe I lost consciousness in that very first moment—and it must have slammed me down on the rocks like some useless object, but by then, gone were the early afternoon and my arrival in the hotel, the last references that, in spite of temporal confusion and dislocation, I could still locate in time with some certainty.

But the sound I never found again.

Of getting back to the hotel I can give only as poor an account as I have of how I wound up on the rocks; both had occurred independent of my will, though I was undoubtedly the sole participant and victim of each: while in the first I had been entrusted to the water, to an entire chain of lucky accidents and, thanks to it got away with only a few bruises, scratches, and black-and-blue marks, not cracking my skull or breaking my arms and legs, in the second instance the force which we like to call the survival instinct must have been operating in me, its determination as raw and violent as the elements; if we were to take what we proudly call self-awareness or ego and, applying a little mathematics, examine what remains of it when it is caught between the forces of nature and those of our inner nature, both of them so immense and independent, the result would be pitiful if not ridiculous, I'm afraid. We would discover how arbitrary it is to separate things: the fact that in an unconscious state we are one with trees and rocks: a leaf stirs only when, and in the direction, the wind blows on it—we may be unique but not superior!—when my hands and feet (not me, mind you, but my hands and feet) were searching for something solid to hold on to among those loose, slippery rocks and my brain, a soulless automaton, was calculating precisely the intervals between the breaking waves, when my body, adjusting each move for a possible escape, knew by itself that for safety it must first slide farther down the embankment and only then straighten up, when all this was taking place, what was left of the haughty, inflated pride with which I had set out for a walk in the afternoon? in those critical moments what was left of the pain and joy the ego can provide, the ego that's busy chasing its memories and toying with its imagination?

Nothing at all, I might say, all the more so because when I had set out on my walk, I believed my life was so miserably hopeless, so over, so terminated and therefore certainly terminable, that the best I could hope for was a pleasant last walk before taking a bunch of sleeping pills; the reason the story I invented along the way turned out so neatly was also that I felt I'd reached the end of something in my life, but my hands and feet and brain, my whole body, came to the rescue: they did their job smartly, decisively, maturely, perhaps even rather too eagerly, and in the meantime the so-called ego could do little more than scream like a little child: "I want to go home! I want to go home!" somebody did seem to be screaming within me, a somebody known as myself, and for all I know I may have been screaming and crying; at any rate, that was the real me; and my desperate, cowardly terror was humiliating, stayed with me, suppressed every other memory; the ludicrous way the storm put me in my place—a storm that I'd tended to consider as a well-painted backdrop, an effective musical accompaniment to my emotions—was matched by the equally ludicrous way my own nature deprived me of my supposed autonomy: the fact of the matter is, nothing happened; I got a little wet— all right, sopping wet, which meant that at worst I might catch cold; the skin on my forehead was lacerated, maybe the flesh, too, just a little, but it would surely heal; my nose began to bleed but then stopped; I lost consciousness for a time but then came to; yet my body, trying to escape, forcefully mobilized all its necessary animal instincts, as if it were in mortal danger rather than merely exposed to mild insults, like a lizard seeing the inevitable end in every stirring shadow; but more important, the body acted as if the ego, fed by its intense emotions, had not wished for death at all; and the knowledge of nothingness not only showed me that all these past experiences I had imagined as so grandly excessive were in fact ridiculously trivial but also intimated that whatever was yet to come would be no more significant; I was exposed, I was but a receptacle of trivialities, and for all my awareness of what was happening to me, or what might still happen, consciousness was completely useless.

Dawn was slowly approaching; outside, the wind raged on.

My clothes were drying on the radiator and I was standing naked examining myself in the mirror of my hotel room, when there was a knock on the door.

I knew it was the police, and I shuddered, not because I was afraid but because I was naked, yet I didn't care that much, I was totally absorbed in the sight of my naked body, and my shudder wasn't so much a response to the knock, a habitual reaction dictated by decency, as an outward manifestation of total inner exposure which at that moment held my attention more than any anticipated event possibly could.

Why did this particular wish surface—the wish to go home—if not completely unexpectedly, then surprisingly and with such far-reaching implications? why did the body, seeking its own safety, choose to save and have my consciousness articulate this word "home" and why did it both seem so inane and yet also carry a most profound meaning, even if I was at a loss to say what?

Before the knocking, I had to touch the bruise on my forehead to feel what I was seeing in the mirror, to feel the mild pain this superficial cut caused, to perceive the sight and its physical sensation simultaneously; then I passed my finger down the bridge of my nose, my lips, my chin, not ever forgetting that the full-length mirror screwed to the closet door reflected the whole body, just as the story of a single touch always has the whole body for both its hero and its setting; though I tried to guide my finger at an even pace, it seemed to linger on my lips, or maybe the effect of the touch went deeper; then I reached my neck; a small lamp with a waxed-paper shade stood on the night table behind me, and in its faint yellow light the mirror showed the contours of my body more than its detailed, full image: proceeding along the arched rim of the collarbone from the shoulder, I descended into the soft hollow formed by the neck muscles where the bones meet, whence my finger would have moved rapidly across the chest hair toward the dip of the navel, and along the abdomen's gentle bulge to reach and firmly grasp the genitals, the most satisfying spot of physical self-awareness; but my body started, acknowledging the knock on the door.

In truth, I hadn't the slightest desire to go home, none whatsoever; in this regard, my behavior on the previous night had been very telling: in the almost totally dark entranceway Frau Kühnert, blanking out the attractive nakedness of her face, pushed her glasses back on her nose, and the faint light from the paper-capped wall fixture behind her, as if reflected in her glasses from the inside, made her eyes disappear; I could barely see her face, but I sensed her unexpected retreat, maybe from a conspicuous shift in her posture; my rebuff, ostensibly a response to her lengthy plea and explanation, alluded to our possible lust for each other and she wasn't going to endure so gross a humiliation, for all her inclination to servility; her neck stiffened, straightened, and now, looking down at me, she seemed to be retreating to the safer and more conventional forms of social intercourse appropriate for the relationship between an attentive landlady and an ever amiable, pleasant lodger; she straightened her back, too, eliminating the slightly stooped posture meant to protect her breasts—she was finding her way back to that tactful formality which had characterized our former contacts; but the moment I felt this about to happen, happening, already having happened, I felt like someone who has suddenly lost control of himself, who realizes that with sheer will he has destroyed something far more important than his will: I'd finally managed to sever the imperious, coarsely sensual bond between us that might have led to hate or to love; a moment ago, with some recklessness either one would have been possible, it was only a matter of decision; but this, this switch to unpleasantly cool formality, was totally unexpected; against my better judgment, I would have liked quickly to return to the dangerous but potentially more valuable form of behavior which Frau Kühnert was ready to abandon, but which became markedly important, given the tension and pressure it produced in my groin, and this importance was being plainly communicated to me—not to the point of a full erection, but more in the form of a threat with a hint of possible extortion; when I told her I was going to disappear for good, I was actually alluding to the possibility of suicide, not to going home; and I wasn't disappointed, for this unclearly phrased, ambiguous statement had exactly the effect on her I intended: she was surprised, though I don't suppose she understood what I really had in mind; the secret intention I had been nursing for months, which had matured into a decision, must have deepened my voice so that I could imply the necessary sincerity and seriousness to draw her back into the magnetic field she had been trying to escape; what I was hoping to accomplish, aside from gratifying my ego, I cannot say—perhaps, in light of my imminent death, I wanted to be pitied, or perhaps it would have been too unpleasant to be left alone with the telegram, though I knew that whatever it said, it could not change my mind; in answering her questions, eager and weighing every possible danger I might be facing, I did not say what I really wanted; I didn't tell her, for example, to leave me alone, that nothing mattered anymore, that she was too late anyway, but if she wanted she could take off her pullover and let me close my eyes at last, I didn't want to see anything, I didn't want to know or hear anything anymore, so let's try to work on a single moment, and why not this one, we should be able to manage that much—but instead of saying that, I reminded myself of a previously attempted solution and I described my intended return home as a reassuring form of disappearance;

of course, this was only another way of avoiding her, and myself, because at that moment the word "home" meant nothing more than a distant hope of no real significance; I used it then as a tactful lie: and here in the mirror of the hotel room was this body now, and though neither its sight nor its palpable feel could convince me of the importance or necessity of its continued existence, yet I could not have named anything to prove my unavoidable presence more than this image in the mirror.

Unexpected as the knocking was, it still seemed as if I had been waiting for it—not surprising, since the circumstances made it inevitable, it had to happen; but when it did, when I heard the knock, I didn't feel like hastening events; I did not rush to get dressed—in fact, that didn't even occur to me; I stayed as I was, undisturbed, absorbed in scrutinizing my body, as if there had been no knocking at all; oddly enough, I suddenly remembered something seemingly very remote: I thought of Thea Sandstuhl, I even had time to recall a single gesture of hers: in trying to trace points where random thoughts converge, we may rediscover the psychic miracle that makes the distant appear close, as if merely a matter of simple, mechanical associations; I thought of the afternoon I became acquainted with Melchior, and the knocking I heard I took to be a direct consequence of his escape; the particular moment that came to mind was when during rehearsal Langerhans had impatiently clapped his pudgy hands and in his unpleasantly high-pitched voice said, "Enough! I told you not to stick that hump so high!" and, tearing his gold-rimmed glasses off his pasty face, flew into a rage; and Thea remained as she was, a prisoner of her own gesture, much as I was now, in front of the mirror; on other occasions, after such directorial interruptions, Thea astounded those watching her with her ability to shift emotional gears with incredible ease and speed: she could be crying, screaming, or gasping amorously in one moment and in the next listen obligingly and attentively to the director's latest instructions; it was as if there were no boundaries between her various emotional states, one flowing naturally from the other, or as if bridging the gap between them, making smooth transitions, posed no difficulties for her, which in turn aroused the suspicion of outside observers that she was not present in any of these situations—though she appeared most subtly convincing in all of them; but that afternoon she overwhelmed us with the slowness of her transition, involuntarily demonstrating in pure form the fine gradations through which we can force our emotions to move from one subject to the next: the voice reached her body like a delayed jolt; Langerhans's admonition had already been uttered, but she, with the contradictory emotion of a moment ago, was still pointing the heavy sword at the bare chest of Hübchen, kneeling before her; she made her move as if she hadn't heard what she had to have heard, giving us a sense of the sharp line dividing inner drives from external pressure; her body gave a start only when the response already seemed late, and only then did it freeze in an attitude of innocent, appealing embarrassment.

She looked lovely in a tight-fitting, richly laced, purple dress which at once emphasized and concealed her body's tense, uneasy lines; her neck and torso tilted a little, as though the director's voice had indeed pushed her, kept her from touching the desirable naked chest before her, from following through on her inner urge to deliver the lover's stab; but she also could not yet do what the director, for some inscrutable reason, wanted her to do: that she slowly lowered the sword she'd been gripping with both hands, its tip clanging to the floor, did not mean she was able to choose between her inner urge and the outside command, but merely that she was sidetracked by a deeply ingrained impulse to obey, turning her response into a clumsy display of obedience; Thea considered herself an intelligent actress and always spoke with contempt of colleagues who, amateurishly, wanted to "live" their parts: "Oh, him, the poor thing, he identifies, he becomes the character, his tears flow so much I feel like scratching his ear to make him stop or asking him if he needs to take a crap; but the audience eats it up, it's grateful to him and wouldn't think of disturbing him, after all he's a true artist, the genuine article, we can see with our own eyes how much he must work and suffer for this noble art, poor thing, how he suffers for us, can't you see, the idiot lives the part for us because he can't do it for himself!" these were some of the things she had said, but now her embarrassed body and unembarrassed glance revealed how much she had been captured by the situation, which had nothing to do with the method of acting that is based on "living the part" yet required of her a degree of inner fervor which, despite her firmest intentions, made her open, vulnerable, oblivious to her professional experience and technique; it was this tension that made her so suitable for the situation created not by her but by Langerhans's crafty aggressiveness.

It was a vicious circle: when Hübchen tore off his rough shirt, the sight of his naked body must have stunned her, caught her unprepared, so she couldn't ignore it, and even though they must have rehearsed that scene at least ten times and might go over it a hundred more times, it would always wind up on the same emotional track chosen by Langerhans, who had, very slyly, also taken into account Thea's abilities and desires.

The knocking on the door of my hotel room now turned to banging, pounding fists.

"If you stick it up so high, then she, too, can see it!" Langerhans yelled, and it was hard to know whether he was truly fuming or this moment was simply a pretext to make the already heavy air of discipline in the rehearsal hall even more oppressive; the makeup man, who liked to sit at the edge of the director's platform, so that in time I had become familiar with his fuzzy, freckled pate, sprang up and ran to the lighted acting area, his white robe fluttering like wings, while Langerhans's anger seemed to subside with each sentence he spoke, until he had regained the whispering and rather mannered speech that was his trademark: "What we need now is for her to see his beauty, nothing else!" he said, still yelling; "We need only his beauty now," he added more quietly, "so that the woman should be willing to spread her legs for him right here, on-stage, do you understand?" he was whispering now, with a soft, dainty motion replacing his glasses on his flat nose, "so it should be much lower, as I showed you."

But the improbably open look in Thea's eyes began to waver and fade, releasing Hübchen's near-naked, let's just say pleasingly proportioned, body; only when the director and the makeup man were already standing next to her to take a better look at the ill-placed hump—and not even then—could she turn away or move; it became almost palpably clear that a very powerful emotion could not find an outlet and she didn't know what to do with it, nobody seemed to want it, she had to wait until it would be repressed or help arrived, just as I was standing there in the hotel room, listening helplessly to the insistent banging on the door, re- alizing that all this time I had been looking at myself with Melchior's eyes; and that's exactly how Hübchen must have felt: he didn't budge either but remained on his knees, looking into Thea's eyes, and then rather awkwardly, foolishly, burst out laughing, braying like a teenager, which anywhere else might have caused embarrassment but here nobody paid attention to real feelings and emotions which, like the chips and shavings of the work being shaped on the stage, were flying in all directions; it wasn't as if Hübchen's body and amazing, creamy-white, hairless skin had aroused ordinary, offstage feelings in Thea—though that would not have been so unusual, because women like to boast, even at the risk of losing out by such statements, that the beauty of the male body has scarcely any effect on them, their contention being borne out, apparently, by the truth that bone structure, muscle definition or the lack of it, even flabby softness have no discernible effect on sexual prowess (one need only note that after penetration the body's external features lose importance and become mere conductors, mediators), though the symbolic value of the visual experience is far from negligible; beauty is the advance payment on desire, an invitation to pleasure, and there is no difference between the sexes in their preference for what is firm, well shaped, supple, and strong over bodies that are shapeless, flaccid, washed-out, and feeble; in this sense the sight of the human body is not a question of aesthetics but of vital instincts: not only could Hübchen's body be called perfect, but Langerhans, with calculated and characteristically almost perverse shrewdness, had Hübchen's trousers made with a low waistband to make it look as if they had slid down accidentally, leaving his bony hips and gently sloping belly bare and suggesting that he wore nothing underneath; and though he wore soft leather boots and the cleverly shortened pants on top, one had the impression of total nakedness, and only at his groin did one's glance stumble on discreet covering.

Thea finally looked at me.

She probably couldn't see me, I sat too far away in the hall, and her glance could not easily pass over the sharp line separating light and darkness there, but the vague feeling that somebody was sitting calmly, watching her, and not without empathy, was evidently enough for her to retreat from unpleasant, all-too-human openness into the more secure role of the actress; anyway, I had the feeling that my sheer presence was of some help; at almost the same moment, a bit later, Langerhans must also have noticed her poignant confusion, and rather gently, but with the professional aloofness of a man who knows that the psychological maintenance of his actors is part of his job, he placed his hand on her shoulder, squeezed it encouragingly, helped her recovery along; and Thea, sensing the warmth of a strange body, suddenly tipped her head sideways without otherwise altering her position in the slightest, touching the hand with her face and locking it between her face and shoulder.

And they stayed that way, their images reflected on the huge, slightly raised glass panel covering the walls of the rehearsal hall.

Hübchen was still kneeling, with the makeup man bent over him trying to remove his hump; Langerhans was watching his actress's face; and Thea, still clutching the lowered sword, rested her head on her director's hand.

The tableau-like scene seemed infinitely tender, but the greenishly sparkling glass backdrop made it look stiff and cold.

It was late afternoon by now, only a few of us were left, and it was so quiet you could hear the hum of the radiators and the gently tapping rain on the roof.

"There's nothing wrong with my seeing his hump," Thea now said; although there was a cooing tone in her voice as she tried to match her emotions to his touch, Langerhans wasn't going to be taken in so easily and cheaply; he withdrew his hand with undignified haste and blushed, as he always did when contradicted: "It seems you still don't understand your own situation, Thea," he said quietly, his voice devoid of emotions not relevant to the subject at hand (it was this voice that made him so detestable and unapproachable): "You shouldn't worry about yourself so much, you know; after all, what can happen? Nothing. Go ahead, don't be afraid to be a little more vulgar, it's okay, we're talking business here, plain and simple. You'll simply sell your body, that crack between your legs, to be exact, because that's all you've got left, that slit. Your life has finally revealed its true nature to you. That's all there is, that hole, that body, and nothing else. He's killed your husband. So what? He's killed your father-in-law. Big deal. He's also killed your father, but that doesn't matter either, because you're scared, because you're all alone. They're all dead, but you're alive, and when he tears off his shirt you can see he's quite attractive. You don't even want to see his hump. So his offer sounds like a good deal all around. Be a slut, my dear, and don't try to be his mother."

"But even a slut could be a mother, have you ever thought of that?" Thea said, even more quietly.

"Go ahead, catch your breath. Take your time."

"You're being very nice."

"No, I'm just trying to understand you."

"But what should I do with all that phlegm? while I'm doing all that cursing it just builds up, almost choking me. What should I do? I think I should be spitting at that point. It was dumb to cut that. I'll choke on it, I'm telling you. What should I do?"

"Swallow it."

"I can't, I just can't."

"You can't spit on the glass, if that's what you had in mind."

Thea shrugged her shoulders. "You still need me?"

"We'll take a short break," Langerhans said.

I got up from the chair on which I had been comfortably swinging back and forth; Thea was heading toward us.

This was the dull part of the day, as always happened when rehearsals stretched into the late afternoon: even if the rehearsal hall's tall, narrow, highly placed windows had not been covered with black curtains, anyone interested in the outside world and looking out through the heavily barred windows would see little besides a few slender chimneys rising above grim walls, darkening in the rapidly descending twilight, and blackened roof tiles across the way, and a sky that more often than not was depressingly, monotonously gray; still, sometimes I'd stand by those curtains for a while, usually after politely offering my chair to Thea, who, when not onstage, liked to sit next to Frau Kühnert at the little table near the edge of the director's platform; my small courtesy toward Thea came in handy because around that time of the day, as late afternoon was turning into evening, insecurity and anxiety took hold of me, nearly suffocated me; we'd call it simple anxiety, I suppose, since I really had nothing to do here, I was only an observer, which after a while proved to be not only exhausting but downright unhealthy; I just had to get up and look for something to do; but the view from the window didn't relieve my anxiety, if only because I went on being an observer—though not of gestures, faces, and accents, which in the artificial light of the cavernous hall had become all too familiar, along with the personal, often secret motives animating them; what I saw from the window, from behind crude iron bars, was a different set of relationships, between walls, roofs, and the sky, and I had nothing to do with them either, except as an observer, yet even here I could see some subtle changes: no matter how relentlessly gray the sky may have appeared, the various shades of light had enough play to emphasize certain details over others, so that the same view in fact was constantly changing, looked new and different; and similarly, under the even glare of the rehearsal lights there were enough surprises to make transparently familiar gestures and responses seem startlingly fresh; in my better moments I could consider myself rich in the accumulated knowledge of these details and the relationships among them, but I had to forgo the natural desire to contribute actively, to participate; my mind may have been producing some very decent ideas, but I had no clearly defined role, no real niche, and this proved to be a fundamental handicap here, where one's place in the strict hierarchy was determined by the role one played, where only rank could give validity and weight to one's observations; in a certain sense I was tolerated only in the chair I occupied, and it wasn't a permanent chair either but an extra one put in for me, temporarily; I was nothing more than an "interested Hungarian," as somebody once said, standing right behind me, not at all concerned that I might overhear this odd characterization, which, come to think of it, wasn't offensive, given its factual correctness, perhaps more accurate than the person who spoke it might have thought; anyway, my situation was not so unusual or unfamiliar; I could have found it highly symbolic that I was deprived of a chance to interfere with the course of events, made a silent witness, an observer condemned to inaction who also had to bear, all by himself, the consequences of his silence and his helplessness, without the chance to blow off steam; I was indeed a Hungarian, in this sense very much a Hungarian: no wonder Frau Kühnert's pleasant attentiveness and Thea's flattering interest were so gratifying.

Thea stopped in front of us, and by now I was holding the back of the chair, ready to give her my seat; there was something characteristically exaggerated in my politeness—I shouldn't have been so afraid of losing that modicum of goodwill she had shown me—but she wasn't ready to sit down yet, she didn't even step up on the platform as she usually did but, rather, she slid her two elbows to the table and without so much as casting a glance at us leaned her chin on its edge, like a child—she had to get on her toes to do this—and then, resting her head on her arms, slowly closed her eyes.

"What a disgusting piddling around all this is," she said softly, without batting her eyelids; she was perfectly aware that her little performance, for all its hamming, was impressive enough to hold us captive; after all, a truly great actress was doing the hamming, by way of relaxing, and it seemed to betray real emotion. Frau Kühnert did not respond, let her go on, and I didn't start for the window, as was my custom, to disappear behind the black curtains, I was curious; she paused effectively, making us wait, then let out a small sigh, giving us time to watch her shoulders gently rise and fall; with her eyes still closed, she lowered her voice even more, making herself barely audible and, as someone yielding to exhaustion but unable to stop the flow of thoughts, continued, savoring her words: "He'll ruin me, he has ruined me, with this disgusting fussing and piddling."

By now the silence in the rehearsal hall was so deep you could hear not only the rain pattering on the roof and the radiators humming but Frau Kühnert closing her prompt book with a real thump; but she must have meant this rather abrupt gesture as only a prelude to another, more sensible move, because it made as little sense to close the prompt book as it did to leave it open: Frau Kühnert came to the first rehearsal with the full play already memorized, as the actors did, and from then on her only job was to enter the various changes in the text, erase them if necessary, re-enter the final version in ink, and make sure the changes were clearly marked in all copies of the script, and to be on the safe side, she had to sit there with the thick master copy, saving her attention and voice for the moments when someone unexpectedly got stuck, when she would feed them their cues with the eagerness of a good student; this happened very seldom, of course, so now, like one who has finally found real work for which she feels inner motivation, she rested her veiny, masculine hand on the closed book a second, and then gently yet eagerly slid the hand onto Thea's head.

"Come, darling, sit down here, rest a little," she whispered, and though her words were loud enough to be heard, people were too tired to turn around and give her a dirty look.

"He wore me out completely."

"Come, our young friend here will give you his seat."

They had their game down pat; Thea still didn't budge; her face, like an open landscape anyone could freely admire, was relaxed, absorbed in itself.

"You ought to give that boy a ring, Sieglinde; why don't you call him for me?" she continued in the same, softer than whispering voice: "Please. The way I feel, I don't think I have the strength to go home. The thought that my old man's been piddling around all day, just the thought of that makes me sick. How I'd like to enjoy myself for a change! Maybe we could go someplace together, I've no idea where. Someplace. And you could call the boy for me, right? Will you call him?"

She seemed to be playing at someone talking in her sleep, maybe over-doing her part a bit in the game; because she had to get Frau Kühnert to carry out a most unpleasant task, she almost went too far.

"I don't dare call him, because the other day he told me not to. He told me please to stop calling him. Not very polite, is he? But if you call him it's different, you might be able to soften him a little. Would you do that for me? It wouldn't take much, just a little buttering up," she said, and fell silent as though expecting a reply; but before Frau Kühnert had a chance to answer, Thea's unpainted lips began moving again: "I'd love to buy my old man a great big garden, and I shall, too, once I have lots of money, because it must be awful for him to sit in that horrible flat all day, just awful—for me it's all right, except right now I don't feel like going home—but for him it must be depressing as hell, he ends up smelling bad after piddling about all day; I mean, imagine, that's all he does all day, sits down, gets up, lies down, sits down again, and that's how he spends his whole life; if he had a garden, he could at least move around while doing nothing; shouldn't I buy him a garden? will you call that boy?"

Our Afternoon Walk
Continued

But after so many digressions, let's return to that afternoon walk—we'll have enough time to deal with what is yet to happen, for it's the past we so often forget, and so quickly, too; let's go back to where we left off, to the moment when, having concluded the fresh-air cure in rather dramatic circumstances, we started on the straight road leading to the station, walking under the giant plane trees.

Here we immediately reached the peak of sensory delights, the gayest hour of the promenade; the trees' long shadows fluttered in the gentle sea breeze, which also carried the soft music of the dance band set up in the open lobby, now bringing the strains closer in unpredictable waves, now turning them into garbled snatches and scattering them into the distance; carriages were rolling toward the railroad station to pick up new arrivals and one could already hear the puffing, whistling locomotive; riders were trotting, alone and in groups, down the bridle path, switching to brisker gallops as they rounded the tidy stationhouse, only to be swallowed up by the dark and dense beech forest whose very name, the Great Wilderness, had a quaint archaic flavor; and the strollers! at this hour everyone whose cure did not call for bed rest was on his feet and out here, was expected to be here and to cover this short distance on foot, to and fro, stopping along the way for a brief chat or an exchange of pleasantries; if one walked with someone more serious or with a more interesting topic of conversation, the distance could be covered more than once and away from the general traffic, but one didn't tarry too long with any one partner, for that might be taken for unseemly eagerness, and here everyone was watching everyone else; one had to be careful that the casual informality—the robust bursts of laughter, the abrupt darkening of brows, the waving of hats, kissing of hands, the knowing chuckles, trembling nods, and raised eyebrows—an informality full of resentments and petty jealousies, naturally, should not violate the familiar conventions and should seem spontaneous, for all its glib artificiality; young boys and girls, more or less my age, trundled colored hoops along the road's smooth marble slab, and thought they were especially adroit if the hoops did not get caught in the folds of ladies' dresses or roll under gentlemen's legs; on occasion, even Heinrich, Prince Mecklenburg, would appear, in the company of his much younger and somewhat taller Princess and surrounded by attendants, and each time he did, the promenade's unwritten rules were altered; outwardly nothing seemed to change except that the apparent naturalness appeared a shade less natural, but the experienced stroller, as soon as he reached the decorative marble urns on their slender white pedestals, could sense that the Prince would be there; the two marble urns with their velvet-smooth cascading purple petunias formed a kind of gateway to the tree-lined esplanade; yes, the Prince would definitely be present today, because backs were a bit straighter, smiles a shade friendlier, laughter and conversation so much softer; soon, though not yet, he would be seen on the arm of the Princess, in the wide semicircle of his attendants, listening attentively to someone, registering every word with grave nods of his gray head; it was improper to seek him out even with a curious glance; he had to be noticed accidentally, as it were, and with the same casual ease we also had to adjust our pace to the rhythm of his steps and seize that fraction of a second during which, without interrupting his conversation, he might honor us with his attention, so that our respectful greeting would not dissolve in the air but might be returned; we had to be alert to avoid any potentially embarrassing thing and to pay attention to proper decorum; and the strollers thronging the promenade were indeed alert, each and every one well prepared: what if the Prince should wish to exchange a few politely pleasant words with me! with my humble person, of all people! and they would watch and listen with mixed curiosity and envy, determined to learn the identity of the lucky person the Prince talked to, and later to find out what had been said.

Mother, who thanks to her upbringing was particularly adept, one might say accomplished, in matters of decorum, accepted Father's politely proffered arm with a gesture worthy of the gentlest wife, and smiling the

loveliest smile of the afternoon walked with him arm in arm, her chest
and back erect, gracefully picking up the train of her elegant mauve dress
with three fingers of her free hand, pressing against him comfortably,
somewhat committing her body to his care; I lagged behind, because I
couldn't stand their bickering, but also catching up and joining them at
Mother's side when I was curious; it seemed to me that these slightly
raised flowing gowns (one never raised them too high, of course) polished
the white marble pavement to a sleek, smooth shine; those fabulous fabrics! those fine silk, lace, and taffeta dresses swishing and rustling, and
dainty shoes gliding smoothly on the bright surface, with the boots tapping
just a little harder! with such activity all around, and Father's permanent
smile, a forced smile to be sure, it was not in the least surprising that
strangers and even acquaintances were unaware of, and from my parents'
posture could not guess, the intense hatred they had for one another: "In
that case we ought to leave immediately! The purpose of our stay here,
my dear Theo, if I'm not mistaken, is not for you to be entertained but
for me to get well!"—in these quiet, frequently repeated scenes Mother
was in control of their emotions; she hated more, and more strongly,
because Father's mere presence was the source of her sufferings; he was
present, yet she could not reach him, she was like one aroused but not
satisfied, while Father seemed completely indifferent (though he may not
have been) to the emotional exertions of this slender female body; it was
Mother's stronger passions and her exceptional skills in handling social
situations that enabled her to take revenge during the most sensitive moments on these afternoon walks—and hers was no ordinary revenge: the
more elegantly she carried it out, the more ruthless she became, she had
the upper hand; but revenge is treacherous; during the momentary lulls
in the complex, well-worn ritual of strolling and chatting, in full view of
the promenaders, she murmured and hissed into Father's ears her sharpest
and nastiest remarks, which Father, because of his less agile physical and
mental makeup, could not possibly return in kind; she did this accompanied by her most enchanting smile.

On that memorable day it wasn't the comment he had made that triggered Mother's indignation, at first restrained and only threatening but
quickly accelerating into a sweeping, all-consuming force: "Or am I mistaken, dear Theo? Tell me! Why don't you say something? You know,
when you're like this, I'd really like to spit in your face!" and it wasn't
because Father, breaking their previous agreement, would not wait for us
to finish the prescribed exercises before sounding his warning that if we

were too slow we might miss the train; in fact, it seemed to me that she tried to provoke the warning by deliberately slowing down her breathing, which I tried in vain to adjust by setting an example of the proper, prescribed rhythm; no, Father's careless and graceless warning was a sign, I'd say an open demonstration, of the ever-present explosive discord between them, a pretext for venting their emotions; I can still hear him uttering that sentence, alluding to a rather simple fact, how his words came out awkward and forced in spite of his efforts to sound casual, how his deep voice slipped into a higher register; but for all his clever dissembling he could not deceive Mother, who heard clearly what he had tried but was unable to conceal: his growing impatience.

It was Privy Councillor Frick who was to arrive on the train, and Father had been waiting for him anxiously for several days; significantly enough, in talking about him they would call him "the privy councillor" or "Frick," carefully avoiding his Christian name even though he was Father's closest and best friend and had been for decades, a childhood friend; as far as I can judge in retrospect, their bond was an unclouded, remarkably strong one, for in spite of considerable differences in character and intellect, their strong common roots evidently determined similar developments, and this was only natural, since they were both the product of and, in the conduct of their adult lives, also fugitives from the same religious institution famous, indeed notorious, for its medieval rigor; their kindred spirits, therefore, may have been a belated testimony to their Spartan upbringing or, just as likely, to their rebellion against it; so if Mother took care that the councillor's Christian name did not pass her lips, this was her way of letting them both know that she had no desire whatsoever to have a personal relationship with a man whose "immoral lifestyle," as she put it, whose cruel and aggressive nature had corrupted and continued to corrupt Father, whose "moral fiber, unfortunately, was much too weak": "Theodor, you behave like a charmed insect near a bright light, that's how you behave! You are childish and ridiculous when the two of you are together, and I am deeply ashamed!" Father, by the way, not only pronounced his friend's first name with almost sensuous delight but also used coy terms of endearment, calling him ducky, sweety, my little pussycat, even my little rotter, though he also preserved the rigid formality of their alma mater: the two of them never used the familiar form of address, and when talking to Mother about him, Father invariably avoided using the councillor's Christian name, to keep her out of the territory of that friendship, out of that warmest of relationships, the very place Mother would have liked to invade even at the cost of destroying it; this was the mysterious region, the forbidden zone, about which neither of them would brook any nonsense.

Once, awakening from my afternoon nap, I myself witnessed the kind of scene Mother would surely have disapproved of: the two men were standing on the terrace in the sunlight; lying on the narrow sofa in the living room, I didn't even have to move to see them through the muslin curtain fluttering back and forth in the afternoon breeze, but they could not see me—it was too good a moment, too rare an opportunity for me willingly to give myself away, and anyway, I was still a bit dazed from sleep—they were leaning against the railing, their arms resting on the stone balustrade, alone in that sun-drenched space, not too close to each other, though their fingers probably did touch on the rough, weather-beaten stone, adding a certain intimacy as well as an element of tension to their tête-à-tête; they stood there facing each other in identical poses, in their lightweight summer suits, as if mirror images; they were even the same height, it was hard to decide who was reflecting whom, maybe they were mutually reflecting each other; "Our instincts, my dear friend, our instincts and our stimuli," Frick was saying even before I opened my eyes, and his voice echoed into my awakening so pleasantly, softly and naturally, as if it were my own, as in the state when we think to ourselves and in our own voice, not addressing someone else; "Even as I stand here and have the honor of looking into your eyes, even this, every moment of our existence! because we are pages that have been filled out, fully written, all of us; that's why we find ourselves so boring! Moral refinement, good and evil, these are all silly, ludicrous notions. You know I don't like to talk about God, I simply don't like this God, but if there is still a place where He can be found, or where He can find us, it must be in our deepest instincts, there He may still reign supreme. If that is your belief, I join you in it, but even here He must be doing the job without the slightest effort, without even lifting His little finger, because He has already set the course, He's nothing left to do except to watch impassively as we act out what He's set into motion, what in fact He has already carried out and inscribed in all of us. All I can say—and I hope I'm not boring you with this improvised discourse—is that moral refinement and consequently notions of good and evil are never found in things themselves but, rather, we are the ones who belatedly place them into things, and the reason philosophers, psychologists, and other useless folk feed us their pitiful fare about these notions being inherent in things is that they

113

consider it too brazen, too simple, and too pedestrian to seek the motives for our acts in our primitive instincts; they are looking for something loftier than instincts, higher than common things, chasing after some noble idea or concept that will make sense out of this disconcerting chaos. But this is nothing but the consolation of the weak! And of course they have failed to notice the inner nature of this chaos; they have told us nothing, or nearly nothing, about the gratifying details of this inner nature, they haven't even considered them. So for them, the things everybody must experience all the time have become improper and indecent. Now when I hear people talk about what is good or what is evil, I think of how I haven't managed to take a good shit today or of needing to let out a good fart, which in terms of spiritual cleanliness is most essential, though I know that in decent company one doesn't do such things. Believe me, moral refinement is nothing more than holding back a fart for a few more moments."

"You are a believer, my pet, how reassuring; I envy you!" Father said this in the same intimately soft voice his friend had used, and all this time not only their heads and bodies remained motionless but their eyes hardly flickered; they were looking straight into each other's eyes as openly as they could, as if this eye contact were more important than any other form of communication; the two pairs of eyes did not even approach the perilous edge of an amorous union, they did not seek that particular refuge: what was actually happening had a much more significant and powerful effect on them, perhaps because they knew that a physical relationship was impossible, and they held each other captive with their eyes, gradually overcoming the sensual excitement two eyes immersed in each other can offer, though at the same time exploiting these natural centers of sensuality, from there to shift their glances just enough to notice the tiny movements in the wrinkles around the lashes, the eyelids, the eye sockets, leading to two identical involuntary and discreet smiles; "Should I express myself more plainly?" said Frick, his question a response to a request never made, and Father said, "It wouldn't hurt," supporting his friend in what I think he wanted to do anyway: they didn't merely venture over the slippery topic of the body but moved with equal ease through the subtler folds of each other's thoughts; did not give in to any possible weakness, and in this sense there was something cold and cruel in their confabulation; try as they might to elude all-powerful Eros, still, in the utter shamelessness with which they observed, controlled, and read each other's mind, and in the meticulous regard they had for each other, crafty Eros did manage to gratify them, and itself: "Look, it may be a bit much to say that it's all between our legs," continued Frick; "But I thought that's exactly what you had in mind," Father retorted. When exchanging such short, clipped sentences, the depth, color, and strength of their voices seemed to adjust to and blend themselves into each other so fully that one had the impression of a single person speaking, arguing, debating with himself: "No, no, far from it! If it were so, I'd be committing the same reprehensible error," Frick said, somewhat louder, but still without much emotion; "Elaborate!" Father said, and his request, like a short pause, remained suspended in midair.

"True to our old habit, let's start with the obvious: here I stand and here you are facing me," said Frick, who now appeared taller than Father because he was slim, though proportionately so, not in the least gaunt—and I don't mean just his body, which I had an opportunity to observe fully on the beach, as he was wearing one of those newly fashionable swimsuits that cling to the body when wet, for his face, too, was lean, the skin adhering to his skull in a smooth, tight fit; he was beginning to grow bald, and to mask this as much as possible—he was quite vain—he had his fine sun-bleached hair cut short in military fashion; "If we swept aside with one grand gesture all the ethical norms drummed into us, the only certainty left to us is this, that we are here, the sense and sight of our sheer existence, that's all we can contemplate, and that is no small thing; and I must admit that unlike the educated dilettantes I referred to before, I am not interested in anything else."

At this point, however, Father gave a quiet laugh, and as this short, not unintentional chuckle bespoke sarcasm, Frick's vehemence slackened a bit, and on his face, surely one of the most extraordinary faces I ever laid eyes on, the strain of concentration eased, loosened by momentary embarrassment, which was remarkable because his face was defined by an inner calm, a natural hauteur, an unruffled superiority, and of course its starkness, as if nature had shaped it in bold strokes, adding neither fussy details nor charming little folds of fat to the skull which carried the face and, let's note this now, to which it would be pared down in death: no matter how quickly Frick spoke, or how much, at times his face struck me as a skull, a death's-head, a grim paperweight on a desk, or as a structure of boiled-down bones, while at other times, as on that day, it was its perfect roundness that caught the eye, the taut, dark-toned skin turned almost black in summer, gleaming on his forehead, the hairline wrinkles neatly tucked away on the close-shaven cheeks, yet not even these dry furrows made him look older than he was, for what stood out in all their brilliance was his huge expressive eyes, cool gray eyes with a piercing, ruthless gaze, their sternness further emphasized by his pointed nose and rather thin lips, though the soft dimple of the chin, like a child's, gave the face an appealing gentleness; "Don't think that the desire for power doesn't imply physical pleasure," he continued, his momentary embarrassment relaxing into a gently sardonic smile; standing motionless, they were still holding each other's unaverted gaze; "On the contrary, the desire for and wielding of power can immerse you in pleasure so deep, or lift you up so high, that the only comparable thrill, deeper and higher still, would have to be that of sexual climax, the very greatest of physical pleasures which each of us ought to reach in the manner best suited to our nature, and that is just what I was getting at, my dear, that everything around us desires, and offers, the pleasure of ejaculation, if we are free enough to note these desires and offers, so it was perfectly sweet of you to interrupt me with your little chuckle, to sidetrack me in this direction, leading to the very essence of things! I don't mind a bit," he said, pausing long enough to catch his breath; "That's right, there's a kind of congenial balance between our senses and our thoughts, between instinct and reason, the balance of counterbalances, if you will; and who is better suited to revel in the pleasures of existence than he who holds power? Power alone can carry him to the limits of the mind, of the intellect; and when he returns from those frontiers, if he can make it back, that is, he can truly indulge his senses, because having lost his fear of perilous extremes and shaken off all moral constraints, he can be equally uninhibited when turning to sensual pleasures, seeking out the extreme limits of that realm as well; and who is freer than the man who delves into the pleasure and pain of his own limited possibilities—limited because predetermined— which he will explore to the utmost, my friend, yes, even if our freedom doesn't allow us to know what these possibilities are for, what anything is for; freedom is indeed limited, but only in that it is never an abstraction but rather the practical exercise of the will, which is fully aware of its own possibilities but which the mind cannot conceive. But why am I blathering on, you know what I mean."

"Another exciting little adventure?" Father asked.

"Something like that," he sighed.

"Tell me about it," Father said.

"An actress," he answered.

"I wager she is blond and indecently young"—thus Father.

"Oh, that's the least that can be said of her!"

And he would have continued, too, describing the affair not just in general terms but in great detail, as I had the good fortune to hear him do on another occasion, but at that moment they had to turn toward the wide staircase leading from the park to the terrace, cutting the conversation short just when it promised to turn most exciting—for, returning from her leisurely afternoon coffee break, Mother had appeared in the company of Fräulein Wohlgast, with a clear air of shared intimacy as they slowly walked up the stairs, and the young lady, in her usual loud manner and somewhat raspy voice, was launching into a playful attack: "Oh, the men," she exclaimed at the bottom of the staircase, her words almost coinciding with Frick's last sentence, "just when we are discussing such weighty matters, too; I am telling you, Frau Thoenissen, there was a time when men held our destiny in their hands; those days, I daresay, are over; while we make plans and reach important decisions, they engage in frivolous chitchat, or am I wrong? will they be honest with us, might I ask them not to tell us fibs just this once?"

But all this happened much earlier, maybe two or three summers earlier than the afternoon I referred to before, at least that's how my memory has preserved it, and since a child's mind can't absorb all the cleverness and foolishness of adults, my imagination has had to fill in the white spots of this scene of long ago.

Much earlier, I've said, alluding hesitantly to some of the more distinctly remembered details: everyone knew that Fräulein Wohlgast had lost her sweetheart in '71, in the war against France; he was said to have been a dashing officer, and she, in patriotic zeal, had vowed to mourn him for as long as she lived, "until the grave and beyond," forever reminding the world of the "infamy perpetrated not only against me but against us!"— and she wore dark gray clothes, no longer black, though every year the gray got lighter, until on a certain afternoon when, thanks to Mother's venomous outpouring, we arrived at the station in quite a state, crossing the splendid glass-covered and at that hour pleasantly cool stationhouse just as the squat engine and its four red cars pulled in, and she appeared in a stunning, lace-trimmed, lily-white dress.

By this time Mother's unanswered, bristling sentences were sticking out of Father like the arrows out of St. Sebastian in some romantic illustration, penetrating deep under the skin, into the flesh, and still quivering in the air: the only sentence he managed to squeeze out was something about turning back, but Mother pretended not to have heard that, and of course everything played into her hands, because there was no time to catch their breath here, either; once again they had to greet acquaintances, had to keep smiling; there was quite a gathering on the open platform, people coming to meet the new arrivals (there weren't that many anyway) and to enjoy the lively spectacle offered by this little marvel of modern science; they acted as if their brief afternoon stroll could be properly terminated only here. I cannot imagine what the spa's guests did for entertainment before this railroad line was built (it connected the charming old town of Bad Doberan, also the Prince's summer residence, with the lovely-sounding Kühlungsborn); anyway, the buzz of conversation died down and, as if sitting in theater boxes, everyone watched in fascination as nimble conductors threw open the doors, lowered the steps—ah, the moment of arrival!—watched the porters, too, as they vanished and reappeared in the clouds of steam emitted by the puffing, screeching engine, hurriedly unloading the heavy pieces of luggage; soon, though, after a few minutes of idle waiting, while words of greeting and farewell intermingled on the platform, at a signal from the stationmaster the steps would be pulled up, the doors slammed shut, and leaving behind the pleasant fatigue of arrival among those who had disembarked and the sad silence of distant longing among those who welcomed them, and with some more whistling and clanging, the engine's puffing gradually accelerating to a steady clatter, the whole brief show, like a momentary vision, would disappear around the nearest bend, and once more we would be left as we were, this time unmistakably by ourselves.

Peter van Frick was standing in the open door of one of the red railroad cars, the first to appear, and surveying the crowd on the platform, he noticed us right off—I felt and also saw that he did this, picking us out of the throng of friends and acquaintances who had come to welcome him—but then he immediately turned away, his face more serious and sullen than usual, his dark complexion more pallid; he was wearing a well-tailored traveling suit that made him look even taller and more slender; as he stepped gracefully off the train, one hand casually holding his hat and valise, with the other he quickly reached back to help somebody else down; who that was we couldn't yet tell, but a moment later there she was, none other than Fräulein Nora Wohlgast, yes, no doubt of it, dressed in white, like a bride; it must have been the first time I saw her in white (and, it must be said, as a result of the rapid and drastic turn of events, also the last): if Frick's arrival was considered an extraordinary event because of the delicate role he had played in exposing the recent double assassination attempt against the Kaiser, about which the vacationers at Heiligendamm had learned only in newspapers and whose precise details and wider ramifications they were now hoping to ascertain firsthand, well then, this dual appearance was an out-and-out sensation, bordering on scandal, though in light of his very special position and his momentary popularity people were willing enough to close their eyes and pretend either not to see what in fact they could not avoid seeing or to make believe it was mere coincidence, and in any event, the reputation of society's darlings is always enhanced, their superiority confirmed, by a little scandalous behavior; they rise above and rule us precisely because they cross boundaries we dare not, but the Fräulein! how could she have wound up on that train, when this very morning she had breakfasted with us at our regular table? and why in white all of a sudden? and so conspicuously white, to boot, which on account of her age she had no business wearing, for she was closer to thirty than to twenty! why this sartorial provocation which seemed so unlike her, why? could it be that she and that inveterate bachelor, the councillor, were secretly engaged, or might he have already married her? prompted by this flood of questions, I looked first at Mother, then at Father, hoping to read the answers on their faces, but Mother's face was unresponsive and Father's showed such shock and agitation that, without realizing why, I automatically grabbed his hand, as if to hold him back from doing something dreadful, and he let me, yielding helplessly, turning pale, ashen, though his eyes, bulging out as if mesmerized, kept staring at the couple who were unmistakably together; his mouth dropped open and stayed open, and all the while we were getting closer, for they were heading our way and we were moving toward them, and a moment later, as if pushed along by the rather exaggerated and overly enthusiastic shouts and exclamations, we found ourselves part of the colorful human ring surrounding Frick, as scores of unfinished, interrupted sentences clashed and tangled above our heads, as they all besieged him, of course, asking about his trip and expressing delight at seeing him, alluding to his "extremely exhausting work" that must have accounted for his "wan" complexion; in this platitudinous atmosphere, overheated by noise and mawkishness, no one could be expected to look at that other face, Father's foreboding countenance, not even Frick himself, but they all had to see and hear Father, who, having snatched his hand from my terrified grip, leaned very close to Fräulein Wohlgast's face and, though he might have liked to whisper, shouted, "What are *you* doing here?"

As if no emotion were powerful enough to penetrate the armor of appearances, there was no outburst and no scandal, nobody screamed and no one became violent, even if the propensity for sudden hysteria lying dormant in human nature may have warranted it, rather, it was as if Father's question had never been asked, or that it was the most natural question in the world put in the most natural way possible, although they knew only too well that Father wasn't, couldn't be, on intimate enough terms with Fräulein Wohlgast to permit himself such a question, and in public, too, using the familiar form of address! or could he be? was something dark and confusing being exposed here? for all I knew, it wasn't just the two of them but perhaps a curious threesome or, counting Mother, a foursome; yet no, it wasn't so, for no one seemed to notice anything, everyone finished their sentences and launched animatedly into new ones, assuring the purity of the proper social overtones produced by the music of their chatter; what is more, I could detect the effect of propriety even on myself, for I suddenly felt so faint I had the distinct impression that the scandal had already erupted, the abyss had opened up, and there was no escape; not only did I feel that we would be falling—that ominous feeling experienced so many times before—but that this was the fall itself, we were in the midst of it! I wanted so much to close my eyes and stop up my ears, but I could do nothing, the sense of propriety being stronger than I, and my having to remain in control, while as for Mother, her performance was simply brilliant: as Frick bowed slightly to kiss her hand, she could even bring herself to laugh heartily, gaily: "Oh, Peter, we are so delighted that you can be here at last! If not for those important affairs of state, we'd probably never forgive you for depriving us of your company for so long"; and in fact there was no stopping now, the situation rolled on: stepping before Father, smiling a self-satisfied smile over the answer he'd just given Mother—"And I shall do my best to make up for lost time"—Frick offered to shake Father's hand, no hugs on this occasion, of course, while Father, speaking even louder than his friend, said, "Affairs of state? Nonsense!" and rather than letting go of the privy councillor's hand grasped it even harder, staring into his eyes with an impenetrable look, and then lowering his voice to a whisper: "You mean a criminal affair, Herr Frick, don't you? which is not so hard to uncover, provided the assassination was well organized."

"You are a witty man," said Frick, laughing deliciously, as if he had just heard the most amusing jest, and once again the situation was saved; members of our little party were now ready to help things along, determined to ward off further attacks from Father, so their chattering grew louder, became a frantic hubbub, until an elderly, highly respected lady, who must have weathered quite a few storms in her time and had ample practice at saving the day, took Frick's arm and cried, "I am going to snatch you away from here, sir," and with that she jolted the whole company out of any lingering shock; becoming aware of the changed mood, people were ready to gloss over the momentary unpleasantness, though the word "scandal" must have still been buzzing in their heads, and though when Mother took Father's arm she seemed to be restraining him, which he needed, for he looked as if he was about to hit someone or start screaming, but the dowager chimed in again: "I know it is beastly of me, but what I have to say is important and should mitigate my rudeness— the Prince, you see, is waiting for you!" and the old lady's pleasantly tremulous voice rose above the din; by then our company began to move, treading on the crunchy gravel path leading to the white stationhouse, and only two of us were left behind, almost abandoned: Fräulein Wohlgast, who, still paralyzed from the earlier situation, could not take advantage of the improved, more favorable one, and I, of course, whose presence made absolutely no difference to anyone.

"Let's get out of here, and quick!" Father snapped, and promptly began walking with Mother in the opposite direction, but an unpleasant white apparition blocked their way, the Fräulein herself, who in this latest confusion somehow ended up in front of Mother and, having cast about in her stunned mind for a plausible explanation, seemed just at that very moment to have hit upon the answer: "You won't believe this, but after breakfast I felt like going for a long walk, and I didn't stop until I got as far as Bad Doberan, and who should I meet there?!"—her chatty tone in the circumstances sounded like an absurd parody—"You have behaved scandalously, Fräulein!" Mother said, with an air of superiority, looking calmly into her eyes, but then Father pushed Mother along, and the two of them swept the young lady out of the way; I hurried after them across the railroad tracks, as in complete silence and almost running, we let the forest trail lead us on, and only after making a detour long enough to count as an excursion, via the marsh, did we return to the spa, well after dark.

Oh, what a terrible night was to follow!

I was startled from my sleep by someone standing in the open terrace door behind the translucent curtain—or was it just a shadow, a ghost?— and thinking that even a flickering eyelid might be noticed, I didn't dare close my eyes again, even though it would have been much better not to see or hear what was to come; the terror of the previous afternoon returned, adding to my fear; and then the curtain did move, and a shadowy figure entered and hurried across the room, in the dark, a night without light, footsteps tapping on the bare floor, then muffled on the soft rug, and I recognized Mother in the shadowy figure, heard her reach the double door leading to the hallway; she must have put her hand on the door handle and even pressed it down, because a sharp click shattered this deepest silence of the night, in which the lazily rolling sea could barely be heard and even the pine trees had stopped whispering, but then apparently she changed her mind, crossed the room again, the high heels of her swansdown-trimmed slippers tapping resolutely, as though she knew exactly where she was going and why, she was wearing her flowing dressing gown, which she must have hurriedly thrown over her nightgown, I could hear the silky rustle; when she got back to the terrace door and stayed there motionless for a few seconds, I wanted to say something, but no sound would leave my throat, just as in a nightmare, except I knew I was fully awake; then cautiously, with the attentiveness of a spy, she pulled the curtain open, but instead of stepping out on the terrace she turned around quickly, hurried across the room again toward the double door leading to the hallway, pressed down hard on the handle, the sound was unmistakable, but the door didn't open, she turned the key, the lock clicked open, yet evidently she thought better of it; without venturing into the hallway, she headed back to the terrace, while the door left ajar produced a slight draft, making the curtains flutter in the dark; I sat up in bed.

"What happened?" I asked very quietly, perhaps too quietly, because of the shock, far greater than mere fright, that seized my neck and throat, but without responding—she may not even have heard me—Mother now walked out on the terrace, took a few steps, and, as if the irritatingly loud tapping of her slippers made her stop, rushed back into the room; "What happened?" I asked again, louder this time; and now she was at the front door again, opening it, and once more turning around, and at this point I simply had to jump out of bed, I had to try to help her.

Moving fast in opposite directions, our bodies collided, and for a moment we clung to each other in the middle of the dark room.

"What happened?"

"I knew it, for five years I've known it."

"What?"

"I knew it, for five years I've known it."

We were holding on to each other.

Her body was terribly rigid, I could feel the tension in it, and though for a brief moment she hugged me and I tried hard to yield to her by hugging her back, I sensed that our physical contact was of no help to her, that my eagerness was in vain, that though I could feel her she could not feel me, I might as well have been a table or a chair she was using to regain her balance and resolve, resolve bordering on hysteria, to propel her on to carry out her will, and still, not wanting to let her go, I pressed my body to hers, as if I knew precisely what she was about to do, what awful act I had to keep her from committing—it made no difference to me what it was, I had no clear idea what it might be, but my instincts told me to protect her and keep her from doing whatever it was she now seemed desperate enough to do—and it felt as though my persistence did affect her, as if she had finally recognized me as her son, as someone who belonged to her, and she bent down and kissed my neck passionately, almost biting it, but the next moment, as if having drawn strength from that kiss and from my quaking body, tore my clinging arms from her waist and pushed me away—"Unhappy boy!" she cried, and ran out the terrace door.

I ran after her.

Instead of heading for the wide staircase leading to the park, as one might have expected, she ran in the opposite direction, stopping at the door of the Fräulein's suite.

Candles were burning within, and their lambent light reached our feet.

The sensation that I was standing on my feet had never been so acute.

Nor the feeling that not only my eyes but my whole body was there only to absorb the sight before me.

I cannot honestly say that I didn't know what it all meant, but neither can I claim that I did.

Because a child doesn't merely have knowledge of what ought to take place at such moments but, shocking though it may be to admit it, may have already experienced it, when squeezing pleasure out of his own flesh; nevertheless, what I was seeing came as such a surprise I am not sure I could comprehend it.

Here the spectacle was created by two strange bodies.

Their nakedness gleamed on the bare floor.

With pieces of white garments strewn all about them, the Fräulein seemed somehow to be lying on her side, her knees drawn up almost to her breasts, her body bending into itself, turning her formidably ample buttocks to Father; seeing them in retrospect, with experienced eyes, those buttocks seem extremely beautiful and "turning to" a most inadequate phrase; she was proffering, tendering, serving up her buttocks to Father, while he more or less squatted, knelt above her, one hand frantically clutching her loose dark hair, as he slammed against her, the convex hollow of his loins thrusting in, clinging to, then retracting from the concave double bulge of her behind; he was inside the perfectly enclosed body, able to ravage it freely, powerfully, yet most exquisitely; today I know how that is—in this position not only can one's member slip to the deepest or, I should say, highest reaches, but the sensitized foreskin, the bulbous glans, the bulging blood vessels, while rubbing against the stiffened clitoris and caressing the vulva, can swab and scrub the tight yet slippery cave of the vagina, making the erection so tumescent, so throbbing, that the organ, having reached the mouth of the womb, the last obstacle, can fill the hollow so fully, so perfectly, that one can no longer tell what is ours and what is hers; in this odd position, therefore, violent entry and tender lovemaking can merge and become one; could anyone wish for pleasure more intense? but on that occasion all I could see was that Father's spine was bending sharply, his buttocks spread almost as if he were about to defecate, and he was supporting himself with his free hand: in the moments of rhythmic disengagement his enormous, slightly updrawn testicles became visible, and then he would lunge again, covering completely the spot that induced such bubbling pleasure in both of them; the Fräulein squealed in a piercing, high-pitched voice while Father's mouth opened—and this frightened me because, as if unable to close it, he let out a deep rattle, the tip of his tongue stuck out, and his wide-open eyes stared into space, but of course I couldn't connect the shriek and the rattle to the carnal delight I was witnessing, because when Father reached the highest point of penetration, when he seemed to find his place at last, he froze, and his whole body, covered with thick patches of black hair, was shaken by an uncontrollable and insatiable trembling; still holding her by the hair, he kept raising and banging her head against the floor, and though this produced in her the most pleasurable shrieks, she also began squirming underneath him, as if trying to escape, so that dropping back from his climax, Father's loins resumed their gentle but firm thrusts, which she greeted with softer, more intimate squeals; then Father yanked her head up and knocked it against the floor with a resounding bang.

If at this moment my enjoyment proved far greater than my surprise, if, forgetting Mother's presence, I focused all my senses on this spectacle and even considered myself fortunate to be witnessing it, it was not a child's openmouthed curiosity that was responsible, or the undeniable fact that I was already privy to such secrets, thanks to Count Stollberg, my playmate at Heiligendamm, a boy just a few years my senior; the truth is that many different, hitherto buried desires, cruel impulses, and inclinations had to clash together into some harmony, as if exposing me, as if the Fräulein, with her squeals of delight, had caught me in the act! and what I saw became an illumination of the senses, a revelation that had to do not only with me or with an abstract knowledge of the act or even with my playmate, whom I came across in the swampy reed bed one day, spread out on the soft soil, playing with himself, or even that much to do with Father, but directly with the object of my admiration and affection: Fräulein Wohlgast.

Could it be that those nocturnal escapades had had consequences, after all? those many nights when on our shared terrace I wanted to be alone but was nevertheless happy to find her and have her draw me to her body redolent with the warmth of her bed and of her restlessness?

Beauty radiated from her body, even though this beauty lay not in the shapeliness of her form and not in the regularity of her features but in her flesh, one might say, in the hot exhalation of her skin, even though in purely aesthetic terms she obviously did not measure up to an abstract ideal; her attraction proved stronger than that exercised by so-called perfect beauties: how lucky it is that we trust our fingers more than we do some insipid aesthetics; I hasten to add that even Mother had not escaped the Fräulein's confusingly profound influence and though always willing to accept tiresome rules, in this case Mother also chose to trust her own judgment; she was quite enamored of the Fräulein, indeed idolized her, even fantasized about being as intimate friends with her as Father was with Frick, and was affected by many of the Fräulein's physical features— the sparkling, impertinent brown eyes, the gleaming, darkly Mediterranean, almost Gypsy-like complexion, with skin taut over wide cheekbones, the tiny quivering nostrils, and the full cherry lips that looked as if a ritual sword had split them in half not just horizontally but vertically as well— was stimulated, galvanized in her company, and in spite of Father's frequent and somewhat teasing warning, "The Fräulein is quite common, really," she put up with her loudness, closed her eyes to her uncouth lack of refinement, and did not seem bothered by the limited intellect whose

physical manifestation may have been the low, flat brow which the Fräulein not only failed to offset with a measure of self-discipline but added
to with her licentiousness; the body lying on the floor I also knew well—
the small, hard, pointed breasts and the waist, which her cleverly cut
dresses made seem much slenderer than it was, and the voluptuous hips,
which those same dresses tended to overemphasize—I knew this body
well, because on those nights, when driven by insomnia and restlessness
she appeared on the terrace and embraced me maternally, with an exaggerated tenderness I now know was meant for Father, I came to be familiar with it, precisely in its disproportionate and unconcealed perfection;
she didn't bother with a robe then, and the sheer silk of her nightgown
conveyed everything unhindered, I could even feel her soft bush below
whenever my hand strayed there, as if by accident, and I could inhale the
heavy fragrance in which I sank and sank.

Thus far, and no farther!

Propriety and good taste demand that we pause now in our recollections.

Because Mother, emitting what sounded like a moan, collapsed in a
faint.

Girls

The garden was huge, like a park, shady, mildly fragrant in the warm summer air; pungent smell of pines, their resin dripping from green cones that snap quietly as they grow; firm rosebuds resplendent in red, yellow, white, and pink hues; and yes, a single, ruffled, and slightly singed petal that could open no further, now almost ready to fall; and the tall, rearing lilies with their wasp-enticing nectar; violet, maroon, and blue cups of petunias fluttering in the slightest breeze; long-stemmed snapdragons swaying more indolently in the wind; and along the footpaths, great patches of foxgloves luxuriating in the flaming brilliance of their own colors; opalescent shimmer of dewy grass in the morning sun; clusters of thick shrubbery arranged in rows—elder- and spindleberry bushes, lilacs, intoxicatingly sweet hyacinths, and, in the deepening shadows, under the forsythias, hawthorn and hazel bushes, the damp rot in which green ivy runs riot, exuding a sour-sweet odor, tendrils and shoots creeping over fences and walls, wrapping around tree trunks, fine clinging roots covering everything in sight in the effort to protect and propagate the mildewy decay on which ivy feeds and which it keeps producing; it's easy to see this plant as a symbol of life: in its dank profusion it consumes twigs, branches, grass, everything, then every autumn lets itself be buried in a red grave of fallen leaves, only to revive again in the spring, rearing its waxen head, navigating atop long, hardy stems; green lizards and pale brown snakes once used to enjoy the cool shade here, and fat black slugs traced their convoluted paths with their ooze, which turns white when dry and cracks when touched; when I think of this garden today, I know there is nothing left of it, they cleared the shrubbery, cut down most of the trees, tore down the gazebo with its green trellis and pink rambling roses, carried off the rock garden, putting the stones to some other use and destroying the vegetation in it: the ferns, the stonecrop, the blue and yellow irises; the lawn went to seed and is now burned out in spots; the white garden chairs probably rotted away and fell apart; the stone statue of Pan blowing his pipe, porous with age, that stayed lying on its side in the grass after a storm knocked it off its pedestal may have been thrown into somebody's basement, and even the pedestal disappeared; the plaster ornaments on the façade of the main house, the openmouthed goddesses rising out of seashells over the windows and the decorative scrolls of the fake Grecian columns were all knocked down and the glass veranda walled in; and during one of the reconstructions they even tore the creeping vine off the walls, the favored haunt of ants, beetles, and other insects; but no matter how much I know about all these changes, and know this garden now lives only in my memory, I can still sense every leaf stirring in it, every smell, every ray of light, the direction of every breeze, know them as well as I did then, long ago, and if I wish, it's summer again, a silent summer afternoon.

And there stands the boy I once was, slight, fragile, not ill-proportioned, even if he feels clumsy and ugly and is therefore reluctant to undress completely even in the summer heat; if he can help it, he won't take off even his shirt and will certainly keep on his undershirt, and prefers to wear long pants even in summer, would rather sweat though he finds the strong smell of perspiration repellent; today, of course, we smile at all this and note sadly that we are never fully aware of our own beauty, which can be appreciated only by others, and we can do so only nostalgically, in retrospect.

There I am, then, standing on the sloping garden path, and it's one of those rare moments when I'm not preoccupied with myself or, more precisely, am so taken up with anticipation that I myself have become an actor in a scene that follows an unknown script, and for a change, I don't even mind not having my shirt and trousers on, and stand here in only my blue shorts so faded from repeated washings they are almost white; I disregard all that, even though I know she'll soon be here.

I am simply there, along with the garden, the street, and the woods beyond the street; I am holding a large slice of bread smeared thick with lard and covered with slices of green pepper. I cut up the pepper myself, careful to leave the veins that make the pepper hot attached to the stem. When I lift the bread to my mouth, ready to bite, I have to press down on the strips of pepper to make sure they don't slip off—of course they always do—but not too hard, or else I squeeze the fat off the bread and get it all over my face.

The sky has turned hazy gray from the heat, the sun is beating down, it may be the hottest hour of the day, not even insects bother to stir, yet on my skin, still moist from sleep, I seem to sense a breeze, very gentle and cool, that blows nowhere else but on this steep footpath.

The lizards have disappeared, the birds are silent.

The garden path leads to an ornate wrought-iron gate leaning against carved stone pillars, past which, on the street, fine shadows are quivering, and beyond them begins the dense woods where the cooler breeze seems to be coming from; I stand there in a daze, enjoying the breeze playfully tickling my skin, but I am also attentive and, let's be honest, aware that it is my self-esteem making me pretend I'm in a dazed, dreamlike state.

If I weren't pretending, I'd have to admit that I have been waiting for her, just as I was waiting for her when in my comfortably darkened room I pretended to be deeply engrossed in my reading; waiting for her even as I fell asleep and waiting when startled out of sleep, waiting for hours, days, weeks, even in the kitchen when I was spreading lard on my slice of rye bread, cutting the pepper, and looking again and again at the loudly ticking alarm clock—I lost count of how many times I looked, as if by chance, glancing casually at the dial, hoping she would also look at her watch just then, at that very second, and get up and leave; she comes this way every day at this hour, at two-thirty, so it cannot be mere coincidence, but all the same, I cannot erase from my mind the terrifying thought that it's all a mistake, that she's not coming this way because of me, that it is only a coincidence, and that she passes by here only because she feels like it.

A few more minutes and then I might start walking toward the fence as if I had some important business there; I give her a few more minutes, a half hour at most, long enough for her to feign indifference and decide to be late, just as I sometimes, to preserve the appearance of my independence, pretend I'm not standing behind the bushes, waiting; I try to ascertain how much time has elapsed, it could be little or much, although I always hope it's little and passing quickly, ever since that one time when she didn't show up at all and I waited until evening, I couldn't help it, kept waiting by the fence way past dark, but she didn't come, and since then I know how fathomless time can be when one is waiting, when one absolutely must wait.

And then she appears.

Like every moment we want to be significant, this one, too, turns out to be insignificant; we have to remind ourselves afterward that what we have been waiting for so eagerly is actually here, has finally come, and nothing has changed, everything is the same, it's simply here, the waiting is over.

By then I found myself standing among the bushes close to the fence, not far from the gate; this was the place, my post, directly opposite the trail that curved gently, almost surreptitiously, out of the woods and onto the open road, concealed by dense shrubbery and the sagging branches of a giant linden tree, a road that was always empty at this hour, so if I stood guard here at the fence, I couldn't possibly miss her, and I did watch every second, my body cutting a passage in the bushes where I got to know every single twig and branch that kept snapping in my face, where I could follow her until I'd bump into the fence of the neighboring garden, and my gaze could follow her even farther, until the red and blue of her comically swaying skirt disappeared in the green woods, but that took a good long time; the only way she could surprise me was by not coming on the wood trail—and she did make sure that our silent game did not become too regular or predictable: sometimes she made a detour and came up the street, appearing on the left where the street suddenly begins to climb and then, just as sharply, dips, a roadway that had once been paved but by now formed an almost continuous crevice because of cracks and potholes caused by sudden freezes, but her trickery was to no avail, I heard her every time, for in that infinite silence, where beneath such irregular and accidental noises as the rustling of leaves, the twittering of birds, a barking dog, or an indefinable human cry, even the keenest, most sensitive ear had trouble making out the uniform murmur and buzz of the distant city, I was familiar with every last detail of both sound and silence, even with the subtle interplay of the two, a highly developed sensitivity to sound that in no small measure was due to my waiting for her; she might decide to come up the street, but she could not fool me, the crunch of her footsteps gave her away, it could be no one else, I knew those steps too well.

That day she chose the wooded path after all. She stepped out onto the road and stopped. If my memory captures her image precisely, and I think it has, she was wearing a red skirt with white polka dots and a white blouse, both of them heavily starched and ironed to a shine, so that the rigid fullness of the blouse concealed the mounds of her small breasts and the stiff cotton skirt swished against her skinny knees. Each piece of her meager wardrobe displayed or concealed different parts of her body, and for this reason I had to keep track of each item—skirts, dresses, blouses, everything that she herself, while dressing and possibly even thinking of me, must have considered extremely important; craning her uncovered neck, she looked around, slowly, carefully, the only movement she allowed herself; peering out from under the mask of her coy reserve, first she looked to the left, then to the right, and while turning her head, her glance would come to rest on me as if by accident, very often for no more than a fraction of a second, and then I tried in vain to catch her eye; at other times she looked at me more boldly for quite a few seconds, and once in a great while for an absurdly long time, but of this I'll have more to say later—in any case, I knew her eyes were looking for me, because if it happened that I wasn't standing at my usual place, if, say, I dropped down on my stomach or stood behind a tree so she would not notice me right away and I could extract some small advantage thereby, then her gaze grew uncertain, her face showed the deep disappointment which I hoped to wheedle out of her with my little game of hide-and-seek, and which, given her reserve and aloofness, could be considered blatant flir-tatiousness; one single glance a day was my due, nothing more, while I stood helpless behind the fence, in the stifling shade of the bushes.

She wasn't beautiful, a statement that needs immediate clarification, for with mixed shame and regret I had to admit this even to myself while, however, she did seem beautiful to me, and once she disappeared in the bend of the street I almost felt I had to be ashamed in front of certain people that the girl I had fallen in love with was not beautiful, was ugly, or, however charitably we'd want to put it, not very beautiful; in any case, the doubt, the inexplicable shame was strong, and since I spent so many days in agonized waiting, I couldn't protest, couldn't prevaricate, in the end had to admit to myself and to say out loud, to shout it to the world— in the hope of regaining my freedom I screamed into the air that I was in love, was in love with her, but only the shouting itself made me happy; when I was through, I couldn't shake the nagging feeling that now I would have to start waiting again, and go on waiting until two-thirty, and when she finally did come, I'd have to wait for her to be gone so that I could wait for her the next day, and that really seemed perverse and even more senseless than trying to avoid meeting Krisztián only to lessen the pain of seeing him.

But if things had to be this way, if I had to see her, then why couldn't she be beautiful at least, that's what I would have wished, for if she were beautiful, then her beauty would have lingered in me even after she was gone and I wouldn't have to be ashamed about my feelings: her beauty in some way would absolve me, I thought; as it was, I was forever entangled in the same agony—today I would call it the agony of longing for beauty, an agony so dark and dismal it must be hidden from the eyes of strangers, just as I had to conceal my love for Krisztián—for different reasons, of course—and still he managed to humiliate me, because my silent love for him made me memorize his quick gestures, his awkward smiles, and his wild laughter, his untouchable sadness, the transparent flash of his green eyes and the nervous twitch of his muscles, and not only did I absorb all this but I made it my own, so that he could surface in me anytime, in the most unexpected situations, as if replacing my body with his and pretending I was he; thus, with a single imagined gesture, look, or smile he could destroy anything that might be very important to me but also help me with problems I would have found hard to solve on my own, so that his constant presence was two-faced, benevolent, or hostile, but always unpredictable; he never left me, he was my crutch, my secret model, almost as if I no longer existed or did only as his shadow: and he was here now, hanging about me, drifting in and out, shrugging, grinning, pretending slyly not to notice me yet watching me all the same; I may have found this girl terribly exciting, her very sight may have swept away my fatuous doubts, but I was not alone, not the only one looking at her, and even if strictly speaking I was, I couldn't form a clear opinion based strictly on my own feelings but was of two minds, influenced by a critical faculty that, in matters of beauty, I found eminently competent; in truth, whose judgment could I trust more than his?

In the meantime, it was still I who was watching her—who else could it be?—I who was waiting for her, happy when she showed up, and I who have seen no more profoundly exciting face and body since, or, to be more precise, ever since and in every woman who appeals to me, I seem to be looking always for what I finally got from her—nothing she actually gave me, but this nothing was painfully real, and later I tried to fill it without even knowing it; today I know that it was beauty, her own unique perfection, which every day she revealed to me, and only me, if only for a few moments, for what is beauty if not the involuntary giving away of what is hidden even from ourselves? and if in spite of this I still couldn't consider her beautiful, then strangely enough it was only because, despite all appearances, I couldn't ever be alone with her, not even for a moment; there were always others standing with me in the bushes who interfered, held down my arms, gave me goose pimples, warned me not to yield to my feelings—maybe they did the right thing, I say philosophically today, mindful of the pain that teaches us what we can and cannot do; and he wasn't the only one who argued against her—absurdly enough, I even experienced the jealousy my phantom Krisztián would have felt, had he loved me, about the real Lívia, and strangely, very strangely, there were several of us inside me who were watching her—I, who would have loved to love this girl, wasn't alone, and even if I wasn't fully conscious of this at the time, the other boys were there, too, disturbing me, standing behind me, watching the same girl, and they didn't think she was beautiful, didn't even think she was ugly—because I believe that besides me no one had ever even noticed her before.

I was the first and only one, and this couldn't but make an impression on her.

I knew she also was ashamed of her ugliness; everything about her spoke of this: her walk, her skin, her compulsively clean dresses, her shy cautiousness, her bashfulness; yet this did not make her weak, but, on the contrary, perhaps made her beautiful, and she let me understand with an earnestness bordering on defiance that, though she might think herself the ugliest of girls she must still come by my spot—and let's add that her defenselessness was made even more emphatic, almost absurd, by the stoic dignity of the poor; all the same, a curious shiver of excitement ran through me when I thought of the cellar where she lived.

She was small, slight of build, fragile, and almost always kept her head lowered, so that her great brown eyes were forever looking up at things, unblinking, and—I think the best word to use here would be deeply— and her short-cropped chestnut hair was held together with two clips, two white butterflies, to keep it from falling into her eyes, which definitely made her look awkward and little-girlish, but I liked her like that; her nicely rounded forehead was visible, testifying to the care her parents must have given her, the concern that she look neat and well-groomed; I could see how her father, while sitting in his porter's cubicle, drew her between his knees and with a handkerchief moistened with spittle wiped something off her face—her father was the school janitor and also the sexton of a nearby church, a skinny, blond-haired man with a little mustache and artificially curled hair, and they lived in the basement of the school; somebody told me that her mother, whom I saw a couple of times emerging from the dark basement loaded down with pots and bags, was helping people out with leftovers from the school lunchroom, and she also fed her own family from there—she was said to be a Gypsy, and she had the kind of shiny rosy brown skin which the summer sun turns just a shade darker, though its winter paleness may be even lovelier.

The snow was almost gone when all this started between us, on a day notable for another reason: the thaw had come late that year after a hard winter; what the sun melted during the day froze over again in the cold of the night, and only gradually, slowly, was it becoming clear that the thaw was finally setting in, that spring was here; first to melt were the cushions of snow on the rooftops and the snowcaps on chimneys, along with the fluffy white strips on the tree branches which wind had hardened into crystals; long icicles sprouting from the eaves during the night dripped during the day, and the cool water made the snow cover around the houses sag; you could break off and lick the fine, cold icicles, specially flavored by rotting leaves in the drainpipes and the rust of the pipes themselves—we loved them; a thin armor of ice hardened on the ground at night, ideal for walking and sliding—it snapped and cracked under our feet, and we could leave footprints in it until, after a few mild days, everything came to life and began dripping, snapping, drying, crackling, trickling, flowing, and the birds began to sing; so the day was one of those wonderfully drippy, mild, clear days with a perfectly cloudless blue sky, and in the long morning recess we all, class after class, had to march down to the gym, line up, and stand in silence, looking straight ahead, not moving, not turning our heads; but impressive as the solemnity of the ostentatious memorial ceremony may have been, you still managed to see the soothing blue expanse beyond the tall narrow windows—without turning your head, of course—from the corner of your eyes, standing in a silence alive with stifled unrest; on the gym stage, its red curtain drawn, all the teachers stood—silent, of course, and motionless.

This was the hour of Stalin's funeral, when the embalmed body was being taken from the marble hall where he had lain in state to the mausoleum.

I imagined it to be a vast hall, enormous and almost completely dark, so huge in fact that it might better be called an indoor arena, a marble hall, yes, I savored the name, but no ordinary huge hall, like a railroad terminal, for instance, but one in which marble columns stand like trees in a dense forest, reaching to the heights, and up there in the heights, it is also dark, the space so immense that the coffered ceiling cannot be seen; no footsteps are heard here, no one may enter and no one dare enter, lest the loud echoes of his steps disturb the silence; and there, at the far end of the hall or arena, he is lying on his bier—I pictured a simple black platform, a bed actually, which one presumes is there but can't really see because not enough light comes through the narrow doorway to illuminate the place; only the marble glimmers softly here and there, the grayish-brown, delicately veined marble, the mirror-smooth columns, the floor, there are no candles, no lights; the image was so vivid in my mind that I can easily recall it even today, with no subsequent, perhaps ironic embellishments; I had the feeling that the whole world partook in the silence, even animals, sensing the ominous human stillness, falling silent in astonishment, for his death was not a passing away but the ultimate, absolute crescendo of solemnity, the outcry of respect, joy, longing, and love that could not be expressed before with such force—only now, in this breathtaking death; and the vision I had was not the least bit altered by the fact that in the gym we could hear the happy chirping of sparrows fluttering around in the eaves and the indifferent cawing of crows; and then I tried to imagine this vast dense silence as the stillness of all the world's humans and animals congealed into one enormous, terrifying silence, tried to gauge it, find some appropriate unit of measurement for it, since we knew of course that at this hour nothing must stir outside either; all traffic came to a halt, cars and trams and trains between stations stopped, people cleared off the streets, and if anyone happened to be out when the sirens began to wail they had to freeze, remain rooted to the spot; and just as different kinds of noises can blend, as the noise of a whole city from a distance can be perceived as a coherent, uniform hum, the different silences had somehow to blend into one, so that in the end it could be heard even in that dark marble hall, the knowledge that the whole world fell silent must penetrate even that vast interior, though he could no longer hear, not even this silence; and what must it be like, I wondered, when one can no longer hear even silence, to be dead? at which point my neat mental picture became rather confused, because I knew he wasn't just dead, not just dead like anybody else, lowered into the grave to rot away, but was different—a secret ointment would preserve and consecrate him, though the whole embalming business seemed so murky and incomprehensible that it was better not to think about it at all; hard as I tried to get my mind to leave this forbidden territory, it obsessed me more than his death, and I had to think about it all the time, about the mysterious embalming process administered only to the greatest of the great, the pharaohs of Egypt; when finally I asked Grandfather about it—perhaps I thought he knew everything because he was so tight-lipped—and also wanted to know why only the pharaohs and Stalin, what possible connection there may have been between their greatness and his, I felt a little guilty because I suspected his answer would be biting and sarcastic, he talked like that about everything; and I was right; rather than allaying my moral uneasiness about embalming, his answer made it even more acute: "Oh, that's a splendid invention!" he exclaimed with a sudden laugh, and, as always when he began to speak, whipped off his glasses: "Well, it's like this, you see, first they take out all the internal organs that decompose easily, like the liver, the lungs, the kidneys, the heart, the intestines, the spleen, the bile duct, let's see what else, oh yes, the brain from the skull, if there was any to begin with, they take it all out; but first they pump the blood out of all the veins, provided it hasn't clotted, because blood is also a perishable item, and when there are no soft parts left, I think they even take the eyeballs out of the sockets, so only the skin, the flesh, and the bones are left, the empty shell of the man, then they treat the body with some sort of chemical, inside and out, but don't ask me what, because I don't know, and after that all they have to do is stuff it and sew it up, carefully, as your grandmother does when she stuffs the chicken for Sunday dinner; well, that's about it," all of which Grandfather said without wondering why I asked the question or who I had in mind, and if he did wonder, he didn't seem very interested, for he said no more, mitigated his brief monologue with not a single word or gesture but simply fell silent, the smile vanishing from his lips and again becoming as glum and matter-of-fact as he had been on the day of Stalin's death, when I had been looking for some black material suitable for draping the school bulletin board and the only thing I could find was one of my grandmother's old-fashioned silk slips, which I proceeded to cut up, unstitching the lace trimming and the straps; seeing me do this, Grandfather remarked, "While you're at it, why don't you take along one of her undies, too?" and as if his next gesture was meant to indicate he was returning to the silent world where he spent most of his days, he shoved his glasses back onto his nose and turned away, taking with him the glance that only a moment ago had seemed interested and cheerful.

But how could anyone in his right mind even conceive of such an answer—it sounded so blasphemous, not just the part about cutting open the great man's stomach and taking out his organs but also the way Grandfather talked about it, so flippantly and irreverently!—surely if there was no way to preserve the body, then it would be best to keep quiet about the whole outrageous procedure, pretend it wasn't true, pretend it never happened, yes, we should have all kept quiet about it, just as I had to keep quiet about, not admit even to myself, what Krisztián had said when we were told of the unexpected, fatal illness, as though the mere fact that I overheard the statement was in itself a grave offense.

My overhearing Krisztián was indeed accidental, merely accidental, and I clung to the word as if for a good reason; yes, of course, that's what it was, an accident to be quickly forgotten, along with so much else, because if I hadn't happened to be the monitor that day and hadn't had to go to the bathroom to dampen the sponge, or if I had left the classroom just a few minutes earlier or later—but that's exactly what made it an accident!—then I wouldn't have heard what he said, he could have said it and I wouldn't have known about it, after all, many things had been said that, fortunately, I knew nothing about, but it did happen, and I did hear it, and almost as if looking for a pretext to avoid it, I kept reenacting the scene in my mind, obsessively, for days, hoping it could be forgotten like everything else, but I couldn't forget it and I didn't find an acceptable pretext either; on the contrary, the episode reminded me of my responsibilities; it seemed irrevocable, not an accident at all but something done willfully, like a retaliation; but then I could take my own revenge, although that was also a trap, because taking revenge would also expose me, my lies, and my futile attempts to ignore everything that had to do with Krisztián, to treat him like air, less even than air, as if he were nothing! to wish him out of my life, as if I had killed him.

And the idea of killing him wasn't a passing fancy but one I thought about, toyed with, worked out the details of: I planned to steal Father's pistol because he had once taught me how to load it and how to handle it, I felt very confident about the technical details of the planned murder: I planned to steal the pistol, which he kept in his desk drawer and once a month cleaned with a rag dipped in kerosene, which blackened his slender fingers, so if he wanted to look up while explaining something to me, he could use only the back of his hand to sweep the hair out of his eyes—it was his cool blue eyes, the penetrating smell of kerosene, and the rather simple rules about handling the pistol that one Sunday afternoon paved the way to my murderous impulse, which I could respond to quite rationally, since I thought the only thing left to be worked out was how to cover up the traces; but now this stupid accident, which I had tried so hard to ignore, frustrated all my designs, exposed my murderous fantasies, revealing to me that I was far too weak and cowardly to become Krisztián's murderer, for I even lacked the courage to report him, for God's sake, after he had inadvertently given me the perfect opportunity, and though the possibility of turning him in did occur to me, of course, I rejected it as soon as I thought of it, for I knew that that would make me unacceptable to myself, that I'd surely feel like a lousy little stool pigeon.

I did feel like a stool pigeon even though I didn't do anything, dreaded even to think about doing anything, wouldn't even tell my mother about it, though I'd have loved to unburden myself, feared being unable to follow the advice she'd give me about how to resolve my quandary; I decided to say nothing, but she must have sensed something and even asked if anything was wrong; no, nothing, I said, since I was also afraid that I might get Grandfather into trouble, because the two reactions, his and Krisztián's, were closely connected in my mind, one as if preconditioned by the other—if Grandfather hadn't prepared the ground, then Krisztián's comment wouldn't have seemed so remarkable, but I knew that when the boys—the friends!—were by themselves they talked of things they'd never mention in front of me; a whole range of opinions and judgments, a tight circle of confidences was and always had been permanently closed to me, and Grandfather's views also belonged to that circle, which I accidentally, unwittingly penetrated and I was now aware of and therefore couldn't simply block out, if only because of my smoldering, tormenting jealousy: this being so, the unwanted knowledge alone, the secret knowledge of what to me were unacceptable judgments, was enough to make me a stool pigeon.

They must have thought I'd watched them go into the bathroom for their conference and waited for the right moment to burst in on them. Naturally, I noticed Krisztián first. He was standing in front of the tar-covered wall of the urinal, his legs wide apart, but what a pose, even while urinating!—one hand on his hip, gracefully bending back his wrist, and his other hand holding his penis, but not like children who copy the gentle touch of their mother's hand, holding their weenie at the base with two fingers, a bit clumsily since the last drops can never be properly shaken out that way and pee always gets on your fingers or your pants, but in the grownup way, in fact just like a grownup, in a backhanded sort of way, grasping his tool between his thumb and his other fingers, loosely, the little finger a bit apart from the rest, away from the stream, cupping his penis in his hand as one would a cigarette in windy weather, and this could have been taken as a sign of sensible modesty, if he hadn't at the same time been thrusting out his hips in such an indecently sensuous manner and spreading his legs so wide apart that his posture seemed to indicate—to whom? to himself? to us?—that he could take pleasure even in this act, could urinate shamelessly and, what's more, had turned it into a fashion that others imitated, and not just the boys in his group but everybody in the class, myself included, though his brazen, open enjoyment was his alone, others couldn't duplicate it; when I opened the door, with the dry chalky eraser in my hand, I noticed Krisztián in this familiar pose, which seemed even more casual because he was talking to Szmodits, who was peeing next to him and talking loud enough to be heard by Prém, waiting in line behind him, and even by Kálmán Csúzdi, who was leaning against the doorpost, smoking; what I really felt like doing at that moment was backing out of the bathroom, but I couldn't, because Kálmán Csúzdi had noticed me, so I walked in, and Krisztián, perhaps because he didn't hear the door open or simply ignored it, went on to finish his sentence: "so finally this sonofabitch is gonna croak, too!" just as, after a brief hesitation, I closed the door behind me.

Prém, a stocky dark-skinned boy, was like an amiable courtier who went everywhere with Krisztián, his wise, all-knowing, and all-forgiving gentle brown eyes seeming always in search of opportunities to be of service to him, and though he was just as nice to me as he was to Krisztián and, as far as I could tell, to everyone else, I felt toward him a deep and implacable hostility bordering on revulsion, and no wonder, considering he had achieved without pain or effort what I didn't have the courage, skill, and, possibly, playfulness to achieve; their bond was refined to the most subtle form of equality, precisely the kind I longed for, like brothers, like twins, even a little indifferent to each other since their relationship was arranged by nature and therefore they had nothing to add to it, also like lovers, since no matter how far apart the two faces moved, they seemed to be able to maintain a link, each always referring in some way to the other, always aware of each other's presence; all the same, Prém, the smaller of the two, was clearly Krisztián's servant (in such relationships the smaller is always the servant)—Prém now let out a full-mouthed guffaw, as if Krisztián had cracked a hilarious joke, even though the sentence had a rather ominous ring, an anxious undertone; I wouldn't have been surprised if Krisztián had smacked him for his too-ready laugh—he sometimes did that, knowing that an underling's exaggerated zeal can detract from rather than increase his superior's authority and therefore deserves punishment; I especially hated Prém's mouth—and those eyes! I hated the soft, alluring submissiveness in those wide-open, slightly bulging dark eyes with their thick lashes—oh that mouth! wild, darkly, savagely red, the lower lips a bit protuberant, in itself not exactly ugly, except that in the smallness of his face it seemed exaggerated and unnatural, and as if he himself were aware of its exceptional size, and of the attractiveness that could not be denied him, he had the habit of licking his lips with the tip of his tongue, taking real pleasure in doing it; his manner of speaking was unusual, too, always leaning over, speaking softly, never looking straight into his listener's eyes but aiming for one of the ears, since he didn't so much speak his words as murmur them, whispered little monologues into one's ears.

Yet I don't think it was only these inane jabberings that amused Krisztián, but also the surprise and befuddlement evoked by Prém's little pranks, which he followed with paternal solicitude, although Prém chose his victims according to his own inscrutable logic: he'd scurry down the hall or saunter alongside the classroom desks, stop abruptly in front of a classmate, lean over with a confident air, and, with a fractured sentence that was but the start of his ingratiating whispering, evoke immediate and intense curiosity or clear consternation; pretending to pay little heed to the response, which he left to Krisztián watching from a distance, he'd just look at his victim very tenderly and begin again: "Sweet little scumbag, have you heard, it's those Hungarian Fascists again, the ones who've been holed up since the war—they broke out of the hole again, it was on the radio last night and again this morning, crazy isn't it, to come out of the hole—" and then he'd stop and fall silent, and the startled query would come: "But what hole?" "Why, your asshole," he'd whisper, and move on as softly and stealthily as he had come; but now, in the bathroom, it was Kálmán Csúzdi who was looking at me, his eyes reddened from the hollow-filtered Russian cigarette dangling from his lips, sizing me up as he would a strange, slightly repulsive object, somewhat sternly, ready to check my every move, sly blue eyes with pale blond lashes in his bright, chubby face, his hands stuck in his pockets; he came to the bathroom only to smoke and be with his friends—his cigarette would soon be passed around, I knew they always shared it—and with his stern attention to me he seemed also to be watching over the others, accentuating their togetherness as if letting me know that any one of them might have said whatever Krisztián had said, they were so completely in agreement; and when the door finally clicked shut, and first Szmodits then Prém turned to me, and Krisztián, without changing his position, looked straight into my eyes, I knew something was going to happen.

The sentence had been uttered, couldn't be taken back, and there was no doubt to whom it referred, the laughter confirmed that.

And if Krisztián had not looked into my eyes the way he did, had he not stood there in that inimitably shameless pose, I'd probably have pretended that I didn't see or hear anything, and, protecting myself from him, would have simply wetted the sponge and gone, without so much as looking again at them, but the blatant openness and provocative artlessness of his stare proved to be an emotional rape against which I immediately had to react, though I'd have preferred not to, my self-esteem demanding it, asserting itself independently, it seemed, without regard for my conscious will; "What did you say?" I asked very quietly, staring back at him, and to hear my voice so calm was such a shock that I was immediately gripped by anxious fear, and when I continued I heard my voice, hoarse and much louder, saying, "Who's supposed to croak?"

He didn't answer, in the uncomfortable silence it was as if I had finally risen above him, and I stepped closer to him, my eyes confidently locked on his, but then something happened that I should and would have anticipated, had not the preceding moment made me so self-assured: completely by surprise, Prém's face appeared between us, one could say that he slipped his most enchanting smile between our two faces, and as I still looked into Krisztián's eyes I was forced to see Prém's bulging eyes, too, and his lips, which he was licking sensuously with the tip of his tongue, and had to hear his voice whispering, "Little snitch, you know how big a horse's prick is? as big as Csúzdi's!" By then Kálmán Csúzdi had already pushed himself away from the door, and his voice was much stronger, huskier: "You can have Prém's dick for lunch!" and at this point, according to the unwritten rules of the game, they should have roared with laughter to lessen the impact of their group performance, but they didn't laugh.

The silence grew more oppressive, as though a shared common fear lay at the bottom of it, made every clever mediation futile, neutralized their numerical advantage, at once confirming and casting doubt on my own superiority, a silence that Krisztián finally broke as he turned to the wall again to fix his pants; "A little more refinement, boys," he said, which may have surprised them more than me, and created an even more troubled silence.

Not knowing what to do next, I suddenly felt the sponge in my hand, which was the only thing that could help now, to step up to the faucet and wet the sponge, after all, that's what I had come in here for.

But when I turned around I couldn't seem to prove to them, not so simply, that that was the only reason I'd come into the bathroom, and all four of them were staring at me, motionless.

I knew I had to get out, this had to end somehow.

An awfully long time seemed to pass before my feet managed to get me to the door, which I opened, but before I could close it, Szmodits growled after me, not much conviction in his voice, "Better watch your step there or somebody'll beat the living shit out of you!" which I couldn't be angry at him for, and which didn't frighten me either, since I knew that this sentence, too, had to be said.

Of course I can't claim that later as I stood silent and more or less motionless in the gym I thought only about this episode and recalled every detail exactly as it had happened, but it did preoccupy me, though there were plenty of other distractions, like the fantasies about the funeral, the discomfort of standing in place, and spring, already present in the blueness of the wintry sky, making itself felt through the tall, heavily barred windows; I thought about the famous corpse, too, with its stomach and chest split open with a single incision and the inner organs removed, ready to be stuffed, but with what? they couldn't very well use straw; I saw the body lying on the dissecting table with the exposed heart, the soft lung, the purple kidneys and intestines next to it, and although I didn't like thinking about it, this still made me happy and I derived some dark satisfaction from having thoughts I knew I shouldn't have, since violating the spirit of the solemn ceremony got my mind off my fears better than anything else might have, for naturally the boys' threat had had its effect, and just when I thought I had nicely forgotten the incident, a totally insignificant detail would suddenly flash before my eyes, the green wall of the toilet or the cigarette smoke, and revive my fear, and when you are gripped by fear and trembling you want to find a clearly identifiable object to go with it: what I most feared was that they'd sneak up on me and jump me, yes, I was afraid of being overwhelmed and beaten to a pulp, though given their numbers my defeat and humiliation was a foregone conclusion, and for days I'd been thinking of ways to protect myself; in the gym, Prém was standing right in front of me, Kálmán Csúzdi behind me and a little to the right, and I could feel the presence of the other two, who stood next to each other way in the back—in short, I was surrounded, though at the moment they couldn't move any more than I could; considering my total helplessness, this enforced immobility was a shield offering a temporary reprieve, though I couldn't help staring at Prém's neck, fearing he might suddenly turn around and slap me across the face, as a signal for the others to pounce.

This was the reason I couldn't forget the moment when I felt someone looking at me; fear made the moment memorable.

But I'm not even sure just how it happened; it's surely one of the most mysterious and baffling sensations when someone is watching us or talking or just thinking about us and we turn, without anything consciously registering, toward the source of attention and only afterward realize why we looked in that direction—we felt it, we say, but can't say just what, as if our senses functioned more subtly and naturally than our minds or, to be more precise, as if our minds can work only with the materials and energies our senses provide and usually the processing is delayed, which makes for constant dissonance and uncertainty, and the question remains: What sort of force, energy, or material is able to span great distances and signal to our senses that that of others is present, what kinds of signals can we receive or broadcast without conscious intention? when all we seem to do is look at the other person, think about him, or make a casual comment very quietly, and suddenly the air is charged, loses its neutrality, and relays clear messages, whether friendly or hostile, and then the most complex form of communication follows; and I don't even think she wanted to attract my attention, which at that point would have been unthinkable for many reasons, so her glance was as unconscious as my turning toward her, two beings staring at each other unconsciously, baring themselves to each other eagerly, shamelessly; needless to say, we had to take care, our teachers were up on the stage, watching, and because of the special nature of the proceedings, they couldn't move either and couldn't yell at us as they usually did, so we were spared "Stop moving back there!" or "Keep still, snotnose, or I'll kick you out on your butt!"—warnings that now had to be communicated with looks only: a twitch of an eyebrow or an almost imperceptible nod warning that unruliness, conspicuous fidgeting, and audible giggles were duly noted and would not go unpunished, all of which made the silence heavier and more ominous than it would have been if they could freely shout at us; but she was one of those who lived inconspicuously among us, never calling attention to herself, much too timid and bashful to risk violating the rules, and it was inconceivable that she'd start flirting with me out of boredom just to amuse herself; I simply didn't know what to make of her look.

For this look, I realized later when I had time to reflect on it, called attention to itself precisely because it didn't seem the result of some childish whim, which became clear to me when, in response to my uncomprehending, questioning glance, her face did not dissolve into a defensive or apologetic smile but remained motionless, her gaze unwavering, with nothing awkwardly solemn about it either, simply serious, and I asked myself, Why is that dumb girl giving me the eye? and my own eyes must have asked the same question, as I thought of the silly line we used to blurt out in similarly ambiguous situations, as a form of defense against embarrassment—"Just keep lookin' if you so smart, come on closer 'n' smell my fart"—and she didn't respond to this either, didn't change, even though my grin must have indicated what I was thinking about, and I almost laughed out loud; in the end, I did notice a change, but in myself, because I couldn't turn away and in fact also became serious, as if, from the slippery slopes of my earlier fear and anxiety and of my lopsided grin, I now had to plunge into an infinitely soft body of gray water where nothing palpably familiar remained except this extraordinarily open gaze, seeking no effect, therefore most effective, meaning to achieve nothing, with no recognizable purpose or wish to communicate, using the eye simply and naturally for what it was meant for—to see, to look—reducing the organ to its basic biological function, a nearly uninvolved possessor of objects in its sight; and this was so unusual yet so similar to everything I had vainly longed for in my relation to Krisztián, because he always found ways to evade me, to stay aloof—oh, how familiar it all seemed—yet I had to be suspicious of her, because the open look of natural possession is separated by only a thin line from the other kind of look that appears when, concentrating on what is happening within us, we do not notice what our eyes are looking at and, the inner occurrence seeming more important, the lens itself cannot decide whether to focus on the inner or outer subject and the face we involuntarily present to the person we are observing becomes impassive and inert; but no, I could detect not a single trace of this self-absorbed blankness; her face remained discreetly closed and inaccessible, but the look in her eyes was like an animal's! no mistake, she was looking at me, nobody else, she saw me, her attention was directed at no one but me.

I saw her through heads and shoulders, standing in the first row, being one of the shortest pupils, while I, not much taller, was in the third row; the distance between us was considerable because boys and girls were separated in the gym, so not only did her gaze have to traverse the wide no-man's-land which, in compliance with school regulations, divided the sexes and where on other occasions the beribboned flag of our Young Pioneer troop was raised with solemn ceremony and the accompaniment of annoying loud drumrolls, but she also had to twist her head and look backward to see me, yet she seemed to be standing very close to me, right in front of me; I don't know how long it took for all my suspicions to dissipate, but after a while her closeness was almost palpable; she was practically inside me, the whites of her eyes gleaming in the wintry pallor of her brown skin, the almost sickly dark circles around her eyes where the veins were so prominent that the brown of her skin seemed to fade into blue; the tiny mouth under the pointed narrow nose, the impertinent little bulges of her upper lip, and her forehead that later was to have a special fascination for me; I grew to love its clear, even brown hue in summer, its delicate spots in winter, when the bone structure appeared in faint outline, softening the shadows in the delicate hollow of her temples and making her hair, pulled back with white clips, even darker, her wild, thick, strong hair, like her eyebrows, arching delicately but asymmetrically, almost comically, above her eyes; that's how she looked then, or rather, that's how I saw her, that's what I saw of her, that and her neck as it rose out of the open collar of her white blouse, the muscles hardening with almost boyish toughness as she turned around, keeping her head low; only later did I begin to notice her body; her eyes were what was important now, and perhaps their immediate setting—her face, but that, too, was soon lost, to be replaced by a warm, hazy sensation, not unlike fainting, a mere feeling, a state of being, a certainty that at this moment she and I were experiencing the same feeling, sharing an identical, most intense state of being which never became conscious and in which there were no thoughts, glances, or bodies but all these fading into blurred outlines and replaced by something that cannot be talked about.

Her eyes were in my eyes, my face penetrated hers, and my neck felt her neck and was keenly aware of the danger, the risk she took by turning around to me, and as if blinking might interrupt the continuity of our shared gaze, we seemed not to have closed our eyes, not even once, and our gaze seemed endless.

We are trying to stare each other down, I thought then, but today, delving into my memories, I find this interpretation derisory; our inner monologues are but feeble rationalizations, deceptions, or, at best, mistakes compared to the dialogues conducted by eyes and faces; of course we weren't trying to stare each other down.

Yet we shouldn't be surprised if strong emotions demand immediate verbal expression, since the mechanism that operates on early conditioning, what we call personality, is compelled to defend itself most vigorously precisely when in its devotion to another it loses its conditioned habits.

I simply didn't know what to make of it all.

I couldn't comprehend what had happened, was happening, or was yet to happen to me, and I didn't know where it would lead us, this powerful, uncontrollable, ultimately unfounded happiness, the ease with which our gaze possessed our emotions, and I began to be afraid again—of her, and of Prém, who might choose this moment, now that I'd found some security with her, to turn around and quick as lightning hit me across the mouth; if he did that so that she saw it, I'd have to hit him back, and that, I felt, given the likely complications, should be avoided at all cost; and I didn't understand why she did this here, why now? since plenty of opportunities for this, or something like this, arose at other times and in other places—it was not, after all, some inexplicable miracle that brought her face so close to mine, and it would be a deceptive exaggeration to claim it was sheer force of emotion that shortened the physical distance between us; no, I had known her well enough to sense her closeness from afar, even with the heads and shoulders between us; this wasn't the first time I'd seen her—although at this moment she really did seem like a stranger we might pick out of a huge crowd simply because we felt lost and in some undefinable way this person struck us as friendly and familiar, as though we'd met and even talked to each other before—so I did know her, and her body, her face, her gestures were all familiar to me, I just wasn't sufficiently conscious of this knowledge or that it might be important to me; I've no idea why, I just hadn't noticed her, though I should have; for six years we'd been attending the same classes in the same school. My senses no doubt had registered her every feature, but impassively, with no emotional resonance; come to think of it, there was no aspect of her quietly modest being that could have been unfamiliar, since during all those years of such close proximity we had to communicate on many levels, and quite intimately, too, because she was on confidential terms with two girls, Hédi Szán and Maja Prihoda, with whom I had an unusual and for me typical relationship—ambiguous but very warm, less than love but far more than friendship; she was rather like a lady-in-waiting to them, a quiet shadow cast on their beauty, a mediator between two rivals, and, in their meaner moments, their maid and servant, a position which, with the dignity of her innate wisdom and sense of justice, she did not seem to resent, being as neutral then as she was whenever the two, with exaggerated solicitude, chose to treat and love her as an equal.

That hot summer afternoon when she stepped onto the main road from the forest path, the soles of her red sandals crunched a few more times and only then did her searching glance stand out in the quivering silence, a moment before meeting my eyes; and I was standing by the fence, among the bushes, as I did every day, hoping for and being terrified of something, not knowing what but feeling that something was going to happen, something had to happen, but also knowing that as soon as she appeared, my fantasies, however innocent, could not be realized; I had barely swallowed the last bite of my bread, and holding the fence with one hand I was about to wipe my other hand on my thigh, smearing the lard, but then our searching eyes met and couldn't part, we kept staring for a long time, without stirring, endlessly, like that time in the gym, except then, without acknowledging it, we were protected by both distance and the crowd, whereas here we were utterly defenseless, at the mercy of our deepening emotions; yet the present moment was as inexplicably accidental as that encounter in the gym, for on many other occasions our eyes, our faces, and our gestures could have been this close, but it never happened, not once after that first time, though we kept looking at each other all the time, kept looking for the chance to gaze at each other from afar and near, though cautiously, stealthily, and as soon as we had the chance, we ruined it almost on purpose, looked away, fled, then quickly looked back to see if the other still felt the same desire, the same pain; once, she ran away and looked back while still running, then tripped and fell but quickly jumped up and continued running; her compulsion to flee made her so graceful and nimble that I couldn't even laugh at her as I would have wished; that early spring morning began to haunt me again, though much had changed since then, if only because without either of us talking about our relationship it could not remain a secret; after a few weeks passed, the word was out that Livia Süli was in love with me.

Actually, it was not so hard to tell, we had given ourselves away already in the gym; after Livia turned discreetly away, her gaze was still with me though she was no longer looking at me, so she was the one who put an end to the moment whose beginning I couldn't exactly recall: first, she simply unfixed her stare, as though it had been a mistake and she'd been looking at not me but Prém, and there was something undeniably flirtatious in how she withdrew her glance; then she turned her head, thoughtfully, seriously, but that, too, for all the subtlety of the motion, was blatantly theatrical! she could stand there, calm and dutiful, ostensibly meeting all the requirements of the silent ritual, as if nothing had happened, as if it had been an accident, an error, yet by turning away she in fact reinforced the effect produced by her glance—what could I do? ashamed of being so vulnerable, I, too, turned away, yet still I felt that I should look back, that something important was being taken away from me—just how important I hadn't even realized until then—though what was truly important was not that I got something from her but that it could be taken away so easily, every minute without her looking at me now seemed wasted, empty, unbearable, a time in which I did not exist; mostly those eyes stayed with me, but her mouth and forehead, too, and I had to have them in front of me, no amount of fantasizing would do, without their visible presence everything would recede to an oppressive, faraway dimness; but for all that, I didn't look back, which took a lot of effort: my face, neck, shoulders, even my arm grew numb, but I didn't want to look, and making yourself not do something is always a struggle, you stretch it until the effort becomes unnatural; the longer I stood there, abandoned, the stronger and more painful my awareness of this altogether impossible sensation, almost as if my body had swelled and swallowed another, my distended skin was covering more than my own body and my brain was beginning to think another's thoughts; the more agonizing this state became, the more offended and angry I got, desperate in need of relief, for the real state of affairs, the true balance of power, seemed perfectly clear: I weighed the opportunities afforded by each passing moment but had to concede, and it wasn't easy, that I didn't have the upper hand; it was she who had both provoked my attention and then abandoned me; therefore, in no circumstance should I look back now, for if I did, it would be clear that she was winning, was the stronger, and it would mean that once again somebody had subdued me, triumphed over me, this servant, this ugly girl, just a girl, a maid, this angry conclusion being not totally unfounded, since she seemed to play the same role around Hédi and Maja that Prém did around Krisztián and Kálmán Csúzdi, so my feelings about the two servants neatly merged, and just for that I vowed that even if she stared at me for the rest of her life, I'd never so much as cast another glance at her, she'd never be able to do this to me again! let her turn blue in the face, let her admire me to her heart's content, let there be someone who follows me and only me with her eyes—and let me pretend it means absolutely nothing to me; but when I finally did look back—I couldn't help it, her burning face made me—I could feel nothing stronger than again that look, that face, looking at me; and if she kept looking, then after a while I could let go, just for a moment, look and then quickly look away, to make her look even harder, feel more painfully my absence, let her know how serious it can be when I take my eyes off her; but it wasn't she looking at me—I was deceived again!—it was Hédi Szán, standing a few rows over, in a perfect position to observe both of us, and no doubt she did, because ever so sweetly, softly, albeit with a hint of malice, she made a face.

Our last class was canceled, we were sent home at noon.

And as we lined up for dismissal, we heard church bells, first only four peals breaking the bright blue silence outside, then the great bell tolling, answered by a clanging smaller one, and then both boomed and pealed as though nothing had happened and it was simply noontime on an ordinary day, no different from any other.

I didn't want to walk home with anyone, get into a conversation, so on the staircase I fell out of line before the others thundered down the steps, unruly and irrepressible, shouting, a pent-up herd squeezing through the narrow doorway out into the open, where one could finally catch one's breath as if breathing for the first time in one's life and where the teachers' hysterical yells no longer made a difference, and I headed for the third floor, which is why Krisztián may have thought I was going to the teachers' room to report him, but in an unguarded moment and very cautiously, lest I be seen, I continued on; past the third-floor landing the staircase became narrow and dusty—since then I've often dreamed of myself ascending those dusty, untraveled stairs, which they obviously seldom cleaned, I am the only one ever to climb these stairs and in my dream this has special significance, for I am doing something forbidden, I shouldn't be here, thick, soft dust rises with every step and is slow to settle, so when I look back I see I've left no footprints, I prick my ears but nothing stirs, it's all quiet, I feel safe, though I know I could get caught, and no matter how alert I am and certain that no one saw me, I still have the feeling somebody is watching, and perhaps I am that somebody, unable to hide my little secrets from myself; anxiously I reach the attic door, which of course is locked; the black iron door was always locked and yet I always tried it anyway, in case someone might have left it unlocked by mistake.

This was my last refuge, the sort of hideaway one instinctively seeks out; I had such a place in our garden, too, also dark, but where the light was blocked by the foliage of a chestnut tree and honeysuckle crawling up the high bushes—it was interesting to watch the struggle of the two, with the bushes letting out new shoots and the honeysuckle, as if waiting in ambush, creeping after them, by autumn covering all the new shoots; here, by the attic, I had a pile of old desks, file cabinets, chairs, blackboards, crumbling old wooden platforms, and the neutral silence of discarded furniture; there, in the garden, my solitary daydreams and a lingering memory of secret games with Kálmán, which I believed to be sinful; moving in the neutral silence of discarded furniture, now bending down, now creeping sideways, I tried to avoid the hard edges and sudden protrusions, and when a bunch of old things began to shift and creak and seemed about to topple, I froze and instinctively covered my head, but kept inching toward the inner sanctum—nothing more than an up-ended old leather couch pushed against the wall with just enough room to slip behind, where I let myself be pressed against the wall by the overhanging cushions, which I clung to and which clung to me; the darkness was total and the leather, as always, cold, until I warmed it with my body.

I closed my eyes, and I thought that now I must kill myself.

I had no other thought.

It wasn't so bad to think about it; no, it was rather nice.

I'll go home, pry open my father's desk, sneak out into the garden, to my private place, and simply do it.

I saw the gesture, saw myself doing it.

I put the barrel of the revolver into my mouth, pulled the trigger.

And the thought that nothing would follow this act for me illuminated, harshly yet benevolently, everything that did follow.

So that I could see it.

As if for the first time I could see, simply and free of any weakening emotions, what my life was really like.

Everything hurt, in my chest and in my neck, there were moments when the top of my head hurt so much it was as if someone had pulled a round hat of pain over it; I shivered, I quaked; this was nothing like the pleasurable pain of self-pity but every part of the body hurting at once with a pain independent of the body, moving around, each stab stronger than the one before, each one making the previous seem like child's play; I wanted to scream and scream and keep on screaming, but I didn't dare, and that's also why I couldn't endure it anymore.

There was nothing new in the thought that I might not be normal, that I was just as sick as my sister, though in a different way, and that she may have been the only person with whom, in our sickness, I had something in common; what was new was the realization that I could once and for all put an end to the pain of trying to be like other people, to these completely futile attempts, since I could never resemble anyone strongly enough to be just like them and there was always a difference, and ultimately I always found myself alone; no one, myself included, ever wanted this difference or whatever it was; and though I may have hated myself for it, with every effort to identify with someone and at the same time lure him into my orbit, I only called attention to this difference, to my illness, to the very thing I wanted to annihilate; with my enticements I only revealed what I wanted hidden; and the realization that this un-bridgeable gulf within me could be done away with by simply killing my body first occurred to me then and there.

She didn't look at me after that.

Yet it seemed to me that only her look might still save me.

If only it could be made to last, if only time wouldn't pass without it, because that look of hers, that ultimate self-revelation, and the way she gazed, the way we looked at each other, might clear up the confusion within me, explain my unfulfilled yearnings, my sins, committed yet ir-redeemable, my endless lies—for I had to lie all the time to protect myself, which was petty and humiliating, and I was terrified, too, of being found out; I was suffering and saw no way to be free of suffering, because it wasn't only that I had to lie, deny myself everything that could give me pleasure, no, none of this: I could never have what I liked, and I had to live as if carrying a heavy, burdensome stranger with me, hiding my real self under this dead weight; in my infinite desperation I did try to share some of my pain with my mother, but so much had accumulated I couldn't possibly tell her everything, wouldn't even know where to begin, and anyway, I couldn't be that open with her, since she had plenty of complaints about me having to do with the very secrets I was hiding from the world, mainly out of consideration for her, a consideration I felt was justified because despite her irritation, her anger, complaints, and even disgust with me, she wished to see in me some unattainable perfection and for this reason was even stricter with me, at times more cruel, than with anyone else; the only thing that relieved the harshness and made it acceptable was that I had my private language with Mother, just as with my little sister, in which we could avoid words we judged irrelevant or meaningless, a language of touching, at times touching with our very tongues, the language of our warm skin, of our bodies; if I earlier mentioned a sickness of mine, I might risk another guess: that perhaps it was her sickness, and my sister's, which in some mysterious way penetrated and permeated my own being; these two disparate yet to me closely related illnesses might have been the consequence of the pervasive imbalance and uncertainty in my immediate surroundings, the physical manifestation of the fact that everyone was sick, which for a long time didn't bother me, which I accepted as the inevitable condition of my life, indeed finding my mother's illness rather beautiful and loving it; she must have infected me with that sense of grandeur one finds in illness while I was holding her hand or gently sliding my own over her bare arm, when I'd sit on the floor by her bed, put my head on her lap, or simply rest it on the sheet and breathe in the smell, the mixture of febrile warmth, sweat, and medicine emanating from her body, from her silken nightgown, a smell that was always there no matter how frequently the room was aired, and listen to her breathing, letting her hover between sleep and wakefulness, until my own breathing took over her strange, soft, fluttering rhythm, the rapid rises and slow falls; I got used to the smell to the point of no longer finding it repellent; sometimes she would speak to me softly, opening her eyes just a little, then closing them again: "You are beautiful," she would say, and I was always as astonished by this phenomenon in the bed as she must have thought my presence most pleasing; there was her white face sunk deep in the white pillows, her thick auburn hair neatly spread out, with strands of gray flashing through around the temples, and her smoothly rounded forehead, fine nose, and, above all, the heavy eyelids with long lashes which she would lift lazily as if in a daze, so that for a fraction of a second her crystalline green eyes appeared, looking at me so brightly and intently that her illness seemed a mistake, an illusion, a game, but when the lashes were lowered and the green eyes were once again covered by the blue-veined flesh of the eyelids, their color an ever-darkening brown, something, I don't know what, seemed to make her sick again, though the gaze remained on her sick face, along with a wan smile on her lips, which was meant for me, a mere hint of a smile, and "Tell me," she'd say at moments like this, "tell me what's been happening," and if I didn't reply, because I couldn't or didn't want to, she would continue by herself: "Should I tell you what I've been thinking about just now? did your sister eat her dinner all right? at least I didn't hear your grandmother yell; I'd rather you didn't stay long today, I feel weak, maybe that's why I thought of the meadow again, I wasn't asleep, I was standing in a great big beautiful meadow and wondering why it looked so familiar, I distinctly remembered having seen it before, and that's when you walked in," and she would stop, take a quick breath, as I watched the blanket on her breast rising and falling; "I probably would never have thought about it otherwise, because when you live, new images take the place of old ones all the time, but for some time now I've had the feeling that nothing's ever happened to me, never, though of course lots of things have, and you know I've told you much of it already, still, it's almost as if they didn't happen to me, they're only so many pictures, and while I'm in the pictures, somehow it's more important, or it says more about me, or it's more like me that I lie here in this bed, that this picture doesn't change, I lie here the same way, and if I look out the window I see the same things, now it's getting dark, now it's getting light, always the same picture, and in the meantime I can traipse around in my old pictures because there are no new pictures to disturb the old ones," sighing deeply, the rising air breaking the rhythm of her words: "I don't even know why I'm telling you all this; you should be able to understand it, still I feel a little guilty telling such things to a child, I'm philosophizing, I guess, which is kind of ridiculous, but I don't think there's anything sad or tragic or serious that should be kept from you, it's simply natural, and I never denied myself anything I thought was natural and I should do it"; laughing at this and opening her eyes for a moment, she would take my hand as if telling me to go ahead and do everything I felt to be natural: "Let's just stay like this now, quiet, all right? I'm tired, and I can't get that picture out of my mind, the one I wanted to tell you about but couldn't, just as you don't tell me much, either, though I always ask you, beg you to tell me things, and I understand perfectly when you'd like to tell me this or that but feel you must keep quiet, I even know what those things are that you keep quiet about, because all we can hope for is that the same kinds of things are happening to both of us, there is no difference, always the same things must keep happening, even the feelings are the same, only the pictures change; we understand each other even if we say nothing, that's how it is, and now let's be quiet for a little while, all right? and then go, darling, all right?"

Of course it wasn't so simple to leave, and I doubt she wanted me to obey her and go; her silence only increased the tension between us, and as if she had meant to add to it, she kept repeating herself, "Go now, there's a good boy, go, will you?" sometimes pressing me even harder to herself, in the guise of an embrace, holding on to me, hoping to delay the moment when prompted by some inner sense of propriety I'd get up and somewhat dazed but also relieved stumble into another room; but not yet—rather than spoiling the moment, I wanted to stretch it out, hold my face in my own breath, which her body had heated, in our common breath that made me feverish, too, and to position myself so that my mouth could brush against the skin of her bare arm, say in the curve inside her elbow, which is an especially soft spot, or her neck, where, in contrast, the mouth could explore the tensing muscles and tendons, and maneuvering further still, making it look completely accidental, pry open her mouth, and with the inside of my lips and the tip of my tongue feel the taste and smell of her skin.

She didn't pretend not to have noticed these amorous gropings, but didn't want to expose my sly little tricks, either; she never made believe that she took them to be the bumbling, simpleminded signs of a child's love or that they made her feel uncomfortable; neither did she retreat behind the protective shield of illness, pretending that only physical weakness made these dangerous excesses of mutual tenderness possible and necessary—no, she didn't do any of this, but responded simply and naturally by softly kissing my ear, my neck, my hair, wherever she could reach; once, burying her head in my hair, she remarked that she could smell the little male animal in my hair, a whole school of itching little males, and that she rather liked it; it was a smell I hadn't noticed before, but from then on searched for, wanting to experience the cause of her fleeting pleasure; all along she was giving me a live demonstration of naturalness, pointing out the natural boundaries of naturalness, because even when she used words to interrupt and thereby cool the ardor of our physical contact, the interruption appeared as natural and appropriate as the contact itself, not a defense or protest but a sensible rerouting of emotions that had no other outlet.

"All right, then," she said somewhat louder, and laughed a little for having come this far, "all right, maybe I'll try to tell you what I couldn't tell you before, listen: what I wanted to say was that I wasn't alone in that meadow; we were lying there in the tall grass, the sun was shining, with hardly any clouds in the sky, only those very light summer clouds that hardly move and you could hear the insects, wasps and bees, but it wasn't as nice as you might imagine, because every now and then a fly landed on my skin, and though I'd move an arm or a leg and it flew away, it would come right back, in the midday heat flies are always that pesky, try it sometime, and it was noon then; it's as if on purpose they won't let you enjoy whatever it is you want to enjoy, all that beauty, they simply won't have it, maybe because they also want to enjoy something just then, your skin, for instance, but again I'm not telling you the story I wanted to tell you; I can feel it myself, it's not for children, especially not you; one should keep quiet about everything, anyway; well, three of us were in that meadow, and there really was such a meadow, we came in a boat and tied it up at a prearranged spot where we were to meet the others, but we got there first and stretched out in the grass, quite a distance from one another, two men and me; and when you walked into the room and I woke up—came to, rather, yes, that's the right word, I hadn't been asleep at all—I was inside the picture, just then I saw the three of us from above, the way you do in a dream, and saw how terribly, how infinitely beautiful all this was then, because everything in the world is beautiful, though for me then it was sheer hell, a stinking swamp, and not because of the flies but because we couldn't decide who I really belonged to."

"And Father?"

"Yes, he was there, too."

"And how did you decide?"

"I didn't."

She may have wanted to say something else but she didn't, as though she couldn't utter another word, not a single word ever again—that's how abrupt her silence seemed.

And I couldn't ask her to go on; we both tensed up, lying there like two logs, or like two stalking beasts frozen in a moment of indecision, not knowing which will first pounce on the prey.

Saying more would have meant going beyond all possible limits; as it was, we had come very close, helplessly skirting, if not actually arriving at, the very last border.

She could not go any further out of sheer tact, and I couldn't have taken any more, so she smiled serenely, beautifully, her special smile for me, but this smile no longer seemed to be a part of a larger whole, a process with a beginning and an end, and I looked at her as one would look at a photograph of a smiling face out of the past, though the moment offered more than the images and random ebb and flow of thoughts evoked by this picture; it may sound like sentimental exaggeration, but this moment was a sudden illumination for me or, anyway, what for lack of a better word we usually call illumination: I saw her face, her neck, the creases and folds of her bedding, but every little detail acquired a story of its own, far richer than I had possibly imagined, and each story possessed a past filled with emotional and visual clues of whose existence I had otherwise been ignorant, and though the stories could not be recalled by ordinary, descriptive means, at this moment I could somehow grasp the clues: for example, there was a picture of me standing in front of the closed bathroom door, late at night, dark, and I wanted to go in but didn't dare, because what I was curious about I knew was forbidden and rightly so, but it wasn't their nakedness—they never deliberately concealed that from me, and I was the one who considered it a secret, the very top layer of the secret; no matter how unself-consciously they might have moved about in front of me, if I happened to see them naked I was the one who couldn't see enough of them, was embarrassed and excited by the delicious sense of peeping, by having to glance at their usually covered parts, which always seemed new and different and which I could never get used to; but what filled me with even more exquisite pain, offended my sense of modesty, and intensified my jealousy of their nakedness was the realization that their matter-of-fact behavior in front of me was part of a piously fraudulent game; I sensed that the two uncovered bodies, whether displayed individually or together, were meant only for each other, never for me, that only with each other could they be truly uninhibited, and I was excluded from their exclusive company, regardless of whether they happened to hate each other at that moment and intended to go for days without exchanging a single word, pretending to be completely indifferent to each other's presence, or whether the opposite was true, that they loved each other and every casual touch and fleeting glance, every burst of unexpected laughter, every knowing smile, bespoke an ineffable tenderness that I could not possibly have anything to do with; I was excluded, bypassed, made superfluous even if they seemed to love me the most at just such moments, with a love that was the overflow of their passion for each other, a treatment that was no less humiliating than being ignored or considered as an unnecessary, bothersome object; so Mother's last sentence, that unexpected confession, whose ambiguity held out all sorts of possibilities but also steered our short conversation toward that tense silence, seemed to illuminate for me the uneven nature of our relationship: she was going to let me have the key to secrets I had tried to unlock whenever

I wished their relationship to be less exclusive than they made it appear, whenever I hoped they would somehow let me squeeze in between them; from inside the bathroom I would hear the sound of water splashing, soft words, and Mother's laughter, a peculiar laugh, so unlike all her other laughs, which gave me the intoxicating feeling that I had stood before this bathroom once before, in exactly the same way, in the dark, in my pajamas, and had been standing there ever since, everything that had occurred between these two indeterminate points in time being nothing but a vague dream, which had a beginning that now, as I was waking, I couldn't remember; and then, in a very different voice, deeper and stronger but preserving something of the playfulness of a high-pitched, squealing laugh, Mother called out: "Who is there in the dead of night, behind that door?" and of course I didn't answer, and thought that maybe the creaking floor had given me away, though I was so careful not to let it creak, or could a physical presence be strong enough to be felt through a closed door? "Is that you, darling? A black raven knocking on my door? Come in, come in, whoever you are!" I couldn't answer, but she didn't seem to expect a reply, for she said, "Speak to me, speak, and come!" practically singing her words, and they were both shrieking with laughter, the water was splashing and purling in the bathtub, spilling onto the tile floor, and I could neither leave nor say something and walk in, but then the door opened.

It was no mistake or a sensory illusion that made me think just now of having stood like this in a doorway once before; Mother's unfinished sentence conjured up part of an even earlier image, only a flash, really, just her feet, her head on the pillows, but enough to make the abyss I could now look into appear even more attractively bottomless, an image that, while standing in the bathroom door, only my instincts could recall— groping blindly for traces of an existing and carefully stored memory, knowing precisely its time and place, savoring its many flavors, and still unable to locate it—but now, unsummoned and unannounced it appeared, hanging into the other image, the pictures of nakedness affirming the connection between the two: when Father, leaning out of the bathtub, opened the door, my astonished face appeared in the steamy bathroom mirror, he loomed enormous, standing in the tub and leaning toward the door handle, his back, like a red blotch, reflected in the mirror streaked with running drops of condensed steam; both my face and his back were in the mirror; Mother was sitting in the water, rubbing her heavily sham- pooed hair; she smiled at me, blinking because the shampoo stung, and then, closing her eyes, she dunked her head to wash out the shampoo under the water; then, as now, I felt the same dazed helplessness, as if the pajamas were my body's only defense against feelings that would otherwise leave me naked, the pajamas were more real than I was, and then, too, I started walking in the direction of a remote, hollow, almost inaudible yet very penetrating voice; it was night, I got up to pee, and heard this voice, unfamiliar but not at all frightening, on a silent winter night lit by a cold moon, when the light refracted by the window frames into sharp angles and planes seems to float, and soft shadows seem to soak up all the familiar objects so that you are afraid to cross the sharp border of light, a voice coming from the hallway; my face turned a frightful blue by the moon, I saw it flash for a second in the hallway mirror, I thought someone was screaming or sobbing, but there was no one out in the hall, the voice was coming from the kitchen; I moved on, guided by my own amazement, my bare feet squishing on the stone floor; nothing, the kitchen was dark, something squeaked under the opening door, but then silence, no one there either; still, I felt or imagined the silence of living bodies, as if not only pieces of furniture soaked in the night were standing there and the quiet I heard was not just my bated breath; then, from behind the open door of the maid's room I heard a deep hoarse rattle, and with it the rhythmic creaking and groaning of bedsprings, each creak and groan and thrust seeming to let loose, from deep inside a throat, a high-pitched, ever-rising scream, a cross between a sob and a shrieking laugh; this was the voice that had attracted me, I wasn't imagining it, after all, and one more step was all it would take to look through the open door, and I wanted to look but couldn't; it seemed that I'd never reach the miserable door, still not there, still far away, even though the voice was already with me, so close, so within me, with all its depths, heights, and rhythms, and I didn't even notice when I finally managed to take that longed-for last step and could also see what I was hearing.

Of course Father did not appear enormous because he really was enormous, in fact he was rather slight and slender; it's things like the incorrect use of the word "enormous" that now make me realize the powerful inhibitions and self-deceptions, over long decades, that I must grapple with when speaking of things one ordinarily doesn't, or perhaps shouldn't, talk about but which, since they are linked inextricably with the so-called inner life of the boy I once was, are unavoidable; so let's take a deep breath and relate quickly, before one's voice flags, that quite apart from that very early incident which for better or worse had dropped out of my memory for a long time and resurfaced unexpectedly and vividly only when Mother told me about the meadow—yes, the memory of Father's body in the scissors of two female legs on the bed of the maid's room did come back, like a well-kept secret that I mustn't tell Mother even now; I couldn't see the face, but I could see that the squeals of pleasure and pain were muffled because with his outspread fingers Father had thrust a pillow over the head below him; the legs entwining his waist told me that this woman was not my mother, how could she be, what would she be doing there? and because we can just as easily recognize a thigh, a foot, the curve of a calf as we can a nose, a mouth, or a pair of eyes, it isn't surprising that I knew those legs were not hers, and it wasn't her voice I heard from under the pillow—I knew very well who lived in the maid's room—what was startling was that I half expected them to be Mother's legs, not as if I had the vaguest notion of what was actually taking place but awareness yielded to unawareness in my assuming that in such close proximity of mutual pleasure there could be no room for anyone but Mother, thus, what I saw before me, no matter how pleasurable and therefore perfectly natural it may have seemed to a small child, was still repellent; yet all this was not directly related to the perception of Father as someone enormous, an impression that was made on me when, in his usual unsmiling, humorless way, he leaned out of the bathtub to open the door and, as he did, also blocked my way with his wet naked body glistening in the strong bathroom light, towering over me so that my eyes were focused on the darkest part of him, his loins, one might say right under my nose; and I knew, saw, and felt that, as always, not a single unguarded glance or move I made would escape his notice; his wet hair clung to his scalp, his forehead left clean and open, and his gaze—normally tempered and sheltered by strands of straight blond hair and thus engagingly attractive, almost beautiful, though his steely blue eyes made it strong and stern, but the thick mass of hair, which he combed straight back but which kept falling forward as he moved, lending him a casual, boyish look—this piercing gaze dominated his face, an open, attentive, cool, and threatening gaze, as if challenging the world, demanding an explanation from it; it seemed that he wasn't only towering over me but forever looking down from some unapproachable peak, from the heights of his undisputable certainties, from which he could afford to tolerate others' preoccupation with petty desires, instincts, gooey emotions, while he watched and judged, even if he didn't often put his judgments into words; viewed from this perspective, straight on and a bit from below, his body seemed perfect, at any rate what we usually call the perfect male body, and I deliberately used this emotionally neutral word, modestly avoiding the slightest suggestion of a natural attraction, so that I needn't call it beautiful, let alone exceptionally beautiful or, perish the thought, overwhelmingly beautiful—by calling it beautiful we'd have to admit being defenseless, at its mercy, and then, by the nature of things, we'd want to be at its mercy, indeed our greatest desire would be to immerse ourselves in it, to travel down the byways of this body, if only by tracing its lines with our fingers, to make our own with our touch what our eyes can only see: the broad shoulders that years of rowing and swimming had turned so firmly muscular that the otherwise charming protrusions of the shoulder and chest bones were barely visible; the firm shoulders leading smoothly, fluidly yet firmly, to the more articulated musculature of the arms and the well-toned, undulating plane of the chest, where the pregnability of the bare surface was both accentuated and toned down by a profusion of blondish hair, more attractive when wet, for the clinging strands encircled the nipples' darkened areolae like improvised wreaths, guiding our glance farther, to follow either the contours of the torso, narrowing at the waist, or the gently rippling sinews sheathing the ribs, and linger perhaps on the firm bulge of the belly, where the dark hollow of the navel and especially the wedge of pubic hair, pointing upward, might impede a farther descent of our glance, but this delay is far from final, because eyes, independent of will, always pick out the darkest and lightest points, they're created like that by nature, as are all our instincts, and so we finally reach the loins, and if we have a chance to linger, if our glance is cautious enough and he doesn't notice—but of course he will, because in a similar situation his eyes would do the same, but he may be generous and pretend he didn't mind, or, if he did he might turn away and put something there, or drop a word, meant to be casual but inappropriate enough to reveal his embarrassment—or, if his knowledge of human nature was so secure that, suspending all moral considerations, he'd simply let us tarry, then we'd love to linger for a while, scrutinizing this rather intricate region, hoping to savor every detail, to assess its possibilities, knowing well that our eyes' journey thus far had been but a deferment, anticipation, and preparation: now we have reached the most intimate object of our curiosity: this is our place, this is what we'd been longing for, only from here can we draw the knowledge necessary to evaluate the whole body; consequently, it would be no exaggeration to claim that even from a moral standpoint we have reached the most critical spot.

As I had once before, I yielded to the desire to hold it in my hands.

It was summer, a Sunday morning, with sunlight already streaming through the white curtains drawn over the open windows, when I walked into my parents' bedroom to crawl into their bed, as was my custom, not suspecting that this was to be the morning I'd have to give up this pleasant habit for good; the bed, the bed in which Mother later lay alone, wrapped in the heavy odor of her illness, which was so hard to get accustomed to, was wide and somewhat higher than average and seemed to dominate the almost empty room, its headboard and frame polished black wood, as was the other furniture—a plain chest of drawers, a dressing table and mirror, an armchair upholstered in white brocade, and a nightstand—yet these, along with the blank walls all around, made the room neither cold nor unfriendly; their blanket was on the floor as if just kicked there, Mother was gone, fixing breakfast most likely, and Father was still asleep, all curled up with only a thin sheet covering his naked body; I still don't know what possessed me to cast off my natural modesty and inhibitions, not even realizing I was doing so or violating some unwritten law; maybe it was just the carefree morning air, with a fine breeze bringing to us the smell of dew from the cooling earth, the gentle currents carrying a taste of the sizzling heat to come, the birds still chattering, and down in the valley, over the city's hum, a church bell ringing, and in the neighbor's garden sprinklers hissing quietly away, and for no apparent reason I felt delightfully mischievous; without giving it another thought, I threw off my pajamas and, stepping across the blanket on the floor, climbed into the bed next to my father, and snuggled up to him under the sheet, naked.

It's true, I might say today, by way of explaining though by no means excusing what I did, that one of the most important things about these Sunday-morning visits was that they should occur while we were still half asleep, so that when waking for real, when it was really morning, wrapped in the warmth of my parents' bodies, I could experience the pleasantly deceptive feeling of waking someplace other than where I'd gone to sleep, so that I could marvel at this self-created little miracle and, semiconscious, imitate the same commingling of time and place that dreams so effortlessly carry out on their own, but while, as I say, this can serve neither to explain nor excuse, it's not negligible either, especially when we bear in mind that the end of our childhood is generally thought to be at hand when these cruel little games vanish in a benevolent oblivion, when every part of our being has learned to suppress our secret desires and dreams, and with grim determination we adjust to the set of paltry possibilities which the conventions of social existence offer to us as reality, but a child does not have much of a choice, since he's forced to adhere almost like an anarchist to the laws of his own nature—and we're ready to admit that we consider these no less real or reasonable—and at this point perhaps does not yet make a scrupulous distinction between the laws of the night and those of the day, and even now we're very sensitive to this will to keep things whole; the child must feel his way carefully between the acceptable and unacceptable; we remain children as long as we feel the urge to keep crossing this border and to learn, through other people's reactions to us and through our often tragic confrontations with our own nature, the alleged place, time, and name of things; at the same time, we must also master that sacred system of hypocritical lies and deceptions, subterfuges, pleasantly false appearances, subterranean passages, quietly opening and closing doors of secret labyrinths which will allow us to fulfill, besides the so-called real desires, our true, even more real desires; this is what is called a child's education, and we are writing a *Bildungsroman*, after all, so, without beating about the bush, and it's precisely the sacred ambiguity of the educational process that prompts us to express our secret thoughts, let's say then clearly that sometimes it's by grabbing our father's cock that we can most precisely gauge morality, whose dictates, despite all our compulsions and good intentions, we can never fully obey; when I awakened again that morning, my naked body lying on his, embracing him in his moist sleep and fumbling in his chest hair, I almost felt as if I were deceiving myself, not him, as if I had to deceive myself to believe that by clinging to his back, his buttocks, entwining my legs in his, I could feel the meeting of our nakedness, yet this was in fact what I woke to in that second awakening, and I was surprised and delighted that in this very brief and deep sleep our limbs had gotten so entangled that it took long moments for my senses to sort them out, and at the same time I couldn't help realizing that it was I who had arranged the awakening this way, consciously, though the act also had deeper, hazier elements, which I was trying to explore and indefinitely prolong, since they felt so pleasant and gave me that sense of wholeness in which desire and imagination can mingle harmoniously with deception and crafty manipulation; and then, without opening my eyes, feigning sleep, playing hide-and-seek with my-self, I began to slide my fingers slowly, very slowly toward his belly, waiting intently for the skin to quiver under my touch, for the spittle in his mouth to glisten, to see if he would just snort once and go on sleeping, but while I was filching this lovely sensation for myself, it dawned on me that I was lying in the warmth my mother had left behind, taking her place—or, the feeling I was stealing, I was stealing from her.

It was as if I had to touch Mother with my mouth and Father with my hand.

And on his belly my hand had to open if it wanted to press down on his firm protrusion.

From there it was just one more downward slide, hindered momen-tarily in his pubic hair, and then I was pressing my palm over his genitals.

The moment had two very distinct parts.

When his body moved, not indifferently, willingly even, and he awak-ened.

And when with a sudden violent jerk he pulled away and let out an ear-splitting scream.

As when one finds a clammy toad in his warm bed.

By morning our sleep deepens, coarsens, and if I hadn't roused him from this deep morning sleep, he might have had a chance to realize that he was the hero of that same *Bildungsroman* in which nothing that is human can be alien, so that on the one hand what happened was not so unusual as to elicit his most violent feelings, and on the other, if he didn't want his impulsive response to have incalculably serious consequences, if he didn't want to elicit a similarly violent response from me but, as a reasonable educator, wanted to achieve a positive effect, he would have acted with much greater understanding and tactful shrewdness, for he must have known what every human being over forty can be expected to know, especially a man, namely, that everyone must at least once, literally or figuratively, symbolically or with one's bare hands, touch that organ; at least once everyone must violate his father's modesty—to keep it in-violable perhaps?—yes, everyone does it, one way or another, even if the ordeal leaves him no strength to admit the act even to himself, the denial being dictated by natural self-defense and a moral sense that surfaces only in extreme situations; but Father was startled out of sleep and because of his first, instinctive move must have felt betrayed by his own nature and could do little else but scream.

"What's got into you? What are you doing?"

And he kicked me out of bed with such force I landed on the floor on their blanket.

For a long time afterward my inner world was ruled by the silence of criminals, the mute, tense silence of anticipation which, as one waits for consequences and retribution, makes the act seem more irrevocable and therefore somewhat wonderful and thrilling, but no punishment was forthcoming; no matter how closely I watched them, I could detect no indication that he even told Mother about the incident, though in other situations when I was caught in some mischief, they always tried to present a united front, though I must say they never succeeded so well that I couldn't discern some subtle differences in their positions; now, however, they professed complete innocence and seemed truly united, acting as if nothing had happened, as if I had dreamed it all, both the touch and the scream, and while waiting for the spectacular retribution I failed to notice the consequence, far more serious than any punishment could have been; looking back now, as a reasonable adult, I ask myself just what sort of punishment I was expecting: a bloody, merciless beating? what kind of punishment can be invented in a case like this, when it seems that a male child has fallen in love with his own father? isn't the terrible, unrequitable, physically and emotionally devastating love itself the greatest punishment? at any rate, what I failed to notice, maybe couldn't have noticed, or what I had to pretend not to notice, was that after the incident Father became even more aloof, carefully avoiding every occasion that might have called for physical contact; he didn't kiss me, didn't touch me, and, come to think of it, didn't hit me either, as though he felt that even a slap might be construed as responding to my love for him; he withdrew himself from me—but so inconspicuously, his reserve so perfect, lacking all outward signs, no doubt some great fear making it so perfect, that I myself sensed no connection between his behavior and its cause, and maybe he didn't either; I even managed to forget the underlying cause, just as I forgot that I had discovered him in bed with Mária Stein in the maid's room—maybe he forgot that, too; the only threat that remained with me was the unassimilable knowledge that this was the kind of man my father was: not enough of a stranger to leave me unresponsive and not affectionate enough to love me; so when he opened the door to let me into the bathroom, what I could read in his unsmiling face, in the blatant nakedness of his body, was this reserve and mistrust, a well-disguised shyness, a fearfulness, and a reluctance, too, indicating that he was opening the door only at my mother's urging though it didn't sit well with him, he didn't find my peeking and eavesdropping so easily forgivable; instead of this daring family coziness he would have preferred to send me back to my bed—"All right, out!" he might have said, and as far as he was concerned that would have been the end of it, but vis-à-vis Mother he appeared to be at least as vulnerable and defenseless as I was with him, which of course was a source of comfort to me, and if there was the slightest hope of my ever squeezing in between the two of them, it could only be through this tiny opening afforded by his willingness to please Mother, to gain her favor, to satisfy her needs; I had no direct way of reaching Father.

"Close the door," he said, and turned around to sit back in the tub, words that for me, still unable to decide whether to go in and still standing motionless in the doorway, were an ambiguous gift but a gift nonetheless, and even the reluctance in his voice, intended more for Mother than for me, could not completely spoil my happiness, because I had won without hoping for victory; and the sight of his body turning sideways was yet another new experience, a striking flash, to be enjoyed and suffered only until he lowered himself into the water; if earlier I said that from the front his body looked perfect, well-proportioned, attractive, and beautiful, I now have to add something that natural modesty makes even more difficult to articulate, or could it be that it isn't modesty at all but the strange desire to see our parents, in both body and mind, as the most perfect creatures on earth, even when they are not? is that the reason that experience forces us to see beauty in ugliness or, if we cannot abandon our inextinguishable yearning for perfection, at least to be more forgiving and understanding of imperfection, learning from the human form that everything seemingly perfect also contains a tendency for the distorted, the twisted, and the deformed? is this, after all, what gives our feelings their unique character and flavor? and not only because no single human being can embody perfect harmony of form but also because perfect and imperfect always go hand in hand, are inseparable, and if, disregarding the most obvious imperfections, we still try to worship a person as perfect, is it simply our imagination playing tricks on us?

When I looked at my father sideways, it turned out that whatever had seemed perfect from the front now appeared misshapen: his shoulder blades protruded prominently from his bent back, he looked stooped even when standing straight, and if I weren't afraid of the word, I'd say he was only a breath away from being a hunchback, yes, a hunchback, which we usually find exceedingly repulsive; I'm convinced it was pure accident that he wasn't, as if halfway through its work nature could not decide whether to fashion an ideal or a grotesque human form and left him to his fate, and he, recognizing this fate, tried to blot out or at least correct the effects of this dark hoax of nature, though his efforts were only partially successful, despite his undoubtedly very real suffering and almost unseemly industriousness and zeal: the body, the human form, however devoutly we may expound in our Christian humility on the externality of the flesh and the primacy of the soul, is so potent a given that already at the moment of our birth, it becomes an immutable attribute.

But with the utter partiality of a lover, I loved this, too, liked inhaling beauty and ugliness in the same breath and experiencing with equal sensitivity and intensity both attraction and repulsion; his imperfections made him perfect to me—nothing could better account for his obstinate seriousness, his formidable alertness, the eagerness with which he went after everything he judged wayward, unlawful, criminal, and therefore ugly and perverse than his slight flaw, his tiny would-be hump, in the absence of which he would have become just another pretty face and no more; but this way he was a man forever on guard, emotionally rather dour, physically somewhat cold (for all his sexual excesses), and very intelligent, as if in the retreat forced on him by his physical attributes, his attentiveness longing for but unable to cope with tenderness had grown so acute that no plan or motive, however cunningly concealed, could escape his scrutiny, and the energy lost in that retreat returned most aggressively in his sensitivity and intellect, enabling him to uncover the subtlest of connections; he was perfect then in trusting his intuition to let his abilities and natural gifts complement one another; one could only rarely discover in him an insincere attempt to be what he was not, and though then I knew very little about what the work of a state prosecutor actually entailed, I couldn't imagine a more appropriate setting for that body; I liked to see him encased in the severity of his dark gray suit, his long fingers gathering up his papers from a gleaming desktop under the glare of chandeliers turned on even during the day, the cut of his suit being perhaps only a slight deception, in the cleverly placed shoulderpads that compensated for the irregular curve of his back; in the long marble-faced courthouse corridors there were usually very few people around, now and then a messenger hurrying past with heavy file folders, and sometimes small clusters of people standing about in front of one of the huge doors, taking not the slightest notice of one another; dignified, dusty boredom prevailed except when clanking footsteps broke the silence and grew louder until in one of the bends in the winding corridor a handcuffed prisoner appeared led by two guards, only to disappear behind one of those huge brown doors and then enter the courtroom; I liked to see his back receding down the dim corridor, in his back rather than in the more ordinary beauty of the rest of his body, where everything that I felt was refined, distinguished, and intelligent in him seemed to be concentrated—to complete the picture, I should say something about his shapely and muscular backside, whose graceful curve was quite feminine, and his firm thighs, and the protuberant veins branching off under the golden hairs of his leg, and the arching foot with its long, delicate toes—but still, it was his back; his walk was soft, supple, vigorous, like that of a beast delighted to feel in the soles of its feet the limber, ready weight of its body, but Father seemed to carry his intellectual burdens and worries, which I imagined had to do with pursuing justice, not in his feet but on his back, as if his strength lay in the curvature of his back, and I so very much wanted to be like him, to possess his imperiousness, his strength, not just the beauty and symmetry leading to and radiating from his loins but his rarefied spiritual ugliness, too, so for a while I tried to imitate his stoop as I walked down the far less impressive corridors of my school the way I had seen him walk in the courthouse.

But then I decided to walk into the bathroom, after all, and I closed the door just as he told me.

He sat back in the tub, and Mother, who just then re-emerged from the water, started laughing; their movements spilled more water onto the floor.

"Just throw off your pajamas and join us," she said, as if this was the most natural thing in the world.

And when I climbed into the tub and positioned myself between their drawn-up knees, the water overflowed again, the bathroom was awash, slippers began to float, which made all three of us laugh.

It was one of those sudden outbursts of laughter, a spontaneous eruption that dissolved the residue of suspicion and fear and timidity in us, canceling out every warranted and unwarranted anxiety, tore that scrim, that veil between external reality and the more powerful inner verities to which I alluded earlier, seemed to liberate our bodies from the confines of their weight and inertia, lifting us into a higher sphere where there is free passage between the reality of the body and that of our desires; there we were, in a tubful of cooling, lukewarm water, three naked bodies—

though only a single mouth seemed to do the laughing, as though the rollicking laughter with its undertones of sly devilry had burst forth from the same giant mouth, as if the identity of our liberated senses endowed us with one common mouth!—and caught between Father's outspread knees, I had my feet between Mother's open thighs under the sudsy and murky water that was gently lifting her large breasts, making them float and bob on the surface; then Father pushed me, and Mother pushed me back, and with each push the water sloshed and overflowed, that's what made us laugh actually, this bit of silliness; at the same time, the giant mouth seemed to be swallowing the three naked bodies, devouring them, disgorging them, and sending them down a dark gullet of pleasure, only to bring them up again in tune with the rhythm of laughter as the laughter burst, rippled, and soared, only to dip and scoop up from still deeper layers of the body the hidden and hitherto unimagined treasures of its pleasure and then, with even greater lung efforts and from an even greater height, to let loose its indigestible joy just as the water kept running over and out of the tub.

But in all fairness, for the sake of truth and completeness, I should correct any impression that my life at that time consisted solely of blank despair, shameful cruelties and defeats, and unbearable, yes, unbearable suffering; to counteract the admittedly one-sided nature of my account I must stress that it wasn't so, really wasn't, because joyful, pleasurable experiences were just as much part of my life, and perhaps the reason suffering leaves a deeper mark is because suffering, relying on the mind's ability to think and therefore brood and mull things over, stretches out time, while true joy, avoiding conscious reflection and confining itself to sensory impulses, grants itself and us only the time of its actual existence, which makes it seem fatefully accidental and contingent, always separate and wrenched from suffering, so that while suffering leaves long, complicated stories behind in our memory, happiness leaves but flashes in its wake—but away with this analysis getting bogged down in the details of details, and away, too, with the philosophy that seeks the meaning of details, though we may need it if we want to ascertain the richness of our inner life, if it is rich why not take pleasure in observing it? yet precisely because this richness is infinite, and the infinite belongs among the incomprehensible things of this world, we are tempted, in our hasty analysis, to pronounce a perfectly ordinary, ultimately natural event to be the root cause of all our injuries, obsessions, mental illness—let's say it, the cause of our disabilities—and we do this because we lose sight of the totality of an event in favor of certain arbitrarily chosen details, and terrified by the abundance of these, we call a halt to our search at just the point where we should go further, our terror creating a scapegoat, erecting little sacrificial altars for it and stabbing the air in mock ceremony, causing more confusion than if we hadn't thought about ourselves at all; happy are the poor in spirit!—so let's not think, let's submit freely and without preconceived notions to the pleasant sensation of sitting on the floor next to Mother's sickbed, our head leaning on the cool silk counterpane so that our lips can rest on the bare skin of her arm; we can feel her delicate fingers in our hair, a slight tremble, a pleasant tingle of our scalp, because in her embarrassment she's dug her other hand into our hair as if to console us, to see if she can lessen the impact of her words with this idle gesture, and though the tingling slowly takes possession of our entire body, what she has said cannot be taken back so easily, since we, too, have suspected that our father may not be our father, and if she couldn't decide between the two men, this suspicion may become a certainty, but about that, understandably, nothing further can be said, so let us be quiet, and then we may feel precisely that everything her words evoked in us as memories—and that have already subsided, however important and decisive they may be—are only in the background of our emotions and true interests, because in the space where we are trying to grasp them and reflect on them, where real events are taking place, there we are completely alone, and they—those two men and Mother—do not and cannot have anything to do with it.

And if what she said didn't leave me cold, it wasn't because it was important for me to know which of the two men was my father, a question that was exciting, to be sure, teasing, titillating in its immodesty, above all, a delicious secret, like the picture I kept in mind of the man I knew to be my father with that other woman in the maid's room, but still, I'd say the question itself was not of primary importance, it could be dismissed, forgotten, relegated to the background, like the broad sweep of the horizon in a painting of a quiet, misty meadow at dusk, in other words, a mere frame that fades away, undeniably part of the picture, but the picture itself, our picture, begins and ends where we are, where we assume our position in it: our view of existence can have only one center, and that is our body, the pure form of being that makes this view possible and provides strength, authority, and security, so that ultimately—I emphasize, ultimately—nothing else should interest us but our body in all its possible aspects and manifestations; Mother's last sentence silenced me and ruled out further questions, mainly because it was like a not quite inadvertent allusion to everything that had been preoccupying me; I couldn't make decisions, yet felt compelled to decide, just as she did— only from her sentence it was already a guilty conscience staring back at me, stemming from an inability to decide, which, I knew, would last a lifetime: I was facing my own future filled with threatening chaos and confusion, though viewing it with the serenity of one who already knew he couldn't hope to decide what is undecidable, in which regard her confession was quite liberating, as if she had sensed that she was going to die soon and, as her last will, meant to warn me not to experiment with making decisions when no solutions were possible and to allow uncontrollable events to be my only joy, as if real freedom consisted of nothing but letting ourselves be affected, without protest, by occurrences that choose to manifest themselves in us; consequently, for me, then, she wasn't like a mother, whom we expect to shield us with the warmth of her body from the rigors of the real world, but like an experienced person who has returned to herself after many adventures and indulgences and is therefore necessarily cruel and cold, a person with whom I had very little to do because common ties are defined by warmth, yet with whom I was in every way identical because, regardless of differences in age and sex, the occurrences within us were identical.

It was as though she was talking about something she could not have known anything about.

Our silence spoke of this, too.

And then I did manage to tell her something about which I had never spoken to her before.

It wasn't real speaking, of course, not a single word being formed or articulated in the deep silence, and lasted only as long as it took my mouth, breathing tiny kisses, to inch its way from the soft curve of her arm up to her shoulder, but "Girls like me very much," I would have whispered in the choked voice of a lover's confession meant just for her, "they like me more than any of the other boys," I would have whispered, as if to prove something, and also a bit ashamed of this surprising, inappropriate, ever boastful declaration, because everything we say out loud about ourselves, even if only to ourselves, needs immediate, disappointingly ambiguous amplification, so I would have said this, because they didn't like me that way—"I know, and I'm ashamed that they like me not the way girls like boys but as if I were a girl, too, which I'm not, of course, I'm a boy, but this difference, this thing that separates me from other boys, I can't help being proud of," and I would have asked her to help me, because I was saying it all wrong and desperately wanted to say it right, and the plural didn't mean girls in general—there is no such thing anyway—but the three of them, Hédi, Maja, and Livia, they were the girls, and in the same way, when I thought about boys I saw Prém, Kálmán, and Krisztián as belonging together; if I had to decide which sex I was more attracted to, buffeted between these two dependent yet separate trinities of the sexes and trying to find my place, I'd have to have said that women and girls were dearer to me though men and boys attracted me more.

I'd have said all this, if it had been possible to talk openly of such matters.

But leaning on Mother's shoulder I remembered what it was like to come from the garden and silently step into the Prihodas' spacious dining room, where their maid, Szidónia, was clearing the table, and to watch for a while, without a sound, as she got down on her knees, her buttocks thrust toward me, to pick bread crumbs off the floor.

Perhaps it was the heavy fragrance of Mother's skin that made me reveal all my secrets to her, things I experienced independently but which still had to do with her, somehow.

And when the maid finally noticed me I put my finger to my lips, warning her to be quiet, say nothing, nobody should know I was here, not yet, I wanted to be able to surprise Maja, and she stayed as she was, motionless, fortunately unaware of the deeper meaning of my precaution, thinking it was a prank, some innocent prank, after all I was such an amusing fellow, wasn't I? and my smile, my playful plea, made her my accomplice; very carefully then, not to make the floor creak, I started walking toward her—Here comes that rascal again, her beaming eyes seemed to say—and, watching me approach, she burst out laughing.

I always had to think of something new; old tricks were good for starters, but I had to devise something extraordinary to heighten the effect, which was not so hard as it first seemed; I had to remain refined in my little acts of rudeness, gauge precisely the opportunities afforded by the given moment.

And in this silence I went as far as not saying hello to her, knew that only the most extreme gestures were effective, sometimes would only nod, but another time would suddenly grab her hand and kiss it, she'd slap me lightly on the back of my head: that is how our contacts remained silent, even when free of playful smacks and cuffs, still more expressive than words could have made them: we were giving, exchanging signals, a form of communication that suited us perfectly, why spoil it with mere words?

No need to concentrate on anything else: I had only to look at the yellow flecks in her gray cat's eyes—I knew that every premeditated and self-conscious move was too artful, therefore patently false—to establish contact between those flecks and my instinctive gestures in order to learn whether I was on the right track or not; now, for example, her loud laughter was a kind of revenge for my imposing silence on her, but she laughed out loud, and that called for reprisal; our furtive pleasures demanded these little reprisals, which gave us a chance silently to kick, bite, scratch, and furiously pummel each other, and then, very slowly, I too went down on my knees—no need to mimic her openly, she got the message!—simply replicating, mirroring, the funny, somewhat humiliating position her body had assumed; I knelt next to her, among the legs of a couple of chairs, as if to say, You are like a dog here, yes, that's what you are, a dog.

Szidónia was a fat girl, her thick brown hair pinned up in a braid, her oily skin glistened, her eyes were bright, and every move she made was disarmingly, awkwardly childlike; there were dark stains of perspiration on her white blouse under her arms; I knew I had to do something with this penetrating, enduring odor: but I am your dog, I intimated, and, sniffing noisily, stuck my nose into her armpit.

Her body dissolved in silent pleasure, she rolled under the table, and I followed the moist, wet smell until she bit into my neck, hard; it hurt.

Now this way, now that, whichever way we played these little games, they were only the antechamber of pleasure.

Because in the inner sanctum, deep inside her room, poring over her books and notes and resting her head on her hand and chewing on the end of her pencil, sat Maja, her bare legs crossed under the table, and she kept swinging them, shuffling them in an irritatingly unpredictable, nervous rhythm.

Thick shrubs grew tall outside her window, old trees lowered their branches like a curtain, the air in her room was always filled with green stirrings, green flickers on the wall, as the leaves outside floated and fluttered.

"Livi isn't here yet?" I asked quietly, making sure I opened with a crucial question, a confession really, letting her know right away that she wasn't that important to me: she may have been waiting for me, and now pretending not to be, but I hadn't come because of her.

She didn't look at me; she always made as though she didn't catch my words the first time, always sat in some contorted position, and not so much read her book as scrutinized the pages from afar, with a certain revulsion and wariness, keeping them as far away as she could, as another person might look at a painting, taking in both the details and the composition as a whole, furrows of concentration creasing her brow, her dark brown eyes round with a constant, level astonishment, all the while chewing and twisting her pencil with her beautiful white teeth, chewing and twisting it again; and if my presence registered in her consciousness this was indicated only by a slowing in the shuffle of her feet under the chair, a less active nibbling on her pencil, but needless to say, these were signs not of inattention but of the most concentrated attention—these monotonous, mechanical motions enabled her to absorb knowledge far removed from her physical being—and if she finally managed to tear herself away from what she'd been so intent upon, she looked at me with the same deep, astonished interest; I must have seemed like another object to her, every object being remarkable in its own way, as slowly, very slowly, she lifted her head, the furrows of her brow disappeared, she had to pull the pencil from between her teeth, her mouth stayed open, and her eager, attentive look did not change.

"You can see for yourself," she said casually, but she didn't fool me, I knew she enjoyed reporting painful news.

"She's not coming today?" I asked, needlessly, only to emphasize that I hadn't come to see her, let there be no misunderstanding about that.

"I'm getting a little tired of Livi, maybe she won't show up today, but Kálmán said we'd see her anyway, because Krisztián is doing some kind of theater."

She might as well have stuck a thorn in me; of course nobody had told me about this, and she knew they meant to leave me out of it.

"We'll see them, then?"

"I guess so," she said innocently, as though the plural included me as well, and for a moment I almost believed it.

"Did she say that I should go? That you should invite me?"

"Why, didn't she tell you?" With just a touch of mock indulgence, she savored my embarrassed silence.

"She did mention something," I said, knowing well she could see through my lie; she seemed to feel a little sorry for me.

"Why shouldn't you come if you feel like it?"

But I wanted no part of her pity. "Then our whole day is shot again,"

I said angrily, inadvertently betraying myself, which of course pleased her no end.

"Mother is out."

"And Szidónia?"

She shrugged, which she did with inimitable charm, raising a shoulder just a little, but somehow this made her whole body sag, reaching the limits of its inertia, and after an indefinable moment of transition she relaxed again, flung her pencil on the desk, and stood up.

"Come on, let's not waste any more time."

She acted as if she really wasn't interested in anything else, but I couldn't shake my anger so easily, and besides, I wasn't quite sure what she was getting at, since all I knew was that once again something had happened behind my back which I had to scream out of my system.

"Just tell me this one thing, will you: when did you talk to Kálmán?"

"I didn't," she said with a gleam in her eye, almost singing the words.

"You couldn't have, because he walked home with me."

"You see—so why don't you just leave it at that?" she said, grinning pertly, eager to let me know she was enjoying my annoyance.

"But may I ask how you found out about their plans, then?"

"That's my business, don't you think?"

"So that means you have your own little plans, right?"

"Right."

"And of course that's where you want to go."

"Why not? I haven't decided yet."

"Because you don't want to miss out on anything, right?"

"I'm not going to tell you, so don't get your hopes up."

"I'm not interested."

"So much the better."

"I'm an idiot for coming here."

There was a moment's silence, then very quietly and hesitantly she said, "Want me to tell you?"

"I couldn't care less. Keep it to yourself."

She stepped closer to me, very close, but the look in her eyes faltered, turned opaque, as though she'd been deeply touched by something, and that fleeting uncertainty made it clear that she didn't see what she was looking at, didn't see me, didn't see my neck, although she seemed to be looking at it, at the bite mark, but that's not what she saw; in her thoughts she was roaming that secret region which she wanted to hide from me and which I was so curious to see, to know, and above all, I wanted to feel Kálmán in her, feel her every move, hear the words she had whispered in his ear; then, hesitantly, as if trying to convince herself I was really there yet not fully realizing what she was doing, she pinched together the collar of my shirt, tugging at it absentmindedly, and lowering her voice to an ingratiating breathlike whisper, she drew me even closer.

"The only reason I am going to tell you is that we promised we wouldn't keep any secrets from each other."

And like someone who has managed to hurdle the first and most serious obstacle posed by her own sense of shame, she sighed, even smiled a little, using this smile to find her way back to my face and, looking straight into my eyes, continue what she had started: "He wrote to me, sent me a letter, Livia brought it over last night, that I should come, too, on account of the costumes, you see, and that we'd meet in the woods this afternoon."

Now I had the upper hand, because I knew that this wasn't the whole truth.

"You're lying."

"And you're completely off your rocker."

"You think I'm a fool and can't tell when you're lying to me?"

I grabbed her wrist and simply yanked her hand off me, she had no business pawing me like that, but I didn't let go of her completely, I just pushed her away—she shouldn't be the one, certainly not with her transparent little lies, to decide just how close we should get—and I made this move though her affection expressed by such proximity, letting me feel her breath on my mouth, and even her dangerous lying that might have deceived just about anybody else pleased me very much, yet it was as if I had realized that the body, seductive and warm though it may be, never wants to possess another without attaching some moral conditions to this possession, and that precisely for the sake of a perfect and total possession, so-called truth is more important than the warm body or its momentary closeness; this truth, of course, does not exist, yet one must strive for it, for this inner truth of the body, even if it turns out to be only provisional, ephemeral; and so I acted like a cool-headed manipulator, deliberately and ruthlessly interfering with the process in the interest of some dimly perceived goal, rejecting the body in the hope of regaining it more completely sometime in the uncertain future.

There is no harsher move than pushing someone away, deliberately, contemptuously: I lost her mouth, I gave up my attraction to her beauty in favor of a deeper attraction, but I did it in a shrewd, calculating way, so that she should be even more beautiful when I got her back, when she'd be all mine, because it was my rival, of course, the usurper, the stranger who was also my double, Kálmán, whom I had to evict from her mouth when I insisted that this perfectly formed mouth should not lie; therefore, I hoped to gain as much through the harshness of my gesture as I had to lose by it.

"Forget it, it's not that important," I said to her mercilessly.

"Then what d'you want from me?" she cried out, choking with anger, and snatched her wrist out of my hand.

"Nothing. You're ugly when you lie."

Of course lying did not change her looks—if anything, her wounded feelings made her more beautiful; again she shrugged her shoulders, as if she were not at all interested in how I happened to see her at any given moment, a nonchalant shrug that was in such stark contrast with what she must have been thinking that she had to lower her lids, chastely, her wide-open, always astonished eyes disappearing behind the lazy, thick lashes, leaving her mouth free to rule her face.

I couldn't have wished for anything more at this point than to watch her motionless mouth: perhaps what made this mouth so unusual was that the upper lip, a perfect twin of the lower one, arched straight toward the little groove running down from the nose to the edge of the lips, without the two usual peaks breaking its rise or the tiny hollows at the mouth's edge interrupting its downward slope; the symmetrical pair of lips formed a perfect oval.

A mouth ready to whistle, sing hauntingly, or chatter endlessly, and full cheeks framed by a mass of springy brown curls all added to her cheerful, carefree, and unself-conscious demeanor; she turned around and without relaxing her narrow shoulders still raised in a shrug headed for the door, but then unexpectedly changed course and, instead of walking out, threw herself on the bed.

It wasn't a real bed but a kind of divan that doubled as a bed where during the day a heavy Persian throw rug covered the bedclothes; it was soft and warm, her motionless body fairly sank in it, clad in the maroon, flower-patterned dress she had filched for the afternoon from her mother's closet, which was in fact a tiny sunlit room with built-in white floor-to-ceiling wardrobes, all filled with pleasant-smelling dresses, one of our favorite places for rummaging and exploration; her bare legs, dangling helplessly from the divan, almost glowed in this stuffy dim room, and what made the sight even more inviting was that her skirt rode up to her thighs, and as she lay there, hiding her head in the protective embrace of her arms, she began to cry, making her shoulders, back, and even gently curving backside shake and quiver.

Her tears didn't move me much, I was familiar with every possible variant of these crying sessions: the simple whimpers, the even, inconsolable sniffling, and the furiously rising huge outbursts that she invariably carried to unbearably ugly, sloppy, snotty crescendos of bawling, followed by slow, talkative denouements, quiet shivers, stifled tremors of exhaustion that made her body spongy-soft and relaxed until, without noticeable transition, she found her way back to her usual self, which was, if possible, even stronger and more confident—and fully satisfied.

This familiarity with her crying styles didn't mean of course that I could deny her my sympathy, for I knew she was capable of crying even when I wasn't looking; she had given detailed accounts of her solitary crying sessions often enough, lacing them with a healthy dose of self-mockery, including the candidly revealing admission that crying, an unabashed and self-indulgent flaunting of pain, was no small pleasure, and what's more, she liked to cry in Livia's company, too, finding her a similarly sympathetic, gentle, somewhat more objective provider of solace than I; still, something about her crying was directed only at me, some playful, exaggerated quality made to order, as it were, a theatricality prompted by my presence; her cries were part and parcel of our mutual dishonesty, an important element in the elaborate system of lies and pretenses that nevertheless had to be enacted with the utmost care and conviction, the very fraudulent games which we played in the guise of total honesty and openness; it was as if with these cries she was trying out, in front of me and for me, the part of the weak, helpless, easily injured, refined woman she would one day become, although in reality she was cold and hard, calculatingly cruel and shrewd, and while in beauty no match for Hédi, she acted so very tough and aggressive, so stubbornly possessive of everything and everyone, that she seemed to dominate us even more than Hédi did with her beauty, although that, too, was a charade, as she must have known I knew; she was rehearsing a role, and those flounced and frilly dresses and silky fabrics for which we both had developed a deep liking were the appropriately feminine, external supports for the role, and stealing them added a further element of excitement to her clandestine acts of transformation, because she wanted to be exactly like her mother; I started toward the divan with the most confident steps, for in my assigned role I had to be strong, calm, understanding, a trifle brutal even, in short, absolutely masculine, a role promising so many play-ful pleasures that, however false it was, I had no problem assuming it.

And perhaps it was this deliberate readiness for falsity that made me different from other boys.

I was so much in tune with the source of her femininity, I had the impression I was just playing at being a boy, and my playacting might be exposed at any time.

As if there was no dividing line between my maleness and my female-ness.

It seemed to me it wasn't I who did this or that, I wasn't the one who acted, but only chose between two pre-prepared patterns of action inside me, one for boys and one for girls, and since I was a boy, I chose the male pattern, naturally, but could just as easily have chosen the other one: I could now ask her, for example, in a rough, no-nonsense voice, what in God's name was the matter with her, though I knew perfectly well what the matter was, and if she didn't answer I could demand even more forcefully that she stop the hysterics, tell her sarcastically that her idiotic bawling and hollering was a sheer waste of time, or I could start swearing and make as though her crying annoyed the hell out of me, which it didn't; or I could switch, take the part of a girl friend and tell her that if she still wanted to see her darling Kálmán, that disgusting fat slob—and that was what she wanted to do, wasn't it?—though I had no idea what she could see in him, his name was enough to make me puke, but if she still wanted to see him, she'd better mind her lovely face and not mess it up with all that disgusting blubbering, because then he wouldn't like her nearly as much as she would like him to; all the while Maja, trusting herself to the undulating waves in the opening movement of her crying, seemed to be waiting for just these harsh words, the precise content of the rudeness hardly mattering, just needing symbolic slaps to prove to herself that she was indeed weak, as I needed to swear to prove I was strong, and as soon as she got these bracing slaps, she released the pent-up energies of a well-practiced performance, turned on her side, lowered her arms, and, switching to deep-throated bawling, finally showed me her face, so contorted by tears and screaming that it deserved some real sym-pathy.

As if there was a degree of falsity where the false began to appear genuine.

"What do you all want from me? Why are you screaming? What do you want? Why? Everybody, everybody keeps tormenting me!" she screamed, her scream turning into a howl that sounded quite real, giving me a perversely wonderful pleasure since her howling had to do with both Kálmán and me: it was her wavering and vacillating between the two of us that was real, though for me it still remained a game I could observe from the outside; but now, rolling back on her stomach, she buried her head in her arms again and began her rise, this time without the slightest inhibition, into regions of higher, truer, more real sobbing; I stood over her, fascinated and mesmerized, as she manipulated, slowly, gradually, with finesse, what may have seemed like a game a moment ago into a passion of suffering, and though her body at first resisted, having no real cause for suffering, and refused to cooperate, now it did, and the clever maneuver worked: sunk deep in the soft bed, she was suffering, she was trembling and writhing, this was no longer just a game; yet still I made no move, still tried to preserve the calm air of a confident male, did not reach out toward her, didn't touch her or comfort her, though the sight truly shocked me, because she kept tearing and biting the blanket and, like an epileptic, jerking and tossing her head while her legs dangled lifelessly over the edge of the bed, and she seemed to be having an attack, trapped in the unrelieved tension between total self-revelation and total self-defense; and my fear, dread, and shocked immobility hiding behind benevolent indifference were more than justified, because I was the one who wanted this to happen, I had provoked it with my words, teased the secret madness out of her so that I could feel my power over her, vanquish, in her body, that other boy within me who was too tenderly and cruelly familiar to make me truly jealous—it was all for me, then, only for me, but that voice! the shrill sobs swelling into screams seemed to be issuing not from a single source but from two different voices, as if behind the pitiful bawling, broken by the rhythmic writhing of her body, there was another, shrieking voice that grew piercingly, unrelentingly, thinner and reedier; it was unbearable, and I felt everything about to crumble and slip out of my control.

And when I lay down next to her on the soft divan, leaning over her and cautiously touching her shoulder, I was not motivated by tenderness or empathy—if anything, she disgusted me, I hated her, and feared she might go on like this forever; and though I knew all crying must come to an end sometime, its effect on me was so powerful, the sight and sound so immediate, that my former experiences failed to reassure me and I thought, Yes, she will go on like this, she won't stop, ever, whatever had been hidden and now surfaced accidentally will become permanent, and

Szidónia will walk in and I'll be found out, and the neighbors will come trooping across the garden, because everybody could hear her, and they'll call a doctor, and her mother and father will come, and she'll still be carrying on in her red dress, and they'll find out that this dreadful thing was all because of me.

"Maja dear."

"Your mother's cunt, that's what's dear!"

"But what is it? Come, don't cry like this. What happened? I'm here. You know I understand. Everything. We promised, remember? You've said it yourself."

"Fuck your promise!" she said, and she rolled back toward the wall, pulling away impetuously, and I clambered after her, just to make her stop.

"I'm not going away, I only said that to get you scared, but I'm not, I promise. I'll stay right here. Come on, Maja, Maja! But you can go. If you want to, you can go. You know I always let you do what you want. Why don't you answer?" I whispered in her ear and tried to hug her, flatten myself against her, hoping that the calm of my body would somehow pass into hers.

But where was my superior manly calm by then! I was also trembling, my voice also shaking, and I didn't suspect that with faultless concentration she sensed everything and that I couldn't have given her greater satisfaction than this.

At the same time my alarmed tenderness instead of calming her frenzy oddly intensified it, and only at this point could I peer behind her madness and ascertain that, as frightful and uncontrolled as the spectacle seemed, there was plenty of sober and calculating sense left in her; I may have drawn her head close to me with a gesture disguised as one of caring attention, planning slyly to put my hand over her mouth so that no more of that sound should come out, but it was no use, we saw through each other, and she could accurately detect the deceit hidden in my gesture; her body tensed up, she flung me off her and began kicking and pummeling me, biting my fingers hard, as she kept on wailing and shrieking; her face was contorted, almost as if it had become a boy's face, hard, angular, and dirty from tearstains; and if at that moment my quaking fright had not been replaced by a bit of cunning, if I had responded to her blows and kicks with blows and kicks of my own, chances are she would have beaten me thoroughly, for though we never fought in earnest, she was probably stronger than I and, in any case, wilder and more reckless.

I didn't defend myself, I didn't even notice when she stopped screaming, what's more, I didn't try to hold her down, and I restrained myself—our relationship never had a more honest moment—I let her claw and bite and kick and scratch and tried to respond to her every move with the gentlest of touches, soft caresses and kisses that bounced off her, given the unevenness of the fight, just as her clumsy, broad-stroked, girlish punches missed me; still, I was the girl and she the boy, in this situation at least, in the way she glowered and bared her teeth and tensed her neck muscles; in the sudden silence that followed, only her loud panting, the groans of the mattress, and the thud of punches could be heard.

She tried to push me away, pressing her fist against my shoulder, off the divan, onto the floor, but when my hand clasped her naked thigh, it was as if her hate-filled resistance and raging fury had suddenly left, unexpectedly even to her, flowed out, evaporated from her limbs, and her body relaxed in an instant; as if seeing me for the first time in her life, she seemed genuinely surprised that I was so close to her and that she liked it; she opened her eyes wide again, no longer whitely insane but familiarly inquisitive.

She held her breath.

As though she was anxious not to let even her breath touch my mouth, not if we were this close, this hot.

The bare skin under my hand quivered a bit, as if she had just realized my hand was there.

And how could my hand have gotten there?

Then she burst into tears again.

As if the closeness and the warmth had brought on the tears, but now there was real pain behind them, a quiet, I'd even say wise, pain.

A pain that had no hope of finding relief in the heat of another outburst, and indeed never turned into a real cry comparable to the earlier one, but remained a quiet whimper.

Still, this voice touched me more deeply than the earlier voices, and I somehow caught it from her: a long-drawn-out whine did leave my throat though my cry could not burst forth but only choked me, because in my chest and in my thighs a firm and eager but also paralyzing force, preventing total yielding or weakening, was pushing, thrusting me toward her; if before I had assumed or suspected she was foisting a nonexistent, imaginary pain on her body, using it to deceive and distract me so that she could obtain my surrender, I now realized this assumption was unfounded, because something was causing her real pain—I was the cause of her pain, the fact that she loved me as well.

I edged closer to her, and rather than objecting to this she helped me by slipping her arm under my shoulder, gently hugging me to herself, and simply to return the gesture I let my hand slide up her thigh, my fingers slip under her panties.

And we lay there like this.

Her burning face on my shoulder.

We seemed to be lolling in some spacious, soft and slippery wetness where one doesn't know how time passes but it's of no importance anyway.

With my arms I was rocking her body as if wanting to rock both of us to sleep.

With my little sister, too, I used to lie like this, in a time beyond memory, under the desk, when I was experimenting with those pins and she, looking for a place to hide and finding it with me, screamed in pain and terror as she flung herself on me, as if by entrusting her pitiful, twisted, and by all appearances disgusting body to me, she was trying to say she'd understood my cruel games and was even grateful to me, since I was the only one who, through those games, had found a language she could use; that's how my sister and I kept rocking each other, half-sitting, half-lying on the cool parquet floor, until we fell asleep in each other's arms in the late-afternoon twilight.

"One day you'll realize you've been tormenting me for no good reason," she whispered later, her trembling lips almost touching my ear, "because you never believe me, but there's nobody I love as much as I love you, nobody."

She sounded like that other voice, out of that long-ago afternoon, straight out of the body of my little sister, a shrill but lilting voice, tickling my ears; it felt as though I was hugging my little sister's formless body, knowing it was slender Maja I was holding.

In the meantime, she kept buzzing and bubbling in my ear, gratefully, softly, unstoppably.

"Like yesterday, I told him he could bully all he wanted, you were my number-one love and not him, I told him straight out; I told him you were good and kind, and not mean like them, and I know he's doing it with me just so he could tell Krisztián about it, I told him he's definitely number two."

She stopped for a moment, as if she didn't dare come out with it, but then, like a whiff of hot air, assailed my ear: "But you are my baby, and I love to play with you so much! and you mustn't be mad when I pretend to be in love with him. He interests me in some ways, yes, but it's all a game, I'm only using him to tease you, but there's nobody, nobody I love as much as you, believe me, certainly not him, because he's a brute beast and not nice to me at all. Sometimes we could make believe you're my son. I often thought I'd like to have a little boy just like you; I can't imagine him any other way but as a sweet, kind, innocent, blond-haired little boy."

She fell silent again, her gushing coming up against real emotions.

"But you can be a bastard, too, you know, and that's why I cry all the time, because you want to know everything and won't let me have my own little secrets, even though you and I have the greatest, the biggest secret of all, and you can't possibly think I'd ever betray you, because that secret is more important to me than anything else, and will be forever. But you keep secrets from me, too; don't you think I know that it's not Livia you're after but Hédi, and that you don't give a shit about me?"

Nothing changed, we kept rocking and swaying, but something urged me to let myself be seduced completely by this voice; it seemed that I was no longer rocking her, but that she was rocking me with her voice, lulling me, and I had to keep us on the threshold of sleep.

"Now you can tell me about it," I said in a loud voice, trying to rouse myself from the pleasant torpor.

"What?" she asked just as loud.

"What you two did yesterday evening."

"You mean night."

"Night?"

"Yes, night."

"Are you going to lie to me again?"

"Well, almost night, late in the evening, very late."

It sounded like the beginning of another digression, which interested me as much as the story itself, but she didn't continue, and I stopped rocking her.

"Tell me."

But she didn't reply, and somehow even her body fell silent in my arms.

Melchior's Room
under the Eaves

With soft lively steps he moved about the large room like someone going through very familiar motions, each step he took making the all-white, ostentatiously white, floorboards creak slightly, his pointed black shoes looking especially worn and battered on this startlingly white floor and on the thick, deep-red rug; he seemed to be preparing an unfamiliar secret ritual or initiation ceremony; rattling a box of matches, he began to light candles and with a politeness bordering on stiff formality offered me a comfortable-looking armchair—would I care to sit?—there was a hint of intrusiveness in these unnecessarily elaborate preparations, his scrupulous politeness notwithstanding, as though he were making it all too clear that he wanted the time we were about to spend together to be exceptionally pleasant and comfortable and with his movements was making me a virtual part of his little plan, as he threw off his jacket, loosened his tie, undid the top buttons of his shirt, and, looking thoughtfully around the room to see what else needed to be done, unself-consciously scratched his chest hair, enjoying himself as though I weren't even there; then he walked through the pretty arched doorway into the entrance hall and fiddled with something there, which mystified me even further, after which soft sounds of classical music swam into the room from concealed speakers, but I didn't want to yield to this fastidiously yet crudely staged atmosphere and chose to remain standing.

He came back to turn off the overhead light, and that surprised me—in fact, to be honest, since I took it as too hasty an allusion to something we were still anxious to hide, even from ourselves—frightened me, though by then candles were burning in sconces and candlesticks and we weren't in sudden darkness, at least thirty tall tapers making the room both churchlike and reminiscent of wartime blackouts, and he drew together the heavy red brocade curtain, its fleur-de-lis pattern glimmering gold in the candlelight, the rich ruffled fabric covering the entire height of the wall from floor to ceiling.

He enjoyed his movements, and because his limbs were long and slim— long arms, long fingers, long thighs in rather tight slacks—his movements were not ungainly; he touched objects with a sensual, even voluptuous pleasure, as if in coming into contact with them even these routine ges- tures caused him a kind of elemental joy, yet in making this subtle, over- subtle play for objects, suggesting cozy intimacy, he seemed to have me in mind as well, as if he had to prove something not only to himself but to me, trying to demonstrate—surely the game was not without purpose— how one could and should live pleasurably in this place, what rhythms were required by these surroundings, to show me in minute detail that this rhythm was as much his own as were the objects themselves; but for all the openness and genuine amiability his moves implied, I sensed a certain tense anxiety, and not only because the less-than-perfect ease of this shameless exhibitionism had a hint of obtrusive familiarity in it, but also because behind the exhibitionist's easy self-assurance, superior air, and secret delight, I couldn't help noticing a certain touchy tentativeness, as if he were watching me from the protected forward position of his superi- ority, trying to see whether I was really interested in the intimate tokens of trust he was offering me, whether he mightn't have made a mistake.

And because I felt this avid, persistent, selfish curiosity in every move he made, however harmonious and confident, however much offered as a revealing confession, his unspoken question was not unjustified, because I did act like someone who couldn't care less about his elaborate show, who'd rather remain within the reliable boundaries of conventional eti- quette and did not even note the secret meaning of his gestures; I was so uninterested in him that I would have liked just to close my eyes so as not to see him open up like this and lay himself bare in hopes of a like response, but he, accurately gauging the nature and extent of my fears, was willing to neutralize the signals with other gestures—in short, was ready to retreat.

But by then we were too far gone, to say nothing of what had led up to this meeting, and an actual retreat was clearly out of the question, for my original mistake was to come up here in the first place and let him stand before me and smile his infinitely trustworthy smile, steady and untroubled, not begging for but offering trust and confidence, its fluttery surface made more sensitively responsive by hidden tentativeness, an all-pervasive smile; it was there in the vertical creases of his lips, in his eyes, but truly inside them somehow, on his smooth forehead, as a shadow in the corner of his mouth, and of course in the ingratiating dimples of his cheeks; so I could not close my eyes, if only because I felt acutely that if I were to do so, or even allow my lashes to droop the least little bit, I'd betray the feeling I'd harbored almost from the very first moment we met, and that would certainly contradict the stiffish posture, a result of my feigned indifference, with which I tried to hide, neutralize, force into the accepted moral order my unequivocal and rapturous attraction to his mouth, his eyes, his smile, the soft depth of his voice, his playfully buoyant walk—he walked as though he were flaunting it: Look, this is how I walk! he seemed to be saying—how was I to curb and discipline my senses, and thereby keep his movements, too, within bounds? no doubt it was foolish, absurd, to hope that in this situation, in this repellently rather than attractively interesting room, the coy game between sense and sensuality might be checked by some inner discipline; I tried desperately to steer my attention out of the trap of his smile to other things, to focus on the room, hoped to divert my attention by looking for other reference points and, by understanding the connection between them, perhaps I could rescue my mind, now very much at the mercy of my body; but meanwhile, I made the unpleasant discovery that my mouth and eyes had involuntarily borrowed his smile; I was smiling back at him with his own smile, his own eyes; I hadn't closed my eyes, yet I became one with him; minutes went by like this, and no matter what I did or tried to do, I was being carried in the direction he chose to steer us; and I knew that if I allowed this to continue and let his smile freeze on my lips, if I couldn't get it unstuck somehow, I'd soon lose what we call the right to self-determination—if only his all-too-knowing, accommodating, yet indecently high-handed determination hadn't bothered me so much!—my only means of escape would have been to find a clever excuse, say goodbye and get out of there, just leave, but then why was I so willing to come up in the first place? or maybe I should just walk out the door without saying a word? but there was no clever excuse for parting, simply couldn't have been, since we both took care to keep the smooth veneer of conventional social intercourse in this perfectly ordinary situation: two young men facing each other, after one of them had invited the other up for a drink; who could find anything objectionable in that? their mutual attraction, stronger than their bashfulness, was slightly embarrassing, but during the course of a serious conversation, when they'd let the power of their instincts manifest itself as abstract thought, the embarrassment would surely disappear, if only this smooth veneer weren't so transparent! as it was, attempts at distraction only enhanced the sense of intimacy, which I both welcomed and tried to avoid and which our mutual tactfulness—I wouldn't offend him and he wouldn't go too far—also strengthened, everything did, and in the end, however ill at ease I may have felt, all my eager concessions and self-deceptions, my glossing over things, my embarrassment, conspicuous stiffness, and forbearance simply boomeranged.

And on top of it all, he kept on talking, rapidly and more loudly than necessary, always following my eyes with his words; to the exclusion of all other possible topics, he held forth on whatever he thought my eyes were curious about; we might say more cynically that he was running off at the mouth, trying to relieve my embarrassment and at the same time keep my forced, trembling smile—his smile on my lips—from somehow reinfecting him; he went on jabbering, buzzing and flirting in a way that made his high-handed, obnoxious complacency unbearable and unacceptable precisely because it was so very masculine, or at least what's usually considered masculine: a mildly aggressive, enticing, instinctively obtrusive, ingratiating, audacious mirror image—what a caricature mirror image!— of the sort of behavior I had never had a chance to observe from the outside, for without giving it a thought, I had indulged in it myself; a disagreeable pose is what it was, a pose one masters sometime in adolescence, considering it very manly; the trick is to talk, talk a blue streak, without saying anything, so that only the form itself, the style, the razzle-dazzle of words can clue one in on the speaker's secret designs: I was surprised, wasn't I, he asked, that he'd painted the floor all white—but he wanted no reply, only to catch my eyes again with his and not let go— he knew, of course, that this sort of thing was usually not done, he said, but that had never stopped him before, and didn't I find it attractive, though? he did, when he'd finished painting it, and was pleased that he wouldn't have to scrub it anymore; the place used to look like a dump, a pigsty really, some old geezer had lived here before—he often tried to picture his old age and feared it, actually, considering that given his aberrant inclinations it would surely be the most critical period of his life, a horrid wreck of a body with still youthful urges lusting after young bodies—anyway, the neighbors told him the old man had died on a urine-soaked mattress in that little room where the sofa was now standing; he hoped fate wouldn't deal him such an old age; in fact, he didn't want any kind of old age; and I couldn't imagine the dreadful state of the apartment when he moved in, filthy beyond belief and so foul-smelling he had to keep the windows open even in winter, and it was still in the air, sometimes he could smell it even now, four years later; anyway, why shouldn't a floor be all white, who said it must always be brown or an ugly yellow? wasn't it a great idea to spread the color of pristine purity over all that smut? and wasn't this, after all, perfectly in tune with the taste of our upright Germans, and he was, if not fully, at least half German.

Only half? I asked, surprised.

That's a long and quite amusing story, he said with a laugh and, as if sweeping an unexpected obstacle easily aside, went right on, with the same fervor, asking me if I had had the chance to make these or similar kinds of observations, because if I hadn't yet, I would surely discover in the future that white could be the appropriate symbol for the defeated German people's national character.

I said it was mostly gray I'd been noticing, and because I felt I should somehow be embarrassed for him, for his flippant tone, my gaze drifted away.

But he followed my eyes: ah, the desk, a nice piece, wasn't it? and the armchairs, candelabra, and rugs, too, all brought over from his mother's, just about everything was from there, a kind of family inheritance, all of it, he looted his mother's place, but she didn't mind, mothers never do, and all this was recent; at first he wanted the place to be white and bare, just a bed covered with a white sheet, nothing else . . . he was blathering away, giving me all this nonsense because he was glad I was there but afraid to say so; shouldn't we rather drink something, he happened to have a bottle of French champagne, chilled, saving it for some special occasion, one never knew when such an occasion might arise, right? how about making our meeting a special occasion and uncorking the bottle?

Taking my bemused silence for acquiescence, he left to get the champagne; the antique clock on the wall struck twelve, I counted the strokes, mechanically, helplessly; So 'tis midnight, I thought, which wasn't too bright but characteristic of my state, for by then my thinking had simply shut down so that pure sensory perception could take control, making me appear as another object in the room without my knowing how it got there, a not unfamiliar sensation, yet never before had I sensed so vividly and thoroughly that the place I was in was as unique as the hour marked by the countable strokes of the clock, because something had to happen here, something that went against all my wishes and that would change the course of my life, and whatever it might turn out to be, I knew I had to yield to it: midnight, the witching hour, never more propitious, I had to laugh at myself, as though I'd never let myself go before, a slight exaggeration, surely, as if I were a young girl debating whether to lose or keep her virginity, as if this room were the last station on a long deferment whose nature and content had been unfamiliar until now; I was fooling myself, still pretending—what pleasure to pretend to ourselves!—that I really had no idea what extraordinary thing might happen or perhaps already had happened here tonight, but what was it?

The candles flickered and crackled, soothingly, beautifully; outside it was pouring, and after the clock struck twelve all one could hear was the even, bubbling rhythm of baroque music and the pelting, pattering sound of the rain, as if somebody had overdirected this scene to be so obviously, so ludicrously beautiful.

Because somebody did stage it, I was sure, not he or I but somebody, or at least it got staged beforehand, as all accidental encounters are; no one plans them or counts on them, and only later, in retrospect, do we realize they were pivotal, fateful; at first it all seems banal, incidental, incoherent, random fragments and flashes to which we needn't attach much significance, and as a rule we don't, for what may be accidentally visible to us from a tangled heap of occurrences, what may hang out and appear as a sign, a warning, is nothing more than some detail belonging to another cluster of happenings we have nothing to do with; a prop in Thea's slightly laughable romantic agony, that's what I thought of him then, because he was the one she spoke to Frau Kühnert about on that dark autumn afternoon in the uncomfortable silence of the rehearsal hall, calling him "the boy," an odd and deliberately derisive appellation, enough to arouse my curiosity; but then it had been more intriguing to try to follow the inner process, the various degrees of transition, that Thea had to follow so that finally she could focus the intense emotions of her just completed scene on some external object, which she ended up calling the boy; as I have already pointed out, Thea, like all great actors, had the special ability to make her inner processes, mixed in with her private life, continually visible and spectacular and, precisely because emotions displayed on the stage are nourished by the actor's so-called private life, one could never be sure when she was in earnest and when she was only playing with something that might mean a great deal to her; in other words, unlike normal mortals, she would toy with deadly serious things and take seriously what was only make-believe, and this interested me more than the seemingly irrelevant question of who the elusive person was whom she labeled "the boy," the person she disdained, hated even, so much so that she wouldn't utter his name, the person she nevertheless didn't dare telephone because for reasons unknown to me, he had asked her never to call him again, for whose closeness, then, right after the erotic desire expressed onstage had become impersonal and objectless, she still yearned so much that she was willing to risk humiliation, and in whose room I would be standing later that same evening—in a sense as her replacement.

In spite of my apprehensions, and they were numerous enough, I had given in to her pleading and nagging and agreed to spend the evening with them: "Come on, don't be such a meanie! why can't you come with us, why play hard to get when I so very much want you to come? oh, you boys drive me mad! you'll get to meet him, at least, he's a remarkable character, and you don't even have to be jealous of him, he's not quite as remarkable as you are, Sieglinde, do me a favor, you ask, too! my asking isn't enough? it's me, me who is asking you, isn't that enough?" she was purring, whispering, playing the girlishly awkward seductress, leaning her light, fragile body against mine and taking hold of my arm; it would have been pretty hard to resist such a playful display of affection, yet what compelled me to go was not curiosity, let alone jealousy—the prospect of observing the two of them in a probably perverse relationship didn't intrigue me either—but because from the moment Thea had managed to avert her lustful and horror-filled gaze from Hübchen's half-naked body and, turning toward us, caught my stare, the almost voyeuristic stare of an overstimulated spectator, I too had been deeply, personally touched by her emotional upheaval, playing itself out in the very sensitive border region of her professional and personal candor: it was impossible to decide whether the scene, interrupted by inveterate directorial rudeness just as it was reaching its climax, might not perhaps continue between the two of us, because to bring it to a halt was impossible, about that there could be no doubt.

Yet ours was a very cool-headed game that no single glance, errant or uncontrolled, was going to derail from its consciously, intelligently charted course; a glance like that could only add spice, introduce another hairpin turn of emotions to make more daring and fiery what was and would continue to be essentially cold, as though haughtily, arrogantly enamored of our intellectual superiority, we had said to each other, No, no! we won't do it! we can easily withstand even these impulsive, involuntary looks, and we won't fall on each other like a couple of animals! we'll stick to the warmest mutual interest, which pays attention to the details of every detail and remains, therefore, in the realm of activities of the conscious mind—unnaturally and anti-lifelike, no matter that it can expose the rawest of instincts—precisely because the interest is so intense that the natural ability to let go, the vulnerability necessary for normal human contact, cannot be realized even for a moment: not so unusual a phenomenon, for we need only think of lovers who, reaching the peak of their mutual attraction with its promise of annihilating fulfillment, cannot achieve physical union until they fall back from that rarefied sphere of inspirited love to a more earthly closeness, until their bodies' pain shrinks the spirit of love to a humiliatingly manageable size; then, in the throes of excruciating pain, they can make their way not to ultimate bliss but to the liberating pleasure of momentary, flashlike gratification, arriving not where they had originally headed but where their bodies will allow them to go.

We were standing under the cheerless neon light of the narrow, characteristically ill-smelling corridor between the rehearsal hall and the dressing rooms, storerooms, showers, and toilets; it was here, in the pungent smell of gluey stage sets, paints, powders, and colognes, sweat-stained costumes and human bodies, permanently clogged drains, worn-out slippers and shoes, melting soaps and damp, used towels, that we first touched; I'd never seen her face so close, and it was as though I was looking not at the face of a woman but at some special, cozy, and familiar landscape whose every byway and hiding place I knew, every furrow and shadow, every memory and the meaning of every movement; looking at this landscape stripped me bare, down to my childhood; Frau Kühnert was still standing there, holding the receiver of the pay phone, distant and offended, but also smugly dutiful: "You see, your requests can be so humiliating sometimes, but there's nothing I wouldn't do for you," for she'd just finished giving us a supposedly objective report of her conversation with Melchior, and "What did I tell you? face it: I'm irresistible!" Thea cried triumphantly, whereupon Frau Kühnert, with a smile of success but still angry, slammed down the phone; Thea was being outrageous, of course, though no more so than usual, hogging every speck of the success, playful to be sure, quite aware of her own weaknesses, but still! Frau Kühnert's resentment wasn't unwarranted, since the kind of conversation she'd just concluded is never easy—convincing someone to do something he has little inclination to do—yet it was fairly obvious that Melchior's accepting the invitation had nothing to do with Thea's being irresistible but that the ruse had worked, the trap had been well set: what Melchior had accepted was not the invitation but the intermediary, Frau Kühnert, whom he hardly knew and did not want to offend; or, more precisely, since he did not yet suspect that Thea had no compunction about gossiping freely about everything—as if being totally open were the price of guarding the really important secrets of her life—and did not wish to publicize the rather cruel way he had been forced to respond to her impulsive and, as I was to learn later, morally dubious onslaughts, he had no desire to let Frau Kühnert in on secrets that, as it turned out, were no secrets to her; Frau Kühnert's reproachful look and offended tone came not so much because of the unpleasant nature of her conversation, not even the quietly vindictive manner in which Melchior had given Thea to understand that her disagreeably persistent efforts were to no avail, that he remained in control of the situation and that he'd come all right, come gladly, but would like to bring along a friend of his from France who happened to be staying with him, to which Frau Kühnert couldn't very well say no, don't bring him, but instead had to assure him effusively that any friend of his would be more than welcome; what really triggered Frau Kühnert's resentment and anger—yet another surprising and unaccountable turnabout—was the very gentle manner in which Thea turned to me during our conversation, clinging to my arm, purring and flirting, to which I responded, naturally enough, with an awkward grin, for what was she doing grabbing and pawing me when she was really after the other one? or did she now want me instead, repeating her earlier double take, when she'd responded to my unashamed glance after she'd had her feel of Hübchen's unashamed body? or did she want both of us at the same time? bring us together just to play us off against each other? prove that she wasn't interested in Melchior, could twist everyone around her finger, anyone, and thus overcome the humiliation she'd suffered from Melchior's rude rebuff, a hurt she felt like a reopened wound during her scene with Hübchen? because she did yearn for youth and beauty, oh yes, and the wound began to bleed even more when she got into that hopeless argument with the director; in any case, the display of what seemed like tenderness, mutual interest, and trust, the picture of us standing there, clinging, our eyes locked, while life went on around us—props and flats were being carried past, somebody flushed the toilet, and then Hübchen marched out of the shower, naked, and headed for his dressing room, but along the way winked at Thea as if to say, rather insolently, "See, you miserable slut, you'll get from this one what you wanted from me just a while ago"—must have really unnerved Frau Kühnert, who did not comprehend the message, or the meaning of our intense look; what's more, Thea didn't even bother to thank her for having been the go-between, couldn't, really, since she was too busy paying attention to me and of course took it for granted that Frau Kühnert was there to serve her.

It soon became clear that Thea only appeared to be paying attention to me—just as I appeared to be listening only to her—which made me feel as good as if it were real and complete, which flattered me; her body was light and delicate and I felt, not for the first time, that I'd like to press it into myself though I knew that it was the kind of body that mustn't be held too hard, its melting softness with its touch of firmness yielded only if we ourselves remained soft and gentle, if we managed somehow to refine and attenuate our own forcefulness; yet she did sweep me off my feet, as they say, and while giving her proof of my rapt, almost obsequious attention, I was really bent on finding out how she did what she did, how she could produce this perfectly exquisite play of appearances, these irretrievably effective situations, and at the same time always remain outside them; where was she, I wondered, when she had no more gestures under her control; then again, I too was only appearing to be as respectfully, almost lovingly attentive as Frau Kühnert thought I was: but this whole business, which in the end turned into a deadly serious game of pretenses, began at the moment when, about six weeks before this little scene in the corridor, Langerhans first led me to the small director's table and sat me down next to Frau Kühnert in his own empty chair—which he never used because during rehearsals he would pace up and down, scratch his chin, whip off his glasses, then push them back on again, as though he weren't even there and was doing something other than what in fact he was doing—at any rate, from that moment on I had been in a state of continuous excitement.

But exactly how and when she showed up at that table I cannot remember, for as soon as I took my place, a place that as time went on I found more and more unpleasant, she was already there—or could she have been there before and I just hadn't noticed?

It's possible she was there from the beginning, or maybe she came over later; either way, I had the feeling from the start that she was there because of me, and this apparent oversight or lapse of memory is but further proof that the mechanics of emotions, about which we are so curious in this novel, are obscured by the very emotions operating in us, so that we can never say anything meaningful about it; it's almost as if every occurrence were obstructed by our own sharply focused attention; consequently, in retrospect, we recall not what happened but the way we observed what happened, what emotional response we had to the event, which itself became hazy and fragmentary under our observation; we do not perceive a happening as a happening, a change as a change, a turning point as a turning point, even though we expect life to keep producing changes and dramatic reversals, for in each change and reversal, however tragic, we expect redemption itself, the uplifting sensation of "This is what I've been waiting for," yet just as attention obstructs the event, change is obstructed by anticipation, and thus the really momentous changes in our lives occur unnoticed, in the most complete silence, and we become suspicious only when a new state of affairs has already got the better of us, making impossible any return to the disdained, abhorred, but ever so secure and familiar past.

I simply didn't notice that from the moment Thea appeared I wasn't the same person I had been before.

As I say, she was standing there next to the raised platform, leaning her elbow on the table, as if I weren't even present, continuing an earlier conversation that for some reason had been cut short; as I looked at the face I knew from photographs and movies, a scene suddenly flashed through my mind: lifting the covers, she climbs into somebody's bed, her small breasts swinging forward as she does—true, she was ten years younger then, but now her looks were completely unfamiliar, like seeing the face of someone very close to us, a lover or our mother, for the first time; what I sensed was a combination of intimate familiarity and complete unfamiliarity, natural curiosity and natural reserve, feelings so strong and contradictory that I couldn't but yield to them all, at the same time pretending to have yielded to none of them, and from that moment on I paid attention only to her and nothing else, even keeping her smell in my nose, while pretending to pay attention to everything but her; oddly, she too acted in very much this same way, though for different reasons that became clear to me only much later, pretending not to notice that my face was but a few inches from hers, that she felt the heat radiating from my face, that it was really me she was talking to; of course she went on talking to Frau Kühnert, nonchalantly continuing their earlier conversation, but shaping her words, modulating her intonation so that I, having dropped into the middle of the story, would find her telling of it interesting precisely because of its bewildering incomprehensibility.

It seemed she had received some frozen shrimp from the other side, from across the Wall, from the western half of the city—this odd, convoluted reference, uttered in the rehearsal hall noisy with preparations for the day's work, made her announcement sound unreal, like a line from a fairy tale or cheap thriller, forcing one to imagine that as soon as one stepped out the door, one would bump into the wall, The Wall, about which we rarely spoke, and behind which were tank traps, coiled barbed wire, and treacherously concealed mines which a single careless step could set off, and beyond the sealed strip of no-man's-land lay the city, the other city, a fantasy city, a ghost town, for as far as we were concerned it didn't really exist; and yet the little packet of frozen shrimp did make it across a border guarded by machine-gun-toting soldiers and bloodhounds trained to kill; actually, they were brought over by a friend, I didn't catch his name but gathered he was a pretty important person over on the other side, and a great admirer of hers; when she cut open the package and emptied its contents on a plate, the shrimp looked to her like pink caterpillars which, just as the poor critters were about to spin their cocoon, a terrible ice age had descended on; she had seen shrimp before, but for some reason—she didn't know why—she now found them disgusting, they turned her stomach, she thought she was going to throw up, what was she going to do with them anyway? and wasn't it disgusting that we gobbled up everything? wouldn't it be nicer if one was, say, a hippo and ate only crisp, tasty grass? but those taste buds on our tongues were filled with mean little cravings, they wanted to taste sharp things and sour things, sweet and tart things, they were ready to burst, these buds, that's how hungry they were, they hungered for tastes that didn't even exist— she was babbling on, unstoppable; what was really indecent in her view was not people fucking in public but people openly stuffing their faces, and she finally decided, even though she still felt nauseous, to proceed as she usually did before cooking, as Frau Kühnert well knew, laying out all the ingredients on the kitchen table, nice and neat, because this way she could actually see the additional flavors alongside each other, could savor all of them with her eyes as well as her tongue, that's what's called stimulating the palate; to her, cooking was also playing, improvising, and the show must go on, not even a good puke could stop it; anyway, she decided to whip up some potatoes first, but not just some ordinary mashed potatoes, mind you, she enlivened the boring taste of spuds, milk, and butter with grated cheese and sour cream, then spread the hot puree on a big plate, scooped out the middle with a spoon, and filled it with the shrimp she had first sautéed in herb butter, and that's how she served it, with a side dish of boiled carrots seasoned with Jamaica peppers and a bottle of dry white wine, and it was heavenly! simple yet heavenly! ordinary yet quite, quite elegant, "like me!"

As she craned her long neck, revealing well-conditioned yet delicate, skinny, and strangely underdeveloped muscles, almost like a child's, as she thrust her head seductively forward, hunching up her narrow, bony shoulders, arching her body like a cat poised to jump, looking long and steadily into everyone's eyes as if challenging them to be part of a play whose stage would be the face itself, its fluid features and the eyes, and whose director, of course, would be she herself, as she did all this, she displayed plenty of studied coyness, no doubt, but not the usual kind; in this game she did not want to be beautiful and attractive, as other people might, in fact she wanted to look uglier than they were and it was as if she had deliberately made herself look unattractive, or rather, as if her body had a different view of beauty, refuting as false and craven the generally accepted notion that a human body or face can be beautiful and not simply a functionally arranged system of bones, flesh, skin, and various gelatinous substances that have nothing to do with the concept of beauty; and for this reason, although she was preoccupied more with herself than with anyone else, she made no attempt to look beautiful, and her purpose seemed to be to laugh at, to ridicule her own longing for beauty and perfection; with a slight exaggeration we might say she loved making a fool of herself; with her ugliness she annoyed, provoked, and challenged her surroundings, like a mischievous child calling attention to itself by being mean and difficult, though all it wants is to be petted and cuddled; Thea's hair stuck sloppily to her well-formed, almost perfectly round head; she herself cropped it very short, "so it shouldn't sweat under the wigs," she said, and without a single remark from me, she would plunge into endless monologues justifying her peculiar hairstyle: in her opinion there are two kinds of perspiration—plain physical sweating, of course, when the body for some reason can't adjust to the surrounding temperature because it is tired, worn-out, overfed, or run-down, and then the far more common, psychic perspiration, the sweating of the soul that occurs when we don't listen to what our body is telling us, when we pretend not to understand its language, when we lie and dissemble, when we are weak, clumsy, greedy, hesitant, and stupid, when, defying our body, we insist on doing something only because it's the proper thing to do—it's the clash of wills that produces the heat, and that's when we say we are soaked in sweat; as for her, if there was anything she wanted, it was to stay free, and therefore she wanted to know whether it was her soul that was sweating, she didn't want to blame it on wigs and heavy costumes, even if what she was secreting was the filth and grime of her soul; of course, all this didn't explain why she dyed her hair, now red, now black, using a do-it-yourself kit, and why at other times she neglected it completely, letting it grow and revealing that if she hadn't been touching it up it would be almost completely gray, but then again, what she had wasn't like real hair but instead a thin, frazzled fuzz with no body, probably no particular color to begin with, neither blond nor brown, a slight fluff on a fledgling's head; about the only thing that lent character to her face was her prominent cheekbones, otherwise her features were rather nondescript, her face was dull: a not very high or broad forehead, a somewhat misshapen pug nose whose tip stuck up too much, staring into the world with two disproportionately fleshy nostrils; the lips were wide and sensuous, but they did not blend smoothly into her face and seemed almost as if lifted from another face and placed in hers by accident; oh, but the voice that issued from those lips, from behind the nicotine-stained teeth! a deep, raspy, fully resonant voice or, if she wished, soft and caressing, or hysterically, piercingly thin, as if its tenderness resided in its roughness, the possibility of a howl lurking in every whisper, while her real howls were full of hateful hisses and whispers, each sound implying its opposite, an impression that her face as a whole also gave: on the one hand, her plain features made her look like a worn-out, emotionally unfulfilled working woman whose many frustrations rendered her dreary and uninteresting, and in this respect it was not very different from the faces one saw during morning and evening rush hours on subways and commuter trains, faces sunk in the quiet stupor of fatigue and uselessness; on the other hand, her skin, with its naturally brown coloring, was like a false front, a mask, with a pair of huge, very warm, intelligent, and darkly glittering brown eyes accentuated by very thin lashes; one had the feeling that these eyes belonged not to this mask but to the real face under the mask, and they did glitter, this is no exaggeration; looking for an acceptable explanation, I thought that perhaps her eyeballs were much larger than one would expect in such a relatively small face, or that they were more rounded, more convex than the average eyeball, and that was quite probable, since one did not cease to be aware of their largeness even when she closed her eyes; smooth, heavy, arched lids slid over her eyes, and the mask, full of wrinkles, turned into a kind of antique map of a lively face growing old; on her forehead the furrows ran in dense horizontal lines, but if she suddenly raised her eyebrows, two vertical lines shot up, beginning at the inner tip of the brows, and cut across the horizontal ones, making it appear as though two diaphanous butterfly wings were fluttering on her forehead; only in the hollows of her temples and on her chin did the skin remain smooth, and even on her nose there was not so much a wrinkle as a soft-rimmed indentation that followed the line of her nasal bone; when she pursed her lips, these dips and grooves prefigured the old woman in her; when she laughed, crow's-feet radiated outward from the corners of her eyes; and if in her youth her skin had been overstretched by her protruding cheekbones, the virginal tightness now seemed to be taking revenge on cheeks that were a veritable parade ground of wrinkles, and to know these wrinkles required close and patient scrutiny, because this was not a confusion of lines but a profusion of details so rich it could not be absorbed with a single look.

"We'll wait for you to change, okay," I said quietly, "and then we can still talk about tonight, but hurry up."

She was still looking at me: the wrinkles of her smile, the furrows around her eyes, the closely meshed curved lines that seemed to relieve the darker, deeper grooves of bitterness and suffering around her mouth were still meant for me, but as she withdrew her arm from mine, slowly, making sure the transition was appropriately considerate, therefore beautiful, a flicker in her eyes already indicated that she wouldn't have time to reward my graciousness; as soon as she got what she wanted she no longer felt she needed to pay attention to it, she was already gone; and though she did want to hurry, it wasn't because I had asked her to, or because she had to change, but because there was something else she had to do.

"I hope you don't mind, but I won't be going with you, count me out this time," Frau Kühnert said, and not even her exemplary self-discipline could hide the hurt and reproach in her voice; by this time Thea had torn herself away from me and was running down the long corridor, only to disappear in Hübchen's dressing room, but she yelled back, "I've no time for you now!"

Frau Kühnert, as if she had just heard a terribly funny joke, burst into an openmouthed laugh, what else could she do? there is a level of rudeness and insolence to which we cannot respond with hurt or indignation, because we sense that it is the manifestation of the most profound affection and, canceling out our other intentions, actually makes us happy; she stepped closer to me, and as if searching for her friend's just vanished presence, she seized my arm impulsively, unthinkingly; as soon as she became conscious of it, her ringing laugh collapsed into an embarrassed grin, and the grin, without the tact or subtlety of a smooth transition, hardened into a groundless gloom.

When I was looking not at Thea's face but at anyone else's, I found every face, including my own, coarse and vulgar, their expressions hopelessly awkward, conveying feelings crudely and obviously; at this moment, for instance, I would have loved to withdraw my arm from Frau Kühnert's hand, and she would have liked to retract her sudden gesture, but we remained in the void left behind by Thea—and didn't know what to do with it. In her confusion, clearly heightened by my own reluctant response, Frau Kühnert addressed me with a crude and verbose openness that was not only unwarranted but embarrassed us so much as almost to unite us, though it was a union neither of us desired.

"Please don't go with her," she said, or rather shouted, squeezing my arm, "I'm asking you not to interfere in this."

"In what?" I asked with a silly grin.

"You don't know this place well enough, and it's just as well, you don't have to know it, but I get the feeling sometimes, and please don't take this personally, I get the feeling that you don't always understand what we're saying, and that's why you might think she was, I don't know, crazy, but please understand that this can't be explained, because it's madness, believe me, the whole thing is madness! I always try to hold her back, I do what I can, but sometimes I must also give in to her, otherwise she couldn't go on playing the whore, because that's what it's all about, don't you see? if she couldn't do it, she would really go crazy, so please, I beg of you, don't take advantage of your position; if not you, it would be somebody else, she'd be doing it for somebody else, can't you hear them in there?"

We could indeed hear wild noises from Hübchen's dressing room, his screams and Thea's shrieks, objects falling over and crashing, skittish giggles, ripples of slightly forced laughter; then the door slammed shut, and for a moment it seemed the little room discreetly hushed up the sound of their secret doings, but then it flew open again; although I understood perfectly well what Frau Kühnert was talking about, the role she offered me suited me fine; after all, is there any event that can't be understood even better, any detail that doesn't contain potentially more significant, further details? if I went on playing the fool, I might just stumble on new details, discover hitherto unfamiliar connections—or so I hoped.

"I'm very sorry, but I haven't the slightest idea what you're talking about," I said, stretching my innocent grin to idiotic proportions and pretending to be a little indignant—offended, too, of course; the strategy worked, because my befuddlement, which always flatters my interlocutors, pushed her in the direction she had meant to go anyway; she felt she could speak freely now, since she was talking to an idiot, and, moreover, she could also release all the anger and frustration that had built up during that telephone conversation: "You don't understand, you just don't understand," she whispered impatiently, her sidelong glances taking in the bustle around us, "that's exactly what I mean, you couldn't possibly understand, and you shouldn't, because I don't want you to, because it's private, but if you really want to know, she is passionately, desperately in love—do you know what that is? have you ever been?—well, she's desperately in love, no, she thinks she is, she's made herself believe she's desperately in love with that boy"—she jerked her head angrily in the direction of the telephone—"and it's not enough that he's twenty years younger, he's even gay, yet she got it into her head that she'll seduce him, because she never loved anyone so much, not like this, I mean she could go to bed with the idiot in that room, with anyone, with you, but she wants him, don't you see? wants him because she can't have him, so there, now you can understand, and I'd really like you to leave right now, please don't be offended, just leave, because then maybe I can still hold her back, I can't bear to see her being humiliated, I just can't, can you understand?"

There was something false in this outburst, for she obviously enjoyed letting me in on something she should have kept and even wanted to keep quiet about, yet her passion was so deep-felt, so genuine, I couldn't ignore it; her abnormally large eyes were bulging at me from behind her glasses, which slid halfway down her nose: the upper rim of her glasses seemed to be cutting in half the watery-blue bloodshot eyes, and the lower half of the eyeballs became frightfully magnified and distorted under the thick lenses; this was the passion of goodness, love, and concern, expressed openly and unambiguously, not to be shaken even by the realization that the expression of goodness also needed a measure of falseness. Frau Kühnert needed, and wanted, to enjoy the knowledge that she was the only one of Thea's friends who was not patently selfish and greedy, who was not prompted by ignoble motives, who accepted her unconditionally for what she was, who truly understood her, and the total understanding of another person, an initiation into her secrets, was, after all, the only real satisfaction one could and should receive in return for selfless giving and attention; her hand, which a moment ago was holding me fast, was now steering me, pushing me forward, and I obediently started walking toward the exit, but at the same moment the two of them were suddenly in the corridor again, flushed and out of breath, still caught up in their pleasurable roughhousing, still panting; with his hand on his crotch, Hübchen was trying to back away while Thea, with a wet towel in her hand, assumed a fencer's posture, and lashing out with the towel, she pursued the little idiot—as they called him among themselves—letting the towel sting whenever it hit his naked body; but when she sensed, like a flash seen only from the corner of her eye, in which direction I was headed, she produced one of her most extraordinary transitions, dropped the towel, and yelled after me, "Where do you think you're going?" and letting her victim get away, she dashed after me.

But what she had intended as a final, victorious assault turned into a quiet farewell.

By the time we got to her car for the short ride to the opera house, to catch the new production of *Fidelio*, it was a subdued Thea who was with us; she rummaged around in the dark for a long time until she finally found in the glove compartment the glasses she needed for driving, and what a sight they were! greasy, dusty, the lenses uncleaned for ages, with one of the sidepieces missing so she had to stretch her slender neck even more, watching every move of her head, carefully balancing the spectacles lest they slide down her nose; it was late evening, the streets were empty, a strong wind was blowing, and in the halos ringing the streetlamps you could see the rain coming down at a slant; none of us was talking; from the back seat where I sat, somewhat discomfited by this silence, I kept watching her.

Now she seemed to be playing no role; it was a rare moment, a welcome intermission, though possibly it was Frau Kühnert's confidential disclosure that made me see her like this, serious, self-absorbed; she was probably dead tired, too, and seemed vaguely distracted, her limbs automatically going through the motions needed to drive, she was paying so little attention that when she was about to turn from the almost completely dark Friedrichstrasse to the better-lit Unter den Linden, she stopped, as she was supposed to, and signaled; the little red light on the dashboard began to flash, but as if an endless stream of cars had filled the avenue and she couldn't cut in, we just sat there waiting as the red light kept flashing and clicking in the dark, fresh gusts of wind whipped the rain against the car door, the wipers squeaked and ticked as they flattened the water running down the windshield; if Frau Kühnert hadn't said, "Maybe we can go now," we might have spent even more time at that intersection.

"Oh yes," she said quietly, more to herself than to us, and then made the turn.

Those few moments, seemingly very long yet also too brief, that dead time before we turned, meant a great deal to me; I had been waiting for it without knowing it, hoping it would come without knowing that I was hoping for such an ordinary moment, a moment of letting go, of imposing no control, and I myself was too tired and too upset to track this moment consciously or even think about it; it was the case of raw and pure senses perceiving raw and pure senses, even though I had only a side view of her face, and her profile, especially with those sorry-looking glasses, wasn't so memorable; still, it seemed that the streetlights reflecting off the wet pavement altered that face or, rather, changed it back to its original form, in part highlighting its surfaces and in part wiping away the fineness of its wrinkles: this was the face I'd been looking for in her, the face I'd seen before but only in flashes because of its mobility; the face in its entirety had always eluded me; the face I now saw was the face behind the mask, the one that belonged to her eyes; this face was even older and uglier, because it had more shadows, and in the color of the streetlights and because of its own inner immobility, it was a dead face, yet the face of a little girl, unformed and taut, whom I had known within myself and loved tenderly for a long time, a beautiful little girl who kept trying out her charms on me; but it wasn't a face out of my childhood or adolescence, even if the moment and the late-autumn downpour did evoke memories and fill me with nostalgia; this little girl was akin to all the little girls I had ever known, yet in her unfamiliarity resembled me more than people I had actually known and only seldom thought of.

This was probably the reason I had been watching Thea for weeks with such reluctance, as well as with a fascinated revulsion, and all the while inexplicably identifying with her, as if without a mirror I could watch myself in her face, and most likely that is why our relationship, for all our eager interest in each other, remained calm and controlled, making us recoil from even the possibility of physical contact—one can never be directly in touch with one's mirror image, however flattering and intimate it is; self-love can be consummated only through indirect means, via secret paths—but at the moment, which I remember more vividly than many subsequent, far more intimate encounters, a seemingly out-of-place image flashed through my mind, blotting out the real image before me: of a little girl, Thea, standing in front of a mirror, serious and deeply studying the features of her face, playing with them, distorting them, not simply clowning but listening to some inner sensation, trying to see what effect her facial tricks would have on her; this was not an actual memory but a fantasy working in visual images that came to my aid; I simply imagined her, and who can say why I had to imagine this particular situation, in which this little girl, opening up the peculiar gap between her inner perception of herself and her own face, struggled really to see herself in the mirror, see herself as somebody else might, anybody, nobody in particular.

What I may have spotted in her then, and I say this now in retrospect, was the creature, or that layer of her personality, on which she built her pretenses, her clowning and hamming, her chameleonlike transformations, her lies as well as her unceasing, ruthless, and self-destructive struggle against them; this was her only secure ground, the nourishing soil to which she could return when tired, insecure, and desperate, the ultimate home front from which she ventured forth with her games and pretenses, a place so safe she could freely abandon it; for her, then, the short ride between the two theaters was but a brief retreat to this hinterland, so that stepping into the lobby of the opera house she could appear before Melchior with her face and body fully restored, offering him her utmost, her true beauty, the picture of her reconstructed self; and her becoming so beautiful again revealed something about the secret roads she had to travel so that onstage she could at will assume and cast off the most wide-ranging human characteristics.

Perhaps it was not a little girl or boy whom I saw in my imagination but a sexless child who had no doubts or misgivings yet, because it couldn't conceive of not being loved and therefore turned to us with such confidence, such faith—this was the child in Thea whom Frau Kühnert loved, whose mother she was—that one could not help reciprocating, if only to the extent of an involuntary smile—and that's how she appeared in the theater lobby, light, beautiful, slender, a bit like a child, ready to meet Melchior, who was standing on top of the staircase with his French friend, towering over the noisy throng of theatergoers; and if Melchior's face still showed a touch of displeasure at the moment when he noticed us, by the time he was hurrying down the stairs toward Thea he began to bask, almost in spite of himself, in the glow of the smile he was receiving from her, with no hint of the mocking cruelty with which Thea had prepared herself for this meeting, no trace of the raw lust with which she had pointed the tip of her sword at Hübchen's naked chest, or of the dread with which she had sought fulfillment in my eyes afterward; likewise, there was nothing to suggest that Melchior was just another "boy" for her, like Hübchen, for instance, with whom she could romp to her heart's content; Melchior was a proper young man, calm, handsome, well-adjusted, unconnected with the theater, a civilian with no inkling of the raging passions she regularly left behind in the rehearsal hall; a very likable young man, jovial, always ready to smile, his bearing straight to the point almost of stiffness, which may have been the result of good breeding or self-discipline; and in the moment the two were approaching each other, it also became clear that we, witnesses to this meeting, simply did not exist.

They embraced; Thea reached only to his shoulders and her thin body almost disappeared in his arms.

Then Melchior gently pushed her away, but didn't let go.

"You look beautiful tonight," he said softly, and laughed.

The voice was deep, warm, ingratiating.

"Beautiful? Dead tired is more like it," Thea answered, looking at him with her head tilted sideways, coquettishly, "I just wanted to see you for a moment."

And after a few weeks had passed, perhaps as much as a month, during which every hour spent alone seemed like a waste of time, we decided to part, we felt we had to; we had to break out of our furtive closeness and go somewhere, anywhere; and if we couldn't part, as we couldn't, we thought we should at least stop spending all our time together here, like this, disdaining and neglecting our obligations and most of the time sitting in this room, under the eaves, a room whose very sight my eyes had a hard time getting used to, because it was at once dreary and stifling; in the candlelight it often struck me as the drawing room of a fancy bordello or some secret sanctuary, the two not being so different; it exuded a cold sensuousness, a curious enough combination of qualities to make one feel ill at ease; it became a more ordinary, livable room only when the sun shone through the filthy windows, showing the fine dust settled on the furniture, on picture frames and inside the folds of the curtains, the fuzz-balls gathered in the corners; the weak autumn light that seemed, because of the flying motes, to be hovering brought with it that austerely beautiful outside world of gray, grim, moldering walls, roofs, and back yards from which Melchior had tried to isolate himself with his softness, his silks and richly patterned rugs and heavy brocades, and to which, by his very attempt to escape it, he remained connected; ultimately, it didn't much matter where we were, we happened to be here and couldn't really go anywhere else, and who cared about the nuances of our differing tastes or about so-called cleanliness? we certainly didn't, if only because this room was the only place that guaranteed privacy, hiding and protecting us; sometimes even going to the kitchen to fix a bite to eat seemed like a big and bothersome undertaking; he had an obsession about always keeping the kitchen window open, and I failed to convince him that odors become stronger in the cold air—he hated kitchen smells and therefore the kitchen window had to be kept open—so we'd sit in the warm room, facing each other; in the morning he made a fire in the white tile stove, I sat in the same armchair he'd offered me the first night I visited him, which became my permanent seat, we sat looking at each other, I liked looking at his hands mostly, the white half-moons of his slender, steeply arched fingernails—I'd scrape their reticulated, hard surface with my own, less tidy, flatter nails; I also liked to look at his eyes, his forehead, his eyebrows, we held each other's hand, and at his thighs, the swell between his legs, his feet tucked in his slippers; our knees touched, we talked, and if I turned my head I could see a slender poplar tree: in the back yard ringed by roofs and bare walls a single poplar tree grew so tall it reached all the way up here to the sixth floor and shot up past the roof, into the clear autumn sky; it was shedding its leaves now, becoming more and more bare every day.

We talked, as I say, though it would be more correct to say that we told each other stories, and even that would not be an accurate description of the feverish urging to relate and the eager curiosity to listen to each other's words with which we tried to complement the contact of our bodies, our constant physical presence in each other, with signs beyond the physical, with the music of spoken sound, with intelligible words, and at the same time to use words to envelop, to obscure the physical relationship; we soliloquized, we gabbed, we inundated each other with words, and inasmuch as speech has a sensual, physical significance in the words' relationship to one another, in tones and rhythms independent of meaning, we used it to enhance our physical closeness, knowing well that words could only allude to the mind, to what's beyond the body, for words may be genuine but they can never tell the full story; we kept gabbing away—interminably, insatiably, in the hope that with our chaotic stories we would draw each other into the story of our own bodies and share that story with each other the way we shared our bodies, and at the same time we seemed to be using the same stories to defend ourselves, to fight our mutual helplessness and interdependence, aware of that ridiculous past tense in which we each had our own history, when we were independent of each other, when we were free! yet with unerring good sense, we didn't make all that much of these stories, not for lack of attentiveness but because we never wanted to tell each other just something but always everything, everything in every moment—an impossible, laughable undertaking—and as a result we got completely lost in each other's stories; the truth is, I have no idea what we could have talked about at such length, I'd be hard put to cite specific sentences, even if now, recalling our entire episode, I can safely say there's nothing about him I don't know, nothing factual, that is; but every one of our stories suddenly had a hundred more parts and sequels, also waiting to be told, nothing could be followed to the end, though we wanted to reach an end and understand finally why he loved me and why I loved him; needless to say, coming from two seemingly wholly different worlds, our stories were concocted from historical, social, cultural, and psychological fragments, a kind of intellectual dialogue in which often a single word could be clarified only by using another hundred, to say nothing of the fact that only he was speaking his native language, exploiting and delighting in this advantage, creating more and more puzzles and mysteries for me as we went along, so an inordinate amount of time and attention had to be devoted to developing a common language, to clarifying meaning; and still what we said was a little shaky, a little tentative, I could never be sure he understood me correctly, while he was forever amplifying, inferring, interpreting; we spent irritatingly long periods clearing up misunderstandings, defining terms, explaining expressions, idioms, grammatical rules and exceptions, but these seemed only playful exercises for him and a sheer waste of time for me; in fact, they were the natural and, in a certain sense, symbolic obstacles to true understanding, cognition, and mastery that could not, and perhaps need not, be overcome with intelligent discourse; just as in the intricate system of a language we invariably reach a point where any insistence on logic will hinder rather than promote mastery, our verbal showers, torrents, and floods also reached their terminal points—one more phrase beyond that point and our glance strayed; distracted, we felt our pulse in our fingertips or noticed the reflection in the other's eyes of a candle's leaping flame, as if the eyes were illuminated from the inside and turned into an inviting blue space, which through the dark gates of the pupils our gaze could enter; he couldn't stand living here, he said, as if talking of someone else, smiling at his own words, he couldn't stand being here! not that it bothered him at all that everything here was supposed to be corrupt, false, rotten to the core, and that every- · thing he touched was twisted and slippery and unreal, no, he was amused by all that, he knew it all too well; if anything, he considered himself very lucky to have been born in a place where a state of emergency had been in effect for fifty years—this was worth pondering—where for half a century not one honest word had been uttered in public, not one, not even when you were talking with your neighbor, a place where Adolf Hitler had scored a knockout victory! where at least one didn't have to bother with unnecessary illusions, because beyond a certain level, a level "we way surpassed," as he put it, he considered lies quite human, quite normal, and he should be permitted the perverse pleasure of not calling a system that ran on lies and fed on lies "inhuman," of not crying "fascist state," as the rest of the world did, for at least this was up front! it was outrageously up front always to say the opposite of what one might be thinking, to do the opposite of what one would like to do, to build on the simple premise that the urge to lie, to cover up, to be secretive and sly, was at least as strong as the urge to be sincere, open, and aboveboard, to seek the so-called truth, which, by the way, we find equally hard to take; and just as humanism tried to institutionalize common sense and reason, fascism institutionalized unadulterated lies, and that was all right too, because, if one wished to look at it that way, it was just another version of the truth, but who the hell cared, anyway, it was all politics, everything he said was, and he didn't give a shit about any of it, not about their truths or their lies, his own included, not a shit about their theories and sentiments, not to mention his own theories and sentiments, about which he also didn't give a shit—not angrily, just mildly amused; he knew all too much about the inner workings of lying not to respect and love it; he considered it a sacred thing, he really did; it was good to lie, it was necessary and pleasurable; he, for one, lied all the time, he was lying right now, every word a lie, so I shouldn't take anything he said seriously but just as a joke, I shouldn't trust him, rely on him, count on him; he knew, for instance, that for all my tact I detested this room because I thought it was a fake; I shouldn't take offense, but he felt I was bourgeois at heart, of an earlier vintage, and I lied timidly, I wrapped my lies in tissue paper; he liked this room precisely because it was a fake, he had made it this way not because he wanted to, he didn't even know what a room should look like to be called really his, he didn't know and didn't care to know! if he left it empty, as he'd originally planned, it still would have looked fake, so between two fake looks he chose this one; he didn't want his room to look the way a room was supposed to look, just as he himself wasn't what he was supposed to be, so let's be consistent in our lies, let's not put the ugly next to the beautiful, the good next to the bad, lies go better with lies, and so on; and the way I lied didn't escape his notice, either: he was taking a stand now, of course, this was a protest, an act of defiance and aggression, in this sense, he must admit, he couldn't deny his Germanness; I need only think of Nietzsche, if I was familiar with his work, of how relentlessly and precisely he rails against a God that didn't exist—he had to laugh every time he thought of it—and thus he fashions Him from His absence, from the desperate anger he felt over His absence; he longs for Him, but should He exist, he'd promptly destroy Him; yes, Melchior wanted to make a show of the fact that he couldn't live here, yet he did, and though he kept bumping into strange, superfluous objects, he knew how to get around them, he was used to them and even liked their falseness; although he didn't believe for a moment that it might be better elsewhere, he was all set to leave, he was simply tired of this place, and he would try to get away, even if it cost his life, which it might, but he didn't give a damn about his life; not that he wanted to commit suicide, but were he to die, now or tomorrow, he'd find it perfectly appropriate; I should try to imagine a life that in all of twenty-eight years had given him only one moment he would call real or genuine, and he knew exactly what that moment was: it happened when he was recovering from an illness that almost proved fatal, and that he'd already told me about when I asked him about the two long scars on his belly, when he'd told me about his two operations; he was seventeen at the time; he climbed out of bed and for the first time after the operation tried to stand up; he had to concentrate just to stay on his feet and hold on to furniture and watch his balance, so he didn't really know what he was doing, didn't notice that the first thing he wanted to get to was his violin, the case was lying on a shelf, all dusty; I couldn't possibly imagine, he said, what such a black case can mean to a violinist! he realized what he was doing when he was already holding it in his hands, ready to smash it—not smash it, really, not destroy it completely, just make it unusable, maybe knock it against the sharp edge of the shelf or punch a hole in it, not that he had the strength to do anything like that! all he saw was a blur, a soft, dim blur, but he heard loud noises, it sounded like a power saw screeching as it cut into wood; he was alone in the house, he could have done anything he liked, but couldn't, really, he was so weak, his own physical condition preventing him from doing what he had so much wanted to do; he barely had strength to slip the violin onto the dark green velvet of the case, and then he collapsed, and as everything seemed slowly to be growing dark he passed out; but what he really did then was to smash within himself whatever that violin had meant to him; the violin, he realized, was not meant to keep alive the wonder his otherwise pathetically provincial playing had inspired in his audience, it wasn't meant to sustain the benevolent fiction with which his mother deceived him and he, in turn, deceived himself and everyone else who admired him as a child prodigy, who thought that playing the violin made him different from other children, finer, more special, one of the elect; he was the prima donna of a dead object! no, the violin existed for itself, it wanted to play itself, fusing its own physical possibilities with those of a human being, and whoever had the gift of genius would always hover on that very fine line where the object ceases to be an object and the player ceases to be human, where the ambition to draw sound from an instrument is no longer personal but is focused entirely on the object itself; and he seemed to be talented enough to realize this, that no matter how diligent and attentive he was, he could never make the violin sing, the only thing he could coax out of it was the deceptive ambition to be exceptional, and he never wanted to do that again, he would never again touch the violin; they all pleaded with him, implored him to play, for they didn't understand; neither did he, not completely, but he could never touch it again.

He had first hung it on the wall back then, in that boy's room of his, because it was beautiful! he didn't want it to be anything else, anything more than a shapely object, let it hang there undisturbed, content, that's why he hung it on the wall here, too, let his violin, at least, remain what it was; though now that he had told me the story, and this was the first time he had ever told anyone, it seemed that what he had so lovingly cherished in his memory might not even be completely true; perhaps he only used it to justify his despair, his cynicism, his frustration, his cowardice, feelings akin to the sudden attack of nerves, the paralysis evoked by an even earlier revelation that he'd also told me about, which happened when he once asked his mother, quite casually, playfully even, whether it was possible that he was not the son of the dead man whose name he carried, since on photographs he had never been able to discover the slightest family resemblance, maybe he was someone else's son, and as his mother she ought to know, he was a big boy now, she could tell him; How did you know? she cried—she happened to be washing dishes and swung around, her face suddenly looking as though it were full of long, wriggling worms; he knew nothing, nothing at all, what should he know? it was as if his own death were staring back at him, his end was literally in sight; and from her cry he understood that, unexpectedly and quite senselessly, the two of them were thrown into a state of mortal danger when, in anticipation of rigor mortis and before any decisive action is possible, limbs and sense organs turn stiff and numb, only the skin quivers a little; he was staring into dead eyes; for the longest time they couldn't escape each other's presence, and until late in the evening they didn't even move from the kitchen sink, because it was there she told him the story of the French prisoner of war who was his real father, a story he'd already told me once; it was after this incident that he got sick, though he didn't think his illness had anything to do with the shock of finding out, or at least that was unlikely; you see, he said, when you don't have a father you make one up; then it turns out you don't even have the made-up one, the only thing you've got is his absence, as with God; and now he knew that this was the reason it had been so important for his mother that he not be like the others—hence the violin!—that he be exceptional, which he wasn't, that he not be German, even if he was; but what he hadn't told me yet—he suddenly thought of it now—was what happened after the hospital: for two months he lay in the ward for the terminally ill where patients kept changing so rapidly that in fact he was the only one who remained terminally ill, no one else was left alive; he enjoyed his rare status while his stomach kept filling up with pus; the doctors saw no reason to perform another operation and just stuck a tube in his stomach to drain the pus, he still had a bump there, I should look at it sometime; they simply didn't know what to do with him; he was a goner, but not the proper kind, because he couldn't even die properly, so after two months they asked his mother, who in the meantime had been going insane and gray with guilt, to take him home; she was wasting away, trembling constantly; she kept dropping things, and her eyes seemed to be asking for mercy, but he, no matter how much he would have liked to, could not forgive her; she hovered over him like a ghost, as though every sip of water she got him to swallow was an acquittal, as if that sin she had committed long ago—I must remember, a German woman with a Frenchman! and though at the time, luckily, she had been spared the punishment for criminal miscegenation, "she did rot in jail for three months with me in her belly"—as if that sin came back to haunt her after all those years, but this, too, was a story for another day; anyway, their family doctor, who visited him twice a week, once on an impulse asked him to open his mouth, let's see those teeth, young man; a couple of weeks after they extracted two of his molars he was fit as a fiddle and he'd never had a problem since, as I could see for myself, so, thanks to those two rotten teeth, maybe we could finally extricate ourselves from the slimy depths of his soul; but all joking aside, he must honestly tell me that he was grateful, yes, profoundly grateful to me, because for the first time he dared say out loud all the things he had learned about himself; to him, I was a little like that dentist who had pulled those tiny Adolf Hitlers from his mouth; I had wrenched something from him, and also solved something for him; while talking to me he began to see things more clearly, things he'd never been aware of before, even if he still couldn't talk about them properly; and since he was by nature incredibly self-centered, he believed this to be the reason I had to enter his life, because all the things he'd told me he could share only with a foreigner; yes, he will go away, that much is certain, he has had enough of being a stranger here, and it's better to leave with a clear head, without reproach and hatred, and perhaps he can thank me for that, because I am also a stranger here.

I must have said something to the effect that he was exaggerating again, I didn't believe I could be so important to him, that wasn't the way major decisions were made.

He said he wasn't exaggerating at all; when thanks were due, one must be properly thankful; and his eyes filled with tears.

Maybe that's when I touched his face and gently reminded him that Pierre was also a foreigner.

But with him he didn't speak in his native language, he said, Pierre was French, and in a way he was French, too, even if his native tongue was German.

French, my foot, I said; he was being overly nice, which was flattering, of course, but I wasn't asking for any kind of proof, he must believe me, I simply felt . . . but what I really felt I could not say out loud.

So I just said that I'd be ashamed to say it out loud.

I held his face in my hands, and he held my face in his, the gestures were identical, yet our intentions seemed to be at odds; it's possible that I didn't even mention my shame, didn't say it out loud, afraid that if I went further and said the word, I would have to be truly ashamed, because he would respond the only way he knew, with cold reserve and suggestive irony, with his perennial, exasperatingly beautiful smile, and then my own embarrassment would spoil something that must not be spoiled at any cost, I would deprive my hand of the warmth of his face, of its smoothness, of the stubble's crackle under my fingers, which I especially liked, though on our first night it had still elicited resistance from me, caused by the dread of the familiarly unfamiliar, a resistance that was also an attraction enticing me to cross the border between smoothness and coarseness on the face of a man, with my mouth to touch another mouth that was also ringed with stubble, to feel the same kind of strength from it that I was imparting to it, as if receiving back not his strength but my own; "Why, it's my father's mouth!" someone shouted in my voice on our first night when he leaned over to kiss me on the lips, and I could hear the scraping and blending of whiskers on our chins, the stubble on our father's chins touching the smooth skin of our forgotten childhood selves! I sank pleasurably into the loathsomeness of self-love and self-hatred, yes, I can see clearly now that we had to stop talking, although we hardly noticed that this was no longer talking; I began to love the self-loathing I had left behind; what I loved about it was that it blotted out everything that would still make me fearful and anxious; with him, I literally stepped over my father's corpse, I could finally forgive him, and although I couldn't be entirely sure which of the two was my father, I was cleansed; they were together now, fused, and there was silence now, only our bodies were talking; a profusion of words was still droning in my ears, because it takes a while for the brain to process verbal stimuli and to store them in their proper compartments and receptacles, and even after the buzz of this sorting operation abated, there remained scraps and fragments that somehow didn't fit in the large storehouse of received information; oddly enough, these strays were unimportant details of some communication:

French death, for instance, was a phrase that meant absolutely nothing, and the gesture, the way I drew his face closer and held his chin in my hands, barely touching the skin of his face with my fingertips, was nothing more than an unconscious means to an unclear end; neither of us could go on talking anymore; earlier, while he was talking, although he held my gaze captive as if in my eyes he had found the only secure point to which he could anchor himself, it didn't seem that he was looking only at me, that I was the only subject of his scrutiny; gazing at me like this allowed him to retreat into himself, to regions where he would not venture alone; but now, his retreat enabled me to enter this otherwise forbidden territory, and the more his gaze became fixed in mine and I became a subject of his gaze, the farther he could push himself away from me—I had to be on the alert—and the farther I could retreat along with him; and because I was with him, he could handle his real subject with even cooler, more cerebral, and elegantly meandering sentences, adorned with an even softer smile; and his real subject was his thoughts, his memories; let's call it by its name: the solitude caused by the sheer existence of the body, the sensation of being alive in a space felt to be dead! and then this smiling coldness removed him so completely from the story of his body that he could see its little episodes almost with my eyes—hence his gratitude, perhaps, for being able to sense, if only in a flash, how dead space might perceive a living form, to sense that even I could become one with that alien outside world; hence the wetness in his eyes, a wetness that produced no tears to roll down his cheeks but only blurred his image of me and obscured that other, more distant sight he beheld; his embarrassment over this physical change pulled him back from that interior landscape; the thing he'd fixed his eyes on turned back into a person, me; to match the speed of his return, I had to back out of his eyes just as quickly, but scared of losing what I had gained, I pressed his knee between my knees and bent forward slightly to touch his face, while he, pressing my knee between his, also bent forward to touch my face.

To touch.

Just to touch, and to feel.

Sometimes we listened to music, or he would read something to me out loud, or I would recite Hungarian poetry to him; I wanted him to feel, to understand the poems, was eager to prove that there was such a language, a language in which I could also express myself reasonably well; he was amused, chuckling occasionally, even letting his mouth drop open like a child when shown a new toy; I was light and carefree; dressed or naked, we fell asleep in each other's arms on the divan in the dim hallway, while outside it darkened and was evening again, another winter evening; candles had to be lit, the curtain drawn, so we could sit there again, facing each other, well into the night, sometimes into early morning, when the room had cooled off; the clock on the wall ticked away peacefully, the candles smoked as they guttered, and we drank heavy Bulgarian red wine out of dainty crystal glasses; hours turned into days, days into weeks, carrying us almost imperceptibly from autumn into winter, when each morning our poplar tree, like its own laced skeleton, drifted into ever softer mists; I would find giving an account of this time as difficult as it would be to answer the question of what right I have to include his feelings in this recollection of a shared past, the feelings of a stranger; on what grounds can I claim that this or that happened to us, when I feel equipped to talk only about myself, to describe with reasonable accuracy only the things that happened to me? there's no answer to the question, or maybe the only answer is that one winter evening I realized just how much we loved each other, if love means the fervor and depth of mutual attachment; yes, that may be the answer, even if just a few weeks or at most a month later we noticed that something had ominously changed in us, in him as well as in me, and kept changing, ever more threateningly, until it reached a point where I had to close my eyes so as not to see him like this and hope that when I opened them again all the disconcerting hints would have vanished, and his face, and his hand in my hand, would be the same as before—at the moment I seemed to be clutching the stump of my own hand—and his smile would be the same, too, because nothing had changed, nothing could have changed; I don't remember exactly when, calendar time meant nothing to us then, but it must have been at the end of November or the beginning of December, my only point of reference is Thea's opening, for which Melchior joined me, though by then they were no longer on speaking terms, so in all probability it was shortly before then, at the height of her pre-opening-night frenzy and panic, that she came up there one evening, hoping to find Melchior alone—I remember supporting her in that hope—but she found only me, and that meeting also made things different, although on the surface nothing had changed; he and I went on sitting in our chairs, just as we had done before, the candles were burning the same way, and it was as quiet as before; the room hadn't changed, the phone didn't ring, neither did the doorbell, nobody wanted anything from us and we didn't want anything from anybody; it was almost like sitting in a gallery above the ruins of a deserted and depopulated European city, with not much hope of being liberated, and though there may have been others out there sitting in similar rooms, it was unlikely we would ever hook up with them; our solitary togetherness, made exciting earlier by our having to hide and pretend, turned unpleasant now, I don't know why; I realized, of course, that it was on my account that he had driven everyone away, locked us in, unplugged the telephone, and would not answer the doorbell, yet I couldn't help reproaching him for it, not openly of course, because every-thing he did he did for me; I tried to block out these thoughts by closing my eyes, but it didn't help; what disturbed me most was the thought that we'd grown so very close, I just had to back off, loosen the bond; it was as if I had just become aware of our closeness and suddenly found it revolting, unbearable; I had to find some unfamiliar ground, something I could not have known before, and neither could he, something that could in no way be his, something unshared; and when I opened my eyes again his face struck me as being a little more distant and indifferent, a stranger's face, and the discovery was both pleasant and painful, because any strange face can raise in us the hope of recognition or the possibility of getting to know it better, but this face was vacant and boring, holding out no hope at all, I'd had my fill of it; I might have gotten to know it these past few weeks, but the knowledge was insignificant, like so much else I'd picked up, because it seemed that no amount of knowledge, not even dangerous knowledge, helped me to find a safe haven within myself, a foothold of devotion and permanence; so it was a mere adventure, then, an unprofitable one, for in the end he remained a stranger to me, as I remained a stranger to him, and I didn't understand how I could have thought him beautiful when he was ugly, no, not even ugly, only boring, a man, one I couldn't possibly have anything to do with—a man.

I hated myself, I found myself disgusting.

And he may have had similar thoughts, or sensed what I'd been think-ing, because he withdrew his hand—at last I was free of that horrible stump—stood up, kicked the armchair aside, and turned on the TV.

This was so deliberately rude, I let it go, I didn't say a word.

Then I got up, too, kicked the chair out of the way, and walked into the hallway.

Almost at random I picked a book off the shelf and, making myself believe I was really interested in it, stretched out on the soft dark rug and began to read.

At first the patterns of the rug distracted me, and the archaic style of the book was no small obstacle either, but then I got into it, reading that the only true temple was the temple of the human body, that nothing was more sacred and sublime than the human form; it was nice to stumble on these words on that friendly, warm rug, to read that when we bow down to man, we pay tribute to revelation in flesh; to touch the human body is to touch heaven.

I tried to understand the concept, inappropriate though it seemed at this moment, and not pay attention to some woman climbing out a window, clutching at the creeping ivy, plaster falling, she screams and leaps; then it seemed that everything would blow over, only one thing bothered me still, that I'd given the armchair such an angry kick; ambulance screeching to a halt, the clattering of instruments, we're in an operating room; it seemed like such an unimportant thing, plain silly, yet I couldn't help feeling I'd been rude; I should have seen what I was doing, kicking the armchair like that, and it wasn't even my chair; sounds of funereal music, the woman must have died, she's probably being buried; I shouldn't have done it, I might have damaged the thing; one shouldn't kick someone else's chair, even if the human body is a sublime temple; he could kick the armchair because it's his; I shouldn't have, yet I did and felt good about it.

Later I asked him in a rather loud voice if I should leave.

Without turning his head, he said I should do as I saw fit.

I asked him if he held anything against me, because I wouldn't want that.

He could ask me the same thing.

I emphasized I held nothing against him.

He just wanted to watch this movie now.

This particular movie?

Yes.

Then he should go ahead and watch it.

That's exactly what he was doing.

The oddest part of all this was that we couldn't possibly have avoided the real issues more objectively; we were more explicitly truthful than if we had said what was on our minds; more precisely, our lies and subtle evasions defined the situation more honestly than emotions might have, for at the moment our emotions were too violent to be true.

I couldn't go away and he couldn't hold me back.

And this bare fact, emerging from the background of his words, proved to be a stronger bond than a pact sealed in blood.

But because of our lies, something, or the emanation of something, perhaps a compelling force that had been there before, moving between us with the naturalness of instincts, now seemed to have abated; it didn't disappear completely, only stopped; at any rate, something was no longer there; and in this absence I sensed what I had felt before.

And I knew that he sensed this, too.

There it was, still flickering like the bluish television screen, almost tangibly filling the space between the room and the hallway, maybe we could still reach it or stop it for good, but it was precisely its vibrating immobility, independent of us, that paralyzed us both, unable to make the slightest move, as if with cool reason it were suggesting that we had no other choice but to accept and endure this immobility, this was the only bond between us, and it was as strong as judgment itself; it was as if for the first time an outsider had shown us the true nature of our relationship—now, just as it was jolted in its course.

In situations like these, we automatically consider and rapidly weigh the most obvious and therefore simplest practical solution; but getting up, kicking his slippers off my feet, putting on my shoes and coat, and leaving seemed impossible, and absurd, for after all, what had happened here? nothing!—so to do all that would have been just too awkward and tedious, it would have taken too much effort and would have been unbearably dramatic. But it was just as impossible to maintain my relaxed pose on the rug, that would have offended my sense of propriety for another reason; after all, I was lying on his rug, and the question of ownership—let's not forget, it's a measure of being at another's mercy—can be more crucial than our emotions, even in the case of true love; I should go away, I should get up and leave, I kept repeating to myself, as if just saying it would make it happen, but I stayed and pretended to be reading, just as he pretended to be watching the screen.

Neither of us made a move.

He sat with his back to me, in the blue effulgence of the TV screen, and I was leaning over my book; though this may be a trifle, it bothered me more than anything else that I was holding myself stiff, because it gave me away; and although he couldn't see me, I knew that emotionally we were keeping track of each other's moves very precisely, so he was as aware of my feigned nonchalance as I was of his forced concentration on the screen; while pretending to be watching that stupid movie, he was actually watching me, and he knew that I knew; nevertheless, something compelled us to play this transparent little game, which was more offensive than any candid response would have been, yet also, despite its seriousness, quite funny, amusing in fact.

I was waiting, biding my time, and thought he would make use of this funny, amusing quality to find the last opening we could squeeze through and escape the trap of our own pompous gravity; to be more precise, I wasn't actually thinking all this but, rather, sensed that behind the tragic pose there lurked an urge to laugh.

Because this was a game, and now it was his move; a clumsy little game of feelings it was, a transparent, trivial game whose rules nevertheless forced us to observe the measures and proportions needed for human relationship; what makes us play this game is our taste for a fair fight and our eternal desire to get even; and precisely because this was a game in the purest sense of the word, I could no longer be indifferent to him or consider him a stranger; I was playing with him, wasn't I, we were playing together, the joint undertaking was bound to temper my hostility; still, I couldn't move, I couldn't say anything, I had to wait; I'd already had my chance and played my best card when I lied and said I didn't have anything against him; now, according to the rules, it was his turn.

The tense anticipation, a moment of truth hovering in the air, the invisible third person who had touched him and had touched me as well, that certain compelling force that was present but no longer functioning— and it was hard to say whether it was emanating from me toward him or the other way around, or was simply hanging in the air, making it so dense that it "could be cut with a knife," as people like to quip—it all reminded me of my first night there; we felt it then, too, when he went into the kitchen to get the champagne.

He had left the door open and I should have heard something, little noises, the refrigerator door opening, the muffled thud as he closed it, the clinking of glasses or his footsteps; but later, when we had drifted too far apart for things to make any sense and as a defense began to review our shared experiences and piece together the fragments, he told me that he had stopped by the kitchen window that evening, watching and listening to the rain, and without knowing why could not move away, as if he didn't want to go back to the room but wanted me to sense the dead silence of his helplessness; and I did, I sensed his expectation and indecision; he wanted me to be aware that the rain, the dark rooftops, the very moment itself were more important to him than I was, waiting for him in his room, though he had to admit that my waiting made him very happy; and it was this feeling, so rarely experienced, that he would have liked somehow to share with me.

He got up and, as if now, too, he was just going to the kitchen, started walking toward me.

Though we couldn't yet tell what we would decide to do, we both felt that the decision, whatever it might be, had already been made.

Then suddenly, as if he'd changed his mind and decided not to go to the kitchen, he lowered himself next to me on the rug, supporting himself on his elbows; he put his face comfortably into his hand, he was half lying, half sitting, and we looked into each other's eyes.

It was one of those rare moments when he wasn't smiling.

He looked at me as if from very far away, not really at me but at the phenomenon I had become for him at the moment, just as I was looking at him the way we look at an object whose beauty and worth cannot be denied, in spite of our resistance, but nevertheless which isn't identical with what we could love; the beauty we saw was not the one he loved, or the one I thought I'd loved.

And then he said quietly, This is what it's like.

And I asked him what he had in mind.

What he had in mind, he said, was what I must be feeling.

Hatred, I said. I could say it out loud, because it wasn't quite that anymore.

Why hatred? would I tell him? could I?

A shock of curly blond hair, a forest of hair, a luxuriant mane; the smooth skin taut over the high forehead with its two pronounced bulges; the soft hollow of the temples; dense, dark eyebrows adorned with some longer hairs; although thinner and narrower over the ridge of the nose, the brows met and mingled with lighter hairs as they curved up toward the forehead and then descended in an even lighter, downier arch into the shell-like indentation of the temples, at once shading and accentuating the finely cushioned eyelids, themselves divided by long, curled dark lashes, forming a living and moving frame around the black centers of the pupils dilating and contracting smoothly in the blue of his eyes; what a blue that was! how strong and cold! and how strange the blue eyes seemed, framed in black on the milk-white skin; and the black dissolving into blond with the greatest of ease; all these intrusive colors! the nose, its spine descending in a straight line to the flaring base, blended at a steep angle into the low region of the face, but with an elegant flourish, curling back into itself, it also encircled the dark little caves of the nostrils, only to continue, imperceptibly and under the skin, and protrude in the form of two delicate hillocks above the lips, connecting, symbolically almost, the inner lobes of the nostrils with the rim of the upper lip, bringing into harmony total opposites: the vertical line of the nose with the horizontal of the mouth, the oblong face, the perfectly round head, and the lips! those coupling slabs of flesh, their rawness barely concealed.

He shouldn't be angry with me, that's all I was asking.

And the only way I could prove that I meant what I'd said was to kiss him, but this was no longer the mouth but just another mouth, and mine, too, was just a mouth, so this wasn't going to work.

Why should he be angry; he wasn't angry.

Maybe it wasn't even his features but the movements of his lips, parting and closing as they formed words, the mechanical motion itself that, for all his calm, exhaled an infinite coolness, or could I myself have been so cold at the time? or both of us? but everything, everything changed! his face, his mouth, mostly his mouth, opening and closing, and my arm feeling the weight of my body, the strain of being in that position turning it numb, and his hand as he propped himself up, as though all this was but the mechanics of that unfamiliar force manifesting itself in the physical properties of our bodies, we might have possessed this compelling force, but our every move was defined by those properties, everything was determined by them; to put it another way, I may feel God residing in me, yet no motion can be other than what is prescribed by my physical form, every gesture must take place within the limits set by this form, which also sets the patterns for that compelling force; thus, the effect produced by a gesture can be only a signal, an allusion, nothing more than the perception of the purposeful functioning of these physical forms; I may take pleasure in perceiving a familiar pattern realized, and take it to be a real feeling, but it's nothing but self-enjoyment; I am not enjoying him, I merely see a form, a pattern, not him, but a signal, an allusion; the only thing we enjoy in each other is that our bodies function in similar ways, his movements elicit identical patterns in me, immediately making it clear what he is after; amusing ourselves with mirrors, that's all we were doing, the rest was self-deception; and this realization then was as if in the middle of enjoying a piece of music I'd suddenly started paying attention to the physical workings of the instruments, to the strings and hammers, and the musical sounds themselves grew distant.

I said I was sorry, but I didn't understand anything.

Why must I understand, he asked, what was there to understand?

I told him not to be angry with me, but there was nothing else I could say; maybe now I'd be able to tell him what I'd kept quiet about last time because I'd thought it was too sentimental, and although he had been most curious to hear it, I'd feared ruining something then; but now, I hoped, he wouldn't be offended, I could tell him that even his movements were not that important to me, it just didn't matter anymore that he could touch me or I him, because whatever we might do—and there was nothing we couldn't do—it had been arranged this way and that's all there was to it! and somehow we had been together, he and I, long before we became acquainted, only we didn't know it; would he believe it if I told him that we had been together for almost thirty years? that was my obsession, my *idée fixe*, and now I could say it: I believed he was my brother.

He burst into hearty laughter, he guffawed, and as soon as I said the word I had to laugh, too; to take the edge off his guffaw, he touched my face with the tips of his fingers, gently, patiently; and the reason we had to laugh, I was laughing, too, was not only that what I had said, in a voice charged with emotion, was embarrassingly gauche—not to mention that it was not at all what I had meant to say—but also that the word itself, "brother," in his language, and in our particular situation, did not mean the same thing it did in mine; as soon as the word slipped out, I noticed my error, because one immediately had to think of the little adjective "warm," which had to be attached to the word "brother" if one wanted to say "queer," *warmer Bruder,* in his language; so what I had said to him, in a voice charged with emotion, was that he was my little faggot, which may have been a witty wordplay, if only I hadn't said it so emotionally, but this way it was like mentioning rope in a hanged man's house, a well-intentioned gesture gone laughably awry, and we did laugh, he in particular laughed so hard his eyes filled with tears, and it was no use explaining to him that in the Hungarian word for brother, *testvér,* blood and body are linked, and that's what I had in mind.

When he had calmed down a bit, and the little afterbursts of laughter were coming at longer intervals, I realized we had drifted even further apart.

He seemed to have assumed again that air of superiority with which he had looked me over on our first night together.

I told him quietly that what I had said before was not what I'd wanted to say.

He held my face, he forgave my silly slip, but his forgiveness, already past the laughter, made him appear even more superior.

What I wanted to tell him, I said, what I really wanted to tell him was something we hadn't talked about before, because I didn't want to hurt him, but now I felt this whole thing to be hopeless, and please don't be offended, I felt I was locked up in jail.

Why should he be offended; there was no reason to be offended.

Perhaps, I said, we should stop seeing each other for a while.

Well, yes, that's why he'd said before that this is what it's like, now I could see it for myself, but then I'd pretended not to understand.

I didn't.

The truth was, he continued, he hadn't thought about it either, for once, with me, he also forgot that this is what it's like, and just a few minutes earlier, when he sensed on my hand that it was over, he was surprised, and terrified; but he assumed that this was how long the thing was meant to last, and not longer; and while he was pretending to watch TV, he had to realize that if I felt that way, he would just have to accept it, and that made him feel better, because—I had to believe him—he knew from experience that two men, or as I was kind enough to put it before, two brothers—and he let out one more tiny burst of laughter, though it could have been a sob, too—two men simply cannot take it for long, and there were no exceptions; what I had tried to do was to force on our relationship the emotional standards I'd been used to with women, and he couldn't help it if I had such a muddled past, but I shouldn't forget that with a woman, which ruled out both of us, it was possible to make something of the relationship even if I knew there was no chance, for no disqualifying circumstance could upset the chances of natural continuity; between two men, however, what you had was always just what you had, no more, no less; and for this reason, in a situation like this, the best thing to do was to get up, stop playing games, find some excuse, and clear out quickly and gracefully, and never come back, never even look back; what I could take with me this way would be more precious to both of us than if I tried to deceive myself; with all due respect, him I couldn't deceive; he didn't mean to rub it in, but he was beyond all that, he knew these routines all too well, so really, the only sensible thing to do was not to give him another thought, ever.

I said he was trying to play the ruthless male, not to mention the fascist, just a little too transparently.

I was being sentimental, he said.

Maybe, I said, but I couldn't express myself properly in this rotten language.

He'd do the expressing for me.

Please, stop acting silly.

Is that what he was doing? he asked.

He could go on acting silly, if he liked.

Did I still know what we were talking about?

Did he?

PART II

On an Antique Mural

The picture I had been keeping tucked away in my notes, the one I would have described in my planned narrative as the multisecret world of my presentiments and presumptions—had I the necessary talent and strength to do it, of course—depicted a delicate, lovely Arcadian landscape with a gently rising clearing among hills that stretched into the horizon, sparse thickets and silky grass, flowers, storm-ruffled olive trees and weather-beaten oaks, a skillful copy of an antique mural I had had the opportunity to admire several years ago during my travels through Italy which, in the full splendor of its bold colors and formidable dimensions, captured the landscape in the very moment when morning slowly rises out of Oceanus to bring light to mankind, and with its infinitely fine light illuminated the dewdrops perched on blades of grass and settled in the hollow palms of leaves, the time of dew, a time when the wind does not rustle the leaves but seems to have abated, a time we think of as eternity, when night has already laid its silver egg but Eros, according to some tales the son of the wind god, cannot yet emerge from this egg and is still in a state of Before, before something, before anything we might call an event, in the moment just before that event but already after the noble act of impregnation and conception, when the two powerful primordial elements, the wild wind and the dark of night, have already coupled; this is a time when as yet there are no shadows, we are still before everything that might be described later as Afterward—this is the nature of a primal morning! and that is why this extraordinary moment should not be confused with, although it may be compared to, that other moment when Helios is about to vanish with his horses and chariot behind the rim of the earth, because then, terrified of mortality and hoping to overtake the departing sun—anything is better than to stay here! not here!—every living thing stretches to the limit of its own shadow and the pain of parting turns everything ruddily fatal, shining like gold; but in this early moment everything is almost lifeless, almost stiff, pale, almost gray, silvery, looming in the dimness, cold, and if just now I mentioned vivid colors, it was only because this silver is of course no longer the silver glow of the night which so eagerly draws into itself all the colors of the world, dissolving them into homogeneous metallic flashes; no, at this hour things have already received their own colors, which is to say these colors have been conceived but are not yet fully alive: the naked body of Pan, at the geometrical center of the picture, bursting with pleasure, shows a rich brown; the coat of the handsome little he-goat at his feet is appropriately gray, dirty white; the grass is an angry green, the oak tree an even deeper green, the stone is whiter than white, and the light capes of the three nymphs are turquoise, olive-green, and red silk; but just as at this dewy border of night and day the nymphs are motionless, having completed their last nocturnal movements but not yet begun the first gestures of their new day, so the colors of their bodies and garb remain within the shadowless outline of their pure forms, and so do the colors of the shadowless trees, grass, and stones, because just as at the border of the End and the Beginning these creatures have nothing to do with one another, each looking in a different direction—making the picture, even on our small copy, seem to grow in size—colors have no relationship to one another either: the red is red for and by itself, the blue is blue only for itself and not because it is to be distinguished from green, which is only green; it is as if the painter of the picture, in his own barbarically simplifying ignorance, had captured the very moment of the world being born, or, more simply, as if with deadly precision he had insisted on depicting the mood of a summer dawn when one is suddenly startled out of sleep without knowing why; one gets out of the blind warmth of bed, staggers out of the house to relieve oneself—that at least if one's already awake—and is greeted by a terrible silence undisturbed even by the dew congealing into dripping drops, and although one knows that in the very next moment the warming yellow of daylight will jolt the universe out of its frozen, mortal state, making it come alive in a new birth, one also knows that all one's experience and knowledge is as nothing compared to the silence of nonexistence, and if up to now one has sought death in the shadows of the day or while groping in the dark of night, one now discovers it, in this colorfully colorless instant, and unexpectedly and with such dreadful ease that the hot urine won't gush out: death lay in the moment that, until now, one has been fortunate to sleep through, one's body kept warm in the embrace of the gods.

And maybe it's not even Pan sitting on that stone: in spite of my careful and thorough studies, I have been unable to determine for sure—maybe it's Hermes my picture represents, which means not the son but the father, no small difference, that! for in that case it is not the son's lovemates whom we see, his frolicking maid-lovers depicted as the three nymphs, but the woman-mother herself: in an ambiguous way, every little motif in the picture refutes its own assertions, so much so that I could afford quietly to suppose—in fact, this supposition is what has excited me—that the painter deliberately did this brave mixing up, showing the father but meaning the son or, conversely, painting the son but meaning to show the father in his youth, and depicting for us the mother as the adoring lover of them both, for this figure in her olive-green cloak at the right side of the picture, with her head lowered, her sparkling eyes following her fingers gliding over the strings of the lyre pressed against her bosom, seems somewhat older, perhaps considerably older than the naked youth, and we must risk drawing this conclusion even if we shudder at the thought that our eyes, prompted by wishful imagination, may deceive us and even if we know well that gods are ageless; of course, when it comes to nymphs, this is not entirely accurate, for their immortality, as evidenced by traditional narratives that have come down to us, is directly proportional to their proximity to the divinities, and consequently there are mortals among them: nymphs of the sea are said to be immortal, like the sea itself, but the same cannot be said about the more common naiads of the springs, and even less so of the nymphs of the meadows, groves, and trees, especially those who live in oak trees and die when the trees die; and if, following the painter's rather confusing hints, we try to guess the age of a particular nymph by examining her face, as her fingers reach for the most distant string of the lyre, her glance measuring the exact intervals between the strings, for she wants to produce an elegant light glissando, we must remind ourselves of the ancient method of reckoning life spans according to which the chattering crow lives the equivalent of nine human generations, a stag has as many as four crows' lives, and three stags' lives add up to a raven's age; a palm tree lives as long as nine ravens, and nymphs, Zeus' lovely-haired daughters, can expect to live as many years as make up the lives of ten palm trees; in this calculation, then, our nymph must have been into her sixth raven's lifetime, so by declaring her older than the naked youth I don't mean to measure her age in human years, and I did not see the tiniest wrinkle on her face—she appeared to be blessed with the wisdom of motherhood, at least when compared to the two other nymphs, who, although closer to the youth, in fact identical to him in age, were untouched by that bliss beyond pain; and I could not exactly tell you why, but her neck also indicated this maternal wisdom, arching out of the rich folds of the cloak draped over her shoulders; oh, that exquisite feminine neckline! which remained bare and white under auburn hair gathered into a loose bun by a silver clasp and seeming so attractively and shamelessly naked precisely because of a few unruly curls, short, frizzy strands falling back onto the flesh—of course this is most attractive, for it is the mix of being dressed and being naked that we like so much; and if I succeeded in describing the nymph's neck in some such fashion, I'd most likely put into words the experience I've preserved in the image of my betrothed's neck, no, not just preserved, but cherished, adoringly, an experience of the two of us sitting next to each other while leafing through a photo album, let's say: she would lean forward a little, to look at some negligible detail in a picture, and I'd gaze at her from the side, quite close, wanting to bend over her, touch her neck with my lips, with tiny kisses barely graze the skin made taut by her movement, dissolve her warmth and smell in my mouth, work my way up to her hair—but I don't, I am held back by a sense of propriety, tact.

When the dawning day melts night's residual silver into gold—oh, if only I could speak of ancient mornings in such phrases!—and fingers pluck the strings, the flurry of sounds will be the beginning; with the dulcet tones of her lyre, the nymph wishes to be first to greet the new day in whose warm light the oak tree casts its pleasing shadow.

For, needless to say, it was an oak tree behind her, gnarled and to our eyes quite old-looking, probably hit by lightning once, because it seemed oddly tilted, though the wind had already ripped out and scattered the withered branches, and in their places new clumps of foliage had sprouted; this not only confirmed my sense that she had to be rather advanced in years but directly indicated that we are dealing with the nymph of the oak who, strumming her lyre in the morning, was none other than Dryope, of whom we know that with her slender body and noble mien she so aroused the passion of the Arcadian shepherd Hermes that the inflamed god spent a long time pursuing her—though let it be said in passing only long in human terms, about three lifetimes, but no more than one-third of a crow's life span—until their love was properly consummated: this was by no means an extraordinary occurrence; we might even say that the nymph, whose name suggests a female creature who turns a man into a *nymphios*, that is, a bridegroom confirming his manhood, did only what she had to do, as did the god himself; nevertheless, the love-child brought into the world of immortals by the beautiful Dryope could not be judged by the standards to which this poor dutiful mortal, almost human girl-mother, had been accustomed.

We don't intend to claim that Dryope was a timid, fragile, easy-to-frighten maid, of course; as we know, she was rather tall, strong-boned, often mentioned as having powerful limbs, and when pursued by amorous gods or men she didn't always flee; from time to time she would also attack, stand firm as if her feet had taken root, immovable like an oak, hiss, snarl, use her fists, and be ready to bite; when on the banks of cool mountain streams she took off her green mantle to wash away her body's sweat, her round arms and her thighs, exercised in running, showed firm muscles, filling out her pearly skin; her breasts, too, were firm, set high by their own, tense roundness; and her clitoris, as would be revealed in the moment of ecstasy, at the height of her pleasure, could grow as large as the phallus of a child awaking from sleep; therefore, it may be said that the god had good reason to wish to soften this hardness, tame this wildness, make tender this toughness; still, when she tore the umbilical cord with her teeth and in the bloody afterbirth between her legs glanced at the blinking, bawling, giggling, kicking issue, she let out a girlish scream of terror and had to bury her face in her hands; and no wonder, how was she to know that there was no cause for alarm, that she had given birth to a god, how could she have known that, seeing only what she could see? at that moment it seemed to her that she had yielded not to carefree Hermes' lust but to a stinking he-goat, for long, coarse strands of hair were growing on the infant's head, two tiny crescent horns sprouted from his forehead at the very spot where in people and in gods the bone protrudes just a little, and his feet—how horrible!—terminated not in soles like ours but in hooves, like a kid's, hooves still soft and pink that in time, we know, would harden most horrendously, would clatter and throw off sparks over stone and turn an ugly black.

Terrified by the fruit of her womb, Dryope sprang up and ran away. Her story ends here, we know no more of her, or of how she fared thereafter, and if we should want to learn more, we must rely on our imagination.

We do know, however, that Hermes found his son in the grass, and not only did the little boy's appearance cause him no surprise but it put him in a prancing good mood; by then the boy stood on his feet, or rather on his little hooves, took a few tumbles, turned a few cartwheels, rolled around and enjoyed being prickled by blades of the dewy grass; then he chased flies and wasps, plucked flowers, tore out and munched on their petals, and with his soft hornlets butted stones and trees, his body tickled with pain; to satisfy his longing for pranks he pissed on a butterfly and shat on a snake's head; in short, creation itself seemed to function perfectly within the small creature; we shouldn't be surprised, then, that with all this, the sight of the son found favor in the eyes of the father; and since fathers tend to view their sons' lives as reprises of their own, Hermes suddenly remembered the morning of his own birth, when gentle Maia had brought him into the world and laid him in his cradle, but in an unguarded moment he climbed out of the cradle and left the cave: outside he found a turtle, fashioned a lyre out of its shell, and with the lyre set out on his wanderings; by the time that even the ears of Helios' horses had vanished in the glowing red rim of the earth—and we know precisely that this was the eve of the fourth day of the lunar month—he had killed two oxen with his bare hands, skinned them, and to roast them quickly invented fire, then proceeded to steal a whole herd of cattle to cover up his mischief before climbing back into his cradle; now he lifted up his young one, just as Apollo had lifted him, and took him up to the gods, so they could delight in him as well.

Dionysus was the happiest to see the new arrival, who was immediately named Pan, for in the language of the immortals this word covers the concept of All, Everything, Universal, and unless we are mistaken, the gods saw in him the perfect embodiment of that word.

With one hand the handsome youth sitting at the center of my picture raised to his lips a panpipe, unmistakable symbol of his panhood, and therefore, according to legend, he had to be the one who led the nymphs' nocturnal dances, and then also brought on the morning; he was a furious, spiteful god who let out his anger, especially when his midday sleep under a shady oak was disturbed; and he was also the friendliest of gods, high-spirited, generous, playful, prolific, fond of merriment, music, and noise; in spite of so many signs indicating that the figure in the picture was in fact Pan, I could not shake the doubt that perhaps he wasn't the great phallic god after all, but then who was he? A satisfactory answer seemed impossible, for not only did he hold in his other hand a leafy staff, which, according to legend, Hermes received from Apollo in exchange for his lyre, but his body wasn't hairy, his brow had no horns, and he had feet, not hooves—unless the shapely billy goat lying at his feet like a watchdog was meant to symbolize everything missing from the god's smooth, anthropomorphic body; we know there are artists who tend to represent as beautiful what is completely ugly, because they're afraid to show the creature named after the universe as hairy, hoofed, and horned—this is but an absurd human weakness, of course, but all the same, I couldn't rule out the possibility that through his laughable weakness the painter had tried, misleadingly, to prettify the history of the gods; on the other hand, one couldn't claim with any certainty that the figure was Hermes, that blasted leafy staff of his notwithstanding, for then why the pipe in his other hand? It was all a muddle, the whole thing, and I probably wouldn't have paid attention to it if sorting it out had not been part of the preliminary studies needed for my planned narrative: I pondered and probed, toyed with and tested my alternatives, self-indulgently playing for time in the process, afraid to tackle my true task, which seemed formidable, and whenever I managed to come to a final decision about something, a new idea would invariably occur to me; for instance: Very well, I mused, let's assume that this figure is neither Pan nor Hermes but Apollo himself, who was also said to have fallen in love with Dryope once and, appropriately, to have chased after her, but because the lovely oak-maid refused his advances, the aroused Apollo changed himself into a turtle and found his way into the hands of the playful nymph; Dryope placed the turtle on her beautiful breasts, where he quickly turned into a snake and under her robe united with her—but this bubble of an idea soon burst, for if that's what happened, how did the lyre end up in Dryope's hand, and the lyre, as I've mentioned before, was made by Hermes after he left the cave on the morning of his birth, which happened much later than the Apollo episode.

My questions and ideas would have remained only questions and ideas if I hadn't found the behavior of the two other nymphs, on the left side of the picture, so peculiar: like the brown-skinned god, one of the nymphs was sitting on a white rock; she was wearing a red cloak, holding a small tambourine in her lap and two drumsticks in her hands, but her face was missing; the paint had simply peeled off the wall, though the position of her body suggested that when she still had a face she was looking straight ahead, she was the one looking out of the picture at us, her gaze, be it severe, forgiving, or gentle, following us wherever we might move in front of the picture; but what piqued my interest even more was the other nymph, standing directly behind the faceless one and wearing a turquoise cloak, the only one in the scene who showed any interest in the youth whom I ventured to identify as Pan; she was the most beautiful of the three nymphs, her face full, her brow clear, her blond hair loosely braided in a crown, her body slight and delicate; she stood there with her hip thrust out just a little and her arms intertwined behind her back, a pose that radiates calm, confidence, and openness; her eyes were huge, brown, and warm, a bit sad, too, sad with longing, and then—I almost yelled out at the joy of discovery—I realized that this same sadness was reflected in the youth's eyes, although his head was turned away and he hardly took notice of the third nymph's wistful glance brushing his bulging chest; over the shoulder of the lyre-strumming Dryope, he was looking out of the picture, and—no mere coincidence—he, too, must have been looking at someone and was likewise being watched by that someone, but that someone was not visible, because he or she must have been standing not here in the clearing but among the trees of the forest.

And it was the forest I was mainly interested in, where this impossible love could be possible, even if it would never really come to pass; it was this love I wanted to write about.

But to return to the picture, hoping to make clear in the light of what follows why I was so preoccupied with it, even though in my story I wasn't even going to mention the mural or any of the characters in it, I thought I recognized Salmakis in the figure of the nymph hidden in the background; while the name further fueled my already inflamed imagination, and feeling as if I'd been given the key to a puzzle, I thought of yet a third, equally complicated story: this is the one, I thought to myself with some satisfaction; as we know, Hermes had another son—a dubious designation, perhaps, for the issue of his union with Aphrodite, if only because according to some genealogies, the two of them had to have been siblings, children of Uranus the night sky and Hemera the light of day, and not only siblings but twins! for we also know that they were born on the fourth day of the lunar month, and therefore the fruit of their love possessed in equal proportions the features of their parents' faces, bodies, and characters, just as when two ample streams converge and, with much splashing and bubbling, flow into one another, and who can separate water from water! consequently, in their offspring there was an equal measure of what our language calls boy and girl but what coexists quite naturally in some gods, and to make this divine mingling of male and female unmistakable, the child was given a name that contained equal proportions of its father's and mother's names, Hermes and Aphrodite.

By now everyone can guess whom I'm thinking of: yes, the newborn was Hermaphroditos, and immediately after his birth Aphrodite entrusted him to the care of the nymphs of Mount Ida, who properly raised the child—we have here another case of a mother abandoning her child, but once we get over our disillusionment, we must see that for the gods this is only natural: every one of them is complete unto himself, this is what they all have in common, the gods are born democrats, one might say; but to continue with Hermaphroditos' story: he grew to be such a dazzlingly beautiful youth that many mistook him for Eros, thinking that Eros must also have been the fruit of Hermes' loins and Aphrodite's womb, which of course was highly unlikely; at the age of fifteen, Hermaphroditos set out on a journey across all of Asia Minor, and wherever he went he kept up his curious habit of admiring all bodies of water, until he reached Caria, where, on the bank of an enchanting spring, he came upon Salmakis.

And at this point our third story also becomes hopelessly tangled; many versions of it have come down to us, and we can sense how time obscures the actual event, but this is the very nature of tales, to indicate the limits of human memory; but if our inferences are correct, we may imagine that at its source the clear spring formed a small pond, and Salmakis, wearing her turquoise robe, was combing her long hair while looking at her reflection in its surface, and when she managed to comb out the tangles of the night, something was amiss: either she did not like the way her hair looked or ripples may have disturbed the water's mirror, so that she began anew, and then kept on combing her hair; today we would call her mad, for she did nothing but comb her hair, that's how she spent her life, and since she was a fountain-nymph, we can't claim that what she did had neither rhyme nor reason.

And just as in any promising human encounter, it is the first moment, the very instant of catching sight and discovering the unexpected presence of the other, that offers the most insignificant, one might say imperceptible, change—no, it doesn't happen accidentally, for in what follows, the two beings, created for and guided to each other by the gods, would recognize themselves in the other, but since each sees his or her own reflection in the other, they are not compelled to do what is so common in everyday encounters, namely, to step out of themselves and, because of the other, break the boundaries of their own personalities; no, the two separate personalities can penetrate each other while remaining intact; what is usually most delimited is now limitless, and later, looking back on this moment that proved to be so significant, one simply has the feeling that one hadn't noted, most curiously, the very thing one had indeed noted most of all; something like that must have happened with the gods as well: Hermaphroditos looked at the water, and to him Salmakis combing her hair in the water's mirror was nothing more than a feature in the infinitely attractive body of water, another of its details, one might say; he saw it, of course, but so many other things were reflected in that water—sky, rocks, white patches of slowly moving clouds, dense sedge— and to Salmakis, intent on her own reflection and on combing her hair, it was of little importance that besides her face, the flash of her naked arm, and the gleam of her comb, she also saw, beneath her own reflection, the silver streak left by swiftly swimming fish or the golden ridges of sand at the bottom of the pond, so for her the appearance of Hermaphroditos' image in the water meant little more than, let's say, when a water spider, its long legs barely sinking into the surface and creating minuscule ripples in its wake, flitted across her reflected face; at that moment Hermaphroditos was not thinking of anything, he was sad, infinitely sad, as sad as he had ever been, and sadness keeps one from thinking in great detail; not only had creation granted him all at once what it grants us only piecemeal, but as a bonus he also received every possible desire; however, he knew nothing of the exciting little games used to attain those desires, because in him all desire was already attained; we might also say that creation had denied him ordinary gratification because he himself was creation's own gratification—hence the sadness, that infinite sadness which, it so happened, reinforced my suspicion that the figure in the painting was neither Hermes nor Pan, both known to be cheerful and wild, and sadness was not one of Apollo's attributes either, for though he was attracted with equal passion to goddesses and divine youths, nymphs and ordinary shepherd boys, we know of no instance when he would have been at a loss at fusing in himself this dichotomous world; no, sadness came naturally only to Hermaphroditos, it was his special trait, I decided, and this was his great moment: without tearing herself away from her reflection, a surprised Salmakis lowered her comb onto her lap; although each saw the other, they were still not looking directly at each other, and

236

then Salmakis thought (what in later stories became the source of much confusion) she was seeing Eros, that it was his beautiful face gliding over hers like a water spider; and Salmakis was respectful enough to fall in love promptly; she was a kind of ancient bluestocking, but the question of why and how it happened was completely irrelevant at the moment when the two reflections overlapped, eyes over eyes, nose on nose, mouth inside mouth, forehead in forehead, and sad Hermaphroditos now felt what he could never have felt before—his two lips stifled a divine roar!— what an ordinary mortal feels when able to reach out of his self and make contact with another—think of it!—and while everything is perfectly still, there is yet thunder and a raging storm, the rumble of rocks crashing into the sea—think of it!—how great the pleasure when a god tears out of his own boundaries! at that moment Salmakis lost her reflection and Hermaphroditos lost the water; they both lost the very things for whose possession they had been created, and so it should come as no surprise to anyone that they could not remain in one another, as we mortals can, even if the legend speaks of a perfectly consummated love.

But when I tried at this point to summarize what I did and didn't know about this mysterious and beautiful youth who over Dryope's shoulders was looking out of the picture, gazing longingly at someone, while Salmakis was watching him, filled with the same longing, and when it also became clear to me that neither of them would ever possess the object of their longing, then all I could ask was: Ye gods, what's the point of it all? if such a foolish question may be put to you, I felt as lost about my own feelings as the figures in the painting seemed to be confused about each other and themselves; stripped of my usual artful deceptions, I had no choice but to recognize in Salmakis' gaze, plain and direct, the gaze of Helene, my fiancée, as she tried with great longing, sadness, and understanding to absorb and make her own my every thought and gesture, while I, accursed and doomed, incapable of love no matter how much I loved her and, like the youth in the picture—alas, my beauty no match for his—not looking at her, not only was I not grateful for her love, but it downright irritated and disgusted me, and I was looking at someone else, of course someone else! and that someone, I might as well risk the highfalutin claim, excited me more than Helene's palpable love, because that someone promised to lead me not into a cozy family nest but into the murkiest depths of my instincts, into a jungle, into hell, among wild beasts, into the unknown, which always seems more important to us than the known, the reasonable, and the comprehensible; yet, while observing this emotional chaos within me, I could have thought of another story, no less plainly and directly out of my own life—to hell with these ancient tales and legends! I could have thought of a sweet-smelling woman whose name I must keep secret so as not to ruin her reputation, a woman who, in spite of my will, resolve, even desires, was at the center of my secret life, standing there as firmly, enchantingly, and coldly as fate is usually depicted in stylish pseudo-classical paintings, a woman who reminded me of Dryope most of all, the one who could not return my love, not with the same burning love I had for her, because she was in love, as deeply as I with her, with the man whom in these memoirs I mentioned rather misleadingly as my kind paternal friend and to whom I gave the name Claus Diestenweg, concealing his real identity because I was determined to reveal that it was not this woman whom he loved, with the kind of fervent love with which I could have loved her or the hopeless love she bore him, but I was the one he loved and wanted with an insane passion; and if on occasion he submitted to the woman's ardent desires, it was only to taste something of my love for her, to be my surrogate, as it were, to partake of something I had denied him; he loved me in the woman, while I, if I wanted to keep something of her for myself, was forced to love him, at least as a friend or a father, and thereby to feel what I would have to be like for that woman to love only me; although this incident took place in my early youth, we became deeply involved in it only after my arrival in Berlin, following Father's horrible deed and subsequent suicide, but then occurred another terrible tragedy which, though it could not eliminate the effects of the first, ended the story of our curious three-some, and then, because I lacked the strength or courage to die, I had to start a new life; but how dreary and empty, conventionally bourgeois, petty and false this life turned out to be! Or could it be, I wondered, that the story in which man is brought closer to what is divine in him is made of just such, or similar, human muddling and confusion, or just such a frightful tremor in the unattainable? is there nothing but tragedy? but then, what's the use of all this accumulated material, research, notes, all this paper, all these ideas? once past tragedy, we tend to admonish ourselves as if we were gods, but of course we're not even close to being gods; consequently, I could not tell who the youth in my picture was and couldn't even understand why the whole thing interested me so much; how could I possibly get beyond what only the gods can get past?

Still, I couldn't get the painting out of my mind.

As if solving a puzzle, considering not only the possible evidence but all the disqualifying factors as well, I concluded again and again that the youth was as beautiful as Eros, his beauty kept me in thrall, yet he could not be Eros, because he was sad like Hermaphroditos, but he couldn't be Hermaphroditos either, since he was holding Pan's pipe and Hermes' staff, then again, I countered, refuting an elusive opposition while fondly observing the youth's phallus, rendered with the delicate strokes found in miniatures, he couldn't really be Pan, if only because the great phallic god is never depicted as being so calmly immodest, his thighs spread apart and seen from the front, we always view him from the side or in a pose that conceals his member, which is logical as well as natural, since from the tip of his horn to the heel of his hoof he is one great phallus, so it would be both impossible and absurd for anyone to use paltry human judgment to decide what this phallus should look like in a painting— small or large, brown or white, thick or slender, dangling sideways over his testicles or stiffening upward like a red bludgeon; in my picture it was more like a handsome little jewel, untouched, like a hairless infant's, like his whole body, whose taut skin glistened with oil; when there was nothing more to ponder, not a single detail which I hadn't thoroughly scrutinized, either with my naked eyes or with a magnifying glass, not a single allusion I hadn't tried to clarify with the aid of scholarly books, to bring light into the dimness of my own ignorance and lack of erudition, I finally realized that it made very little difference to me who was portrayed in that picture; it wasn't their story that interested me, for the stories of Apollo, Hermes, Pan, and Hermaphroditos flow into one another like all the things I had intended to reveal about myself, and that, after all, is as it should be, and it wasn't even their humanly fallible bodies that interested me; it was the subject of my planned narrative, which seemed to be identical with that in the painting and was most clearly present in the eyes of its figures, eyes which, though bound to their bodies, were no longer corporeal, their gaze being somehow beyond their bodies, transcendent; well anyway, to pursue this line of thought I should have set out for the place where the youth's gaze as well as mine were directed, the woods, to see who was standing among the trees, who was it whom this youth loved so much and so hopelessly while he was loved just as hopelessly by someone else? what was this all about? well, we were back at the original question again, but I realized I couldn't make my own life's no doubt foolish questions more momentous by concealing them in some antique mural, because they would keep crawling out from the wall—all right, then, enough! let's talk about things as they are, no pretense, let's talk about what is ours—our own body, our own eyes; I shuddered at this thought, and at the same time I discovered something I'd been blind to up to then, though with a magnifying glass I had gone over the youth's calves, toes, arms, mouth, eyes, and forehead repeatedly, with my ruler measured the angle and direction of his glance, and with intricate calculations identified the spot where the mysterious figure had to be standing; what I hadn't noticed, simply failed to notice, was that the two ringlets falling on his forehead were actually two tiny horns, that's right, which means that he must be Pan after all, yes, Pan, no doubt about it, except this certainty no longer interested me in the least.

And neither did the forest.

Standing at dusk by the window of my flat on Weissenburgerstrasse—feigning even to myself a certain absentmindedness, so that I could always retreat into the wings of the curtain without having to feel ashamed about spying—to be able to witness undisturbed the scene that took place twice a week, I felt the same gently fluttering excitement I had when studying the painting, because, just as in a classical story where there's always an objective, down-to-earth designation of the time and place of the occurrence, however abstracted and rarefied the human events being dealt with, I could be sure that the little interlude on my street would always take place not only at dusk but on Tuesdays and Fridays; my own excitement arrived according to this timetable, I could feel it in my throat, in my belly, and around my groin, and I could no longer tell which image was more important, the one of the antique mural or the one I'd call real and could see come to life by looking through my window; at any rate, this is where I would have begun my narrative, with this scene, though I would have liked to leave out the observer and his creative feelings, so similar to sexual arousal; I didn't want to treat the story as if someone were actually witnessing it, but instead indirectly, as it unfolded of itself, always the same way, repeating itself, beginning with the arrival of the horse-drawn wagon: on nearby Wörther Platz the gas lamps were already burning, but the lamplighter still had to traverse the square, with his forked pole uncover the peaked glass bells, and with the same long fork turn up the bluish-yellow flames before he got to our street; it wasn't dark yet, daylight still lingered when in the shadow of young plane trees lining the street, and just in front of the entrance to the basement butcher shop across the street, the closed white wagon came to a halt and the slim coachman, after throwing the reins over the shiny brake handle, jumped off his seat; in winter, or if a cold wind was blowing, he would quickly pull two horse blankets from under the seat and spread them over the horses' backs, so that while the scene was taking place the sweating animals wouldn't catch cold—this bit with the blankets was omitted in the mild weather of spring or fall or when the ruddy twilight of a warm summer evening still played with the breeze among the trees and on the blackened roofs of the mean tenements; then he would take the whip and, after first cracking it against his boot, stick it next to the reins; by this time the three women would be standing on the sidewalk near the wagon, but since I was watching from my fifth-floor window, from the shadow of the roof, the wagon blocked my view of their shapely figures; moments earlier the three heads had popped up, one after the other, as the women emerged from the depth of the steep staircase leading to the basement; the heaviest of the three, by no means fat, was the mother, who, from a distance at least, hardly looked older than her unmarried daughters, more like an older sister of the twin girls, who in build and movement were perfectly identical, and only from close up could one tell them apart by the color of their hair, one being an ash-blond, the other's blond hair darkened by a tinge of red, but they had the same, somewhat blank blue eyes set in the full, white expanse of their faces; I knew them, though I had never made it down to the cold bowels of their white-tiled shop; once in a while I had seen them on the street when during their lunch break they went for a stroll in the square, arm in arm, their skirts swaying evenly around their waists, or when I peeked through the barred cellar window and they, like two wild goddesses, were standing behind the counter, their blouse sleeves rolled up to their elbows, carving bloody chunks of meat; and thanks to my good old landlady Frau Hübner, who cooked for me and who bought cold cuts and other meats there, I knew everything about these women, everything that could be gleaned from kitchen gossip; not that I wanted to include in my story those intimate details known to everyone on our street; what interested me was the mere unfolding of the scene, its mute choreography, as it were, and the series of exciting relationships it intimated.

The wagon came from the main slaughterhouse on Eldenaerstrasse.

The coachman could not have been more than twenty, just slightly older than the two girls, and hadn't yet lost the adolescent resilience that long years of hard physical labor would surely rob him of; his tanned skin had a healthy sheen, his hair was so black it seemed to glitter, and a profusion of wild, dark chest hair curled out of his always unbuttoned shirt; the three women looked even more alike on such occasions, because they all wore bloodstained smocks over their dresses.

As the young man strode to the back of the wagon, he gave each of the women, the mother included, a gentle slap on the face; they had been waiting for this, anticipating the pleasurable warmth of the rough hand on their cheeks, and now fell in behind him, giggling, touching, pinching one another as they went, as if to share among themselves what each of them had just received from the young man; he opened the wagon door and, throwing a large blood-spattered sheet over his shoulder, began to unload the shipment of meat.

The women carried the smaller pieces, shank, ribs cut in long strips, heads split in half, and haslets—livers, hearts, kidneys, and the like—in blue enamel dishes, while the coachman, with an exaggerated ease meant to impress the women, lifted and carried down into the cellar pigs cut in half and whole sides of beef; well, this is where the real plot of my story would begin, for they were apparently all working attentively, efficiently, at a nice even pace, yet they kept finding opportunities to touch one another, push, jostle, and bump into one another; moreover, under the pretext of assisting him, the women managed to touch the bare skin of the coachman's chest, neck, arm, and hand, and when they did, they relayed their pleasure in the touch, as if they were parts of a chain—sometimes they'd cling adroitly to his body for a while—but it was clear that, no matter how slyly or eagerly they did all this touching, this was not the object of the game, which, once accomplished, would satisfy them, but rather as if it was just an introduction to a more complete, purer form of contact, a more elaborate game they had to prepare gradually; but I was not given a chance to see this next phase, because they'd often disappear inside the basement shop for long periods, sometimes as much as half an hour, leaving the wagon full of merchandise open and unattended; occasionally dogs with bristling hair and cats dazed with hunger would appear on the scene, sniffing at the spilled blood and shreds of meat, but oddly enough they never risked climbing up or jumping into the wagon; there I stood, behind the drawn curtains, in the twilight dimness of my room, waiting patiently, and if the four of them did not appear for a long time, then in my imagination somehow the basement opened up, its walls fell away, and they, shedding their bloody clothes, stripping down to bare skin, reached that Arcadian meadow—I don't know how, or I should say

I do, of course I do! I pictured a subterranean passage that led them under the city and out into the open, where the two images simply merged, observation slipped into imagination; they were pure, innocent, and natural, and this is the point where my story of that coarsely beautiful man and the three women really becomes involved.

One reason I didn't like Frau Hübner barging into my room without knocking was that while observing the Tuesday and Friday twilight tableaux, or while concentrating on my fantasies about its absence, I experienced such a powerful arousal that to calm myself, and also intensify my solitary pleasure, I had to reach inside my trousers and touch myself; I would not move away from the drawn-back curtain; letting the fear of being discovered increase the tension, I stayed put and gently wrapped five fingers around my hard member pressing against my robe, doing it, of course, like a discriminating connoisseur, simultaneously cupping the soft testes and the blood-stiffened shaft in my warm palm, as if seizing at its source, at its root, what would soon erupt, and at the same time, with a certain amount of cunning self-control, I continued to pay strict attention to the events of the street, then to the silence, the absence of any action, and now and then to the unsuspecting passersby; I wasn't interested in quick gratification; delaying it kept me on the edge between the real spectacle and creative fantasy; the sudden rush of shuddering ecstasy, the convulsing spurt of semen would have deprived me of the very thing that, with the help of endless and timeless fantasies of pleasure, had nourished the body's delight in itself; delaying bliss is the way to prolong it; by touching my own body I could feel the pleasure of other bodies; I'd say that in this way my hour of shame had become the hour of communion with humanity, the hour of creation; consequently, it would have been most unpleasant if at such a moment Frau Hübner had entered my room; and it wasn't just the street I saw, I was there with them in the cellar, I was the man and I was also the three women, in my own body I felt their intimate contacts, and my imagination shifted the scene of their ever more serious game to that particular clearing, for that was where they belonged, the coachman became Pan, mother and daughters turned into nymphs; and there was nothing high-handedly false about this, because I had no doubt that this lovely meadow was very familiar to me; my imagination wasn't leading me to an unknown place; it merely took me back in time to a place that lived in my memory as one of the scenes in our summers at Heiligendamm.

My antique mural could only vaguely remind me of this realer-than-real place.

If you let yourself down the side of the embankment, constantly slipping on the loose rocks, and then followed a well-trodden trail, shielding yourself with your arm to keep the sharp-edged sedge from poking you in the eye, and then waded through the marsh, you came to a tiny bay where, as I've already mentioned, I had once surprised my childhood playmate, the young Count Stollberg, lying on the soggy grass, playing with his tool; he was lying on his back, with his pants pulled down to his knees, his head thrown back, his eyes closed, and his mouth open; the rhythmic movement must have made his beribboned sailor's cap slide off his head and it was caught in a clump of grass, its blue ribbons dangling in the water; he raised his hips in a gentle arch and spread his thighs as far as his pants, stuck over his knees, allowed; with rapid jerks of his fingers he kept yanking the foreskin of his little penis—everything about him was small and well-shaped; pulling back and releasing his skin, he seemed to have a tiny red-headed animal appearing and disappearing in his hand; his tense face was riveted to the sky, and I had the impression that with his arched torso, open mouth, and tightly shut lids, he was having some sort of discourse with the heavens, while with bated breath he was most deeply engrossed in himself; when indignantly, shocked by my own agitated reaction, I asked him about it, he very willingly and in his charmingly affable way proceeded to initiate me into the pleasant ways of squeezing pleasure out of one's own body; nothing bad had happened, he said, no reason for me to be angry, and in fact I should join him, and further, we should look at each other while doing it, that would make it even more enjoyable; at any rate, as I was saying, after a ten-minute walk on this trail you could reach the clearing, still breathless from the stifling silent air of the marsh, where suddenly the landscape would open up, and in the distance you could see the forest that bore the quaint name of the Great Wilderness and where, had I ever succeeded in writing my story, I would have taken my four characters, using clear concise sentences as their guide.

After this encounter, because of our shared secret, I was not only more deeply drawn to the boy but also afraid of him, almost hating him; still, we often took that trail to the clearing, a trip that to me also meant a kind of flirting with death, because I could never stop thinking of what Hilde had once whispered to me, as if she knew exactly what she was saying and why, how precisely she touched a most delicate nerve with her warning: "Whoever strays from the trail into the marsh is a dead man."

But we kept going back just the same, though of course we needed an acceptable excuse to disappear periodically into the sedge; since Dr. Köhler had his snail farm in this clearing, we had a chance to look around, watch the snails, and chat with the servants or with the scholarly doctor himself about the life cycle of snails, thus finding the perfect cover for our favorite pastime; the snails became our accomplices, and no doubt it was from the mire of these early lies that my ghosts arose, the ones I was frightened enough to describe to my father.

I realized that to write my narrative I first had to straighten out my own life, to break open and reveal every layer of my self-deceit.

But time, minutes and hours, resolved nothing; my body became my worst enemy: so many conflicting desires lived their separate lives in it that my head was unable to follow them, or to keep them under control by tempering them with reason; I could not establish within myself a suitable balance of sense and sensuality that would find its proper expression in clear, lucid words, the only possible system of communication for me; but this was not to be; consequently, the thought of doing away with my body stayed with me like a faithful friend all my waking hours; and yet the reason this never became more than a tempting thought was that my longings, imaginings, desires, literary ambitions, and the tension of little secret gratifications gave me such an abundance of pleasure, the pleasure of my own body, that to deprive myself of them would have seemed plain foolish; claiming that suffering was also pleasure, I allowed myself to take risks, to go too far, and that was the reason I had to keep imagining my own death, which would relieve the strain—indeed, I got so used to enjoying my suffering that I could no longer tell when I was genuinely happy; for example, on the morning of my departure, when my fiancée and I were lying in each other's arms on the rug and my glance strayed to the black leather case in which I'd carefully packed all the material I had collected for this story, even there and then, at the very moment the fluids of our bliss were flowing together inside her beautiful body, the first thought that occurred to me was that right now, this instant, I should drop dead, croak now, no better time than now to cease, to evaporate, and then I'd leave nothing behind except a few self-consciously mannered pieces of prose, a few glib sketches and stories that were published in various literary journals and would very quickly sink into oblivion, and the open, patent-leather case, which, in the form of raw and to others indecipherable notes, contained the real secrets of my life, that is all—except perhaps for my seed in her body uniting with her egg at that very moment.

Now if some unauthorized stranger were to rummage through my things and go over my papers ... well, this stranger, this secret agent who'd appear after my death to make out a report about me based on the papers found among my effects had often cropped up in my dreams; although he was faceless and of indeterminate age, I found his immaculate shirtfront, stiff collar, polka-dotted necktie adorned with a glittering diamond pin, and especially his rather shiny frock coat all the more characteristic and significant; with long, bony fingers he rummaged expertly through my papers, occasionally lifting a page close to his eyes, giving me the impression that he was nearsighted, though I didn't see him wearing eyeglasses; he perused a sentence here and there, and I noted with satisfaction that he derived completely different meanings from the ones I had hoped my sentences would imply; no wonder I had managed to fool even someone like him; after all, I made sure that my fleeting ideas, fragmentary thoughts, and hasty descriptions were jotted down so that my papers remained well within the bounds of middle-class propriety, counting also on the possibility that dear old Frau Hübner, taking advantage of my absence and driven by simple curiosity, would likewise look through the pages piled on my desk; thus I became an unauthorized stranger to my own life, because seeing myself as a criminal, a miserable misfit, I still wanted to remain a perfect gentleman in the eyes of the world, I myself became that shiny frock coat, the starched shirtfront, and the tie pin, the irreproachably inane form of bourgeois respectability; secretly, and proud of my own slyness, I figured that if I used a private code when recording my accumulated experiences, then, since I possessed the key, I'd always be able to open the lock of the code; but as might be expected, the lock turned out to be foolproof, and by the time I finally came around to opening it, my hands, trembling with anxiety, simply could not find the keyhole.

That is how some things remained a mystery forever, my own secret alone; no, I'm not too sorry about it, after all, whatever doesn't exist, what no one has declared a public and consensual secret, should be of no interest to people; and so the reason I took with me to Heiligendamm those two little booklets by Dr. Köhler about the *Helix pomata*, the common edible snail, remained a puzzling mystery, as did the question of any possible connection between these snails, the above-described insignificant street scene, and that splendid antique mural.

The snails Köhler describes so dryly and dispassionately in his books were consumed by the dozen each morning by guests at the spa; raw, ground to a pulp, the snails together with their shells were lightly seasoned and sprinkled with lemon juice; eating them like that was as much part of the cure as were those breathing exercises at sunset; these snails—classified by the doctor according to their shape, build, habitat, and characteristic traits, and grouped into species and subspecies—are amazingly solitary and at the same time very lively little creatures in whom the slightest contact with other snails produces profound terror; it takes them hours—which in their terms may mean days, weeks, even months—to ascertain with their feelers, and later, on a higher level of certainty, with their mouths and their undulating undersides, that they are indeed suited to one another, and there is no need, because of some compelling and disqualifying reason, to crawl on, disappointed, in search of another potential mate; in principle, any snail can couple with any other—in this sense they are nature's most favored creatures, being the only ones to preserve and act out nature's primeval unisexuality, being androgynous, like plants, their bodies possessing qualities that we humans can only vaguely recall, which perhaps explains their exceptional fineness and timidity; each one is complete in itself, and therefore two complete wholes must find each other, which must be an incomparably more difficult task than simple gratification; and when they do unite, in complete mutuality, simultaneously receiving and fulfilling each other—Köhler's description is at this point most detailed, his prose most impassioned—they cling to each other with such force, and no wonder, this is the strength of the ancient gods! that the only way they can be separated, experimenters tell us, is by literally tearing them apart; but like the characters in the mural, the snails would not have appeared in my narrative; studying their physiology was also part of my preliminary research, material that nourished the work but would not be found in the finished product; secret ingredients like this can be found in abundance in any work of art worthy of the name; or perhaps they would have appeared but only in some incidental, seemingly unimportant image, as some symbolic device, say, sliding past on a large fern leaf at the edge of the forest, or on fragrantly decaying leaves on the forest floor; there might have been a pair of them, and we'd noticed them just as they touched each other with their seeing tentacles.

Yes: every step I took, whether toward vile death or in my longing for the happiness afforded by vileness, carried me to this forest.

It was not a dense forest, but when finding one of its trails and letting it take you randomly among the trees, you quickly realized why popular lore referred to this woods as a wilderness; no one ever came here to mark the trees with white chalk or chop them down, clean them carefully of their branches and cart them away; nobody gathered brushwood here, picked wild berries or mushrooms at the edge of its snail-inhabited clearings; it seemed as if for ages, for unconscionably long ages, nothing had happened to or in these woods except what we might call the natural history of flora and fauna, which of course is no small thing: trees come into leaf, mature, live, and, after slowly passing centuries, die away; under their foliage, germinating, sprouting, and growing at the mercy of sunbeams the leafy boughs let through, there is an undergrowth of shrubs, bushes, ferns, creepers, runners, and climbers, grass, nettles, a thousand different weeds, garishly colorful and sickly transparent flowers, all taking their turn according to the changing seasons, until the thickening foliage completely deprives them of light and they perish, yielding their places to moss, lichen, and fungi that prefer cool dimness and, thriving on decay, sustain the life of the ground's spongy surface; there is silence here, and the silence is also ancient, and thick, because undisturbed by the wind; the air is so redolent that within a few minutes you'd be overcome with a feeling rather like a pleasantly soothing swoon; and it is always warmer here than out in the real world, a hazy warmth that makes one's skin moist and slick, like the body of a snail; the trails here are not real paths, trod and beaten down by human steps, but the life of the forest shapes these passages, whimsically, gracefully, unpredictably, as gaps in the continuous story of the ground's surface, pauses that only our resolute human intelligence would dare name, for it has learned to disregard other, perhaps much more important occurrences, and is accustomed simply to cut through the thick of things and, in its own doltish way, make use of nature's silence.

You'd find here gullies in which pebbles and stones roll and clink together; stretches of level ground where driving rains have spread crumbled clumps of dirt; long runners of soft moss, or patches where the layers of fallen leaves are so thick that their decaying mass cloys even the wild mushrooms; you could walk here, though not quite unimpeded, because the natural passageway may unexpectedly be blocked by a bush rising out of a warm spot in a pool of sunlight, or by a thick trunk of a fallen tree, or a huge, pointed, smooth lava rock, ingeniously called a "findling," conjuring in our imagination something between a found object and a foundling; according to local legend, giants of the northern seas strewed these rocks about the flat coastland where, after the battles had subsided, these peaceful forests arose.

Deep-green dimness.

Occasional scraping sounds, a thud, a crack.

One cannot tell how time passes here, but so long as you can hear the twigs snapping under your feet and you feel that it's your silence that is being disturbed by each snap, that means you're not quite here yet.

So long as you wish to get somewhere, to a place that is yours—though you don't know what that place is like—so long as you refuse to be led by the paths opening up before you, you are not quite here yet.

Behind the loose curtain of the thicket a tree seems to move, as if someone who'd been standing behind it now stirred, just as you keep stirring from behind something and then being covered again by the thicket.

Until it all looks beautiful to you.

Everyone can see you—anyone, to be more precise—and yet you are still covered; no, I couldn't succeed in describing the forest; I would have liked to have talked about the feel of the forest.

So long as you carry with you the turns and bends, forks and obstacles of the trails you've left behind, you can find your way back to where you started from, and in your fear you look at the plants as you would at human faces, taking them as signposts, assigning them shape, character, and histories of their own, hoping that in return for that they'd lead you back—so long as you do that, you are not quite here yet.

And you are not quite here yet even when you realize you are not alone with them.

I would have liked to have talked about the creatures of the forest as Köhler did of his snails; I would have borrowed his style.

When you are no longer aware of yourself or, more precisely, when you know time has passed but not how much or how little, and you don't really care . . .

And you stand there without knowing you are standing; you look at something but don't know what; and for some reason your arms are spread as if you were yourself a tree.

No, this story could never have been written successfully.

For you can feel what the tree in all probability cannot feel.

And you have heard all the rustling and scraping sounds but did not realize you were hearing them.

When you know that you are here, but not when you got here, because you have lost all the clues.

But so long as you keep listening for and trying to remember lost clues, you are not quite here yet, because you believe you are being watched.

And then it flits by, between two trees, and quickly vanishes, a flash of blue in a field of green.

You start off, unaware of having started off, but you cannot find it.

So long as you make a distinction between trees and colors, so long as you look to the names of things for guidance, you are still not quite here.

So long as you think you only imagined seeing the flitting creature as a blue flash in a field of green, and you follow it, cautiously, and no longer care about the path, about branches slapping you in the face, you don't hear the crunch of your footsteps, don't notice you've fallen, you get up and run after it, nettles sting you, thorns prick and scratch you, but all you want is to catch it, yes, the one that keeps disappearing but always reappears, to make sure you see it, though it occurs to you that you shouldn't yield to the temptation.

So long as you still want to make a decision, so long as you are thinking about it, you won't be able to catch anything; they'll keep eluding you, they can smell your sour odor from afar.

Now it's there, standing in a small depression, and if you don't move, then, among the silently stirring leaves, you can make out its eyes as they flash into yours, though this is no longer the same being but another, maybe a third one, someone, anyone, because you let time pass in the mutual gleam of your eyes while you notice that the creature is naked, and so are you.

So long as you wish to reach its nakedness and bend the branches to have a better look, so long as you want its nakedness to touch yours and thus make it your own, and for this purpose you are ready to move from your spot even though you have found the creature you've been after, then you are still not quite here.

It's gone.

And so long as you keep searching for them, yes, the ones you managed to alarm with your clumsiness and sour smell, so long as you hope to meet them again and all the while keep grumbling that you should have been more clever and more cautious, you are still not quite here, and nobody will be able to reach you.

But chance comes to your rescue, because you have come far enough inside to be a little bit here.

You turn around, and what you had seen in front of you before is now behind you; on the soft green mossy stream bank, the creature is lolling on its stomach; you let your eyes run over its back, rise on the curve of its round buttocks, and then roll down on its shapely legs; it nestles its head in its arms, looking out from there, and this gives you such joy that not only your mouth breaks into a grin but even your toes begin to smile and your knees laugh; and by then you don't feel like moving, because you've found your place here: that laugh is your place on this earth; and then you notice that the eyes are not looking into yours, that there is a third creature in the picture, there in that small depression in the ground, the one you thought had vanished completely, and they are looking at each other; they are the ones, you think to yourself, who could teach you what you need to know.

They are looking at you the way you'd like to be looking at them.

But you are still not you, you still let your thoughts stand in for you; until you learn not to do that, you are not quite here yet.

Your snooping startles them, they spring up and melt into the thicket.

Just as their gaze makes you take cover.

And then for a long time you see no one.

So long as you want to find them only for yourself, the forest remains silent.

But this is already a different kind of silence; this silence has eaten itself into your skin, and the laughter must reach your bones.

When even your smell becomes different.

Grass Grew
over the Scorched Spot

The tiniest move could have broken this peacefulness, so I didn't even feel like opening my eyes; I was hanging on to something that had become final between us then, in the shared warmth of our bodies, and I didn't want her to see my eyes, to see how frightened I was of what was to come—it was good like this, let fear be mine!—of my body I felt only the parts her body could make me feel: under the rucked-up silk dress the moist surface of her skin touching mine—that was my thigh; at the level of her neck my own breath mingling with the whiffs of stifling odor rising from her armpits; I felt the hard edge of a hip that may have been mine, its hardness the hardness of my bone; I felt my shoulder and back because of the weight of her arm as she very slowly lifted it away, but even then my shoulder and back still felt the arm, for somehow even the receding weight left an impression in the flesh and bones; and when she also raised her head a bit to take a better look at the bite mark on my neck, I was glad to be able to watch through barely raised eyelashes, not exposing my eyes; all she could see was the quiver of the lids, the flutter of the lashes; she couldn't imagine how scared I was, and we hadn't even begun, but I could see her in almost perfect clarity, looking at my neck, yes, I could fool her so easily; she looked at it long, even touched the spot with her stiff finger; her lips parted, edged closer, and kissed it where it still hurt a little.

As if she were kissing Szidónia's mouth on my neck.

We lay like this for a long time, her face on my shoulder and my face on her shoulder, silent and motionless—at least that is how I remember it today.

Perhaps our eyes were closed, too.

But even if I did open my eyes I could see only the patterns of the rumpled bedspread and her hair, the tickly ringlets on my mouth.

And if her eyes were open, all she could see were the green afternoon shadows stirring silently on the vacant expanse of the ceiling.

I may have dozed off for a short time; maybe she did, too.

And then, so softly that my ear felt more the thrusts of her breath than the sound of her voice, she seemed to say that we should get started.

Yes, we should, I said, or meant to say, though neither of us moved.

There was nothing to stop us now, and who would have thought that the greatest obstacle we had to overcome would turn out to be ourselves?

Around this time of the afternoon Szidónia usually disappeared, visiting neighbors, going on a date, or just taking time off for herself, and so long as she didn't tell Maja's parents about the afternoon adventures of their daughter, she could be sure her own little illicit absences would not be discovered; and they not only covered up for each other but also shared their intimate experiences and adventures, like girl friends, disregarding the seven-year difference in their ages; once, inadvertently, I overheard them, barely able to catch my breath at my unexpected good fortune: with her hair undone, Szidónia was swinging back and forth in the garden hammock, confiding something to Maja, who, fully engrossed in the story, sat on the grass, giving the hammock an absentminded push now and then.

What we should have got started on, what we both wanted to begin, was the search that, once we did begin—our own compulsion making us shake and tremble—was so grave and dark a secret she didn't mention it to anyone, and I'm convinced she's been quiet about it ever since, just as I've never spoken about it to anyone, ever—let this white sheet of paper be my first confidant!—not even to each other did we mention it, we merely alluded to it, dropped hints about it; it remained a silent event in our lives, and in a certain sense we blackmailed each other with the fact that we had a secret so terrible it could not be shared with anyone, binding us together more fatefully than any form of love ever could.

And what is that mark on your neck, she asked, her whisper no more than a breath.

This red one, here.

For a moment I didn't know what she was talking about, thought she was just playing for time, not wanting to get started, but I also needed more time just then.

Oh, that mark? it's nothing; she bit my neck, that's all, I said, and I didn't have to say who, she knew; and I was very pleased that the teeth marks were still visible and that she'd noticed them.

From the shade of the apple trees, the hammock swung lazily into the light.

I've never forgotten that afternoon, either.

And with her mouth sunk into me, as if her lips had fallen asleep, we stayed that way.

As the hammock swung into the light and the two tightening ropes tugged the trees, Szidónia's voice grew stronger; the leafy crowns of the apple trees rustled, the branches strained and moaned, and then, as the hammock swung back, she lowered her voice, which not only lent a curious, almost panting rhythm to the story but for no logical reason amplified certain of her sentence fragments, while others became barely audible whispers; her voice swung back and forth, the unripe apples kept shaking on their stems; I was standing behind a round shrub, a boxwood, enveloped by the warm fragrance of the little oily green leaves, listening to Szidónia talking about some streetcar conductor, and the rhythm of her voice, growing alternately loud and soft, seemed to be in direct contact with Maja, because she pushed the hammock as if in immediate response to the story—more vigorously or more gently, speeding up or slowing down the pace, now shoving it furiously, let's get on with it! now barely giving it a tap, anyway rather unpredictably; the conductor was short, with big, bulging, bloodshot eyes, his forehead full of pimples, "big as my fingers," Szidónia was saying, "red and bumpy," which made Maja squeal and give the hammock a good shove, though interestingly enough, the emotional tones of Szidónia's delivery oddly suggested complete detachment—she talked about everything with the cheerful smile of someone for whom details are very important but never very meaningful, let alone decisive, each detail being important simply in and of itself; she took the Number 23 tram, getting on the last car, where she liked to ride because "it jerks and bounces"; the tram was almost empty; of course she sat on the shady side; she was wearing her white blouse with the picot-edged light-blue collar which Maja liked because it hugged her hips so nicely, and the white pleated skirt which at home she was allowed to wear only on holidays like Easter, because it soiled so easily, and whenever she sat down in it she spread a handkerchief under herself; besides, it was hard

to iron all those pleats; it was warm in the streetcar, and this conductor—
he may have been a Gypsy, Szidónia thought, Gypsies have such bulging
eyes—rolled down all the windows, every last one of them, using one of
those hand cranks; it took him a long time, because the crank kept slipping out of its slot; then he sat down opposite her, quite a distance away,
actually, on the sunny side, put the crank back into his conductor's bag,
and began staring at her; but she pretended not to notice him, as if she
had to close her eyes because of the wind blowing in her face; what she
liked best was when the tram was going really fast, because that scared
her, especially around sharp bends; once she got on a roller coaster with
her godmother's younger sister and she thought she was going to die right
there and then; and there was this other man in her car, watching the
conductor watching her, but she kept forgetting about them, because she
was really looking out the window, or she closed her eyes and thought of
other things; but she did not get off, kept on riding, and the conductor
kept changing his seat, moving closer to her; of course she took a look at
his hands, he didn't have a wedding band; though she didn't find him
attractive she liked his jet-black hair and the hair on his arms, he was a
bit dirty-looking; and she was curious to see what would happen, whether
he would have the nerve to speak to her, especially while the other man
kept looking at them.

I could actually see her thick brown hair getting dry in the heat of the
afternoon; when I'd begun watching them from behind the hedges, it still
clung wetly to her bare back and shoulders; she was wearing a white linen
undershirt and a lace-trimmed petticoat; the vestee, as she called the little
shirt, fastened in front with tiny snaps and held down, almost flattening
her aggressively large breasts, but it left bare her back, her broad shoulders, and her strong fleshy arms; as the hammock kept rising into the
light and falling back into the shade, the drying strands of hair on her
shoulders and back gradually came unstuck, at first only at the edges,
fluttering and gliding in the wake of each swing.

Then finally, she went on, after riding like this for a good long time
they got to the last stop, except she didn't know it was the last stop, and
the conductor, sitting opposite her but much closer, now stood up, and so
did the other man, to get off, though he was still looking at them, wondering what would happen; he seemed a decent sort, wore decent clothes,
a white shirt and black hat, and had a small parcel with him, probably
food, because the wrapper was greasy, and yet he looked hungry, but not
drunk; then the conductor told her that it was the last stop and to his

regret they'd have to part company; and she laughed at him, saying there was no need to part, she'd take the return trip with him.

This made both girls laugh, a brief, dry, I'd say colliding laughter, a meeting and sudden breaking off of two separate laughs; Maja stopped pushing the hammock and with a quick move gathered her skirt between her thighs and, still sitting, leaned stiffly forward; the hammock was slowing down, and in the girls' silence it continued to rock Szidónia's body gently for a little while longer; I felt I had come upon their innermost secret; they looked so familiar and at the same time I was seeing them for the first time; Maja's eyes seemed to be thrusting, retrieving, and rocking Szidónia, while Szidónia's softly swaying glance kept Maja in a charmed immobility; but it was not only that with their looks they held each other in this position, but that their faces also remained fixed in that short, dry, somewhat sarcastic burst of laughter; no matter how different those two sets of silently parted lips, wide-open eyes, and raised eyebrows, the sharing of their secrets made the two girls alike.

When the hammock was only barely swinging, about to stop, Maja grabbed Szidónia with both hands and gave her a mighty push; there was cruelty and fierceness in the movement, even a touch of wickedness, but not directed against Szidónia so much as sent forth with her, and Szidónia, flying back into the light, resumed her story, her loud voice resonating with the same touch of wickedness.

On the way back, she said, the conductor went on talking to her, but she wouldn't respond, only listen, look at his bulging eyes, get up suddenly to change her seat, playing this little game for a while, as the conductor would also get up, follow her, not listen, go on talking and talking; no one else got on the streetcar for a long time, and the conductor told her about how he, too, was from the country and lived in a workers' hostel and how much he wanted to find out her name; she didn't tell him, of course; and he said he'd fallen in love with her the moment he saw her, she was the kind of girl he'd always been looking for, and she shouldn't be afraid of him, and wanting to be honest with her, he'd tell her right away that he just got out of jail a week ago, having served a year and a half, and all that time he hadn't been with a woman, but she should hear him out, he was completely innocent; he was an illegitimate child, his mother had a friend, a boozing good-for-nothing whom his mother had sent packing and never wanted to see again, even though she had another child by him, a little girl, and the conductor loved this little sister of his more than his own life, and since his mother was a very sick woman, with a bad heart, he had to raise the little girl, a sweet child with golden hair; but the man kept coming back, whenever he ran out of money or had no place to sleep, he would come and kick in the door, he even smashed in their window a couple of times, and when he couldn't have his way he would beat the sick woman, call her a whore; and if he, the conductor, tried to stop him, then the big lug would beat him up, too; one night, after they'd bathed the little girl and put her to bed, he was doing the dishes and accidentally left a knife on the table; it wasn't a big knife but very sharp—he used to sharpen all their knives—the man showed up again, and it was the same old story: they wouldn't let him in, but then the neighbors started yelling that they'd had enough of this, and so his mother finally opened the door, he came in and started after her; as she was backing away from him, she reached the table and tried to hold on to it, and as she did she felt the knife; she snatched it up and stabbed the bastard, and then, to make sure his little sister wouldn't lose her mother, he confessed to the crime, but at the trial it came out that he wasn't the one who'd done it, because the door was open and the neighbors saw everything; so he was sentenced to a year for perjury and for being an accessory to a crime; and now he was asking her not to get off the streetcar without giving him her address at least, he wasn't asking for a date, but he didn't want to lose her, and anyway, from now on he wouldn't stop thinking about that pretty face of hers.

Maja sprang up from the ground because she could push more easily when standing, took two steps back, spread her legs, dug in her heels, and pushed Szidónia so hard that it looked as if she'd meant to turn her over completely, which was of course impossible; the apple trees groaned and creaked, their crowns trembled, but up there, in the light, the hammock always came to a halt and, pulled back by the weight it carried, came swinging back with equal force; and Szidónia, catching her breath and shouting from the speeding hammock, continued her story.

Well, if he really wanted to see her again, she told him, he should take this tram on Saturday afternoon to Boráros Square, change to Number 6; yes, but he was on duty Saturday afternoon; well, change shifts with somebody, take the Number 6 to Moszkva Square, change to Number 56, and then get off at the cog-railway station, walk up Adonisz Road, and at the end of the stone fence around the first house he'd find a trail leading to the forest, he couldn't miss it, he'd see three tall pine trees, he should walk right into the forest and keep walking until he came to a large clearing and she'd be waiting for him there.

The only thing was, she'd already made a date for the same time with Pista, Szidónia was now shouting.

I, too, knew this Pista.

But she said she was curious to see what these two would do with one another.

Maja could contain herself no longer; her whole body tautened with excitement, and I could sense that the tension would soon reach a point where she'd have to tear herself away from Szidónia's story; she was still pushing the hammock, then suddenly covered her face with both hands, as if she had to laugh as hard as Szidónia was shouting, but no sound came from her, she was only shamming this laughter, for her own benefit, and for Szidónia's; the hammock kept flying of its own momentum, and Maja seemed determined to continue the game, false or true: once she started it, she had to go on; pressing her hand to her stomach, she nearly doubled over with this silent laughter; convulsing, she sank to the ground, slipped her hands between her thighs, which she kept pressing together, and looked up at Szidónia as if she were about to pee in her pants.

In patches, the skin on her neck and face turned white, her body seemed glued to the ground, and I knew she was ashamed of herself, but her curiosity must have been equally deep and eager, because her mouth was open and because, begging all at once for mercy and for more of the story, her eyes were flashing wildly among the tall blades of yellowing grass.

But Szidónia did not wait for the hammock to stop; she sat up, grabbed the taut ropes on both sides, and, thrusting out and pulling in her bare feet, she began to pump herself forward and backward, as on a swing, the effort making even her wrinkling forehead turn red though her voice remained soft and steady, and the smile, with her teeth continually exposed, did not leave her face for a moment, which must have been painful for Maja to bear.

By the time she got there, Pista was waiting; she hid in the thicket where the trail dipped, on that flat rock among the bushes where they often found discarded condoms—yes, Maja knew where that was—a very good spot from which you can see everything, but from below no one can see you; she was squatting on this flat rock, didn't dare sit down, ready to run away should something unexpected happen; Pista was not in uniform that day, he wore a blue suit and a white shirt—the reason she'd not told Maja about all this before was that she was afraid of the possible consequences; anyway, Pista was lying in the grass, on his back, smoking, his neatly folded jacket next to him on the ground, he was such a neat fellow; he was planning to take her dancing later on; for a long time nothing happened; Pista wasn't getting impatient, and there was no noise of any kind, nothing to make him think she was coming, only the sun shining very brightly, and once in a while he shook himself, a fly must have landed on him; this made her want to laugh up there on the rock, but she wouldn't; she began to think that the conductor might not show at all, because she heard the cogwheel train stop, move on, and still he didn't come; anyway, a whole hour went by, because he came with the next train; Pista kept smoking and twisting and shooing away the flies, and once in a while she did sit down on the rock.

That's what he always did, that Pisti, pretend not to hear her; he'd always do that, and then she'd sneak up on him and kiss him, but even then he wouldn't pull his hand out from under his head and wouldn't throw away his cigarette; with his eyes open he'd pretend he didn't see her, and then she had to go on kissing him on his mouth, his face, and his neck until he couldn't stand it anymore, and then he'd kiss her back, and pull her down, and by then she couldn't get away no matter how hard she tried, he wouldn't let her, he was very strong: now the conductor was there, and he stopped; he was still in uniform, with his conductor's bag slung over his shoulder, who knows, maybe he just simply left his tram for her; he looked around to make sure he was at the right place and then, very quietly so Pisti wouldn't hear him, he backed away, back among the trees; she couldn't see him anymore, though Pisti sat up.

From her place she saw that Pisti couldn't see the conductor but the conductor could see Pisti, and Pisti must have sensed that.

Because Pisti acted as if he was just getting up, having rested there for a while, and was now ready to go on; picking up his jacket, he was on his way; but as soon as he got as far as the trees, he suddenly turned around and kept staring at the spot where he thought the conductor must be hiding.

And then she, squatting up there in the stifling heat, felt that she had suddenly got her period, and she had no panties on.

You're an idiot, you're a complete idiot, Maja said.

Slowly the conductor ventured out of his hiding place, not completely, for a while he just stood there, under the trees, listening for noise, adjusting his leather bag and rubbing his forehead, all those pimples, and he was very nervous, thinking maybe he was at the wrong place after all; and then he started walking, not noticing that Pisti was watching him.

In the meantime, she had such cramps she thought she was going to burst; she reached under her skirt and felt that everything was bloody, it was gushing out of her and, since she was crouching, trickling down her behind and dripping onto the rock; she didn't know what to do, she couldn't very well stand up; when the conductor reached the middle of the clearing, suddenly Pisti also stepped out into the open and started toward him to cut him off; luckily she had a handkerchief with her; she folded it, twisted its edges, and then stuffed it in; but she still couldn't wipe the blood off or budge from her place; and she was sure Pisti had figured out she had a hand in all this, she was still pretty sure even though he never said anything about it to her; and now he was headed straight for the conductor as if he didn't even see he was there; whenever it was hot, Pisti would hook a finger into the loop of his jacket and sling it over his back; anyway, the conductor could no longer turn back, even if he wanted to; he stopped, and so did Pisti; all she could see was that he yanked the jacket off his back and smacked the conductor across the face with it, and when the conductor doubled over and put up his hands to protect himself, Pisti hit him on the back of his head with the hand he had the jacket in, hit him hard, so hard that the conductor just crumpled up, tripped over his bag so stupidly the change spilled out all over the grass.

She thrust out her beautiful bare feet and pulled them under herself, but she was sitting too deep inside the hammock to pump; the hammock barely swayed to and fro.

And then Pisti left, just like that, without even looking around; and she never told him she'd seen the whole thing, but she's pretty sure that if she ever ran into that conductor again he would probably beat her.

Maja sat up, the mysterious dignity of her face and bearing somehow reflecting Szidónia's calm and infinite satisfaction; for a long time they did nothing but look at each other, silently and a bit dreamily staring straight into each other's eyes, and to me this silence was far more telling than the story I'd just heard; each time Szidónia thrust out her feet she almost brushed Maja's face, but Maja did not bat an eye; it was as if now, in this silence, something more important than the story was happening, or assuming a recognizable shape, something that moments earlier I'd felt to be a secret, their secret, and it may have been nothing more than Szidónia's urge to tell all this to Maja and Maja's urge to listen.

Down in the valley, cradled by gently curving mountains, the city hovered in the bright summer mist.

260

And then, in a curious voice I'd never heard before, Maja began to speak.

The white shimmer of houses and the blurred outline of jumbled roofs and towers on the Buda hills were all so peaceful and distant.

But what kind of handkerchief did you use, my dear? Maja asked.

Beyond the gray strip of the lazy river, the mist of smoke and dust of the Pest side stretched into the horizon.

Maja's voice was sharp, offensive, a falsetto not her own.

What d'you think? Szidónia answered languidly, her voice deep; with her outstretched toes she was poking Maja's face.

That's just what I'm asking you, my dear, what kind of handkerchief?

A bloody one, Szidónia answered and on the next swing of the hammock shoved her foot into Maja's face.

So it was my little batiste handkerchief you shoved up in there, wasn't it, Maja said, her voice rising to a higher register, though her face was enjoying the touch of Szidónia's sole, and for a moment, full of pleasure and satisfaction, she closed her eyes; don't deny it, it was my little handkerchief, the one with the lace!

What was most peculiar was that the smile had vanished from Szidónia's face and Maja wasn't smiling either; they were content, pleased with each other, very much alike now, or maybe their sudden solemnity made them resemble each other; whatever was happening did not seem too serious.

Maja was sitting on the grass, her feet under her, thighs spread apart; holding her spine straight and throwing her head back a little, she kept pushing the soles of Szidónia's feet, not too hard, with steady, even movements; they were no longer looking at each other, so I couldn't tell what would happen next.

That afternoon, too, Maja was wearing one of her mother's dresses, an absurdly long, loose-fitting, lace-trimmed purple dress, whose shoulder pads hung down almost to her elbows; her distorted voice also reminded me of her mother's, though perhaps the dress made me think that; anyway, the two girls carried on their dialogue so rapidly and easily that I could see they were indulging in a familiar, well-practiced game.

The sun was beating down on my neck; it was their silence that made me realize I was there, too, and I was hot, as though until now I hadn't been aware of my own presence.

I had no idea how long or how cautiously I'd been hiding behind the hot green boxwood; there was really no need for all this spying and listening, actually, because at other times they felt free to discuss adventures like this right in front of me or even with me, asking my advice, which I gladly gave; I could have stepped forward at any time, and nothing would have happened if they had noticed me, the only reason they didn't being that they were too involved in the story; the ball-shaped shrub was so dense that if I really wanted to see anything, and I most certainly did, I had to stick my head out; nevertheless, I couldn't bring myself to leave my ludicrous hiding place; I would have preferred to disappear, evaporate, or maybe rudely disrupt the scene, end it by throwing a stone at them; I could have used the spigot only inches from me and the red garden hose lying right there in the grass like a snake, but it would have been hard to pull over the nozzle and turn on the water without their noticing; if I could just wreck that annoying strange intimacy of theirs! which I could share only by not stepping forward, by their not noticing me; I could deceive myself, but in every moment, and every little fragment of each moment, things were happening here that in my presence never could; I was stealing from them, though I had no idea what; and the excitement was also unbearable, the shame of acquiring something I could neither use nor abuse, for it was exclusively theirs; the confidence they'd shown me was illusory, fraudulent, they'd given me mere morsels of confidence but in truth deceived me; they'd never let me come into their real confidence, because I was not a girl, and now they were talking about themselves, among themselves, and it seemed that I was robbing them of something.

Choosing the most shameful escape route, I was about to back away so I could sneak off, disappear, never to return, hoping to reach the garden gate unnoticed and be able to slam it shut really loudly, but just then, using both feet, Szidónia caught Maja's neck in a vise, and simultaneously Maja grabbed hold of those powerful feet and tried to pry them off her, and the hammock swung back, so that Maja lost her balance and was dragged along on the grass; it was now impossible to see just what was happening, and as they were pulling, pushing, clawing, and kicking at each other, with hands and feet, suddenly Szidónia tumbled out of the hammock right on top of Maja; Maja cleverly slipped out from under her, sprang up and started to run—by now they were both shrieking, letting out terrific screams—and Szidónia took off after her; they were like two rare butterflies, flitting and flashing into and away from each other, Maja's loose purple dress billowing against the wings of Szidónia's rising and falling waist-length hair streaming above the white undershirt as they plunged down the garden's steep slope, at the bottom of which they finally crashed into each other and, I did see it, kissed each other, but in the very next moment, grabbing each other's hands, their bodies arched, they were whirling round and round, and they kept it up for a long time, until one of them must have let go, because they flew apart and went sprawling; they stayed there on the grass, panting hard.

It wasn't me Maja liked but the mark Szidónia's teeth had left on my neck.

Later, when those lips began to stir on my neck, the unexpectedly coarse friction sent shivers down my back, the sudden chill making me feel how our bodies were intertwined.

I'm bleeding, said the lips resting on my shuddering skin.

And while curled in my mother's lap, my lips resting inside the crook of her elbow, where under the skin there were yellow and blue splotches caused by the frequent taking of blood samples and where the much-abused vein was such an invitingly tender place for the mouth, I should have told her about this, too, and somehow I had the vague feeling that I had.

Maybe the touch itself told her the story, for I gave her back what Maja's mouth had given me on the spot where Szidónia bit me.

But as much as I would have liked to talk about it, I could never put into words this painful confusion of touches, impossible even to begin the story, because each touch had to do with many other touches, and Krisztián's mouth was also part of the story.

Well, come on, I said, but we didn't move.

I could tell she enjoyed whispering into the skin of my neck; I shouldn't be angry with her, she said, the reason she was so nervous before was that she was bleeding and that always made her very nervous, as I probably knew, and that was another thing she'd never tell anyone else, ever.

On days like that she's very agitated, and much more sensitive than I can imagine, and she needs to be loved, otherwise she'd start crying again.

And I should have removed my finger from her underpants; under the weight of her body my arm fell asleep, and what I took to be sweat, moistness of skin, was probably blood; and my finger was in it, I suddenly realized, I was dipping it in her blood, but I did not move my finger, I didn't want to be rude, I sensed I had to guard a feeling in her which I myself could never feel, and I did envy her for that bleeding; I stayed the way I was, letting my arm grow more numb, and most of all, I didn't want her to know how much she had upset and terrified me, how I feared getting menstrual blood on my finger.

The truth is, I wasn't exactly sure how this whole bleeding business worked, and she might have been lying to me, for all I knew, making it all up just to be more like Szidónia.

I wouldn't want her to cry now, would I? so I shouldn't make her.

I had to be careful not to move, not to let her body feel that I knew it was all a sham, that whatever she was saying or communicating with her movements was not meant for me, and whatever I felt to be mine just seconds ago was not mine at all; she had deceived me again, and the only reason she had given anything to me was that I happened to be there, at hand, and the one she would really like to do this with she couldn't, wouldn't dare.

I should love her, she said, the way she loved me.

And I was cheating, too, of course, because I'd come to her house not because of her, not to play detective, but in hopes of finding Livia there, yes, Livia, whose very name was now abhorrent to me, whom that afternoon I had waited for by the wall, in vain, since once again she didn't show up, and I couldn't stand it anymore, I just had to come, I had to see her, if only for a second, and if she would look at me again, the way only she can look! but with her it's different, I couldn't even bring myself to speak to her, let alone touch her.

At the same time, in spite of our cheating bodies—feeling in Maja what Kálmán should be feeling, and involuntarily giving of myself what I should have given to Livia—it was so good, so infinitely good to hear Maja whisper into my neck, to smell her body, to feel her blood, her weight, my arm growing numb, and our body heat, and in the dark joy of betrayal to know that again I was coming into possession of something that did not belong to me and that there was no deception from which I'd be able to spare myself.

That I could think of Livia at all just now, not of her so much as of her absence, made me feel that I had hurt her feelings irrevocably, dragged her into the filth in which I liked to wallow, and that I hated her for not showing up.

I just know I'll be a whore, Maja said.

But this sentence wasn't hers either, she was merely echoing one of Szidónia's exclamations; like a lifeless stone that drinks up the heat of the sun and then breathes it back into the night, she had drunk in and breathed back into my neck echoes of the words of Szidónia, whom she desperately wanted to resemble, whom she clung to, whom she kissed, whose every move she adored, and this indecent behavior reminded me so much of Krisztián, and the memory was so painful, that it was like someone sticking me with a pin; last night, she went on in the same breath, because she didn't want me to interrupt and say something hurtful, well, maybe it wasn't night yet, but pretty late, everybody had gone to bed, and Kálmán again climbed in through her window; just imagine, he must have been crouching under her window all that time until the lights were out; and he scared the life out of her, she had almost fallen asleep, and she couldn't even scream she was so terrified, and he was begging her right here by her bed that all he wanted was to sleep here for a little while, sleep by her side, nothing more, and she must believe him, would she please let him in; imagine waking up to somebody wanting to get into your bed with his cold feet; but she didn't let him in, she pushed him away, and Kálmán just cried and cried, so much that in the end she had to comfort him, rotten bastard! she had to promise that one day she'd let him in, except that she never will, never, did I understand? yes, she'd be a whore, but she'd never do it with him, never! still, she'd promised she would, but only to get the hell rid of him, because he kept crying and she wanted to be nice to him; she stroked his head and his face, while he held her hand and cried some more; she told him she'd scream if he dared get into her bed, and would he please stop kissing her hand, because she really hated that; and she wanted him to get lost, her hands were a mess, tears and snot, he was really bawling something awful, and she had to swear she loved him; she said she'd scream and then her father would come running and would beat him up, so he should be reasonable and leave like a good boy and then she would even love him a little.

And I felt as if my brain had been flooded by a hot surge of blood blotting out her voice, turning me deaf, peeling away her arms, sweeping away her whole body without a trace, and all the while the touch of her lips and her breath kept sending cold shivers through me, one shuddering wave after another.

Now that she'd confessed this whole thing to me, she said, because I had a way of forcing things out of her, she hoped I was satisfied.

But now I hated her as passionately as I hated Livia for not showing up, hated her for being Maja and not Livia, as much as she must have hated me in her bed the night before.

I know you kissed him, I said to her, and I heard my voice rising out of this hatred.

No, she didn't, and would I please stop tormenting her.

She couldn't possibly understand that at that moment I thought I was kissing Krisztián, because once again I wanted to be Maja kissing Szidónia on the mouth, I saw it, and I was being consumed by a terrible envy, because she led a more daring life, yes, and Szidónia kissed her back and at night Kálmán climbed into her bed; she squirmed in my arms, grateful for my assumed, definitely misunderstood, jealousy; but it wasn't Kálmán I was jealous of, it was her and Szidónia; I hated her for aping Szidónia so shamelessly; perhaps because I never imitated Krisztián so shamelessly I could never know what was true and what was false, never know whether good things are born of truth or falsehood, never know what was permitted and what was forbidden.

Just before I drowned in that dark abundant flood of blood, Livia's pale little face flashed before me again, or rather, her absence made me recall that March morning when I promised myself not to look at her anymore yet kept glancing at her even after Hédi Szán had begun to watch us, when it seemed that my stare made Livia teeter, crash through the ranks, and fall headlong to the polished gym floor; the girls started screaming, but nobody moved, we just kept watching her; then came the sound of pounding feet, people rushed in and quickly carried out her limp body, her feet in white socks dangling in the air.

It all happened so fast, we hardly had time to notice it, and then there was really no moving in the ranks, not a sound uttered, but this silence no longer had to do with the solemn ceremony.

And even if no one knew it, that gigantic eye did, knew it and saw it: I was the one who caused it all, I was the culprit.

What Maja told me, what I had supposedly forced out of her, didn't make me at all happy; on the contrary, I felt humiliated by her openness and thoughtless confession, and though the betrayal of their secret increased momentarily a sense of closeness with her and she was palpably in my arms, what I really wanted was to come between them, to oust the other boy, to squeeze him out, and in a way I did; I also wanted to know what it was that Kálmán did to her, hoping to learn from that what I should be doing, and further, to find out what was going on behind my back all the time! were those boys really as irresistible as they'd have me believe with their lewd chatter? the way they talked about girls always seemed false; and all Maja could convey now, with the desperate tones of her revelation and the heat of her coarseness breathed onto my neck, was that Kálmán, though in some ways more daring, loved her with the same hopeless devotion with which I loved Livia—trying to have her always in sight while she kept me bound to herself by permanent rejection; she was only toying with me, I was sure, and when the time came she would betray me—affecting an air of self-conscious, shameless superiority—to someone she didn't even much love; in my jealous rage, and it was choking me, I imagined that while I lay cozily with Maja in her bed, Livia was lying somewhere with Krisztián, talking about me.

It was as though Maja's mouth were whispering Livia's treacherous words into Krisztián's neck.

I told Maja she'd better be careful, her darling little Kálmán might be crying and all, but she ought to know better than to believe him; and I enjoyed hearing how soft and calm my voice sounded.

Just what did I mean? she asked.

Oh nothing, I said, nothing special, only she'd better be careful.

But why?

That I wouldn't tell her.

That wasn't nice of me, since she'd already told me everything.

She just shouldn't go into the woods tonight, that's all, I said.

But why not?

She shouldn't, that's all I can say, I said, I had my reasons.

Who was I to tell her what she should or shouldn't do? but she didn't say that, by now she was shouting, and she pushed me away.

My finger slipped out of her panties and I could finally free my arm, numbed by the weight of her body.

Of course she could do as she pleased, I said, I merely meant to caution her, because Kálmán had told me a thing or two which I wouldn't care to repeat just now.

We both sat up quickly and, without moving, began staring at each other, letting our looks do the wrestling; it was impossible to parry the dark sparks of her eyes, smoldering with hatred and indignation, and I didn't really want to. Our legs were still entwined, but her upper body, thrust toward me, was stiff and arched with fury, while mine stayed relaxed and apparently calm, because I meant to overcome her ferocious stare with the gentle superiority of treachery; at last I was master of the situation, or so I thought; I could finally vanquish, both in her and in myself, something that had long been tormenting me; true, my shrunken moral self whispered, it would take an act of base betrayal, but I could triumph! still, I was surprised by the sudden reversal in the situation; it made me falter, lose confidence, for what I had meant to divulge about Kálmán, moments earlier, in the heated intimacy of our closeness, what I'd hinted at so insidiously, slyly, as if I had nothing less than absolute knowledge of the facts, now, as we sat and looked at each other face to face, no longer seemed possible to say out loud; it had become hideous, unnatural, shrinking back into itself; in the ordinary light of that average-looking room of hers, I couldn't have told myself what it was: a momentary, careless flash of memory in the darkness of my own inner dialogue, a seemingly innocent image waiting to be revealed, one for which there were no words and which had quickly to be forgotten, the whole thing resembling the way my body deceived me then, in that situation; and today, when looking around from the high ground of my age and experience as I write these lines, it is with no small pleasure that I recall that very special, one might say fateful, early confusion of body and soul; I see this little boy, deceived by his soul and lured into a trap by his body, who only moments earlier, lying in the arms of a little girl, felt so strongly the blood rushing to his head and throbbing in his temples—what a strange coincidence that she was just then speaking of her bleeding!—but deafened by the bloody pounding of the little girl's words hadn't noticed, still wouldn't notice, that the process itself, the urge to dominate the other, the fevered struggle to gain true inner power as well as to overcome the true inner forces within him, had heated his blood and not only flooded his brain but just as strongly reached down to his groin; between the girl's lap and his own hand, his member stiffened, referring back to that sudden flash of an image he would have liked to blurt out as a clincher but simply couldn't bring himself to utter.

Then again, Maja didn't seem too eager for me to tell her anything.

But what? What did he tell you?

Our own forbidden games, the mere mention of the woods, the scene of Szidónia's adventures, was enough to give weight to my warning.

No, not that; don't! she seemed not so much to beg as shout at me; her eyes narrowed protectively, full of suspicion, hatred retreating into their brown depths.

Love wants no knowledge; her mouth opened.

And I did not answer, lest her glance stray between my legs; I tried to hold on to her eyes with mine, in case my pants showed what I was feeling.

What I was going to tell her about was Kálmán and me lying on that flat rock shielded by the bushes above and Kálmán doing what I, too, wanted to do, but didn't dare touch his until he touched mine; when my arm crossed his, reciprocating his move, and we were holding each other's—oddly enough my fingers did not feel his to be as hard as I felt mine in his hand, though they both seemed equally erect—that's when Kálmán said in a hoarse voice, and that's what I should have said out loud before, that one day he was going to screw Maja for sure.

That's what he said.

Then, trying to stall for time and to distract her from my own shame, I said that one day I would tell her, because I told her everything, but not now; and I was afraid she'd notice how red I was with shame.

But I knew I could never ever tell her about that.

It wasn't fear of disgrace that held me back; to push him out and take his place I'd have felt myself capable of any disgraceful act.

If somehow I had been able to lift that sentence from the situation in which it was uttered, if only Kálmán's hand hadn't been clinging to my member, if only I hadn't felt in it the heat of that white rock; but by revealing Kálmán's secret intention to her, I would have exposed my own falseness.

I could not remove myself from the context of that sentence, could not tear myself away from him, because his sentence referred not so much to Maja as to him and me.

And I couldn't tell her about that, because our physical contact was not the overture but rather the concluding movement, the closure, last stop, in our relationship, the furthermost point two boys might dare to venture in a realm off limits to girls, indeed a forbidden zone within that realm beyond which even boys must not go; and it is a credit to Kálmán's wonderful and accurately functioning instincts that at this terminal point of this perilous zone not only did he dare hold on to his innermost desire, which was to ascertain that another boy's body felt as his own body did and felt it the same way, but also, with his characteristic bravado, he linked the act of touching another boy with the ungratifiable desire he felt for a girl, turning the unsatisfiable into satisfiable, another's pleasure into his own; it was his way of placing side by side two secret realms revolving within each other that could never really unite.

What he said he might do to Maja was more like an apology for what the two of us were doing at that moment.

And also an obvious allusion to what Szidónia had tried to do with him, which he had already told me about.

We should not be appalled at this; we all know from other, more mundane aspects of our lives that to endure the terrible solitude of being different we seek solace and support in what makes us the same as others.

Girls also have their own separate realm we can only spy on, sniff around, circle the borders of, or, as secret agents, penetrate and even learn about some of its important areas, but the inner sanctum, that secret zone, must forever remain hidden.

The only way I could have told her everything was, of course, if I had been a girl, if as a girl, I could have spied on myself and that other boy, watching "them" with the unknowing, trusting eyes of a girl; and since I wanted so very much to be a girl, it seemed that only a thin, translucent membrane separated me from being a girl, or rather from being also a girl; I had an overwhelming desire to break through, work my way through, this thin membrane, for I hoped that then I'd reach the light of a world without shadows or falseness, find myself in an idyllic clearing; consequently, the way I wanted to identify with Maja—to turn into a girl, in other words—was by betraying my boyness; but since I could not tell her that story about me and Kálmán, I could not become the spy of that other realm—and she wouldn't want me to be one—my silence and my shame thrust me back among the boys.

A not insignificant detail of our emotional life was the fact that, as a result of our parents' political trustworthiness, we were privileged to live adjacent to the immense, heavily guarded area that contained the residence of Mátyás Rákosi.

When coming home from Maja's house, I often chose not to walk along the wire fence of the huge tract of land where everything was ominously silent—nobody used this street, which, nicely shaded by foliage spilling over the fence, actually cut the forest in half—and the air itself stood still and the only thing you heard was the crunch of your own footsteps; the armed guards were nowhere to be seen, although we knew well they could see everything from their underground bunkers or observation points camouflaged by trees and shrubs; none of our movements went undetected; with their periscopes and telescopes they could follow me, bring me up close, or accompany me on the street; if to shorten the trek home I did take this street instead of walking through the woods, I felt these watching eyes very strongly; more precisely, it was not their watchfulness I felt, I'm not sure one can actually feel that, but somehow my own watchfulness was redoubled because of their presumed presence; I saw

myself unsuspectingly walking along the street, taking in what my unsuspecting eyes were taking in, and at the same time I was watching
suspiciously, along with the unseen guards, my own suspiciousness
wrapped in an unsuspecting nonchalance; this was similar to what I felt
when something disappeared in school and in the awful atmosphere of
general suspicion I felt that I was the thief! but on this street the unseen
guards made me feel as if I were an assassin or a spy unable to conceal
his real intent, and I felt how this strain, this exercise of historical proportions in watching oneself being watched, made my skin crawl every
time, I felt it distinctly on my back, my arms, my neck; I walked on this
street as if expecting a shot to ring out at any moment, I knew I mustn't
get too close to the fence, this ordinary-looking, somewhat rusty wire
fence, and I was terribly afraid of the dogs, which I dreaded even more
than the gimlet-eyed guards.

And it wasn't just we children who were terrified of these huge watchdogs but the grownups, too, and regular, civilian dogs like Vitéz, Kálmán's
otherwise formidably aggressive black dog, whom we simply couldn't
sweet-talk into coming out of the woods and onto that road; if we tied a
rope around his neck and tried dragging him along, hoping they'd go at
each other and we'd see a horrific, bloody fight to the death, he would
crouch, flatten himself against the ground, stricken with terror, the hair
on his spine would stand on edge, he'd whimper, yelp, and no amount
of yanking, pushing, dragging, teasing, or coaxing could arouse his fighting spirit; in the meantime, from the other side of the fence, those enormous beasts would regard our clumsy efforts with stony indifference.

And because of this—though my mind did comprehend the need for
these dogs—the whole protected area became something like a focal point,
the living nucleus of all my fears.

The untouched forest on that side of the fence seemed exactly like the
peacefully silent oak forest on this side, the real, free forest, our forest; it
seemed exactly what a forest ought to be, with dried and broken branches,
wind-torn treetops adorned with clumps of mistletoe, toppled tree trunks,
broken roots sticking out of the gritty soil, nearly ossified giant lips of
tinder fungus thriving on decay, deep dark hollows everywhere, shimmering cushions of moss, tender saplings, slender and delicate, burgeoning
under the protection of ruffled groups of ancient but healthy oaks;
horsetail and fern spinning out from beneath soft, century-old layers of
fallen leaves; ephemeral green undergrowth in spots warmed by sun rays
slashing through the foliage; the purple crest of corydalis fluttering in the

breeze along with blue bunches of fragrant grape hyacinths; the white umbrellas of the poison hemlock rocking on high, jagged petals wide-open now; yellow blades of meadow grass and bluish-green wild quick grass; the shiny-leafed marsh marigolds in damp crevices; in the shadow of craggy rocks the waxy-green cyclamen that never bloom in these parts; in the sunny spots, fuzzy leaves of wild strawberry, and tiny bell-shaped flowers on the thick stalks of Solomon's seals, peeking and nodding between the ribbed leaves; oh, and the shrubs around the big oak trees, the hawthorn that can thicken into a tree when it has enough room to grow, the hearty spindleberry bushes, and, most of all, sprouting and climbing in the impenetrable prickly thicket, lots of dewberry vines producing by autumn their pleasantly tart fruit—and still! in spite of all this, the practiced eye could tell immediately that on the other side of the street, behind the wire fence, it was not the same forest; no twisted and toppled tree trunks there, torn and fallen branches were carefully removed by busy hands, perhaps after dusk, when one can still see a little in the afterglow of the opaque sky, or stealthily at early dawn, because I never saw anyone work there, in fact I never saw a human figure there at all; the bushes grew more sparsely and had been thinned out, and since fewer leaves fell at summer's end, the grass could grow taller and in wider patches; in short, this was a carefully tended forest designed to appear wild to unsuspecting observers; I never understood why, since the deception was obvious, given the two-meter-wide strip of land along the fence cleared of all living growth, with overturned soil covered with fine white sand, and on the surface of the sand traces of the same secret gardeners' handiwork, grooves left by the teeth of rakes, and it was also in this strip that the watchdogs made their appearance.

When I turned off Istenhegyi Road and started up the gently rising slope of Adonisz Road, it didn't matter if I crossed over to the other side and never took my eyes off the silent bushes behind the fence, I could never be alert enough to see them appear; they materialized out of nowhere, silently and unnoticed, one at a time; I knew they rotated the dogs on and off duty as they did the unseen guards, powerfully built, well-fed German shepherds with darkly spotted, sand-colored, sometimes grayish fur, and tapered shaggy tails, the eyes in their projecting muzzles appearing benign and wise, pointed, acutely sensitive ears registering the slightest vibrations of hostility, mouths nearly always open, with fleshy glistening red tongues sliding up and down to the rhythm of their constant panting, revealing the white cusps of fang-like back teeth; and all they did was follow me, faster when I quickened my steps, slower when I slowed down, of course making not the slightest noise, their huge pads sinking silently into the sand; and I had long ceased to experiment with stopping, because if I did they'd stop, too, turn their snouts toward me and just watch; their look, their eyes, were the most terrifying things about them—excited, keyed-up, yet completely impassive, eyes like two pretty balls, and at the same time you could see that under their thick fur the muscles were wound up like coils, ready to spring; and not only did they not emit a sound—no yelp or growl—they didn't even pant harder; Kálmán learned from Pista, because Pista was a guard on the far side of the restricted area, at the Lóránt Street gate, and he not only talked to Kálmán sometimes but also let him have some of his hollow-filtered Russian cigarettes, which they ended up smoking in the school bathroom during the long morning recess; anyway, it was Pista who said that this was when the dogs were most dangerous, and one should never take one's eyes off them; it didn't matter that they had been trained for any eventuality, in fact, the more rigorous their training, so the trainers had said, the more unpredictable their nervous system would become; they knew and understood everything, Kálmán reported, but were nervous wrecks, the trainers themselves feared them; they had muscles of steel, that's the phrase he used, muscles of steel, and they could hurdle a not-too-high fence like that from a standing position, which was the reason there was no barbed wire on top; supposedly the trainers asked that the barbed wire be removed because the dogs' tails might get caught; their commander refused at first, it seems, claiming that without the barbed wire the fence would not conform to regulations, and finally Comrade Rákosi had to intervene personally, because the dogs were extremely valuable; even within the compound they were led about on leashes, and it was impossible to befriend them; they would not accept food or candy from anyone, wouldn't even sniff at it, it was as though you weren't there, they looked right through you; and if anyone tried to provoke them by kicking the fence, something that would make any other dog go crazy, they would simply bare their teeth as a warning; they were trained not to get riled up needlessly; when they made a mistake, however, they were beaten mercilessly with sticks and leather straps; if you did nothing but look into their eyes, without moving, they wouldn't know what was happening or how to react, and that's when you could see they were nervous wrecks; they might be beaten for jumping unnecessarily, but they couldn't always control themselves and they'd jump, catch their victim from behind, go straight for the nape of the neck; so they kept following me—to be more precise, after a few steps abreast of one another, it seemed I was following them; they were trotting on their sandy strip one step ahead of me; at the top of the incline we came to a sudden turn, the fence also followed the curve of the road, and there began a long, straight stretch; with their tails up, the dogs led the way, and if I behaved, that is to say if I didn't hurry or fall behind, if fear did not make me break into a run—that wouldn't have been a good solution, since on that straight stretch past the turn I would have had to race for about three hundred meters accompanied by the dogs' frightful barking—if in spite of all my shame and humiliation, hatred and urge to rebel, I complied with their demands, if I did not stop, run, slow down, or speed up, and was even careful not to breathe too loudly, and if I managed to suppress any gestures and emotions they might construe as obtrusive, just as they tried to curb their nervousness and, as a result, the tension of our mutual suspicion became stabilized, then, after a while, our relationship became more refined, not so threatening: I did what I was expected to do, and the dog, becoming almost indifferent to me, did what it was supposed to do; but if coming from Maja's place I wasn't in the mood, or wasn't mentally prepared, to play this game—for it was a game after all, a kind of experiment, a not altogether harmless balancing act at the edge of self-control and dependence, self-discipline and independence, a sort of political gymnastics—then I chose the shorter and in many ways more pleasant route, right near the three tall pines, the very landmark Szidónia had mentioned to the streetcar conductor, I would take the forest trail and would peer back at the canine guard on duty from behind the safety of the dense shrubbery, noting with considerable satisfaction the perplexed and disappointed look on its face as it stared after me; I was quickly concealed by the woods, though I knew the guards' binoculars could follow me even here; the trail rose sharply as I moved farther in; at times I chose this path even after dusk, knowing well that there might be darker, not to say more ominous dangers lurking in wait for me there, yet I felt I could cope with these dangers more easily and confidently than I could with those rotten dogs.

At that time this was still a real forest, perhaps the last large, continuous spot of green on the map of hills and mountains ringing the city, the last reminder of the original natural harmony of soil and flora which the expanding city slowly encroached upon, altered, and devoured; today, this area, too, is full of high-rises; of the forest only a few clumps of trees have remained—hardly more than nondescript garden ornaments.

I do not regret the loss; there's nothing in the world with which I have a more intimate relationship than ruination; I am the chronicler of my own ruination; even now, when making public the destruction of the forest, I'm recounting the history of my own destruction, looking back once more, for the last time, and I confess not without emotion, on the seemingly endless yet so very finite time of childhood, a time when nothing appears more unalterable than the richly grooved bark of a luxuriant old tree, the peculiar twists of its roots, the communicated strength with which the tree accommodates and also clings to the soil; in a way, childhood perceptions have no firmer assurance and support than nature itself, in which everything militates against destruction and destruction itself speaks of permanence, impersonality, continuity.

But I don't wish to weary anyone with too finely drawn reflections on the relationship between a child's arbitrary perceptions and the spontaneous life of nature; I believe it is true that nature is our greatest teacher, but it teaches only the wise among us, never the dullards! so let us continue on that lonely forest trail leading to the clearing, and let us also take a closer look at how the child is walking, relying on the profound knowledge in his feet, familiar with every dip and bump of the ground, even with the stone that in the next second might knock against the tip of his shoe, prompting him to stretch out his next step; familiar with the dense air, and the direction of wayward breezes against his face, his sensitive nose telling him if anyone has passed by recently and whether it was a man or woman; only his ears deceive him once in a while: he hears a muffled sound, a crack, a thud, a cry, something resembling a cough, and he stops; to be able to go on, his eyes must skip over his fears, over frightening presentiments, and, at times, over shadows that seem to be moving; yes, he must step over dire warnings and horrific imaginings.

Then the trail melts into the tall grass of the clearing, his bare feet are anointed with dew, now he is accompanied by soft rustles and whirs, the summer sky is still glimmering above him, but except for him nothing appears to be moving, and that seems unreal to him; then a bat flits by silently, returns to circle above him, but he's reached the upper end of the clearing and stepped back in the woods where the trail continues, now branching off into two, and he can go on up the hill.

At the top, an abandoned road marks the end of the forest, and Felhő Street is only a few steps away, and that's where Hédi lives, in a small yellow house opposite the now darkened school building; at this hour Mrs. Hűvös closes the curtains and is ready to turn on the lights.

From Hédi's window you can see Livia's.

This time, though, at the fork I took the other trail.

No matter how late I got home, no one ever asked where I had been.

The forest was not so dense here, I could make out the ridged roof of the Csúzdi house; the feeble rays of the porch light projected long pale spots and strips into the dark forest; the effect was friendly, reassuring, revealing something about the attractive solitude of the house; and taking this route home I could be almost sure to find Kálmán still outside.

I was still far away, but his black dog already yelped into the silence.

The house stood in the middle of a rectangular piece of land cut out of the forest, with a cornfield in the back and a large orchard in front; they called it a farm—an impressive, very old frame house whose simple front, in the manner of the building style favored by the original owners, ethnic German wine growers, was adorned by a raised open porch, protected by the overhanging gabled roof; under the porch a heavy double door opened to the wine cellar; at the other end of the spacious yet intimate brick-paved yard a similar but lower frame house served as stable, garage, and barn; in the middle of the yard, enclosed by a simple hedgerow, stood a large walnut tree and, a little farther on, a tall, hard, tightly packed haystack; it all seems incredible today, but back then, on the rocky and clayey slopes of Swabian Hill, this low mountain so close to the city, there were still these peasant homesteads, cut off from the world, living out the last phases of their existence.

Lazily, Kálmán's dog came down to the hedgerow to greet me, not barking or jumping up on me as it usually did, staring absentmindedly, with occasional swipes of its tail, waiting for me and, as if to signal that something unusual was afoot, leading me across the yard, ambling pensively.

It was warmer here; stones were exhaling the sun's warmth and the dense hedgerow kept the cool forest air from penetrating the yard.

At the time the Csúzdis still had a horse, several pigs, two cows, some chickens and geese; the dovecote over the hayloft echoed with the cooing of turtledoves; one after another, a pair of swallows alternately nose-dived out of their nest built under the eaves, one flying out as the other headed homeward; around this time, at dusk, the yard resounded with the noise of animals, seeking calm and rest as they prepared for the night, and the warm, still air was filled with the powerful smell of urine, droppings, and fermenting manure.

Surprised, I followed the dog, and soon saw the yellow light of a kerosene lamp, which seemed strange in the bluish twilight; Kálmán was standing in the open door of the pigpen, watching something intently, something the raised lamp lit up in the dark.

The flame flickered and smoked under the glass, its yellow light licking Kálmán's bare arms, back, and neck.

From early spring until late autumn, as soon as he got home from school, Kálmán would kick off his shoes, pull off his shirt and trousers, and lounge about in his long johns all day, and as I had occasion to observe, he also slept in them.

A deep rattling sound was coming from inside the pigpen, which soon rose into a high squeal, suddenly stopped short, and after a brief pause reverted to a deep-throated rattle.

But he didn't look funny in his black long johns, his strong legs and muscular buttocks filling them out completely, the creases and folds of the fabric, faded into gray from washing, hugging his large body and accommodating all its possible moves, stretching over his stomach, bulging around his crotch, fitting itself to him like a second skin, making him look naked.

The dog stopped listlessly in front of the pen, wagged its tail, and then, as if it had changed its mind, decided to get behind Kálmán and settle down there on its hind legs as it let out a somewhat nervous yawn. ·

In a stall separated from the other pigs, a huge sow was lying on her side; Kálmán had raised the lamp so high that the light was partly cut off by the door frame, and at first all I saw were her teats sprawled on the sloshy floor and her rump turned in our direction—the sounds were coming from the darkness.

I wanted to ask what was happening but decided not to.

Certain questions one had better not ask Kálmán; he wouldn't answer them.

He must have been standing there for a long time, that's why he was resting his forehead on the door beam, staring into the pen, motionless, almost indifferently, but I knew him well enough to recognize this look as a sign of tension near the breaking point, if not the point of explosion.

And as I stood next to him and watched what he was watching, the sow's eyes and open snout began to emerge from the dimness; we listened to her rattling, the sudden breaks in her breathing, the whistling of her narrowing and expanding nostrils that became a sharp squeal; and all this time she was trying to stand up, though her short, thrashing legs seemed unable to find the ground, as if a great force were holding her back; her thick skin rippled helplessly over the heavy layers of fat on her foundering body; contradictory impulses made all her muscles twitch at once; then suddenly, without even looking at me, Kálmán thrust the lamp into my hand and climbed into the stall.

I tried to hold the lamp straight; the glass cover was hot, and if the kerosene sloshed a little over the wick, the lamp started to smoke and the flame blackened.

Kálmán must have been afraid a little, because he flattened himself against the partition of the pen, ready for any eventuality.

Maybe he was scared the sow would get angry and bite him.

But then he grabbed hold of the pig's head, at the base of her ears, scratching her, trying to calm her, and though the animal gave an angry grunt, he managed slyly to keep her head flat against the floor, so that with his other hand he could explore, and not too gently either, the mountainous belly and sunken hollow of her flank; to this she responded with expectant silence.

And then he made another curious move—until then I hadn't noticed that under the darkly wrinkled anus, her fully dilated vaginal cleft, like a huge multilayered set of pink lips, spilled out of her body and hung, swollen, clean, firm, silky, and smooth, over her rump streaked with feces and urine; Kálmán now passed his finger ever so carefully over this live, burning crater of flesh, and the responding quiver of her rump was just as delicate as his touch had been, but then he quickly backed out of the stall and obliviously wiped his finger on his thigh.

The animal seemed to be looking straight at us.

Impatiently Kálmán grabbed the lamp from me; the pig's watchful eye dissolved in the darkness, she was quiet for a few seconds, all we could hear were the restless grunts and stomping feet of the other animals in the adjacent stall; and once again Kálmán leaned his forehead against the splintery beam.

It's been an hour, her waters broke at least an hour ago, he said.

It would have been silly to ask what waters.

And they left her here, just upped and left, he said, the words erupting with such force that the lamp began to shake in his hand, the glass knocking against the door beam, and he cried out again, desperately, but his body remained stiff, the tension wouldn't let the tears come, he tried to swallow but choked; they left her here alone, he repeated a third time, even though they knew, they knew and still they left, the bastards.

The sow's rump twitched on the slick floorboard, her head fell back and flip-flopped, then slipped along the floor, because she kept opening her mouth as if gasping for air, and it was horrible to hear no sound issuing from her despite the cramped straining.

Something was happening inside her that was not ending.

He must get his father.

Kálmán's father and his two much older brothers were bakers; the bakery where they worked used to belong to them, so Kálmán, being the son of a former property owner, was considered a "class alien," as was Krisztián; the men would leave in the afternoon to prepare the dough and light the ovens, and return early the next morning, after the bread had all been baked and delivered; his mother also left the house after the two cows had come back from the pasture and she had milked them; she had a night job cleaning wards at János Hospital.

So we were both free; no one at home ever asked me where I was off to, and Kálmán was left alone every night.

At our feet, the dog was switching its tail and whimpering quietly.

Kálmán shoved the lamp into my hand again, and he seemed hesitant—I thought he was going to run for help, after all, which would have meant leaving me there, alone and helpless, with this horrible thing; I would have liked to say, You stay here, I'll go—or just go without saying anything—but now the pig was slipping and sliding so quietly that Kálmán decided to climb in again.

I moved closer, to give him more light; I wanted to do it right, though I had no idea what he could possibly do, or whether he knew what one was supposed to do in a situation like this; but somehow I trusted him, he'd know what to do, even if at the moment he looked as though he didn't—when it came to plants and animals, he knew everything; to me the sight was so incomprehensible, the feelings it aroused so confusing, and the suffering (which, because of our helplessness, immediately became our own suffering) so overwhelming, giving us neither time nor strength to escape, that I was grateful to him for not leaving me there, for trying to do something, in a way doing it for me, so that all I had to do was hold that lamp straight.

He crouched behind the animal's rump and for long seconds did nothing.

In the stench and stifling heat it was getting harder and harder to breathe, but that didn't bother me then, because I sensed the presence of death, though I knew I was witnessing birth.

And then he slowly lifted one of his hands, raised it from his lap, oddly, tentatively, with a pensive look on his face, his fingers loosely crooked, and slipped the hand through the thick folds of those swollen rosy lips; I could see his hand disappear up to his wrist.

This made the animal twitch, and she was finally able to breathe; when the next contraction wrenched her body, the sound she emitted was not so much a rattling as a retching one; she was kicking and slobbering, and snapping her teeth, as if ready to bite Kálmán.

He yanked his hand free, but could not get away while still crouching, I was blocking his way, standing with the lamp in the narrow doorway, too scared to jump back quickly; he plopped down on his butt, right into the muck.

But the pig dropped her head back, her mouth still open, hawking and gasping in irregular bursts, snapping at the precious air, and from below bristled lashes, her light-brown eyes seemed to be fixed on Kálmán.

I could feel the even panting of the dog on my leg.

As the sow lay there, looking at Kálmán, I saw that the whites of her eyes, bulging almost completely out of their sockets, were all bloody.

By then Kálmán wasn't trying to figure out what to do—he was also watching those eyes—he got on his knees, sank his hand again into the animal's body, and as he slowly penetrated farther, paying no attention to slipping and sliding in urine and shit, he laid his body on the animal's swollen side, pressing down with his full weight; they were looking at each other all the while and breathing together, because as he pressed down, the animal exhaled smoothly, and when he lifted his body slightly, she inhaled helpfully; his arm was inside her, up to his elbow, but then, as though hit by an electric shock, he jerked out his hand and, his whole body shaking violently, he began to yell at the top of his voice.

He was yelling something but I couldn't understand what; I heard him yelling words but couldn't make them out.

The sow squealed, slid farther on her rump, gasped for air, her feet stuck out, stiff, and she squealed again, so shrilly, so long, and so loud it sounded like a human scream; she writhed, then stiffened again, but some-how her body preserved—more precisely, it refined—the rhythm the two of them had found before; and not for a second did she take her eyes off Kálmán, she remained fully alert, and his eyes were also glued to hers, even as he raised his soaked, gooey arm, illuminated by the lamp, and held it before him as if it were some strange object, and just as abruptly as he had started yelling moments before, he now fell silent; if I were to say the sow's eyes were pleading for help, if I said she was begging him to do something and was also guiding him toward that goal, if I said she was grateful to him and urging him on, with her willingness reassuring him that Yes! Yes, we're on the right track, let's keep going! then with my sentimental human notions I'd be defiling that direct raw but by no means brute sensual power that I suppose only an animal's eyes can convey.

The pig responded to his screams with squeals of her own, and he answered her silence with silence.

In spite of being apart now, they stayed together.

The depth of the open vaginal orifice was frothing and bubbling with spasms and thrusts whose rhythmic repetition was like breathing or the beating of a heart.

He reached in again, back to the very spot that had made him recoil before, but this time matter-of-factly, the way we return to familiar places when necessity compels us.

Simultaneously he turned his head away from the sow in my direction, but he closed his eyes.

The animal was quiet now, as if to oblige him by holding her breath.

It seemed he kept his eyes closed because he was doing something inside and did not want to see anything, the better to feel what he was supposed to do.

And then he pulled out his hand, slowly, wearily, got on his knees; his head slumped forward and I couldn't see his face.

It was still quiet, the animal lay motionless, but then, as a delayed response to his manipulation, her side began to undulate, then her whole body was moving in waves from the pressure and the gasping, and at the end of each spasm she let out an alarming squeal that died away in the stifling stench of the narrow pen.

She won't make it, he said, she can't do it, he said quietly, as one who could not be moved even by this undulating suffering because he already saw what lay ahead, he could see all the way to death; and though he did not move away, he stayed put, there was nothing for him to do.

But whatever was happening in the animal's body was far from over.

For in the next instant something red appeared in the heaving folds of that slit, and he, shrieking and wailing like the pig, jumped to grab it; immediately he fell silent, because that something, as if a strange bone had gotten into the sow's flesh, slipped out of his fingers; he grabbed it again, and again it slipped out.

The rag, he screamed, and this was meant for me, yet I felt that a very long time, important and precious time, went by until I grasped that there must be a rag here somewhere.

A sudden paralysis, a grievous failing at this moment, might keep me from finding the rag.

There was no rag.

It was as if suddenly I had no idea what a rag was, had lost the meaning of the word, in my own language! and in the meantime that thing—Get me a rag!—slipped out of his hand again.

He was howling at me.

And then the lamp's glass cover almost tipped over; I was going to look outside, and the lamp accidentally knocked against the door beam, and in fact the rag was there, I could see it, the dog was beating it with his tail, but I had to catch the glass first.

It didn't break—what an accomplishment! a victory I haven't experienced since!—and I could make a grab for the rag, too.

Two tiny cloven hooves were sticking out.

He wrapped the rag around them and pulled; he slowly backed away, still squatting, while the pig pushed and squealed.

It's the struggle that is long, the event itself unnoticed.

The little body slipped out so smoothly that Kálmán, still squatting, couldn't retreat fast enough; he plopped down on his butt, and between his spread legs there it was: the palely glistening lifeless body of the newborn, inside the glassy sac resting on the filthy floor.

I think all three of us stopped breathing.

The mother was the first to move, I think; she lifted her head as if wanting to see for herself, to make sure the thing had indeed happened, but she sank back from sheer exhaustion, though just as her head hit the floor some new excitement of elemental force coursed through her body, a happy force, because it made her nimble, adroit, quick, resilient, and inventive—which one would never have expected from such a large ungainly animal; she managed to shift her weight and turn over slightly, the long umbilical cord allowing for the movement, so that the piglet still between Kálmán's legs hardly stirred; grunting and snorting jubilantly, she leaned closer, sniffed her baby, trembled with joy at recognizing its smell, and then with two sharp snaps bit through the cord; while Kálmán maneuvered his way out of the pen, sliding clumsily on the seat of his pants, the sow got up, sprang up really, and began licking and prancing around the little body, grunting as she impatiently prodded it, poked it, lapped it up almost, until it finally began to breathe.

When about an hour later we shut the pigpen door and the wooden bolt slid quietly home, there were four piglets sucking on their mother's hot, milk-filled, purple-red teats.

The summer night was silent, dark, and full of stars.

The dog followed us.

Kálmán went to the back, dropped his pants, and took a long leak.

I was alone in the middle of the yard, with only the dog standing next to me.

There, in the manure pile, Kálmán also buried the afterbirth.

There was nothing left for us to say, and I felt that we would never need to say anything to each other again.

It was more than enough that I could stand there while he relieved himself, listening to the long, cascading sounds of his rich stream.

Because when the first of the litter was already out and he quickly got out of the stall, and I stepped aside, raising the lamp high, there was a single moment when our eyes locked, and while our movements crossed, our looks were caught up in the sameness of pure bliss, and that moment grew so long, became so intense, that real time seemed to have slipped away, as if everything that had still remained trapped in us from the struggle could break free only in our sudden oneness; it was the insanity of a grin that the lamp was illuminating: our faces were very close, his eyes vanished in the grin, I could see only his mouth and teeth, his sharply protruding jaw, his drenched hair matted on his forehead, and the sudden appearance of his face so close to mine made me realize that this face was a double of my own, because I was also grinning to myself with the same eager, insane grin, and it seemed that the only way we could break out of the frozen time of our grin and truly enter our oneness was if we were to fall on each other.

If for the sake of this oneness we would love each other.

And it still wouldn't have been enough; even with that we couldn't have measured up to the pig's victory.

Instead, we broke into a dialogue.

Into the laughter of words.

I almost broke the glass, I said; the little thing must have been lying in the wrong position, he said; and I asked him why he started yelling like that, what the hell was he yelling about; his father couldn't have done it better, he said; first I thought the pig was only sick, I said, and it was lucky about the umbilical cord, and I didn't know where the rag was; that was one smart pig, he said.

The dog was running about the yard, yelping and running, round and round it kept running in ever widening circles, which was also part of the same kind of conversation.

The porch lamp shed a sober light on us.

In a daze, exhausted, we made our way slowly up the steps.

Water was still steaming in a pot; while waiting for the afterbirth to come out, I had put it on so he could wash the pig's teats in warm water.

He went to the table, pulled out a chair, and sat down.

First I looked at the things in the kitchen: the white enamel stove, the apple-green cabinets, and the pink eiderdown on a narrow cot, then I put the kerosene lamp on the table; because we left the door behind us open, there was a slight draft and the lamp was giving out more smoke than light; then I also sat down.

There we were, just sitting and staring into space.

God's prick, he said quietly after a while.

We weren't looking at each other, but I felt he didn't want me to go yet, and I didn't want to leave.

And his swearing, sounding like someone making quiet amends, was addressed to me.

Kálmán seldom cursed and, unlike the other boys, rarely used foul language; I can recall only two other instances—when he talked about Maja, saying what he would do to her, and the thing he'd told me in the school bathroom.

That I could eat Prém's prick for lunch.

That last one remained with me like a stinging insult, like a wound that wouldn't heal; I forgot it, but could not forgive it.

By blurting out that seemingly harmless obscenity, he joined forces with Krisztián and Prém, but could he have done otherwise? no matter how much it hurt, I couldn't really blame him, for I sensed in his act the permanent and in many ways exciting uncertainty inherent in all human relationships; for it seemed to be the way of the world, or maybe the spirit of our times, that you could never tell your friends and foes apart, and in the final analysis everybody had to be considered an enemy; it was enough to recall the fear and hatred I felt while passing by the fence of that restricted area with the dogs to make me realize I had no idea where I myself belonged; and there was the pain of knowing that because of my father's position the other boys labeled me a stool pigeon even though I had never betrayed anyone; but Kálmán, by allowing himself to join the other boys with that statement, betrayed the deepest secret of our friendship—even if the others could not have known what he meant when he'd said I could eat Prém's for lunch, couldn't have known what he was alluding to, but still! as if he had said in front of all of them, which was more than shameless betrayal, that I'd once held his in my hand; he said it as though I had no other wish in the world than to eat it for lunch! as though what had happened between us hadn't been by mutual consent, as though he hadn't himself initiated it.

He got up, kicked the chair out from under him, and took a bottle of brandy and two glasses from the kitchen cabinet.

He denied the act with the same unthinking courage that he'd displayed when his hand had reached toward me that time.

To avoid embarrassing himself in front of the others, he renounced his own most intimate gesture; but now, as if trying to make up for his betrayal by those swear words, he seemed to be thanking me for being here.

Which released such a flood of emotion that the less said about it the better.

And I could not tell any of this to Maja, just as I could not talk about girls while resting my head on my mother's arm.

Without a word, the two of us got drunk on the brandy.

If one could learn the most important things in life, one would still have to learn how to keep quiet about them.

We sat there for a very long time, staring drunkenly at the kitchen table, and for some reason, after his swearing, we didn't look into each other's eyes anymore.

Even though those words cleared up everything, for a lifetime; above all, they spoke of ultimate loyalty, of how no one could ever forget anything.

He started fidgeting with the lamp, trying to put it out, but though he lowered the wick the flame would not go out, it only started smoking even more; and then he took off the glass cover so he could blow out the flame, and while he was blowing it—he had to make several attempts and he started laughing because he couldn't hit the flame, always blowing next to it—the hot, smoke-darkened glass slipped out of his hand, fell, and broke on the kitchen floor.

He didn't even look down.

It felt good to hear the sound of breaking glass shattering into a thousand pieces.

Later, it seemed to me I was quite alert as I drifted into this pleasant state of feeling good, or as I simply got lost among my own thoughts, though I couldn't have said what I was thinking about or whether I was thinking at all; the feeling of sensations dulled by drunkenness had become this state of thinking without thoughts, and I didn't notice that at one point he got up, put a large wash bucket on the floor, and poured the leftover hot water into it.

The image wasn't blurred, only distant and uninteresting.

And he simply kept pouring the water.

I'd have liked to tell him to stop pouring, enough.

Because I didn't notice that he was now pouring some other water into the bucket.

From a pail.

And I also failed to notice when he threw off his long johns and stood stark naked in the wash bucket; the wet soap slipped out of his hand and scooted under the kitchen cabinet.

He asked me for the soap.

I could hear in his voice that he was also drunk, which should have made me laugh, except I couldn't get up.

The water splashed and sloshed, and by the time I managed to get up he was already scrubbing himself.

His wasn't nearly as large as a horse's, but rather small, solid, and thick; it always stuck out, overlapping his balls, pushing out his pants; he was busy soaping it now.

I was already on my feet, and realized it hurt, really hurt, that I'd never know whose friend I really was.

I don't know how I made it from the table to the wash bucket, the decision must have carried me unnoticed over the time necessary for the trip; I was standing before him, motioning to him to give me the soap.

This closeness, past love's passion, was the kind I had longed for with Krisztián, this nearly neutral feeling of brotherhood which I had never managed to reach with him and which is as natural as seeing, smelling, or breathing—the genderless grace of human affection; and perhaps it's no exaggeration to speak of the warmest gratitude here, yes, I was grateful and humble, because I got from Kálmán what I could never hope to get from the other, and what's more, I didn't need to humiliate myself or be grateful to him; gratitude was just there all by itself, simply because he was there, the way he was, and I was there, just the way I was.

He looked at me hesitantly, tilting his head a little, trying to look into my eyes, but could not catch my glance, yet he understood me immediately, because he thrust the soap into my hand and crouched down in the wash bucket.

I wet his back and began scrubbing it carefully, I didn't want it to be dirty.

I knew the only reason Prém said that idiotic thing was because his was so big; Krisztián sometimes asked him to show it to us and we would stare at it, laughing with pleasure at the possibility that it could be so big.

I was indescribably happy that Kálmán was my friend, after all.

I got a whiff of the pigpen's smell rising from his sudsy back; I had to rinse him really well.

And the only reason Prém had said what he said was to stop Kálmán from getting close to me, to make sure he remained their friend.

But the soap slipped into the bucket, sank, and disappeared between his spread legs.

That minute I hated Prém so much, I just had to go outside for a breath of fresh air.

My foot felt something soft.

I hated him so much that I felt ill.

It was the dog, sprawled out on the porch and sleeping peacefully.

My hands were still soapy.

I was lying on the ground, and someone must have turned off the light, because it was dark.

The stars had disappeared, the muggy night was silent.

For a long time I thought I should be going home now; go home; I could think of nothing else.

But in the distance the sky flared up with lightning, followed by sounds of rolling thunder.

And then my legs were carrying me, my head was pulling me, my feet felt a path that was leading to some unknown destination.

As the rumbling thunder brought the flashes of lightning closer, the air itself swirled and thickened, the wind howled into the tree crowns.

Only when my mouth felt something hard and cool, the taste of rust, only then did I realize that I'd gotten home: below, among the trees I could see the familiar windows all lit up, and this, then, must be the gate, its iron hinge must be in my mouth.

It was like entering a place that was already familiar for the first time, as if I had seen before what now seemed so strange.

I had to look well to see where I really was.

In the cool of the gathering wind, large warm raindrops began to fall, stopped, then started again.

I lay there for a while, in the light under the window, and wished that no one would ever find me.

I kept watching flashes of lightning slide down the wall.

I didn't want to go inside, because I loathed this house, yet it had to be the one and only place for me.

Even today, while attempting to recall the past with as precise and impartial perspective as possible, I find it difficult to speak objectively of this house where people living under the same roof grew so far apart, were so consumed by their own physical and moral disintegration, were left to fend for themselves, and only for themselves, that they did not notice, or pretended not to notice, when someone was missing, their own child, from the so-called family nest.

Why didn't they notice?

I must have been so totally unmissed by everyone that I didn't realize I was living in a hell of being absent, thinking this hell to be the world.

From inside the house I could hear the fine creaks of the parquet floor, other small noises and faint stirrings.

I was lying under my grandfather's open window.

Grandfather switched day and night around, at night awake, wandering through the house, and during the day dozing off or actually sleeping on the couch in his darkened room, and with this brilliant stratagem making himself inaccessible to the rest of us.

If there was a way for me to know when this mutually effective and multifaceted disintegration had begun, whether it had a definite beginning or when and why this commodious family nest had grown cold, I would surely have much to say about human nature and also about the age I lived in.

I won't delude myself; I do not possess the surpassing wisdom of the gods.

Could it have been Mother falling ill?

That was certainly an important turning point, though in an odd way her sickness seems to me to have been the consequence rather than the cause of the prolonged decline; in any case, the family glossed over her illness with the same lies—so vile in their seeming benevolence— they used about my little sister's condition, or Grandfather's asthma attacks, which, according to Grandmother's confidential revelation, no treatment, diet, or medication could remedy because they were simply hysteria.

And all he needed was a bucketful of cold water on his head, she said.

But it would have been as unseemly to talk about the physical manifestations of this slow decay as it would have been to mention why Grandmother never talked to Grandfather, who in turn refused to say a word to Father, the two men passing each other, day after day, without even a greeting, each pretending the other didn't exist, even though Father was living in Grandfather's house.

Maybe it's fortunate, or unfortunate, that to this day I cannot decide what is better, knowledge or ignorance; no matter how much I tried to live their lies and find my place in the system of falsehoods, contributing to the smooth operation of the system's fine mechanism with effective lies of my own, and even if I could not see what had set it all in motion or what was covered up by what, still, over time, I did gain some insight into the layers of deception; I knew, for instance, that Grandfather's illness was real and quite serious, and that any one of his attacks might prove fatal; as Grandmother gravely and passively watched them, I felt she was actually waiting for his death, which could happen any time; and I also knew, of course, that my little sister was incurable, was born braindamaged, and so she'd remain, but the circumstances of her birth or conception—the cause of her condition, if indeed there was one such thing—were shrouded in the conspiracy of my parents' guilty conscience, which is why they were compelled to talk constantly about the hope of finding a cure, as if with their hope they were trying to mask an awful secret which no one must ever find out; it seemed as though every member of my family used lies to hold the other members' lives in his or her hand; and because of an inadvertent gesture of mine, I also knew that what Mother was recovering from was not a successful gallbladder operation.

I was resting on her arm, watching her breathe, and all I wanted to do was touch her neck, smooth my hand over her face—and that's why I'm talking about an inadvertent gesture: she was not asleep, only her eyes were closed, and as I clumsily reached toward her neck, my finger got caught in the cord of her nightgown—it wasn't tied properly or it just came undone—and the light silk material slid off her breast or, more precisely, in that fraction of a second I thought I saw it slide off and saw her breast, that is what I was supposed to see there, but in fact what I saw in place of her breast was a network of ruddy scars, the traces of many stitches.

I heard a clicking sound; someone quickly shut the window above me.

The storm could not have come at a better time; I lay there hoping the downpour would drive me into the ground and I'd be dissolved, absorbed, but instead, the cool rain sobered me up.

I scrambled to my feet, to knock on the window and be let in.

To my astonishment, Grandmother's terrified eyes looked back at me from within the room; on the couch Grandfather was lying on his back with his eyes closed.

While I was waiting at the door, my pants and shirt soaked through, it was pouring, thundering and lightning, and by the time Grandmother finally let me in, my hair was sopping wet.

But she didn't even bother to turn on the light, didn't say a word, and without paying any attention to me hurried back into Grandfather's room.

I followed her.

But she didn't hurry back to help him; she immediately sat back down on the chair she'd risen from a moment earlier; she was in a hurry to be present when the expected finally happened.

The rain sluiced down in great sheets on the large glass panes, in which a continually flashing blue light illuminated the mysteriously blurred images of trees; approaching rumbles made the glass tremble; it seemed that all the heat preceding the storm had been trapped in this room.

Grandfather's chest rapidly rose and sank, a still open book hung from his hand as if ready to drop, but he seemed to be holding on to it, clutching the last object connecting him to this world; his face was white, glistening with perspiration, and more pearly beads were gathered in the stubble over his mouth; his breathing was very fast, whistling, drawn-out, labored.

The light coming from under the waxed-paper shade of the lamp on the wall above Grandfather's head illuminated his face, as if to ensure that there would be nothing mysterious in his struggle; Grandmother sat motionless in the shadow, in the warm and friendly dimness, peering out, a bit tense, full of anticipation.

Her posture was as stiff as the back of the chair she was sitting on.

Grandmother was a tall, straight-backed woman, a dignified elderly lady, though today, as I backtrack in time, I confess I thought her much older than she actually was; she couldn't have been more than sixty at the time, almost twenty years younger than Grandfather, which I characteristically, having a child's concept of time, did not think such a large age difference then; I saw them both as equally ancient, resembling each other in their antiquity.

They were both lean, bony, and taciturn to the point of virtual muteness, and this, too, I saw as an inevitable, concomitant sign of old age, although they must have become taciturn for very different reasons and their separate silences did not have the same quality: Grandmother's implied a slight hurt, a constantly and emphatically communicated hurt, suggesting that she remained silent not because she had nothing to say but because she was deliberately depriving the world of her words, and would continue to deprive it, this was her way of punishing it, and I dreaded this punishment; I don't know what she was like in her youth, but in searching for the causes of her resentment, I had to conclude that she could not have coped with the fundamental changes that affected their way of life if she hadn't been able at least to flaunt her sense of having been wronged—the changes were simply too great for her—and as a young girl she had been much too pretty not to have believed that she'd be the world's pampered child until the day she died; for a few years after the war they used to be taken into town in a black Mercedes; always gleaming like a mirror and reminding me of a large comfortable coach, it was driven by a solemn-looking chauffeur, properly uniformed, his cap complete with ribboned visor, but of course they had to sell the car, and for years I covered my school texts and notebooks in now worthless stock certificates; once you removed the perforated coupons, the snow-white reverse side was ideally suited for this purpose; and then, unexpectedly, Grandfather closed his law office on Teréz Boulevard, as a consequence of which they had to let their maid go, and for a time after that Mária Stein moved into the maid's room until she, too, disappeared from our lives; finally, to complete the disaster, in the year when most private property was nationalized, Grandfather voluntarily, and without previously consulting Grandmother, surrendered all claims of ownership to their house; Grandmother was so unprepared for this, as Mother once laughingly told me, that when she found out, several weeks after the fact and quite by accident, she simply fainted—after all, the house had been her entire inheritance—and when they finally managed to revive her (it was Mother's older sister Klára who managed to slap some life into her) she imposed the worst possible punishment on both herself and the family: she refused to say another word to Grandfather, ever; what was most ludicrous about this was that Grandfather kept on talking to her, as if unwilling to acknowledge her silence; and in truth, her wounded feelings had to be taken seriously, because she wasn't born to be maid and nurse to three hopelessly ill and two mentally unhinged people—she was convinced that Father and I were not completely normal, and no doubt there was some truth in that; she was not cut out for such tasks, having neither the feeling nor the strength for them, even if she did carry out all her duties efficiently, conscientiously, with all the dignity of her wounded pride, while Grandfather's situation was just the opposite: he may have been silenced by his own inexhaustible patience and uncanny sense of humor; with him it wasn't a matter of wounded pride; more precisely, he did not consider himself the wounded party, it was just that he came to look upon the business of the world as so absurd, crazy, trivial, dull, and transparent that out of sheer consideration he didn't want to offend anyone with his opinions; to such an extent did he dismiss as not serious things others considered dead serious that he learned to hold back his natural responses in order to avoid dispute, and from that, I imagine, he suffered at least as much as Grandmother did from her wounded pride.

Bitter traces of his ironic smile hovered around his lips even during his attacks, as if behind the protection of his closed eyelids he were making fun of his own gasping and choking, considering the futile struggle his body was waging against him as a pitiful if unavoidable mistake: the body would not, still it would not, let happen what must inevitably happen.

Grandmother observed this struggle rather angrily, if only because his peculiar frivolous ways made him an exasperating patient; he would have liked to die but couldn't; therefore he didn't entrust himself to his nurse but, with a kind of ultimate wisdom, offered up his body and soul to the force his faith told him held sway over him, withdrawing from the merciful, worldly benevolence of treatment; he made human attempts to cure him look frivolous.

But from Grandmother's wounded vantage point this attitude must have seemed as though he was going through all this, this ungratefully long agony, all this fuss, only to annoy and offend her to the bitter end.

At the same time, as far as appearances were concerned, there was nothing shameful, awkward, or shabby in this struggle, in their tug-of-war; they both gave it its proper due.

I never saw my grandparents in scanty, slovenly, or even casual attire: they were always meticulously, impeccably dressed; although he never left the house, Grandfather shaved every morning, wore only white shirts with starched collars, silk cravats tied in big, bulky knots, crisply pressed, wide-bottomed trousers, and short beige corduroy housecoats; Grandmother washed dishes, cooked and cleaned in slightly elevated, morocco-leather house shoes, in narrow-waisted house robes that flared, bell-like, over her ankles; depending on the season and occasion, they were made of cotton, silk, soft wool, or dark rich velvet, and they graced her figure as exquisitely as evening gowns; she did not look at all ludicrous but, rather, stern and dignified, moving about cautiously, squeamishly touching the objects that had to be dusted, as if by accident, smoking one cigarette after another; she engaged help only for the strenuous chores like spring cleaning or doing the windows or waxing the floors; "I'll have a girl in for that," she liked to say at such times, just as she would "have" a taxi or streetcar take her, rather then "taking" a taxi or "getting on" a streetcar. She had Kálmán's mother do our laundry; once a week she came to pick up the dirty clothes, and returned them clean and pressed.

That night, in the short pause between two long whistling gasps, Grandfather said something like Air! Window! but we couldn't quite make out the words, so garbled were they by his convulsive breathing. And Grandmother did get up, but instead of opening the window she turned off the lamp over Grandfather's head and sat back in her chair.

It must have been around midnight.

We are not going to open the window for him, she said in the dark; I don't feel like mopping the floor in the middle of the night, and there's plenty of air in here, plenty.

Whenever I was with them she spoke to him as if she were speaking to me.

And then we went on waiting in the dark for his attack to subside, or for something to happen.

Despite the long night vigil, I awakened quite early the next morning.

It was a remarkable summer morning, quite remarkable: the rising mist of last night's storm made the sky a clear, downy blue, with not a single cloud; the wind was blowing in fierce gusts.

High, way up high, it blew, who could tell where, with an even boom, a ceaseless howl; in mighty swoops it ran through the trees, bending their crowns into itself, struck the bushes and lashed across the shimmering grass, shaking, rattling, and tearing apart things in its path; for the duration of this onslaught, the sounds of the whirling, colliding, rustling leaves, the sounds of cracking tree trunks and crashing, groaning branches harmonized with the howl on high, made everything terrestrial slide, vibrate, and flash because the wind jolted light and shadow from their natural positions, out of their plane, dislocated them, and while the wind could illuminate and rearrange things, it could not make a permanent new place for them in time, before the onslaught was over, and only the rumbling in the blue firmament remained, bringing nothing, fulfilling no expectation—as a thunderclap would in the wake of lightning—and with the next downward swoop it began all over again, unpredictably, again bringing neither clouds nor rain, neither bringing back the storm nor disturbing summer's tranquillity, being neither cool nor warm, the air clear, in fact becoming clearer and less humid, no swirling funnels to churn up the dust, one could even hear a woodpecker tapping; still, it was a storm, perhaps it was pure force, dry and empty.

A raging fury to which we yield uneasily, fearfully, a bit ruffled, like birds that at times like these let themselves be buffeted by the harmless wind.

It was good that the wind was blowing, and it was also good that the sun was shining.

My little sister was already in the garden, standing on the steps leading to the gate, her hand clinging to the rusty iron, her head dangling, heavy and helpless, down to her breasts, her long white nightgown ballooning out in the wind.

With a mug of warm milk in my hand, I stepped out of the house into the wind, slightly annoyed to find her there, because I knew that if she noticed me I'd have a hard time getting rid of her; this was never easy, and the truth is that no matter how willingly I played with her, my ultimate goal in those little games was always to shake her off somehow.

But so early in the day the danger wasn't too great, for after walking Father out to the gate, sometimes she'd just stand there for a whole hour, not budging, sunk in her sadness.

Sometimes her misery put her in a state of such numb immobility that not even Grandmother could drag her away, although Grandma was the one person she truly feared.

My little sister had a very reliable internal timetable; trusting her un-canny secret sense, she could feel, to the second, when Father woke up in the morning, and then, giggling merrily, she'd climb out of bed, walk him to the bathroom, and position herself by the sink to watch him shave; this was the high point of their relationship, the moment of fulfillment in the love life of my little sister, a rapturous joy repeatable and repeated daily: Father stood in front of the mirror, and as he began to lather his face with the shaving brush, a low hum would issue from his throat; the foamier the shaving cream became under the brushstrokes, the louder his hum would grow, as if he was pleased with his ability to whip up such nice, firm, tastefully towering mounds of foam out of nothing; my little sister would imitate his noises, and when he was finished with the lathering and his hum had grown into a loud, singing bellow, he'd suddenly fall silent and she'd follow suit; in the welcome pause of silence Father would rinse out the brush, replace it on the glass shelf, and with a ritual gesture raise high his razor; with bated breath my sister would stare at Father's hand, and he'd watch her eyes from the mirror; while emitting a pleasurable moanlike scream, and repeating it with each stroke, Father would stretch his skin with his finger, plunge the blade into the foam, get down to the business of removing the stubble underneath, their game being to pretend the razor was hurting the foam, though it also made it feel good, and my sister joined Father's sounds with squeals of pleasure and pain of her own each time the knife sank into the foam, and afterward she watched excitedly as he got dressed, and sat next to him, buzzing and babbling, while he ate his breakfast; but when he got up from the table and wiped his mouth with a napkin, ready to leave, which meant this wasn't Sunday, when the quick wipe would be followed by a leisurely smoke, then the cheerful look on her face was replaced by one of panic and despair; she clutched Father's hand, his arm, and if it so happened that he had forgotten to set out the papers he was going to take with him that day, he had to drag the silently clinging child across the hallway, into his study, and back again; Father enjoyed the shaving game, but this was a bit much, and he'd often lose patience—under his controlled smile he'd flinch and grouse about the circus he had to go through every bloody morning, at times he'd be on the verge of hitting her, but always recoiling from the thought, he then became even more indulgent; by the time they reached the front door and parting was inevitable, my little sister would plunge swiftly from the heights of desperate rage into the resigned indifference of sorrow: she'd let Father take her hand, and hand in hand they'd walk all the way to the garden gate, where his car, engine running, was waiting for him.

Who could say why I started walking toward her now, when my aim was to avoid her and not disturb her in her grief, which at the moment suited me just fine; in any case, I had no idea how jealous her unconditional devotion to Father had made me, nor that it was this jealousy that made me seek out her company, because, willy-nilly, we were compelled to share the object of our mutual affection.

Just as I grew close to Kálmán because of our mutual affection for Maja.

She was holding on to the gate; I sat down on the steps and sipped my milk, making sure none of its wrinkly skin slipped into my mouth; what I was really doing was enjoying, with the most insidious humility, the grief emanating from her body.

The body really does emanate its emotions, but you have to be close to feel it.

What I actually sensed was a distorted version of the grief that the absence of Father's naked body had evoked in me, an absence that would forever remain in me.

After a while she turned to me, followed my movements, which made me drink my milk even more slowly, so it would last longer; in general, I pretended not to know, see, or feel her presence, and in so doing I instinctively hit her where it hurt most: I reinforced her sense of abandonment.

I kept this up until she completely transferred her sense of abandonment to me, hoping to find solace in my mug, in the milk.

I didn't have to wait long; she reached for it, but I raised it to my mouth and took another sip.

Letting go of the gate, she took a step toward me—more precisely, toward the mug, toward the sip of milk, toward the instinct of drinking.

She was standing over me, and between us this amounted to a conversation.

I was still pretending not to notice that she wanted my milk; as if by chance, I slid the mug between my raised knees and guarded it there.

When she reached for it, I lifted it from between my knees, out of her reach, openly withdrawing it from her.

She let out a single whiny sound, that hateful sound with which she waited for Father every afternoon.

For not only did she sense instinctively when he got up in the morning, she also had a secret intuition about when he would return at the end of the day.

In the afternoon when I'd be waiting for Livia, usually between four and five, no matter what she was doing my sister would suddenly become cranky and irritable and let out this strange, drawn-out whiny sound, as of joy heralded by pain, and she went on repeating it until she began to cry in earnest, rocking, driving herself into crying, actually not real crying, there were no tears, more like an animal whimpering, which she kept up as she wandered through the house and roamed the garden, clutching the fence, until Father arrived.

Come to think of it, the only time my little sister did not give way to these displays of joy, rapture, pain, and sorrow was when the family was together, when everyone was present after our Sunday dinners.

But now, because I didn't feel like listening to her crying anymore, I stuck my index finger into the mug and lifted out the skin.

This bit of silliness made her laugh; she plopped down next to me on the step and opened her mouth, indicating that she wanted it.

I dangled it like bait, even lowering it into her mouth, but when she was about to slurp it up with her lips and stuck-out tongue, I pulled it back; we repeated this stunt until she again made a face as if to cry, and then I let her have it along with my finger.

She sucked it off; to increase her pleasure, I put the nearly empty mug in her hand, and behind her back sneaked through the gate and ran off, so by the time she realized what had happened, she'd see nothing but the empty street.

Kálmán was standing on the trail.

This was the trail that led from their farm, above the cornfield, into the forest; he had a stick in his hand, pointing it at the ground, but seemed to be doing nothing else with it.

The wind was scraping through the deep-green corn leaves, making a shrill sound; the forest was booming.

What was he doing there, I asked him when, still panting, I reached him up on the hill, I had to scream almost to outshout the wind; but he said nothing, slowly turned his head toward me and stared at me as if he didn't exactly know who I was.

Right before his feet, in the middle of the trail, a dead mouse lay on its side, but Kálmán wasn't touching it with his stick.

I had no idea what was eating him; when I had quietly looked for him earlier in their yard—no shouting was allowed then, his parents and brothers were asleep—everything seemed fine; he'd already let out the geese and the chickens, the stable was empty, and in the pen the little piglets were busy suckling at the teats of the sow, sprawled peacefully on the floor.

When I stopped in to see how she was doing, she raised her head, gave me a long series of grunts; she recognized me, was happy to see me, and it was this silly feeling I wanted to share with Kálmán, that their sow loved me.

A little way off, his dog kept circling a bush, stuck its nose roughly into the layers of fallen leaves, scratching feverishly, and then ran around the bush some more until it hit a spot that must have promised some important and exciting find but that it couldn't get to, and began scratching and digging again.

And then, thinking I'd found a way to make him talk, I quickly squatted down on the trail, because I suddenly discovered that he must have been looking at the maggots toiling around the carcass of the mouse; his silence annoyed me, and maybe because of the wind, I don't exactly know why, I felt too energetic and excited to adjust my mood abruptly to his; at the same time I couldn't very well ask him what was bothering him, you didn't just come out and ask a thing like that.

I definitely couldn't, if only because whatever was bothering him was serious enough for him to ignore my helpfully inquisitive gesture; he pretended to be standing there by chance and even seemed embarrassed at having been looking at the dumb bugs; his posture, standing motionless, implied that I was mistaken to think he'd actually been doing something before I got there; he wasn't watching those insects at all, he had no intention of doing anything, none whatsoever, he was just hanging around, wanting to be alone, and he wasn't interested in anything; I might be an eager beaver, of course, but he didn't need me, I might as well buzz off, instead of pretending to be so interested in those bugs, he could see right through me; wasn't it enough that the wind was blowing like crazy and the sun was beating down so hard and his dog had gone nuts, so why didn't I just get the hell out of there?

But I didn't, which was a little humiliating, since staying there with this kind of rebuff and indifference made no sense, but I didn't budge.

And why was I there all the time, why did I keep coming around, anyway? but where should I have gone? and if I hadn't gone over to his house, wouldn't he have come to mine? because whenever I got stubborn and dug in my heels or got really offended, or my humiliation was too deep to get over with just a shrug of the shoulders, then he was sure to show up, grinning as if nothing had happened; and I also knew full well that he showed up not just because of me but somehow to prevent me from going to Maja, and the reverse of this, if not quite so emphatically, was also true: I kept going over to his house to see if he wasn't at Maja's.

This was the difference between us: he'd put up obstacles, hold inspections, divert and impede my actions; I merely checked things out, wanted to know what was happening, and if I didn't find him at home and his mother couldn't tell me where he was either, and after roaming the forest in the hope that his disappearance was only a mistake and I'd find him but didn't! then jealousy made my whole world turn a little black, not so much because of Maja as because of Krisztián.

Imagining that while I stood there alone, helpless and miserable, they were playing together, conveniently forgetting about me, making it clear I meant nothing to them.

But Kálmán couldn't have had any inkling of this.

Just as it never dawned on him that if he managed to elude my vigilance and slipped over to Maja's, my jealousy wouldn't be nearly so intense as his when I did the same, because it bothered me much less what he might have done with Maja; put more precisely, I wanted to know about it, but it gave me pleasure, painful pleasure to be sure, that in a relationship which didn't mean all that much to me he was my stand-in, and that when I was there I became his substitute—and I found this act of substitution immeasurably exciting.

It was as if in Kálmán and me Maja loved not two different individuals but a single one who couldn't be fully embodied in either one alone, and so when she talked to me, she was invariably addressing Kálmán as well, and when she was with him, she would also want to be with me a little; whether we liked it or not, we always had to endure the presence of the other, play the role of a stranger for her, a stranger who had become familiar because of these games yet whose strangeness prevented the longed-for consummation and fulfillment, because no matter how provocatively she may have been playing the whore, showing off with the superficial characteristics of one, Maja remained more like a yearned-for object of desire for both of us; and she couldn't be the real Maja either, not for him, not for me, not even for herself, because whatever she was looking for in him or in me, she could find only in the two of us together, yet she was also searching for a one and only, and because she couldn't find him she suffered, and aped Szidónia's unbridled licentiousness; in the process, she became a kind of symbol of femininity for us, which we felt we should measure up to with our budding masculinity—we couldn't have known then that it was precisely with these games of substitutions— experimenting on, learning from and about one another—that she would lead us to where we had to go; all in good time, nature bids us be patient, even if patience must be extracted from a would-be lover's passionate impatience.

I thought that in this confusing game I, and only I, could come out the winner, because even if something irrevocable happened between the two of them, something more than a kiss—and of course I also wished to have that "more" myself—even then, even beyond that, Maja and I shared a deeper, darker secret: our clandestine searches, and Kálmán couldn't possibly come between us, with his love or with anything else; there was nothing he could do that might disturb our very special relationship.

And even if that "more" did happen, I would have benefited from it somehow; Maja would have returned some of it to me.

Kálmán and I kept a hold on each other, cunningly and ardently we held on, wouldn't let go, and compared to this fierce embrace, which pervaded every moment of our lives and in the hours of jealousy seemed deadly, having touched each other's member seemed rather trivial, and if not trivial then only a consequence of our rivalry.

But after the experience we'd shared the night before, I felt he could do anything to me and I wouldn't be offended, or do something I'd done on other, similar occasions, like telling him, "Up yours, motherfucker," and then taking to my heels, resolving an unpleasant situation by running away; I could outrun him, but had to be sure my words hit him only when I was already in motion, because his reflexes were faster and he might be able to trip me.

On the other hand, I felt that his moroseness and anger had nothing to do with me, he just felt that way in general because something bad had happened to him, and even if I could not learn the cause of his trouble, I wanted to help, for it occurred to me that he was like this because of Maja; I wanted us to do something that would take his mind off whatever it was.

I started picking at the dead mouse with my fingers; the bugs immediately stopped moving, waiting to see what would happen next, but didn't run away, were unwilling to let go of such rich booty.

These bugs brought to mind something else we had in common.

Sometimes, because of Livia, and with nothing special to set me off, I, too, would be overcome by dejection, gloom, apathy, disgust, feeling as if I were huddling at the bottom of some dark, slimy pit, and if somebody peered inside I'd be enraged, full of hatred, murder in my heart, wishing the intruder dead, out of existence.

My fingers felt something soft and squishy; death had left the little mouse's eye open; a small incisor protruded from its mouth, and under the tooth there was a tiny drop of clotted blood.

I was expecting Kálmán to growl at me to stop poking at the dead animal; he didn't like people picking at things.

Once, he beat up Prém because of a lizard.

It was a beautiful green lizard, its head turquoise, not too big, pitifully skinny from the winter cold, and young, which you can tell by looking at its scales; it was springtime, when lizards still move lazily, and ours, atop a tree stump, was soaking in the sun; sensing our proximity it moved over a little, which was hard for it, and also it didn't like giving up the warm sun for the cold shade; its wise eyes stared at us for a while, then weighing its need for warmth, it must have concluded that we had no hostile intentions, so it lowered its eyelids, entrusting itself completely to our goodwill, which is when Prém couldn't control himself anymore and grabbed at it; and although enough survival instinct materialized for the lizard to slip through Prém's fingers, the tail remained behind, a watery drop of blood marking the spot where it had snapped off, it was thrashing by itself, writhing on the tree stump; and then a screaming Kálmán pounced on Prém.

But now, not even my poking could get a rise out of Kálmán, I couldn't get him to say anything to me, and the bugs resumed their labor as the shadow cast by my hand began to recede.

Whatever I knew about carrion bugs, as about so many other animals and plants, I knew from Kálmán; it's not that I was completely insensitive to the world of nature, but the difference between us, I think, was that he experienced natural phenomena as events of his own nature while I remained an observer, felt excitement, revulsion, disgust, fear, and rapture, which lead directly to the urge to interfere, but Kálmán always remained calm, calm in the deepest, broadest sense of the word, as when someone is overwhelmed by the darkest grief or most radiant joy and instead of protesting gives himself to it, not trying to hinder the expression of his emotions with fears and prejudices; he remained calm with the neutrality of nature, which is neither empathetic nor indifferent but something else: I suppose that is what emotionally courageous people must be like! and maybe this was why nothing ever disgusted him, why he wouldn't want to touch anything that did not touch him, why he knew everything there was to know about the woods, the scene of our daily rovings; he was quiet, slow to move, but his eyes took in everything, his gaze was unerring, in this realm he brooked no opposition of any kind, here he was lord and master, though he did not want to rule; it was this intuitive, sensory awareness that made him irresistible, as on that early Sunday afternoon when he showed up at our house, appearing unexpectedly in the open door of our dining room, looking, from the adults' point of view at least, somewhat hapless and comical, as we sat around the table, in a cozy family setting, over the remains of our midday meal, listening to my cousin Albert: my Aunt Klára's son, a slightly chubby young man with a bald spot, whom I admired for his self-confidence and winning superiority and despised for his slyness and stupidity, was just then in the middle of a story about an Italian writer named Emilio Gadda; Albert was the only so-called artist in the family, an opera singer, who therefore had the chance to travel a lot, a rare privilege in those years, and was full of strange and colorful stories which he was quick to relate in his mighty bass—the pledge of a promising career—though always affecting a measure of modesty; he peppered his anecdotes and off-color witticisms with little melodies, singing while he spoke or speaking while he sang, giving us brief musical quotations, as if to imply with this curious habit that he was so much an artist that he couldn't afford even in pleasant leisure hours to neglect exercising his precious voice; but when Kálmán appeared in the doorway, barefoot and in his flimsy shorts, Albert interrupted his story at once with a loud, affected guffaw: how charmingly ill-mannered can such a grimy ragamuffin be! he said, and the others laughed along with him; I was a little ashamed of my friend and also ashamed of feeling ashamed, but without a word, not even hello, he told me to come with him right away, he was driven by something so strong he paid not the slightest attention to the company present, behaving as if he saw nobody but me, which I have to admit had a certain comic effect.

The bugs, though hindered now and then by a clump of dirt or a big pebble, quickly bored their way under the carcass; they used their jet-black pointed heads as shovels, spinning in the protection of their armor-like shell, and the dug-up dirt was thrown to the rear by their tiny many-jointed feet; first they dug a proper trench around the dead mouse, then scooped out the soil from under it so that the carrion sank below the surface of the ground, and then, using the dug-out dirt, they carefully buried the animal completely, leaving not a trace; and as I then learned from Kálmán, that's why they are called necrophores, burying beetles; their work is hard, and since the corpses they bury are immovable giants compared to their own bodies, it takes many hours to complete the job; of course, the work is not without profit: even before they begin their labor they lay their eggs inside the carrion, where the eggs will hatch; as the larvae mature, they consume the decomposing body, and eventually chew their way out to the light of day—that's their life.

That Sunday, when Kálmán came to call for me, they were burying a field mouse, which was a much easier piece of work, despite the field mouse's larger size, since here, around this wood mouse, the ground was not only hard because of the trail but also full of stones.

Nine carrion beetles were on the job.

The hard shells of their backs were marked by two red stripes running crosswise, and on their necks and abdomens fine yellowish hairs protected their delicately articulated bodies.

Each insect worked within a clearly defined area, yet this was clearly a concerted effort; if one of them came up against a stone or a too solid clump, it stopped, as if to summon its mates, and the others also stopped; then they all began scurrying around the object causing the difficulty, touching it with their long, hornlike feelers, appraising the situation, and then, as if to discuss the problem and reach a decision, they touched each other, and several of them got down to work, chewing from different sides, burrowing under the obstacle, making a common effort to remove it.

While I was watching the beetles and trying to figure out what had got him so upset, Kálmán told me, out of the blue, that Krisztián had knocked the milk out of his hand on purpose.

I didn't know what milk he was talking about.

But he kept insisting that Krisztián had done it on purpose, it was no accident, he meant to do it.

Only I did not understand what had been done on purpose.

Last night, Kálmán said breathlessly—after he managed to tear himself away from his obsessive insistence on Krisztián's hostile intent and was ready to answer my repeated questions—last night, and he'd forgotten to tell me this before, they decided to camp out—yes, I knew, Prém had this large army tent—and a little while ago he brought them fresh milk, and then Krisztián did this stupid thing: Look, he said, there's a fly in the milk, and as Kálmán looked down, Krisztián hit the bottom of the jug, knocking it out of his hand, and of course the jug broke, and this was something Kálmán would not forgive him.

He was serious; in the terrible noise of the strong wind I almost had to read his lips, and he wasn't even looking at me, he was looking off somewhere as if ashamed to speak, or ashamed at not being able to keep this to himself, at complaining; but as I pictured the scene, the crude little trick that works every time, I couldn't help seeing him as the milk hit him in the face, and I burst out laughing.

It was as if Krisztián had tried to please *me* with this trick, although I'd never have thought of taking my anger out on Kálmán.

Yet my laughter, I realized as I heard it, would seem like revenge, pleasantly gratifying revenge, an abuse of Kálmán's trust; still, I could not help myself, I had to laugh: still crouching over the hardworking beetles, I looked up at him; the mark Krisztián had left on his innocent, strong face, in his offended yet still candid gaze was plain to see, and it made me feel so good to be able to read Krisztián's handiwork on his face that I couldn't, and didn't want to, stop laughing—it's a good thing we don't always know what we're doing! grabbing my legs below the knees, I tipped over and dropped on the trail, rolling with laughter as I thought of how Krisztián had knocked the milk into his face, crash! the jug shattering into smithereens, the milk splashing all over; at the same time I saw the shocked and indignant look in Kálmán's eyes as he watched me convulsing with laughter, he couldn't possibly comprehend this, how could he? the only reason Krisztián could manipulate him so cruelly and tyrannically was that this was a language of bullying and cruelty Kálmán could neither speak nor understand, while not only did I speak and understand it but it was my sole common language with Krisztián, the language of achievable superiority, of acquirable power; this was our innately common language, all right, even if we tended to watch from a distance our different means and strategies in using it; and right now it was a delight to be able to communicate with Krisztián in this secret language at Kálmán's expense.

What was I laughing at, he asked, looking at me with his transparent blue eyes; what's so funny? he repeated somewhat louder, now he'd get it from his mother, it was a fine glazed jug.

A glazed jug, yet! reveling in the liberating effect of spoiling and destruction, I had to laugh even harder, and precisely because you don't know what you're doing but are free in that you're doing it unknowingly and unintentionally, I had to do something more: my joy was so intense that laughter alone didn't suffice, and his mere existence, the sparkle of his blond, brushlike lashes, could only increase the pleasure of my laughter, now bordering on hysteria, and still this wasn't enough; letting indecency run amok, I needed to draw Kálmán into the merriment, to share my pleasure with him, not to mention that at that moment laughing for me was but kissing Krisztián on the mouth; so as I was rolling around the ground next to the dead mouse, laughing even at my own laughter, I suddenly grabbed his feet, which surprised him so much he toppled onto me.

That was it: the joking, the laughter, the kissing, the joy of unforeseen revenge all ended when, still falling, he seized my neck with both hands and Krisztián's mark vanished from his face without a trace, and although I quickly locked my arms around his back and arched my body to throw him off with one heave, my laughter had obviously released a current of obstinate and implacable hatred in him so powerful that I had neither the strength nor the skill to subdue it, and I realized, with the last spark of rational thought in me, that I'd have to resort to more treacherous, baser tactics, though to do so right away would have been shameful—first I'd have to struggle, display courage and resourcefulness, flaunt my manhood, abide by the allegedly civilized rules of properly declared hostilities; but I couldn't shake him; he was squeezing my neck so hard that the sound of the wind began to fade, darkness was descending on me, like a red rainfall, his body was becoming unbearably heavy; I gasped and choked, and I got angry, but what was that compared to the raging hatred directed not only at me or my laughter but also at Krisztián—I could clearly sense this even at the moment when he fell on me—for humiliating him so; his innocent, good-natured, patient, considerate self went haywire, he wanted to choke me! get back at me for the injury received from Krisztián and take revenge on me for Maja, too; no, there was nothing funny about this, he meant to stifle me, to knock the laughter out of me for good, along with Krisztián and Maja; he pressed down on me with every ounce of his body, which was both an advantage and a disadvantage: I couldn't kick him in the balls, couldn't move my legs or move him, but for a moment I could catch my breath, and that loosened his grip on my neck, and I tried to use that favorable moment to break the stranglehold by yanking my head out of his hands, so I began knocking my forehead against his head; the two skulls collided with terrific force—a whole shower of stars—and I couldn't capitalize on the advantage of my desperate counterattack because I was dazed and in pain, and I missed my chance: he still had me pinned down, and to incapacitate my head, he struck my face with his elbow; all I could do was jerk my head sideways; I felt my nose begin to bleed, and my open mouth was touching the dead mouse! do criminal statistics include records of children murdering other children? but I'm sure he wanted to kill me—no, I'd better qualify that, he didn't want to, I don't think he wanted to do anything just then, for

raw fighting instincts had displaced will, intention, and premeditation—
and if I hadn't felt the dead mouse on my lips, the limp little body all
but dangling into my mouth! if this humiliation, which took the fight out
of the realm of the usual daily horseplay, hadn't mobilized the deepest,
most artful cunning—when, sensing complete physical defeat, one is ready
to try anything, seek the most desperate solutions—I'm sure he would
have killed me, I don't know how, maybe choking me or bashing in my
head with a stone, though that wasn't the uppermost question in my mind
at the moment, I had no question at all, there was nothing, everything
we might call the controlled function of the conscious mind had vanished,
dissolved in the haze of the battle; in a split second, in a flash, the prank,
the childish swagger, the game of rivalry and provocation had turned into
a life-and-death struggle, an extreme situation in which the mind can
summon the body's untapped resources precisely by rejecting all means of
moral control as unnecessary, throwing off all restraint, no longer wondering whether what is possible is also acceptable, considering the body's
capabilities no longer from the standpoint of conventional moral order, as
a supervisor might, but only and exclusively from that of its own survival:
in a sense, that's a matchless vantage point, God looks the other way at
such moments, a wonderful lookout point for the memoirist, even if the
inevitable lapses in conscious functioning keep us from remembering specific decisions, specific questions, and answers from our inner dialogue,
and we can recall only random images and chaotic feelings, for in that
state the mind has no purpose other than to preserve the body and
therefore has no will either, so what is left is a bare shape which, being
unaware of itself, is not even our own; more precisely, we are no longer
in control of it, and it is making decisions about and for us; it's no accident
that poets so delight in singing of the connection between love and death,
for never do we experience our body's autonomy so purely as when we
fight for our lives or in the moment of love's consummation, when we
experience our body in its most primeval form, with no history, no creator,
obeying no law of gravity, without contour, able to see itself in no mirror,
having no need for any of this, becoming a single, explosive dot of pure
light in the infinity of our inner darkness; so I wouldn't want to give the
impression that at that moment I was thinking about what I was doing;
no, it is only now, out of the shards of pure sensation preserved by memory, that I am trying to assemble this pretty little series of actions—which
also happens to reveal some of the dark spots of my character, and of
course I realize that as soon as I say dark spots I am exercising the mem-

oirist's inevitable moral judgment, nothing but the moral distortion of the story, after the fact, similar in nature to the way we view great wars in retrospect, ennobling what is ignoble, adding the moral requisites of courage and cowardice, honesty and treachery, steadfastness and dereliction, but then, it is our only chance to retrieve the amoral period of a state of emergency, tame it, refit it into the humdrum morality of our placid daily life; if in my pain I had closed my mouth, I'd have bitten into the mouse, with the blood from my nose dripping on the tiny body, and the possibility of this must have struck him as so bizarre, so repulsive, yet also so sobering that for a fraction of a second he relaxed his grip: there was something odd about this momentary relief, maybe a touch of uncertainty, but it held out no promise of escape, merely opened a crack through which the soul could witness the total defeat of the body; no, in this very short interval I did not think of Maja, although being defeated by Kálmán might also mean I'd be at a hopeless disadvantage with her; when you taste defeat, when the soul is in flight, you grasp at the very thing you had abandoned, which in this case was laughter, and I simply had to laugh, more freely and brazenly than before, but silently, and out of this bubbling, frantic laughter, which mocked his murderous intent, his victory, his strength, and made me feel his skin and the warmth of his bare body, directly out of this perfidious and hideous laughter flowed the movement of my hands: I tickled him, and the joy of seeing his reaction caused me really to bite down on the dead mouse, at the same time as Kálmán grabbed my head with both hands and began banging it against the ground, which didn't bother me, because the treachery of the soul had handed me the key to the situation: I kept laughing and tickling him, I was retching and spitting, he could have held my hand down only by rolling off me, which would have robbed him of his victory, but he couldn't take the tickling; he banged my head hard four times, very quickly, I felt as if a sharp stone had torn into my skull, and then he began to howl; I tickled him and he howled, how he howled! starting out as a cry of victory, exploding out of the deadly force pent up in him, and now feeding on itself, then at its loudest, at the peak of his triumph passing over into a whimpery laugh; his skin, his twitching body, his very flesh tried to repel this laugh, but the howling had become a kind of defense mechanism: on the one hand he tried to scare me with it, and on the other he hoped it would help him get over the unwanted laughter, but as he tried to evade my tickling fingers and abruptly arched his body over me, I was able to complete the move begun but thwarted earlier: I managed to get up, thrusting out my hip and kicking against the ground at the same time, while he, enervated by the tickling, giggled and whimpered and let himself be turned over, and we kept on turning over and over, screaming, laughing, clinging to each other; tugging and pushing each other we rolled off the trail and into the bushes, and by then his dog had turned up, greatly excited, barking and snapping at us, and that definitely determined the kind of outcome our fight would have.

And then I started running, rejoicing in the elemental pleasure of running, with the wind against my body, heading straight for the thicket, and he quickly took off after me; I knew he mustn't catch me, for although my running, my having to flee from him, was an admission of his victory, it was also a way of striking back, of getting even; with his dog running after us, the race was turning into a game, a reconciliation, a mutual acceptance of a tie in the contest; and then, like a young male animal fresh from a successful struggle for his female, exhilarated by my victorious escape and enjoying the swiftness of my body as I bobbed and weaved among the trees and ducked the lashing branches, the resiliency that gives running the sense of freedom, delighting in the sudden twists and changes of direction, I did think of Maja, saw her running, fleeing from Szidónia across their garden and down the slope; it must have been our laughter, the inner similarity of the image, that made me think of her, and I felt as if I were Maja because my tactics, my stratagems were not those of a boy, and there was Kálmán, tramping, clattering, panting right on my heels, the dry twigs cracking under our feet, the branches and leaves swishing, brushing, flying against our bodies; he couldn't catch me, though; I quickened my pace, wanted him to feel my superiority in the increasing gap between us; and that's how we reached the clearing at whose farther edge, but still under the trees, the boys had set up their tent.

When I suddenly stopped and turned back toward him, he was shaking, not laughing at all; his face was pale, which gave his tanned skin a strange, blotchy look; he was trembling all over, and we were both out of breath, panting into each other's face; I wiped my nose with my fist and was surprised to see it bloody; I reached back to find that blood from my ear had trickled down my neck, but I was too excited to pay any attention to that now, and I saw that he was excited, too, although we looked into each other's eyes with seeming indifference.

I knew he knew what was afoot, I could sense it while we were still running; we understood each other.

Seeing the blood made him a bit uneasy, scared even, but by wiping my fist on my pants I showed him that this was of no importance, I didn't care, and it shouldn't bother him either.

It was a good thing that because of the wind they couldn't hear us running; I motioned to Kálmán that we should hide behind a bush and he should do something about his dog; from the thicket we watched them in silence.

The dog kept watching us, not understanding the reason for this sudden stop; there was a danger that it might give us away with its movements or bark at us in its disappointment.

And the only way this thing could work was if they remained completely unsuspecting.

The tall grass of the clearing was undulating in bright, shiny waves.

If everything stayed the way it was.

Krisztián was standing at the lower edge of the clearing, holding a long, leafy branch in his hand and working on it with his characteristic intense concentration and flippant elegance; he was using a bone-handled knife, a veritable dagger he was very proud of, for it allegedly used to be his father's; he was stripping the branch of its leaves, probably making it into a skewer. Not far from him, Prém was sitting up in a tree, saying something to him that we couldn't make out because of the strong wind.

Sounded like something about bringing more planks.

But Krisztián didn't answer, he'd only look up absentmindedly from time to time, letting Prém go on, holding the branch away from his body and aiming at the spots where in tiny nubs the leaves join the branches, flicking his blade to make the leaves drop off.

It occurred to me that I had never before seen them alone like this, although from their hints, casual remarks, and vague allusions I knew they were inseparable; but no matter how closely I had watched them or tried to figure them out, everything between them remained a secret, their hints and allusions expressive of an intriguing collusion; it seemed that there was them and then there was the rest of the world, or rather another world, completely separate and inconsequential, peopled with dull, inferior strangers; and if anyone tried to get close to them, they'd accommodate the intruder for a while, like two ballplayers perfectly attuned to each other's thoughts and intentions, playing politely and graciously, if only to keep themselves amused; their shared life, thus hidden from others, may have been the source of their self-assurance and sense of superiority; one had to assume that theirs was the true life, the splendid real life we all long for, which remained and had to remain hidden, since they were its sole keepers.

How I longed for him, how grievously he was hurting me; I wanted him to be mine, or at least mine, too; I fantasized about that life and about being a part of it.

Their tent stood under the trees; I saw a blue bucket lying on its side, a shovel stuck into the ground with its handle rising straight up, a woodpile prepared for the evening campfire, tall grass swaying gently in the wind, and farther away, the red spot of a blanket spread on the ground; and Krisztián, standing on the lower part of the clearing, slapping at his back, probably shooing away a pesky fly, and Prém sitting in the tree— there was something so ethereally calm and serene in this picture as to suggest a secret, mysterious message, but I hoped to discover even more exciting secrets about them.

Kálmán cautiously bent down, picked up a stone, and threw it quickly, aiming accurately so he wouldn't actually hit his dog.

The stone struck a tree, the dog didn't budge; it kept watching Kálmán as though it understood him, but apparently it understood something else and only wagged its tail once, lazily; I detected a certain indignation in this.

Kálmán hissed angrily at the dog, motioned to it to go home, get lost, and to show that he meant it, he picked up another stone; he was still pale, still shaking.

And then slowly, reluctantly, the dog started to move, though not to where Kálmán was pointing but toward us, and strangely enough, as it moved, the light of curiosity and attention in its eyes which we had seen only moments before began to die out; it abruptly changed direction and, ignoring Kálmán's angry hissing and brandishing of the stone, trotted out from under the trees into the clearing; frozen, we stared after it; for a while it disappeared completely, and we could only follow the line where its body broke the rippling waves of the tall grass, only see its black back resurfacing near Krisztián's feet; he looked up, said something to the dog, the dog stopped, even let Krisztián scratch it with the tip of his knife, then trotted into the woods.

Seeing Krisztián so unsuspecting, not even bothering to glance our way to see where the dog was coming from, assuming it must simply be wandering about, filled us with such a sense of victory, such elation, that Kálmán raised a clenched fist and we silently grinned at each other, the grin looked kind of odd on his pale face, especially since he still hadn't stopped shaking; he seemed to be struggling with an inner force unable to break out of him and now made more powerful by that triumphant gesture of his fist; his neck was pale, too, and though the skin on his body didn't change color, it seemed shriveled somehow, matte and chilly, as when covered with gooseflesh, making it seem as if another boy, a stranger, was standing next to me, yet because of my own excitement I didn't attach special importance to this at the time; after all, is there anything a child wouldn't consider natural? anything he couldn't comprehend? shaking, pale, lusterless, he lost the familiar shape of his easygoing, good-natured self, although he seemed stronger, better proportioned, perhaps even more beautiful; yes, I'd be on the right track if I said that it seemed as if, along with the fatness, the softness that lent him a genial air had been dissolved, and the petulant, tense vibration of his naked muscles bespoke an already transformed being; he was more beautiful but also distorted: his bluish-red nipples seemed larger on the muscles of his chest, which kept twitching feverishly; his mouth seemed smaller, his eyes expressionless, and innocence seemed to have been supplanted by a kind of stiffness, which emphasized the anatomical aspects of his body and threw them into sharper, more striking relief; yes, we could contemplate the laws of beauty: if he were still alive, then, ever curious about the principles governing beauty's functions, I would question him about the secret cause of the physical change, but he died, before my very eyes, in my hands almost, on the night of October 23, 1956, which was a Tuesday; so I can only surmise that the emotions released by our fight, by his defeat and victory, made him confront feelings that, being unfamiliar, his body could not struggle against; he began to run and I ran after him, and if I said that the idea of running had been mine, I must also say that actually doing it was much more urgent for his body; we ran carefully, watching every step, trying to make no noise, seeking each secure foothold with an attentiveness sharpened by excitement, swiftly deciding on a slight detour so Prém wouldn't notice us from his tree.

That's how, having gone around the clearing, we finally reached the famous spot, that jutting rock, where we had once touched each other and where, hiding behind the tall thornbush, Szidónia had watched Pista fight the conductor and in her excitement begun to bleed.

When I look at it today, it is not some great rock but a rather ordinary, not even very large flat stone that, ravaged by the elements and assailed by tree roots, is crumbling into separate layers; and when I recently found myself at this place again, it was surprising to realize that children, in their blissful ignorance, may consider a rather exposed spot or sparse thicket to be the safest of havens.

Krisztián must have finished preparing his stick, he said something, but we couldn't hear because of the wind, and Prém, thrusting his body away from the tree, dangling, his feet groping for a branch, began to climb down.

This was the right moment, or rather, we couldn't delay any further.

I rushed out first, I wanted Kálmán to follow me, the all-compelling, ready impulse could be restrained no longer; if I had let him he would have started out too rashly and I desired the more subtle effects of a surprise.

With long leaps we quickly gained the tent and slipped in unnoticed, fairly sliding on top of each other as we did, it was a surprisingly spacious, dark tent, its thick canvas letting in no light, also warm, and although we could have stood up, we chose to crawl on all fours; in the stuffy darkness I could immediately distinguish Krisztián's delicious smell; through an open flap on top a single beam of light fell into the tent, somehow making it seem even darker; we kept bumping into each other's hands and feet, we were blinded by both the darkness and the light as we moved about, touching objects in our way; I can still hear Kálmán huffing and puffing like an animal; hard as I try, I remember little else besides this groping and crawling in the stifling excitement of the heat and darkness, and the sharp ray of light hitting the back of Kálmán's neck, and his heavy panting; I don't know, for example, how long all this lasted or whether we said anything to each other—probably not, there was no need; I knew what he wanted and what he would do next and he knew the same about me; we both knew why we had to touch these precious objects which almost made us cry out with joy, objects which in a moment would be sent flying out of here! and still, we were alone, each of us locked in his own feelings, in the very center of what we had assumed was that secret, real, and conspiratorial life; I think he made the first move by knocking the entrance flap up to the top of the tent; anyway, I remember that first it made the tent light, and then I heard a thud as the kettle crash-landed after a great, arched flight; a flashlight was next; at first we were tossing things out one by one, whatever came to hand, the harder and more fragile the better! we hurled, smashed, shattered, pulverized them one after the other; after a while we didn't have time to pick out just the good ones, and we dug into the soft stuff, frantically heaving out clothes, sheets, sacks, blankets, bumping into each other in frenzied haste, for by then we saw them running up the clearing toward us, Krisztián with his stick and knife; there were still plenty of things left in the tent, but even in my feverish zeal I made sure that the more delicate items like binoculars, an alarm clock, the slightly rusty hurricane lamp, a tuning fork, compass, and a cigarette lighter were flung as far and in as many directions as possible.

I had to yell to reach Kálmán, and I did, at the top of my voice; I was also tugging and pulling him to come on! because stones were beginning to hit the stiff canvas top; Prém was running and throwing stones, with devilish agility running, bending down and throwing without breaking his stride, but Kálmán was so caught up in this orgy of destruction he saw nothing, heard nothing, and I thought I'd have to leave him there, though that didn't seem plausible, so I kept nudging and pushing him and still he didn't notice that they were almost on top of us and that Prém had overtaken Krisztián; we had no time left, I had to make a decision, so I sneaked behind the tent and, holding on to branches and roots, constantly looking back to see why he was taking so long, started to climb up, trying to reach that miserable rock and the safety of the large bushes; Kálmán stopped right in front of the tent, stood up straight, and stared them in the eye; they were only a few steps away; then Kálmán bent down and with a leisurely saunter circled the tent, pulling up every single stake, kicking the looser ones free with his feet, and only after he'd pulled up the last one did he take off, running and then climbing after me.

The tent collapsed the very instant the boys reached it, and the sight clearly stunned them; they may have had some idea about what they were going to do, but now they just stood there, panting, helpless.

In the still booming wind I could hear the crunch and then the falling of pebbles dislodged by Kálmán's feet as he scrambled his way up toward me.

Their defeat was so spectacular, so final, their losses so considerable, they simply couldn't move, couldn't yell or curse, couldn't chase us; a single look couldn't possibly take in the extent of the destruction, and any move or word would have been an admission of this total defeat; they simply couldn't find an appropriate response, which gave us further satisfaction; in spite of our retreat, we were in a position of perfect advantage: we were above, looking down at them from a well-hidden, protected observation post, and they were below, in a fully exposed open space; as soon as he was next to me, Kálmán threw himself flat on his stomach to avoid being a target, and we lay there quite still, waiting; victory was ours, but its possible consequences were unpredictable, and for this reason I can't say we savored it for long; it was as if we ourselves were reappraising the dimensions of our deed; I was now shocked both by the sight of it and by my own presentiment that we had crossed a barrier into the forbidden, not with the treachery of our attack or the unexpected termination of a friendship—we could always find a nominal justification for that—but with the real destruction of real objects; we shouldn't have done that, we couldn't just simply return from that and resume our customary games; so now something even more dreadful, something fateful was yet to happen, it was no longer a game; by smashing those objects, we had exposed the boys to unpredictable parental intervention; however justified our retaliation may have been according to the rules of the game, by doing it the way we did, we had in effect turned the boys in; our victory, therefore, was an act of treason, and it put us outside our own law, too, for not only had we administered justice but we had exposed them to the reprisal of the common enemy; we knew only too well, for instance, that Prém was beaten nightly by his father, and it was no ordinary beating: his father set upon him with a stick, a leather strap, and if Prém fell down, his father would go ahead and kick him, too; the hurricane lamp and the alarm clock belonged to his father, Prém had taken them without permission, I knew that, and I also thought about it the very moment when I'd heard them break to pieces; still, it was our victory, and we were not to be deprived of its momentary advantages by petty ethical considerations or the shock induced by the extent and possible consequences of the destruction, if only because our victory had given them a moral superiority we couldn't possibly endure.

They didn't look at each other, just stood there motionless above their collapsed tent; Krisztián was still holding his stick in one hand and his knife in the other, which in light of their stinging defeat looked ridiculous rather than ominous; their faces were also completely motionless, and it didn't look as though they were exchanging secret signals to ready themselves for a counterattack but that they realized it was all over; their necks were stiff, Prém was closing his fist as if still holding the stone he'd hurled at us moments before; but if it was all over, what then? I didn't know what Kálmán was thinking, I myself was weighing the possibility of an immediate, unconditional, and silent withdrawal; we had to extricate ourselves somehow from this impossible situation, back off, slink away, quit the battlefield in a most cowardly fashion, if necessary, forget about our victory, and the sooner the better; but Kálmán quickly got up on his knees and, realizing what a wonderful arsenal he had been lying on, scooped up a fistful of pebbles and stones, leaned out of the bush, and without even aiming began throwing them.

With his very first stone he hit Krisztián in the shoulder; the others missed.

And then, as if pulled by the same string but in opposite directions, the two boys ducked and took off, one to the right, toward the woods, the other to the left; they disappeared among the trees at the edge of the clearing.

By doing this, not only did they blunt the attack and confuse us, the attackers, but they also dispelled the illusion that in their defeat they didn't know what to do.

It may not have been written on their faces, but they had some kind of plan; this running off was a planned move, not a flight, which they must have prepared right before our eyes, only we couldn't comprehend their secret signals; and this meant, of course, that there was a special bond between them, after all, something that could never be broken.

What an animal, what a prick, I muttered angrily, what did he have to throw those rocks for? using a word that ordinarily I'd never have used, but now it felt good, because it was part of my sweet revenge for everything.

Kálmán stayed as he was, on his knees, still holding the stones in his hand; he shrugged his shoulders lightly, which meant there was no reason to get excited; the curious pale splotches vanished from his face and he wasn't trembling anymore; he was content, calm, and gave me a friendly look filled with a kind of witless superiority born of hard-won victory; his mouth relaxed, the savage glint left his eyes, though in this newfound amiability there was a certain amount of contempt for me; with a wave of his hand he indicated that those two were probably trying to surround us, and it would be highly advisable to stop grumbling and turn around, because we had to secure our rear, too.

But I was so angry at him, hated him so much, that I wanted to fall on him, or at least knock those lousy rocks out of his hand; it was on account of his precious glazed jug, I realized, that he'd turned Krisztián into my enemy for good; I got to my knees and began cursing him; and just then two black butterflies floated by between us, their fluttering wings almost touching his chest, then they flew upward, around each other, and passed by my face; I didn't tell him what I really wanted to, that he was an ignorant hick, instead I grabbed his hand, but it turned out differently than I intended; I don't know what happened, I found myself begging him, Let's get the hell out of here, even called him Kálmánka, which only his mother did, and that made me feel more disgusted; I told him the whole thing was so stupid, and who the hell cared, anyway, and what more did he want, and if he didn't come I'd go by myself; but he just shrugged his shoulders again and coldly withdrew his hand from mine, which meant I could go whenever I wanted to, he didn't care the least bit.

Fuck you, I said to him—and it was for Krisztián's sake that I said that.

Actually, I'd have loved to tell him we shouldn't have done this, except I couldn't forget so fast that it was originally my idea, and a disgraceful act cannot be put right by another act of dishonesty; he was also important to me, but not like that, surely not like that! and besides, the moment of victory was not a good time to remind him of the horrid way he'd got back at me; I preferred my own quiet disgust.

But not leaving made me feel even more disgusted with myself; inert, I turned over to lie on my stomach and kept my eyes on the forest to see if they were coming.

In a way I was grateful to Kálmán; by staying with him I managed to salvage some of my honor, and my cowardice would be put in the right perspective, at least between the two of us; I was even more grateful that he didn't take advantage of this, said not a word, even though he understood, perhaps accepted for the first time, how important Krisztián was to me and that he, Kálmán, was of no account—I saw his acknowledgment in the form of a jeering glint, hardly more than the flash of a sideways glance.

The sun beat down on us mercilessly, not even the wind could relieve the heat, the rock was hot, and nothing was happening save for the flies swarming; we should have accepted the fact that they weren't coming, though they might charge out of the woods any second, because I was sure they wouldn't leave matters unavenged. I could have yelled, They're coming! it even occurred to me not to warn him, let them come, let them do with us what they would! with the trees groaning and creaking in the wind, cracking and snapping with each gust, branches bending and foliage sweeping forward then springing back, gaps opening and closing between the bushes, light flashing irregularly as it tried to elude the pursuing shadows, it wasn't hard to expect the sound of running feet, to see spying faces among the leaves, bodies advancing from or retreating behind tree trunks; but nothing happened, no matter how much I hoped to win back Krisztián by betraying Kálmán; they weren't coming. And I had to stay on the overheated rock, on the lookout, alert, all according to some unwritten code of honor; stay with him, though he didn't mean anything to me, I didn't care about him. To take my mind off things, I began to collect stones and lay them out in a neat row in front of me, as if to prove to myself that I was ready for combat—should the need arise, the ammunition was to hand—but I tired of this, too, and there was nothing else to do; whenever Kálmán stirred and my foot accidentally touched his shoulder, I pulled away; I didn't enjoy the warmth of a strange body.

Of course we also had to figure on their returning with possible reinforcements; one of them might still be nearby, keeping an eye on us, while the other ran off to get help; yet all I could think of was Krisztián's knife, that he might surprise me from the back, and this made me feel even more strongly the scorching sun on my back and the futile cooling efforts of the wind.

It was around noontime, though the midday bell that would reverberate through the woods hadn't yet been rung; the sun was directly overhead, its blaze felt as if it were right on top of us; if it were not for the wind blowing so strongly, it would have been impossible to endure that hour of idle waiting; all that time I spoke to him only twice, to ask if he saw anything, because I didn't; but he didn't answer, and from his stubborn silence I could surmise that our bodies lying next to each other on that hot rock were gripped by the same desperate, pent-up fury; anxiety held our fury at bay and vice versa, the sharp point of hatred was blunted by fear, though this restrained yet somehow still freewheeling emotion was no longer aimed at the other boys but at ourselves; it was no ordinary fear, not a fear of being beaten, surrounded, overwhelmed, defeated, because by now it was clear we didn't have a chance, and having no chance reduces one's fears; the problem was that during the time passed in uncertainty we ourselves, or rather the peculiar feeling lingering between us, destroyed our advantage; this is the fate of victors who finish the job left undone by the enemy; our bodies, our skin, our very silence carried on a withering conversation during that anxious, uncertain hour, and it became clear to us that our victory was not only morally dubious but also unacceptable for simpler, more pragmatic reasons; we couldn't agree even on the significance of the victory, since it meant something different to each of us, and little by little we began to sense the limits of our friendship, to understand that without the other two boys our momentary alliance simply didn't exist; we could rebel against them, and during a brief period of plotting and acting against them might have felt our relationship to be as strong as theirs, but it could not cope with our victory or sustain it; there was a secret lack here, we could not measure up, Kálmán and I could only be accomplices at best, for we lacked the very harmony—of being complementary and suited to each other—for which we had attacked them, which I envied and found so irritating, which proved as impregnable as a rockbound fortress; and it was with the magic radiance of this harmony—yes, magic radiance, I'm not afraid of the phrase—that they drew us into their friendship and ruled over us, and we appreciated the good that came from this arrangement; and now we had squandered this good, exhausted and shattered it; it wasn't them that we had destroyed but our relationship! Kálmán's rightful place was with them; his easy calm complemented their nimbleness, his lumbering wisdom was a proper match for their resourcefulness, his benevolence a mate to their cruel humor; I was on the outside and could get close to them only through my friendship with Kálmán, like a cool observer of a triumvirate who, by standing on the sidelines, reinforces their cohesiveness as well as their hierarchy—Krisztián was at the top, of course, by virtue of his irresistible charm and intelligence, which had to be accepted, no rebellion should or could topple it; he lived in us, being with him was our life, and perhaps I even had a need to suffer because of him, for something good did come of it, something real and whole and workable; what I understood right away—that we were fatally defeated in the very moment of our victory and that along with my pains I'd lose everything that was any good in my life—took Kálmán longer to comprehend, though now I sensed a message sent out by his body that it was no use lying here, no use waiting, that we were defending our honor for nothing, since even if we managed to defeat them, which was just about impossible, the broken order of the world could never be restored; there'd be no new order, only chaos.

Look, he said suddenly, quietly, choking with surprise, and though I'd been waiting for just such a sound or signal, it came too suddenly—in the desert of endless waiting the slightest stirring of even a single grain of sand seems sudden and unexpected—and I perked up, but this wasn't the same voice, not his pugnacious voice but his old one, a joyful voice expressing fond surprise at seeing what he'd anticipated all along, as when during our rovings he'd spot a fledgling bird fallen from its nest or a hairy caterpillar or a tiny porcupine among the dry leaves: I had to sit up to see what he was referring to.

There it was: down where the winding trail, rising sharply from the street and hidden by two big elder bushes, ran into the clearing, there among the windblown leaves was a flash of white, then something red, a bare arm, a blaze of blond hair, bobbing, moving closer, then popping out from behind the bushes: the three girls.

They were moving steadily up the trail, sticking close together, slightly blocking one another; they must have come in single file on the trail and now, having reached the open field, were jostling one another a little, full of small movements, leaning to the side, throwing out their arms, chatting and giggling; Hédi, the one in the white dress, was holding flowers—she loved picking them—and, leaning back, kept brandishing them in front of Livia, behind her, even stroking her face with them, gently, teasingly; then she leaned over to Maja and whispered something in her ear, though it seemed she meant Livia to hear it, too; Livia, whose skirt was the red spot we'd seen before, leaped in front of the other two, laughing, and as if wanting to carry them along with her momentum seized Maja's hand; but Hédi grabbed Livia's hand and waved her flowers in Maja's face this time; and then they stayed this way, hand in hand, their bodies almost pressing together, advancing slowly, taking very small steps, first Hédi, Livia in the middle, then Maja, completely absorbed in one another, and at the same time exchanging words, moving in an unknown formation, hovering along on the rhythm of their continually crisscrossing conversations, their faces and necks leaning close to and away from one another, their progress in the windswept, wildly undulating grass at once swift and majestically measured.

The sight itself wasn't so unusual, since they often walked this way, hand in hand, clinging to one another, and it also wasn't unusual that Hédi should be wearing Maja's white dress and Maja Hédi's navy-blue silk one, though because of the differences in their build the dresses didn't quite fit them; Hédi was taller, rounder, "stronger in the bust," they'd say among themselves, the mildly judgmental words referring only to how the dress made her look; I always paid close attention to such remarks, eager to learn whether they had a rivalry similar to the one found among us boys, but they weren't concerned so much with the difference in breast size as with the right place for the bust seam, which they debated with great seriousness and adjusted with little pulls and tucks, even unstitching and basting it anew; and although this managed to lay my suspicion about rivalry to rest, I still felt it wasn't quite unfounded; anyway, Maja's dresses "unflatteringly" flattened Hédi's breasts, but it seemed that the not-quite-perfect fits, the continually mentioned differences in build, was what made swapping dresses so attractive for them; however, they never swapped clothes with Livia and were very sensitive to the pride she took in her clothes, so while they tried on her dresses, they never insisted on wearing them; her wardrobe was rather shabby and limited in any case, though they always found her things "adorable" and eagerly outdid each other in lending her scarves and bracelets, pins, belts, ribbons and necklaces, things that would "show Livia off," as they put it, and that she accepted with engaging bashfulness; even now she was wearing a coral necklace Maja filched from her mother whenever she wanted to wear that white dress; the two girls did not seem to mind that these uneven exchanges tended to favor Maja, because most of Hédi's casually loose-fitting dresses looked quite good on her; at least in our eyes she seemed more grown-up in them, like a woman, her gangly awkwardness vanishing in their ample material; in fact, it seemed that our overlooking the unevenness of these exchanges eliminated the actual, hurtful differences which caused so much jealous rivalry between them and from which Maja suffered so much, Hédi being the pretty one, the prettier of the two, or, more precisely, the one considered pretty by everybody, the one everybody fell in love with; whenever the three of them were out together she was the one everybody looked at, behind whose back grown men whispered lewd comments, who was felt up and pinched in dark movie theaters or on crowded streetcars, even when Krisztián was with her; she cried, felt ashamed, tried to hunch her back so that her arms would cover and protect her breasts, but all in vain; and women were crazy about her, too, praising her hair especially, touching it like a rare jewel or digging into it with their fingers; with her soft blond hair falling in great shiny waves over her shoulders, her smooth, high forehead, her full cheeks and huge, somewhat protruding blue eyes, she was the "prettiest of them all," which hurt Maja so deeply that she always brought it up, kept dwelling on it, extolling Hédi's beauty more loudly than anyone, as if proud of this gesture, hoping that people would correct her exaggerations; what made Hédi's eyes especially interesting and dazzling were her long jet-black eyelashes and equally dark eyebrows, the precise curve and density of which she controlled and maintained with the help of a tweezer, plucking out hairs she considered superfluous—a very delicate operation which I saw her do once: with two fingers she stretched the skin above the eye; while working with the tweezers, snipping and plucking the stray hairs, she kept glancing at me from the mirror, explaining that although thin eyebrows were the current fashion and some women plucked them out altogether and drew new ones in with a pencil, "like that cook in school, that monster," a truly fashionable woman wasn't supposed to conform blindly to everything new but had to find the proper balance between her own assets and the prevailing trends; now Maja, for instance, often made the mistake of wearing something that, though very much in fashion, didn't look at all good on her, and if she said something about it to her, Maja would be gravely offended, which was childish; as a matter of fact, her eyebrows could use some plucking but she said it hurt, well, it didn't hurt that much, and anyway, if one had brows as thick and ugly as Maja's, one should use hair remover, which didn't hurt at all, and she should use it on her legs, too, which were terribly hairy; and the reason she didn't want to make her own eyebrows too thin was because that would make her nose look even bigger, and it was big enough as it was, so in the end she'd lose more than she would gain; her nose, skinny and slightly hooked, might indeed have been a bit large, she had her father's nose, she once told me, the most Jewish feature of her face, otherwise she could pass for a German, even, she added with a laugh; she'd never known her father, was too young to have remembered him—just as Krisztián had no memories of his father—he was "deported"; the word made as profound an impression on me as that other phrase about Krisztián's father, who "fell in battle"; and I liked running my fingers over her nose, because then I felt I was touching something Jewish; in any case, the color of her skin made up for this tiny flaw, if one can call flaw the irregular which is so organic a part of beauty; her complexion complemented her beauty, made it whole, though not fair, as one might expect in a person with blond hair and blue eyes but with the hue of a crisp, well-baked roll, and it was this color, full of tenderness, that created the harmony of perfection out of her sharply contrasting features; and I haven't even mentioned her round shoulders, her strong, slender legs that touched the ground so softly, her narrow waist and mature, womanly hips, on account of which she was once sent home with a note from her teacher for supposedly wiggling them too much; Mrs. Hűvös came flying into school and was heard screaming in the teachers' room that they'd do better to curb their own filthy imaginations than scribbling such revolting notes, and teachers like that ought to be "banned from the classroom"; Hédi's exquisite perfection did not just make her special among us but made her a distinctive and provocative beauty, a true beauty; with the help of these swaps, sometimes she sought relief from this image of perfect beauty, the swaps being all the more attractive, since Maja's dresses were nicer and more interesting.

They were coming from Maja's house and were on their way to Livia's or Hédi's, and chose this route as a shortcut, or to give Hédi a chance to pick flowers; she was assertive and narcissistic enough to advertise that she looked good picking flowers, just as she looked good playing the cello or having refined, pretty things around her; her room was full of little mugs and glasses and tiny vases; she picked fresh flowers every day and kept the withered little bunches for a long time; she was forever chomping on some plant or other, a blade of grass, a leaf, a flower; she never folded back the edge of a book page or used a bookmark, but placed a flower or, in the autumn, a colorful leaf between the pages; if you borrowed a book from her and weren't careful, a whole dried-up arboretum was likely to fall from its pages; she also took cello lessons and played her large instrument quite skillfully.

She played her cello at school functions, and once asked me to go with her into the city, where she was supposed to perform at some Jewish social event and didn't want to travel alone, especially since she'd be coming back late at night; she was also worried about her expensive instrument, not to mention all those insolent men; actually, Hédi lived in the city, in Dob Street, not far from the Orthodox synagogue, in a gloomy old apartment house on whose ground floor was a hostel for workers, who washed themselves in the courtyard in huge wash buckets; Hédi's mother, whom I hadn't yet met, had sent Hédi to live with Mrs. Hűvös over in Buda, partly because of the fresh air—Hédi supposedly had weak lungs—and partly because Mrs. Hűvös had a big vegetable garden, kept animals, and her food would be richer; but Hédi told me this was just an excuse and the real reason she became a "foster child" was that her mother had a lover, a certain Rezsö Novák Storcz, whom Hédi "couldn't stand, with his smarmy manners"; her mother wasn't home but left a note tacked to the door telling Hédi that they'd be waiting for her at the party, and also what dress she should wear; I probably remembered all this because Hédi wore the same dark navy-blue silk dress that afternoon which Maja had on now, in the woods, and Hédi's mother had some reason to object to it then: we were standing outside their door on the depressing gallery, the inner balcony running along the apartments, and it suddenly occurred to me that her father must have been deported from this very spot, an appalling nightmarish scene it must have been, thickset characters hauling off a live human being as if he were a piece of furniture, a couch or a cabinet; now all I could see were gleaming brass door handles, the pretty, old-fashioned brass buttons on bells and nameplates, the walls showing traces of bullets, alterations, badly done repair jobs, smaller holes close together in the soot-blackened plaster, left there by bursts of machine-gun fire; it was autumn and still warm, rays of the sun were sliding languidly down the slanted roofs, and down below, workmen stripped to the waist were washing up, splashing each other playfully, the whole courtyard, decorated with oleanders, resounding with their cries; in a kitchen somebody was beating eggs, through an open window we could hear choral singing coming from a radio; pressing the huge black cello case between her knees, Hédi read her mother's note as if it contained some dreadful news, read it several times, turned pale, seemed incredulous; I asked her what it said, even tried to peek, but she pulled it away, and then, sighing deeply, reached down to get the key from under the doormat.

In the spacious apartment, dark and cool, the doors were tall and white and they were all wide-open. Hédi ran straight to pee; deathly silence; the windows facing the street were shut, fringed wine-red velvet drapes hung over the heavy lace curtains fully drawn; everything in the apartment seemed layered, piled up, and invitingly soft: dark-toned hangings on the silver-patterned wall, on which were hung gilt-framed landscapes, a still life, and a painting of a nude woman illuminated by the scarlet glow of a fire in the background; striped red runners were spread over the carpets, and the flowery slipcovers of the deep armchairs and the straight-back chairs all had lace antimacassars; from the ceiling of the central room, where I stood waiting for her, hung a chandelier, wrapped like the mummy of a frightful bloated monster in a white protective cover twisted in a knot at the bottom; everything was spotless, unpleasantly, too neatly, permanently arranged—glass, brass, silver, china, mirrors, everything polished to perfection and, at least in the dim light, mercilessly free of dust.

It took a long time for Hédi to return; I had missed the sound of her trickle but heard the flush; when she came out I could tell she hadn't gone to pee but to have a little cry; she had the look of someone who has just put an end to something that was terribly important but was now over and done with; "This is the sitting room," she said, wiping her eyes again, for the last time, though there were no tears, only redness from rubbing, "and that's my room over there," she said; her pain must have been the kind she wanted to get over quickly, yet as much as she tried to smile at me, I felt she didn't want me to see her struggle, would have preferred me not to be there.

She seemed to turn very quiet in that apartment, indeed said nothing after that, but opened the big black cello case, took out the instrument, and sat down with it by the window; she tightened the bow, tested it, applied resin, took a long time tuning, while I had a chance to walk around the apartment: each room opened into another, and it was easy to imagine someone being hauled out of here, but what could not be imagined was that every night, in the completely darkened bedroom that gave onto the courtyard, this Rezsö Novák Storcz was doing something to her mother that Hédi had said always "got on her nerves."

I got back to the sitting room just as she started playing; the piece began with soft, long, deep strokes of the bow; I loved to watch her tense, absorbed face, her fingers feeling the long neck of the instrument as she quickly attacked a chord, held down the strings, her fingers quivering; then, in reply, came rapid, plaintive sounds dying quickly, higher and higher notes, reaching a level from which, with unexpected shifts and the blending of two positions—highs and lows, long and short notes played simultaneously—the melody should have emerged, leading to a clear statement of the theme, but she missed some notes and after several tries, she stopped playing, obviously annoyed.

The annoyance was for my benefit, though she pretended I wasn't in the room.

Leaning the cello against the chair, she stood up and started for her room, but changed her mind, came back, effortlessly picked up the instrument by its neck, and carefully placed it in its case, put bow and resin into their compartments, closed the case, and stood silently in the middle of the room.

For some reason I didn't say anything either, just kept watching her.

She would flop today, she said; no wonder she couldn't concentrate, she said; it was bad enough that her mother dragged along that idiot of a disgusting beast everywhere she went, she said softly, with such hatred that her body trembled, even though her mother knew, knew damn well, that just seeing him drove her to distraction; at least she should have the decency not to bring him to her performances, because that really made her unbearably nervous; all of which seemed very strange to me, since I'd never heard anyone speak with such open hostility about their own mother, and it embarrassed and shamed me; I would have liked to protest, ask her to stop, I felt I was being dragged into something I wanted no part of; she couldn't stand it anymore, she went on, she couldn't stand this man sitting there, staring at her! and as though that weren't bad enough, she said with a bitter laugh, he always has to butt in about what she should wear—Yes, yes, your little white blouse, Hédi dear, and that pretty navy-blue pleated skirt—so she'd look ridiculous and ugly! she hadn't worn those things for two years at least, because she'd outgrown them, but she pretended not to notice, hoping that slimy animal wouldn't be staring at her.

Furious, she loosened her belt and began unbuttoning the little red buttons on her blue dress—the belt was red, too—and when she reached her waist and under her hand I could see bare skin, I thought of turning away, because she didn't seem to be taking off her clothes for me, she was simply undressing, but then, with a single move, she slipped out of her dress and stood before me in the dim light, wearing only her panties and white sandals, holding her dress turned inside out, her hair slightly tousled.

And she said quietly not to be scared, she'd already shown them to Krisztián; and then we fell silent again, just standing there, and I don't know when the distance between us slipped away, all I wanted to do was touch her; she didn't look so beautiful with just her sandals on, looked rather awkward with her dress hanging from her hand, but her breasts, her breasts were calm, the two nipples looking at me; what I do remember after that—without recalling whether she started in my direction or I in hers, or maybe we both took a few steps—is the deliberate way she let her dress drop to the floor, as if she had sensed her own little-girlish, almost laughable awkwardness, and, to appear more daring and shameless, put her arms around my neck, but in a way that kept me from seeing what she had offered up to me; I was overwhelmed by her skin, by the breezy smell of her perspiration, and with an unconscious move I hugged her, even though I would have preferred to touch her breasts; the situation could have been ludicrous, since she was at least a head taller than I, but I wasn't thinking about that then—it was painful not to have my fingers touch what my mind so badly desired.

Not from the touch of her arms or skin but from the movement of her breasts did I feel that she quickly and softly kissed my ear; then she laughed and said that if she couldn't have Krisztián, she'd steal me from Livia; but I wasn't interested, because all I wanted was her breasts, the flesh, I don't quite know what, the way they were touching me, their softness or their firmness, but she was careful not to press too hard against me, wanting the tender flesh to remain between us, keep us apart; and with that laugh she let go of me and, leaving her dress on the floor, walked into another room, taking her breasts with her; I heard her open a closet door, and it was as if all this had never happened.

And when Maja had whispered in my ear earlier that she knew all along that I loved only Hédi, the reason I hadn't protested—or insisted I loved only her, Maja, or told her I loved neither her nor Hédi but Livia— was that I would have liked Maja to steal me from the other two.

They got as far as the middle of the clearing when all three of them stopped at once, looking around somewhat foolishly, realizing at last that something odd and unusual had happened or was happening here, something dangerous they suddenly didn't know how to cope with; when I'd first sat up and noticed them, it even occurred to me that Krisztián might have sent them, this could be a trap, the trick we'd anticipated, but their genuine bewilderment made it clear that their showing up here was purely coincidental, and as astonishing as that seemed, I felt it was beautiful, simply beautiful; it was fascinating to see the three girls frozen in their tracks and listening, each in her own way, each in a different direction, their high spirits ebbing away as they grasped one another's hands even more tightly.

Their physical intimacy had always intrigued me, the mutually tender ways they touched, held hands, chased about, in constant bodily contact, put their arms around and danced with each other, and kissed so freely; the way they exchanged clothes, as if giving themselves to each other or lending some very precious part of themselves; the way they combed out, curled, and set each other's hair, polished each other's nails, put their head on the other's shoulder, lap, or chest, and cried unabashedly when they were sad, shared their happiness, locking themselves in a clinging embrace with every part of their bodies participating—all this evoked in me a desire beyond envy or jealousy which I could hide but, shameful as it was, could not suppress or restrain; and I tried, hard, for I knew that Father was forever on the lookout, noticing and censuring every so-called girlish gesture of mine, perhaps he, too, had something to fear, I don't know; at any rate, I saw, I had to see, that a perfectly innocuous gesture was enough to fill me to the brim with this desire, which may explain why I wanted to be a girl, and indeed often imagined being one, to have some unequivocal legal grounds for these unpunished contacts, even though I sensed far more impulse, fear, constraint, habit, and routine in the apparent freedom of the girls than I could admit; and whenever my longing for uninhibited constant bodily contact did not completely cloud my mind, I realized, of course, that this contact was but a parallel version of the same passionate rivalry that existed among us boys, even if we weren't permitted to touch one another physically or had to find complicated, tiresome, and often humiliating pretexts to do so, resort to trickery, outsmart one another just to share among us our most elementary emotions; I couldn't ignore, and in fact bitterly envied the profound attraction that made Krisztián want to fight with Kálmán all the time, choosing the uniquely boyish form of fighting, which girls never used; girls entered into physical fights only when in dead earnest, and then they would scream, tear, scratch, and bite one another; between us boys the game of fighting, unimaginable among girls, always erupted for no apparent reason, simply because we wanted to touch, hold one another, feel and possess the other's coveted body, and only this kind of playful fight could legitimate our desires; had we expressed them as openly as girls did, embraced and kissed as they did, had we not camouflaged the true intentions of these physical rivalries, the others would have called us fags, because clearly I was not the only one watching his step, the others were also very careful not to cross certain boundaries, although you could never be entirely sure what the word itself meant, it had a mythic character, like almost all our curse words and imprecations, implying a desire for something forbidden; for example, we say "eat my dick," because it's forbidden, or we say "motherfucker," alluding to another taboo; to me the word meant a prohibition against an entirely natural impulse, the meaning of which was only vaguely illuminated by a remark Prém dropped once, which he'd heard from his brother, who, being six years older, was considered an authority, according to whom "if you let a guy suck your cock, you'll never be able to screw a woman," a statement that needed neither comment nor explanation; it made it quite clear that everything faggy or having to do with faggots or faggotry endangered masculinity, the very thing we were striving for; in another sense, the whole notion was beyond the grasp of a child's mind; for me it meant one more of those disgusting, mean things adults did which one was never keen on following, but the word failed to stamp out the impulse, the lively desire, camouflaged though it was by the innocence of our playful fights, it merely held in check the desire that among boys constantly seeks expression; as I've said before, I wasn't alone in this; for instance, Krisztián would creep up behind Kálmán, throw his arms around him, and wrestle him to the ground, or—and this was one of their favorites—they'd grab each other's hand

and keep pressing, squeezing, and bending it, the rule of the game being that no hand must be seen above the desk, and you weren't allowed to rest your elbow on your thigh—in other words, one arm had to wrestle down the other in the air; they'd turn red, grin, and, straining for support, would hold their bodies stiff by pressing their locked knees together; the object here was not to beat the opponent, as in a serious fight, but to get a lover's taste of his strength, agility, and resilience, to enjoy the preeminence of sexual sameness, and fulfillment meant the tender meeting of two like strengths; in the same way, with the tender intimacy of the girls, one could feel a certain amount of unpleasant, irksome falsity, although not so clearly or emphatically as with us, but when they were walking about hand in hand, giggling, whispering, gossiping, or dressing, consoling, teasing, or caressing one another, I couldn't help feeling that this degree of direct bodily contact was permissible only because it was merely the outermost layer of their bond, friendship, and alliance, a kind of necessary guise, like our playful fights, contact that seemed not to express real feelings but rather to demonstrate a secret conspiracy or even conceal a deadly hostility; this became especially obvious to me after the incident in the gym when Hédi accidentally discovered that Livia and I had been staring at each other, and of course she made sure word got out: that Livia and I were in love, for by doing this, she not only exposed Livia to common talk but delivered her up to me, and further, by spreading the rumor that Livia had fainted in the gym out of love for me, she saw to it that this act of deliverance became public knowledge; interestingly enough, Hédi's machinations did not make Maja jealous; on the contrary, she showed great enthusiasm, forever trying to arrange for Livia and me to be alone; yet it was clear that with their acts of kindness and maternal solicitude, Hédi and Maja would not let go of Livia; their kindness was a trap, their solicitude a noose, and what's more, buried in their approbation were underhanded concessions with which to get into a more confidential relationship with me, as if they knew that ultimately this would only confuse me, as if this had been their express goal from the start; they got me Livia, but on no account was I to be able to choose among the three of them: Livia could be mine, but only in the way and to the extent they allowed, and Livia had no objections to the arrangement, because the alliance the three of them had forged, for and against me, the conspiracy itself and their bond, was far more important to her than I was, or, more precisely, she knew it was in her own best interest not to let this secret alliance unleash their own fierce rivalry, not to let open hostilities between them make me take sides, and everything should stay as it had been: undecided, ambiguous.

In the clearing, Livia was the first to adapt herself to the new situation; she slipped her hand away, bent down, and with no little astonishment picked up the wounded alarm clock; she said something and giggled, maybe amused that the clock was still ticking, for she was pointing at it; at that moment she seemed to be the wildest of the three, but the other two paid no attention to her, and she proceeded to pick the pieces of broken glass out of the frame of the clock's face and drop them on the ground one by one; she seemed to be enjoying herself immensely; then she put the clock on her head, balancing it carefully, wearing it like a crown, and, self-possessed, stepping out majestically, she moved on.

The other two girls, more sensible, were still standing in place, hesitating, looking and listening, one to the right, the other to the left, and only when with an adroit gesture Livia wrapped the red blanket about her shoulders did they begin to move—maybe because the gesture was a kind of signal.

They ran after her; when Maja wanted to wrap herself in the white sheet, which she picked up on the run, a mild altercation ensued, for Hédi also wanted the sheet, and they tugged it back and forth; I assumed that Hédi thought the sheet would go better with her white dress, the one she had borrowed from Maja, and though the problem seemed to be solved with amazing speed, it became clear that the argument wasn't just over the sheet, over who would get it first, but there was a need to establish a pecking order appropriate for the current situation: the sheet went to Hédi, who on the strength of her beauty always got her way, which made Maja retreat into quiet petulance; the sheet became a train of the white dress, Maja helped tuck it in under the red belt, so now Hédi was the queen, Livia a sort of lady-in-waiting, and Maja the humiliated maidservant who, naturally, lifted the train all wrong, for which she received a kick, and that finally determined her place in the hierarchy.

They did all this quickly, like a well-trained team, but not at all seriously, acting it out, one might say, as if they were only playing at playing, and yet we couldn't laugh at them because, on the one hand, their silliness was so uninhibited and shameless and they were enjoying it so much, and on the other hand, they were very much out of place on this turf; we watched them with bated breath, too shocked to realize that in our hopeless situation they were our saviors.

But I also thought they were obnoxious for meddling in something that was none of their business.

Now they were marching in single file, led by Livia, with the red blanket tucked under the collar of her blouse, the alarm clock on her head, Hédi's train raised high by Maja, who picked up one of the castaway pots she stumbled on and humbly, smiling maliciously, placed it on Hédi's head; they kept perfecting their procession until they reached the collapsed tent.

I must have understood what they were doing at the very moment they themselves realized, without exchanging a single word, what it was they were supposed to be playing.

It had to do with a big book Livia had, *Great Ladies of Hungary*, which she often took with her to Maja's house—they liked to peruse it together—which had a mournful illustration depicting the dream of Queen Mária, widow of King Lajos, in which she searches for her husband's body among grisly corpses and bloated carcasses on the battlefield of Mohács.

Livia began to move in this dreamlike manner, and the other two quickly caught on and followed suit: they stretched their arms to the sky and walked as in a dream, without touching the ground; to show pain and grief, they raised their hands to their breasts, crying, like the queen in the picture with huge teardrops rolling down her pale blue cheeks.

In front of the tent Livia fell to the ground with her arms still outstretched, the alarm clock fell off her head and rolled away, and she enacted this little scene so the effect would be truly funny.

I didn't find it funny at all; it was disgusting to see her clowning like that for the benefit of her two friends.

Kálmán's mouth dropped open, stupidly; I wanted to step in, ruin the performance, put an end to it.

The two girls looked at Livia, commiserating, leaning over her, blinking their teary eyes, comforting her, and then they reached under her arms and tried to help her up, but now that she had found it, it was with great difficulty that the queen could be torn away from the body of her slain husband.

And when they did tear her away and led her off, supporting her on both sides, just as in the picture, Livia finally found her way into the part: for a few moments the clowning became a true performance, some real feelings appeared in her acting, her performance as a woman out of her mind, her eyes rolling and turning inward, thrusting out her hands and, though seeking the support of her helpers, lurching stiffly forward so the two others had to hurry along, because she was propelled by frenzied pain; before long, the spectacle turned my disgust with Livia into astonishment; she surprised me, caught me unprepared, and just as in the movies when something heartrending or awful on the screen made me want to scream or cry or even get out of the theater, I had to remind myself that it was only an act and therefore the truly felt emotions in it were not real, but in that very instant Maja pulled out her arm from under Livia, moved away, and began to run, which made the two other girls lose their balance and get entangled; Hédi, who couldn't see because of the pot on her head, rammed into Livia and pulled her down, and Livia sought support in Hédi's falling body; noticing none of this, Maja kept running toward the neatly stacked woodpile, most likely attracted by the matches placed next to it, and while the two other girls were rolling around with laughter, she squatted down and put a match to the pile.

A loud scream went up from among the trees, Krisztián's; like an echo, the reply came from the other side of the clearing, Prém's; then Kálmán began to scream, and I also heard myself screaming.

With this exultant harmonious battle cry, blasting through the still raging wind, we swooped down on the girls, Krisztián and Prém advancing from either end of the clearing; with sounds of crashing and crackling we hurled ourselves forward, dirt rolling down and stones flying in our wake; to the girls it must have seemed not that they were being surrounded by four different screams but that they were being hit by a single elemental blow of nature.

The flames tore swiftly into the dry twigs, the wind immediately stirred up the light, darting tongues, blowing them out in long stretches, then sucking them in again; Maja threw away the matches and ran to the other two for cover and then back again; the girls sprang up, and by the time we got there, the whole pile was ablaze.

The three girls took off in three different directions, but they were surrounded, had no escape; without knowing why, I went after Hédi, Kálmán chased Maja, and both Krisztián and Prém went after Livia, who was off like a shot; Hédi was running down the hill, one of her sandals flew off her foot, which she ignored, she threw her head back, her blond hair streaming in the wind, the white sheet sweeping the ground after her; I thought of stepping on the sheet and making her trip, and I didn't know what was happening behind us, the only thing I saw was that Maja had almost got to the trees when Kálmán managed to grab her; just then

Livia began to squeal and scream so loudly—and there was no playacting in that—that Hédi abruptly changed direction and, while my momentum stupidly made me run past her, had time to swerve around and start running back up the hill to help Livia.

They were entangled in one whirling mass, twisting and grappling on the ground, the wind whipping long flames over them; like a lunatic, Hédi threw herself on them, screaming, perhaps to let the struggling Livia know she was there, ready to help, and I threw myself on top of Hédi, even though at that moment I could already see what was happening: they were pulling off Livia's red skirt, there it was under Krisztián's knees. It couldn't have been hard to get the skirt off, it was held only by an elastic at the waist, but now it looked as though they wanted to tear off her blouse; while Krisztián used his knees to pin down Livia's naked lower body to keep her from kicking, Prém, kneeling above her head, was trying to restrain her flailing, protective arms and get the blouse off; the completely incredible circumstance that Prém had no underpants on I noticed only at the very moment I was jumping on Hédi's back; Livia kept her eyes shut tight and kept on screaming; above her face, directly above her face, dangled Prém's famed member, flapping, swinging, swaying to the tune of the furious struggle, almost touching her face.

And even though I saw this, I still wanted to help the boys; I tried to get Hédi off Krisztián's back, which wasn't easy, since she was now scratching and biting.

In the end, this rather dubious help from me was totally superfluous, because as soon as Krisztián sensed that Hédi was on his back, clinging to him and sinking her nails into his shoulder, he let go of Livia and with one violent jerk of his back threw Hédi off, so powerfully that she slid down and turned over; Prém stopped, too, but when Livia tried to slither out from under him, he once more snatched at her blouse; I don't know whether the buttons had been ripped off earlier or popped off now as she sprang up and fled, but in any case her breasts were visible; Krisztián grinned at Hédi, something made him shake his head, his beautiful dark curls, and smartly feinting, he managed to slip away, because Hédi was again screaming and trying to attack him, while Prém started running after Livia—but actually to get his shorts, which he'd thrown away before—who, clutching her blouse to cover her breasts with one hand and her red skirt in the other, sprinted for the trees; Kálmán, who was just coming out of the woods, returning from his apparently unsuccessful foray, stopped, surprised, to watch Livia in her pink panties disappear;

"You're an animal, an animal!" Hédi screamed into Krisztián's face, her voice choking, her scream turning into tears, but he somehow looked past this outburst, as though their love no longer mattered to him, his glance grazing mine, and I felt I was grinning just the same way he was; there were long scratch marks on his forehead and chin; he stepped toward me, we grinned into each other's grin, and, with Hédi standing between us, looked into each other's eyes; then he stepped around Hédi, lifted his arm, and with all his might slapped me in the face with the back of his hand.

Everything went black, and not because of the slap.

I seemed to have seen Hédi, who couldn't possibly have understood the reason for the slap, trying to defend me, but Krisztián pulled away from her, shook her off, turned, and started slowly for the fire swirling in the wind.

And I probably turned my back on the scene then and let my feet carry me away.

Kálmán was standing under a tree, looking at us impassively, Prém was pulling on his pants, and Maja was nowhere to be found.

Prém later claimed he'd been taking a crap when Maja lit the fire, but I didn't believe him; when you take a crap you pull down your pants, you don't take them off; but after what had happened it wouldn't have made any sense to tell him to his face that he was lying.

I also found out later that Kálmán had almost managed to catch Maja, but to get to her would have had to hug a tree trunk; he wanted to kiss her, but Maja spat into his mouth, and that's how she got away.

It took many a long week to get over this incident. We didn't go to each other's house; I barely dared leave our garden for fear of running into one of them.

By the end of that summer, though, things had got back to normal, more or less, if only because Krisztián began to hang around Livia, perhaps to win Hédi back by making her jealous or perhaps because he really got a good look at Livia that afternoon or because he wanted to make amends for assaulting her; anyway, he'd wait for her and walk her home from school; from her window Hédi must have seen them leaning against the schoolyard fence, engaged in conversation, long, absorbed, cozy conversation, for she complained about it to Maja, who, just to torment me, told me about it, on the pretext that she'd once again found something suspicious among her father's papers, something quite new, which I'd better go over to look at; she called urgently on the telephone, but in fact she hadn't found anything interesting or, rather, useful; it was a neatly folded copy of a memorandum in which her father requested the Minister of the Interior to confirm in writing that he'd acted on the minister's express verbal instruction when he had had a tap put on the telephone of a certain Emma Arendt.

Maja wanted to gossip, to see how I'd react to this new development, and the excuse came in handy, since I'd been looking for a way to patch things up between us, so I went over and pretended to be not the least interested in what was going on between Livia and Krisztián; we also decided that in the future we wouldn't talk about important things over the telephone, because if her father was told to listen in on certain phone conversations and if there was indeed such a listening device, then quite possibly our phones were tapped, too.

On my way out I saw Kálmán standing outside the front door; he turned red and said he just happened to be passing by—from the time of that incident we all began to see through one another's lies, yet stubbornly went on lying—and Kálmán and I walked home together, because he couldn't find an acceptable excuse for staying, having to be consistent in his lie; on the way I found out he had made up with Prém and Krisztián, the opportunity for which had been provided by the military maps Krisztián had left at his house; in short, by summer's end, slowly, not quite smoothly, and in a somewhat altered configuration, the old relationships were more or less re-established, but they could never regain the strength of the old closeness, no longer had the old flavor and fervor.

In his clever, cunning reasoning, Krisztián went so far as to call what happened that afternoon in the woods a piece of theater, and by using that phrase he tamed it; what's more, he planned more performances on the original site: we'd clear away the bushes under the flat rock, that's where the stage would be, and the girls would sew the costumes; at first he wanted to leave me out of the production, but the girls wouldn't let him—it seemed that even our differences meant something to them—so he finally relented and suggested I write the text; twice I went over to his house to discuss the details, but we only ended up fighting again, then he decided we didn't need any text; he wanted to do something dealing with war and I had a love story in mind, which doubtless resembled too closely our real-life situation; by stubbornly insisting on my version, I talked myself out of a job, because the girls far preferred playing amazon-like warriors to inamoratas.

The afternoon I visited her, Maja was getting ready to go to a rehearsal for one of these performances—I wasn't invited—but of course there could be no more performances, not after that unique, true performance born of a series of coincidences, the one we'd do well to forget; subsequent ones were prevented by other, strange coincidences, because without our feeling the changes in ourselves, our childhood games had come to an end once and for all.

But sometimes I still walked through the forest just to feel, for myself only, the thing we were so afraid of.

The following spring grass grew over the scorched spot.

And now, after what turned out to be a lengthy digression—so long that it's hard to tell what we had digressed from and to what—it's time to return to the point where we left off our recollections; it's to Maja's rumpled bed that I should return, to her open mouth, to her slightly alarmed yet hate-filled, loving eyes, as she simultaneously wanted and didn't want me to tell her what I knew about Kálmán, and there I am, unable to tell her what I want to tell her; desire, will, and intention falter and stumble on the strict dividing line between the sexes; something made itself felt, something with a will stronger than mine, like a law or an erection; at the same time, the mere mention of the woods was enough to make her lose heart, frustrate her designs, interfere with and even cancel some of her plans, and I could do all that without betraying my own smoldering jealousy.

That afternoon we were going to go through her father's papers, and there was nothing to stop us from getting down to business as soon as I arrived; her mother had gone shopping downtown, Szidónia was out on an early date, yet we had good reason to tarry: we were scared; now I should find my way back to our dark secret, mentioned only in hushed voices, I should tell about it, about how we conducted our searches, sometimes in my house, sometimes in hers, and I should remark, objectively, that it was more dangerous in my place, because Father knew all about my penchant for spying and snooping and kept his desk drawers locked.

It was one of those tricky locks, locking the middle drawer locked the rest as well, but the tabletop could be lifted with a screwdriver, and then the lock simply snapped open; Maja and I were convinced that our fathers were spies and were working together.

This, the most dreadful secret of my life, I have never told anybody before.

There were enough mysterious elements in the behavior of both men to make our daring supposition not altogether implausible, and we were constantly on the alert, searching and collecting evidence.

The two men had only a nodding acquaintance, or more precisely, we assumed they only pretended not to know each other well; we would have thought it more appropriate, and also more suspicious, if they didn't know each other at all; sometimes their travels—of unknown purpose—coincided, but we were suspicious even when they didn't and one of the men would leave just as the other returned.

Once I had to deliver a heavy sealed yellow envelope to Maja's father; on another occasion we both witnessed a particularly suspicious scene: Father was coming home, in his official car, and Maja's father, in his car, was on his way into the city; on busy Istenhegyi Road the two cars stopped, the men got out, exchanged what seemed like routine pleasantries, then her father handed something very quickly to mine; when later that evening I asked Father what Maja's father had given him—the question was a kind of cross-examination, of course—he told me to mind my own business, and laughed suspiciously, which I promptly reported by telephone to Maja.

If we had found a piece of incriminating evidence, like a cryptic note, some foreign money, a strip of microfilm—we knew from Soviet films and novels that there was always some incriminating evidence, and we went from cellar to attic looking for it—if we had found some tangible, incontrovertibly incriminating evidence against them, we swore to each other that we would report them, because if they were spies, traitors, we'd show no mercy, let them perish! and our mutual oath could not be broken because this mutual intrusion into our parents' lives made us fearful, terrified of each other, and so we kept searching feverishly, hoping to pick up a trail, stumble on a clue, get the thing over with; there was crime in the air, that much we knew, we felt it in our bones; and if there was crime there had to be evidence; at the same time, and equally, we feared being proven right, a fear we had to hide from each other because showing concern for our respective fathers might have been construed as a violation of our oath, a betrayal of our principles; so we stalled and dallied, deferring for as long as we could the moment of possible success, of possibly coming upon some proof positive.

The moment would have been wonderful, and awful; in my fantasies it implicated only Maja's father, and Maja behaved so heroically that only a single tear of anger and frustration glistened in her eye.

And that afternoon, in our fear, we got so entangled in each other's soul and body that we mercifully forgot all about our original goal, our secret, the solemn vow, and the search itself, although we knew we couldn't completely get away from them: our political alliance had revealed a mysteriously deep, to us incomprehensible, erotic pain and thrill which proved more powerful and more exciting than our unfulfillable spiritual and physical desires.

But to return, to pick up the thread of the narrative, even if my narrator-self hesitates at this point, and of course also urges itself to carry on, yes, please continue! go on! yet it fears, even today it fears, that the siren voices of charged emotions may lure it toward further digression, explanation, self-justification, self-exposure, an even more scrupulous unearthing of details, just to avoid this one subject! the analytical part of the self would find this justifiable, because without further detours it is even harder to explain why two children would want to denounce their own fathers, why they would suppose their fathers to be agents of an enemy power—what kind of enemy power, anyway, and who was the enemy of whom?

It would be overhasty and no less vulgar if I explained that our secret political alliance gave us the hope that by exposing these two men, whom we loved with the most ardent physical love above everyone else, by sending these fathers to the gallows, we could unburden ourselves of this impossible love; and in those years denunciations like these were not considered only the result of childish fantasies: the imagined scenario, like a broken record, kept going around and around in our minds.

But this was it: what had to happen did happen, and there was to be no more delay; Maja pulled her foot out from under my thigh, helping herself with her hand, slipped out of our closeness, quickly and mercilessly, as when one is compelled to cut something off, got up, and started for the door.

From the middle of the room she looked back—her face was red, splotchy, and most likely as hot as I felt mine to be; she gave me a strange, soft smile—I knew she was heading for her father's study, but I waited for my emotions to subside; again she was the stronger, which made me feel as if she had torn herself from my body, a feeling that would not subside, because as she was standing there smiling, in the middle of the room filled with flickering green shadows, I heard myself think, in Kálmán's voice, I should have screwed her; it was as if in his stead I had bungled something he had been waiting for in vain.

And the reason I called her smile strange is that it had neither disdain nor mockery but, if anything, perhaps a touch of sadness, meant more for herself than for me: a wise smile, a mature smile that tried to solve this seemingly insoluble problem not with the superficiality of force but by sensibly accepting the notion that when you are unhappy in a given situation, when you get no satisfaction from it, then you must, without repudiating anything, change it.

The slightest change in our situation holds out hope; even a restless little stirring can offer hope.

And this is so even if the new situation, like the one Maja was now offering to me and to herself as she headed for the other room, seemed at least as insoluble, and ethically as disastrous, as the previous one; still, it was a change, and change has an optimism of its own.

There I sat on her rumpled bed, my heat still feeling hers, all that heat and energy which ultimately had been conducted nowhere stayed in me, in the bed, in her, while the room looked back at us impassively, coolly; I could not break out of that heat to obey her summons now, and not only because my body wasn't presentable but because her smile generated new waves of gratitude and realization in me.

Today this realization seems more like obtuseness, and I think the reason I felt such great but by no means obligatory gratitude was that she was a girl, and though I didn't feel like poking around in her father's papers, I knew I was going to follow her.

It was as if she knew better, knew that our secret search would produce the same aching excitement in our bodies that could not be gratified before.

Then without a word she left the room.

I never loved her as much as I did then, and I loved her because she was a girl, which may not be so great a foolishness as it at first sounds.

When after long minutes my body was finally ready to move, to shift position, and walking through the deserted dining room I entered the study, she was standing by her father's desk with her back toward me, waiting—she couldn't start without me.

The enormous desk, with many drawers of various sizes and compartments in various positions, unattractively dark and unadorned, took up almost the whole room, looking like an old, overweight animal on short thin legs.

I shouldn't close the door, she told me quietly but impatiently, her tone almost hostile; it was fairly late, which meant her parents might be coming home soon.

She needn't have said that; we always left the door ajar, to give us some cover but also so we could hear approaching steps; the study was like a mousetrap, a dead end, the innermost room in the apartment, a kind of pit, as it were, from which there was no escape; you could leave here only by backing out, invariably bumping into an overstuffed chair as you did.

No matter how much we tried to discipline ourselves, as soon as we sneaked into this room our breathing turned loud, choppy, almost whistling, and we had to hold things too firmly, too deliberately, to hide our trembling movements, but the effort betrayed us anyway, making each of us vulnerable to the other, and that's why we spoke hostilely even when there was no reason for it, and somehow, in here, we each considered every move made by the other to be clumsy, wrong, sure to spoil everything.

It's hard to say which one of us was in greater danger; in her house, she was, I suppose: any incriminating evidence found in this room would have exposed, first of all, her father; consequently, irritated as I was, I felt I had to be more considerate with her than she might be with me; on the other hand, if we were caught red-handed, I'd be far worse off, because I had even less right to touch things in this room than she did, which is why I positioned myself so that if I heard footsteps I could be the first to slip out; even if it meant abandoning her, I had to have that slight advantage.

Of course I was a little ashamed of this attitude, but didn't have the courage to give up my advantage; I projected the worst possible scenario: if I heard footsteps only at the last minute, I'd quickly grab and hold the doorknob, like someone just standing there, observing her, not touching anything but the doorknob; I admit, even as an imagined scene this was very cowardly.

Yet our frantic excitement, the almost intolerable tension, could not be allowed to affect our activity; there was to be no haste but painstaking precision, infinite circumspection, we could not behave like amateur burglars who ransack the whole house looking for money and jewelry and then clear out leaving a huge mess behind; the nature of the work was such that we couldn't expect quick results and there was no detail we could afford to overlook; so in spite of all our excitement and impatience, we learned to exercise self-control, to be humble and meticulous, and we turned ourselves into expert sleuths.

Regardless of its boring familiarity, we first had to inspect the area under investigation, a procedure with a definite order, if not rules of its own; at their house she directed the work, while at mine it was my job cautiously to pull out the drawers—in each case the host had to assume responsibility for the operation's physical aspects—and together we had to ascertain whether there were any notable changes since the last search; generally two weeks, sometimes a whole month went by before we could reinspect each desk, a long enough period for substantial changes in the contents of some drawers: objects and papers might disappear, temporarily or permanently, the old contents might be differently arranged, or entirely new objects might replace the old ones; in this respect we had a harder time at her house, because her father, while not exactly untidy, was not nearly so neat and methodical as mine, who did not make our job harder by carelessly reaching into a drawer or poking around impatiently in another or pulling out something from the bottom of a pile.

To start with, Maja quietly pulled out the drawers while I watched over her shoulder, pulled them out one by one, without haste but not slowly either; we were familiar with each other's ability to observe, the pace with which to record what was observed; we knew how much time we each needed to take in the object as well as the direction of our search, to fix in our minds a picture of the drawer's inside, its overall shape that would enable us to make quick comparisons; and it was at such times that, without saying a single word, we had our most professional debates, touching on the very essence of our work; what was at stake was the integrity of our voluntary work as agents, and the heavy political responsibility that went with it: once in a while we might have pushed back a drawer too quickly, without noticing (or, worse, pretending not to notice) possible changes in its contents; at such moments the other person, with a mere glance, ordered a halt and demanded a correction; our roles changed according to the location—in my house she kept an eye on me, here I was the fussy one, though we made sure the control remained impersonal, and wanted to keep it skeptical but not mistrustful, overlooking the regrettable and unavoidable fact that, instinctively, against our better judgment, we were each protecting our respective fathers, which of course could prejudice our work; a drawer whose contents looked suspiciously different or that had been obviously gone through nervously, or the mere sight of a new batch of papers or an odd-looking envelope was enough to make us edgy, and it was the job of the other, acting as controller, to get us over this edginess so characteristic of amateurs, and to do so subtly and delicately, with the sober gravity of a glance reminding us of our commitment to professional honesty and objectivity, helping us overcome our intrusive albeit understandable filial bias; at the same time we couldn't seem sarcastic, aggressive, or rude; in fact, sometimes, for the sake of our ultimate goal, we'd even be slyly complaisant and act as if we hadn't noticed something the other one didn't want or dare to notice, and point it out only later, as if by chance, unexpectedly, and then pounce on the crucial item with all the rectitude of true conviction.

Only after these preliminaries could the real work begin: the close examination of notes, letters, receipts, papers, and documents; we never sat down but stood next to each other, in the shared sphere of each other's heat and excitement; we read the stuff together and in unison, devouring with greedy curiosity what were for the most part routine and boring, or fragmentary and therefore largely incoherent, pieces of information, and only when it was clear that the other didn't understand or might misunderstand something and therefore draw the wrong conclusion did we break the silence with a few whispered words of explanation.

We were not aware of what we were doing to each other and to ourselves; in the interest of our stated goal we didn't want to acknowledge that as a result of our activity a feeling was forming, like some tough stain or film, a deposit on the lining of our hearts, stomachs, and intestines; we did not want to acknowledge the feeling of repulsion.

Because it wasn't just official and work-related documents that we came across but all sorts of other material that we did not mean to find, like our parents' extensive personal romantic correspondence; here, the material discovered in my father's drawers was unfortunately more serious, but once we put our hands on it and went over it thoroughly, painstakingly, with the disinterested sternness of professionals, it seemed that by ferreting out sin in the name of ideal purity, invading the most forbidden territory of the deepest and darkest passions, penetrating the most secret regions, we, too, turned into sinners, for sin is indivisible: when tracking a murderer one must become a murderer to experience most profoundly the circumstances and motives of the murder; and so we were right there with our fathers, where not only should we not have set foot but, according to the testimony of the letters, they themselves moved about stealthily, like unrepentant sinners.

There is profound wisdom in the Old Testament's prohibition against casting eyes on the uncovered loins of one's father.

Maybe if we had uncovered this forbidden knowledge separately, each of us alone, we might have been able to conceal it from ourselves—forgetting can sometimes act like a good comrade; but our situation was exacerbated by our attachment, this passionate and passionately suspicious relationship which went far beyond friendship but had not reached love; we got to know these secrets together and, let's not forget! while still sexually unsatisfied: the very object of these secrets was passion and its mutual gratification, and as we know, a secret shared by two people is no longer a secret; with her full knowledge and approval I read through letters written by a woman named Olga and also by her mother, both women writing from the height of emotional and physical rapture, cursing, berating, extolling, admonishing, fawning, and above all imploring her father not to abandon them, and, in keeping with the conventions of such love letters, decorating their words with encircled teardrops, locks of hair, pressed flowers, and little hearts drawn in red pencil; though old enough to sense the raw power of passion, in our aesthetic squeamishness we found all this very repugnant; with my approval and eager assistance, Maja had a chance to acquaint herself with the stylistically more restrained letters that János Hamar wrote to my mother and the ones my father wrote to Mária Stein, but my father and mother also wrote letters to each other in which they discussed their feelings about being caught up in this inextricably complicated foursome; and since all this was revealed to both of us, we should have made some judgment, or at least have appraised and characterized the information, put it in its proper place; needless to say, this went way beyond our moral strength—which otherwise we thought quite formidable.

How could we have known then that our relationship reenacted, repeated, and copied, in a playfully exaggerated form—today I know it followed a diabolical pattern—our parents' ideals and also their ruthless practices, and to some extent the publicly proclaimed ideals and ruthless practices of that historical period as well? playing at being investigators was nothing but a crude, childishly distorted, cheap imitation; we could call it aping, but we could also call it an immersion in something real, for Maja's father was chief of military counter-intelligence and my father was a state prosecutor, and therefore by picking up on hints and remarks they dropped, we were both initiated, almost by accident and definitely against their will, into the professional pursuit of criminal investigation; more precisely, for us it was turning their activities into a game that enabled us to experience their present life and work—which we thought was wonderful, dangerous, important, and, what's more, respectable—and also to bring their past closer, which, judging by the contents of those drawers, was filled with adventure, real-life dangers, narrow escapes, false papers, and double identities—we could see their youth; and if I were to go a little further—and why shouldn't I?—I'd have to say that they were the ones who blessed the knife with which we sought their lives; in this sense, we not only suffered for playing our games but also took great delight in them; we loved being serious, we basked in the glory of our assumed political role, not only filled with terror and remorse but bestowing on us a grand sense of power, a feeling that we had power even over them, over these enormously powerful men, and all in the name of an ethical precept that, again in their own views, was considered sacred, nothing less than the ideal, self-abnegating, perfect, immaculate Communist purity of their way of life; and what a cruel quirk of fate it was that through it all they were totally unsuspecting, and how could they have guessed that, while in their puritanical and also very practical zeal they were killing scores of real and imagined enemies, they were nurturing vipers in their bosom? for after all, who disgraced their ideals more outrageously than we? who put their ideals more thoroughly to the test than we, in our innocence? and since we also harbored the same witch-hunter's suspicion toward them and toward each other, which they had planted in us and bred in themselves, with whom could we have shared the dreadful knowledge of our transgressions, whom? I couldn't talk about things like this with Krisztián or Kálmán, nor could Maja discuss them with Hédi or Livia, for how could they have understood? even though we lived in the same world, ruled by the same *Zeitgeist*, this would have been too alien for them, too bizarre, too repulsive.

Our secrets carried us into the world of the powerful, initiated us into adulthood by making us prematurely mature and sensible, and of course set us apart from the world of ordinary people, where everything worked more simply and predictably.

These love letters referred openly and unequivocally to the hours in which, by some peculiar mistake, we had been conceived—by mistake, because they didn't want us, they wanted only their love.

For example, in one of her letters to my father, Mária Stein described in great detail what it was like to be embraced by János Hamar and then by Father. In her letter, and I distinctly remember this, it was the stylistic value of the word that troubled me most; I would have loved to understand "embrace" as a hug, a kind of friendly hug and squeeze, but of course there was no doubt that the word alluded to something else, which for a child was a little like watching an animal in heat that suddenly starts speaking—interesting but incomprehensible; the letters Mother got from János Hamar before I was born were no less ardent; this was the same János Hamar who then disappeared from our lives as mysteriously and unexpectedly as Mária Stein did; neither of them came around anymore, and I was supposed to forget them, because my parents wanted it that way; Maja, on the other hand, was visibly pained by the fact that her father was still seeing this Olga woman, even though as far as her mother knew, the affair had ended long ago; Maja was forced to become her father's silent accomplice, though she loved her mother more.

I imagine the archangels covered God's eyes while we pored over these letters.

We made things somewhat easier on ourselves by quickly dismissing the letters as unimportant and silly—how could respectable, middle-aged people scribble such smutty things to each other?—thus extinguishing the flames of our interest, which had been fanned by our own nature, we went about even more desperately looking for crimes that did not exist, at least not in the form we imagined.

Except I couldn't take it anymore: there was nothing premeditated about my decision; it was a sudden and complete indifference toward the whole business, a feeling that these drawers with all the papers in them no longer interested me; they had before but now for some reason didn't, and I must leave.

While the setting sun still shone outside, a soft dimness was already spreading within; it was nice, and somehow made the large desk loom even larger and more gloomily, and in the fine layer of dust covering its smooth dark surface, I could see Maja's telltale fingerprints.

And there was something else: a strange, unfamiliar, and infinitely light sensation that I in fact existed, not irresponsibly but in full awareness of my responsibilities, and that I should stop doing what I was doing, and it would be not cowardly to stop but, on the contrary, an act of courage; I was still bothered by how tensely and crookedly she drew up her shoulders, that movement bothered me, and so did the traces our search had left behind; it may have been the feeling of being conscious of my body, that earlier erection provoked by her nearness, which now removed me from the childish games that we had transformed into a seemingly serious activity; I don't quite know what it was, except I felt that I must break out of this, and now! it seemed that all I wanted was that these lovely, slender, restive shoulders of hers—I did love it that she looked so impossibly thin in her mother's dress, I liked them more than Hédi's fuller, broader shoulders, which would have no trouble filling out such a dress—yes, I wanted these shoulders to relax, to be like, like . . . but just what they should be like my wish failed to spell out; and if I had said anything then, if I had said that I didn't want to go on, her probable reaction would have been quite different from what I wanted.

And I also knew I would lose her, something would come to an end, but this knowledge caused me neither pain nor fear; the feeling was as if, within me, what would occur between us only in the next moment had already come to pass; some things had to come to an end, and one need not regret them.

But I did not want to be rude to her; this had gone too far, but still, I mustn't end it rudely.

Somebody's coming, I said quietly.

The hand with which she had just pulled out the bottom drawer stopped for a moment; she listened, then quickly pushed the drawer home, but since there was not the slightest noise to be heard, it was the sound of my voice rather than the situation that made her wonder; she couldn't understand why I was lying so obviously as to give myself away; it wasn't a decent thing to do.

And as if she'd just been slapped in the face—which she wouldn't have minded as much—she looked up, her hand still on the drawer.

It's nothing, I thought somebody was coming, I said a little louder; to make it more believable, I should have shrugged my shoulders, but I indicated I was still lying, and deliberately, by leaving my shoulders motionless; in the meantime, my eyes followed the subtle change taking place in her as the result of an emerging but still unfocused emotion; she blushed as if embarrassed, and at the same time the very thing I hoped for actually occurred: her whole body was relaxing, and as she crouched there in front of the drawer her shoulders relaxed.

She didn't understand me, but she didn't seem offended.

I have to go home, I said, sounding pretty dry.

Had I gone crazy? she asked.

I nodded, and sensed the feeling of lightness growing stronger, because I felt no need to explain anything and there was no point in spoiling this feeling.

Because it was so fragile, I was afraid it might vanish altogether and then everything would be as difficult as it had been before; this feeling had to be treated with care, and this game of maintaining my inner balance had to do with the fact that I couldn't just suddenly turn around or back out of the room, I had to do it so that she would wish it, too, or at least so it wouldn't happen without her, even though she'd stay—at least that's how I felt.

Come with me, I said, because suddenly I wanted to be magnanimous.

She stood up very slowly, her face lingering near mine; she looked serious; in her surprise she opened her mouth just a little, wrinkled her nose and forehead, as she did when she was reading and wanted to understand from a distance what was there in front of her eyes.

But I immediately felt it was impossible; she had to stay, and that was a pity.

You chickenshit, she said, as if she had opened her mouth only to close it again so I wouldn't see that she understood everything.

She understood all my hidden motives; the smile she saw playing on my lips—I didn't want to smile but felt it anyway—filled her with such hatred that she turned red again, because seeing my treachery made her feel ashamed for me.

What the hell was I waiting for, then, she said, I should go, get the fuck out of there, miserable coward that I was, what was I standing there for like a prick?

My head began to move toward the mouth spewing the invectives, I wanted to bite into it, and as my mouth, my teeth, reached the light playing on the dark skin of her spitting mouth, before making contact, she quickly closed her eyes, but I didn't close mine, because I was involved not with her but with my own feelings; I saw that as her lips stirred under my teeth, her eyelids were trembling.

I wanted to stop her mouth with my teeth, but those warm, soft lips, parting curiously, seemed to be longing for my mouth, and we drew back, simultaneously, because her mouth sensed the sharpness of my teeth.

And when I stepped out the garden gate and began walking up the hill, I would have liked Kálmán to be there waiting for her again; I imagined motioning to him casually: Go on in, she's all yours; this could happen only in my imagination, because in reality they were far from each other, everyone was far away, and at last I was alone with my own feelings.

It was as if nature had unveiled to me the feeling created by the union of two bodies.

Today I know that this peculiar, powerful, and triumphant feeling began to germinate when my body made me experience what "girl," a word familiar to me for thirteen years, really meant, and the feeling blossomed to fulfillment the moment my body made me refuse any further rummaging through those drawers; I took this feeling with me that day like a rare treasure, to be shielded, protected, and kept out of harm's way, submerged so deeply in myself that I didn't notice where I was walking, I was merely putting one foot before the other, as though my body was not mine but that of this feeling; coddling this feeling, my body kept walking on the familiar street, in the summer twilight, between the shores of the forest, only vaguely aware of being accompanied, behind the fence of that restricted area, by the watchdog on duty; and my body felt neither fear nor aversion, since this wonderful feeling was there to shut out everything obscure, secretive, and forbidden; today I know that as the afternoon turned into dusk that day this feeling caused a complete change in me: it did not want me to know or understand what I could never hope to know or understand, it kept me from plunging to the depths of despair and revulsion and at the same time let me know where my place was among the world's creatures, which, for a body, is certainly more important than some ideals and their degree of purity; I was happy, and if I didn't believe that the feeling of happiness is nothing but concealed remembrance I'd say I was happy for the first time, happy because I felt that this sweet tranquillity, surfacing so suddenly and guiding my every move, had extinguished all my pains, conquered them once and forever.

It extinguished them with a kiss, and it is also true that in that kiss there lingered the memory of another, grievous kiss; at that moment, on Maja's lips I said goodbye to Krisztián, said goodbye to my childhood, feeling strong, omniscient, as one who, annealed by dread and sorrow, can size up all his possibilities, understand the meaning of words, rules, regulations, one who need not go on searching and experimenting; this was the nature of my happiness, or this is what made me happy, even though this feeling, which seemed to explain and resolve so many things, was nothing else, nothing more than a reprieve of the body, necessary for its own self-defense and granted to us for only a brief moment of transition.

That is how our feelings look out for us, deceiving us so as to protect us, giving us something good, and while we hold on to our momentary pleasure, distracted by happiness, the evil is quickly taken back, which is not really deception, because every evil feeling leaves a residue behind.

I am talking about a momentary reprieve, though Maja and I never again played detective; my precious feelings, my final shrinking back, my blissful defense mechanism ended our perverse activities, and our relationship also broke off almost completely; we no longer knew what to do with each other, because what could be more interesting than mutually perverting the emotional ties we had for our respective parents, and since nothing was more exciting than that, we pretended to be offended, barely saying hello to each other, so that under that pretext we could forget the real reason for our anger.

And I would have forgotten about the whole affair, and in the meantime maybe a whole year had gone by.

When, on an innocent afternoon in the earliest spring, having returned from school, I saw that strange coat hanging on the rack in the foyer, and the chain of events that followed reawakened in me a world of secret feelings, suspicions, and forbidden knowledge which, following the wrong path but enjoying the dark pleasure of our reckless games, Maja and I had acquired.

Our silly searches were also dictated by a singular feeling, hinting and intimating that despite our environment's aggressively maintained appearance of wholesome well-being, something was not quite right: we looked for reasons and explanations and, finding none, discovered the frightful agony of doubt, became well acquainted with a feeling which, in a way, was the emotional form of the day's historical reality.

But how could we have understood, how could our childish minds have conceived that in our feelings the most complete form of truth was made manifest to us? we were after something more tangible, something to hold in our hands, and that is how our feelings were guarding us against our feelings.

We couldn't have known yet that destiny, which would eventually also reveal to us the palpable contents of our feelings and explain in retrospect the connection between seemingly disparate emotions, always travels in roundabout ways, arriving secretly, inconspicuously, and quietly, and one need not rush it; it cannot and should not be rushed.

It arrives one afternoon very late in the winter, almost like all other winter afternoons, announcing itself in the form of a strange overcoat with an unpleasant, musty smell, shabby-looking, and only one of its buttons resembles the buttons on Krisztián's coat, maybe its color is also like that of his coat.

The dark coat on the rack could mean only one thing: a guest had arrived, an unusual guest, because it is a stern-looking coat, quite unlike those that usually hang on the rack; it cannot be the doctor's or a relative's, which would have a different smell; this is more like a coat emerging from the depths of imaginings, from the distance of anxieties, from oblivion; I heard no strange noises or anyone talking, everything seemed as usual, so I simply opened the door to Mother's room and, without fully comprehending my own surprise, took a few steps toward the bed.

A strange man was kneeling in front of the bed, holding Mother's hand and bending over it as it lay on the coverlet; he was crying, his shoulders and back shaking, and while he kept kissing the hand, with her free hand Mother held the man's head, sinking her fingers into the stranger's short-cropped, almost completely white hair, as if wanting to pull him closer by his hair, but gently, consolingly.

This is what I saw when I walked in, and like a knife tearing into my chest the thought hit me: So it's not just János Hamar, there was another one! oh, the hatred welling up in me! but I did take a few more steps toward the bed, driven now by hatred, too, and saw the man lift his head from Mother's hand, not too quickly, while Mother abruptly let go of his hair, leaned forward, raising herself slightly off her pillows, threw me a quick glance, and, terrified that I might have just discovered her repulsive secret, told me to leave the room.

But the man told me to come closer.

They spoke simultaneously, Mother in a choking, faltering voice, at the same time her hand rushing to her neck to pull together her soft white robe so I would not see that her nightgown was open, too, and then I knew immediately what they had been doing; she had shown him, she'd shown her breast to the stranger, her breast that had been cut off, she had shown him the scar; the stranger spoke in a kind, soft voice, as if he were truly glad to see me come in now, unexpectedly, at the wrong moment; in the end, embarrassed and confused by the contradictory signals, I stayed where I was.

A slender shaft of late-afternoon sunlight pierced the window, outlining with wintry severity the intricate patterns of the drawn curtains on the lifeless shine of the floor; and it seemed that everything was booming, even the light; outside, the drainpipes were dripping, melted snow from the roof sloshed and gurgled through the eaves so loudly it sounded amplified; leaving Mother and the stranger in the shade, the shaft of light reached only as far as the foot of the bed, where a small, poorly tied package lay; as the man straightened himself, wiped the tears from his eyes, smiled, and stood up, I already knew who he was, though I didn't want to know; his suit also seemed strange, like his coat on the rack outside, a lightweight, slightly faded summer suit; he was very tall, taller than the János Hamar preserved in my memory, the man my turbulent feelings did not want to recognize, these booming emotions were trying to protect other emotions; he was very tall, his face pale and handsome, both his suit and white shirt wrinkled.

He asked me if I recognized him.

I was watching a red spot on his forehead and saw that although he had wiped his eyes, one of them still had tears in it, and I said no, I didn't recognize him; I didn't want to, and somehow there was something totally unfamiliar about him, though the real reason I said no was that I still wanted to hold on to the lie with which my parents for years had eliminated him from my life; I hoped that insisting on this lie would keep him away from Mother.

But my adored mother did not or, rather, would not understand my insistence, and she lied again, she felt she had to, and with her lie she pushed me away, crushed me; she pretended to be quite surprised that I didn't recognize this man; she was doing this for his benefit, with this pretended surprise trying to suggest that it was only my forgetfulness, and not them, she and Father, to blame for erasing this man from my memory; the excitement of her own lie dried and choked her voice; it was repulsive to listen to it then; today, however, having recovered from the shame of my powerlessness and from the deep wounds of childhood injuries, I rather admire her self-discipline; after all, I did come in at the most dramatic moment of their reunion; what else could she have done but seek refuge in a familiar role; she felt she ought to play the mother now, a mother speaking to her son; she very quickly wanted to change back into being a mother, her face underwent a complete alteration as a result of this mental exercise: a strikingly beautiful, red-haired woman was sitting in that bed, her cheeks flushed, her slightly trembling, nervous fingers playing with the cord on her bedjacket—she seemed to be choking herself with them; this woman seemed a stranger, her voice phony, as she refused to believe I'd so quickly forgotten this man, the man I hated, but her lovely green eyes, narrowing and fluttering, betrayed how completely defenseless she was in this painful and embarrassing situation.

And this, in fact, made me happy; I'd have loved to come right out and say she was lying, shout to the whole world that she was lying, deceiving everyone, but I couldn't say anything, because I was stifled by the constant booming in my ears, and tears that wanted to spill from my eyes were trickling down my throat.

350

But the stranger, who sensed nothing of what was happening between me and Mother, burst into a loud resounding laugh and, as if coming to my aid and neutralizing the tone of resentment in Mother's voice, said, "It's been five years, after all," which made it clear to me how long had passed since his disappearance, and now I was touched and consoled by his voice and by his laughter, he seemed to be laughing off those five years, making light of it all; as he began walking toward me, he indeed became familiar; I recognized his easy, confident stride, his laugh, the candor of his blue eyes, and, most of all perhaps, the trust I could not help having in him; my defensive and self-protective attitude was gone.

He embraced me and I had to surrender; he was still laughing and saying that it was five years, not exactly a short time; his laughter was meant more for my mother, who kept on lying, saying they had told me he was abroad, which of course wasn't at all what they had really told me: only once did I ever ask them where János was, and it was she, not Father, who said that János Hamar had committed the greatest possible crime and therefore we must never talk about him ever again.

She didn't have to tell me, I knew, that the greatest crime was treason, and therefore he was no more, didn't exist, never had, and if by any chance he was still alive, for us he was as good as dead.

My face touched his chest: his body was hard, bony, thin, and because I automatically closed my eyes, submerging myself in that loud booming, withdrawing into the only refuge my body could provide, I was able to feel a great many things in his body: his tenderness radiating warmly into my body, the excitement of his joy still unable to break free, his lightness, and also a wound-up, convulsive strength that seemed to cling to his sinews, bones, and thin flesh; still, I did not yield completely to his embrace, I could not tear myself away from my mother's lies, and the way I trusted his body seemed much too familiar, harked back to a buried past, spoke to me of the absence of my father's body and, somewhat more remotely, of the pains I'd suffered for loving Krisztián; his body spoke to me of the perfect security provided by a male body and the repeated withdrawal of that security; reopened the past of five years earlier when I could still touch anything with absolute confidence; precisely this excessive openness of feelings made me undemonstrative in his arms.

I could not deny and absorb time any faster; I couldn't have known that the time of fate cannot be stopped; they began talking above my head.

Why should they lie, he was saying, he'd been in prison.

At the same time Mother mumbled something about not being able to explain to me exactly what that meant.

Then he repeated, more lightly and playfully, that yes, he'd been in jail, that's where he'd come from just now, straight from the slammer, and although he was talking to me, he meant the mischievous undertone for Mother, who, finding some possibility for evasion in this playful tone, assured me that János hadn't stolen or robbed or anything like that.

But he wouldn't let her have her little detour and retorted that he'd tell me about it, why not?

But then Mother's voice, deep and filled with hatred, pounced on him, challenged him to tell me if he felt he must, which meant of course that she was forbidding him to say anything; she was trying to protect me and to invalidate him.

It felt good that she hadn't thrust me away from herself, after all, that her protective voice was lashing about behind my back, even if this odd sort of protection quickly pushed me from the threshold of knowledge back to the dark realm of suppressed information; the stranger made no reply, their argument remained suspended above my head, and though I felt I must know, had the right to know, his eyes told me hesitantly that perhaps now was not the time; gripping my shoulders firmly, he pushed me away from himself so he could see me, take a good look at me, and as I followed his glance sweeping over my face and body, I felt time opening up in my body, because the sight before him, me, with all the changes and growing, made him happy and infinitely satisfied; his eyes seemed to devour the physical changes my body had undergone in five years, with great delight making them his own; he shook me, slapped me on the back, and for a brief moment I, too, could see myself with his eyes, and I was hurting terribly, everywhere, in every part of my body that he now looked at, his glance hurt me, because I felt as if my body were deception itself; he was enjoying it so much yet I was standing before him unclean, and that hurt me, hurt me so terribly that the tears stuck in my throat broke out in a quiet, pitiful whimper; he may not have noticed it, because he planted a loud smacking kiss on each of my cheeks, almost biting me, and then, as if unable to get enough of my sight and touch, kissed me a third time; that's when Mother behind us told us to turn away because she was getting out of bed; by then I was sobbing, making gurgling and rattling sounds, and after the third kiss I clumsily, the clumsiness caused by my emotions, touched his face with my mouth, that musty smell on his face, I was touching this erupting pain of mine to his face;

but he didn't care, roughly he yanked me to himself and kept me pressed to his body, and of course he cared, he cared for me because he wanted to drink up my sobbing with his own body.

The booming seemed to gush out with my sobs; I didn't know why I was crying, I didn't want to cry, I didn't want him to feel, or for the two of them to see, what was happening, because it was my impurity that was flowing out of me in those tears; and while I was still struggling with myself, entrusting my body to him, the turbulence in his body came to an end.

Tenderness seemed to be carried along by capillary-like tributaries, by swift underground rivulets, and driven out of the honeycombed darkness of the body, it surfaced as inert strength, strength of the arms, the loins, as a trembling of the thighs; nothing more was happening, nothing was changing anymore; he was holding me in his embrace with the gentle strength of his tenderness, and at the same time his sources had dried up, nothing more was flowing from him into me, he became like silence itself.

I don't know how long Father had been standing in the open door.

I had my back to the door and was the last to notice him—when the vanishing tenderness made me realize that something had happened behind my back.

Above my head he was looking at Father.

Mother was standing in front of her bed, about to reach for her robe flung over the back of the armchair.

Father had his coat on, his soft gray hat was in his hand; his straight blond hair fell over his forehead but he did not push it back as he usually did with his long, nervous fingers; he was pale, looking at us with clouded eyes; he didn't seem to be really looking at us but at something incomprehensible located where our hugging bodies were standing, at an apparition, or at nothing at all, as if he could not possibly understand how this apparition had gotten here; maybe that's why I thought that his always clear, stern gaze was dimmed—his expression made almost idiotic—by his own astonishment; his lips kept trembling and he may have wanted to say something but then changed his mind because the words wouldn't come.

The cooled-off tear smudges on my face were now superfluous; the silence of the men was so deep and immovable that I could feel my own superfluity in my limbs, or perhaps what an animal feels when escape is made impossible by not only a perfectly constructed trap but its own paralyzed instincts.

Slowly he let me go, languidly; one lets go of an object with such indifference; Mother did not move.

A great deal of time must have passed like this; all those five long years must have passed by during that silence.

What I had learned about Father while rummaging through his papers seemed trivial compared to what was now becoming visible on his face; perhaps once again it was something I should not have seen: his body shrank somehow, his figure—I always thought of him as tall and slender—sagged under the weight of his coat; his comportment, the strength of his proud bearing, seemed to be illusory now; all these changes produced a curved back and stooped shoulders, and he had difficulty holding his head up, it was wobbling, hovering helplessly above his coat, because not only what he would have wanted to say but couldn't made his lips tremble—the trembling radiating to his nostrils, eyelids, and eyebrows, knitting his forehead in deep furrows—but also another force was stiffening his head in a twisted position, and what his mouth wanted to say was stuck in his windpipe, in his shoulders; always an impeccable dresser, Father now looked disheveled, his tie twisted to the side, the tips of his shirt collar standing straight up, his coat and the jacket under it both unbuttoned, part of his shirt slipping out of his pants over his belly, so many signs of frantic, undignified haste, embarrassment, and agitation, but of course he couldn't have been aware of them; I still don't know how he got the news—to all indications János's arrival at our place was completely unexpected—but I imagined that the moment Father heard the news he jumped into his car, he must have been both overjoyed and devastated, his soul, if there is such a thing, silently split in two, while at the command of his instincts he tried to maintain the impression that he was still a whole person; two irreconcilable emotions must have been raging in him with equal force, that's what made his face twitch, his head float and wobble.

But so far I've spoken only of the strength and rhythm, the dynamics, of emotions, that ebb and flow in which their colors and directions manifest themselves, their pulse and breathing, but by no means the emotions themselves, only one of their many characteristics; what really must have happened in him I can only approximate with a metaphor: he became a child and an old man, as if these two ages had yanked his features in two different directions; he turned into a very offended child whom up to now the world had pampered with false appearances, whose good mind had been nursed into idiotic complacency, and now that this same world had revealed its cruel face to him and he didn't like what was happening, wasn't used to it, the child withdrew from reality into sulking, into hurtfulness, into hate-filled, sniveling regression, unwilling to see what he saw, hurting to the point where he should have been whining and whimpering with pain, which is why he tried so desperately to force himself back into the world of comforting appearances, wanting to be coddled and nursed again, to be dumb and complacent, to stick his thumb back into his mouth, to have his mother's nipples; consequently everything I had once seen as clear, bright, and pure, the sternness of moral behavior reflected in his face, now seemed to be exposing their sources: inane, childish trust, and the fact that he was holding on to somebody's hand; his mouth and nostrils quivered, his eyelids fluttered, his brows twitched like a child's, and all this superimposed on adult features made his face look malformed and freakish; I glimpsed within the ravaged face of this man the child who had never managed to grow up; at the same time, the child seemed older than his years, his pale face was full of shadows; he had turned into a very old man so utterly shattered, crushed, pulverized by real, cruel, bloody, criminal phenomena hiding behind the world of appearances that nothing in him was still innocent, his life force was barely flickering; now he knew, saw, and understood everything, nothing could catch him unprepared, and anything that did was but the recurrence of something that had happened before, and thus behind the fine veil of his intelligence and insight there was a weary boredom rather than affection or love; he seemed to be thrashing between the extremes of his childhood and old age, between his past and his possible future, and being unable to find the noble expression appropriate to coping with the situation, his face simply fell apart.

And János Hamar kept looking on, calmly, almost moved, seemed to be peering out at Father from a strength reduced and clinging to his bones, looked at Father as if at the erstwhile object of his love, as if smiling at his lost past, with the soft expression we use when we're trying to help someone, to identify with him, urging him sympathetically to go ahead and say what's on his mind, we'll understand his feelings, or at least we'll try to.

I was certain, or rather my feelings were certain, that János was my real father and not this ridiculous figure in the clumsy, oversized winter coat; that's when I suddenly remembered that János's hair used to be dark and thick, and the only reason I didn't immediately recognize this real and profound inner closeness which I had always carried with me was that the color of his skin had changed, too, having lost its lively brown hue, and was now clinging, white and wrinkled, to the powerful bones of his face.

Mother's face, the most mysterious of all, confirmed my feelings about the men; without having moved from her place or having picked up her robe, she came and stood with her face between the two men.

And then the trembling mouth belonging to my father with the winter coat finally thrust the first sentence out into the silence; he said something to the effect of, You've come to see us, then.

On the other man's face pain rolled over the smile, and when he said he'd come against his will and couldn't help it, the smile and pain united again, and he continued: his mother had died two years ago, as Father must surely know, of course he went home first and found out from the people who in the meantime had taken over his apartment.

We didn't know, said my winter-coated father.

But then, in a very sharp, shrill voice, almost like a saw stuck in a knot of wood, Mother shouted, That's enough!

Again there was silence between the two men, and while my mother added—her voice deep and choked, sounding as if taking revenge on someone—that they did know but hadn't gone to the funeral, I felt all my strength flowing out of me, which is why I couldn't move from my spot.

Everyone was quiet, as if they all had retreated into themselves and also needed to gather their strength.

All right, János said a little later, it didn't matter; and the smile vanished completely from his face, only the pain remained.

This made my winter-coated father feel stronger; he moved finally, started for János, and although he didn't do anything but walk with his hat in his hand, making no other gesture, it still looked as though he was going to embrace János, who, as if alluding to his pain, apologetically raised his hand, imploring him not to come closer, to stay where he was.

He stopped, in his winter coat, his hair shone as it caught the slender shaft of sunlight, and I don't know why, maybe because of the unfinished movement, his hat fell out of his hand.

We must get over this, Mother whispered, as if trying to take the edge off János's rebuff, and then repeated even more quietly that they must get over this.

They both looked at her, and the way they did showed that both were hoping that she, the woman, would help them.

And this one look brought them together, made them a threesome again.

Except that here no one could help anyone; after a little while János turned away, it must have pained him that they were again three; and as soon as they felt János could not see them, the other two exchanged a hateful glance, some kind of signal, behind his back; he seemed to be looking out the window, listening to the water dripping in the drainpipe, watching the bare branches swaying in the wind, and a sob broke from him, a whimper, tears spilling over the brim of his eyes, but just as quickly he pushed it all back, swallowed it down; Yes, all right, he said, I know, he said, and then he broke down completely, and Mother began yelling at me, What was the matter with me, couldn't I see I had no business being there? and like a madwoman she shrieked at me that I should get out!

I would gladly have obeyed her, but I couldn't, just as they couldn't take another step toward one another but all stood in their places, too far apart to cross over.

So you want to settle the account, after all, Father said, too loudly, for at last he could say the words he'd been afraid to say earlier.

No, no, I'm sorry, János said, wiping the tears from his eyes with his fist, but, as before, one eye remained filled; I'm sorry, it's not you I came to see, I did come to this house, but not to see you! and then he said that my father had no reason to be afraid, there wasn't going to be a show-down, why, he couldn't even talk to Father; and if he planned to wipe out Father's family, he would go about it differently, wouldn't he? but either way, from this moment on, no matter how unpleasant it might make their reunion, or however uncomfortable it might be, my father had better get used to the idea that János was here, was alive, hadn't rotted away in jail, and would say whatever was on his mind; Didn't he think, my winter-coated father asked very quietly, that he, too, had something to do with it?

With getting him into jail or with getting him released? János asked.

With getting him released, of course.

No, frankly, he didn't think so; as a matter of fact, because of certain circumstances, he had reason to believe just the opposite.

In other words, János thought that Father was responsible for the first.

Unfortunately, János said, he couldn't forget the circumstances; five miserable years hadn't been long enough for that; only the dead could conveniently forget things; those responsible should have done the job more thoroughly, with greater foresight! making sure no one was left to remember.

Would he be good enough to tell him just what circumstances he was alluding to, my winter-coated father asked.

At this point Mother let go of her robe, as if something terrible had happened inside her, hunched over, placed both hands on her stomach, and pressed down, trying to stop whatever was going on inside her.

No, he didn't think circumstances were right to discuss trivial details.

No, don't! not now, Mother whispered to them, not now!

What did he mean trivial details, his honor was at stake, and Father demanded, most emphatically demanded, to know the circumstances János was hinting at: Come on, out with it!

János remained silent for a long time, but this was a charged silence, unlike the earlier one; turbulent emotions seemed to have had a purging effect on Father, helped him to regain his equilibrium, to put his feelings back on the smooth, well-worn track of conviction, and this gave him strength, though behind the brittle guise of regained strength he was still fearful and humbled as he kept on listening to the words of the other man, who, because of the quarrel that had erupted between them and against his will, was now strangely less self-assured; as he tried with elaborate and carefully chosen words to keep his contemptible opponent at a distance, all the tender sentiments vanished from his face, gone was the lovely pain caused by the shock of his sudden freedom, the news of his mother's death, his passionate reunion with us, not to mention the sight of Mother's mutilated body, which in itself would have been enough to turn a man into mush in the maw of fate; unlike Father, János reacted to the argument by casting off the burden of his sentiments and now seemed ready to resume the fight naked, with nothing to protect him; he struggled, he wanted to smile, but he was struggling not with his emotions but with the freedom the gods had inflicted on him; pain made the wrinkles around his eyes contract and deepen, with a bit of fanciful exaggeration one might even say that Mentor was standing next to him, urging him on; he became somber, the wrinkles relaxed, and he grew weary but not weak, with the weariness of a man so confident in his own truth and in the justice of his cause—way beyond the personal, this was nothing less than part of universal truth and justice—that he was already bored by, and found superfluous, the very process of having to present evidence; at the same time, from a moral standpoint, this struggle could hardly seem elegant, since only he, and he alone, could have truth on his side—

after all, he was the victim; and although this was the role that in his freedom he was most loath to take on, the fight could not be avoided—indeed, they were already in the midst of it; for several minutes they'd been speaking in that secret language only they could fully understand, the language of alertness and suspicion, of constant readiness and accusation, whose sources and origin Maja and I had tried to trace while playing detective; this was their language, their only common weapon, the language of their past, which János, unless he was determined to annihilate himself, could consider neither irrelevant nor useless; he hated their shared past, and so he was looking for a chink in the armor, a phrase, a piece of information, with which he could still avoid his former self.

Look, he said, drawing out the word as if with this one word he could gain precious time for himself, you must know much better than I what you may or may not ask of me, but first of all, don't shout at me, don't try so desperately to be right! and second of all, please let me ask you, like this, very calmly, that aside from my so-called case—because in our relationship that case no longer makes any difference—tell me, how many death warrants have you signed? I'm curious, purely for statistical reasons.

Father remained quiet for a while, but they kept looking at each other, their eyes locked; and now it was Father's turn for fancy language, saying that he did not consider the question justified, since János must know that he could not have signed a single death warrant, that wasn't part of his job, therefore the question, at least in this formulation, was inappropriate.

Oh, of course, sorry! he'd completely forgotten about that—he begged Father's pardon.

That's right, Father said, he too drawing out his words, as a prosecutor he might ask for the death penalty in a given case, but as is well known, two members of the people's tribunal and a people's judge brought in the verdict as they saw fit.

Why, of course, János cried, that's how it is, this jurisdiction, these legal proceedings, it's all so complicated, Father should forgive him, but he always got lost in them, got everything all mixed up.

Yes, that's how it is, and one shouldn't mix it all up.

Well, in that case, everything's all right!

I would have liked very much to get out of there, but I didn't dare move the air in the room.

Because he was of the opinion, Father continued ominously, slowly and quietly, that based on their former acquaintance, and he didn't know which one of them had been more radical, János wouldn't have acted differently in a similar situation; he would have discharged his duties to the best of his beliefs, wouldn't he? and therefore he saw the roles they had been assigned during the past five years as the work of mere chance.

Their voices were lowered to the level of whispering, of hissing, while Mother also kept up her whispering: No, don't, not now, I beg of you, not now.

There, you see, János whispered, I would have forgotten about the role of chance, but even if it was a series of chances, they've become facts which now, for some reason, seem to bother you, why? why this ludicrous display of emotion? if that was my role, as you say, then it's all right, we're all set; I'm over here, and you're over there, and there's nothing I want to tell you, you understand?

He was ready to tell him everything he knew, everything, Father said; all he was asking now—asking, not demanding, because he really had no right to demand—all he was asking was that János tell him what circumstances he had been alluding to earlier.

Because your honor is at stake, János said.

Yes, my winter-coated father said, my honor.

It got very quiet again, and in this quiet I started for the door; the silence made Mother open her eyes, because she wanted to see what was happening in the silence; I walked past her, right in front of her eyes, but she didn't notice that I could walk again.

You're conducting my interrogation very skillfully, János said, but then you really know me, you know almost more about me than I do myself.

What was he talking about? Father asked.

He wasn't talking about anything, and he didn't want to talk to him about anything at all.

This I heard as I was on my way out, but I couldn't actually leave, because Father began to scream; it was as if the earth itself was shaking and everything that man had ever built on its thin crust was going to collapse, crash, crumble; the sound was that of crying and wild yelling, the kind of male sobbing that's only a breath of self-discipline away from murder; pressing his hands against his temples so he wouldn't murder the other man, or maybe to keep his head from splitting open, he was crying and screaming, But why? why like this? I can't stand it! I can't! and he went on screaming that János didn't understand anything, how could he ever tell János about the nights spent waiting, when he thought he was going to be next, when he felt completely alone; yes, he was ashamed, but didn't understand; no, he wasn't ashamed, just didn't understand why his best friend, who made him die a thousand deaths, didn't want to talk to him.

You are disgraceful, ridiculous, you are disgusting, János said clearly and calmly.

I was holding on to the doorpost, to the white wood.

But why, why? he can't see it, he can't stand it anymore, it hurt so much.

When you walked in here, János said, and I looked at you, I thought there was enough decency left in you—no, not decency, just common sense—to take a look at what you've done.

Father's hands dropped, for an instant his breath seemed to stop, his lips were parted by the child's pain that erupted with those murderous manly sobs; still, I felt that these were not signs of weakness, his body remained strong.

It was as if this body were telling him that his life was nothing more than a minute curiosity and nothing mattered except what this other body was telling him.

All right, János said gravely, let's get it over with, and with his big blue eyes growing even bigger he looked into Father's blue eyes, and every last wrinkle on his face relaxed; order returned to his face; but I don't want you to misunderstand, he said, listen: on the second day, and you should know very well what the second day means in there, they showed me a piece of paper signed by you, a confession stating that when I was released in May '35 I'd told you, in tears, that I couldn't take the beatings anymore, and Sombor and his fascist thugs got me to work for them as an operative—he faltered for a moment and took a deep breath—and you took it on yourself not to report me because I was crying so hard, he said, and under some pretext you let me lie low for a while so I'd have nothing to report to my new handlers; no, this is not a confrontation, not a settling of accounts, I'm not calling you to account! he shouted, but when I prevented our operation at Szob and Mária was caught because of me, then you became convinced I was working for them, after all.

But that's ridiculous, Father said, everybody knows we worked together in our hideout for two whole months after that.

From the second day on, make that the third day, János corrected himself, because he'd needed a bit more time to grasp things, he admitted everything, anything they wanted him to.

But he never signed any statement, Father insisted.

Not only did he sign it, he even corrected the typos, as always, as János remembered his friend and his meticulous ways.

No, no, there must be a misunderstanding; he never made out a deposition about János, nobody ever asked him for one.

You're lying, János said.

I was holding on to the smooth white doorpost, hoping it would help me slip out of the room, and I almost made it, I was almost out.

János, believe him, he's telling the truth now, I heard Mother's faint voice.

He is lying, János said.

At that moment, without the sound of her footsteps announcing her, Grandmother appeared, our bodies nearly colliding in the open doorway.

No, János, I would know about it, I heard Mother say inside the room; I wouldn't have let him, János; but nobody ever asked him to do it.

Grandmother had come from the direction of the kitchen, and her face was flushed with the steam and vapors of cooking, with the gentle expression of bashful triumph and anxious anticipation that is inscribed on a housewife's face only when cooking is not a bother, not a burdensome daily chore but a myriad of tiny conditioned gestures and moves, when peeling, grating, lifting the lids, tasting the food, yanking pots off the fire, scalding, rinsing, stirring, and straining receive their true, lovely, and festive meaning from the heightened attention and dedication of the cook, because sitting in a distant room, a beloved guest is waiting for the meal, and now that it's all ready it must be announced, but will they really like it? and it was clear that she wasn't coming straight from the kitchen but had first stopped in the bathroom to fix her hair, touch a powder puff to her face, and put on a little lipstick; she probably changed, too, so as not to bring the kitchen smells with her; she was wearing the silver-gray corduroy housedress that went so well with her silvery-gray hair, and now, as she hugged me for a second to avoid our crashing into each other, I got a whiff of her freshly applied perfume—two dabs behind the ears, always.

It was unlikely that she hadn't heard the last few sentences spoken in the room, and even if she hadn't caught their meaning, filled as she was with the excitement of her own activities, it was impossible that she wouldn't have sensed from the intonations, just from the way the three of them were standing—far apart, frozen in place, stiff in the grip of their emotions—the awesome tension in the room; but she was not to be distracted, and with a deliberate but not rude gesture she swept me aside, in her high-heeled slippers she stepped quickly into the room, and with a solemn face, as though she were blind and deaf or incredibly stupid, made her announcement: Come on, everybody, dinner's on the table!

Of course she sensed what was going on, but with her gentility and fastidiousness, her long stiff waist, puritan humorlessness, fuzzy upper lip, and chiseled, somewhat dry features—at the moment made more lively and feminine by the kitchen heat and the excitement of János's presence—Grandmother was like an antediluvian creature of bourgeois decorum; she came, and with the cruelty of her obtuseness she plowed through events and phenomena of human life that, in her view of the world, could not be reconciled with the demands of propriety and dignified behavior, as if to say with her superior air (in which there was nothing aristocratic because she was not above but only bypassed the things she was critical of) that what we cannot find solutions for is better left unacknowledged, or at least we should not let on that our eyes see everything, and with the illusion thus created we ought to facilitate the inevitable unfolding of events, and we ought to deflect, stall, wait, let ride, and evaluate things before taking action, because action is judgment, and that is a very tricky business! as a child, I was terribly disturbed by this attitude, disgusted by the lying it implied, and a very long time had to pass before, in light of my own bitter experiences, I made its wisdom my own, before I understood and could sense that seemingly phony, willful blindness and feigned deafness require much more flexibility and understanding than openly demonstrated sympathy and helpfulness; her approach assumes more considerateness and a greater allowance for human fallibility than so-called sincerity, a more forthright, truth-seeking response, does; her mode of behavior is a way of curbing innate aggressiveness and hasty judgment, albeit at the price of another kind of aggressiveness; at that moment she must have been in her element; without batting an eye she entered the room as if it were a drawing room in which guests were making small talk while sipping aperitifs; just how fully aware she was of the seriousness of the moment became apparent when, without giving herself time to catch her breath, she turned to Father, expressed surprise at seeing him there—we'll need another setting— and in her most casual manner, in a kind of chatty, slightly military tone, told him he should take off his coat, wash up, and then let's go, yes, everybody, she wouldn't want the food to spoil! and she had already turned to János, to whom this playacting was addressed, the performance meant to say that no matter what happens, we are a normal, loving, smoothly functioning family; perhaps it wouldn't be inappropriate to interject here that the last qualifier points to the wise moral of bourgeois propriety, to its practicality, which was that life must remain functional at all times and at all cost; this won't be much of a lunch, just something I've thrown together, she said, smiling; she looked at János for a long time, giving him a chance to collect himself, then gently touched his arm and told him he couldn't possibly imagine how happy she was to see him.

My grandmother's staunchly resolute dissembling in itself could not have cooled emotions which had reached the boiling point, or steered them to the calmer waters of reason and understanding; in their present state, it was not only difficult to see how these murderous emotions, which required clarification, could be cooled from one minute to the next, since they all desperately needed to arrive at the truth, but was also conceivable that Grandmother's obvious falsity might be the last straw, and all the anger, shame, despair, suspicion, and pain that had erupted during those few moments, seeking solace in a palpable truth, would now rain down on her head; Mother turned red with hatred for her mother, as if she wanted to yell at her to get out! or to fall on her, grab her by the throat, and smother that detestable false voice, but she was prevented from yielding to the impulse by their moral code, my parents' the exact opposite of Grandmother's, whose essence lay in making the finest, most subtle distinctions among the means of their tactics and strategies in pursuit of a certain end, between their legal and illegal conduct, and in making these distinctions they must remain appropriately discreet and unpredictable, which is what ensured them of moral superiority and practical power; therefore, any extreme manifestation of word or gesture, would be tantamount to treason, a betrayal of their mutual trust; they wouldn't allow themselves to express their emotions freely, the inner conflict of their secret lives had to remain a secret; this was the restricted area they guarded with the same conspiratorial means they had used to set it up, they had to settle everything between themselves and totally exclude a hostile and suspicious outside world; for me, the most remarkable thing about this whole scene was the way the two modes of behavior—nourished by two totally opposite motivations and with dissembling and illusion for their common ground—wound up blending peacefully into each other.

Of course, later they continued where they had left off, but for the moment Father, as if really in the midst of some frivolous chitchat, said yes, of course, he'd wash up promptly, he was on his way, and this was a kind of warning to Mother, whose face turned even more deeply red, but she readily reached for her robe, if only to turn away so she could hide her face, trembling with rage; she said she'd have to change, she wouldn't want to come to the table in her robe, she'd hurry, it would only take a minute; and the nervous twitch of embarrassment on János's face quickly dissolved into a smile, as if by this rapid change he was protecting what had to be kept secret; this was habit, too, the conspiratorial smile matching most precisely the genuine joy, expressed with phony exaggeration, which Grandmother had beamed at him; in their own way both smiles were perfect, since by hiding their feelings both Grandmother and János managed to produce real emotions.

He wouldn't describe himself as happy, exactly; János grinned, and reciprocated Grandmother's touch by touching her arm, but he was glad to be here, of course, though he couldn't quite comprehend just what was happening to him; Grandmother's face assumed a properly sympathetic expression: your poor, poor mother, she said with real emotion, her eyes welling up; there was a real kinship between them now, producing, most likely, the same emotional cliché, namely how sad it was that his mother couldn't have lived to see this day, but the cliché was effective enough, and because they were looking for a possible common ground, the sigh, the pitying intonation, the misty eyes harked back to the first time they had broached the subject, soon after János's arrival; this, then, was the closing of the subject, its quiet and heartfelt burial; Grandmother composed herself and gently, consolingly, as if embracing his dead mother as well, took János's arm.

I did not move; nobody was paying any attention to me anyway; Father disappeared and Mother went to change.

Ernő must be beside himself with excitement, Grandmother said with a laugh, he's so anxious to see you.

And they started for the dining room.

János, who adopted this convivial, conversational tone easily, was somewhat embarrassed about his oversight and asked a little too eagerly, How is Ernő? which made his voice ring false.

How clearly the mind can see now what back then was absorbed by the eyes as gestures, by the ears as sounds and stresses, and by memory, who knows for what reason—all stored away.

Hearing this stray tone in János's voice, Grandmother suddenly stopped before the dining-room door, as if she had to tell him something important before going in, withdrew her arm from his, turned to face him, and with eyes slightly dim with age looked up at him; all the brilliance she had forced on her eyes moments before was gone, replaced by sadness, fatigue, anxiety, and still she wouldn't say what she really wanted; she changed direction, pretended to be distracted, and grasped János's lapel, which she tugged with the apparent embarrassment of a young girl; this seemed like something serious again but was only a further hiding of something inexpressibly real.

Just when János felt that his features were safely under control, when he thought he'd found the only (properly false) voice to suit the situation, the discipline of his face broke down, nearly fell apart, and all the suppressed excitement, not of this moment but of the earlier moments, rose to the surface, the wrinkles around his mouth and eyes began to twitch and vibrate, and he seemed to be dreading what Grandmother might have wanted to say but wouldn't, although he knew what it might be.

You know, Grandmother then said very slowly, almost whispering so no one else would hear, he's been a very active man all his life—she pronounced the word as *actif*—he could never stay put, and now this whole thing—I don't know much about politics, and I don't want to say anything—but this thing has also destroyed him, this helplessness! and your tragedy caused him much suffering, too, I know, although he never talks of it, or of anything else, he just keeps to himself, not saying anything, and that's how he lives his life from one attack to the next, he's driven everybody away, doesn't talk to anybody; Grandmother's whispering grew ever more passionate, and signs of her own deep hurt began to appear on her face, for she really wanted to talk about her own grievances; that man couldn't be helped anymore, he didn't want anyone's pity.

János stroked Grandmother's hair, not as if he was comforting a silly old woman, but as a bashful, faltering attempt to reach out.

Grandmother laughed again, wanting to elude the true meaning of János's gesture; So that's how things are, she said, come on, she added, and opened the door.

But she opened it only for him, she didn't go in; she and I watched this meeting through the open door.

And he most certainly needed all his presence of mind to accept as natural the sight that was waiting for him, which caught him unprepared.

One can bear life's vicissitudes only because our reflexes do for us what should be done with one's whole being, which in turn gives the impression that the body is not quite present when it is indeed present, and that's how our feelings protect us from our own feelings.

It was clearly visible on his back, his protruding shoulder blades, and his neck reduced to skin and sinews, that it wasn't he, János, who stepped into the room, because he was shocked and rooted to the spot; it was his humane duty that borrowed his legs and brought his body into the room.

In the dining room, the chandelier glowed brightly above the long, elaborately set, festive table, and my grandfather was standing behind his chair, feeling ill but fighting it, grasping hard the back of the chair, not even looking up, his gaze somewhere between the cream-colored china, the silver flatware, and the crystal glasses, but in fact he was listening to his own breathing, seemed almost to be looking at his breaths; his fragile face was dark, and above the two deep hollows of his temples, high on his arched forehead, whose sternness was relieved by the smoothed-down waves of his feather-light white hair, two thick blue veins protruded; he had to pay attention to every single breath, how to inhale and exhale, making sure it all went smoothly, not to let choppy breathing slip into an uncontrollable attack; he was an ancient but still beautiful man; at the other end of the table, my little sister sat on her chair on a stack of pillows, all dressed up in a smart blue outfit with a round collar, her hair neatly combed; deeply engrossed, and totally undisturbed by the opening door or the approaching stranger, she kicked the table with evenly paced kicks and banged her little tin plate with her spoon; naturally her mouth was open.

Grandfather slowly peered out from behind his glasses, he hadn't lifted his head yet, his gaze did not want to reveal more than what he was feeling, but that was so much, and so true, that what he could say with words would be much less, and so he couldn't really lift his head, but the artificially prolonged whistling of his breathing began to subside, his face grew even darker, his forehead turned whiter; he had things under control.

And with his glance he immediately perceived unease in his guest's eyes; he didn't smile but remained serious, and yet something appeared on the surface of his eyes that we might call cheerfulness, and with this cheerfulness he was helping along János's eyes.

Somewhat playfully, tilting his head sideways, he threw a glance at my little sister as if to say to János, You see, that's how she is, and I'm standing here, making sure she's allowed to bang on that plate to her heart's content; yes, that's what he seemed to be saying, giving János a chance to take a good look at her so he wouldn't have to pretend not to notice what he couldn't help noticing.

Then their eyes met again, and while my little sister continued banging on her plate with her spoon, they slowly began to walk toward each other; they grasped each other's hands, two old hands holding two mature hands over the head of an idiot child; and then I could see János's face again, which had returned to its former look; the two men held each other.

I thought a lot about you, Ernő, said János after a long silence.

If that's true, Grandfather said, then there was nothing more János could possibly tell him.

He had no choice, János said; besides, he had plenty of time to think.

As for himself, Grandfather said, he'd been preparing for eternity; he didn't think, didn't hope, that it would be over one day, or at least that he would live to see it, though he should have known.

Known what? János asked.

Grandfather shook his head, didn't want to say, and then, as if the thing they had meant to cover up—not for fear or shame, just wanted to—erupted from them, they fell on each other and stood for a long time hugging.

When they separated, my sister stopped her banging and watched the two men, her mouth wide-open; a small sound issued from her, not clearly of fear or happiness; behind me, Grandmother sighed and hurried back to the kitchen.

And they just stood there helplessly, their arms dangling at their sides.

He'd begun to understand a lot of things, János said, so many things that he'd almost become a liberal, would you believe that, Ernő?

What d'you know! Grandfather said.

Can you imagine that?

Then maybe you should run for office in the next election.

And one pair of hands again grabbed the other pair, and the two men literally laughed in each other's face, coarsely, loudly, knocking against each other in their drunken laughter, and then the laughter suddenly drowned in silence, which must have never left them, not even during their laughter, which had been there all along, biding its time.

I was still standing in the door, unable to tear myself away or to follow the events with my body and make it enter the room; I suppose this is the state we describe as being beside oneself; I had to turn away; I saw my little sister, still clutching her spoon, with her big head tilted, who was staring at the men; now with little giggles and a grin, now with drooping lips and whimpering sounds on the verge of sobbing, she also seemed to be experimenting, trying to decide what would best suit this unusual occasion; she could experience any emotion now, most likely experienced a great many, could perceive the situation as friendly, just as easily feel it to be hostile, and because she was not choosing between fine shades of emotion and was perhaps terrified by the impossibility of choosing, she began a dreadful bawling.

Which anyone who had never lived in close proximity to a mentally defective child might have considered the capricious creation of chance.

Later, it was Father who had to push me to the table; I was so paralyzed by my sister's bawling I couldn't make it there on my own; I remember using the excuse that I wasn't hungry.

Grandmother came in with a steaming soup tureen.

As precisely as my memory has preserved the events leading up to this meal, it has buried just as deeply those that followed it; I know, of course, that memory mercilessly retains everything and I do admit my weakness: some things I don't want to remember.

Like how Mother's face slowly turned yellow, a very dark yellow, I could actually see it happening, but she kept pretending there was nothing wrong, and that's why I didn't dare say anything to her or to anyone else.

Or what happened earlier, when she came in wearing her navy-blue skirt, a white shirt, showing off her long, pretty legs in high-heeled lizard shoes which she saved for the most special occasions; as she hurried over to my little sister, I saw a colorful silk scarf tucked under the wide-open collar of her blouse; I hadn't seen her dressed for months, and that scarf showed just how much weight she had lost, she looked as if she had been put into the clothes by accident and the scarf was supposed to hide the weight loss; when my little sister behaved like that, it was best not to touch her, so Mother crouched down next to her and made a bunny rabbit from the napkin.

And the way János was watching all this.

And how Father yelled, Get her out of here!

And how, as she was dragged out, the silence of the three men remained behind, and how her screams faded away.

And the feeling during the hours that followed, that somebody had to be silenced, and the silence, and the voracious eating.

And how the end was so long in coming; the thing was not going to end, kept lasting, there was still more of it no matter how much everyone tried to eat it off their plates; and how everything that occurred to any of them as a solution or possible evasion, everything was part of the end that wouldn't come.

And then they shut themselves in another room, and only random words and stifled cries could be heard; but I didn't want to draw any conclusion from these scattered words; the message, to me, was the same.

And it must have been late at night when I took the screwdriver, I didn't turn on the light and didn't even close the door behind me—there was no point in being cautious anymore, and in fact I didn't much care what I was doing—inserted the screwdriver between the desktop and the drawer, raised the top, the lock snapped open, and just as I was taking the money out of the drawer Grandfather walked across the dark room.

He asked me what I was doing.

Nothing, I said.

What did I need the money for? he asked.

No reason, I said.

He stood there for a while longer, then very quietly told me not to be afraid, they were just straightening things out among themselves. And then he left the room.

His voice was calm and serious, and this voice, as if coming from a different source, this reasoning of his, coming from such a different way of thinking, exposed, showed up for what it was, what I'd intended to do; for a long time I stood in the dark room, thus exposed to myself; Grandfather wrecked my plan, yet also put me at ease a little; the money, two hundred forints, I put in my pocket anyway.

I left the drawer open, with the screwdriver on top of the desk.

I also remember that I fell asleep that night with my clothes on, which I noticed only the next morning; during the night somebody covered me with a blanket; at least I didn't have to get dressed in the morning.

And I mention this not to be amusing but to point out with what trivial little advantages one is ready to console oneself at a time like this.

And when I came home from school, the two coats, Father's heavy winter coat and that other coat, were still hanging on the rack; and I heard the men's voices from the room.

I did not eavesdrop.

I don't remember how I spent the afternoon, though I vaguely recall standing in the garden and not taking off my coat all afternoon, I stayed just as I was when I'd got back from school.

I remember it growing dark as some kind of mitigating circumstance, a red twilight with a clear sky, the moon was up, and everything that had thawed out during the day now refroze, snapping and crackling under my feet as I cut across the forest.

Only when I got as far as Felhő Street up on the hill, and saw Hédi's window, the closed curtain and the light inside, did I become conscious of the air, of the piercing cold I was inhaling.

Two little girls were coming down the darkening street, pulling and yanking a sled that kept getting stuck in the dips and mounds on the icy roadway.

A hell of a time to go sledding, I said to them, the snow had just about melted.

They stopped, gave me a dumb look, but one of them tilted her head a little, stuck her neck forward angrily, and said very quickly, That's not true, on Városkúti Road there's still plenty of snow.

I offered them two forints if they went in and told Livia to come out.

They didn't want to do it or didn't understand, but when I took a handful of change from my pocket and showed it to them, the one with the big mouth took a few coins.

I'd taken the money from János's coat before I left the house; I just scooped it all out, every last coin.

They dragged the sled with them across the schoolyard; I kept pointing and yelling to show them which door to take to the basement.

It took them a long time to maneuver the sled down the stairs, but at last it was quiet, the horrible grating and scraping sound stopped; they just had to drag that rotten sled with them, the little jerks, fearing I might steal it; for a long time nothing happened, and I was about to leave—I decided several times that I wouldn't wait anymore, I didn't want Hédi to see me—when Livia appeared, wearing sweatpants and a blouse with its sleeves rolled up; she'd been washing dishes perhaps, or mopping the floor, and was now lugging the sled up the stairs.

She wasn't so surprised to see me standing by the fence; she put the cord in the girls' hands, they could now pull it themselves, which they did, and again the sled made terrible sounds as it scraped along the slushy schoolyard, but they also kept looking back, whispering and giggling, curious to see what the two of us might do.

Livia strode across the yard with deliberate steps, she seemed cold, kept slapping her shoulders, stooped over a little to protect her breasts from the cold; when she heard the giggling, she gave the girls such a stern look they shut up and tried to get away as fast as they could, though their curiosity slowed them down.

She came very close to the fence, and the warm kitchen smell emanating from her body and hair enveloped my face.

Those little idiots, now at a safe distance, yelled something back at us.

I said nothing to her, but she could see I was in big trouble, that's what she was seeing in my face; and my eyes were glad to see what her face had brought from their kitchen—the perfectly ordinary, warm and friendly evening—and we both felt that this was almost like that summer when I always waited for her by the garden fence and she'd come and walk past me, except now I was the one outside the fence, and this belated switch of positions pleased us both.

She pushed her fingers through the fence, all five fingers, and I immediately leaned my forehead against them.

The lukewarm tips of her fingers barely touched my forehead, and when my face also wanted to feel them, she pressed her palm on the rusty wires and through the spaces my mouth found the warm smell of her hand.

She quietly asked what had happened to me.

I'm leaving, I said.

Why?

I said I couldn't stand it anymore at home, and just came to say good-bye.

She quickly withdrew her hand and looked at me, trying to see on my face what had happened, and I felt I had to tell her, even though she didn't ask.

My mother's lover is more important to her, I said, and I felt a short, stabbing pain, as if hitting a live nerve, but what I'd said could not be expressed any other way, and so even the pain felt good.

Wait, she said, truly alarmed, I'm coming with you, be right back.

While I waited for her, the short stab-like pain passed but left behind a queasiness, because, although less intensely, the pain caused by my not-exactly-precise sentence was still coursing through my body, spreading, branching out inside me, reaching every nerve, every cell, with some kind of sensation, like the root of a thought, swinging at the tip of each nerve ending; yet there was nothing more, or closer to the truth, that I could tell her; the pain ran its course and was subsiding, but at the same time—more significantly than the pain and in apparent tune with the beating of my heart—my brain kept repeating the words "with you, with you," but I didn't understand how she could come with me, how she could even think about it.

By now it was almost completely dark, the yellow glow of streetlamps softened the cold blue darkness.

She must have been afraid I'd leave, because I didn't have to wait long before she came running, her coat still unbuttoned, holding her scarf and red cap in her hand; but she stopped and carefully closed the gate, the lock was missing, it had to be fastened with a piece of wire.

She looked at me expectantly, and this would have been the time to tell her where I was going, but I felt that if I did, it would be all over, the whole thing would seem impossible and absurd, like saying that I wished to leave this world—which in fact was true; when I had pried open the desk drawer, for a moment I had hesitated between the money and the pistol, but this was something I couldn't tell her.

I did want to run away, for good, but we were no longer children.

With a beautifully peaceful, circular motion she wrapped the scarf around her neck, waiting for me to say something, and because I didn't, she pulled on her cap, too, and just looked at me.

I couldn't tell her not to come, and against my will I squeezed out the words, Come on; if I hadn't said that, my decision would have become meaningless even for myself.

Thoughtfully she looked me over, not just my face, and said I was pretty stupid not to wear a cap and where were my gloves; I said I didn't care; she purposely didn't put on her gloves and gave me her hand.

I grasped the small warm hand, and we had no choice but to get started.

She was marvelous for not asking any more questions, for not asking anything, for knowing exactly what she had to know.

Walking along Felhő Street, hand in hand, there was no need to say anything; our hands were talking excitedly, about something entirely different, naturally enough; when one hand feels the warmth of the other and finds its place inside the other, it's a good sensation, but also unfamiliar, and the palm gets a bit scared; then, with little squeezes, the fingers come to help, and the reluctant muscles of the palm relax into the soft frame of the other palm, fit into its dark shelter, and that seems so right that with great relief the fingers clasp each other, closely entwine; but this poses a further complication, because the very pressure of the hands keeps them from feeling what they really want to feel.

The fingers should be completely relaxed to the point of having no will of their own; they should just be, wanting nothing, and they should be allowed to stay entwined; but then a light, playful curiosity surfaces from the fingertips: what's it like to touch, to stroke, to want to feel, and yes, to want the tiny little cushions of that other palm, to go down into the little valleys created by the clasping fingers and in gentle brushings against and cautious retreats from the skin to explore the other hand, until slowly and gradually these contacts are transformed into a firm grip; and then I was deliberately squeezing her hand hard, pressing her into myself, let her ache, too; and she cried out—but of course it wasn't too serious— just as we began the steep climb up Diana Road.

We didn't look at each other after that; we wouldn't have dared.

Hands is what we were then, because it seems that the pain was serious, after all; offended and hurt, her hand wanted to pull out of mine, but my gentleness wouldn't let it, and with diminishing force we glided down from the peak of her little pain to a quiet reconciliation, which was so final that all previous struggle and play lost their meaning.

We continued on Karthauzi Road, and though I had no set route in mind, I led her instinctively and confidently in a direction I felt proper, which would take us to my uncertain, distant destination, which I'd picked out with a rather childish self-assurance; still, I don't regret my impulsiveness; but for her hand, the feeling that we could not change the situation would have paralyzed me; if I had been alone, if her hand hadn't forced me to take responsibility for my impulsive, senseless adventure, I would certainly have turned back at some point, the remembered warmth would have lured me back to the place whither, in my right mind, I could never have returned; but with her hand in mine, there was no turning back; and now, as I reminisce and follow the two of them with my sentences, I can only keep nodding like an old man: yes, let them go on, good luck to them; their foolishness, I must admit, is very dear to me.

Above us, on the still snowy embankment, two lit-up but nearly empty cars of the cogwheel train passed by; only a few people were trudging along the road, meaningless shadows of the world we had left behind.

We carried our shared warmth in our clasped hands. When the two hands rested motionless in each other for a little too long, it seemed, not only because of the cold but also because of having grown used to each other, that one hand began to lose the other; it was time to change position, but carefully, so the new hold wouldn't upset the peace and calm of the old one.

At times our two hands fit so well, found such a natural and balanced position, that it was hard to tell which one was mine or where exactly was hers, whether I was holding hers or the other way around, which caused the vague fear that I might lose my hand in hers, a fear that then became the reason for shifting position.

The strange shadows were gone, we were alone; the crunching of our hurried, perhaps too hurried, steps echoed into the ill-lit road, into the darkness the moonlight conjured out of the bare trees; we heard dogs barking, sometimes in the distance, sometimes close by; in the air—so cold that the fine hairs in our noses froze with every breath, a very pleasant sensation—we could smell the acrid smoke of chimneys; on the left side of the road, in the gardens below, snow was glimmering in large patches; the smoke was coming from these mostly darkened villas.

There was a full moon that night, and walking up the Swiss Steps we came face-to-face with it; there it was, glowing at the top of the steps, as if its motionless round visage had been waiting just for us.

This interminably long set of steps confused our hands; on the flat road our steps had automatically assumed a harmonious rhythm, but now either I pulled her or she pulled me, and it wasn't even the stairs disrupting the rhythm, for we still managed to stay together on them, but the interim landings; every third stair was followed by a landing that took four steps to cross; on one of these, in the middle of taking the four flat steps—I was actually counting them—she asked me where I wanted to go.

She didn't ask where we were going but where I wanted to go, and asked it as if the question were part of her heavy breathing, and therefore the wording didn't seem crucial, so I didn't have to stop.

To my aunt, I said.

Which wasn't quite true.

But luckily she didn't ask me anything else, and we kept climbing the stairs, still not looking at each other, which was just as well.

Perhaps a half hour went by, and when we reached the top we looked down, as involuntarily one always does from the top.

And as we did, to see how far we had come, our faces brushed against each other, and I could see that she wanted to know, but I had nothing to say, or rather, it would have been too complicated to tell her, and then, both at once, we let go of each other's hand.

I started walking, she followed me.

Rege Street is mildly steep here; I quickened my pace, fleeing from having to explain things; and then, after a few steps taken in this state of nervous estrangement, she reached out her hand to me.

She reached after me because she already knew, and I could feel it from her hand, that she would leave me, and my hand did not want to make her stay, it wanted to let her go.

We kept walking on the treeless hilltop, past the hotel's long wire fence, and where the fence ended, the city's last lamppost waited for us with its yellow light in the blue darkness, as if illuminating the outer limits of our possibilities; the road ended there, only a trail led farther, nothing but a few lonely oaks and sparse shrubs; and after we left this last yellow light behind us, I sensed that at any moment my hand might let go of hers.

We walked on like this for another half hour, maybe a little less.

We were inside the deep Wolf Valley, whose high rims were covered with untouched, bluish snow; snow crackled and crunched under our feet; and there it finally happened.

She stopped; I immediately let go of her hand, but she held on to my open palm and looked back at me.

She kept looking, but could not see what she wanted to see, couldn't see the lights we had left behind; we were deep inside the valley.

She said I should go back with her.

I said nothing.

Then she let go of my hand.

She said I should put on her cap, but I shook my head; it was silly, but I didn't want to wear a red cap.

Then at least I should take her gloves, she said, and pulled them out of her pocket.

I took them from her and put them on; they were knitted woolen gloves, nice and warm, and red, but that I didn't mind.

This frightened her, and she started begging and pleading; it wasn't for her sake but for her parents', and no, it wouldn't be a sign of weakness; she said all sorts of things, speaking quickly and quietly, but the valley snapped up even these tiny sounds.

The echoing sounds made me shiver, and I felt that if I let a single sound escape me and it echoed like that, I'd have to turn back myself.

She was scared, she said, scared to go back alone; I should walk her back a little way.

A little way, way, said the valley quietly.

Quickly I started off, to continue, to make her stop talking, but after a few steps I stopped and turned around; perhaps like this, from here, it might be easier for both of us.

We stood like that for a long time, from the distance we couldn't see each other's face anymore, it was much better this way.

For me it was better if she went back, yes, to let her go, and perhaps she sensed that for me it wasn't at all a bad thing if she went back; she began to turn away, slowly, and then she turned around completely and began to run; she was sliding on the snow, looked back and ran, and then I kept looking at her for as long as my eyes saw what they wanted to see; maybe she turned around again, or stopped, or walked faster, or ran, a dark little spot hovering over the blue snow, until she disappeared altogether, though I still seemed to be seeing her.

For a while I still heard her steps in the snow, and then I only thought I heard them; they were no longer footsteps but the cold breeze fingering branches, echoes of creaking, snapping sounds, secret crackles; still, I wouldn't move from my spot, waited for her to be gone, walking her back in my mind, away from here, wanting her to disappear completely.

A tiny, cold scraping in my throat still hoped she'd turn around; and if she did, then she should reappear just about . . . no, not yet; now, now the little spot should appear! but nothing did.

And I was glad I was rid of her, because this did not mean that I'd lost her, on the contrary, this way I'd possess her for good, precisely because I had the strength to stay alone.

The road was waiting, and I did take it, though I don't think it would make much sense to describe the details of my flight.

My foolishness had me believe that I was the story, and this bleak cold night merely its setting, but in fact my real story played itself out almost independently of me or, more precisely, occurred parallel to my own little adventures.

It was eight in the evening when we'd left home, I remember hearing the church bell, and it must have been a little before ten when she got home, just about the time I left behind the cliffs of Ordőgorom and reached the wide plain that starts at the foot of the mountain; I was glad to see the dim lights of Budaörs, which were far away, but it wouldn't be hard to stay on course in their direction.

I found out later that she sneaked into her room unnoticed, threw off her clothes, slipped into bed, and was almost asleep when they discovered her; they turned on the light, started yelling at her, but not wanting to give me away, she said she'd had a headache and gone out for a walk; then she started to cry, her mother slapped her, and she was so afraid of what might happen to me that she told them.

By then I had reached Budaörs via a long, dark, winding road that was hardly more than a pass, very like an unpaved trench, with frozen cart tracks; tall thickets on either side gave some protection, and it seemed warmer there than in the open field, but also spookier, because I never knew what might be lurking around the next bend, and also because I kept thinking I was going in the wrong direction, and by way of consoling and encouraging myself I decided that if I did reach the distant lights I'd pay for a night's lodging somewhere, I had the money, or simply ask to be allowed in for the night, but reaching the first village houses brought no relief, because a dog dashed out from one of them, an ugly, frostbitten mutt with a stringy stump for a tail, and it kept following me, yapping and snapping, with every step I took I had to kick so it wouldn't get at my pants; it kept baring its teeth, snarling and yelping, and that's how we passed by the village inn, where they were just pulling down the shutters; two women and a man gave me a long stare, wondering why the dog was following me like that, it looked suspicious to them; and I quickly gave up the idea of looking for lodging there.

In the meantime, Livia's father put on his coat and went over to my house.

It must have been around midnight when I left the village and when Livia's father rang our bell.

With its legs spread wide apart, the dog stood barking away, in the middle of the street leading out of the village, which sloped slightly, while all around us the crisp outlines of silent hills were etched against the shimmering sky; I realized the dog had stopped following me, wouldn't snap at my legs anymore, and I was safe, I was all alone, incredibly happy to be able to breathe freely; as the barking turned into a long, soft whine behind me, I marched out of the village so jauntily that I even forgot how cold I was, and of course the excitement and the walking were warming me up a little.

At home they were waiting for the ambulance to take Mother to the hospital.

Livia's father was standing in the hallway, telling them what had happened, when the ambulance arrived; János went with Mother so Father could stay home and call the police.

Having lost track of time, I kept dragging myself along the silent road and didn't even realize that what I now wanted to hear, with all my young and immature being, was the sound of an approaching car, which first I thought I'd flag down and, whatever its destination, ask for a lift, but since I was afraid to do that, I got off the road, stepped into a ditch, into ankle-deep snow, and waited for it to pass.

It zoomed by and I thought they hadn't noticed me, but then I heard the screeching of brakes, of wheels, and the car spun around on the slippery road, banged against the shoulder that was slightly higher than the road, and, rebounding, slid into a stone marker; the engine stopped, the lights went out.

After the sounds of screeching, skidding, and banging, there was a split second of silence, then the two front doors flew open and two dark coats were running toward me.

I tripped and slid down the side of the ditch, and then started running on the frozen ground of a snowy meadow, spraining my ankle in the effort.

They grabbed me by my coat, near my neck.

You little motherfucker, you; almost wound up in that ditch because of you!

They twisted my arm behind my back; they both held on to me as, pushing and shoving, they dragged me to the car; I didn't protest.

They threw me on the back seat—bash your head in if you so much as move!—and had a hard time starting the car, so they kept up their swearing the whole way, but it was so nice and warm inside, my body tingled, and in this tingling softness and with the droning engine, the swearing slowly receded and I fell asleep.

It was getting light when we stopped in front of a big white building, they showed me the dent on the bumper—they're not gonna be the ones to pay for it, that's for sure, and they'll teach me not to fall asleep at a time like this.

They took me upstairs and locked me in a room.

There I tried to pull myself together; I wanted to think up a story I could tell, but I had to rest my head on the table.

For a while the table felt too hard, I tried to cushion it with my arm, but that was also too hard, and then it turned soft.

A key turned in the lock, I must have fallen asleep, after all; a woman in uniform stood in front of me, and behind her, out in the corridor, I saw my grandfather.

In the taxi, just as we made the turn from Istenhegyi Road to Adonisz Road and drove past the high fence of the restricted zone, he told me what had happened during the night; it was as if not a single night but several years had passed in the interim.

It was a bright morning, everything was melting and dripping in the sunlight.

Mother's bed was covered with a striped bedspread, as it had been years ago, before she got sick.

The way it was covered made it feel as though she no longer lived here.

And my feeling did not deceive me, for I never saw her again.

Description of
a Theater Performance

Our poplar tree was holding on to its last leaves, which had to turn their deathly yellow before they could fall; they rustled in the breeze—too slight to disturb the arching branches, which merely trembled now and again—twirled and twisted on their short stems, bumping into one another.

It was sunny outside and the flickering, twisting spots of pale yellow made the distant sky even bluer; you could see deep into the mistless blue, as though eyes could distinguish between far and near and one weren't staring into a void that ended somewhere only because it wasn't infinitely transparent.

It was pleasantly warm in the room, the fire humming quietly in the white tile stove, and with our slightest move the smoke of our cigarettes sank and rose in thick, sluggish layers.

I was sitting at his desk in his comfortably wide armchair—he always let me have this special corner of his room—working on my notes, which really meant that while staring out the window through the softly curling layers of bluish smoke, I was trying to recall what had happened during rehearsals the day before, superimposing image on image.

There are gestures and words the meaning and motives behind which we comprehend all at once, and we also notice the minute irregularities that at the moment of occurrence may seem contingent and accidental, cracks and chasms of imperfections that separate the player from the play, the actor from his role, and that the actors, in accordance with the strict rules of their craft, would somehow like to bridge, as if to eliminate the sad truth that total fusion, total identification, does not exist, even if it is the ultimate desire of many a human endeavor.

Already while jotting down my notes, which I was doing rather mechanically, I had realized that the principle I was really interested in, if there was a principle, was to be found not in the obvious, logical unfolding of events, in describable gestures and meaningful words—although these were very very important, for they embody human events—but rather in the seemingly contingent gaps between the words and gestures, in these irregularities and imperfections.

He sat a little farther away, typing steadily, lifting his fingers from the keys just long enough to take a quick drag on his cigarette; he couldn't have been writing a poem, for the typing was too even and uninterrupted for that, perhaps it was a script for one of his radio programs, though this wasn't likely either, because I never saw him bring home notes or papers from the studio or take anything back with him from home; he moved empty-handed between the two main locations of his life, as if deliberately isolating one from the other; his legs stuck out from under the table, which must have made for discomfort in sitting, but this way the streak of sunlight slanting in from the tall window could warm his bare feet.

And when he felt I was staring out the window too long, he said, without looking up, that we ought to wash the windows.

His toes were long and as attractively articulated as his slender fingers; I liked pushing my fist gently into the arch of his foot and with my tongue touching each toe, feeling the sharp edge of each nail.

I never took notes right after a rehearsal; I waited until late in the evening or, if I managed to get up early, the next morning; to see more clearly the source of, and reason for, the effect a given scene had on me, to gain a better perspective on it, I had to free myself from the effect itself.

I didn't answer him, though the idea of a joint window cleaning did appeal to me.

This note-taking began as a kind of idle diversion, a solitary mental exercise which often filled me with guilt, especially when riding home in the crowded city train, jostled by grim throngs of commuters; I would often think I was enjoying the privileges of the intellectual elite and decide I simply had to stop playing the observer condemned to inaction and should at least try to profit from the bitter fact that for several years

I'd been not an active participant in so-called historical events but rather their pathetic victim and in this sense a part of the faceless crowd—significant or insignificant, it hardly mattered which—an alien, self-hating element, maybe just a giant eye with no body to go with it; yet when this mental exercise became a regular routine it did have an effect on my daily life.

On casually filled pages, out of comprehensible and therefore not wholly uninteresting notes, the picture of a performance in preparation began to emerge; thus, without my noticing the changes occurring within me, I found myself so deep within the labyrinth of my uncertain and risky undertaking, allowing me to experience vicariously the lives of a group of strangers, that it was no longer just a personal obsession to describe the performance down to its minutest details, every word and gesture, each latent and overt connection, to follow the process of realization, to become its chronicler, to respond to their work with my own, which, after all, is the indispensable condition of human fellowship, but within the small community whose activities my notes hoped to follow I also found a place for myself, however peripheral, a role to be played that gave me the joy of having an identity, if only in relation to the people in that theater.

It was Sunday morning, a day of rest, and since it was his turn to make lunch, every once in a while he would kick the chair out from under him, go into the kitchen, come back, and resume banging on his typewriter.

I seem to remember dropping a remark to Frau Kühnert about my notes, which she mentioned to Thea, who, in her usual overeagerness, must have passed on to the others, for I began to notice that they were more cautious with me, indeed took precautions, trying to talk to me differently, more coherently and confidentially, as if they each wanted to shape the image I'd create of them.

I asked him what he was writing.

His last will, he said.

The truth is, I hadn't noticed how deeply I was being affected by the seemingly insignificant and uneventful times we spent together, by his place not merely being familiar but becoming a home, and that I no longer asked what home meant but thought I knew.

He asked me what I was thinking about.

It was quiet—I didn't remember when but at some point he had stopped typing, which meant he had been staring at me staring out the window at the tree and the sky.

As I turned to him and told him I wasn't thinking about anything, I could tell from his eyes he'd been watching me for quite some time; a smile had gathered on his mouth.

You must have been thinking about something, at least about nothing itself, he said, chuckling a little.

No, really, I wasn't thinking of anything, just watching the leaves.

It was true, I wasn't thinking of anything worth formulating in words, and in any case, one doesn't think in thoughts; it was a pure sensation to which I was yielding unconditionally, without thinking, with no tension between the peaceful sight and my body's comfortable position, between perception and the perceived object, and this is what he must have noticed on my face, body and soul in a state that might even be called happiness, but his question made this sensation rather fragile, and I felt it needed protecting.

Because what he'd been thinking, he continued, was that I might be thinking of the same thing, which was that maybe we should stay like this for good.

How did he mean that, I asked, as if I hadn't understood.

The smile vanished from his lips, he withdrew his searching glance from my face, lowered his head, and, pronouncing the words with difficulty, as if we had exchanged roles and now it was he who had to speak in a foreign language, he asked if I had ever thought of the two of us in this way.

Some time had to elapse before I managed to utter the word that in his language makes a deeper, throatier sound: yes.

He turned his head away and with a delicate, absentminded motion raised the paper in the typewriter, and I looked out the window again, both of us being silent and motionless: as fervent as our shyly voiced confessions had been, so charged with fear was the silence that followed— one would want to hold back one's breathing in this kind of silence, even the beating of one's heart, which is why one hears it and feels it all the more.

He asked me why I hadn't mentioned it before.

I said I thought he'd feel it anyway.

It was good to be sitting far from him and not to look at him, since a glance or physical proximity might have shattered what we had, yet the situation was becoming dangerous because something final and irreversible would have to be said; the sharp beam of sunshine streaming through the window seemed to raise a wall between us through which the words would have to pass; addressing the other, we were each talking to ourselves; we seemed to be sitting in our separate rooms in the shared warmth of our single room.

If I had thought about this before, he pressed on, how was it that it had occurred to him only now?

That I didn't know, I said, but it didn't matter.

After a short while he got up, but didn't kick the chair out as was his wont, rather he pushed it gingerly out of the way; I didn't look at him and I don't think he looked at me, and he was careful not to cross the beam of light that was now a wall between us as without a word he left for the kitchen, and judging by the weight and rhythm of his steps he was walking in order to reduce the tension generated by our words but, not letting down his guard, taking his caution along with him.

And the cozy, familial silence became more significant than the allusive words wrapped softly in silence and suppression, because the words alluded to something final, to the possible end of our relationship, while the wrapper of silence alluded to circumstances known to both of us that, contradicting the meaning of our precisely and reticently spoken words, denied the very possibility of an imminent end, and the fact that we could communicate in a language of allusions whose aesthetics we could share gave the impression, at least to me, that of the two options the possibility of our continued relationship was stronger; I think he remained more skeptical and cautious.

As soon as he left the room, I was overcome by a strange, humiliating restlessness; my movements became independent of me, the compulsion to move and at the same time to restrain movement made me play out, in the covert and overt language of gestures, the emotional struggle unexpressed in our dialogue: I couldn't take my eyes from the poplar tree, kept fidgeting and scratching—all of a sudden every part of me felt like getting out of there, I was itching all over—rubbing my nose and smelling my fingers, sniffing the nicotine on the skin, I didn't light up, though I'd have liked to, in irritation I flung my pen on the desk as no longer needed, but right away started groping for it in the pile of papers, picked it up again, kept pressing and twirling it, hoping it would help me get back to my notes, though at this point I couldn't have cared less about those idiotic notes; I wanted to get up, to see what he was really writing, what sort of last will it was, but I stayed put, didn't want my changing of place to disturb the stillness of some unknown possibility, felt I had to protect something I would be better off getting over, something I should somehow evade or wriggle out of.

That's when he came back, which immediately reassured me, being on the alert, waiting eagerly to see what else might happen, what else there was in us to be said out loud, to be known only when actually spoken or soon thereafter; but my new calm was only a grotesque mirror image of the earlier restlessness, since I still couldn't turn to him—I wasn't calm enough—wanting him to believe that nothing had changed in me while he was gone.

The soft patter of his bare feet betrayed the tiny change that had taken place in him, not hesitation or kind consideration, as he had shown earlier, but increased attentiveness, an absorption in his own quickening footsteps, perhaps an objectivity he'd gained in the kitchen when with the help of a dishcloth he lifted the lid off the pot of cauliflower cooking in its salt water; the water had come to a violently bubbling boil, the steam hit his face, and though the cauliflower seemed soft enough, he nevertheless took a fork from the drawer and carefully poked it to make sure that the white rose-like heads did not fall apart—with this kind of cauliflower, if it is overcooked, that can easily happen—and only after that did he turn off the gas under the pot; sitting in his room I'd heard or thought I heard, seen or imagined I saw, every move he made, and in his footsteps I sensed that these routine gestures had taken back some of that emotional effusion which in me had rather unpleasantly intensified.

He stopped behind my back and lowered his hands to my shoulders; he did not hold my shoulders but simply let the weight of his hands rest on them; I felt not the slightest tension in his muscles, no body weight was communicated through his hands, which made the gesture rather friendly but guarded, too.

I leaned back and looked up at him; that palm-size area on my skull that so enjoys the caressing softness of another's hand—a spot not sufficiently appreciated for its sensitivity—was touching his belly; he looked down at me, smiling.

What's going to happen to us? I asked.

Now he did grip my shoulders just a little, squeezing some of his strength into me; Nothing, he said.

Just enough strength to take the edge off the meaning of that word.

This area of the skull with its peculiar nature is called the fontanel in an infant, and even after the bones fuse and harden, the spot continues to respond to stimuli as sensitively as if it were still a piece of throbbing purple-veined tissue, in some respects even more sensitively than our sense organs, because it seems to specialize in reacting exclusively to either friendly or hostile stimuli, perceiving them with unerring accuracy; I wanted to be aware of, wanted to feel, this area of my skull, and I pressed the spot against his stomach with the same force with which he was grasping my shoulders.

Articulating his words carefully, he said I had to understand, and I certainly mustn't misunderstand, that it was no accident, could not be construed an accident, that until now I'd kept my thoughts to myself about what we mentioned earlier; but he wouldn't want to tell me how to lead my life, wasn't taking back what he'd said before, either, which would be silly; he wouldn't want to influence me in any way.

Looking up at him I laughed, and said I had to laugh, because if he really meant that, then he should have behaved differently from the beginning.

The smile moved from the corner of his eyes back to his mouth; for a while he stared into my eyes, then, across the back of the chair, he pressed me to himself.

It was too late, he said.

For what? I asked.

Just too late, he repeated, his voice deeper.

The position of our bodies, with him looking at me from above and with me looking up at him, as the fragrance of his voice reached me with his every word, seemed to give him more security.

What did he mean, I asked, he had to tell me.

He couldn't tell me.

His white shirt was open to the waist, the gentle warmth his skin exhaled on me was like a memento, its odor containing at least as many meaningful particles as a word or an intonation, a gesture or a glance, except, unlike sight or hearing, smell works in our minds with more insidious and mysterious signals.

He didn't want to tell me, I said.

That's right, he didn't.

Very gently, I peeled his arms away, but now he leaned closer, gripping the armrest of the chair, so the wings of his unbuttoned shirt touched and enclosed my face; in this position our faces came very close, although I would have wanted not his body to speak but his mouth, for him to say not with his body but with his mouth the opposite of what his mouth would have said and what he couldn't say with words.

And so as not to comply with this impossible demand, he kissed my mouth, angrily almost, and I let him, couldn't do otherwise, and in the soft warmth of his lips, under their hard little grooves, my lips did not move.

I should go on with my work, he told me, and he'd have to finish his, the meaning of his kiss now matching that of his words earlier, both intended as a conclusion.

He wouldn't get away so easily, I said as he was about to walk away, and held on to his hand.

It's no good insisting, he said, much as he would like to tell me, and I must understand that he really did, he couldn't help himself, didn't want to know what the next moment would be like, didn't want to know, wasn't interested, that's the way he was, it would make him sick if we started talking seriously about this, and what did I want from him? should we chat about rearranging the apartment? or should we, now there's an idea, go to City Hall and declare our serious intentions? we'd be a great hit with that! perhaps we should plan for a nice little future together? let this be enough, what we had, why wasn't it enough for me that he was happy, all the time I was with him he was happy? he'd say it, if I wanted to hear it, but that's all there was, he couldn't do more, and I shouldn't spoil things.

All right, but he had wanted more before, he'd wanted something else; he talked differently, not like this, why was he taking it back now?

He wasn't taking back anything, that was only my hangup.

I told him he was a coward.

Maybe, maybe he was.

Because he never loved anybody and nobody ever loved him.

Talking like that wasn't exactly attractive.

I couldn't live without him.

With him, without him—these were idiotic phrases, but what he was telling me just a few minutes ago was that he couldn't either.

Then what did he want?

Nothing.

He pulled out his hand from under mine, a movement that perfectly matched his last word; he walked away, to return to what may have been the only secure spot left for him in this room, his typewriter, back to the task that he'd set for himself and that he had to complete, but in the middle of the room he stopped, under the slanting sunbeam, his back to me, and now he, too, looked out the window, up at the sky, as if enjoying the warmth of the light, basking in it, and through the white shirt I could see the outlines of his slender body, whose fragrance was still with me.

And in that fragrance was the memory of the night before, and in that memory all the morning-after recollections of all previous nights.

And in the night, the glimmering darkness of the bedroom, and in the darkness the luminous spots of closed eyes, and in the flashing, flickering patches of light the smell of the coverlet, the sheets, the pillows, and in them, too, signs of what had gone on before: the chill of the room being aired, and in the hot, dry clouds of foaming detergent and steaming iron, his mother's hand.

And under the covers our bodies, and in our bodies our desire for each other, and in the afterglow of sated desire our sprawled bodies on the crumpled bedding, the skin, the vapor of the skin pores, and in the pores the moisture of secretions, the cooling perspiration settling in body hair, the pungent sweat in curves and bends, the smell of vehicles, offices, and restaurants trapped in the tangled strands of wet hair, and in the accumulated smells of the city the sea-salt taste of odorless semen, the bitter taste of tobacco in sweet saliva, food dissolving in saliva in the warm cave of the mouth; decaying teeth, and scraps of meat, fruit skins, and toothpaste stuck between the teeth, and from the depth of the stomach, alcohol reverting to yeast, the cooling fervor of the body in the solitude of sleep, and the fluids of dreams' indefinable excitements, the cool awakening, bracing water, soap, mint-scented shaving cream, and, in yesterday's shirt flung on the back of the chair, the day that's just past.

All right, then, I said, at least now there'll be something we won't be able to talk about, I like that.

Oh, I should shut up.

A little girl was yelling in the courtyard, calling her mother, who of course didn't hear her or didn't want to, and I envied the little girl, perhaps because she was born here and therefore didn't have to leave, or for her desperate and innocent stubbornness, with which she refused to accept being ignored; her high-pitched shouts became more and more hysterical and nerve-racking, then stopped as suddenly as if somebody had strangled her, and only a bouncing ball could be heard.

He sat down at his desk and I knew I mustn't look at him anymore, for he was getting ready to speak, and if I looked he might not.

I picked up my pen and found the last word of my manuscript; it was on page 542, which is where I'd have to continue.

He hit a few keys; in the silence we decidedly missed the little girl's screams, I had to wait until he typed a few more lines when, just as I'd expected, he began to fill the silence, speaking softly, saying we had two months left, and I couldn't possibly be serious about not going home.

I kept staring at the image evoked by the two last words on the paper—"empty stage"—and asked him why he was so damn defensive, what was he afraid of? a question that of course couldn't hide the fact that I could not or would not give him a straightforward answer.

He'll keep in mind what I just said, he continued, as one who'd finally hit upon tangible proof of my true intentions, won't forget it and will try to live with it.

With malicious pleasure we eyed each other from across the shaft of sunlight separating us; he was smiling triumphantly at having exposed me, and I borrowed some of his smile.

Then I'll come back, I said, without being in the least sarcastic, because I didn't want to let him off the hook.

I'd find the apartment empty, then, since I should know by now he had no intention of staying in it.

Idle fancies, I said, how could he possibly leave this place?

Maybe he wasn't as much of a coward as I thought he was.

So he had been making plans for a nice little future, except not with me.

To be frank, he had been planning something; he was going to vanish before my departure, so I'd have to leave without saying goodbye.

A wonderful idea, I said—maybe it was his smile, flashing ever more sharply from his eyes with every spoken word, or maybe it was the fear or joy evoked by this smiling emotion bordering on hatred, but I found myself laughing out loud and saying, Congratulations.

Thanks.

Grinning, we looked into each other's eyes, distorted by grinning, a look that we couldn't escape, so ugly we couldn't make it worse either.

It was odd that he didn't seem ugly and distorted to me as much as I did to myself, seeing myself with his eyes.

There was nothing remarkable about this moment, hour, or day, it was like all the others we'd spent together, except this was the first time we had put into carefully chosen words what we had been looking for ever since that evening when, led there by fate, we wound up sitting next to each other at the opera, although what we felt as so extraordinary that evening kept on presenting and formulating itself always as if for the first time; perhaps one might say that what we were looking for in each other was the ultimate in feeling at home, and every word and gesture seemed to be a form of new discovery in the course of our search, but we couldn't possibly find what we were looking for, because the true home of our longing was the search itself.

It was as though we were trying to deepen and somehow make permanent an already extreme emotion, a bond which can and does exist between two human beings but with which there is not much more that can be done, and perhaps the reason was, as he once had tried to explain, that we were both men, and the law of the sexes may be stronger than those of individual personalities; at the time I wasn't ready to consider or accept this, if only because I felt the freedom of my individuality was at stake, my selfhood.

That first moment encompassed all our subsequent moments, which is to say that in all that followed something of that first moment persisted.

As he stood with his French friend in the dimly lit lobby of the opera house, in the midst of the milling theatergoers on the stairs, I felt I knew him, and knew him from long ago, not just him but everything about him: not just his well-cut suit, his loosely knotted tie, his tiepin, but also his casually dressed friend, and even the relationship that so clearly bound them together, although at the time I had only the vaguest notion of what a love relation between two men might be like; yet the sense of familiarity gave the meeting a quick lightness, an inexplicable closeness we feel only when everything seems so natural that we ask no questions, just let down our guard and don't even know what is happening to us.

When he slipped out of Thea's embrace, which his friend obviously found too effusive and not at all to his liking, we shook each other's hand, not any differently than any two people would in such circumstances; I told him my name and he told me his, while I heard his friend introducing himself to Frau Kühnert and Thea—in the manner of a tough guy, giving only his double first name, Pierre-Max—repeating it twice in succession; only much later did I find out that his family name was Dulac.

After that handshake we didn't pay much attention to each other, yet the inner compulsion of our feelings so shaped the situation that while walking up the red-carpeted gleaming white staircase—I was conversing with his friend and he was chatting with Frau Kühnert and Thea—we seemed to be steering each other with our shoulders; though our bodies did not touch, from that moment on they became inseparable, they wanted to stay close to each other, that's how they proceeded up those stairs, our bodies doing their job so assuredly that we didn't have to pay special attention to our closeness, which was neither surprising nor controllable, setting itself immediately on the right course, with aims and possibilities of its own—about which, as it turned out later, only I had certain misgivings—so he was free to go on chatting without having to look at me, and I didn't have to look at him either, because by then I had gained so much confidence from being close to his body and to its fragrance that I could also converse freely with the young Frenchman walking on my left.

But I wouldn't call this a collusive or complicitous feeling, being much darker and deeper; to use an analogy, I'd say it was as if one was arriving in the present after a quick journey from one's own faraway past, and the present is as improbable and dreamlike as a city that at the moment of arrival one moves about in dazed—no, the meeting had none of the excited cheerfulness and joy peculiar to erotically charged little conspiracies, unless it was the much deeper joy of a long-awaited homecoming.

Actually, what made the moment special for me, and perhaps that's the reason I remember it so well, was the stir Thea created, being a well-known and celebrated personality who attracted the audience's curiosity, which was extended to us as well in the form of furtive, sidelong glances, everybody being eager to see, to know, in whose company and with what sort of men the famous actress was making her appearance here, and we, four very different non-celebrities, must have seemed rather unusual, almost scandalous in this formal, overdisciplined setting.

Thea was onstage here, too, playing the offstage role of famous and notorious actress; and let it be said to her credit that with the most economical means she managed to pretend she noticed none of the eager, respectful, sometimes envious and contemptuous glances, since she devoted all her attention to Melchior—behold, this is the man! she declared by her gesture as she leaned lightly on Melchior's arm, rewarding him with almost the same adoring look she was getting from her admirers, and adjusting her own face—bony, Oriental-looking, no makeup—to look just as pretty as her audiences were used to and always expected to see, of course looking for some protection as she gazed with those narrowed, impishly smiling eyes into his, protection to help her stay incognito—make it so she wouldn't have to look anywhere else! no, she didn't want to mind her steps, she'd go anywhere she was led—though all along she was leading him, in her long, tight black skirt slit to her knees, her dainty spike-heeled shoes, her slightly translucent lead-gray silk blouse, more fragile and vulnerable, altogether more shy and modest-looking than she was in any of her other roles.

She spoke in a voice deep and warm with feeling, softly but volubly, her hushed tones keeping the content of her words from the earshot of the curious, spoke only with her mouth, while her smile, perfectly disciplined, mimicked flawlessly the artless mimicking of social banter, smuggling into her act some of the tension we'd left behind in the rehearsal hall, thriftily using her unexpended energies to reduce and deflect the elemental joy and passion evoked by Melchior's mere presence, by the proximity of his body, but however sparing her histrionic means, or because they were so masterfully pared down to perfect proportions, no one could ignore her presence; people stopped, turned, followed her with their looks, whispered behind our backs, clandestinely or quite openly stared into her face, jabbed each other, pointed fingers, the women checking out her clothes, ogling her supple walk, the men affecting cold indifference, imagining kneading her breasts gently or wondering what it would be like to feel her slender waist or slap her shapely round behind; in a word, they all had her; while she was walking up the stairs, seemingly fully absorbed in her man, her audience, each in his or her way according to his or her taste, made as though she were their exclusive property, their lover, their younger sister, and we, too, gained attention, becoming in the spectators' eyes professional extras in this little scene of Thea's procession.

Prompted more by the situation than by genuine curiosity, and feigning ignorance and surprise, I inquired of the lanky, dark, tousled young Frenchman how he happened to be here; we were still walking up the stairs as he leaned over to me with an expression at once friendly, reticent, and condescending, with his surprisingly narrow, flatly cut eyes in which there didn't seem to be much room for the eyeballs to move freely, which is perhaps why his gaze was so rigid and piercing, but what I really wanted to know was what Thea was buzzing so lullingly into the ear of the man whose closeness my shoulder, arm, and side were registering.

The Frenchman answered in perfectly idiomatic though heavily accented German that he didn't live here, at any rate not in this part of the city, but liked to hop over, and did so frequently; our invitation couldn't have come at a better time, because he'd meant to see this performance, but frankly, he didn't quite understand why I was surprised, why shouldn't he be here? for him this world was not nearly so alien as I might think, on the contrary, he felt more at home here than in the western part of the city, for he was a Marxist and a Communist Party member.

The cleverly manipulated rhetoric of his reply, the unmistakably antagonistic edge on his assertion, the touchiness with which he discovered in me a possible adversary, his self-righteous tone, his flippantly insolent though hardly lighthearted demeanor, his rigid and provocative stare radiating both narrow prejudices and something attractive, youthful, combative—all this I found so remarkable that I took up the challenge right away, though a heated political debate in these coolly, lifelessly formal surroundings seemed out of place: teased by contradictory impulses, I had a strong urge to laugh: what kind of drivel was he trying to palm off on me? his statements struck me as a pleasantly irreverent joke might, an impression only intensified by the childishly defiant expression on his handsome face and the animated elegance which another culture gave his appearance, which, judged by local standards, was rather slovenly: a thick, soft, slightly threadbare sweater, not quite clean, a fire-engine-red woolen scarf wrapped twice around his neck and tossed over his shoulder, attire that the gathering audience, scrubbed to the required level of festive cleanliness and therefore looking pitiful and lacking style, scrutinized with such shock and disapproval you could almost hear the indignant groans, but I didn't want to offend him, if only because I, too, scrutinized by the same audience, felt obliged to remain collected, and so I smiled politely, somewhat superciliously, and without bothering to take the sting out of my words replied that he must have misunderstood my surprise, since no rebuke or calling to account was intended and I considered it a privilege to meet him, it was just that in this eastern hemisphere during the last six years—and, I emphasized, for at least six years—I hadn't met anyone who'd call himself a Communist and claim careful personal consideration as the reason for being one.

Just what was I getting at?

With the superior air of a native I said I wasn't getting at anything, but he could check the arithmetic.

If I was referring to the spring of '68, he said somewhat less confidently—I, enjoying my advantage, nodded that that's exactly what I'd had in mind—and he stared into my eyes, waited for me to stop nodding, and then continued all the more vehemently, he did not believe that the lesson to be learned from those events was to give up the struggle.

The ringing, slogan-like phrase issued so innocently from his youthfully soft lips, so engagingly, strongly, and therefore convincingly—Thea was meanwhile vilifying her director to Melchior—despite the implied question of what sort of struggle he was talking about, struggle against whom or what? that I lost the presence of mind for a proper answer, staggered by the humor of the situation, and in the lull, at once comic and serious, I could hear Thea's unceasing chatter—Langerhans would make a splendid ambassador in, say, Albania, or maybe only a good stationmaster somewhere, well, all you had to do was look at him, the way he kept pushing his glasses up and down his pug nose, the way he dug his stubby fingers into his greasy hair, he reminded you of a large sheet of white paper with nice round stamps on it, he could bang away all day with his official-looking stamps, blues and reds and who knows what other colors, but for God's sake he shouldn't be directing! and this was no exaggeration, no joke; Melchior knew the scene, yes, Act III, Scene 2, the one with the privy council, now that scene had become the only one worth watching in the whole production, that awful council session, with six impossible characters sitting around this huge table, he'd had this impossibly long table made especially and picked six of his lousiest actors for this scene, and Melchior could just imagine how much those poor suckers must enjoy doing it, how grateful they were to Langerhans for the opportunity, but that's what made the scene! the way they sat there shuffling their documents and scratching themselves, and stammering, and chewing their nails, Langerhans chewed his nails all the time, too, disgusting!—and these six weren't even eager to go home like everyone else, it made no difference to them, they'd been waiting thirty years for these tiny parts, for thirty years they hadn't understood a thing, and now it was certain they never would, and just try to imagine, but he'll see it for himself, the whole thing was so incredibly, stupefyingly boring you could fall off your chair, and this was the only thing Langerhans could come up with, this boredom, because what a woman was really like or what she could want from a man he hadn't the foggiest, this bloodless theater bureaucrat.

After a slight hesitation the young Frenchman said he was sure we were thinking about and talking about two entirely different things; he was thinking, naturally, about the Paris of 1968 and I, just as naturally, of the Prague Spring.

Or if Langerhans did have the foggiest about such matters, it was bound to be common, indecent, gross, she'd tell Melchior a little story about that, a racy little adventure, actually.

It wasn't the first time he'd encountered this kind of unpleasant, though from a historical perspective quite insignificant skepticism, the Frenchman continued, and he refused to believe that the Russians' clumsy military action could cast any doubt on the incontrovertible truth that this part of the world was the home of socialism, and then he mumbled something irrelevant about ownership of the means of production.

The thing happened between the two of them—she had to blush about it in retrospect—when they finally reached the point of not knowing what to do with each other, and she decided that she was going to tease the man out of Langerhans, wanting to see what he was like, whatever happened.

To me, this kind of demagoguery was at least as amusing as my skepticism was unpleasant for him, and I didn't really think, I said, that he'd be talking about "clumsy military action" if a foreign army had crushed the student riots in Paris.

It was usually mindless aristocrats who referred to revolutions as riots, the Frenchman said.

Just as it was usually obtuse ideologues who believed that the end justifies the means, I replied.

We both stopped on the staircase while they continued on, though Melchior, as if I were holding him back with my shoulder, quickly turned around before taking the next step, and I could see that the Frenchman, however irritated, was still enjoying what I not only did not enjoy but found disgracefully painful, ludicrously unnecessary, having let myself be dragged into a conversation like this in which I wasn't even expressing my own opinion or, rather, was mouthing a fraction of my own nonexistent opinion, since I had no whole opinion, since the all-too-thin membrane of self-discipline had been ripped open by the seething of raw, deeply repressed emotions, by my willful blindness, by something that knows only the language of the senses, which we ought to hide rather than show, and consequently I was angrier at myself than at him, while he seemed to feel so comfortable with his impossibly lanky body and impossible views that he didn't even notice these people staring at him so indignantly, so enviously! people among whom he supposedly felt at home but who saw him with his uncombed hair and dirty red scarf as a buffoon, as a living mockery of their lives and miserable ambitions, though the real clown, I knew, was not he but I.

It seems, he said calmly but testily, that we were speaking in entirely different languages.

It seems that way, doesn't it? I said, but since he felt so at home here,

I went on, no longer able or willing to contain my irritation, hadn't it occurred to him that while he could freely come here from the other side of the Wall, we weren't allowed to go over there?

I said this a little too loudly, and the two women stopped, if only because Melchior's arm slipped out of Thea's hand, and they all turned around, Frau Kühnert's eyes flashing with fright behind her thick glasses—careful, they seemed to be saying, every word can be heard—but I couldn't stop, and though I was mortified I went on, he shouldn't be too surprised, I said to him, if our notions of individual freedom made us speak in different languages.

But then Melchior, with schoolmasterly authority, stepped between us, shaking a finger at me in mild admonition: I should be careful, he said, his friend spoke with the words of a Robespierre, a Marat, and of course I had no way of knowing that I was talking to a fearless revolutionary.

Completely frustrated with myself, and with the last breath of my ridiculously envious anger, I said that was precisely the reason I was talking to him.

You mean you're one, too? Melchior asked, cocking his bushy eyebrows in mock alarm and disbelief, having a little fun at his friend's expense.

Why, yes, of course I am, I said, grinning up at him out of my anger.

The common ground we found in the intimately conspiratorial tone of his voice promptly relieved me of my shame, for he well understood my feelings, understood my shame, and knew how to dissolve it, with his understanding drew me to himself, distancing himself from his French friend; because of him I could breathe again.

But now unexpectedly the Frenchman broke into laughter, silent laughter, maintaining his aloofness, standing apart even as he laughed, his aloofness being meant for Melchior: the two of them were no doubt beyond such debates, beyond the point where they could reach a pact or agreement, which itself may have become a pact, but now, regarding Melchior and me, as if he were brushing away the filth of our cynically supercilious common stance and, with it, the disgust we had evoked in him, he waved his hand, dismissing us, shooing us away, rubbing us out of his space, indicating that we were frivolous and irresponsible, unworthy of further debate.

And there was something of a heroic pose in his bearing, in the way he threw back his handsome head and at the same time turned it away from us, while our carriage somehow remained servile despite our shared victory.

And then an old, gray-liveried usher, an apparition from a bygone era, with a look of complete attentiveness fixed on and meant exclusively for Thea, flung open for us the doors of the former royal box.

From there, from a height of nearly four meters, we could look down at the orchestra level with its curving rows of crimson and white seats, at a sea of pink faces, an animated expanse still stirring, rippling, then suddenly coming to rest; beyond the rigidly classical proscenium arch with its Corinthian columns and gilded capitals we could see the huge open stage: under the cyclorama painted steely gray to suggest the dawning of a dreadful day, grimy towers and jagged fortress walls loomed, enclosing a prison courtyard still sunk in the cheerless night; from here, darkly yawning passageways led to an even grimmer world of subterranean dungeons; farther back, in the vaulted caves of barred cells carved into the massive walls, one could sense the shadowy presence of human forms.

Nothing moved, yet everything seemed to be alive: there was a sudden gleam, perhaps the weapon of a guard, and the clang and rattle of chains heard over the peaceful uniform murmur of the audience and the bright flourishes of musicians tuning their instruments; and a little later, way upstage, deep in the impenetrable shadow cast by the brooding towers, the pink of a woman's dress seemed to swish by, and a breeze appeared to be carrying the snatches of a melodious offstage command, and indeed there was a breeze, because whenever a stage this size is open, and before the audience's warm breath has had a chance to heat up the vast space thus created, one can always feel a kind of cool breeze blowing from the stage, smelling faintly of glue.

Inside the empty box we engaged in a silent round of politeness over the seating arrangements; from behind a façade of good behavior and courtesy we were sharply observing one another's complicated intentions, indicated by looks and careful gestures—the task was clear: a hard-fought battle had to be brought to a peaceful conclusion, and it was a matter of no small importance who would wind up where—I would have liked to stay near Melchior, which was his intention, too, but I couldn't separate myself from the Frenchman or he from me, for this would have announced too harshly that we were incompatible not only ideologically but physically, found each other's proximity irritating, unpleasant, even repellent, an emphatic mutual rejection that would have hurt Melchior's feelings, which I didn't want to happen, yet at the same time it was so evident that Pierre-Max and Melchior were a couple and that neither Thea nor I had the courage to come between them, though Thea, who had after all organized this whole theater party because of Melchior, wasn't going to yield her place next to him for anyone, while Frau Kühnert, although seemingly unconcerned for the moment, nevertheless let us know in her diffident and unassuming way that we were all just part of the scenery to her and she wanted nothing to do with us: she was most definitely going to sit next to Thea, no discussion about that, which again put me in an awkward position, because sensing Thea's silent displeasure over my loud, tactless, uncooperative behavior, I'd have liked to end up between her and Melchior so that, without having to give up Melchior, I could also somehow mollify her, but of course this was not viable, since I had no right to separate the two of them.

There it was before us: five chairs made up the front row of the box, and our task seemed to be to take the gently entangled strands of the various relationships and smooth them out according to the positions of these chairs.

Of course, in situations like this it's always the rawest impulses that go into action: self-interest sets the true proportions of feelings for others, sets the sounds of raw feelings ringing out under the silly cover of "consideration," and sets the center of those feelings around the dominant victorious persons: from our cautious and polite movements two deliberate signals emerged, two brief phrases with the appropriate gestures to go with them: Come on! Melchior said in French to his friend, who until then had been watching the awkward byplay like a neutral bystander, Yes, please, please, an annoyed Thea said coolly to me.

And now it was perfectly clear that as much as Melchior might have objected to this meeting, Thea was right, after all, or more precisely, her sixth sense did not fail her when she had insisted on it, for she could insist only on something that Melchior must also have wanted.

It wasn't out of politeness or thoughtful consideration for Thea that Melchior so quickly and unceremoniously gave up being close to his friend but because he was attracted to her; he had to choose, and in choosing he was guided by the realization that he and Thea were the dominant persons here, the rulers, meant to be at each other's side, belonging together.

Thea also had designs on me, romantic ones with the intent of possession; we were both constantly aware of the other, but what between us remained only groping and sniffing teetered on the verge of fulfillment between the two of them; their relationship was by no means as one-sided as Frau Kühnert would have liked me to believe, not to mention that the age difference between them was not twenty years, as she would have it, but no more than ten, which made them a strange couple but not a ridiculous one; either way, the moment they made their decision, it became clear that to their ruling duet we provided only a royal escort and nothing could make me forget this, not even the pleasant discovery that in the ceremonial lineup I was assigned a slightly better position than the Frenchman.

Since I wasn't particularly adept at perceiving the subtler signals sent out by another male, I may have been led astray by Frau Kühnert's emotional revelations, and those streams of attraction I seemed to have sensed with and in my shoulders may have been not for me at all but emanations of Melchior's feelings for Thea; we were both in the same orbit around her.

This is how we finally took our places: the Frenchman, now locked in his silence, took the inside seat, I sat down next to him, with Melchior on my right, then came Thea, followed by Frau Kühnert, who, by the way, was the only one to get everything she wanted.

I was careful not to touch even accidentally Melchior's elbow on the armrest we shared; however, as befits wise rulers, he sensed right away that I was ill at ease in the seat he graciously yielded to me, that depriving the Frenchman of his rightful place gave me no satisfaction, and that I also felt the sting of jealousy on account of Thea; it seemed I laid claim to someone who not only wasn't mine but whom I did not even desire as far as I was consciously aware, yet here I was feeling hurt and jealous, I didn't want to lose her yet I was losing her, she was being snatched from me before my very eyes, and I'd have to compete for her with another man; as if wanting to complicate the already painful situation further, Melchior placed his hand on my knee and, smiling, looked into my eyes for a brief second, during which our shoulders touched, then made a face, withdrew his hand, and, as if nothing had happened, rearranged his smile and quickly turned back to Thea.

With that smile stirring on his lips he was apologizing to me for the unpleasantness of what had just taken place, and this was only an introduction to a deeper meaning of his smile, for he drew me into his huge blue eyes where the smile opened up even more and conveyed to me that the man he was parading here as his friend, his alibi, his protective shield, so he shouldn't be completely at Thea's mercy, that man meant, well, something to him, but nothing serious, I needn't worry or make much of it, and let's consider it settled between us; in other words, with that smile he betrayed his friend, abandoned him, yet managed to dig into me even more deeply, his grimace clearly implying that I should rest assured, yes, this woman was clever and manipulative, she was crazy about him and he found her irresistible, too, when she was being her foxy self, yes, by puckering her shapely lips she was mocking the situation no less than herself, which made her charmingly supercilious, but no reason to get excited about that, either, since he had no intention of seducing her, and let that be settled between us, too, between two men.

Neither his gesture nor his expression could remain unnoticed by the people they were meant for; all the same, his unabashed openness and falseness—because more than at any other later time when lulling my own jealousy I would believe him, at this moment I felt his confession was false—his brusqueness, crude interference, and betrayal made a very unfavorable impression, yet strangely I had neither the strength nor the emotional wherewithal to reject his unbecoming and unethical confidence but I sat there numb and rigid, disgusted by my position, pretending to be looking at the stage but in fact glancing to the left and to the right, like a thief, to see how much of this the others might have noticed, yet truth to tell, enjoying the riskiness of our situation.

My guilty conscience was whispering to me that were I to take seriously his silent communication I'd be stealing him from two people, from someone I didn't know and from someone I'd be deceiving despicably in the process, and my anxiety swelled into alarm—needless, because the Frenchman couldn't have noticed anything, he was leaning forward with his chin on the velvet-covered banister, watching the noisy audience below, and as for Thea, even if she did see Melchior's hand on my knee, she couldn't have found it significant; only Frau Kühnert's look issued a kind of warning: I could go ahead and do what I would, there was no way to escape her watchful eyes, she was there to protect Thea's interests.

Traces of Melchior's smile and grimace stayed with me while I also leaned forward in my chair, wanting to move away from both of them, and put my elbow on the banister; I didn't want to feel the emotional confusion radiating from the warmth of his body, to think he had addressed me with real words in a real voice; his voice seemed to be lost in some echoing space, swirling in a vast, dark, empty hall.

The applause first broke out in the upper gallery, then directly above us, and became thunderous when the conductor appeared in the little door leading to the orchestra pit, sweeping over the orchestra seats, reaching all the rows, and just then the lights went out in the huge crystal chandelier hanging from the heavily ornamented domed ceiling.

His voice was familiar, warm and deep, suggesting strength and self-confidence but also knowing not to take itself seriously, to be playful—not for the purpose of putting on a false front, but to keep a sensible distance—deepening to a good-natured growl; I had no idea where I knew that voice from, and I didn't bother to search my memory or explain why it felt so familiar and close, yet it kept streaming and swirling inside me, ringing, rising, grumbling as if testing its pitch and various ranges within, trying to find its place in the grooves of my brain, looking for the very spot, the nerve cells, the tiny space where its previous utterances were stored, a carefully sealed and, for the moment, inaccessible compartment.

When I had first arrived in Berlin, about two months before this performance, a room had been rented for me near the Oranienburg Gate, in the first corner house on Chausseestrasse, a tiny sublet on the fifth floor of one of those hopelessly grim, gray, and ancient apartment buildings; of course there was no city gate anywhere near, the name alone remained from an old city map, the name of something that history quite literally swept away, knocked off the table and cast into the fire, and if I say grim and gray, I haven't said much, because in that part of the city, at least in the sections where the ravages of war had not destroyed reminders of things as they once had been, this was how all the houses looked, grim and gray, but not without style, provided we do not limit style to mean conventionally decorative but allow that every human construct carries in itself and absorbs into its image the material and spiritual circumstances of the act of building; that is the style of any structure, that and nothing more.

And style includes destruction as well—like building, destroying also forms a continual chain in human history, and wartime destruction, in this district at least, was not quite so complete as in others, where nothing remained standing and where between the brand-new buildings only winds of emptiness blew, since here the cracks could be filled, the skeletons of fire-gutted houses could be fleshed out with new walls, enough stones were standing to offer crude shelter and protection from inclement weather, so it made sense to pile new stones on them, enough remained of the pre-destruction foundations, which were familiar, reliable, and therefore most attractive, and though the walls raised on them, patched up and reinforced, could not duplicate the prewar look, the old streets and squares kept their spatial configurations, the city's former layout, its spirit, was somehow carried over, even if nothing but mere traces could be detected of its lively, ostentatious, at once frugal and lavish, frivolous and grave, energetic and voracious style.

The guts of the old style, the principles of yore, the dead visage of the old order showed through the new style of the façades.

The intersection of Hannoverstrasse, splendid Friedrichstrasse, Wilhelm Pieck Strasse (formerly Alsatian Strasse), and Chausseestrasse, which once had formed a pretty little square, was now in this sad resurrection more dead than alive, nearly always deserted and lifelessly silent, an empty hull of different times piled one on top of another, with only a streetcar rumbling through now and then, in the middle of which an advertising pillar stood, left over from the old days, its belly ripped out by shrapnel; in the filthy plate-glass shop windows, blinded by dust, you could see the clock on the pillar top reflected; its glass cover long smashed in, it defied time by not showing it, or more precisely, it showed time arrested, since it clung to the half past four of a long-ago day.

And down below, under the pavement's thin crust, subway cars rumbled past at regular intervals, their clatter heard and felt under our feet, roaring in and out, their rumble dying away in the deep tunnel, but one couldn't get to these trains, since the stations that had escaped destruction were walled off; in the first few days I didn't know what to make of these unused stations on the little traffic islands along Friedrichstrasse, until Frau Kühnert was kind enough to enlighten me: this particular line, she said, connected western sections of the city and didn't belong to us, that's how she put it, so there was no point looking for them on the new maps, they weren't there; I didn't understand, and Frau Kühnert offered to explain, if I'd be willing to listen: Suppose I lived in West Berlin, I was a westerner, all right? say I got on the train at the Kochstrasse station, the train would pass under here, there was a station right under us; it would slow down, but couldn't stop, and simply pass through this part of the city and wind up in the so-called western sector, where I could get off at the Reinickendorf Station—it was that simple, did I understand better now?

It's our own city that we truly understand; in a strange city, even with the finest sense of direction and a thorough topographical knowledge of the place, street names and locations like east and west remain abstract, the street names conjuring up no images or the images lacking lived experiences, but I did understand—for that I didn't have to be a native— that something was under the streets that really wasn't, or rather, we had to pretend it wasn't, there, something allowed to live only in memories of the city as it used to be, yet part of the entire city's lifeline even today, which meant that it did exist, but only for those on the other side, who couldn't get out at the heavily guarded walled-up stations, if only because phantom trains have no stations, and in this way these people were at least as nonexistent for us as we were for them.

I said I understood almost everything, but why did the trains have to slow down at these nonexistent or, rather, existing stations? why the guards? what sort of guards were these, anyway, from here or from there? and since these stations were sealed off, what were they guarding, and how did they get out at the end of their shift? yes, I did understand, more or less, only I found it less than logical, or the logic of it escaped me.

If I continued to use this sarcastic tone, Frau Kühnert said with a native's offended pride, she wouldn't answer any questions in the future, and that finally shut me up.

And somehow this was also the style of that fifth-floor apartment on Chausseestrasse: as you walked through its ornately carved massive brown doors into the entrance hall the size of a reception room, you could smell the aroma of that same style; the entrance hall was completely empty now, and the darkened parquet floor, its worn-out strips replaced with ordinary plywood, creaked at every step, yet you could easily imagine a lighter, finer creak, muffled by rich Oriental carpets, while under the bright light of chandeliers a buxom chambermaid hastened to the door to let in elegantly attired ladies and gentlemen; plain-floored, winding passageways connecting the kitchen, the servants' quarters, the pantry and lavatory led to the masters' living space—five spacious interconnecting rooms whose elegantly arched windows now looked out on one of those cheerless new façades; I was put up in what used to be the maid's room.

From my window I could see only a dividing wall blackened with soot, so close it kept my room almost completely dark even during the day, and my accommodations could be described as extremely modest: an iron bedstead, a creaking wardrobe, the usual table covered with a stained tablecloth, a chair, and on the wall at least twenty neatly framed diplomas that for some reason had ended up in this room.

If, reclining peacefully on my bed, I stared out the window long enough and let my imagination go, on the map of that black wall I could follow the path of huge flames as they must have swooped down from the burning roof, accompanied by thunderous sounds of crackling, crashing, crumbling, could almost feel the wind, or windstorm, of that day as it was stirred by the fire, the enormous conflagration that left these traces for posterity, for me: protruding, peaked stains, colored by soot, where darting tongues of flame had licked the wall, which survived it all and remained intact.

I tried to consider this tiny room temporary in every respect, and to spend in it as little time as possible; and if it happened that I had nothing else to do, I undressed, climbed into the tub-like bed, plugged up one ear, and stuck the earphone of my small transistor radio into the other so I wouldn't have to hear the noises of people in the other rooms; four small children lived in the apartment, along with their grandfather, their invalid grandmother, their father, who'd come home drunk almost every night, and their pale-complexioned mother, who seemed heartrendingly young next to them, whose fragility, harried look, warmly expressive brown eyes, and feverish energy reminded me a little of Thea, or rather the other way around; it was as if Thea were telling me, in one of her older roles, who she would really be if, just once, she could give a full account of herself.

So I ended up listening to radio programs I never intended to tune in to, didn't really listen to them, but stared out the window, and I can't even say that I thought of anything in particular, simply let my body lie suspended in a rootless, transient state, not wanting it to have memories of its own.

And then slowly, gradually, approaching from afar, a man's voice penetrated my consciousness, still fighting off memories, a deep voice, pleasantly soft, smiling or laughing, which is to say that as the man spoke I could almost sense, almost see, the imperturbable good cheer ruling this unknown face, and after a short while I caught myself listening, not so much to what he said as to how he said it, and wondering who he might be.

He was interviewing a prewar chanteuse, a real old-timer, chatting with her lightly and amiably, as if they were sitting over a cup of coffee and not in front of a microphone, which the old lady had probably forgotten was there, because she kept giggling and gabbing away at phenomenal speed, at times actually cooing as if to a baby, which made their intimate tête-à-tête almost visible; and it wasn't just superficial chatter either, for they interspersed their conversation with old recordings, and the man seemed to know all there was to know about the songs, the circumstances of their recordings, the period that had become so fragmented and became the past, the real subject of their conversation, the vibrant and captivating, frivolous and cruel metropolis whose life was now being evoked by the old woman's girlish giggling and cooing; the man knew everything but never flaunted this, on the contrary, cheerfully letting himself be corrected, friendly little humming and growling sounds indicating his assent, or openly admitting his mistakes, though with certain intonations holding out the possibility that it might be the elderly lady whose memory was somewhat erratic, but again, there was nothing offensive about this, because his gentle, filial affection and scholarly dedication simply embraced and beguiled her; when the show was over and I learned he'd be back again next week, I felt as if all my physical and intellectual needs had been satisfied; I pulled the earphone out of my ear and quickly turned the radio off.

The following week at the same time he did come on again, but to my great surprise he didn't talk at all; in this program famous opera singers sang popular songs, he played vintage recordings of Lotte Lehmann, Chaliapin, and Richard Tauber, and all he did was announce names, nothing more; in spite of my disappointment, this made me happy, for he was modest and became talkative only when making his guests talk, I was hoping he wouldn't spoil the first impression, I wanted him to be consistent.

And he was, but I never heard him again, forgot all about him; one evening I went out to the kitchen, probably to get a drink of water, and the young woman of the house was there, peeling onions—she, too, was away during the day, I seem to remember her saying that she worked in an asbestos factory, and because she had small children she always got the day shift and did her cooking in the evening—so I sat down next to her and we talked quietly, which meant that I was talking and she hesitantly responding, thrusting each word reluctantly out of her mouth, while she went on peeling onions; I went as far as to risk the question whether she'd mind if I took down all those diplomas, just temporarily, while I was using the room.

The knife stopped in her hand, she glanced at me with her warm brown eyes, and for this brief silent moment her face remained so soft and calm that I returned her glance without any suspicion; I enjoyed looking at her, she was beautiful; the only thing I found odd and not quite comprehensible was the way she pulled up her narrow shoulders, as a cat does with its back when getting ready to purr, and at the same time lowered her hand, with the knife in it, into the bowl of water in front of her; she seemed about to break down and cry, or as if her whole body might begin to convulse, but instead, with her eyes closed, she started screaming at the top of her voice directly into my still unsuspecting face, using words that were strangely literary, stilted, complicated, and, for me at the time, mostly incomprehensible, hurling at me all the hurt that people like myself caused her: Who do these people think they are that they can just come here and do as they damn please and push us around, these filthy foreigners, these shitty little Vietnamese and rotten niggers, that she should have to work even on her Communist Sunday off! they don't care, they've got the nerve to come here, they've got the gall, and expect her to clean up their shit! and now they won't even let her be in her own apartment, not for a moment, they stick their tongues into everything, stink up her pots and pans, just what the hell do they think, who are they anyway, and who are we to them? she'd had enough of not knowing where the hell these people came from, not that she cared, she couldn't care less, but they wouldn't even learn that when they shit into the toilet bowl, the fucking brush is there for a reason, to scrub off the shit coming out of their foreign asses.

As soon as she mentioned the Vietnamese and the blacks, I stood up and because I really did want to help her, I would have liked to put my hand on her trembling shoulder in an attempt to calm her, but the mere possibility of physical contact made her body recoil violently, her screaming climbed higher and higher into shrill squeals, and she began groping so frantically for the knife floating in the bowl among the cut-up vegetables that I thought I'd better pull my hand back, and fast; having completely lost my linguistic presence of mind—the words wanted to slip out in my native tongue, and I was literally snatching them back with my tongue—I stuttered, and mumbled that she shouldn't get excited, if she liked I'd move out at once, but my quiet words only added oil to the flames, she kept on screeching, the pitch climbing ever higher; I left the kitchen, she followed me with the knife, and screamed her last words into the blackness of the cavernous hallway.

Inundated by waves of applause, the conductor finally took his place, looked to the right, looked to the left, arched his back, and, as if getting ready to swim, raised his arms into the light beams over the music stands; silence fell on the theater, a warmly expectant silence; onstage cold dawn was approaching.

Leaning very close to the Frenchman, I whispered into his ear: As you can see, we are in prison; in the soft dimness his face remained motionless.

I did catch his surprise, lasting only a split second, before the thunder of the overture's first chords seemed to beat back the surging waves of applause, pound them into us, shatter everything showily theatrical, sweep it all away, silence it, shut it out; the four crashing chords, as the earth split open, seemed to make all our strivings petty and laughable; and then, following a consummate silence, the breath caught at the sight of horror in the gaping abyss was released through the mouth of a clarinet in a soaring melody of longing that began in the depths and rose tenderly, lovingly, yearning for grace, was taken over by gentle bassoons and imploring oboes, still rose, seeking freedom; and though the sigh is thrown back by the craggy walls of the abyss, like a furious thunder, the sigh itself swells, gathers strength, now flows like a river, fills the holes and cracks of evil fate, the whole abyss; but roar and rage as it may, sweep away crags and stones, it is helpless, its strength is that of a mere brook against the powerful force that allowed it to swell, the one that rules it, the one that it can never overcome—until that bugle call; from somewhere, from above, from far away, from outside, the familiar, long-awaited yet unexpected, unhoped-for bugle call is sounded: triumphant redemption itself, the simplest, ludicrously symbolic redeemer, the sound of freedom in which the body can strip itself, as it does with bothersome clothes when making love, down to its bare soul.

When the overture ended I finally felt free to move; until then it would have seemed improper, but now the Frenchman and I leaned back in our chairs at almost the same time; he grinned at me, pleased; we both approved of what we'd just heard, and with this joint approval peace was restored between us; a thin strip of light fell through the openings of the fortress wall—morning—a thin strip of stage sun lit up the prison yard.

Later that Sunday morning we didn't have much to say to each other: Melchior was ashamed of his grin, his little acts of cruelty, and we exchanged a few words when we set the table for lunch, but we ate quietly, studiously avoiding each other's eyes.

We hadn't yet finished our meal, there was still a bit of cauliflower, some mashed potato, and a piece of meat on his plate when the phone rang, and looking annoyed and mumbling under his breath, he dropped his knife and fork, though there was just enough curious anticipation in his quick response, the way he reached back for the phone, pretending to be irritated, to make clear that his grumbling and annoyance were meant for me; he was apologizing to me in advance.

Still, in all fairness, he didn't like it when our meals were interrupted, because eating together was first of all not the taking of necessary nourishment but the performance of a ritual that gave significance to the time we spent together and dignity to our relationship.

I never asked him, or myself, how he ate when I wasn't there, but I don't imagine it was very different; most likely he set the table with the same meticulous care, but probably without making such a point of it, or being so demonstrative, a conclusion I came to after our weekend visits to his mother, in his native town, when during those meals among the old furniture of the dining room, I could sense from each gesture, from the tidiness of the table setting and the manner in which food was served, the several-centuries-old Protestant eating habits—frugal, giving each bite its due—that were second nature with them, a tradition that Melchior not only continued but in my presence deliberately exaggerated with his discriminating fastidiousness; but that Sunday, as we ate in silence, I could observe his movements for the first time, the rhythms of his chewing and swallowing, as if through a keyhole, because we were trying so hard to retreat into and isolate ourselves, not disturb the other with our presence, that we were each in separate and complete solitude, and then it became clear to me that his systematic and elaborate ways, his exaggerated decorum and solemnity, which extended to every meal, indeed to every so-called routine activity, were not so much signs of some affectation whose origin and nature I could not fathom and therefore tended to misunderstand as something meant for me, more precisely for us—the exaggeration being there for extra emphasis, that with his ceremoniousness he was marking the time we spent together, measuring and consecrating it, that with every move he made he was gauging our time, counting back from a terminal point that could be ascertained and calculated to the day, down to the hour; and he wanted to celebrate each moment, make it as festive and as aesthetically pleasing as possible, so that when it was all over between us, in a time beyond the terminal point, each moment could become an easy-to-recall, tangible, usable memory.

A candle was burning in an antique silver candlestick, which he put on the table not only because of its beauty and festive look but to avoid having matches or a lighter on the white damask tablecloth for our after-dinner cigarettes; no mundane object should profane the artificially created flawlessness that meant to shut out this world he felt to be alien and despicable; he put flowers on the table, and we pulled our damask napkins from monogrammed silver napkin rings, he would allow no ordinary wine bottle on the table, and though it was not necessarily good for the wine, before the meal he transferred it into a decorative crystal flask; yet there was nothing stiffly formal about our meals, as one might expect as a consequence of this meticulousness; he ate with gusto, chewing each bite carefully and helping himself to huge portions, and if I left something on my plate he'd polish that off, too, down to the last crumb; and without ever becoming drunk or even tipsy, he guzzled his wine from a tall glass.

It was Pierre on the phone, and after swallowing my last bit of food and looking for an excuse to leave the room so as not to disturb them, I began collecting the dishes; they were talking in French, which had an electrifying effect on Melchior having nothing to do with Pierre's person; I won't deny the possible influence of my jealousy, but at such moments he looked to me a changed man, became eager and ambitious, gave up his natural attractiveness for an acquired casualness, turned into a kind of model student who in hopes of the teacher's praises is willing to sing a whole octave higher than his own range, and while the whole class is in stitches even holds his neck differently so he can pronounce each word properly, pursed his lips, pushed the words out, not so much pronouncing as thrusting them out, kneading them, motivated by the desire to sound as perfect as he can while speaking a foreign language and by the need to find another potential self that only flawless pronunciation and phrasing could coax out of him; seeing him like this made me feel a bit ashamed for him, but also reminded me of similar behavior of my own; he leaned back comfortably, settling in for a long chat, motioned to me to leave his plate on the table and not to take away his glass either.

In the kitchen I arranged the dirty dishes on the table next to the sink but didn't wash them—I wasn't so permissive or magnanimous as to leave them completely to themselves—I could have gone to the bedroom, but didn't, and when I went back, they were still chatting, or more precisely, Pierre was talking for what seemed like a long time, with Melchior listening and smiling and absentmindedly picking crumbs off his plate and licking his fingers.

I opened the window and leaned out, not wanting to understand even the few French words I did catch, but letting him know I was there.

In this game, this ambitious linguistic game of his, in which he tried to raise part of his personality and shift it into a different identity, there was a subtle message for me, but after our conversation earlier that morning, my ears registered its subtleties in a new way.

The more he succeeded in adopting the cadences of the foreign language and losing the intonations and accents of his own, which had eaten themselves into his face, his lips, his throat, his posture, the further he moved from the ease with which one speaks in one's native tongue, which was natural, because one never speaks in perfect sentences or with flawless diction in one's own language but chatters away freely, obeying some strong inner purpose and personal sense of equilibrium, the perfection expressed being rather the innate one of a linguistic community, its infinitely broad yet inviolable consensus; in one's own language even a clumsy sentence includes the extremes of total abandon and strict constraint, freedom within the commonly accepted bondage, and in this sense there's no mistake or false intonation, can be no linguistic error, for every mistake or lapse or false turn is an allusion to something real, a mistake, a falseness; but with him it was different: the more imperfect and unnatural he became in this strange, mimicking perfection, the more perfectly he acted out the message that I, who knew him only in his native tongue and in the gestures and demeanor that were part of it, didn't really know him at all, that he was not to be identified with himself, because here he was, I could see for myself, capable at any moment of this kind of metamorphosis, and I shouldn't trust the person I thought I knew, he was two different persons with two different languages, who could choose at will between the two, so try as I might to pin down his emotions, or blackmail him with myself, and especially with Thea, it wouldn't work, a part of his soul would always be free, off limits to me, in a whole different world, a secret realm I couldn't even glimpse, there was no use being jealous, because if he didn't love this particular Frenchman, he must love the Frenchman within himself who was his real father and in whose language his own soul could and wanted to speak; I might look upon his life as a distant accident of history, but I was too dense to understand anything, didn't understand that this fatal physical and spiritual split was his real story, that over the German father he had to choose the French father killed by the Germans, his soul over his body, his body over his mother tongue, not only because that man was his real father—who could possibly care about the sperm of an unknown man!—but because the justice of the story demanded it, he had to reject the German father whom he hadn't had a chance to know either, whom he loved, whose picture he would stare at for hours, whose name he carried, and who in a trench or in some snow-covered field had frozen to death.

And if up to that time even the moments of tension between us had been pleasant, this drawn-out telephone conversation excluding me in more ways than one managed to render them unpleasant; for a few more minutes I let my face be warmed by the feeble winter sun—it had been receding since midmorning and was now only a thin strip of light on Melchior's eyes and hair and on the wall over his head—then I withdrew into the study, took out the blanket from under the pillow, lay down on the sofa, turned to the wall, and, like someone who has finally found rest and solace, wrapped myself in the soft blanket, for perhaps he was right: I didn't take his story quite seriously, and considered his undying hatred for Germans a form of self-hatred stemming from very different causes, just as he shut himself off from the heartrending story of my life, at times shedding real tears over it but in the end making the cold remark that he saw in it nothing but merely the personal, and of course in that sense moving, consequence of the final collapse of anarchistic, communistic, socialistic mass movements caught in the struggle between two superpowers, we were both unfortunate products of that same collapse, two odd mutants, he said, and laughed.

Slightly offended, I reminded him of the special aspects of Hungarian history, offended because of course nobody likes his entire existence to be seen as the symptom of a disease, even an aberration of European proportions, but all my arguments proved futile, he stuck to his guns and launched into a comprehensive geopolitical analysis in which he elaborated on his theory that the 1956 Hungarian uprising—he said uprising, not revolution—was the first and most substantial symptom, one might even call it a turning point in contemporary European history, signaling the collapse and liquidation, the practical demise, of all traditionally motivated struggles, and while at the time the Hungarians appealed very heroically but just as foolishly to a traditional European ideal, that ideal, as it turned out, no longer existed, all that was left of it were a few slogans and a few Hungarian corpses.

Several thousand dead and executed people, I put in reproachfully, my own friend among them.

These ideals and principles, he continued as if he hadn't even heard me, had ceased to be viable with the end of World War II, except that Europe, ashamed at having been unable to defend itself but also euphoric in victory, failed to notice that at the Elbe River the soldiers of the two great powers were already representatives of two superpowers, embracing over the charred corpse of Hitler.

Whatever the aim of the struggle—national self-determination or social equality—to the new world powers it was all the same, he said, because in their respective spheres of influence, reshaped in their own image, they both strove to thwart independent development.

What on the one side meant a return to pre-democratic conditions, suppressing all attempts at democratization or national independence, and to which, I should please note, the other superpower, espousing principles of freedom and self-determination, gave its ready blessing, that very same thing meant on the other side keeping in check all practical achievements stemming from and spread by the movement of bourgeois emancipation, denying them room to grow and flourish, forcing all radical initiatives inspired by the principles of equality before the law, of social justice, into the Procrustean bed of conservatism, to which the superpower on the other side, championing the cause of social justice, gave equally ready blessing, because, for one thing, it too was basically conservative, and also because it felt that any social transformation based on ideals of equality would threaten its own hierarchical practices.

That's how it is, he said, somewhat amused by his own political philosophizing; taking advantage of a momentary, hesitant pause in which he seemed to gather further strength from his own thinking and self-mockery, I expressed my doubts about so crudely equating the two superpowers, whether in intention or practice.

And I shouldn't think, he went on, ignoring me again, that he hadn't heard our little debate as we were walking up the stairs in the theater; he was listening to Thea but heard it just the same, and thought that in our little verbal duel the breakdown of traditional European aspirations was even more evident than it was in the so-called political arena, where crude rhetoric and overcautious diplomatic phraseology tended to blunt the edge of real conflict or push it to absurd extremes; we were being ridiculous, we didn't need a Wall, we kept snarling like mad dogs, not interested in guessing or inquiring what really was happening on the other side, forgetting completely that the Wall was erected to make us bark at each other.

At least three times they said goodbye and then started talking again, so engrossed in each other they couldn't let go; they must have talked for at least forty minutes, and I not only sensed but understood that having retreated behind the protective screen of another language, Melchior was talking about me, gossiping, or, in the squabble going on between the two of them, using me to his advantage—they were jabbering, arguing, fighting, and gabbing like old hags—fuming silently, I huddled under my blanket, hoping that on the waves of his annoying, nasal singsong I might drift off into a light sleep, for I wanted everything to fade away into the distance; if I had to be alone, then let me be really alone.

His arguments seemed persuasive enough, even more so because, unlike me, he never got worked up, never exploded or flew into a rage, not even when his analyses touched on the most sensitive subjects, as if he were short on excitability but long on being cool and reserved, with an uncanny analytical ability, highlighted with ironic overtones, sticking to his own self-chosen matter at hand; but for all that I almost always remained distrustful of his showy theories, for he gave me the impression of a man who talked this way because at each crucial point in his life he had avoided, and still continued to avoid, himself, so that all he did was analyze the evasions with an unerring, seamless logic which he used to conceal his open, bleeding emotional wounds.

True to myself, I paid attention not so much to what he was saying as to the more revealing stylistic elements of his delivery, tried to absorb this emotional block, this ironic, cool, conscious maneuvering with which he distanced himself from himself, tried to understand it by pressing forward to a point where the evasion might occur, gaining a foothold on the slippery soil where his being, the system of his gestures, might be deciphered and he would become touchable, but it was like moving among shadows, for all his gestures remained emphatic allusions to something else, his external features, his smile, his voice, even the people around him were allusions, including Thea, whom he desired yet rejected, and Pierre-Max, whom he no longer desired but was unable to give up, not to mention that I myself was also no more to him than an allusion.

In a foreign city a visitor's eyes, nose, tongue, and ears make extremely curious, and for the natives incomprehensible and hair-raising, connections between the orderly or disorderly layout of streets, between houses—including façades and the feel of the insides of apartments—and their inhabitants' build, dress, behavior, and pace of actions and reactions, because in a strange city the familiarity of routine is absent, the so-called inner and outer natures cannot be separated as sharply as in our home city, where we are used to distinguishing between what we believe to be external constraints and what we assume to be our inner drives; in a foreign city the essential and the trivial merge in an impenetrable blur, a stone façade and a human face, a staircase and the people climbing it become one; colors, smells, lights, kissing, eating, lovemaking—all flash before us, though we cannot know their origins and histories, and their impact is all the stronger, lack of awareness and knowledge transporting you back to the paradisiacal state of a child's urge to observe and discover, a sensual state of unaccountability! perhaps this is the reason why twentieth-century people like so much to be on the move, the comforting, familiar state may be the one they are searching for as they roam about, singly, in pairs, or as part of a herd, in foreign cities all over the world; weighed down by duties and responsibilities, they want out, and this may be the only universally accepted state in which, with no particular danger, they can breach the thick wall erected to isolate the events of one's unconscious childhood from the experiences of what one believes to be conscious adulthood: what infinite joy, what bliss, to be able, once again, to trust oneself to one's nose, taste buds, ears, and eyes, to one's elemental and undeceivable sense organs!

No matter how persuasive his arguments may have been or how self-tormenting and vindictive his theories and assumptions—and therefore apparently not self-hating—according to which he wasn't even German but a fraud who wallowed in his own lies, and since this was the only truth he could squeeze out of himself here, he had to get out, no matter what he said; his apartment, to me at least, exuded the same peculiar style that I felt, for example, in the opera house rebuilt and somewhat remodeled after the war, and not only did the exterior and inner spaces of this opera house evoke in me a mood very close to the one I experienced on Chausseestrasse, in that grand apartment turned workers' flat, but as every important public building in every city is meant to do, it too represented workaday experiences raised to an abstract architectural level.

I knew a few things about this city, but of course no more than one might learn by casually perusing a guidebook: because of my interest in the theater, I knew, for example, something about the history of the opera house, the circumstances in which it was built and then several times rebuilt, I knew that Prince Frederick—Frederick the Great for the historically minded—eagerly sought out the company of his favorite court architect, Knobelsdorff, and while still a young prince presented him with plans to reconstruct the future state capital; when he ascended the throne after the death of his father, Frederick William, often remembered as the Soldier King, nothing could prevent him from embarking on an ambitious building project, which was preceded by the inevitable demolitions and destructions, so in flagrant violation of existing laws, the modest town houses along the Unter den Linden, all different in height and width and architecturally undistinguished—built during the reign of his dour and passionately hated father—were simply erased from the face of the earth to make room for sumptuous, uniform five-story dwellings styled after Venetian palazzi, whose façades nevertheless seemed to look at their surroundings with cold aversion; in the end, all this factual information served no purpose except to enable me, with increasing freedom and abandon, to make connections between things that Melchior found nearly impossible to follow.

I knew that of the public edifices planned for the Unter den Linden and meant to represent the court, the opera house was the first to go up; like all the buildings designed by Knobelsdorff, who followed Palladio's and Scamozzi's principles of architectural forms, it had to be an imposing, well-proportioned structure in the classical style, behind whose simple exterior of geometrical lines and symmetrical proportions every whim and fancy of both builder and patron could explode in the exuberant, lush rococo of the interior, running wild in the white, gold, and purple of its asymmetrical adornments; the site chosen for the theater was a vast open tract, cleared of all former buildings, between the city walls and the old moat (which is now a small winding street still called Festungsgraben).

It was as if someone had accidentally opened an old, dull-gray, squarish, military foot locker, only to find inside it an exquisite music box standing on a jasper base, decorated with sparkling precious stones and dancing figurines, and playing charming little melodies.

The soft, thick, deep-red carpeting on the white floor of Melchior's apartment, the white-lacquered furniture, the heavy folds of the floor-length silk drapes with their gold lilac design, the white wallpaper on the smooth walls, the baroque mirrors, the graceful candelabra, the antique-yellow glow of the tiny flames trembling with each gust of draft, sending up spiraling strips of thin smoke—to me, all this represented the same dazzling strangeness between exterior and interior; in that box of an apartment, originally built for maids and workmen, tucked away on the top floor of a crumbling, turn-of-the-century apartment house that still bore the pockmarks of shelling and the untreated machine-gun wounds of the last war, I felt the presence of that same earnest, constrained aloofness, that same aristocratic aversion to what is external, what is real in the here and now, which I sensed in the historically significant shrine to music and song, the repository of the city's cultural past.

For some reason the builders had been in a hurry, wanting to break away from the hated past as rapidly as possible, so it took barely two years to complete the theater, so extraordinary for its day, used not only for operas but also for social gatherings and festivities, for which reason Knobelsdorff put kitchens, storerooms, servants' quarters, and washrooms on the ground floor, where the lobby and box office are today, and above them three large halls, one behind the other, so that with the help of the available technical equipment, with levers and traps, the three theater spaces of auditorium, stage, and backstage could be turned into one vast hall—no wonder the contemporary world was in awe! and even after repeated renovations and remodeling, this three-way division was preserved to this day.

And so, when I interrupted Melchior's coolly delivered confession about being a man of lies, careful not to offend him, I tried to share some of these observations with him, telling him I found nothing false in the way he had furnished his apartment but, on the contrary, saw in it a unique fusion of bourgeois practicality, proletarian contentment with bare necessities, and aristocratic aloofness, in which all the signs and elements of the past were present, albeit shifted from their original places, a peculiar, warped system of animate and inanimate traces of the past and present mingling with one another that could be found all over the city; he listened, looking at me askance, and though I felt I was straying into an area where he couldn't and wouldn't even want to follow me, I went on, pointing out that to me the overall effect of the apartment was neither intimate nor attractive but very truthful and, above all, very German, and without knowing how things were on the other side, I'd be willing to guess that all this was uniquely local in character, and therefore it wasn't so much my brain as my nose and eyes that objected to his reflections on his own people and to his statements, which, to me, smacked of self-hatred.

It was enough, I said, to take a good look at the refurbished opera house, where the latest reconstruction made the gods and little angels disappear, knocked out the walls between boxes, and, by considerably reducing the use of gold and ornamentation, seemed to sterilize the past of the theater's interior, leaving only stylistic reminders, rococo emblems along the front of the balconies and up in the cupola, the idea being to cool the sensual, overwrought exuberance of the former decor and bring it in line with the studied simplicity of the theater's exterior, architecturally a sound idea, preserving the past even while destroying it, preserving, more specifically, its grim and ugly orderliness, thus matching perfectly the prevailing atmosphere today, in which the aim was to satisfy only the most basic needs of the people; anyway, I said, there seemed to be a constant threat of secret contagion, because everything here stank of some powerful disinfectant.

It was this wariness about the past, these stylistic twists of simultaneously preserving and obliterating it, that I also noticed in people's homes: in this sense I didn't think Melchior could completely isolate himself from anything, but in fact was repeating, involuntarily imitating, what others were doing: dragging his ancestors' bourgeois furniture into a proletarian flat—and doing so to flaunt his eccentricity—was not very different from how that proletarian family lived in the Chausseestrasse apartment, designed originally for ostentatious haut-bourgeois life.

He didn't quite understand what I was getting at, and as we sat facing each other in the candlelight, I could see on his face how he was struggling, quietly, to overcome the hurt he felt.

If I was so well versed in the history of German architecture, he said, not to mention the soul of the German people, then I must also know what Voltaire jotted down in his diary after meeting Frederick the Great.

Just what he'd thought: I didn't know.

Still sitting, he leaned forward a little and, with the tenderness of confident superiority, placed his hand on my knee, and while he talked he kept looking into my eyes, taking pleasure in mocking both me and himself, smiling a small, supercilious smile.

Five feet two inches tall, Melchior said, in playful imitation of a schoolmaster, the king had a well-proportioned but by no means perfect build, and because of his self-consciously rigid posture he looked a bit awkward, but his face was pleasant and spiritual, polite and friendly, and his voice was attractive even when he swore, which he did as frequently as a common coachman; he wore his nice light-brown hair in a pigtail, and always combed it himself—he could do it rather well—but when powdering his face he sat before the mirror never in his nightcap, gown, and slippers but in a filthy old silk dressing gown—in general he eschewed conventional attire, for years he traipsed around in the unadorned uniform of his infantry regiment, was never seen wearing shoes, only boots, and didn't like to put his hat under his arm as was then the custom; despite his undeniable charm, there was something unnatural in the details of his physical appearance and his behavior; for example, he spoke French better than he did German, and was willing to converse in his native tongue only with those who he knew spoke no French, because he considered his own language barbaric.

While he was talking, Melchior grasped my knees, leaned all the way forward in his armchair, and when he finished he planted conciliatory kisses on my cheeks, by way of having arrived at another station of his instructions; I remained unmoved, for now it was my turn to be distrustful and offended, and it was a little annoying but also amusing to realize that no argument or theory, however daring and powerful, could knock him out of the saddle of his obsessions.

I became increasingly convinced that if I hoped to get anywhere with him I should not fight him with arguments and theories but surround him with the simpler language of the senses, but just what pathetic result I was after, and how clumsily, wrongly, and foolishly I went about achieving it, I shall relate at a later point; he kept nodding, his forehead almost touching mine, but wouldn't take his eyes off me for a moment.

Well, he said, well, well, he repeated, as if finding the subject disagreeable, poor old Fredericus, he too must have had good reason to cling to his opinions, to speak of barbarism, to knock down what his father had built, and he must have had good reason also to affect that awkward posture, and incidentally, was I familiar with the story of Lieutenant Katte?

I said I wasn't.

In that case, hoping to advance my knowledge in Germanology, he would tell me.

Sometimes I had the impression we were conducting a kind of experiment on each other, without knowing exactly what its purpose was.

Our armchairs faced each other; he leaned back comfortably and, as on other occasions, put his feet on my lap, and while he was talking I'd knead and massage his feet, which gave our physical contact an unnecessary rationality, a pleasant monotony; he turned away for a second, the wineglass caught his eye, he took a sip, and suddenly there was a change in him—the expression with which he looked back at me was serious and pensive—but this had to do not with me but with that elaborate story which he was probably reviewing in his mind, quickly pulling it together before actually recounting it.

The strange prince is eighteen years old at this time, Melchior began, he will be twenty-eight when ascending the throne and embarking on his grandiose building project, but now, after an especially exhausting quarrel with his father, he simply disappears from the palace.

They keep looking and looking for him but can't find him anywhere; when bits of some servants' confessions are pieced together, a picture emerges: the prince must have escaped, and his escape had something to do with a certain Hans Hermann von Katte, a friend of his and a lieutenant in the Royal Guards.

At the head of his entourage, the king himself sets out in pursuit of the fugitive prince—and I should try to imagine what the poor queen must have gone through while waiting for their return.

The entourage returns on the morning of August 27 from Küstrin, but no one is willing or able to provide information regarding the prince's whereabouts; by late afternoon the king himself is back.

Beset by worries and the most terrible premonitions, the queen hurries to meet him, and as they are quickening their steps, almost running toward each other, just as their eyes meet, the king, livid with rage, exclaims: Your son is dead!

Worn out by the long wait but still hopeful, the queen is struck by these words as if by lightning, and she begins to scream, her words barely coherent: How? why? how is this possible? could Your Majesty be your own son's killer?

But the king does not even stop with the queen, who seems to have turned into a pillar of salt, and simply tosses off his reply that this wretched fugitive was no son of his but a common military deserter who deserves to die, and trembling with rage he demands to see the prince's box of private letters.

Wasting no time trying to unlock it, with two blows of his fist the king smashes the box open, grabs the papers inside, and rushes off with them.

In the palace everyone is cowering, fleeing the king's wrath; the queen hurries over to her children's chambers, but presently the king turns up there, pushes aside the children, who are about to kiss his hand, and practically tramples them with his boots as he runs toward Princess Friederike, who is standing a little way off.

Without so much as a word, he strikes her face with his fist three times and with such force that she immediately collapses, and if not for Fräulein Sonnefeld's presence of mind and remarkable agility in catching the fainting body, she would have cracked her skull on the edge of a large wardrobe.

But the king's fury knows no bounds; he wants to trample on the prostrate body of the princess and is prevented only by the screaming queen and the children, who fling themselves on the inert body, shielding it with their own bodies, absorbing the stomps and kicks of the king's boots and the terrible blows of his cane.

In her memoirs, Princess Friederike writes that their desperate situation at that moment was indescribable: the king's swollen face—he was given to apoplectic fits anyway—turned blue and purple, he was nearly choking on his own anger, the look in his eyes was that of a cornered, crazed beast, his mouth frothing with gobs of spit spurting from his throat, while the queen kept flailing her arms helplessly, like a huge bird, emitting the most painful screams, and the younger children, racked by sobs, lay next to her and clung imploringly to the king's legs, even the youngest, who at the time was no more than three years old, and the two ladies-in-waiting, Frau von Kamecke and Fräulein Sonnefeld, just stood there stock-still, not daring to move or utter a sound, and she, Friederike, whose only offense was that she loved the prince with all her heart—and bore testimony to this love in the letters which had now been found—was the most wretched of them all, her face bathed in cold sweat; even when she came to, her body was flushed and shaking uncontrollably.

For the king not only assaulted her brutally but heaped his most abominable threats on her, blaming her for the disintegration of the royal house, for being the one whose deceitful, conniving, and amoral machinations had thrust the family into the abyss of misfortune and misery, she would pay for it with her head, with her head, he yelled, and he included the queen in his threats, and since in his fury he forgot he'd already declared the prince dead, breathing into her face with the most bloodcurdling and blasphemous cries of vengeance, he swore he'd have his son executed, he'd die on the block, the king huffed, on the block.

It seemed that nothing could check his colossal, vindictive wrath, but then a small, fretful voice announced that Lieutenant Katte had been apprehended.

This had a somewhat sobering effect on the king, or more precisely, those around him watched him turn away from them, realizing that he did so only because mere mention of that name fanned the flames of his vengeance even more violently, and now the wild beast that had wreaked havoc only in his cage was loose; soon he would have enough proof, he said caustically to the queen, for the hangman to prepare for his job, and with that he rushed from the children's chambers.

But he couldn't yet pounce on his new prey, because in his cabinet room the lords von Grumkow and Mylius, waiting for him, were ordered in a choked, breathless voice, in a hideous whisper, to conduct Katte's interrogation; his confession, he decreed, whatever its content, was to be used to initiate proceedings against his son; he briefly summed up the facts of the case and announced that the prince was not only a traitor, an accursed criminal, and an oath-breaking deserter but a hideous worm, a monster, a freak of nature, undeserving of any kind of mercy.

That is when Lieutenant Katte was led in, a slender, twenty-six-year-old youth with large eyes and a handsome face that was now, of course, deathly pale, who immediately fell on his knees before the king; the king just as quickly seized him and violently tore the cross of the Knights of St. John from his neck and then proceeded to kick him and beat him with his stick until he was out of breath and the youth's body lay inert at his feet.

As the permanent Grand Master of the Knights of St. John, the Prussian king had the right to tear away the Knights' cross from the neck of a man such as Lieutenant Katte.

But to continue: with a pail of water and somewhat less violent slaps than the king's, Lieutenant Katte was revived enough to confess, and the interrogation was begun.

Katte answered all the questions put to him so honestly, displayed such moral courage and utter devotion to his ruler, that his conduct evoked the admiration not only of his interrogators but of the king himself.

He confessed knowing about the prince's plan to escape, and because he loved the prince with all his heart and soul, he had been fully prepared to break his oath of loyalty to the king and follow his friend, but he had no knowledge as to which court the prince had intended to escape, and also, did not believe that either the queen or Princess Friederike was privy to the escape plan, since he and the prince had kept it completely secret.

After his interrogation he was stripped of his uniform and given only a cloth apron, and, like that, almost naked, was made to march across town to the central guardhouse, where a court-martial was to sentence him, but its regular members were loath to take a stand in such a delicate matter and drew lots to pick the twelve officers who would have to carry out the unpleasant task.

Count Dönhof and Count Linger were of the opinion that a more lenient sentence was in order, but the others, appreciating the utmost gravity of the offense, recommended that both Colonel Fritz—the king had forbidden them to refer to the heir apparent by any other name—and Lieutenant Katte be put to death.

When the death sentence was read to him, Katte calmly declared his readiness to submit to Providence and to the will of his king, because he had committed no wrong, and if he had to die, it must be for a noble if to him unknown cause.

A certain Major Schenk was ordered to return the prisoner to the citadel at Küstrin, where the heir apparent was also being held.

They arrived at nine o'clock in the morning, and Katte spent the rest of the day in the company of a priest, talking to him about his life of debauchery, for which he now confessed the greatest remorse; he spent the whole night in fervent prayer.

In the meantime, the execution platform was erected in the citadel's square, to be level with the prince's cell; on the king's direct order the cell window was enlarged, cut all the way to the floor, and the new opening, through which one could actually step out onto the platform, was, for the time being, draped with a black cloth.

The noisy construction took place in the presence of the prince, with nine masons and seventeen carpenters working under several overseers, so the prince quite naturally believed they were making preparations for his execution.

At six minutes before seven o'clock in the morning, the commander of the fort, Captain Löpel, entered the prince's cell, informed him that it was the king's wish that he watch Katte's beheading, and, having brought with him a brown suit, asked the prince to disrobe and put it on.

When he finished changing, the black cloth covering the opened wall was removed, and the prince could see the newly and very professionally built scaffold.

Three long minutes went by, and then his friend, wearing an identical brown suit, was led forth, while at the same time the prince was asked to step up to the opening in the wall.

The strikingly identical suits made such a shocking impression on the prince—in no small measure because he knew it had to have been his father's idea—that he was ready to cast himself into the courtyard gaping below, but they pulled him back and held him by the arm; later, nothing would induce him to part with this suit, and for three years he wore it day and night until it was in tatters.

When they pulled him back, he began to weep and wail, imploring those around him to delay the execution, for pity's sake; if his life was to be spared, he must write to the king at once; he pleaded and protested, he was ready to renounce everything, the crown, his own life, if that would save Katte's, they must allow him to send his plea to the king.

Ignoring his sobs and screams, they proceeded to read out the sentence.

After the last word had been spoken, Katte, who was also being held by his arm behind his back, stepped closer to the prince, and that's how they looked at each other for a silent moment.

Merciful God, the prince shouted, how great a misery you have given me! my sweet, my dearest, my only friend, I am the cause of your death, I, who would so wish to take your place now.

They both had to be held firmly, as Katte, calling him my dear prince, said in a feeble voice that if he had a thousand lives he would sacrifice them all for him, but now he had to depart this vale of tears, and with that he knelt in front of the guillotine.

He was allowed to have his own servants accompany him on his last journey, and now one of them offered to put a blindfold on him, but he very gently pushed away the trembling hand holding the kerchief and, lifting his eyes heavenward, said, Into Thy hands I commend my spirit.

The two headsmen placed the condemned man's neck under the blade, the two servants stepped back, and in that instant the prince fainted and sank into the arms of his attendants.

They laid him on his bed, but not until midday did he regain consciousness.

At the king's instruction, Katte's mutilated body had to stay on the block, in the prince's sight, until late in the evening.

When he came to and looked out from his bed, the prince saw the stump of the neck sticking out from the naked torso and the bloody head in the basket.

His body was racked with fever, and he began to wail so piteously, making sounds so piercing, that for a moment the sentries on the ramparts looked at each other in alarm, then he lost consciousness again.

Lieutenant Katte's body was placed in a casket that evening and buried in the fortress wall.

Crouching near the wall of his cell, the prince cried for two weeks, now and then accepting a little water but refusing to take food, and even after his tears dried, he remained silent for months, and when he spoke again, he said no, he wouldn't take off the brown suit, and when the brown suit turned to shreds on him, the pain crawled under his skin.

In my anger I must have dozed off by the time they finished talking on the telephone, because it was the motionless silence in the room that woke me.

I imagine that after he hung up he stayed in his chair for a while, ruminating; I could hear only his silence, the segment of lingering silence in which he sorted out and stored away what had been said and heard, and for this reason it seemed that what I was hearing was not the silence of his presence but his absence.

And after my startled awakening I must have sunk back even deeper into that state of slumbering that hovers on the border of sleep and wakefulness, because the next thing I knew Melchior was pressing himself against the wall and squeezing me out a little as he climbed under the covers.

Trying to settle in, he squirmed and wriggled some more, very slowly and considerately so as not to wake me, but I didn't feel like giving up my place or making the closeness inviting, and I let him have only as much space as he could squeeze out for himself, I didn't open my eyes, I pretended to be fast asleep.

For a while he lay motionless, pressed to the wall, with my drawn-up knees against his belly; I could have relaxed a little, making believe I moved in my sleep, but because I was awake I continued all the harder to fake being asleep.

I could let him have a little room, he said out loud, exposing my pretense and letting me know he knew I was awake.

I was trying to loosen up, not to be so obvious about my shamming.

Sticking one of his arms under my neck and hugging my back with the other, he wanted to pull me to himself, but my drawn-up knees made that impossible, giving him neither the intimacy he was looking for nor enough space to rest comfortably.

For a while he seemed to be reconciled to his discomfort, to the impossible position of his body, and stopped squirming; resting his forehead on my shoulder, he began to breathe with a quiet, even puffing and wheezing, as if trying to breathe himself to sleep, then suddenly he let out a growl and pulled his arm from under my neck; Just you wait, he said, I'll show you, and with that he yanked the blanket off both of us, pushed himself away from the wall, and slipped off the couch.

He was getting undressed, I heard the swish of his shirt, the pants being unzipped, how he quickly threw all his clothes on the floor, then he leaned over me, fumbling around my waist and unbuttoning my pants, grabbing them at my ankles to pull them off while I made no move on my own, my body simply yielding to his forceful movements; he peeled the socks from my feet, reached under my behind, and raising it a little pulled off my underpants.

To get to my shirt he had to crawl back, creep back on his knees on the inside of the couch next to the wall, and since the point of the game was for me to pretend to be asleep, he now had more room to maneuver, because when he yanked off my pants he also straightened out my legs and now they had to stay that way—moving, like pulling up my knees again, would have been breaking the rules of the game.

He had to pull out my hand, which I'd stuck under the pillow, straighten and lift my arms, and pull out the shirt from under my back and shoulders, and he had to fight my body weight with every move; he was panting, grunting, and moaning, also part of the game, though I really had let myself become such a dead weight that his job couldn't have been easy.

And while he planted himself firmly on the soft sagging couch and, with his knees spread wide apart, leaned over me, I was assailed by the raw smell of his body: clothes hold in body scents and isolate them from the outside world, but when they are removed, the subdued exhalation of the body, like a swollen river from behind a dam, surges forward in wild and abundant streams.

He pitched the shirt he'd just pulled off me somewhere, and then, with a sigh, sank down next to me; my arms were still raised over my head, my out-turned wrist was touching the wall, in this way giving him a little room on the pillow as well, and he pulled up the blanket caught between our legs and spread it neatly over my back, then tucked it behind his own; from the window left open in the living room we felt waves of a cool breeze, and emitting sounds of pleasure, he used the blanket to wrap us tight into the heat of our own bodies and then, slipping one arm under my neck again and hugging my back with the other, he lowered his head onto the pillow, next to my face.

I didn't open my eyes; there was one more prolonged moment, full of expectations, before body would touch body; lying parallel and turned to one another, each waited for the other to give up his moral principles as they are expressed in decisions and intentions, because it wasn't my clothes he had peeled me out of but rather my hurtfulness, my pride, and my anger, my resolve that if I couldn't stay with him I'd want to be all by myself; and even though in this game of undressing it was my passivity that had enabled us to come together again, pretending that my limbs were lifeless betrayed a lack of conviction, a reluctance to give up my advantageous position or give in to his closeness, his smell, and his warmth; and of course all this harked back to our morning conversation, which had been cut short when we grinned at each other our most obnoxious grin.

But his activities were no less ambiguous either, for the more determined and purposeful an activity, the more clearly it betrays its true intent: he was bowing to my will, not exactly apologizing but, swallowing his pride, trying to make amends, and for him, this act of getting intimate, this undressing ceremony, meant that his emotions, best conveyed to me through our bodies, made him perform the gestures of the most Christian humility, which was by no means an act of abasement, any more than the ritual of washing a person's feet is, and if after all I wasn't going to reciprocate the gentle aggressiveness of his humility, then he had no further move to offer, that was the limit beyond which there were only unyielding moral principles detached from the flesh.

And then I did move my raised arms, slipping one under his neck and wrapping the other around his back; at the same time he pried open my knees with his, slipped his thighs between mine, his head was on my shoulder, his groin over mine, and thus our two bodies, turned completely toward each other, met along the full surface of their skins.

And this meeting was so abundant in instincts, emotions, and intentions that the fractional moment in which skin touched skin, heat reached heat, and smell mingled with smell to make a closer fit physically impossible was like a deep, painful groan of happiness and good fortune, eliminating distance and division; that's how parallel lines must feel in infinity.

The harmony of the two bodies expressed in this single touch, bridging their differences and bending their moral reserve, was as powerful and wild as physical fulfillment, yet there was nothing false in this harmony, no illusion created that just by touching, our bodies could express feelings that rationality prevented us from making permanent; I might even say that our bodies coolly preserved their good sense, scheming and keeping each other in check, as if to say, I'll yield unreservedly to the madness of the moment but only if and when you do the same; but this physical plea for passion and reason, spontaneity and calculation, closeness and distance, took our bodies past the point where, clinging to desire and striving for the moment of gratification, they would seek a new and more complete harmony.

Our bodies' uncertainty became the only certainty, and that was good enough; desire-filled body watching the body's lack of desire; and the more satisfaction each body found in this watching, the more relaxed they both became, the more comfort they found in each other; I may have fallen asleep a few minutes after he did; just before falling off, I could hear the breeze ruffling the poplar's yellowing leaves, and his ever more regular, even breathing.

We slept in each other's arms, with his chest on mine, thighs pressed together, his head on my shoulder, his hair in my mouth, our legs entwined under the blanket; we had to be this close not only because the couch was very narrow but also because the hard horsehair mattress slanted down on the side and we had to hold on to each other even in our sleep so as not to fall off.

We were startled out of our sleep at the same time: like someone shrinking back just when he is about to sink into an even deeper sleep, his body shuddered along the length of mine, giving me a start, too; under the pressure of his head and shoulders, my own shoulder and arm had gone to sleep and were now aching; looking instinctively for a more comfortable position, which the body always does, I moved away from him.

Our bodies parted, at the same time feeling the peaceful closeness and harmony in which they had rested until now; they didn't separate completely, just far enough so that a bit of cooler air, part of the outside world, could penetrate the space between us, making us more aware of our bodies' heat.

I think we opened our eyes at exactly the same moment, and because his head slid off my arm and dropped to the pillow, we looked into each other's eyes from very close up.

Since our every little move and sensation remained identical, they became our own because we saw them reflected in each other; I caught the same look in his eyes—I might call it a neutral look—with which I felt I was looking at him.

We both had had an equally deep and short sleep, which blotted out time, so that our consciousness was somewhat puzzled as it was trying to return to where it had left off, the resulting look in the eyes being not necessarily a sign of muddleheadedness, in fact possibly of very sharp, keen awareness; I imagine this is the way babies look at the world.

I could see in his eyes that this was just what he was seeing in mine; there was no trace of conscious thought for either of us, and the next moment we both broke into a smile, and this, too, was strikingly similar, one originating in the other; I smiled his smile and he mine, which in turn elicited a like response from both of us, turning bashfully away from this unexpected and unwilled intimacy, we bowed, more precisely, lowered our heads resting on the pillow, making forehead touch forehead.

I didn't close my eyes and don't think he did either, or if he did, he probably opened them again soon after.

The eyes, though retaining some of the neutrality of the first wakeful moment, became alert again, ready to return to former activities, and now shifted downward, into the darkness under the covers; the glance penetrated the feelings as it enjoyed the view of a wedge-shaped configuration, observing it from above.

Our two divergent bodies formed the sides of this wedge: two chests, one of which, his, was hairier; two bellies, appearing a little sunken in this position, one of them taut and flat, the other just slightly bulging; and down below, in the narrower part of the wedge, the nestlike softness of the testicles filled out the angle formed by the entwined legs, and the genitals, one, his, larger and longer, and the other, mine, rather comically limp in its shrunken state, were lying on each other as peacefully as did our intertwined arms above.

The geometric shape could not be perfect, though, if only because of our different builds, and I was also lying a little bit higher: our feelings, too, were similar rather than identical: he was more comfortable, I think, his lower body weighing hard on my thigh, and unless I wanted to paint too idyllic a picture—and why would I?—I'd have to confess that my thigh could hardly wait to be rid of the weight, but in spite of this minor discomfort, we lay there in almost perfectly identical positions; and as we did, aware of and watching this symmetry, the two genitals that had been resting on each other, as if coaxed by our eyes and the geometrical arrangement of our bodies, began to rise, ever so gradually, smoothly; swelling, filling up, lengthening and thickening, their heads crossed, collided, mutually impeded, and then bumped past each other, gaining the feeling of mutual momentum needed for a solitary erection.

The symmetry and simultaneity became clear, unequivocal, and at the same time comical, because what we saw was real, though it also allowed us a glimpse into the workings of our senses, into the almost impassive mechanism of our instincts: forehead bumped into forehead because we turned away so quickly and simultaneously, as if suddenly discovered or exposed by someone, and then we burst out laughing—again at the same time.

Judging by the sound of it, it wasn't just a plain laugh but a guffaw.

An eruption of joy and coarseness, a burst of joy over the coarseness that a stiff penis, by its very nature, provides in any and all situations, the joy of "See, I'm a man," the joy of a living organism expanding, the ancient joy of belonging to the community of males, the joy of life's continuity; and it was also laughing at the coarse mechanism of exposed archaic instincts, which is called culture and which leads to doubling the enjoyment of raw instincts, because I feel what I feel in spite of the fact that I know what I feel—and thus I feel more than what I can possibly know.

With our guffaw we transformed into sounds the coarseness and violence inherent in joy, especially in shared joy, a form of communication which, transmuted by humor, promised a more powerful pleasure than the prospect of consummating the act—and one always grabs for the larger chunk of pleasure, or at least tries to, so I roughly pulled him to myself, and he just as roughly pushed me away; like two crazed animals, we began fighting on the couch.

In reality there's no such thing as perfect symmetry or total sameness; a transitional balance between dissimilarities is the most we can hope for; although our scuffle wasn't at all serious, it did not turn into an embrace, for the same reason that he had pushed me away: up to that point, wishing to keep up the pretense of perfect symmetry, I had accepted the less comfortable position so he could rest comfortably in my arms, but that was like telling him he was the weaker one, which, in turn, was like telling him he wasn't as much of a man as he'd like me to believe, forgetting for the moment that letting him have the better position gave me much more pleasure; yet precisely because there is no perfect symmetry, only a striving for it, there can be no gesture without the need for another to complete it.

The fight turned into a real one; though we both tried to keep it playful, it became increasingly rough, and it boiled down to a question of who could push, shove, squeeze, or throw the other off the couch, gaining a decisive and incontestable victory. The blanket got caught between us and then must have slipped off; naked and sweaty, we kept pummeling each other as much as the cramped space would allow; laughing when we started, we slowly turned silent, only now and then emitting what we imagined to be battle cries, trying to threaten each other with the sound of certain victory at any moment; we tumbled over each other, biting and scratching, thrusting our legs against the wall, straining against slippery skin, against shoving and twisting hands; the couch creaked, the springs moaned and groaned, and in all probability he was as happy as I to see that in this struggle for victory all the real pain we had caused and all the hostility we had felt toward each other rose to the surface out of some hitherto unseen netherworld.

Our bodies, which only moments earlier had given such symmetrical and palpable proof of their desire for each other, now found—without our noticing the change or the moral dangers hidden in it—a different kind of occupation, just as elementary and passionate, and this change completely transformed our feelings, turned them inside out, I might say: my muscles and bones, without the tenderness of desire, were now communicating with his muscles and bones in the language of violent emotions.

Until with a huge thud I wound up on the floor.

I tried to pull him down with me, but he punched me in the face, and then, pushing against my face, worked himself back up on the couch.

He was on his knees, grinning down at me; we were both panting, and then, since neither of us knew what to do with our respective victory or defeat, he suddenly flipped over and lay on his back, and I also lay on my back, on the soft carpet; in the sudden silence we kept breathing, waiting for the panting to subside.

As I lay there with my arms spread wide, and he lay up there also breathing hard, with his arms spread wide, he let his hand hang down, maybe inviting me to touch it; I didn't, I let it hang right in my face, that's what made it nice, the lack of touch, this little gap that could be closed at any time; it seemed to me I had seen the ceiling before, the way the late-afternoon light, broken into three separate strips by the arched doorway, was chasing the shadows cast by the swaying branches outside; I had seen this dead hand before, twisted on its wrist; incredibly, everything happening now seemed to have already happened to me here once before.

At the time I neither found nor looked for an explanation, though the image was not so far from my feelings that I couldn't have reached it, but sometimes the mind, keeper of all memories, does not provide the place of a stored item, only hints at it; for some reason the mind would not call the desired item by its name, and it's very considerate of the mind to be in no hurry to spoil an otherwise enjoyable situation by clearly identifying secret data relevant to it.

Perhaps if I had reached out and held his hand.

For twice in a row, as if compelled to free himself of some deathly anxiety, some choking, harrowing pain or insane joy, he let out a howl so powerful it made his whole body contract, as if all his strength were being forced into his chest and throat, he roared, he bellowed himself into the silence of the room, which hit me as unexpectedly as any blow or grace of fate would; long seconds must have passed while, unable to move or to help, I watched the agony of the large, prostrate male body: the truth is, I thought he was playing, still fooling around; his hand was still hanging down, his eyes were open, glazed over, staring into space, and his feet were flexed.

Now he rose slightly; his chest, filled with air, heaved and quivered, the heaving and quivering coursing through his whole body and then rippling back; I saw he wanted to scream a third time, perhaps hoping to expel what he'd failed to eject twice before, because if he couldn't, his heart would break.

Maybe the reason I couldn't move or help was that he looked beautiful.

And not only was he unable to scream the trapped air out, but all the oxygen seemed to have been used up by his lungs, now swollen to bursting, and no fresh air could enter them; to keep from choking, his body tried to straighten out, jump up, run off, or maybe just sit up, but without enough oxygen it had no strength, only reflex motions seemed to be at work, struggling with themselves, until the straining muscles finally squeezed out a sound, high-pitched but clearly coming from a great depth, a whimper, a broken, breathless whimper that grew longer and stronger as he managed to take in more air.

Shaking, looking ugly, racked by bursts of loud sobs, he wept in my arms.

We do well to praise the wise inventiveness of our mother tongue when it speaks of pain as something ripping open; language knows everything about us; yes, we do make caustic remarks, our hair does stand on end, and the heart does break; in these set phrases language condenses thousands of years of human experience, knows for us what we don't know or don't want to acknowledge; with my fingers, with my palm on his back, I did feel that something inside, in the hollows of his body, really had ripped open, as if the membrane of a mucous organ had been slashed through.

My fingers, my palm could see into the living darkness of his body.

Something ripped open with each new burst of his sobbing, and still there was more to be ripped open.

Years were ripping out from under the membrane of time.

In a half-sitting position he leaned toward me as, perched on the edge of the couch, I clumsily pulled him to me, and with his forehead on my shoulder, the hot waves of his sobs flowed down my chest, his nose was pressed to my collarbone, and his lips, wet with snot and saliva, were clinging to my skin, and of course I whispered all sorts of tender nonsense into his ear, trying to calm and console him, and then did just the opposite: sensing not only that my body could give no strength to his but that any show of so-called selfless love would only divert or stifle the pain that had to come out, I told him to cry, yes, he simply had to cry, and with my voice as well as with my enervated body I tried to help him cry.

How ridiculous all our intellectual babble had been.

For the first time I could feel what I already knew, that behind his cool sobriety he was clinging to me with all his might, in the brief pauses between sobs his lips were glued to my skin, his pain turning this contact into bites, though he meant them to be kisses, and for the first time I could feel that there was almost nothing I could give him; with this realization I was actually brushing his hands off me, which he felt was only natural but in turn made me want to try the impossible.

By the time he'd calmed down a little and the pauses of his childish sniveling had grown longer between the fits of sobbing, an aging little boy's face was sitting atop his mature man's body.

I laid him down, tucked him in, wiped off his smudged face, including the snot—this was a face of his I didn't want to see—sat at the edge of the couch, holding his hand, doing what the stronger one is supposed to do, and even enjoyed a little the illusion of being the stronger one, and when he calmed down completely, I picked our clothes off the floor and closed the window.

Like a very sick child who feels the caring presence of his mother, he dozed off and then fell into a deep sleep.

I sat in his chair, at his desk, where in the growing darkness my pen lay untouchable on top of my notes on a performance; I kept staring out the window; by the time he began to stir and opened his eyes, it was completely dark.

The tile stove in the meantime warmed up the room again; both of us were depressed, and quiet.

I didn't turn on the light; my hands found his head in the dark and I said we could go for a walk if he felt like it.

He said he didn't feel like it at all, and didn't know what it was that had happened earlier; what he'd really like to do was go to sleep for the night, but we could go for a walk.

This city in the middle of a well-kept park which is Europe—to continue and amend with my own impressions his fascinating line of thinking—struck me more as a unique memorial to irremediable destruction than a real, living city, as a frighteningly well-preserved ruin of romantic park architecture, because a truly living city is never the mere fossil of an unclarified past but a surging flow, continually abandoning the stony bed of tradition, solidifying and then flowing on, rolling over decades and centuries, from the past into the future, a continuum of hardened thrusts and ceaseless pulses unaware of its ultimate goal, yet it's this irrepressible, insatiable vitality, often wasteful and avaricious, destructive yet creative, that we call, approvingly or disapprovingly, the inner nature or spirituality of a city's existence; but this city, or at least the sector of it I had come to know, showed none of these alluring urban characteristics, neither preserved nor continued its past, at best patched it up, sterilized it out of necessity or, worse, obliterated it, ashamed; it had become a place to live in, a shelter, a night lodging, a vast bedroom, and consequently by eight in the evening was completely deserted, its windows darkened; from behind the drawn curtains only the bluish flickering of TV screens reached the street, the puny light of that small window through which its residents could glimpse another, more lively world across the Wall; as far as I could tell, people preferred programs coming from the other side, thus isolating themselves from the locale of their own existence much as Melchior did or tried to do, and for understandable reasons preferred to peek into that other, improbable and titillating world than take a look at themselves.

And if at such a late hour, or later, in the dead of night, we descended from our fifth-floor nest to the lifeless streets below, our echoing footsteps made us feel our loneliness, isolation, and infinite interdependence more acutely than we did in the apartment, where behind locked doors we could still pretend we lived in a real city and not on top of a heap of stones declared to be a war memorial.

Some more advanced mammals, like cats, foxes, dogs, wolves, and the like, use their urine and excrement to mark out territory they consider their own, which they then protect and rule as their homeland; other less developed and less aggressive animals like mice, moles, ants, rats, hard-shelled insects, and lizards prefer to move about on beaten tracks, in ruts and burrows: we were more like the latter group, compelled by the almost biological conditioning of our cultures, by our reverence for tradition, and by our upbringing, which could be labeled bourgeois; we flaunted our finicky tastes, our penchant for refinement, and, with a hesitant intellectual relish rooted in our affinity for fin-de-siècle decadence, chose only those routes that in this city could still be considered appropriate for a leisurely old-fashioned walk.

When one's freedom of movement is restricted, then in the very interest of maintaining the appearance of personal freedom one is compelled—in keeping with one's needs—to impose further restrictions on oneself within the larger restrictive limits.

In our evening or nighttime walks we made sure never to wander into the new residential areas, where we would have come face-to-face with the palpable form of the coercive principle that lacked all notion of human individuality and that considered people, quite pragmatically, beasts of burden and, mindful only of the bare necessities of rest, procreation, and child care, packed them into grim concrete boxes—No, not that way! we'd cry, and choose routes where one could still see, feel, smell something of the city's ravaged, continually deteriorating, patched-up, blackened, disintegrating individuality.

I might say that we took our walks through the stage set of individuality's Europe-size tragedy, though in the end we could choose only between the bleak and the bleaker—that was the extent of our freedom.

For instance, if we walked down Prenzlauer Allee, an empty streetcar would clatter past now and then, or we might see a Trabant chugging along, its two-stroke engine belching noxious little fumes—and of course Prenzlauer Allee was a tree-lined avenue, an *allée* in name only—after a good half-hour stroll we'd come to an empty lot as big as a city block, riddled with bomb craters and overgrown with weeds and shrubs, going around which we'd turn into Ostsee Strasse or, better yet, Pistorius Strasse farther up, and pass the old churchyard of the parish named after St. George, and after another twenty minutes through various winding side streets, we'd reach Weissensee, or White Lake.

This small lake in whose murky, polluted water sluggish swans with filthy feathers and attentive wild ducks swam after crumbs thrown by passersby, was surrounded by a cluster of trees, the remains of a formal garden of an elegant summer palace that used to stand there, replaced now by a nondescript beer hall.

That Sunday evening we took a shortcut through Kollowitz, formerly Weissenburger, Strasse, the street where, in my increasingly complicated tale, I had placed the residence of the young man who arrived in Berlin in the final decade of the last century and who, in my imagination, based on Melchior's stories, seemed to resemble me a little, and from Kollowitz Strasse we turned into Dimitroff Strasse.

Of course Melchior had no inkling that living alongside him I was leading a double life, indeed multiple lives; ostensibly, I also thought this route ideal for a peaceful stroll for the same reason he did, namely that after a mere ten minutes the broad curve of Dimitroff Strasse seemed to pull you into the winding little alleys among the trees of Friedrichschain, Friedrich Park, but for me this wasn't pleasant at all, because under the impenetrable evening shadows cast by the trees, lurid little scenes were unfolding in my imagination.

During those weeks, after morning rehearsals, I also spent more and more time traipsing around with Thea.

Being autumn, it got dark rather early; the long hours spent in the artificial light of the rehearsal hall, the twilight meanderings with Thea in the open spaces outside the city, the evenings and nights spent with Melchior—these tightly compartmentalized my days, so tightly that sometimes while touching Melchior I caught myself thinking of Thea, and it happened the other way around, too: I'd be sitting peacefully with Thea in the cool grass near a lake and suddenly would miss Melchior so much that his very absence would conjure him up in my mind's eye; leisurely, and unknown to each other, the two of them kept flowing into and out of each other, creating a strange and baffling chaos that my imagination found hard to keep in check, a strange world that imperceptibly isolated me from my past and from my future—but that at least was a welcome blessing.

And anyway, who is to tell what's strange? suppose that after a rehearsal someone, anyone, an actor or observer, finally leaves the theater at three o'clock in the afternoon and steps out into an ordinary, truly unremarkable, sunny or gloomy, windy or rainy street and stands among rationally constructed houses inhabited by real-life people, while on the sidewalk all kinds of other people, attractive or ugly, cheerful or dejected, old or young, well-dressed or dowdy, all propelled by the same drive as if constantly listening to the invisibly ticking time, hurry about their business, carrying shopping bags, briefcases, packages, run errands, walk in and out of buildings, drive their cars, park and get out of them, buy and sell, greet one another with feigned or genuine pleasure, and then part with loud words, angrily or indifferently or perhaps with a painful sigh;

at the corner sausage stand they dip their hot wurst into mustard and bite into it so the juice squirts out, while aggressive sparrows and pigeons puffed up in agitation wait for the falling crumbs; streetcars packed with still more people, and trucks groaning under the weight of mysterious loads, clatter across the background of this picture which, as one comes out of the theater, seems frighteningly improbable, as if it weren't the spectacle of real life, because the movement, beauty, ugliness, happiness, and indifference seen here, on the street, are neither symbols nor condensations of real, complete attributes or states of being nourished by truly experienced feelings: even if it allows its participants the highest possible degree of awareness, a street scene is real precisely because it is unaware, cannot possibly be aware, of its own reality, and the pedestrian hurrying down the street—a professor of psychology, a muscle-bound laborer, a cruising hooker—is a little like the professional actor who naturally and most appropriately adjusts his expressions and movements to his surroundings, which means that on the one hand, assuming his streetwise persona, he neutralizes himself, blends in, observes very keenly and sensitively the subtlest moral rules of public behavior, and on the other hand, he takes into account the prevailing light conditions and air temperature, and, while preserving the rhythm of his own body and conforming to that of the general traffic, pays attention to time—his own, that is: only for a brief segment of time are his movements regulated by the street's shared circumstances and consensual principles, only for the fleeting moments it takes to pass through this common existence; here nothing is done or left undone with the whole course of life in mind, unlike on the stage, where, as the rules of tragedy or comedy demand, the smallest action must include the whole of life, birth, and death; and since in all probability time is also perspective, the person on the street has only a very narrow and very practical perspective on himself, which is why the real world seems so improbable to one who steps out on the street with his eyes still used to the greater, anyway more universal, perspectives of the stage.

Wearing her short red wraparound coat, the kind that used to be called a coolie jacket, Thea would quickly cross the street toward her car, and with the hand holding the keys she'd wave back invitingly and insistently: would I like to come along? a gesture implying a request for me to get in the car, and also a curt signal to the others that the two of us had things to do on our own, which is how she meant to help me part with the rest of them, though she must have known I was always ready to go with her.

Some days we'd take Frau Kühnert home to Steffelbauerstrasse, and other times we'd simply leave her in front of the theater.

When someone walks out the stage door of a theater, alone or with others, at three o'clock in the afternoon and suddenly finds himself in this dumb state of improbability and realizes, moreover, that it's still light outside, then he can do one of two things: he can walk right into this humdrum, unpromising, sad world that nevertheless has a more tangible perspective and more measurable time and, instead of pondering the relationship between reality and unreality—which is what he should do—quickly go get something to eat though he's not hungry, drink something though he's not thirsty, go shopping though he doesn't really need anything; in other words, by falling back on basic life functions and consumer needs he can artificially readjust to the reality of a world operating with small prospects, even smaller insights, and minuscule perspectives; or he can protect, defend, hold on to his dazed incomprehension in this so-called real world and try to escape from the cold, restrictive scenery of time—even if he has nowhere else to go.

I couldn't or maybe didn't want to understand that I was living in the reality of improbability, though the signs were there, right in front of my nose, in Thea's every gesture and also in mine, undefined but present in our daily experience, but I didn't dare call that experience reality.

I was a wholesome child of my age, contaminated by the dominant ideas of the era, who also waited, along with the others, for the opportunity to seize the true, genuine reality that contained everything personal and ephemeral but was itself impersonal and not ephemeral, a reality that various theories, newspaper articles, and public speeches kept referring to, which had to be seized, which we had to strive for, but about which I had a very guilty conscience, because no matter where I turned I found only my own reality; and since the ideal, supposedly perfect, and complete reality was nowhere to be found, I considered that my own, however crude or cruel or pleasurable but for me perfect and complete in every way, was not reality but the reality of improbability.

Interestingly, I felt and knew exactly what I was supposed to feel and know, yet was forever asking myself what reality was—if my improbable reality wasn't reality, then what was I in this whole false existence?—and although the still-sensible part of my mind kept asking questions, in the end I came to believe that my improbability was not reality, that I was some strange transition between the actual and the real, and the ideal reality was up there somewhere, out of reach, ruling my life against my will, ideal and tyrannical, which I could never be a part of and could not touch, for it did not represent me, it was so powerful and great I couldn't even be worthy of its name, being but an unreal worm; yes, that's what I would have thought of myself if I'd been capable of such extreme self-abasement; and since despite my protests I did think of myself in those terms (without realizing it), the ideological rape used by the era achieved its most profound goal with me: I voluntarily relinquished the right to be my own person.

Thea did not deal in ideas—or, more precisely, they were embedded in her instincts—and I don't believe she gave them any thought, which was exactly why she was so violently opposed to the kind of acting that relies on identifying with or trying to become the character to be portrayed; she wasn't willing to cheapen the improbable experiences of her own sensuous reality, everything that's alive and visceral in a human being—and that is also the matrix of all ideas—to a mere formula and fit it into the uncomfortable narrow bed of an aesthetically prepared, cleverly confining form that others have declared to be, or by some convention accepted as, reality, an approach that for her would have been shamelessly false and ludicrously untrue, and she never had to ask where she was, for she had to be present in her own gestures, an incomparably riskier task than making a sentence or piece of dialogue your own: unaffected by the scruples of the age and using herself as a free human being, she demonstrated what was common to us all, and she knew she didn't have, couldn't possibly have, a single tendency or trait, a single expression of her body or face, that we wouldn't all instantly recognize and share.

Whenever I spent the afternoon with her she managed with her gestures to lift me, almost to thrust me out of the rut of my self-deceiving ideas, and she did this not with a single gesture but with everything she instinctively chose from her inner freedom and allowed to materialize as gestures.

Ultimately, in many respects, Thea and I were quite a bit alike.

Unlike Frau Kühnert, or Melchior for that matter, who used their bodies, their very lives, to block the way leading to hidden and surprising depths, Thea and I felt that it was only down there at the roots clinging to the silt of the senses, at the origins, that we can obtain the life of our bodies.

I also felt that though I might be dull, clumsy, mean, ugly, cruel, fawning, given to intrigues, or anything that from an aesthetic, intellectual, or moral standpoint might be considered inferior, I could balance this aesthetic, intellectual, and moral inferiority, as well as my moral turpitude, with the firm belief that my instincts were infallible and incorruptible: I'd feel first and know second, for I wasn't a coward, unlike those who know first and only then allow themselves to feel, according to the prevailing norms, and therefore knew intuitively and incontrovertibly what was good or bad, allowed or forbidden, because for me the moral sense was not imposed by a knowledge independent of feelings; I fought as single-mindedly as she for the right of the senses, wanted to use her as a means as much as she wanted to use me, wanted also, defying all taboos of mundane conventions and moral standards, to explore the innermost currents of the relationship among the three of us, and, like her, refused to accept the hopelessness of our situation, because then I would have had to admit the error of my supposedly unerring senses, my moral failure.

Strange as it may seem, one would rather let one's head be chopped off than come out with the admission of such a failure.

She always had trouble with the ignition, cursed it, called her car a piece of shit, kept grumbling she'd have to grow old struggling with such shitty contraptions.

And it was also strange that I thought myself free when I was with Melchior, yet with him I was drowning in the story of my body.

From the clutter of the glove compartment or, not infrequently, from the crack between the seats, she would extract her awful glasses, with one earpiece missing, place them on her nose, and keep them there by throwing her head back a little, at the same time managing to get the car started, and from that moment on, her movements were defined for me by a rather endearing chaotic combination of eager dilettantism and flamboyant inattention: on the one hand, she'd pay no attention to what she was doing, let her mind wander and lose contact with the road and with whatever was happening under the hood and indicated on the dashboard; on the other hand, catching herself drifting off, which often got us into truly dangerous situations, like a frightened little girl she would try, of course too abruptly, to correct her movements, while her glasses, falling forward or slipping off, always hampered her in these corrective maneuvers.

Still, I felt quite safe next to her; if I saw, for instance, that she hadn't noticed an upcoming sharp curve or, ignoring the dividing line and heavy oncoming traffic, crossed into the other lane, all I had to do was remark quietly on how smooth or wet the road was, how straight or winding, and she'd make the necessary adjustment; an odd kind of security, I admit, but then I sought personal safety in realms far more profound than that of traffic conditions; in this situation, I first of all had to be ready to give up my life, to say, Well, what the hell, if I die, I die, and trust the comic aspect of her driving style, which clearly showed that she had too much faith in her life to be concerned with the petty demands of traffic, she was busy with other things, she couldn't die so silly and senseless a death: without mixing God or Providence in, she sought to demonstrate with her movements that no one ever died of carelessness, death was always something else, even if its direct cause appeared to be carelessness or inattention, no, this was so only in the newspapers, in reality no precaution or alertness can help us, no amount of attention will prevent our little accidents, we cut our finger, step on broken glass, on a shell, a nail, always by accident, but we do not die by accident; I completely agreed with this, as well as with her other conclusions about life, even if in doing so I held on to my seat more tightly—a visible display of being both able and unable to renounce life, which was funny enough to be enjoyable.

Bouncing and bumping on our seats, the car puffing and sputtering, we sped out of the city.

If on the eve of my final departure from Berlin I hadn't destroyed all the notes I took at rehearsals, I'd have a daily record of the changes I felt were taking place in Thea; toward the end she spoke less and less, grew more quiet and dignified, and we generally rode in the car without talking.

Destroying my notes, burning them in Melchior's white tile stove, had a great deal to do with Frau Kühnert: seeing that my relationship with Thea had become more intimate, she lit into me with the seething anger of barely concealed jealousy, but also with the slyly submissive honesty of one bowing before the inevitable, and let me know that what I took to be a singular exciting change in Thea was nothing of the sort, nothing worth mentioning, oh, how sick and tired she was of all this talk about change, luckily for me I hadn't noticed that I was only a tool in Thea's hand, something she needed in her work, she was using me, didn't I see, and when the time came she'd discard me, luckily, she repeated, because this way, at least I relieved her of some of her burdens, actually replaced her for a while, she had known Thea for twenty years, might say she'd been living with her for that long, and so could tell me precisely, with the accuracy of a train schedule, in fact, down to the day, hour, minute, what Thea would do next, and I should know, she said, that if she hadn't noticed how attached Thea had become to me, she wouldn't be so frank with me.

For first rehearsals she always shows up quietly, solemnly, unapproach-
ably, Frau Kühnert went on, trying to charm me with her Theaological
knowledge, leaning very close to me, speaking almost into my mouth;
though she was never truly beautiful herself, I'd have to agree that she
was always able to create indescribable beauty around her, out of nothing,
if we want to be blunt about it; before the first rehearsal she'd do something with her hair, dye it, cut it, let it grow, and wouldn't talk about it
to anyone, not even to her, spending every free moment with Arno, with
whom she was in love again as she'd been in her youth, she'd rush home
to him, go on hikes and excursions with him, which Arno, being a professional climber, could certainly do without; and she'd become a regular
Hausfrau, making jam, cleaning and painting the apartment, sewing
dresses, but by the end of the second week of rehearsals or the beginning
of the third, she'd start with these impulsive getaways, just like now, with
me, she'd wave her over and they'd ride someplace where she would get
soused, behave like any man at his worst, pick fights, sing, belch, quarrel
with waiters, fart, throw up all over the table, Frau Kühnert had seen it
all, I couldn't tell her anything new, she'd had to pick her up and take
her home from some of the most awful places imaginable, and then the
next day either she'd send word she was deathly ill, not to expect her, she
felt terrible about it, but the doctor said it might take months to recover,
a nervous breakdown or an attack of ulcers, something very serious, no,
she didn't want to talk about it, it was very personal, a feminine problem,
probably a tumor in her uterus, she was bleeding buckets, and she had a
kidney infection, her vocal cords were inflamed, or she'd drag herself to
the theater, bearing up well, thank you, so well that in the middle of
rehearsals she'd have a crying fit and offer to quit the role, and then of
course they had to plead with her, tell her how indispensable she was,
console and beg her, and she would let herself be persuaded but then sink
into the darkest depression, and that was no longer a joke, she couldn't
get up, couldn't get dressed, let her hair get all greasy and stringy; and
whenever this happened, Frau Kühnert even had to cut her finger- and
toenails for her, but through it all Thea felt terribly guilty about letting
down her friends and colleagues, who were all so sweet and nice and
talented, she ought to be grateful, she would say, to be working with a
fine director like Langerhans, who could bring out the best in her, the
very best.

She would become attentive, buying presents for everyone, there was
nothing she wouldn't do for you, she would want to have a baby though

she was getting bored to tears with Arno, who spent all his time puttering about in that dreary high-rise flat of theirs when he should have been up in his real world, on top of mountains; if she could only buy him a little house somewhere with a garden, she felt sorry for him all right, but even more sorry for herself for having to live out her life with someone so miserable; and she, Frau Kühnert went on, had to fight her every afternoon, almost coming to blows as she practically shoved her into her car to make her go home, and if she had an evening performance, not only would she not go home but she would roam the streets with someone until morning, or sleep with some stranger, fall in love, or want a divorce because she'd had enough; she'd keep babbling and showing off, trying to captivate everyone, male or female, it didn't matter, and she'd begin to hate those who wouldn't respond, because maybe they were also in the throes of getting into their roles, she'd make rehearsals difficult for them, threaten to denounce them, and then the others would start hating her, too, torment her and denounce her, because I shouldn't think for a moment that this regularly repeated process was only her specialty, they were all like that here, this was a madhouse; but now we were into the next phase—so, as I could see, there was no change here at all—when Thea had to retreat; with opening night fast approaching, she put herself on hold, because she realized she was all alone once again, no one would or could help her, or rather, she should use the raging emotions stirred up by real, living people only onstage and if she used them offstage she'd end up destroying herself; and she wasn't at all as intuitive and spontaneous as I might think, but managed her resources very carefully, calculating and using them with great economy, because in the final analysis she didn't care about anything except what happened onstage, how she'd bring things off there, so if I really insisted on seeing some changes in Thea, I should see only that each new role demanded a different way of arousing her crazed emotions, and an infinite number of ways were possible; she herself did not exist, no matter how hard I tried, I could never see her; now, for example, in her current role, what I saw was not her but the difference, that clear gap or whatever, that separated Thea from the cold calculating bitch onstage who, even while standing over the dead body of her father-in-law, wanted to remain queen, which a sane person would never do; what always made Thea different from her own self was that she kept looking for herself in roles that didn't really suit her; she herself was nothing but a giant absence, a blank, and if I really meant to be of any help, I must never forget that about her.

But since I did not want to be of any help, in anything—it must have been my attentiveness and exaggerated politeness, my obliging, nearly servile humility that gave Frau Kühnert the wrong idea—my behavior stemming from an acute interest, which I was flattered to see Thea showed similarly in me, and if there was anybody I wanted to help, it was Melchior, which is why I felt I was using Thea and not the other way around, Frau Kühnert did not succeed in disillusioning or offending me, because I was shrewdly and obsessively determined to reach the moment of my desired goal, taking into account that its circumstances might be shaped by the characters of the two women, and went about considering and anticipating these eventualities with the cool detachment of a professional criminal preparing for a really big job.

All the same, it took some time before I could predict on any given day whether we were going to give Frau Kühnert a lift or just leave her at the theater, since Thea never said a word about where we were going, as if she didn't know or knew so well she didn't have to say it, the important thing was to go away from here, be somewhere else, alone, or rather with me, which for her had become a peculiar form of solitude: if we were going to end up at the Müggelheim Ridge, near the Köpenick Castle, or in the nature preserve south of Grünau, or in Rahnsdorf, then we'd take Frau Kühnert along and drop her off at Steffelbauerstrasse, which was on the way—of course Thea may have chosen these destinations with Frau Kühnert in mind in the first place, as a polite gesture toward her friend—but when we headed west, toward Potsdam and the gently flowing Havel River, or east, toward Strausberg or Seefeld, then we simply forgot her at the stage door; Thea would only wave goodbye to her, sometimes not even that, which Frau Kühnert, wrapped in the indifference of her jealousy and deep hurt, pretended not to notice, just as Thea pretended that her little wave or lack of it was the most natural gesture in the world.

These acts of betrayal were not without consequences, but as far as I could see, they were consequences their friendship could easily withstand.

Basically, I had no reason to doubt anything Frau Kühnert told me about Thea; after all, she had known her longer, more intimately, and from a different perspective, but she didn't necessarily know her better, because she knew her only as well as one woman might know another; the hidden little currents and secrets, the subtle signals of her gestures, words, and body which Thea sent out meant exclusively for men, Frau Kühnert could see only as an outside observer, while I, an initiate, instrument, or victim, could experience them on my skin, in my body; anyway, our perspectives on Thea were entirely different, and besides, I knew Frau Kühnert well enough to find my way around the labyrinth of her intentions, to understand the method and meaning of her exaggerations.

I had to conclude, for instance, that when it came to years she invariably resorted to overstatement; just as the age difference between Thea and Melchior wasn't twenty years, neither was it true that she had known Thea for so long—it was only ten years, yet these little lies and exaggerations aside, I had no reason to doubt her credibility, and my feelings told me that, for her, brazen lies and exaggerations no less than scrupulous honesty were all part of the same elaborate and formidable—in its passion rather moving—emotional strategy.

Her superstitious insistence on the magic number wasn't necessarily the result of cunning female rivalry: the reason she said twenty years instead of ten was not to put her friend in her place or at least in the right age bracket—it's true she was a few years younger than Thea but far less remarkable in every way—and was the same reason she was so frighteningly candid with me, shamelessly betraying their friendship by calling attention to Thea's age and revealing the agonies and craziness that went with her profession as an actress: Frau Kühnert was alluding to biological, aesthetic, and ethical realities she hoped would keep me away from Thea.

And I couldn't help noticing that these realities, even if I hadn't attributed much importance to them, did succeed in dampening my interest, thrusting me back from the role of emotionally involved participant to the castrated one of observer; Frau Kühnert stepped between us at a crucial moment, when our mutual attractions were about to converge, and, with her jealousy poured into a seemingly innocuous monologue, ventured into enemy territory, which according to the rules regulating the war of love between men and women she had no business entering.

But with great skill and nearly mythic calm Thea managed to drive back these unwarranted incursions.

No strategic move or subtle emotional maneuver by Frau Kühnert went unnoticed by Thea, who was always on guard, like on that windy late October afternoon when Frau Kühnert got hold of me in one of the narrow passageways connecting the dressing rooms, to pant and whisper at me the emotionally enthralling and professionally quite well-done grand monologue about the process of creating a role and maintaining a distance between actor and character, and when Thea emerged from her dressing room, it took only one look at her friend's flushed face for her to know what had been going on and what had to be done about it: putting her quick wits and absolute power over her friend to immediate good use, she grabbed my hand, turned on Frau Kühnert with the words You've been yakking to him long enough, and—brushing her face against Frau Kühnert's, which may or may not have been a peck of a farewell kiss, and if it wasn't, well, it was only because she had no time—she was off, had to run, with me of course, she got me out of a very tight spot by literally pushing me out the door, which was both an act of revenge and a deliberate humiliation from the standpoint of Frau Kühnert, who with the kiss she did and did not receive was left in a state of outraged shock and utter physical helplessness, as though she'd just been stabbed through the heart; I could almost see blood spurting from her chest.

Thea was carried across the street by the momentum of her resolve, but as soon as we were in the car I could see that the little scene had upset her and put her in a bad mood.

She said nothing until sometime after we got out again—I don't remember which way we left the city because, as I did with Melchior when he was driving, I relied completely on her knowledge of places, and in this way every feature of her face, every move she made, became part of the unfamiliar landscape I was always delighted to rediscover; first we sped down an almost empty highway, then unexpectedly she turned off onto a dirt road, where the area's unusual flatness under the sky's silent dome was relieved only by the soft outlines of occasional woods, razor-sharp outlines of lakes, canals, or other bodies of water, and the dirt road we were driving on seemed to be leading straight to the center of the earth's flat dish; the car rattled and jerked and began to cough as it tried to make it up a very gentle rise; not wanting to push her luck, Thea let the motor die and engaged the handbrake.

Once we were out of the city, it didn't really matter where we ended up.

It was one of those deceptive inclines that will have you believe, with their long, gradual rise, that they won't take much to climb, yet by the time you get to the top you're out of breath; from the dirt road a narrow well-beaten trail led to the top, then although it disappeared near the flat crest, it seemed to continue somewhere up in the sky, appearing to the eyes like a gentle invitation the feet could not resist; sinking her hands comfortably into her coat pockets, Thea proceeded slowly up the hill, lost in thought, while I looked down, wondering who trod here before us and packed the dirt so hard, and also trying to figure out how such trails are formed.

I seemed to be stuck with having to ponder the useless questions of how one ensnares the world in the net of one's secret desires and how one becomes captive in the net cast by others.

The westering sun appeared for brief moments behind enormous, swirling, spiraling, dark-gray clouds, through the opening between which the sky's dome shone through in yellows, blues, and reds; a strong wind was blowing, but since it had nothing to cling to on this flat terrain except us, the whole landscape appeared to be silent.

Only now and then could the sound of birds be heard; long, blurry shadows and deeply burning cold lights streaked by.

In the mistless air, the distant horizon with its gentle curves and dips appeared to the eye sharp and close up, and our bodies sensed the air's chill in a similar way; it wasn't an unpleasant cold, because it nicely encircled each limb, gave strength and vigor to our movements.

It's in the northern regions that one experiences this, where the clear transparent cold has a way of isolating the body's warmth, which can then transmit its inner energies, endow one's acts with firmness and simplicity.

She stopped for a moment, I followed a few paces behind; being closer to her in the infinite distances of this vast open space would have seemed out of place; she didn't wait for me to catch up, only turned around to make sure I was still there before walking on, and then she said, You must never be angry at her, Sieglinde is a very decent girl, and she is always right, always, in everything.

When we reached the top of the leisurely sweeping rise, beauty stretched its new face before us with such serene majesty that words would only have marred it.

From here the trail descended more precipitously to the softly undulating land directly below, beneath a sheer drop, as if pulled down by its own immense weight, where deep in its lap it harbored a shimmering little pond, while farther on, bright strips of farmland and dark-crested woods stretched to the horizon, the intimate grandeur of their smooth lines made even lovelier by the orbs of a few solitary bushes.

For a while we stood on this seemingly lofty though rather low hilltop, admiring nature's spectacle from that well-known pose of casual strollers who usually report, in emotion-filled voices, with phrases like No, it was so beautiful, so infinitely beautiful, I thought I could never tear myself away, I had to stay to the end of my days! which, whether we like it or not, is also an admission, full of nostalgic pain, that much as we may like such a spectacle of nature, we don't know what to do with it, can't identify with it, we'd love to but can't, it's too vast, too distant, we ourselves are too alien in it, maybe too alive, and maybe in death we'll be able to move away and look for a different vantage point, perhaps the ultimate one, though we really ought to stay here because, with or without us, this is nature's ultimate landscape; then, after taking that steep trail down to the pond, to the more reassuring and more prosaic level, where the view was no longer so infinitely beautiful and inhuman, Thea stopped and turned to face me.

Sometimes I could scratch her eyes out, she said in a very calm, deep, earnest voice.

As if with her voice she were continuing the tranquillity of the wind, the clouds, and the undulating lines of the land; the sound of her voice was also twisting and winding, though in the opposite direction, back to the very near present.

But if she wasn't there for me, she said, I might have done myself in long ago.

And now, lurking in her voice, there was a nostalgia tinted with some self-pity, for which the beautiful setting had to be responsible, for it filled us both with a kind of anguished yearning, and she had to break with that, too, for she didn't really feel sorry for herself, she always did what she wanted, what her life as an actress demanded, and whatever self-pity she did feel could be neither expressed nor shared; amused by her own insurmountable curiosity, she broke into a sarcastic smile and came out with the question, after all: What sort of gossip was Frau Kühnert spreading about her this time?

I was taken aback by the smile, her pettiness was out of place in this sublime setting even if she knew it, and I didn't feel like answering her, for to betray Frau Kühnert just then would have run counter to my plans; Nothing special, I said, and, opting for the safety of a general observation, added, Though I've never met anyone who's had a chance to observe, in such a primal form, how a role takes shape within an actor.

Her response to my evasion was a wry smile; Within any actor or within me, she asked.

An actor, yes, any actor, I said.

No, there was nothing primal in what she did, she said reflectively, but I had the feeling she was wondering about my refusal to give her a straight answer; True, she went on, she was unschooled and uncouth, but also intelligent enough to know a lot about a lot of things; and then her face reverted to her sarcastic smile.

Did Sieglinde tell me, by any chance, she asked, that she sometimes let herself go completely and was capable of doing the most dreadful things? she could have, of course, they were so close she knew all about her gutter behavior.

I looked at her quizzically, but she only nodded, perhaps wanted to go no further; she put her hand lightly on my arm.

There were only two people in her life, she said, everything else was just one big stupidity, no matter what she did, she'd always go back to them, and they would never let her go.

I know, I said.

We looked at each other for a long time, a little as we had looked at the landscape before, because I did know what she'd meant and she could be sure I knew; this was the moment when she neutralized not only Frau Kühnert's emotion-driven maneuvering but also my machinations, the emotional dishonesty with which I tried to further Melchior's interests.

Two human beings were standing in a landscape breathing with a life infinitely greater than theirs, and they understood each other, not with their minds or emotions, for in this understanding the central function was assigned to that naturally accepted given to which we hadn't paid much attention before, neither intellectually nor emotionally, namely, that she was a woman and I was a man.

The moment exceeded our abilities and intentions, alluded to our natural differences and the one and only possibility of reconciling them, and thus, overriding all our efforts to remain composed, terribly embarrassed us both.

She didn't let the embarrassment deepen but quickly removed her hand from my arm, gave her shoulder a funny little shrug—at once a coy gesture of surrender and withdrawal—turned, and, now completely in a different time dimension than the city we'd left behind, but also turning away from the landscape, she continued walking along the trail toward the distant woods.

Table d'Hôte

Despite my valiant protest, my fiery and effervescent senses are at the mercy of raw forces we usually refer to as base or dark and, if I'm permitted a rather common term, downright obscene, and even in more refined terms they are no less than filthy, evil, deserving of the greatest contempt and harshest punishment; let's hasten to add that all this is not without justification, for everything I'll be compelled to talk about now is indeed related to the unclean end products of bodily functions as well as to the relief and gratification accompanying them; but no less justified is the question: do or do not these raw forces live inside us as do our discriminating moral sensibilities, whose inevitable task it is to fight them? but whether I consider the impure a part of me or alien to me, whether I accept the challenge and take up arms against it or with a weary shrug submit to it, it does exist—whatever I do, I cannot but continually feel its undeniable power, like some pornography of divine origin; if I manage to keep it at bay when awake, then it assails me, treacherously, in my dreams, flaunting its infinite power over my body and soul, there is no escaping it, and to try is to fail, as I learned on the night of my arrival in Heiligendamm, and let that be a lesson! no matter how much I was trying to be rid of my many worries that night—my foolish reflections on my artistic work, the dark yet exciting memories of my parents and my childhood, the arduous and unsettling journey, the equally unsettling though tender and touching farewell to Helene—no matter how much I tried to escape into a long, deep, restful, purifying sleep, it startled me again, although this time rather gently, not treating me as cruelly as at other times when it would appear, let's say, in the image of a naked man offering me his erect phallus, but announcing itself in a most innocent dream image, its appearance no more than a gentle reminder of my help-lessness.

Loud, strange footsteps were reverberating in a familiar, wet street; the night, mysterious and flecked with the glimmer of gas lamps, enveloped me as smoothly, softly yet firmly, as only a loving woman's embrace or a dream can, and so I sank with it, hardly against my will, surrendering completely to the beauty of the darkness accentuated by the golden halos around the lamps; and since this nocturnal street scene was not far from turning into a person, yes, from becoming Helene herself, although noth-ing indicated directly that the scene was her embodiment, still, quite freely, without fear or reticence, my senses and emotions blended into and spread throughout this scene as if it were Helene, as though I were be-latedly bestowing on her the very feelings which while awake—over-whelmed by the force of circumstances—even at the wildest moments of our ecstasy I was compelled to withhold from her and of course from myself as well.

It was as though the greatest good, the highest, most complete and splendid good was about to overpower me, and I had to hand over every-thing I had; indeed, it had already taken everything from me, devoured me, I was it and it was me, yet still it had more to give and so did I, much more skill; it was on the way to this good that my strong footsteps were resounding, this was the street of the good, the night, dark, and lights of the good, and I felt that the more I gave the more I had left to give; and it was all very good, even if my footsteps seemed to echo back to me from a cold, hollow space.

But from here I could see it, for the nature of the good now made itself visible; and I simply slipped out, emerged from the bothersome noise of my footsteps, to reach it; now I could feel that there was something better than the good, and whatever was waiting for me could only be better, for if I could walk right through all this good so easily and freely, then redemption, for which I had yearned so while lying at the bottom of my suffering, and that unpleasant clatter of footsteps had to do with suffering, could now come to pass without special fuss or ceremony.

And the love, oh, the love granted me now was great indeed; to love the cobblestones of the street as the cambered light highlighted and ab-sorbed each and every one of them, to love the raindrops ready to fall from the branches, to love those sinister footfalls, too, and the gas jets dancing over the water collected at the bottom of the glass globes, to love the darkness for allowing me to see the light, and the cat that scurried by like an unexpected shadow, to love the soft tracks its paws left behind in the night, to love the glistening surface of the slender, finely wrought lampposts and the sound of that rusty creak the ear could hardly register in this loving daze.

And the eyes searched in vain.

For it was like a bubble, could burst any moment.

The creaking sound grew stronger, and leaving the clatter of my feet behind me on the stones, I was headed toward it; a metal door would make such a rusty sound when creaking in the wind, but there was no wind! I was hoping this would be the last clatter, after which nothing more could disturb the thick silence of the dark, but I was still walking and each step produced a new sound.

And then I saw myself approaching.

How could I spare the darkness from these noises?

There I was, standing behind the steel door blown open by the wind, standing in the stench and following intently the sound of those footsteps.

The wind slammed the door shut with a harsh grating sound, hiding me behind it, but the next instant it flew wide-open and I once more saw myself waiting there.

But where was I, anyway?

The place was not unfamiliar even if I could not locate myself in it exactly, which is why the question: Where? persisted; the possibility of being at once here and there made me so anxious I wanted to cry out, and would have, too, had I not been wary of disturbing the darkness with a loud cry, for I was still walking on the street of the good, and knew I was, I wouldn't let anyone deceive me! yet this street led me straight to that door, the bare trees and the wet lampposts were standing there like road markers, I couldn't change course now, I had to reach the steel door that evoked too much shame, desire, fear, curiosity, and humiliation for it to be unfamiliar; its secrets I would have liked to hide even from myself, yet there I was, in the same old spot, waiting for myself in the heavy stench of tar and urine, and I must have stood there for quite a while, because the foul smell had penetrated not only my clothes—whatever happened to my hat?—but my skin as well, it was emanating from me, even from my hair, so there was no point in slipping away, there was a finality about my being there; I had arrived.

And then somebody, the one ruling over my dream—for in spite of everything I knew this was a dream, no need to get excited, I could wake any minute, though someone in control of the dream wouldn't let me— only I could not remember who this person might be, although his voice sounded familiar as he whispered that he was waiting behind the door, and no matter that I still felt the calm bestowed on me by my contact with the good, there was nothing to be done, nothing, because all that, he whispered right into my ear now, had been only to entice me: the dark was waiting for me.

Nothing to be done.

So I kept walking, not surprised at my trembling; I was afraid, but it seemed there was no degree of fear or anxiety I could not make myself adjust to; I protested, of course, tried to protect myself, but it was as if that certain force were compelling my body, now writhing in protest, to admit and accept all the secret desires it had tried to conceal, to acknowl- edge the terrible burdens it had to carry all these years, and this struggle made the way long, and my footsteps grew fainter; though the clatter was still there I no longer felt the ground securely under me, and like an epileptic falling into a fit I lost control over my limbs and felt gurgling saliva gushing from my open mouth; I kicked and thrashed and panted, but nothing changed; the grim little structure with its opening and closing, creaking and squeaking black mouth was waiting for me; with clearly human sounds it creaked and groaned and panted in the middle of a clump of bare bushes.

It just sat there, squat and motionless, etching sharply its ornamental entablature into the night sky, while I wouldn't even dare cry out; I kept walking.

No wonder, then, that the next morning I was quite exhausted, worn to a frazzle, as they say, as if I hadn't slept all night, though I must have slept very deeply to feel so dazed; still, in my frustration, I would have liked to go back into the dream, because maybe it was precisely there and then that what should have happened did happen, but my room in the meantime became much too bright, its features too sharp, as if outside, behind the drawn curtains, snow had fallen; it felt cool, almost cold; oc- casionally I heard soft footsteps in the hallways, and from the breakfast room downstairs came the even clatter and clang of dishes, snatches of conversation; a door creaked, then the same door that had wakened me during the night slammed again, there was the brief laughter of a woman; all these friendly, soothing sounds reached me softly, from a distance, but

I didn't feel like getting out of bed, for all those pleasant morning sounds, familiar to me from childhood, bade me resume a life whose apparent ease and leisure was now not at all to my liking; no, I shouldn't have come here, after all, I said to myself, irritated, and turning over to the other side and closing my eyes, I tried to sink back into the warmth and the dark the dream had offered; but back where?

Snatches of the dream were still hovering about, it didn't seem too hard to return to it, and the man, too, was still standing there in front of the pissoir's gleaming, tarred wall, still in the pose of handing me a rose, which I didn't want to take from him because the grin on his puffy white face was so repulsive, and interestingly the rose looked blue, purplish blue, a firm, fleshy bud about to burst open; and now it was offering itself to me most insistently, as if morning had not yet come, as if I were still there, lingering with it in the night.

And then, in the open door between the bedroom and the sitting room, I saw standing before me a young valet with flaming red hair, standing there quietly, steadily, attentively, his friendly brown eyes following every little movement of my awakening, as though he'd been there forever and even had a good idea of what my dream had been about, although it was probably his soundless footsteps or his mere presence that had startled me out of my slumber just now; he was a strapping young lad, his healthy robust build more like a porter's or a coachman's, his thighs and shoulders about to burst the seams of his trousers and green frock coat, a quiet unobtrusive presence that reminded me of my own duties, as if he had clambered out of my dream or from a place even deeper within me, and also made me think of our servant back home and, once again, of the memory-filled night I had just gone through; I sensed the same stolid calm and rough-hewn dignity emanating from his body that I used to feel in Hilde's presence, so while feasting my eyes on the boy's freckled face and also suppressing a powerful yawn, I grumpily repeated the sentence, by now completely superfluous: No, I should never have come here; but if not here, where? I wondered, and this hulking body pressed into the wrong clothes seemed so comical, as did his flat nose, his freckles, his childishly open curious eyes, and the solemn air with which he stood there waiting for my order, and my own grumpiness, now that I was fully awake, also seemed so inappropriate and foolish that I burst out laughing.

"Will you be getting up now, Herr Thoenissen?" the valet asked dryly, as if he hadn't heard my laughter, which might have been rather over-familiar.

"Yes, I think so. Anyway, I should."

"Will you have tea or coffee?"

"Perhaps tea."

"Shall I fill the washbowl now or after the tea?"

"Do you think one should wash every morning?"

He was silent for a moment, his expression unchanged, but he did seem to understand something.

"And will you be taking your breakfast downstairs or shall I bring it up?"

"No, no, I'll go downstairs, of course. But isn't it rather chilly here?"

"I'll see to the fire right away, Herr Thoenissen."

"Yes, and how about giving me a shave?"

"Of course, Herr Thoenissen."

He disappeared for a few minutes, an opportunity I should have used to get out of bed and relieve myself—I suspect he took his time to give me a chance to do just that, for among themselves men are considerate that way, I wouldn't call it politeness but, rather, a brotherly appreciation of the embarrassing fact that in the morning an overfull bladder often causes an erection, and to jump out of bed in such a state would mean presenting whoever was there with the sight of a deceptive function of biological processes; we'd have to let him in on something whose true nature we ourselves don't fully understand and for that reason deem rather shameful—in any case, I delayed getting up and when he wheeled in a cart and quickly closed the door behind him I was still lying in bed or, rather, having tucked the pillow behind my back, was half sitting, making myself very comfortable, as if I knew that by getting up I would interrupt, or send in a different direction, an event which promised to be perfect in itself and at the moment was far more important to me than easing some physical discomfort; the pressure in the bladder cannot artificially be relieved, but the erection will subside if we divert our attention from it, and with it the last trace of the dream's sensuous excitement will perhaps also fade.

These were some of the things I was thinking about while he quietly busied himself around me, rolling the serving cart up to my bed, treading softly on the carpet, and making certain the dishes on the glass-topped cart did not rattle; I felt I was watching a feline, a silent predator, disguised as a valet; the event of the moment, which held me in its grip and which I found pleasing, was the series of his movements and gestures refined to the point of imperceptibility: without dripping a single drop on the gleaming damask napkin, he poured out the steaming tea and asked if I took it with milk—I don't know, should I? I said, but the deliberate audacity of my reply did not bother him; he acknowledged it and at the same time intimated that he was in no position to answer this question, the decision rested entirely with me, but whatever I decided would certainly meet with his approval, the manner of which would be neither submissive nor indifferent but would reveal, in a purely neutral form, the embarrassing perfection of readiness to meet any wish and at the same time take into account my possible eccentricities, which he might find hard to follow; with stubby fingers he folded back the napkin covering a basket of crisp rolls, and after handing me the teacup and the sugar bowl with its silver tongs, he was gone—I don't know how he did it, I didn't even hear his retreating footsteps, he simply left, sensing I had no further need of him.

Though at the moment there was no one I needed more.

When after the first sip of the hot tea I looked over the rim of my cup, he was back, carrying firewood in a big wicker basket, and he knelt down in front of the white tile stove, positioning himself so as not to turn his back to me completely, I could see him in profile while he cleaned out the stove and started the fire; with one half of his body he remained at my disposal, ready to let me be if I wished or to respond to my slightest indication of need.

The rolls were warm and fragrant, drops of water glistened on the little balls of yellow butter resting in a bed of fresh strawberry leaves; when I gave the cart a slight nudge with my elbow I saw the raspberry jam dotted with tiny seeds quiver in its dish.

If my childhood had not been burdened with so many dark unpleasant memories, if the image of my mother, even as a memory, had not been so coldly distant, I might have thought that what was beckoning to me from this little scene was a long-lost feeling of security, might have said then that in those wholesome rolls, steaming tea, fresh yellow butter, quivering jam, I sensed a peaceful order of things that assures us that once we awaken from our dreams, however frightful, our world—at whose center we ourselves sit, in the bed warmed with our own bodies—not only will be there, spinning securely according to its own immutable laws, but will struggle mightily to satisfy our needs and desires, will heat our room with the trees of the forest, with no cause for alarm, fear, or anxiety; but the truth is that even as a child I had sensed the brittleness, falsehood, and illusory nature of this order; and later, my passionate search had led me to people who were not only ready to expose it but whose declared purpose was to end it, end all deceptions and bring about genuine well-being and security, even at the price of blowing up this shaky corrupt order and incurring a heavy loss of life, so that afterward, on the ruins of the old, they could build a new world fashioned in their own image; I might say, then, that while my eyes, tongue, and ears savored the pleasures of the morning's unchanged old-fashioned order, my mind's eye viewed its own joys, reminiscent of its childhood, from the greatest possible distance, and as it did, I suddenly grew old.

How far this white bedroom lit by bright sunshine seemed from the rooms of bygone years, the dim rooms of my youth where I spent my time in secret company with Claus Diestenweg, hatching plots to bring down the hated old order and build a new one; and how very close it seemed, I thought, to the rooms of my childhood which never really existed in this pristine form.

A fleeting change of mood is all it takes, and we feel, to quote the poet, that time is out of joint.

It was almost as if the man now lying in bed, slightly disillusioned and still perturbed by dreams yet casually sipping tea, had to cope not with three successive stages of a single life but with the lives of three different individuals.

A puff of smoke blew out of the stove, then the fire flared up, painting the valet's face red and continuing to blaze, it seemed, in his hair.

The smoke made him squint; he wiped his tearing eyes and for a moment stared into the clearing, now smokeless fire.

"What's your name?" I asked him quietly, still from my bed.

"Hans," he answered, and as if momentarily forgetting his dutiful attitude, he did not bother to turn toward me.

"And your family name?"

I was glad to have a valet here with me, yet at the same time, having just slipped back from my earlier life, I was ashamed at being glad.

"It's Baader, sir," he said, his voice back to the earlier, proper tone, and there seemed to be no connection at all between the two voices.

"And how old are you?"

"Eighteen, sir."

"Then I will ask you, Hans, to congratulate me; as of this morning, I am thirty years old."

He stood up at once.

He broke into a grin; his beautiful almond-shaped eyes disappeared in the soft cushions of his eyelids and cheeks still like a child's; above formidable teeth his gums flashed pink, almost like raw flesh, which in redheads are always in attractive harmony with their complexion and hair color; sweetly, almost as if I were his contemporary standing next to him, a chum he was about to jab playfully in the chest, he swung out his arm toward me, but the gesture was so blatant and therefore so inappropriate that he became embarrassed, blushed, his whole face turning flaming red, and he could not speak.

"Yes, today is my birthday."

"If we had known, Herr Thoenissen, we would have observed it properly; still, allow me to congratulate you!" he said, smiling, although the smile was no longer meant for me but for himself, pleased that he had managed so cleverly to extricate himself from a delicate situation.

And then there was silence again.

And when in this helpless silence I thanked him, something happened between us which I had anticipated, waited for, tried to help along, for naturally, my thanks alluded not to his congratulations, which I had more or less forced out of him and which in themselves were rather ludicrous, but to him, him for being so perfect and for moving me deeply with his perfection.

He stood there silently for a moment, as I lay motionless in my bed, he bowed his head, humbled and helpless, and I kept looking at him.

And when, moments later, he asked if he could now bring the water, I motioned him to go: this was the boundary beyond which lay the forbidden realm that I shouldn't have wanted us to enter; at the same time, something also came to an end between us, because the intimacy forced out of the moment was now exposed, and sharing anything between us was out of the question, I remained master and he servant who had to fend for himself, be clever in dealing with me, most probably as disgusted as he may have been moved, understanding our inequality enough so as to spoil any pure game of intimacy between us; it was an experiment, then, to want to touch something that had nothing to do with our assigned roles, and I had nothing to lose, since with my advantage it remained my experiment and, I had to admit, for me it was humiliatingly one-sided; yet I couldn't resist the experiment's temptation, because I enjoyed my advantage, enjoyed his defenselessness and enjoyed that he had to endure it precisely because he was a servant, what's more, could even enjoy my own humiliation given his; so our little story continued on its own accord, almost completely independent of me; it couldn't be stopped.

Standing astride my spread-out thighs, he wet my face with a porous sponge that still smelled faintly of the sea; with a slow, circular motion of two fingers he applied the shaving cream and with the soft shaving brush whipped it into a thick lather over my stubble; of course our bodies were very close; with his free hand he had to hold or support my head and put his palm on my temple or forehead now and again; I had to guess his wishes from his movements, follow them, help them along; his knee would occasionally touch mine, but he had to focus all his attention on my face, while I kept an eye on his every move; he held his breath a little and so did I, both of us trying not to breathe into each other's face, a mutual restraint that only intensified the scene unfolding between us, which was about to reach its climax when, having done with the preparations, he pulled the bone-handled razor from its case, ran the blade a few times over the strop, stepped between my legs this time, placed his index finger on my temples, pulling the skin nice and tight, ready for the blade, and then, for one moment, looked into my eyes.

With a single decisive stroke he drew the razor down the left side of my face, I could hear the fine crackle of my whiskers as they parted from the skin, chuckling inwardly at my own nervousness, because no matter how readily we may present our face to the razor and try to be very relaxed about it, fear for life makes the facial muscles tense and knotted, so we want to see that the razor hasn't gotten stuck somewhere and then slipped and cut the skin, our eyes almost pop from their sockets with curiosity, and at the same time we must continue to exude trust, since otherwise we might hinder the work and thus increase the danger, ourselves becoming the cause of a little accident as unpleasant for us as for the man with the razor, because if the skin is injured, suddenly raw hatred spills out from under the disguise of the intimate physical proximity and mutual attentiveness; he'd hate us for our annoyingly unpredictable skin, which makes a mockery of his skill and experience by having whiskers in swirling clumps, or simply hiding little lumps, not to mention peak-headed pimples, that get in the way of the razor; and we'd hate him for his clumsiness and, most of all, for having put ourselves thoughtlessly into his hands; and the mutual hatred only increases when, looking in the mirror and seeing blood trickling down, we both have to pretend it's nothing, and he begins to whistle in embarrassment and with a wild gesture wrapped in the guise of helpful routine picks up the styptic pencil and, causing more, stinging pain, even takes revenge on us; but so far nothing untoward happened; from the way he smeared the lather on his stretched-out finger and from there flung it into a little bowl, I could tell he was experienced; he turned my head and after stepping even closer, so that my nose almost brushed against his shirtfront, starched to an armorlike stiffness, and I could feel his slightly bent knee very close to my groin, he just as decisively shaved the right side of my face; but despite the barber's skill and experience, his almost surgeonlike precision, the skin remains tense and taut, we feel it quivering on our face, and the most sensitive areas are yet to come, the complex chin region, the neck, the throat, to say nothing of the fact that while he is jumping about brandishing the razor, the thought does occur to us: What if he should accidentally cut off our nose or ear, such horrors have been known to happen! but looking at him like this, from below, with upturned eyes, for all the attractive charm of his youth and strength I found his face somehow much too soft, and this exaggerated softness could be seen only from this angle; on his skin, under which you could sense a layer of white fat, the reddish fuzz had hardly begun to sprout; he'll never have to shave, I noted with satisfaction, he'll remain hairless like a eunuch, which you could also see in his large nostrils and capriciously curving mouth—he was biting his lower lip as he delicately worked away on my chin—in a few years' time he'll probably grow a second chin, I thought, his big frame will run to fat, he'll pant and wheeze under the burden of his huge mass, and as my throat anticipated the ticklishly sensuous pleasure of the razor's touch, when he'd stretch the skin away from my Adam's apple and run the blade, smoothly and dangerously, over it, I lifted my hand so he couldn't see, and waiting until he got there, not before, and even then making it appear as though I did it from fear, without moving a muscle in the rest of my body, I placed my hand on his firm thigh.

The smooth muscles under my hand were hard, incredibly powerful, my palm was at a loss on them, seemed weak and insignificant, as if I were touching him in vain, for not only did this reveal nothing of his inner nature, it didn't even let me touch the surface, as if this surface, which of course I could feel, were only a cover on the real surface, a protective armor hard to the point of insensibility; this is what I could have thought if I had thought of anything, for it was clear that just as I could not register any reaction in his eyes and mouth or other features of his face bending over me, now I could not do so in his flesh either, no embarrassment, no consent, no rejection; his skin, face, and muscles remained as neutral as all his movements had been; I was the one who wanted to make this cruel neutrality my own, I reacted to him, not he to me; he didn't feel me, seemed not to understand me or, more precisely, didn't think there was anything to feel or understand.

It always seems pointless to make sweeping statements, but still, I have to say that never in my life, not before or after this incident, have I made a more senseless gesture.

By making it, though, I felt I had reached the peak or the bottom of my strange inclinations.

I couldn't just pull back my hand, anyway the gesture couldn't be undone; at the same time I felt nothing, even though I left my hand there; still working on my neck, he was untouched, as if my move had been only a figment of my imagination, which of course couldn't possibly reach him.

I wouldn't have minded if he had slit my throat at that moment.

If with a barely audible crack the razor had cut through the delicate cartilage.

And I couldn't close my eyes, waiting still for a telltale sign.

To shake into the bowl the lather accumulated on his finger he had to turn aside, which was the only reason he moved his thigh away from my hand.

The orphaned hand, a strange stump still part of my body, was empty, left hanging in the air.

He dipped the sponge in the water and, supporting my head with his arm, washed off my face.

In the meantime I could finally close my eyes.

"This is a cursed place, sir!" I heard him say in my darkness.

By the time I opened my eyes he was again leaning aside to throw the sponge back into the bowl, and there was no telltale sign.

"Some eau de cologne?" he asked, without turning around.

His perfect poise, seeming neither offended nor reproachful, cheered me, for it was as though together we had relegated my failed overture to the world's great junk heap of futile experiments.

"Yes, why not."

At the same time it also occurred to me that his strange statement may have been a secret allusion to those frightful nocturnal noises, the cries and shrieks that woke me from my first sound sleep, with which, for all I knew, he may have had something to do.

In which case my gesture was not an insult and may not have been completely in vain.

Holding the back of my head with one hand, pressing his little finger to my neck and sinking the others into my hair, he used his other hand to splash alcohol on my face.

He fanned my face with a cloth to make the alcohol evaporate more quickly—at such moments we always feel especially refreshed—and for the first time in a long while we looked into each other's eyes.

He must have known something, the place may have been cursed, but the little event I had managed so successfully to force out of ourselves now made the place of my memories cozy and intimate, suggesting I wasn't mistaken, after all—his glance remained dispassionate—yes, I'd be just fine here, the fire crackled away cheerfully in the stove, and I could hardly wait for him to gather his things and leave; as if driven by a slight fever, I was ready to pounce on my black briefcase, snap open its lock, spread my papers over the clear desk, and get to work, even if my bitter experiences warned against haste; things are never so simple as our desires would like them to be; one must delay things, one should skim the foam of tension from the bubbling brew of sensations, let it thicken and mellow, for the moment is never ripe when it appears to be! so when at last he closed the door behind him, I first stepped up to the window, then drew aside the white curtains, and the splendid sight indeed cooled me off.

I had a whole hour to myself before the little bell would sound, calling the guests to our commensal breakfast.

The autumn sky was bright, the slender red pines now stood motionless in the park, the night winds having died down completely, and although I could not see the sea from here, or the promenade along the shore, or the bathhouse, or the wide road leading to the station, or the seawall, marshland, and woods behind, yet I knew they were there, within reach, everything that could be important and painful was there.

I saw a few fallen leaves on the decorative tiles of the terrace.

Yes, everything was here, and therefore I could afford not to be here but in my imagined story.

To forget everything.

But wasn't this feeling of lightness nourished by the hope—so lovely because unrealizable—with which I was deceiving myself that, having finally broken free of my future bride, now this young obliging servant was near me and I could summon him any time I wanted to? but then wouldn't I again be caught between two human beings?

Where, then, was my yearned-for solitude?

The thought unpleasantly linking the two of them in my mind was a pain at the pit of my stomach.

Why were they here, crowding me even in my solitude?

My mood did not darken, though; on the contrary, I was like someone who suddenly glances at his own body with a stranger's eyes and finds its proportions pleasing, not that he doesn't see its flaws and imperfections, and realizes, finally understands, that a living form is always delineated by the relationships among details which are shaped by unalterable processes; the imperfect has its own laws, which is what is perfect in it; functioning itself is perfect, existence is perfect, the unique and unalterable order of disproportions is perfect—why was this made clear to me only now, on my thirtieth birthday, I wondered, why at this mysterious turning point in my life? after all, ever since I could remember, ever since I had become aware that one's body has a life of its own, I had suffered from a sense of always being cast between two things, two phenomena, two people, as though between two crushing millstones! this was part of my earliest memories! for example, when, divided yet unshared, my body was between those of my mother and father on our long late-afternoon walks on the waterfront promenade, my parents may have been full of mutual hostility and murderous rage toward each other—because their bodies were irreconcilable—yet I not only felt identified but wanted to identify with both of them; I neither could divide myself between them nor had any intention of doing so, even if they had wanted to tear me apart; and indeed, I may have been torn apart, for my features, build, and character were undecided between them; I took after both, and after others as well, many others; only for the sake of simplifying things do we speak of a dual division, a dual likeness, for in reality I also resembled my dead forebears, who lived on in my features and gestures; but now it made me quite happy that these two people, my bride and this valet, strangers to each other, wound up so disturbingly close in my thoughts, for how could I possibly decide, know for sure, or have a say about what I was permitted or not permitted to do if I knew nothing about the origin of anything? how could I share what was unsharable in me? everything is permitted, I decided: yes, I'd be the most obstinate anarchist, and not only because fortuitous events in my youth had led me into the company of anarchists (and those years couldn't simply be dismissed, nor the fact that it wasn't high-minded goals and intellectual aspirations that made me join them), but also because I have always been an anarchist of the body, believing that there is no God besides the body, and that only a completed physical act can redeem my body, when I can feel the infinite abundance of my possibilities.

And you know what you can do with your morality.

For me, the valet's temperate thighs, and seeing the tarred wall of the pissoir while dreaming of my fiancée's loins, were no frivolous adventures.

Later, when I walked into the dining room and my eyes were hit by a sudden burst of morning sunshine, flashing and sparkling on the myriad surfaces of glass, mirrors, silverware, and china, not to mention people's eyes, I felt in my limbs this fresh morning brightness, a cozy well-being, the superiority of rebelliousness, and was glad I could immediately share it, look into those eyes with it, and glad that the sea was there, outside the window, still dark and rough from last night's storm, still foamy but gradually subsiding.

And if anything interested me, it was the filthy immorality of this rotten God.

And now I was glad that I had to observe some of those detestable rules of civilized conduct, which I looked down on with the awareness of my superiority, in the knowledge that I was once again in possession of my body.

I found it an infinitely beautiful piece of pious hypocrisy that I, who only two days earlier had made love to my fiancée on the floor of my apartment and a short while ago had felt up the thigh of a valet, was now standing between the open wings of the dining-room door and, blinded a little by the dazzling light, with impunity smiled my most polite smile while listening to the hotelier, a portly, jovial, bald little man, none other than the son of the onetime owner, yes, that's who it was—when we were both children, he would often knock down the sand castles young Count Stollberg and I had built on the beach, and not only that but, being a few years older than we, had also beaten us mercilessly for daring to protest—this same man, in a loud and solemn yet congenially paternal voice, was now introducing me to the other guests, and I kept bowing in every direction, making sure everyone partook of my glance, just as they kept nodding, making certain their glances were polite enough and did not betray curiosity.

At luncheon and supper everyone could choose from the abundant selection of food and sit at one long table to emphasize the more informal, familial character of these meals, as opposed to dinner, which was served more ceremoniously at five in the afternoon and at which we dined in small groups at separate tables; now there was no need to wait until everyone arrived; with the help of waiters posted around the table, guests could start eating as soon as they sat down, and in this regard nothing had changed in twenty years—I wouldn't have been surprised to find Mother at my table, or Privy Councillor Peter van Frick, or my father and Fräulein Wohlgast—the very same elegant silver flatware made the same clanging sound on the pale-blue, garland-patterned plates, although they must have gone through several sets since then; the heavy silver serving dishes were arranged with the same casual artistry, offering their varied courses in the form of a quaint relief map dedicated to good taste and designed to titillate the palate: firm heads of light-green artichokes dipped in tangy marinade, lobsters red and steaming in their shells, translucent pink salmon, rows and rows of sliced glazed ham and delicately braised veal, caviar-filled eggs, crispy endives, golden strips of smoked eel on dewy lettuce, various pâtés shaped in cones and balls—game terrine with truffles, fish mousse, pâté de foie gras—slender pickled gherkins, slabs of yellow Dutch cheese, bluefish in aspic, tart, sweet, and pungent sauces and creams in cups and dainty pitchers; mounds of fragrant warm toast, fresh fruit in multitiered crystal shells, crayfish of various kinds and sizes, quails baked crispy red, tiny sausages still sizzling in a pan, nut-filled quince jellies (of which I could never have enough as a child), and of course there were the warm fragrances filling the room, the evanescent whiffs of perfumes, colognes, pomades, and powders released with every gesture, and the harmonious music of crackling, swishing, jangling, splashing, and clinking rising above and submerged in the waxing and waning din of chatter, laughter, sighs, giggles, and whispers; had one decided to stand aside for a moment to find a secure spot in this well-ordered confusion, one would feel as though one were about to cast oneself into a turbulent icy river: gaze already cloudlessly vacant, obliging smile already on his lips, occasionally freezing into an unpleasant grin, and in his muscles the stirrings of pompous self-awareness, necessary if one is to abandon cozy solitude and make contact with others in a safely inconsequential maneuver, because one knows that here anything might happen, even though the public setting precludes the possibility of anything meaningful; nowhere do we feel the pleasant and unpleasant theatricality of our existence, the reality of peaks and valleys in our falseness and in the noble obligation of lying, as we do in company, when everyone is as politely vague as we are elusive, the strain of simultaneous attack and retreat making them vague and unreachable, and this, in turn, makes us feel drained, tired, and superfluous when on our own, and at the same time gratefully light-headed, too, for at the secret bidding of our desires things happen which in reality do not.

And as faultless as our entrance may seem, it's always accompanied by something unpleasant which at such moments looms as an insurmountable obstacle or an acute embarrassment: sometimes the form and surface of our body, because no matter how carefully we draped it in the folds of our clothing, when terrified at being unable to find the place we had hoped to find in the gathering, we suddenly begin to feel awkward and ugly, our limbs too short or too long, perhaps because we want to be light, graceful, and attractive, really perfect; and then it may seem not the body but our ill-chosen, old-fashioned, or perhaps too fashionable suit that's embarrassing, a collar tight to the point of choking, a garish cravat, a sleeve too small at the shoulders, the seat of our pants stuck in the crack of our buttocks, not to mention the inner sensations that come on so strongly at just such moments: fine perspiration on the forehead, above the lips, on the back and in the armpits, or a parched throat, moist palms, a stomach that begins to rumble, rebelling against the contrived little social games, and bowels which seem always to choose these occasions to release malodorous winds caused by nervous digestion; and of course there is always somebody in such company whose mere presence is irritating, and we are ready to dispense with every reasonable consideration to give vent to antagonistic or perhaps amorous but in any case raw emotions, which must be restrained, of course, just as the sound of those foul winds from our lower body must be held in, because that is what the game is all about: to conceal everything that might be real, while making everything appear as convincingly and charmingly real as possible.

Perhaps it's a boon in such situations that one has no time to dwell on their unpleasantness and must let the fixed smile immediately give way to polite words.

It's as if a large pear had been shoved up our rectum and with the help of clever sphincters we must keep it in balance, neither sucking it in nor expelling it, which I must confess is how I feel in company, as I'm sure many other people do, as though we sense each other's presence in our constricted rumps—an unseemly matter, however shameless we may be.

As the waiter (wearing the same kind of green tailcoat as the valet) led me to my place, I was shocked, nearly rooted to the floor, to see at the table the two ladies who had been on the train with me.

But there was no time to deal with this, because as I took my place between my two immediate table companions, who were already conversing, I also had to glance at the others, which meant that even before the meal began, and because it was communal, I had to offer my face and eyes for their close inspection, which is always a very critical moment.

The man on my right was striking, with almost completely gray-white hair, sleek youthful skin, luxuriant bushy black brows, a thick mustache, a full mouth, and darkly flashing eyes framed in an aggressive smile, and he immediately captivated me: I wished I'd sat across from him instead of next to him; in a slightly strange accent, he asked me if I had arrived yesterday during that awful storm; at first I thought he spoke in a dialect I was unfamiliar with, but as he went on—telling me that after three days of the furious storm everybody complained of sleeplessness, naturally enough, because a storm, especially near water (in the mountains it is quite different, he knew from experience), plays havoc with one's nervous system, causing irritability and flaring tempers—I slowly realized he wasn't speaking in his native language, since he had a problem matching the tenses of the verbs in various parts of his sentences.

"It's all the more pleasant to see the morning sun again in all its splendor! isn't it glorious?" chimed in the man on my left, loudly, his mouth full, waving before my face a bite-size prawn on the tip of his fork, and he went on to explain that I shouldn't misunderstand him, he had nothing against the hotel's cuisine, it was splendid, glorious! but his taste ran to simpler fare, no sauces and spices for him! and if I wanted to taste something truly glorious, I should follow his example, the seafood here was fresh, crisp, tasty, and as you bite down it's glorious! you can feel the sea on your tongue.

Although he muttered "splendid, glorious," several more times later on, too, he seemed to be talking not so much to me as to the food he put in his mouth, because no matter how quickly and eagerly he made his food disappear, however pleasurably he crunched and chewed and ground and masticated the tasty morsels, it seemed it wasn't enough merely to satisfy his taste buds and he had to resort to voluble commentary to feel the certainty of total eating pleasure; around his plate lay little mounds of skin, bones, shells, and gristle, and later I saw that in spite of the waiters' efforts, carried out with a bemused, nearly devotional zeal, the greatest possible disorder surrounded his place setting, because he was always spilling, splashing, knocking over, or dripping something; his abrupt movements made his napkin slide off his lap, sometimes he had to retrieve it from under the table, there were crumbs everywhere, not just on the tablecloth but on his black and no doubt dyed goatee, on the wide lapels of his morning coat, on his less than spotless necktie; but all this did not seem to bother him at all, for only some minor accidents, say a piece of meat sliding out from under his knife, elicited apologetic gestures, and through it all he kept on chattering, with great gusto letting his sentences blend into his chewing and chomping, his Adam's apple bobbing up and down as he swallowed, while his face remained strangely motionless, unsmiling and tense, his wrinkled skin sallow and unhealthy-looking, his alarmed, deep-set eyes darting nervously in their shadowy sockets.

There must have been twenty guests sitting at the long table; only one setting, right across from me, remained untouched.

The younger of the two ladies was eating with her gloves on, which of course one couldn't help noticing, and as I looked at those unnaturally tight white gloves, I felt faint with the same weakness I'd felt the day before when, in our compartment on the train, she had so mercilessly revealed to me the secret of her hands.

I took my time unfolding my napkin—I knew I wasn't going to eat much at this meal—and sensed the furtive glances at my face, eyes, suit, and necktie.

I turned to the gray-haired gentleman on my right, who, incidentally, couldn't have been much older than I; he had broad shoulders, a thick neck, and a compact body; he wore a loose-fitting tan suit that went very well with his swarthy complexion, a somewhat lighter vest, and a lightly striped shirt, the sort of ensemble that was just becoming fashionable for daytime wear; in response to his earlier comment, I told him that I, too, had experienced some of the storm-related stress he spoke of, because, oddly enough, I was awakened by someone's shouts or screams, though it was conceivable, I continued with a candor surprising even for myself— most likely attributable to his confidence-inspiring looks—that no one was actually screaming and the sound was part of my unpleasant dream; in any case, I joined the ranks of those who complained of sleeplessness, although the first night at a new place, as we all knew, was never a reliable measure of one's true state; but by then he wasn't looking at me, seemed not to be hearing me anymore, a studied inattention in which there was something unpleasantly professorial, reminiscent of people who dole out their gestures, comments, and even silences with an air of all-knowing superiority and infallibility, thereby requiring us to be ingratiating, open, and sincere, using our own weakness to bolster their fragile egos; in the meantime, the man on my left was holding forth with what seemed like great expertise on methods of smoking and curing ham, a topic to which I had nothing to contribute, but so as not to appear indifferent, and to please him a little, I asked for a helping of prawns.

The older of the two ladies—whom I'd recognized on the train only after several hours of being together, when she fell asleep with her mouth open and her head kept drooping sideways—was not eating at all but watching her daughter do so, sipping her hot chocolate for the sake of appearances, I suppose, so she wouldn't seem completely idle.

And then I also started on my food.

"We can count on you, can we not, Councillor, to accompany us as soon as possible after breakfast?"

The old lady's voice was deep, husky, masculine, matching her large, bony frame, which made her dainty, lace-trimmed dress look rather like a stage costume.

"I confess I am getting impatient."

The two women sat inseparably close, closer perhaps than one might have deemed proper, and I had the impression it was the mother who needed this physical closeness, just as on the train when she almost fell on her daughter's shoulder though their bodies never actually touched.

And I recalled the contempt and considerable disgust with which the daughter had watched her sleeping and fitfully snoring mother.

Or could her contempt have been directed at me?

"By all means, madam, that's exactly what I've had in mind," replied the prematurely gray gentleman on my right, "of course, as soon as possible, though I must say that in the given situation anything is possible."

And again I had the feeling that the daughter was actually watching me, performing for me, avoiding my glance, of course, as I was avoiding hers.

"And may I be so bold as to inquire if you still remember the dream which you considered so unpleasant?" asked the gray-haired gentleman in his sleepy voice, turning to me suddenly.

"Indeed I do."

"And may I ask you to tell it to me?"

"My dream?"

"Yes, your dream."

For a moment we were both quiet, just looking at each other.

"I'm a sort of dream collector, you see, with a butterfly net, running after other people's dreams," he said, flashing his attractive teeth in a broad smile that was withdrawn the very next instant, as though his sullen black eyes had penetrated inside me and found something deeply suspicious; there was a glint of discovery in the dark of those eyes.

"But you mustn't think for a moment, Councillor, that I am rushing you!" said the old lady now, whereupon he turned to her as abruptly as he had to me a moment earlier—he seemed to enjoy making these sudden, unpredictable moves.

"It's also possible, of course," he said in the same sleepy, absentminded tone, "that the crisis was brought on only by the stormy weather, and just as the elements have subsided, the distraught organism will also come to rest, and do not consider this merely as vain reassurance, my lady, for there is good reason to hope that that is just what will happen."

I was only picking at my food, I didn't want to overburden my already constipated bowels.

I had missed my morning ritual, which I forgo only in extreme circumstances, and now it was for the third time; first there was my fiancée's unexpected visit, then the journey, and that morning the pleasant appearance of the valet, so for three days I had had no normal bowel movement.

"Well, how is it?" the man on my left asked.

"Oh, really splendid!"

And I couldn't tell which one of my two needs was more important, literary activity or the common daily evacuation, but with the passing years, I had to realize that in me the most abstract intellectual and the coarsest physical needs were so hopelessly intermingled that I could satisfy one only by satisfying the other.

Giving me his undivided attention now, the black-goateed gentleman watched me chew and swallow my food, opening his mouth and pursing his lips, a little as mothers do, moving their own lips to help their little tots gum their food, and then he looked around triumphantly as if to say that, as we can see, he was again right about something.

Usually, after getting out of bed in the morning, still unwashed and unshaven and with only a robe on, I head straight for my desk; if memory serves, I acquired this habit back in my parents' house after my father's terrible deed and even more dreadful suicide, when hours had to pass before I could start the day, since, without being aware of it, for years afterward I lived in the torpor of his story: I often found myself on the banks of an immense, majestic river, and if I didn't want to be swept away in the powerful current I had to grasp at brittle, dried-out branches of willows on the shore and pull myself from the silt, and as I did, I saw the gray, gurgling current twist and cradle and rush away with uprooted trees and dead bodies.

Sitting at my desk, staring out my window at the rooftops across the way and sipping my chamomile tea, I'd pull over a sheet of paper absently and jot down a sentence or two, casually, without much thought.

Hilde and I no longer had any secrets from each other; there were only the two of us left in the house; we rarely went out; the neglected summer garden was growing wild around us; sometimes we fell asleep in each other's arms, but without this closeness causing any sexual excitement; she was in her fortieth year then, I was nineteen; I knew that my father had violated the innocence of her warmly yielding body and then for years afterward used her, like an object, for his pleasure; and she knew she was holding in her arms the grown son of that beloved man who a few months earlier had raped, mutilated, and killed her niece, a rare beauty, a delicate girl-child whom she had brought into the house to help with the domestic chores.

Stories, curious little tales composed with no lofty intention, emerged from the sentences, while I waited for the slowly cooling bittersweet tea to loosen my bowels, sentences with which I could make myself forget the night that had just passed.

It happened that on one such morning I successfully relieved myself, thanks to Hilde's tea, but since the act always took a long time—I had to be careful not to squeeze it out too quickly or with too much strain, because that would leave a lot of it inside, and the powerful excremental smell stuck to my silk robe and my skin—I emerged from the toilet trailing the odorous cloud of my little daily victory, and then I saw Hilde standing before me, disheveled, uncombed, the blouse ripped from her chest, her eyes crazed, her lips literally bitten through; she hurled herself on me, gathered me close into her arms, sank her teeth into my neck, and then let out a howl the likes of which I had never heard coming from a human being; it came from deep inside her, with a force to split my ears, and she kept up the howling into my body until her own large frame buckled and she collapsed, dragging me with her to the stone floor.

The young lady stopped chewing, her gloved hands lowered the utensils to her plate.

She eyed the goateed man with the same mixture of contempt and disgust with which she had watched her mother on the train when the old lady slumped over and fell to snoring, but now I couldn't help noticing that this look of contempt and disgust had a certain flirtatious element, seeming a challenge rather than a snub, and when I glanced curiously at my neighbor I noticed that his mouth had stopped moving, too, and only his pointed beard was still quivering slightly with the effort to control himself, for the haughtiness of the young woman's gaze was forcing his own deep-set eyes to calm down, stop darting; they were not only most deeply engrossed in each other but also playing a game.

At the same time, the dignified old lady leaned toward me and apologized for having been forced to talk to the councillor about so weighty a matter, a wholly inappropriate topic at the breakfast table, she realized, and if she still preferred not to go into detail—the others at the table knew well, unfortunately, what she was referring to—it was only out of consideration for me, I must believe her, she did not want to disturb my surely cheerful mood with her troubles, she wanted to spare me! her words to the councillor were meant only as a reminder, she hoped that I would understand.

It was as if she and her fussing had stolen from me those few moments during which I had to assure her that I did understand fully and then had to thank her, producing one of my most obliging smiles, after which I found it hard to look back at the two, who in the meantime of course had gone on playing with each other—even more openly, I could just feel it, since they no longer had to worry about my inquisitive glance; I could see from the corner of my eye, even while listening politely to the mother, that her daughter had resumed chewing, having mesmerized the aging, vain man with the flirtatious disgust radiating from her rosy cheeks, but now she chewed with an amazing display of mimicry, copying his movements, chewing wildly, eagerly, imitating his insatiable appetite, making her chin quiver as if it were a beard, and this was only the beginning of their game, because the man, as if he'd just discovered how beautiful her face was, had no intention of being offended, the eagerness of his chewing simply shifting into his eyes, producing the leer of a shameless lecher, offering gratification—his deep-set, slightly squinting eyes seemed perfectly suited for this purpose—which, in turn, appeared to have a hypnotic effect on the girl; with their jaws locked for a moment, they looked at each other over the devastated table, and then the man started chewing again, carefully, demurely, almost girlishly, inviting her to chew along with him for a few ravenous beats; unbelievable as it may sound, they kept chewing and swallowing together, although there was nothing more in their mouths to chew or swallow.

But I had to stop watching them, because other startling events began to take place in the dining room, one after another at a frantic pace: in the glass-paneled door appeared a young man whose clothes alone were enough to raise eyebrows, and I had just raised my teacup to my lips when the councillor, on my right, still affecting a sleepy calm, made such a sudden, uncontrolled move with his elbow that I almost spilled my tea on the elderly lady, who was leaning forward to tell me something.

The young man flipped off his soft light-colored hat and handed it to a waiter standing nearby; a golden crown of hair, a mass of long blond curls, nearly exploded from under the hat; instead of a jacket, the young man wore a bulky white sweater and a matching scarf wrapped around his neck a few times and slung over his shoulder—clearly not a sign of good upbringing—he must have just returned from a brisk morning walk; his face reddened by the wind; he was cheerful, somewhat impudent, judging not just from his attire but from his whole attitude, his springy walk and open smile; while the councillor and I excused ourselves for the near-mishap, the young man hastened to his chair, nodding in all directions—he appeared to be on friendly terms with everyone—smiled, giggled, unwrapped his funny scarf and put it on the back of the chair, and the elderly lady across the table, who first became aware of the young man's presence by noticing the amazement on my face, now beamed at his lanky figure and seized his wrist with her ring-studded hand.

"Oh, ce cher Gyllenborg," she exclaimed, "quelle immense joie de vous voir aujourd'hui!"

He drew the ring-studded hand to him and kissed it gently, the gesture being at once less and more than gallant.

By then a waiter behind us whispered something into the councillor's ear, and at the same time the hotelkeeper appeared in the doorway, looking shocked, and then with a dumb expression in our direction seemed to be looking for our reaction to something that was about to happen.

Before taking his seat, the young man hastened to the delicately slender older lady enthroned at the head of the table. She leaned back in pleasurable anticipation of a kiss and offered up her clear brow framed by an elaborate silver-gray pompadour.

"Avez-vous bien dormi, Maman?" we heard him say.

At this point the councillor rose, kicking the chair out from under him with such force that it would have fallen over had a waiter not caught it, and dispensing with all etiquette, he dashed out of the dining room.

His squat figure had almost vanished in the dimness of the lounge beyond the glass door when he evidently changed his mind, turned, for a moment he and the hotelier stared at each other, and then the councillor rushed back and whispered something into the elderly lady's ear, who was none other—at last I can reveal it—than the Countess Stollberg, the mother of my childhood playmate and also the mother of the gloved young lady.

I had known this all along; I could have revealed my identity on the train but chose not to, because then inevitably my father's name would have come up, and in view of what had happened to him, I would have found it impossible to talk about him.

There was no one in the room now who did not sense that he was witnessing not just an unusual but a very grave event.

Suddenly there was silence.

The young man was still standing next to his mother's chair.

The two women rose slowly, and then all three of them hurriedly left the room.

The rest of us remained in the silence; no one wanted to stir; some clinking was the only sound to be heard.

And then in a voice touched with emotion, the hotelier announced that Count Stollberg was dead.

I stared at the prawns on my plate; perhaps everyone was staring at his plate; the young man stopped in front of his untouched place setting and picked up his scarf from the chair—I could see all this without taking my eyes off my plate.

"Bien! Je ne prendrai pas de petit déjeuner aujourd'hui," he said softly, and then added, somewhat inappropriately: *"Que diriez-vous d'un cigare?"*

I looked up at him, astonished, because I wasn't sure he was talking to me.

But he smiled at me and I stood up.

PART III

The Year of Funerals

I couldn't cry; the last time I cried was about a year and a half earlier at my mother's funeral, when the frozen clumps of earth began raining down on the coffin, knocking and rumbling, echoing inside it, and I felt the rumbling in my brain, in my stomach, in my heart, the dreadful noise knocking apart an inner peace of the body I hadn't even known before, making me aware—abruptly, with no warning—of the misery of my physical existence.

And if up to then no crying, emotional upheaval, fear, joy, or shock could touch this darkly unconscious inner peace, from then on everything seemed to function as if turned inside out: colors, shapes, surfaces, and textures that could be described as beautiful or ugly simply lost their meaning, yet the stomach went on digesting with nervous spasms when food was shoved into it; the heart beat cautiously, as if looking out for itself, to pump the blood through the veins; intestines grumbled reluctantly, stinking as they twisted with irritation; urine stung the skin it issued from; with each breath the raw pain of having a body wanted to escape the lungs but couldn't, and remained within; and this anxiety— for no physical function could expel the soul's oh so profound pains— made me hear my own breathing, which sounded as if any minute I might gasp my last breath; I was nauseated by my own physical existence, yet every nerve in my body was trying to gauge what was happening inside me, or what else might happen, though outwardly I remained calm, impassive, nearly indifferent to everything around me, and of course I couldn't cry, either.

From time to time, however, something did break to the surface, like phlegm coughed up, and each time this happened I hoped that the warmth of the tears would take me back to the radiant oblivion of childhood, where the gentle strength of an embracing arm can offer consolation; but it was that very thing, that embracing warmth, that was missing, and what forced itself through from time to time was not crying but bursts of cold, wrenching shivers that no one would have noticed had anyone cared to watch me, because they passed quickly and with scarcely an external sign.

Actually, I was playacting, even finding pleasure in my new role; it pleased me that I was burdening no one with complaints about my physical and mental anguish.

On the afternoon about which I'd like to speak, now that I'm nearing the end of my story, I was lolling in bed and aware—if it's possible to describe the state of fatal anticipation with such an intimate word—of silence, a silence in which one feels the total absence of grace; that's the kind of silence that pervaded the house as the cloudy December twilight was descending, softly, heavily; considering the state I was in, this was the most welcome time of the day, since light repulsed me at least as much as did the sensations of my own body or darkness itself, and only the dimness of dusk promised relief; all the doors were wide open, no one had turned on the lights anywhere in this suddenly alien house where, because of the coal shortage, the radiators were only lukewarm, and now and again Aunt Klára's powerful voice reached me from the distant dining room, as she kept up her unrelenting dialogue with Grandmother's silence, which had become more or less permanent: the day Father took my little sister away from her and put her in an institution somewhere near Debrecen, Grandmother had stopped talking; although I could not make out the faraway words, not that I was listening especially, my ears did register this curious, one-way, emotional pulsation that, in another sense, seemed to echo my mother's voice, as if something of hers had lived on, something familiar and vaguely reassuring.

This was the twenty-eighth day of December in the year 1956; the reason I remember so clearly is that the next day, the twenty-ninth of December, was the day we buried Father.

When the doorbell rang for the second time, I heard footsteps, the door opening, and muffled words; a short while later, not to make it too obvious that I didn't care who might be coming or what else might happen that day, I sat up in bed; Hédi Szán was standing in the doorway.

If I wanted to be more accurate, I'd have to say that an awkward creature with arms much too long dangling at her side was standing there, a human form in the dimness reflecting off white walls, a little girl dressed as a woman, a frightened child who bore little resemblance to the beautiful, captivating, grown-up, womanly Hédi I had once known.

She stood there in her mother's fur-collared coat, an ancient coat fished out of mothballs, but everything she had on looked wrong, and she appeared to be exhausted, in need of sleep; her hair—that luxuriant, beguiling golden mane that used to flow and bounce with every step she took, its thick strands rippling with her slightest move, that fragrant forest I so enjoyed sinking my fingers into—was now hanging down like a piece of strange fabric, a limp and colorless frame for her face; her skin was chapped by the cold, she seemed to shiver with fright, looking as if she had got into a predicament against her will; perhaps she was very much like everyone else in those days.

But I wasn't really interested in her loss of beauty, the beauty she perhaps never possessed, or in her coat; it was the look in her eyes that hurt so much, seeing her so frightened and unsmiling; I smiled at her so she wouldn't see my own pain; it was her helpless empathy that hurt, that pathetic attempt learned from adults to wade into other people's suffering without feeling the suffering itself.

I felt my whole being recoil from her in protest and dread, because I knew why she had come.

Still, there was one calming aspect of her appearance, rather appropriate to the circumstances: she was wearing hiking boots and thick socks folded down at the ankles.

She said hello and I must have done the same, though I remember only my forced smile, because I wanted to give her one of those bright, carefree smiles that used to be ours, to smile at her as if nothing had happened and nothing could happen so long as we both had this smile; we took a few steps toward each other, then stopped, hesitated; it seemed odd and repulsive to both of us to meet this way, in roles that made us remember, and remind one another, of all that had happened; there had been too many tragedies, too many deaths; to get over the hard part, I laughed and said it was really nice of her to come, after all, we hadn't seen each other since my mother's funeral.

My laugh seemed to increase her fright and she must have taken my words as a reproach; her big eyes welled with tears—who knows how long those tears had been in the making! and to hold them in, and also to keep me from rebuking her further, she threw back her head defiantly, her hair flowing through the air almost as in the old days; no, that's not the reason she had come, she hadn't lost her mind completely yet, she didn't want to hurt me, there was nothing she could say to me, anyway, she just came to say goodbye to us—that's how she said it: to us—because there was a fairly promising opportunity the next morning: someone had agreed for a reasonable price to take them as far as the border town of Sopron, and there they would see, she said, and shrugged her shoulders; she had gone to Livia and to the Hűvöses, and at Livia's nobody was at home, so if I saw her I should tell her—well, just what to tell her?—on second thought, just tell her that she was here and that she left! and since she had come through the woods, she thought she'd drop by Kálmán's, too; then she fell silent and waited for me, her eyes pleading, imploring me to make her believe the unbelievable, and quickly, too, because there was a curfew and she had to get home.

And then she couldn't stop talking, and forcing her tears back, she rambled on about the situation, explaining things in great detail—but about the important thing, the one thing that touched us both most deeply, she said not a word, almost as if trying to protect us; still, she changed, was transformed back to her old self, not beautiful, but strong, which may have been what we had thought of as beautiful in her before.

Yes, I said.

I had to utter this dry, unemphatic yes without a confirming nod, while looking straight into her eyes so she couldn't get away from it, though I felt how cruel it was, even savagely pleasant, to tear someone's foolish hope to shreds, a hope that can't deal with unalterable certainties, cruel even when the other person knows all too well that the yes can never become a no, that it will forever remain a humiliating yes.

There was no need for us to elaborate on this yes; she told me the bare essential—they were leaving the country—and from this terse announcement, which I must say didn't affect me all that much, I also grasped that owing to some possibly tragic occurrence not all three but only two of them were leaving; she used the plural, but without the usual rancor or peevish, childish spite; my ears missed the intonation that used to refer to her mother's lover, who had come between mother and daughter; we didn't have much time, but regarding the lover the possibilities were clear: either he had died or was lying wounded somewhere or maybe had left the country himself or been arrested, because if he had disappeared from their lives for other, personal reasons, the hatred for him would have been there in her voice, and the two women setting out by themselves, entrusting the lover to the care of impersonal history, for me became as much a part of the realm of insensitive yeses as everything Hédi had been able to learn in the past few hours about my own fortunes, and about Kálmán's death, had become for her.

In other words, my yes meant I knew she knew everything she needed to know about Kálmán and about me, there was nothing I needed to add, just as she didn't have to elaborate on her story, for she must have known I knew all I needed to know.

Wide-eyed—no, with eyes opened wide—we looked at each other, or more precisely, we weren't looking at each other but in each other's eyes we were staring at that mutually understood, impersonal, volatile, and for some reason profoundly shameful yes, which could only allude to death and to the countless dead, perhaps in each other's eyes we were looking at the shame of the survivors, the facts that needed no explanation yet were inexplicably irrevocable, looking in each other's eyes as if we needed to gain time, despite our fretful haste, enough time for the glint of disgrace to fade from our open eyes, but fade into what, where to? into talk, clarification, recollections, and explanations? but what was there to recollect or explain if in the moment of saying goodbye we couldn't have a common future and there was nothing to be salvaged from our common past? and if neither of us could even cry, how could we possibly reach out and touch in a truly human way?

So we remained silent, not because we didn't have anything to say, but because the indescribable number of things that needed to be said became incommunicable in our shared despair and shame at our hopelessness; only by severing the bonds of mutual understanding could we escape the shame of our common fate and make an effort to forget.

That living taciturnity became our common future; for her it lay where she was fleeing to, for me here, where I was staying, a not very significant difference; our features were locked into themselves, self-protective and tactfully hiding their own pain, and our eyes, which even in their indifference were caressing and soothing one another, despite their understanding were now forbidden to find the common ground that glances can share; this was going to be our new bond: the will to end it all, even though we were still alive! all this we still had in common, in spite of everything, and we knew we did.

It wasn't just her, it was impossible for me to tell anything to anybody, I couldn't, and I didn't want to.

What died in me was the need to talk to others, rotting away along with the bodies of my dead friends, and she was going away.

The chairs were there, standing around the table in the darkening room, four forlorn chairs around the table, and it occurred to me that I ought to ask her to sit down, as was proper, except that along with those chairs—on which she had never sat, by the way—there also stood between us all those afternoons when she would fly into my room and, without stopping her flow of words, throw herself on my bed and lie there stretched out on her back or stomach.

I asked her, as if this was the most important of all questions, about Krisztián, what would happen to him now that she was leaving, and we both knew this was only my effort to spare us from dealing with the truly crucial questions.

A tiny wry smile appeared around her immobile mouth, wise and sardonic; she must have thought my evasion too crude, too sentimental, superfluous, and she said she had taken care of all that, a supercilious smile on her arching lips; they hadn't seen each other for a long time, she continued, shrugging her shoulders, letting me know she would not say goodbye to Krisztián—another thing, I thought, that would remain unfinished and painful; she would write to him from the free world, she said sarcastically, quoting the phrase so familiar from radio programs broadcasting messages from refugees; besides, the thing they had between them was rather childish anyway, though Krisztián was no doubt handsome, and then suddenly, openly, emerging for a moment from behind her cynical look, she flashed her teeth in a harsh, coarse smile and said I could have him! uglier boys now appealed to her more, which meant, she was sorry to say, that I was also out of the running.

If she hadn't said that, if she hadn't blurted out the words and made them public between the two of us, if with her laughter she hadn't exposed this most profound secret of mine, which I so longed to put out of my mind, if with this exposure she hadn't disgraced the bond that was our past, then she probably would have found it much more difficult to leave the country; today I think I understand this better.

But then, as we watched each other's defenseless eyes from the dreadful shelter of our stiffening faces, this new shame made the mutually understood yes of the earlier moment turn into a final, irrevocable no.

Any remaining sense of fellowship would have been too painful; a denied one did not hurt, and could be forgotten.

Later in life it often happened that in the faces of complete strangers I'd see Hédi's, distorted and ugly, as she was saying goodbye; it would happen in the most mundane circumstances when I'd see around me immobile yet vibrant faces that even in their hostility could arouse deeply intimate emotions, and while I felt that no matter how much I might try to listen, to give myself to them, to trust them, some inner aversion, a paralysis brought on by vestiges of true feelings despite all the denial, would hold me back, a painful numbness somehow familiar from the far past, and over the years my face changed accordingly, as if an additional face had grown to cover over my own—distrustful, incapable of giving, frightened, made aggressive by constant fear for itself, trying to appear too hard to hide what was too soft, saying yes and no at the same time and doing even that reluctantly, with neither affirmation nor denial wanting to get entangled in any kind of fellowship—and it was as if I saw my own distorted face in all those selfish, hesitant, hurt, sly, apparently attentive looks, in those craftily conciliatory faces with their feigned joviality, which could attack or snub you at any moment, eyes quickly avoiding a stranger's glance, trying to avoid the shame of being unable to make real contact; later, when I began to think about these matters, I had the impression that everyone, without exception (though variously influenced by this persuasion or that affiliation), carries in his face the events of the past they would like to forget and make others forget by hiding them behind artificially altered, deliberately cryptic features.

For this reason I did not think it an accident that after that all-too-quickly forgotten farewell, whose duly deserved pain was denied us, many many long years had to pass, nearly my entire youth, before I could break the mutually agreed-upon silence and for the first time—not counting this written confession, perhaps for the last time, too—begin talking about it, and talk with the same compulsiveness with which I had been keeping it to myself, and talk to a stranger, a foreigner, someone who could have only the vaguest notion about it, and do this in a foreign language, standing in a Berlin streetcar; and there, once I began, it all came up with raw force, like bloody vomit.

It was Sunday, evening, another autumn, when the warm air was already suffused with a mist you could feel—it had a taste, and a metallic smell—and the lit-up streetcar clattered along in its leisurely way in the dark city already deserted despite the early hour.

As was our custom, we were standing in the empty car, because there, under the pretext of holding on to the straps, we could hold hands without attracting attention; we were on our way to the theater, and—I no longer remember how we got on the subject—Melchior began to talk about the 1953 Berlin uprising, when on the morning of June 16, under overcast skies, two zealous Party workers were proceeding unsuspectingly to Block 40 of Stalin Allee, then still under construction and later renamed Karl Marx Allee, to tell a discontented and of course starving group of brick-layers, carpenters, and roofers why raising the work quota was an absolute economic necessity, but somehow that morning the workers did not seem to comprehend what was so clearly comprehensible—of course it was a nasty morning—and, what's more, demanded that the new quotas be immediately rescinded, and then they chased away the two indignant and angry agitprop men, in fact were close to beating them up, and then about eighty of them began marching in closed ranks toward Alexanderplatz, chanting newly made-up slogans; listen to this one, Melchior said: "We are workers, no more slaves, Berliners to the barricades!"

The emotions erupting in the crude rhyme of the jingle, which Melchior found prosodically flawless, and his evocation of the little group of workers growing into an unstoppable human tidal wave; the open platform of the autumn streetcar bathed in yellow light; Melchior's palm, having lost some of its loving sensitivity, resting more lightly on my hand—and no wonder: any love dipped into history lightens by an amount equal to the weight of the historical moments it displaces, the streetcar's clanging little jolts, the taste on my tongue of the warm yet sharp evening air, the sardonic curl of Melchior's lips smiling to keep his distance from himself and his story, the conspiratorial emotions tempered by sparks of humor in his eyes, the familiar old slogans that sounded even more ominously factual when spoken in a foreign language—phrases like "agitprop," and "production quota," and "economic interests of the people"—all these things stirred something in me, I don't quite know what.

I sensed this as I used to feel the excitement and tension of being constantly on the alert: in my feet and in my hands, and also in my face, as if it had freed itself from its old paralysis.

I was thrust back, moved off dead center, given an unsought, not even consciously desired release; in Melchior's narrative the ever-swelling Berlin crowd had not yet reached Alexanderplatz, but my own Hungarian streetcar was already stalled in the midst of a dark throng on Marx Square in Budapest, at the spot where the tracks, screeching softly under the wheels, curve in a gentle arc onto Szent István Boulevard.

Laborers abandoning their scaffolds, housewives on their shopping rounds, students, street urchins, office workers, shop assistants, ordinary onlookers, loafers, dogs too, probably, the procession caught and swept everybody along, Melchior continued with hushed excitement; having swollen to such an enormous size, the crowd seemed to lose direction and then shouts went up: "To Leipziger Strasse, to Leipziger Strasse!" which suddenly became the common will, the current shifted, and the marchers headed toward the government buildings; then two Party workers appeared in front of them, planted themselves in the middle of the still empty street, and tried pathetically, with their bodies, to hold back the angry human tide, which, by then twelve thousand strong, propelled by its own mass and volition, was spreading calmly: "Bloodshed must be avoided!" yelled one of the Party workers; "Don't go to the Western sector!" shouted the other; and the crowd, as if letting out a collective sigh, came to a momentary halt; "You're not going to shoot at us, are you?"—words heard from the first rows, and "If you cross over, we shall!"; later, people said that only two words, "bloodshed" and "shoot," registered with the crowd and rippled through the square within seconds, and then, with the force of helpless rage they surged forward, because their own words were "bread" and "decent wages" and therefore they had to sweep the Party workers out of the way.

We were holding on to the railing, hungrily taking in the spectacle from the slowly moving streetcar, and could see only the tops of people's heads, a not only unfamiliar but completely incomprehensible sight; it was warm in the big, poorly lit square, though it wasn't only the unseasonably balmy air that generated the heat but also masses of people jostling, swirling, trampling on bits of newspaper and torn leaflets, coming from all directions in pairs or in packed, endless columns, singly or in groups, shouting slogans, waving flags, walking every which way, giving the impression of being in complete chaos and at cross purposes, yet the various clustering and dispersing groups seemed to hinder no one, but on the contrary, as if unafraid of colliding with or being impeded by anyone, people proceeded confidently, even at a leisurely pace, to their goal, a whole city having poured out of its houses, factories, restaurants, schools, and offices; here and there you could see policemen standing at the edge of the sidewalk, quite far apart from one another, looking listless and indifferent but mostly helpless and superfluous, for they wouldn't have known what to do with the flood of people streaming through the freshly opened cracks and probably didn't intend to do anything, which created the strange impression that contradictory goals and intentions are permissive toward one another because in them (or above them) is a guiding principle more powerful than any single one of them, an invisible force unifying everything, just as all the shouting and singing, all the jubilantly chanted slogans and jingles ferociously belted out, all the tapping, pounding, shuffling of thousands of feet turned into one wild yet cheerful rumble, as light as the fine edge of the warm evening mist, though even in the impersonal, uniform hum of the huge mass, in its evenly rising and falling sounds, one could distinguish isolated participants who did not want to be part of anything, who simply stared from the sidelines, considering it their mission to be mere observers, or those who hadn't decided whether to join in or hurry on silently and unobtrusively with their strictly personal business, laden with packages and shopping bags, fumbling with curious, restless children who had to be dragged out of harm's way.

With a slight jolt the streetcar came to a stop, the conductor signaled the end of the run by turning off all the lights, and we jumped off; I was there with two of my classmates whom I had very little to do with before (or after) this evening: a tall, strong boy with a beautiful face, István Szentes, who for some reason was always angry and pouting, often hitting out before thinking, and Stark, who kept blinking his sad, deep, dark eyes, and who wanted to be in on everything but was always afraid of retaliation, who seemed to be driven by an unquenchable thirst for experience.

Listen, fellas, he kept repeating now, I think I'll go home, I guess I'll be going home, he said, and then he stayed with us.

But this is what made the situation so wonderful, so great, so extraordinary: the moment we jumped off the streetcar we were caught up by the irresistible force of the crowd and joined a group of young workers who were singing "Red Csepel Island, lead the struggle, Váci Road, jump in the fray!" and their "Váci Road" became a full-throated, tuneless roar, as if they were eager to let everyone know, not just the crowd but, via the dark autumn sky, the whole world, that that is where they were coming from: straight from dingy, industrial Váci Road, in fact straight from the showers, with their hair still wet; now that we were in the thick of things, no longer watching from above or outside, there was no question as to where we were going or why, and it wasn't as if we couldn't extricate ourselves from the crowd, for no familiar force kept us there; of all possible routes we chose the crowd's precisely because in those hours its exhilarating sense of liberation left open all possibilities, allowed for everything, and with all possibilities thus open, one is free to choose anything, even what occurs accidentally, at random, the only condition being to keep moving, and by satisfying this most elemental need, the body's natural impulse to move, I associate myself with everyone around me, I am coming with them just as they are coming with me.

And so it happened that my two classmates, with whom I yielded to the dictates of chance and found myself in this enormous crush, suddenly became very close to me, defined and helped express my own feelings as if discarding all my old inhibitions and resistance, making them useless and laughable, became my friends, lovers, and brothers, as if they, and only they, could make all these other faces familiar, faces that, even without my knowing them, were no longer strange to me.

It was this peculiar, curiously stirring feeling that Stark put into words: he was scared of something he liked, he wanted to run away from feeling good about being there, so Szentes, to let us know that he, too, was in tune with these feelings, and also to stifle Stark's inevitable second thoughts, grinned broadly and slapped Stark on the back, and though it was a hard slap, all three of us acknowledged it with a burst of laughter.

In those early evening hours the crowd had not yet swallowed me up, made me disappear within it, trampled me underfoot, or taken away my personality as it did so often afterward, but generously allowed me to experience—in the most elementary condition of my body's life, in the act of movement—my kinship with others, what is common to us all, let me feel that we were part of one another and that, all things considered, everyone is identical with everyone else, and rather than all this making the crowd faceless, as crowds are usually described, I received my own face from the crowd just as I gave it one myself.

I was neither stupid nor uninformed, knew well where I was and had a good notion of what was happening around me, was so involved that in the next few moments I experienced the movement and emotions of the crowd as something intimate and familial, and thus we were marching and laughing when from the direction of Bajcsy-Zsilinkszky Road the open-hatched turret of a tank appeared, accompanied by the deafening grind and screech of its tracks and the deep rumble of its engine; at first it seemed as if the steel barrel trained on us was being floated above us by the heads in the crowd, though quickly enough bodies pulled aside, cutting a wide path for it; steps slowed down or quickened, and silence prevailed, the ambiguous silence of wary anticipation; yet the tank's approach, like that of a huge wave that might engulf us all, was greeted by a triumphant roar from the crowd, because in the bluish-brown cloud of fumes we saw that unarmed soldiers were standing inside the open turret or sitting around its rim, waving to convey peaceful intentions, and in the overwhelming noise we could pick out individual words, fragments of sentences stumbling over one another: "brothers," "boys," "the army's with us," "Hungarians"; Szentes was also catching some of the words and roared them back so fiercely it was as if for the first time in his life he could tear out his anger by the roots, as if he had been finally liberated, cleansed; "Don't shoot!" he cried, and just a few steps away we saw the soldiers waving and grinning, I didn't shout and had good reason not to, but grinned back just the same, and around us young workers with wet hair responded with similar grins, blaring in unison at the soldiers: "If you're a Magyar, you're with us!" to which unseen heads replied from a distance: "Petőfi's and Kossuth's people, all together, hand in hand!"

In those days Marx Square was still laid out with sparkling dark cobblestones, and as the tank changed direction with a cumbersome yet graceful quarter turn, heading for a space between two stranded streetcars in the middle of the square, the stones threw off sparks under the grating tracks; there was an earsplitting crunch, and then silence, though this time it was the silence of excited anticipation, as when on a soccer field everyone's favorite center forward manages to pull out of a hopeless situation and let loose with a powerful kick, the crowd was holding its breath of collective excitement, for it was unclear whether the space between the two streetcars was big enough for the tank; eyes were involuntarily measuring the gap, both dreading and wishing for the possible clash of the two masses of metal, as if they sensed what was still to come that evening and would surely happen—the inevitable—but as the delicate operation was accomplished successfully, the silence turned into an even more jubilant victory cry, a release of primal joy, and now I found no reason to withhold my own shouts; the tank clattered off toward Váci Road.

We moved on, but after a few steps there was another halt, an unanticipated bottleneck, and we could only shuffle forward, almost in place, progress reduced to barely a crawl; in front of the Album of Smiles photo studio an immovable throng of people was jamming the broad curving sidewalk and the roadway itself was blocked by abandoned streetcars, but the crowd showed no signs of impatience.

In front of the lit-up window of the photo studio, a slight woman in a raincoat was standing on a crate; actually, all that could be seen was the slender silhouette of a female figure rather high up, because only her feet were blocked by the bobbing heads of her listeners, straining to hear; her immobile body seemed tense with anger, she was throwing her head back, shaking it, turning and thrusting it in all directions, piercing the air as with a dagger, as if she were yanking all her movements out of her chest and belly; her long hair streamed, collapsed, floated around her, and she didn't fly away only because her stubborn defiance kept her feet glued to the crate. Szentes jabbed my leg with his wooden drawing board, urging me to look: he was taller than I and noticed the woman first, but just then Stark began reading off a list of demands from a handbill he had fished out from under a forest of feet: "Five: away with obstructionists; six: down with Stalinist economics; seven: long live fraternal Poland; eight: workers councils in factories; nine: agricultural recovery, voluntary cooperatives; ten: a constructive plan of action for the nation"—we could barely hear the woman's voice, but Stark interrupted his reading and, as if this were the most natural thing in the world, joined the woman by mouthing the words along with her, "...as they sink into hell, with mast and sail broken, in tatters hang..." and it did not surprise me, on the contrary, it filled me with warm waves of satisfaction that the patriotic poem so well known to all of us was being recited by a relative of mine— the woman on the crate was my cousin Albert's ex-wife, from the town of Győr—to whom about a year and a half earlier I had wanted to run away, somewhat foolishly but with a confidence in her that had no real basis, just to escape from my own home and my parents.

However silly this may sound, I'll say it: the moment I heard her, I was reassured that I wasn't alone in this crowd with my special personal and family history, that everybody was here with his or her unique situation, and these peculiarities could not challenge or doubt one another, for then all the feelings that had become common to us would have had to be challenged, too, so it didn't even occur to me to go over to her or to tell the others that I knew her, it remained my own pleasurable little secret and ultimate proof that I was at the right place; little Verochka— as my mother waggishly called this budding actress—was up there de- claiming her poem and I was down here, one of the marchers; she was as much entitled to her place as I to mine, even if I refrained from shouting with all those who now had every right to shout, like Szentes, for example, who, knowing full well who my father was, had lit into me during an argument just a few weeks earlier—purple with rage and ready to strike, he screamed into my face that "we lived in a chicken coop, d'you hear? in a chicken coop, like animals!"—or like Stark, who lived near here, in Visegrádi Street, but was now choosing not to go home, who also a few weeks earlier had offered to let me use his drawing pen when the item was unavailable in the stores, but because their apartment was locked, we had to go to the synagogue next door to find his mother, a cleaning woman there, who came with us and opened the door of the ground-floor apartment where the table was already set for two, with only a tiny pot on the stove; my embarrassed protestations notwithstanding, I had to eat my friend's mother's lunch, because she let me understand, with infinitely refined humility, that she knew who my father was; nevertheless, we all got along, each of us carrying his own burden, and I had the right to feel what the others felt, especially since no one had challenged it; in any case, I earned this right, even if my own particular situation seemed to contradict it, because I most carefully distinguished between the concepts of revolution and counter-revolution and did so from the moment I recognized Verochka in that woman on the crate, and because I was neither uninformed, insensitive, nor stupid; I was sure, I knew, that this was a revolution, that I was in the middle of it, in the middle of a revolution which Father, if he were here, would surely recognize; and I also knew he couldn't possibly be here, I had no idea where he could be, he probably had to be hiding somewhere, much to his shame, but if he were here he would tell me that this was exactly the opposite of what I thought it was, he'd call it a counter-revolution.

The words "revolution" and "counter-revolution" occurred to me in their precise, clearly understood forms, guiding me through the thicket of emotional distinctions and identifications that until then had seemed terrifying, stifling, and hopeless, two words whose meaning, weight, and political significance I had learned so early, so precociously, from the conversations and debates among my father and his contemporaries, yet I want to stress that at that moment—and for me this was the revolution—I thought of these words not in their terms, not as a pair of antithetical political concepts borrowed from their vocabulary, but as something intensely personal, as if one of them was his body and the other my own, as if, each of us with his own word, we were standing at opposite ends of a single emotion generated by a common body; This is revolution, I kept repeating, as though I were saying it to him, uttering the word with dark vengeance, gratified to get even with him for everything, not quite knowing what, to which he could respond only with his own word, the very opposite of mine, and therefore I did not feel any distance between us, did not feel that he was removed from me but just the opposite: his body, caved in on itself, stooped, looking pitiful ever since my mother's death, that body the mere sight of which had evoked my fear of dreadful futility, his broken body in which—even after the previous June, after the public disgrace of being suspended for his role in some political trials— he had managed to find enough defiant energy to conspire with some suspicious characters he now called friends, that body was, strange to say, as close to me as it had been when as a small child I had climbed on his beautiful naked body, completely naked and pretending I was part of his dream, and, driven by a secret desire to discover our sameness, reached between his thighs; now I was more cool-headed, knowing well that, physical identity notwithstanding, differences were differences; and here I was, marching with these people I hardly knew yet felt to be brothers, for somehow they meant the same to me as Krisztián had, whose father was killed in the war, and Hédi, whose father was taken to a concentra- tion camp, and Livia, who had to live on scraps from the school kitchen, and Prém, whose father was a drunken fascist, and Kálmán, who was branded a class alien on account of his father, and Maja, with whom I had searched for evidence of treason in Father's papers so that she and I, deceived by our innocence and gullibility, could immerse ourselves in the filth of the age, an abomination that could not be forgotten, something we must still try to put behind us; while marching with these people I presumed their fear, call it worry or concern because I knew what they might be up against, having read the faces of my father's friends gathering at our house; at the same time I also had to fear for Father's racked and tense body, which had grown wild with fever, had to protect it from the flood I was becoming a part of, but knew that I no longer could, knew that I didn't want to resist my own erupting emotions.

We pressed ahead, jostled our way out onto the boulevard.

Defining myself in terms of concepts—my grandparents' strict moral concepts that regulated emotions and passions to fit their middle-class way of life, my parents' more elusive ideological and political concepts—was a not unfamiliar exercise expressing well the kind of upbringing I had, and so it was natural that the self-definition with which I tried in this crowd to separate, indeed sever myself once and for all from my father, quickly changed me back into a small child, for my concern about him, the child's need to identify with him, sympathize with and understand him, proved to be the stronger bond, since ultimately it was with his concepts of myself that I had to justify being here, in this crowd, now, in this situation—or was it our shared grief over Mother's death? as we were finally thrust through the bottleneck and began to run to catch up with the people in front of us—the most elemental need in a crowd is to close ranks—my stuffed schoolbag kept knocking against my legs, my drawing board and long T-square flapping awkwardly from side to side, subtracting something from the revolution, reminding me of my helplessness and confusion, trying to make me admit that this was not for me; each tug and knock seemed to be tapping out this message as rhythmically as they had tapped out revolution just minutes earlier; I felt I had to get home, if only to be rid of these bothersome objects; no problem, I kept telling myself, we were moving in the right direction, I was running among people who did not appear to be bothered by thoughts like mine; I'll get across Margit Bridge somehow, I told myself, and then get on a streetcar, though I was sure I wouldn't find Father at home.

What also seemed reassuring in this plan was that my home was far away, well outside this area that was becoming dangerous even emotionally, up on the hill, far above the city.

And I guessed right: he turned up only a week later, and until then we had no news of him, not even a telephone call, nothing.

It happened on a late afternoon while I was standing with Krisztián in front of our garden gate; it was on the twenty-eighth or twenty-ninth of October, and we were discussing the makeup of the new government—no, it was the twenty-eighth, now I remember, because I had a loaf of bread under my arm, it was the day the bakeries reopened, a Sunday, the first time Kálmán's father's bakery had fresh bread again; Krisztián was telling me how he had managed to get back from Kalocsa, giggling nervously as he told the story, and I knew that the giggles were meant to cover up our efforts not to talk about Kálmán; the year before, after a long struggle, Krisztián had gotten into a military academy; his greatest wish had always been to become an officer, like his father; they happened to be in Kalocsa, on fall maneuvers, when the revolution broke out, and the cadets were simply let go, right in the middle of the field; of course, they had to get rid of their uniforms, because people kept mistaking them for members of the National Security Service, and it was right about then that suddenly Krisztián said, Look, there's your father! and sure enough, down by the hedges, where our garden adjoined the restricted area, Father was hurling himself over the fence.

Embarrassed and blushing over his embarrassment, Krisztián said goodbye; I'd better be going, he said with a last giggle, and I understood well that he didn't want to witness this clandestine homecoming, so he left quickly in the descending dusk, and that was the last time I ever saw him; in the meantime, Father was hurrying up the hill, but instead of cutting across the lawn he followed the curving path of bushes along the edge of our garden and came up under the trees; from a slight jerk of his head I could tell he had seen me; he looked not at all the way I had imagined him during those anxious days of his absence, and I knew, as somebody once told me, that nothing ever is the way we imagine it; he was wearing somebody else's clothes: under a thin raincoat he had on a light summer suit, crumpled and ragged-looking and spattered with mud though it hadn't rained for a week; his face was covered with heavy stubble, and I would say it was almost calm except that his body seemed soft, turned light and pliant by some curious inner excitement that was neither fear nor bewilderment, there was something of a wild animal's resilience and sprightliness in him, and I also noticed he had gotten even thinner over those past few days.

The white summer suit was the first thing I touched, even before he had a chance to kiss me, an involuntary move, and I don't know how one's eyes can distinguish one white summer suit from all other white summer suits, but I was quite certain that he had come back wearing János Hamar's suit, the same suit János Hamar had worn when he came to see us straight from jail the previous spring, the suit he'd had on when years earlier two strangers had asked him to step into a black limousine in front of the Office of Restitution, the same suit in which he knelt by Mother's bed five years later, only hours after his release; this meant that he and Father had been together, again, and he must have lent Father his suit, must have helped Father, maybe helped him hide out, perhaps they even fought together in that armed group Father and his friends had organized a few months ago; when I abruptly extricated myself from the embrace of this summer suit, I happened to say something that prompted him to slap me twice in the face; he hit me unerringly, the movements of his arm and hand loose, coldly, with a force that nearly knocked me over—but more about this later, I told Melchior, it wouldn't make sense just yet.

I was talking to Melchior's eyes.

One of his hands was grasping mine on a leather strap, and with his other hand he was holding another strap, so that his raised arms opened wide the wings of his coat, shielding our faces, our hands, the secret gestures of our forbidden love from the other passengers; our faces were very close, close enough to feel each other's breath, but I was talking not to his face and certainly not to his mind but to his eyes.

And not even to a pair of eyes; what remains with me is the image of a single enormous eye hovering in the breath of my own words, a single beautiful eye, obliging yet twinkling with an inner urgency, and also concealing its light of comprehension each time it blinked, resting, waiting behind the beautiful fluttering membrane of its lid, seeming uncertain, groping, and suspicious; and each time it reopened, it would spur me on, impelling me to forget all the small details because he wanted to see the larger perspective; as it was, there were too many things to take in at once: not only did he have to imagine unfamiliar characters, orient himself in unknown locales, reconcile uncertain time frames, follow a very personal, therefore disjointed account of events which up to then he knew only from rather generalized historical descriptions, but he also had to contend with the unpleasant addition of my linguistic lapses, to deduce from my excited, often incorrectly used phrases just what it was I really wanted to say.

It had happened the previous summer, I told Melchior, about three weeks after Father had been suspended from his position as state prosecutor: one Sunday morning about thirty guests arrived at our house, filling the street outside with their parked cars, all men except for one young woman who came with her father, a glum, sickly-looking, elderly man who, rocking in a chair, said not a word during the entire meeting, waving his hand once to silence his daughter when she was about to say something.

I made use of a little family byplay to sneak into Father's study, where the assembled men were smoking, standing about in small groups, arguing or simply chatting; they seemed to be old friends having one of their get-togethers; after a short while Father stepped into the kitchen to ask Grandmother to make coffee, but as luck would have it, Grandfather was there, too, and before Grandmother could respond with a reluctant but obliging yes, Grandfather broke their years-long mutual silence and, turning red and gasping for air in sudden irritation, told Father that unfortunately Grandmother had no time to make coffee, as she was on her way to Sunday services, and if Father insisted on offering coffee to his unexpected guests he should serve them himself.

Father had indeed made his request as a boss would do to his secretary, so the response caught him by surprise, all the more so since it was perfectly obvious that Grandfather wasn't refusing an innocuous request on Grandmother's behalf but simply found it distasteful to have any close contact with that group of men; It's all right, Father stammered, he appreciated the concern, and as he hurried out of the kitchen, pale with anger, he did not notice me tagging along, or maybe the unpleasant interlude made it difficult for him to object to my presence.

In any case, I positioned myself near the door leading to my room, where the young woman in her attractive dark silk dress was leaning somewhat uncomfortably against the doorpost.

I could tell from Father's vigorous yet controlled stride, from the sharp thrust of his stooped shoulders, from his hair falling over his forehead, or perhaps from the determined air with which he pushed his way through the smoke-filled room, that he was getting ready for something extraordinary, something he'd had his mind set on for a long time; he shoved his armchair out of the way, took his desk keys out of his pocket, opened a drawer, but then, as if suddenly uncertain, did not pull it out but slowly lowered himself into the chair and turned toward the company.

The sight of this change in his movement and the look in his eyes spread like a tremor throughout the room; some of the men fell silent, others lowered their voices, still others looked over their shoulders and purposely finished their sentences or even began new ones, while Father sat motionless, staring vacantly into the air.

And then, with a motion that started slowly but suddenly turned quick as lightning, he yanked out the drawer, grabbed something inside, and, with his fist, from which the grip of the pistol was sticking out, shoved the drawer home, pulled his hand back, and slammed the pistol down on the empty desktop.

One loud bang, followed by silence, an offended, pitiful, dazed, indignant silence.

Outside, the trees stood still in front of the open windows, and one could hear the intermittent hiss of the sprinklers, the water hitting the lawn.

Someone laughed nervously into the silence, a few uncertain laughs followed, there was a very young army officer there, maybe a colonel, a round-faced, smiling man with a blond crewcut who in the stunned silence stood up, leisurely took off his gold-braided uniform jacket, and, smiling amiably, laid it over the back of his chair; a general shouting began, but the officer, as if hearing nothing, quietly sat back down on his chair and in the general uproar calmly began to roll up a sleeve of his white shirt.

Now they were shouting at Father, pleading with him to stop this nonsense, addressing him by his Party code name, Millet, letting him know how well they realized what he was doing, how they sympathized with his outburst, however hysterical and irrational, but he ought to stop it and come to his senses.

No, no, the events of the last few months had finally restored his senses, Father said without raising his voice or looking at anyone, and this was followed by another silence, hollow yet grating; as a matter of fact, he added, the reason he had asked them to come was that he was still hoping to find a few men in this country who, like him, had managed not to lose their good sense.

Fully aware of his dignity, returned to him by the men's silence, his professional confidence marked by his smoothly flowing sentences, he remained seated comfortably in his chair, his hands on the armrest; he did not wish to create a scene or to give a lecture, he went on very quietly, it was a simple, sentimental human impulse that made him remind those present of their obligations which all of them had taken on themselves, not here and not now but for a lifetime, and, he smiled before continuing, in the present political situation he couldn't see how anyone could possibly ignore these obligations; he wasn't looking into anyone's eyes, his smile seemed to be meandering among the faces with that inexplicably sharp glance which always terrified me, which I took to be the sign of madness or deliberate cruelty or maniacal paranoia; he had a very simple proposal to make, he said, speaking without a pause now, the words rolling out as if from a recording, after due consideration he had concluded that to prevent a possible counterrevolutionary takeover, they should establish an armed group totally independent of the army, the police, and the security forces that would be accountable only to the highest echelon of the government.

The last words hovered in the air, then froze between the two potentialities of unqualified endorsement of a self-evident idea and vehement rejection, and only then did pandemonium break out—everything from deliberate and accidental knocking over of chairs, pounding on tables, slapping of knees, bellowing, hissing, yelling, shrieking, hostile whistling, guffaws and laughter of all kinds, although some of the guests remained quiet, and the young woman thrust herself away from the doorpost, seeming to want to say something, her face flushed with indignation, while in the middle of the room the colonel was slowly turning his round, smiling face this way and that; the sad-faced elderly man stopped rocking his chair long enough to silence his daughter with a wave of his hand, and then resumed.

I must confess, I told Melchior sixteen years later in that Berlin streetcar, that I hadn't found the scene at all painful, on the contrary, rather enjoyed it, it made me happy, and not only because—rational consideration notwithstanding, which I'm sure I wasn't capable of at the time—I was impressed by Father's regained prestige, determination, and reckless resolve, qualities that to an adolescent boy are always attractive and admirable regardless of their motivation (even Prém, whose fascist father beat him with sticks and straps, was proud of how strong that drunken beast was); no, my satisfaction had a quite different source: I knew something about Father those men could not have known; they weighed what was happening in political terms, and I weighed it emotionally, I knew that for all his insistence on not wanting to, he was creating a scene, mad performance being the only possible way to escape his own madness, to externalize his innermost insanity, for he was insane, so why shouldn't I have been happy to see this unexpected, purging release; ever since Mother's death, more precisely since János Hamar's return, he had been struggling with this madness; only a few days earlier we had been sitting in the kitchen having dinner when he suddenly looked at me, and I could tell he was seeing not me but someone or something else, something tormenting him, the compulsion to overcome which grew so powerful that his mouth, though full of food, dropped open and he began screaming at the top of his voice, half-chewed bits of food squirting out of his mouth and spattering all over the table, all over my face, and tears streaming from his petrified eyes: "Why, why, why?" he howled at me as I sat leaning against the white-tiled kitchen wall, "why, why?"—he could not stop himself, and as I struggled along with him in that howl, he fell silent just as abruptly as he had started screaming, and it wasn't my touch or hug that calmed him, not my hand or the proximity of my body, I don't know what made him stop, maybe he just resigned himself to being defeated by that someone or something within him, because my hands and body told me he was feeling nothing, he was hard as stone, was no longer there; his head sank into his plate, into the soggy vegetables, as if part of the humiliation he had to endure was soggy vegetables on his plate.

Melchior let go of the strap and motioned with his head that it was time to get off.

We were standing on a square, at the end of the line; the streetcar moved on, making the tracks shriek as it slowly turned, taking its lights with it from behind us; we should have started toward the Festungs-graben, where, among drab little houses, the festively illuminated theater stood, one of the few buildings to have survived the war unscathed, though the lovely little park around it had been completely destroyed.

Others were headed in the same direction, too—black, spit-shined men's shoes, the hems of cheap evening gowns sweeping the pavement and getting caught on gilded high heels—but we stayed there for a while, as if waiting for everyone to leave so for a few moments we could have the dark square all to ourselves.

The feeling that we must be alone now was palpably mutual.

It was also strange, I continued after we started walking down the dark street toward the theater, that Father always made the mistake of calling Marx Square by its old name, Berlin Square—meet me at Berlin Square at such and such time, though as soon as he said it he'd correct himself, I mean Marx Square, under the clock; the only reason I thought of this now, I explained, was because that Sunday they couldn't agree on any-thing, they kept on shouting and arguing for hours without making any sense, until the young woman in the silk dress began to speak despite her father's warning signal; they seemed unable to decide what they really thought of Father's proposal: on the one hand, they accused him of fac-tionalism, sowing discord, some even yelling conspiracy and calling him a provocateur, demanding to know whose agent he really was, telling him they had no choice but to report him; and on the other hand, they ad-mitted the situation had indeed gotten out of hand, State Security had been forced into a corner, the police were unreliable to begin with, the army officer corps was visibly disintegrating under constant, intolerable political pressure, something had to be done before it was too late, before even ordinary criminals were let out of the jails; if yesterday everybody had been an enemy, today everybody was everybody's brother; the most trustworthy Communists were being vilified, people were looking for scapegoats and finding them, directives went unheeded or never reached their destination, everyone was raking up the past, fishing in troubled waters, even the glorious Communist past, even the Spanish Civil War, was open to scrutiny, the whole Party apparatus was full of opportunists and obstructionists, miserable hacks and pen pushers were demanding freedom of the press, nobody worked anymore, public order had virtually collapsed, people were wrapped up in their private affairs, cynically serv-ing two masters, and on top of all that were the enemy's subversive activities; in a word, the country was becoming ungovernable, and for this very reason every firm measure seemed a provocation, unity should not be destroyed by new factional strife, yet who had the right to talk of unity if they themselves could not agree on a proper course of action, it would be irresponsible to incite the various organs of the state against each other, not dissent but confidence had to be strengthened, which all depended on the right kind of propaganda, radical measures only added oil to the fire, the press had to be curbed, anyone with plans like Father's was playing into the hands of the enemy, after all, you can't piss against the wind, when a house is on fire you don't put it out by pouring oil on it; throughout all this, Father sat motionless, saying not a word; but now he was not looking at his friends as from afar, his glance wandering among the faces, but with a vaguely satisfied, friendly smile he gazed at them like one who has finally reached his goal, come home, behavior which made the situation much more complicated: those who were hostile neither to him nor to his proposal might wonder whether he wasn't a provocateur, after all, sitting there so calmly, having used the pistol trick to make people come clean; and his most vociferous accusers might ask themselves how he could stay so calm, so impervious, unless he was indeed backed by people in the highest places, and what did he know that they didn't, while they had unthinkingly revealed their most guarded cards?

And he spoke again, very quietly, but only after rising suspicion had overtaken the group and the shouting had died down, the angry gestures became hesitant; no, the reason he had asked them here, he said, his voice measured and self-assured, was not to debate whether his proposal was necessary or not but to discuss how to execute it.

The unheard-of audacity of this statement immediately dispelled their suspicion, for only someone speaking with the force of his own convictions could be so outrageously imperious; his words again required silence.

Thinking only in political and ideological terms, busy looking for tactics and strategies they believed to be consistent, these people failed to realize that Father had silenced their suspicion not with brilliant reasoning, convinced them not with bold strokes of logic but with the insanity of his argument; an insane man was seizing the reins.

He was about to say something else when the young woman next to me suddenly spoke up, throwing out her arms in a warning and imploring gesture, her fingers trembling in the air as she begged the men's pardon— I was surprised at the strong, resonant voice that came out of her fragile, emotion-filled body; listening to the arguments, she said, she had the impression that she had dropped in not from another country but from another planet; frankly, she didn't know or much care where the members of this esteemed company lived, but in the country where she lived the restoration of a free and democratic government, elected by secret ballot, would be a more appropriate response to the crisis than the deployment of a provocative armed force, and they should not forget that she was not the only person in the country who held this view.

While she was speaking, trembling with emotion, her father stopped rocking in his chair, planted his feet firmly on the floor, and stared ahead with impassive approval as if he knew exactly what his daughter was going to say, even when the period would come at the end of her last sentence.

Unheard-of, this was simply unheard-of, as if an outrageous impropriety had taken place, one that must not be answered or acknowledged, seen or heard, it was beyond anything debatable, it had to be dismissed immediately, except the proper action to do so was lacking; they all sat there stunned.

The woman's father let his chair rock back now, and it swung down with what sounded like a deliberate thud, a reply of sorts, as if to say enough is enough! then he rose ceremoniously, suggesting that he might be able to defuse the situation, walked over to Father, placed his hand on his arm, and addressed him, not too loudly or too quietly, making sure everyone heard him: he thought Father's idea was well worth considering, he said, certainly worth detailed discussion, but perhaps later, as part of a larger debate, or better yet, in a smaller, more intimate setting; so many arguments and counter-arguments had been heard just now, he believed it would be premature, indeed impossible, to form a definite opinion; when he got to this point, many of the others started talking again, too, involuntarily assuming his reasonable, delaying, wait-and-see tone, and speaking as if nothing untoward had happened, everyone anxious to move on to other subjects or, if they had to stay with the one at hand, ready to switch to different, less confrontational attitudes.

Some of them got up, cleared their throats, began to gather their things, lit up last cigarettes, went out onto the balcony, exchanged furtive little glances in allusion to what had been said, here and there giggled, acted precisely as people of varied opinions would act at a not very exciting official reception.

Although it may appear that all this did not amount to much, I told Melchior while we were still walking, very soon afterward I had a definite indication that the debate that Sunday was not a total fiasco and, what's more, that the young woman's words might have helped the debaters clarify their own views; a few days later Father and I made a date to meet at Marx Square, to buy a pair of shoes, I think; I waited in vain for an hour and a half; when he finally got home late that night, his clothes and hair reeking of cigarette smoke, he told me he had had to attend a meeting of historic importance and could not leave it; he sounded anxious but also hopeful as he begged my pardon; this unusual, talkative politeness led me to believe that while he might not have prevailed at the meeting, at least he had not suffered another defeat—we got an additional respite from his madness.

I stopped talking, abruptly, as if I had something more to say but had no idea what I could add or how I had got entangled in the story, which suddenly seemed false, alien, and far removed from me; we kept walking, listening to the even sound of our footsteps, Melchior asked no questions and I was glad I didn't have to say another word.

And in this silence punctuated by our footsteps which was not really silence but the absence of appropriate words, I felt that everything I'd said until then was nothing but idle talk, just words, an impenetrable and superfluous heap of empty words, foreign to me, not bending to my tongue; it was senseless to talk without the proper words, and there were none, not even in my native vocabulary, that would lead somewhere in this story, nowhere to go in the story, for there is no story when compulsive memory continually bogs down in insignificant details or details imagined to be meaningless; at that moment, for example, in my mind I was wandering about the old Marx Square in Budapest waiting for Father, and of course he didn't show up, and still I couldn't tear myself away from there—but why would I tell Melchior about that?

One can only tell the story of something, and I wanted to tell him everything, the whole of the story all at once, to transfer it, place it in his body, vomit it into this great love of mine, but where did that elusive whole begin and end? how could it be created in a language that had nothing to do with my body and weighed so heavily on my tongue?

I had never talked about these events before, not ever, not to anyone, because I had not wanted them to turn into an adventure story, what was not a story should not be turned into one, it would be better to bury it alive in the crypt of memory, the only fitting and undisturbed resting place for it.

In that dark Berlin street I felt I was desecrating the dead.

And isn't silence the only perfect whole?

We were walking side by side, shoulder to shoulder, head alongside head, and in my distracted state I failed to realize that talking to him had become difficult because I had been talking to his eyes, and now the eyes were no longer there.

And at the same time I also felt that our echoing footsteps, our well-matched leg movements, taking us closer and closer to the theater, were also curbing my storytelling urge; no problem, then, the story would end, remain unfinished anyway, and just as well: we'd go to the theater, enjoy the performance, and whatever was still left of the story I would simply swallow, and at least the shame of talking about these events would also remain incomplete.

Thick shafts of floodlights, misty around the huge reflectors, ripped the building out of the autumn evening, and the theater stood before us in the cold blinding blaze like an ungraceful cardboard box; when we stepped into the naked light where people, slightly blinded, hastened to partake of an evening fare that promised release and oblivion, I still wanted to tell Melchior something, something interesting, something funny, anything that would bring a closure to this frustrating walk.

You know, I said without thinking too much, for I was still wandering about that old square, this Marx Square, which Father always called Berlin Square, which was memorable for another reason, because while I was waiting for Father, a group of drunks staggered out of Ilkovits, a notorious dive known all over the city, and among them was a sorry-looking old whore who came reeling over to me, I thought she wanted to ask me something so I turned toward her; she took my arm, bit my ear, and panted seductively that I should go with her, she'd love to blow me, free of charge, and she was sure I had a sweet little cock.

She was right about that, I added, laughing, trying to be funny.

Melchior stopped, turned to me, and he not only did not smile but gave me his gravest, most motionless look.

In embarrassment I continued: she was no fancy lady, only a two-bit whore, she said, but I had nothing to fear, she knew better than anybody what adorable little gentlemen like me liked to have done to them.

With his impassive face Melchior indicated displeasure, but then took both my arms by the elbows, and as his face drew close to mine a tiny smile appeared, not around his mouth but in his eyes, but this had to do not with my evasive little joke but with his determination that right there, in the middle of this floodlit square, in plain sight of people hurrying to the theater, he was going to kiss me, quite passionately, on the mouth.

This soft, warm kiss gave birth to many more tiny kisses, enough of them to cover my closed eyelids, my forehead, and my neck; his lips, with their rapid slides and thrusts, seemed to be groping for something; I don't think anybody noticed, or, having noticed, paid any attention, though I must say they missed a great moment; but then our arms, protectively thrusting us apart, fell to our sides and we stood there looking at each other.

Then I got back that one, single eye.

He laughed, or rather his strong, wild, white teeth flashed from his soft mouth, he motioned to the entrance and said, We don't really have to go in.

No, we don't.

The show could go on without us.

It sure could.

But that single eye, at that moment, in the midst of the crowd, was telling me something very different.

Well, that's the end of the story, I said.

He smiled back at me, mysteriously, calmly, beautifully; I did not fully understand that smile then, for it was not his usual, steady, inescapable smile, the one I at once loved and hated; but I had to obey it, I had no choice; perhaps for the first time in our relationship he fully possessed me.

He must have acquired a part of my personality—a cherished or despised part, it was all the same—that until then he had not encountered or could not account for.

I had the feeling I'd better go on concealing my face with words.

He did not move, making us look as if we were quarreling.

In his smartly tailored dark suit, his clasped hands holding the wings of his open raincoat behind his back, his upper body slightly bent forward, Melchior was standing before me in the harsh bright lights, and as if compelled to entertain serious doubts about something, he narrowed his eyes to mere slits, almost making them disappear.

Several people were looking at us now, but whatever they may have been thinking they were wrong.

Let's go home, I said.

He shrugged his shoulders slightly, seemed ready to go, but that made it impossible for me to move.

I'm sure I have to tell him all this, I said, with an uncertainty caused by feeling powerless, so that he'll understand why I couldn't leave that crowd back then, in Budapest, and go home; the whole thing wasn't so interesting, and it hardly mattered, but I was sure that now he'd understand.

And then I didn't want to say anything else.

He understood, of course he did, he replied impatiently, though he wasn't at all sure that he had understood what I wanted him to understand.

It would have been easy to say something, anything, to break the painful silence that followed, painful because in truth I did want to continue but couldn't, though I did not wish to retrieve that part of my personality he had got hold of and now so eagerly possessed—and this in turn warned me that I couldn't just tell him anything I wanted to; and the reason I couldn't continue was not that I had to utter some terribly important and profound truth but that, on the contrary, an unfamiliar bashfulness was keeping me from recounting perfectly ordinary events, a kind of modesty, more dangerous than that of the naked body, checked the flow of words, for any of my personal experiences would seem hopelessly contingent so many years after the fact, petty, silly, laughable when compared to the events that silent historical memory had endowed with the grandeur of true tragedy.

I certainly didn't feel I should judge the final results of those events, yet it seemed just as wrong to talk only of the drawing board knocking against my legs or the T-square slipping out of my overstuffed briefcase as I kept running.

Still, those objects had been part of my personal revolution, for their weight, bulk, and clumsiness forced me to clarify for myself a question which, from a mundane superficial standpoint, seems silly and insignificant, since in the overall evolution of those events it was then and now unimportant whether one blond high-school student could extricate himself from a crowd of about half a million people or stay where he was; but bluntly speaking, the question for me then was whether I was capable of, or felt the necessity of, patricide; and that was no longer just an insignificant question but, rather, one that, one way or another, must have occurred to everyone in that crowd on that fateful Tuesday evening.

More precisely, if the question had really occurred to people in so crude and oversimplified a form, then none of us could probably have been there, marching side by side, with the commonality created by the heat of our bodies, heading in a direction dictated by an unfamiliar force; instead, horrified by our complicity and denying the power that molded us into a mass, each of us would have fled in panic back to our well-tended, miserable, or plush abodes; we wouldn't have been a crowd, then, but an enraged horde, a reckless mob, rabble bent on senseless destruction; in the final analysis, humans, not unlike animals in the wild, yearn for peace, sunshine, a soft nest, a chance to multiply; man turns warlike only when he cannot ensure the safety of his mate, his home, his food, his offspring, and even then his first thought is not to kill!

That is how it was at that hour, too, in the balmy evening air; we showed our combativeness only in that we were marching together, so many of us; of course our marching was directed against something or some people, but it wasn't yet clear what or who these were, everyone could still think what he wished, bring along his own private grudges, ask his own personal questions without having to come up with definite answers, and if anyone did come up with one, he couldn't know how the others would respond, which is why he spoke in slogans, yelled, or re-mained silent.

There wasn't a single thing seen or heard that evening that was not in some way significant: every taunt, every slogan, every line of poetry, and even silence itself turned into a mass-scale testing of, and search for, my personal feelings, points of contact, similarity to and possible identification with others.

An object—a T-square, a poem, the national flag—gives us a surface for our thoughts; on such surfaces we conceive of things that otherwise could not be put into words, and in this sense objects are but the tangible symbols, the birthplaces of inarticulate instincts and dark, unformed emotions; they are never the thing or event itself, only the pretext for it.

I couldn't stand the glare of the floodlights any longer.

If I could have talked to him, or at least to myself, about this, I should have said that after we managed to press through the human bottleneck on Marx Square and ran to catch up with the others, something in me changed irreversibly; I simply forgot that moments earlier I'd wanted to go home, and it was the city that made me forget it, turning stones into houses, houses into streets, and streets into well-defined new directions.

And from that point on things followed the course dictated by the law of nature: a spring wells up from the ground, branches into streams, flows into rivers rushing toward the sea; it was this poetic and this simple! obeying the attraction of the larger mass, human bodies propelled themselves out of the noisy, gaily seething side streets toward the boulevard and pressed themselves into the larger crowd there; Verochka must have ended her improvised recitation with the resounding line "Those who never knew, there's no more excuse / Learn now what it's like when the poor cut loose," because with the force of a cork popping free, to the rumble of running feet, people were rushing at us from behind, thrusting us forward, all of us sweeping along in the direction of Margit Bridge; yet even this did not mean that these countless individual wills—all at different temperatures, igniting one another with sheer friction but in the absence of real fuel causing only sparks that flared and quickly died—could heat up to a single common will, yet a change did occur, and everyone must have sensed it, because the shouting ceased, there was no more laughing, recitations, speeches, or flag waving, as if crowding into this one and only possible direction, everyone had retreated into the smallest common denominator of the moment: the sound of their own footsteps.

The massive fullness of this sound, the relentlessly even, rhythmic echoing that now filled the deep canyon of Szent István Boulevard, was strong enough not to lessen but to increase the feeling of fellowship, a feeling further intensified by the sight of people clustered in wide-open windows all around; separated from us, they were waving to us, were with us, and we, down on the street, were also with them up there; the crowd began to feel its own weight and strength, and developed with each step a slower, heavier solemnity.

Broad Szent István Boulevard begins to climb near Pannónia Street—today's László Rajk Street—and at Pozsonyi Road gently slopes as it runs onto Margit Bridge; on ordinary days this slight rise and downward slope can hardly be detected, and if I hadn't been in that huge crowd that evening I wouldn't have noticed it either; one simply uses one's city, unaware of the peculiarities of its streets and squares.

At the foot of the bridge, at this little incline, two streams of people met, coming from opposite directions and with very different dispositions, which immediately made clear why our steps had to slow, our ranks become more solid, solemn, silent: we were going up the gentle incline while opposite us people were coming down from the bridge, a crowd that was stronger not only because of its potential energy but also because it seemed more organized, cheerful, homogeneous and youthful, the people looking as if they had already achieved a significant victory; they came arm in arm, singing, belting out rhymed slogans to the beat of their feet, and without breaking ranks swept around the foot of the bridge, cutting a wide path across the intersection, turned onto Bálint Balassa Street, marching in orderly rows; our groups, ascending, tighter but more disorderly, cohering with so many mismatched personal impulses, had to merge into the opening and closing wings of this unending huge fan of people, we had to push our way into the available spaces, increasing our disarray as we went for any crack, any opening.

There are moments when the sense of brotherhood makes you forget all bodily discomfort and needs: you are not tired, love no one, are neither hungry nor thirsty, neither hot nor cold, don't have to relieve yourself; these were such moments.

While we were running, Szentes told us that these were university students coming from Bem Square; the ranks closed around us, we were in them and although we momentarily upset their orderly ranks and unity, we caught their upbeat mood; everyone began to talk, people coming from different places, in different moods, eagerly exchanged views, compared notes, addressed strangers as friends; we learned who had spoken at that other assembly, what demands had been made and how they'd been received; and we told them about the tanks, the soldiers, the workers from Váci Road and the army being with us now; this heated exchange of information and mixing of the two groups made for a certain diffusion, but the somewhat lax procession found cheerful new strength and vigor.

This is how we marched toward the Parliament.

Assuming that I must have a different view of what was going on but not wanting to expose me publicly, Szentes leaned close, making sure that Stark wouldn't hear—in our excitement our faces almost touched—and whispered, There you are, now you can see for yourself, this system has had it.

Of course I see it, I said, and jerked my head away, but I don't know how all this is going to end.

The dark dome of the Parliament was now straight ahead of us; the illuminated massive red star on top had been installed only a few months earlier.

I must have looked pretty funny with my drawing board, my bulging schoolbag, and my self-consciously solemn expression, trying to reconcile the extraordinary events of the evening with my peculiar family experiences, because my apprehension regarding the future so surprised Szentes that he had to laugh; in that very instant, as I tried to figure out what his laugh meant, somebody threw his arms around me from behind and a hand, firm and soft and warm, covered my eyes.

He's at it again, drawing conclusions, he's at it again! it was Kálmán, shouting and jumping for joy, waving his arms, in the middle of a bunch of uniformed baker's apprentices with three flustered high-school students facing him; but we couldn't stand around, we all had to move on.

By the way, I lost my drawing board at the foot of Kossuth's statue; Kálmán climbed up and I climbed after him, we wanted to see the people filling up the square, as earth-shattering shouts went up: Turn off the star! turn off that star! and then, in the blink of an eye all the lights in the square went out, only the star shone on top of the dome, a rumble of discontent raced though the crowd, followed by whistles and boos, and then silence, and in this silence people raised newspapers over their heads and lit them into torches; like a whirlwind sweeping across a huge field, the flames flashed and leaped, flooding the square in light, dying quickly, but flaring up again and again, spreading, glaring in spots, a white conflagration turning into yellow waves, blinking, flickering into red, and falling in glittering crystals at people's feet; a few hours later I left my schoolbag at the corner of Pushkin and Sándor Bródy Streets, where it stayed on the empty pavement where Kálmán, just as he was about to bite into a piece of bread spread with jelly, dropped to the ground to avoid a burst of rifle fire coming from the rooftops; I even thought how quick and clever he was to duck, I thought his face was smeared with jelly.

If later, when Hédi was saying goodbye and looking at me pleadingly, expecting me, an eyewitness, to confirm what still seemed unbelievable, if I could have talked about this, or if she herself hadn't been convinced that talk was futile, then I should have talked about that strong, soft, and warm hand, the palm of a friend's hand, and not about the ultimately useless fact that he died, that it was the end of him, he was dead, and we dragged him across the street into the lobby of a house, and then into an apartment, though it was of no use, he died on the way, or maybe before that, on the spot, but the man who helped me and I both pretended that by dragging him like that we could make him live a little longer or that we could revive him; his whole body was full of holes, but one had to do something, so we carried him, his dead body, and as we did, his blood was dripping, dripping, trailing us, it wet our hands and made them slippery, his blood lived longer than he did, he was no more, he was dead, his eyes were open, and so was his mouth in his mangled bloody-jellied face, he was dead, and all there was left for me to do that evening was to tell his mother, who worked in Szent János Hospital; and then, a few days later, two months before his suicide—with János Hamar's light summer suit in my hand—I had to call my stealthily returning father a murderer; and that, too, I did as I was supposed to.

It wasn't about my friend's death, or about any of the other deaths and funerals, or the cemeteries glowing with candlelight and all the candles of that autumn and winter that I wanted to talk about, but about the last touch of his living body, that I was the last one he touched, and how he was holding that lousy slice of bread with plum jelly he'd gotten from a woman, a woman in the window of her ground-floor apartment at the corner of Pushkin Street who was slicing bread, spreading the slices with jelly out of a jug, and handing them to everybody passing by; I should have talked about the unmistakable smell and feel of Kálmán's hand, about the uniqueness of muscles and skin, of proportions and temperatures, that enables us to recognize a person, about the soft, warm darkness that suddenly makes us forget every historical event and with a single touch leads us back from the unfamiliar into the familiar world, a world full of familiar touches, smells, emotions, where it's easy to pick out that one unique hand.

And to make him understand me, at least some of all the things I'd been telling him, I should have told Melchior about the very last, happy little coda of my story: on that cold, harshly lit Berlin square in front of the theater I should have told him about the soft darkness settling on my eyes in which I recognized Kálmán's hand!—or was it Krisztián's? no, it was Kálmán, Kálmán!—should have talked about this last little remnant of childish pleasure, and since I had no free hand, what with the drawing board in one hand and my schoolbag in the other—which later I lost— I had to use my head to break free of his clasp, I was so overjoyed that he should be there, about as unexpected and unbelievable as when you look for a needle in a haystack and actually find it.

Silently Melchior watched my silence; there was something to see in that, I suppose.

And on that December afternoon, too, it wasn't I who moved first but Hédi; she lowered her head.

She wanted nothing more to do with our mutual silence over recent events, or with the agreed-upon no with which we denied them; she asked me to see her out.

Even at the front entrance of the house we did not look at each other; I looked at the darkening street while she poked around in her pocket.

I thought she wanted to shake hands, which would have been odd, but no, she pulled out a small, shabby brown teddy bear; I immediately recognized it as her and Livia's mascot; Hédi squeezed it a couple of times, then told me to give it to Livia.

And when I took it and her hand accidentally touched my fingers, I had the feeling that everything that might stay here of herself she wanted to entrust to Livia and me.

She left and I went back into the house.

My grandmother was just coming out, probably escaping to me from the annoying, consoling chatter of Aunt Klára.

She asked me who that was.

Hédi, I said.

The blond Jewish girl? she asked.

Dressed in black from head to toe, she stood motionless and expressionless in the dimly lit foyer in front of the closed white door.

She asked if anybody had died in the girl's family.

No, they're going away.

Where to? she asked.

I said I didn't know.

I waited for her to start for the kitchen, letting her pretend she had something to do there, then I went into Grandfather's room.

It had been a month since anyone had entered it; without Grandfather it had become dry and musty, nothing stirring the layers of dust.

I closed the door behind me and just stood there for a while, then put down the little teddy bear on his table, where books, notes, and writing implements, the excited traces of his last days, lay scattered about.

On the third of November he began working on an election reform plan, but could not finish it by the twenty-second of November.

I recalled his story about the three frogs that fell in a bucket of milk: I couldn't possibly drown in such an awful, sticky mess, said the optimistic frog, and while talking, his mouth stuck together and he drowned; if the optimist went down, why wouldn't I, said the pessimistic frog, and promptly drowned; but the third frog, the realist, did the only thing frogs can do: he kept treading milk until he felt something hard under his feet, something hard, dense, and slightly bluish, from which he could push off; of course he didn't know he had churned butter, how could he, he was only a frog, but he could jump out of the bucket.

I had to take the teddy bear back from the table, I felt that leaving it there would be a mistake.

The only thing I knew about Livia was that she went to study glass grinding; once, about two years later, walking on Práter Street, I happened to look through a basement window propped up with a stick; a group of women were sitting behind shrieking, grinding wheels; Livia was among them, a white smock casually unbuttoned at her chest; deftly she was working a stemmed glass on her wheel; she was pregnant.

The same summer I got a letter from János Hamar, a very friendly letter mailed from Montevideo; he wrote that if ever I needed anything I should let him know, I should write to him, he'd like to see me as his guest, but I could stay with him permanently if I liked; he was posted there as a diplomat and had a pleasant, easy life; he was staying for another two years and would gladly go on a long trip with me; I should answer him at once for he, too, was all alone and didn't really want anyone anymore; but the letter arrived much too late.

I continued to believe that everyone who was still alive would eventually return, slip back quietly, cautiously, but I never saw any of them again.

When years later I came across the little teddy bear, I looked at it; it hurt too much; I threw it away.

In Which He Tells Thea All about Melchior's Confession

On our evening or nighttime walks, on whichever of our usual routes we chose, our matching footsteps always resounded like a strange hostile beat in the darkness of the deserted streets, and our conversations or silences were never so all-absorbing that we could free ourselves of the constant, rhythmic beat even for an instant.

It was as if the city's houses, these sore sights, these war-ravaged façades, had kept close track of our harmless footsteps, but when they echoed them they echoed only what was hollow and soulless in us, and if up there, in that box of an apartment under the eaves, we'd chat freely, then down here on the street, where we had to bridge the gap between the bleak surroundings and the intimacy of our emotions, our conversations tended to become heavy, took on a tone of responsibility that is usually referred to as cool frankness.

Up there we hardly ever talked about Thea; down here we did so often.

Prompted by my emotional duplicity, I manipulated these conversations so that I'd never be the first to mention her name, always approaching the subject carefully, circling cautiously around it; when her name had already been mentioned and Melchior was talking about her but got stuck because he became frightened by his own unexpected association of ideas, or recoiled from his too passionate statements about her, then with sly and calculating questions, interjections, and comments, I'd helped us stay on the trail that led back to his murky past, to continue our progress in that foggy landscape from which he tried so adroitly, with all his intellectual resourcefulness, to isolate himself, even at the cost of causing serious emotional harm to himself.

But on my afternoon or early evening walks with Thea, I had to resort to tactics that were exactly the opposite of those I used with Melchior, because roaming the flat, windswept countryside around the city or sitting on the shore of a good-sized lake or on the banks of a canal running off into the horizon, watching the surface of the water or just staring into space, the very spaciousness of the landscape ensured a free intimacy of expression, a clear separation as well as mutual interdependence of sentiment and passion, for nature is not a stage set, is slightly surreal for eyes used to struggling with unreal surroundings, and does not tolerate petty little human comedies with exclusively urban settings; as I continually diverted and sidetracked Thea, my covert intention was to maintain her feelings for Melchior in a state of tension and at the same time prevent her from being honest with me—that is, talking to me about him openly.

I found this arrangement just right for achieving my secret goal.

But we talked about him even when we didn't, and I experienced the suppressed excitement a criminal must feel when getting ready for action, just listening, watching, stalking the scene of his intended crime, convinced he need not do anything, need not interfere in the order of nature, it's enough to have discovered how the system works that has created the prevailing situation; his prey will fall into his lap as a gift from the situation itself; and with both of them I did nothing but continually and consistently maintain this kind of situation with my suggestions and insinuations.

Drop by drop I infused in Thea the seemingly improbable hope that despite all appearances Melchior was within her reach; in Melchior, with the subtlest of means, I tried to eliminate the blocks that stood in the way of his dormant yet sometimes powerful and aggressive sensual impulses; oddly enough, though understandably, Thea never became truly jealous of me, for in her eyes, indeed in her entire emotional system, she saw me as the only physical, bodily proof of her hope for Melchior, which, however vague, was impossible to abandon; and Melchior was intellectually dazed by the possibility that through me he could get to know something he hadn't known before; what's more, he knew I couldn't be completely his until he possessed this other thing as well.

Lovers walk around wearing each other's body, and they wear and radiate into the world their common physicality, which is in no way the mathematical sum of their two bodies but something more, something different, something barely definable, both a quantity and a quality, for the two bodies contract into one but cannot be reduced to one; this quantitative surplus and qualitative uniqueness cannot be defined in terms of, say, the bodies' mingled scents, which is only the most easily noticeable and superficial manifestation of the separate bodies' commonality that extends to all life functions; true, the common scent eats itself into their clothes, hair, and skin, and whoever comes into contact with the lovers will enter the sphere of this new physicality, and if the outsider has a sensitive and impartial enough nose not only will he come under the magic spell of the lovers—put more simply, under their influence—not only will he receive a part of their love, but it's also possible that once inside the lovers' private bubble and led by his own olfactory sensations he will become aware of meaningful borrowings, transferences, and displacements in the gestures, facial expressions, and intonations that are the peculiar physical manifestation of the lovers' emotional union.

The place between Thea and Melchior that I was unable to occupy on our first night together at the opera did in fact become mine later on; all I had to do was let Thea enter a little way into this private bubble of ours and from then on the two of them could communicate with each other with my body as conductor, because without being aware of it I took Melchior with me on my afternoon walks with Thea, and if she took part of me for herself, as she had to if she wanted to maintain her emotional balance, then she took a part of Melchior as well, and this was the same in the other direction, too: if Thea gave me something of herself, then Melchior had to sense the lack or surplus thus created, and he did: when I returned to him from my walks with Thea, he would sniff around me like a dog, making scenes of jealousy that I couldn't lighten with horseplay and joking; we had to restore the upset balance and put things back into their right proportions between us, which of course again meant touching Thea somehow.

I never found out what happened between them at the opera, the answers they gave later to my questions were evasive, letting me understand that they both thought their encounter a shameful defeat, but I realized that every defeat was a prelude to a new offensive, so if I wanted to help along the disintegration of their relationship—and I did, believing it was the only chance to ensure decent conditions for Melchior and me to survive—then I had to make sure I understood the situation precisely.

I cannot explain my motives for an honorable retreat in any other way except to say that I was utterly lost in this relationship, both terrified and exhilarated by the knowledge that I, a man, an individual with a specific psychic and sexual makeup, was now intimate with another not of the opposite but of the same sex; and inasmuch as this was so, as it was possible to be so, if in spite of all prohibitions we were allowed to have this relationship, then it must make sense, it must! the idea of love's indivisibility filled me with such excitement that I felt I was reinventing the laws of nature or discovering a deep secret; for if this really was so, then I was really me, I thought triumphantly, a man, a complete being, an indivisible whole, my sex being only one aspect of this whole, and did it follow, then, that this whole could remain whole only in love? and could the ultimate meaning of love be one indivisible whole clinging to another indivisible whole? and should my connection to another be the choice only of my irreducible self, whether I chose someone of my own or of the opposite sex? but however comfortingly my questions were leading me on, I still had to contend with the painful realization that though I might have chosen one who was like me, he was not me but someone else, though the same sex as I, still not me; thus the pleasure and revenge of direct contact with sameness hit home forcefully, making clear that even in one of my own sex I could not make my own the otherness of another man, a bitter realization that so intensified the hopelessness and futility of my whole life, my past, and all my strivings that, yielding to the part of myself that yearned for stability rather than confrontation, I decided I'd better run away from the place, go home, and in this case home meant something old, dull, familiar, and safe, everything that home means when one is abroad.

I wanted to go home, and he knew it; I didn't explain or give reasons, and he didn't ask for any; with the immeasurable superiority of his pain, he let me go, but as if to beat me to my departure, he also wanted to leave, to return to his barely abandoned despair, to escape; I wanted to get back to the safety of my homeland, he to the uncertainties of his desires; and this was as if with a parallel change of locales—which, being parallel, would not allow us to tear ourselves away from one another— we had wanted to take revenge on each other for our own personal stories, and to besmirch each other with the considerable amount of grimy history that met and clashed in us, except that this was no longer a game, a harmless lovers' quarrel; escaping from this place could have dangerous, life-threatening consequences, a prison term at the very least, in those years only a very small percentage of escape attempts ended in success; we didn't talk about this either, Melchior being very mysterious about it, also tense and irritable; he must have been waiting for a sign or message from the other side, and certain indications led me to believe that it was Melchior's French friend, that self-proclaimed Communist, who was making the arrangements for his escape.

Trusting in Melchior and Thea's mutual attraction, especially in Thea's subtle forcefulness, I figured that if I wanted to hasten the disintegration of their relationship that would enable Melchior to forget his senseless escape plan, which for me was rather unpleasant, since I could not morally support it, then I ought to stay as neutral as a catalyst involved in a chemical process that, having no valence of its own, can never be part of the new compound and falls away.

Needless to say, my scheme violated their privacy, in a sense was a sort of emotional crime, but since it seemed workable—its feasibility was clear to all of us at our very first meeting—I went on with my schemes and plots, assuaging my guilty conscience by telling myself that it was they who wanted it, I was only helping them; success would prove that I wanted only what was good for them; this was my way of saying to myself that I wanted not only to remain honest but to win.

Of course I couldn't be sure the plan would work, and I had to keep going back, all too frequently, to our first meeting, and review every moment, every tiny detail of that evening; and the more often I replayed it in my mind, the more it seemed that in the cold, distant space of the stage, in the bodies of singers moved by the music streaming from the orchestra pit, a wild, emotional chaos arose that was closely analogous to the one overwhelming us as we sat in the plush box.

Without formulating a single thought, then, the events sensed with my shoulders, seen with my eyes, and heard with my ears, occurred in duplicate, becoming their own metaphors, and they affected me in a way I can describe as nothing less than an emotional earthquake; later I could not escape the memory of this profound effect, even if I hadn't intended to exploit it for my own purposes; today I'd say that the smooth, hard ground of my emotions, packed firm in the thirty years of my life, moved under my feet, the magma of instincts was jolted, edifices erected with the stones of mastery and knowledge and self-protecting morality began to crumble during the heartbreaking overture; entire streets of allegedly omnipotent experience suddenly shifted, and almost as if to prove that emotions also had material substance, in the throes of struggling with contradictory emotions arising from a familiar unfamiliarity, I began to sweat so profusely I might as well have been chopping wood, yet I was sitting motionless;

as often happens, I pretended I was being carried away by the music, but that did not help either, for like any obvious lie, it made my body, used to self-discipline and self-denial, swim in sweat.

It would seem that by the age of thirty one achieves a certain deceptive security; it was this security that began to fall apart that evening; but the moment before the collapse, all my edifices held their original forms, although not at their usual places; nothing remained at its original location, and therefore these forms, symbolizing their own emptiness, were unaware of the tectonic forces they were now exposed to; my feelings and thoughts were in their old, cracked forms, squeezed between old borders, wandering on worn paths, and simultaneously were the empty symbols of these very forms; in this landslide I was given a moment of grace: in a single bright flash before the moment of collapse I caught a glimpse of life's, or my own life's, most elementary principles.

No, I did not take leave of my senses, not then and not now as I grope for a string of metaphors to help me approach my feelings at that moment; I sensed quite clearly that what for me was a real prison, the prison of my senses and ideas, for the Frenchman on my left was merely a stage set smelling of greasepaint; after all, the only thing that was going on was that in that stage prison uncouth Jacquino was pursuing charming Marcellina, who had no use for his bumbling masculine charms because she pined for Fidelio, and this apparently kind and gentle young man—who was really a woman in disguise, working hard to free her beloved husband, Florestan, languishing in an underground dungeon—without too much thought, though with rueful sadness, Fidelio put up with Marcellina's misplaced affection so as to attain her politically and personally commendable goal, thus perpetrating the most outrageous or hilarious fraud of all: pretending to be a boy while she was a girl, which of course proves nothing except that the end justifies the means, since everybody loved or would love to love somebody else, but somehow managed to find their true loves, so we could suspend our moral considerations; in the meantime, my shoulder could not and did not want to break free of feeling the shoulder of the man on my right, whose indecent proximity surprised, humiliated, and frightened me no less than his turning away did, offending my vanity; and though I knew that this turning away was temporary, a transparent love ploy, and that he was using Thea as shamelessly as Fidelio in her male disguise was using charming Marcellina's not altogether pristine sentiments, for she should have noticed that that was no man in those clothes! Melchior, with his convenient bisexual approach, exploited and turned to his own advantage what in all this ambiguity was quite real, Thea's real feelings; by withdrawing attention from me, he was actually calling attention to our closeness, which he could do convincingly only by really turning away, by displaying real or potentially real feelings for Thea, giving her what he took from me; and this was just what was happening onstage, where Fidelio had to become a real man, a perfect prison guard, and pretend to seduce Marcellina, in order to be able to free her true love from captivity.

I felt, then, that Melchior was showing Thea something surprising and genuine in himself that had been hidden even from himself, and because I sensed his emotional turmoil, his boyish helplessness, I felt what Thea must have felt, and as she responded to his advances the only way one could in such circumstances, with sighs, altered breathing, glances, I felt that what was going on between them was something of complete mutuality.

In my intricate jealousy I didn't want Melchior, feared him, found his closeness intrusive, or, I should say, I didn't want only him, for I felt that my own desire, mediated by his body, was taking me toward Thea; it would be fair to say that I yielded to Melchior's approach to the extent that it allowed me to approach Thea.

This went on for the entire length of the performance: the closer Thea got to Melchior, the closer I got to her and the more and more palpably I felt his physical presence; I kept feeling I should put my hand on his knee, which surprised me, since as far as I knew it had never in my adult life occurred to me that I could put my hand on a man's knee and have the gesture suggest anything other than harmless friendship, yet I had this almost uncontrollable urge to touch him, and thought of this not only as a seductive gesture, a single gesture with a double purpose, to let him know that his advances were being returned, but also, at the moment more important, as a move with which to draw him away from Thea so that I could regain her for myself.

If then and there I'd thought of anything at all, I'd have thought of my adolescence; of course a great many thoughts crossed my mind, but not that; even if I hadn't thought of my own younger years, I might have reflected in general on the experiences accumulated during adolescence, which one hastens to forget, after one's harrowing initiation into adulthood with its fierce pains and hard-won pleasures.

I should have recalled that in the dreadful needs of adolescence the only way to escape the paralyzing and frustrating sensual urges, gropings, ignorance, is to choose the communally prepared, sanctioned, and delimiting forms of sexual behavior that, though not coinciding with our own preferences—by definition, predefined practices limit our personal freedom and at that age we find them excessive, burdensome, and morally unacceptable—help us within limits to find an optimal middle ground, ways of loving that enable us, by keeping to accepted sexual roles, to fulfill ourselves in another individual who also is undergoing similar crises in self-control; in return for the loss of our real needs and wants, we offer each other the almost personal, almost physical intensity of a passable sex life, and not even the gulf that opens up moments after physical fulfillment, not even the terrible void of impersonality seems unbridgeable, for the most impersonal union may produce something very personal and organic—a child, and there's nothing more real, organic, or complete than that; a child for us, we say to ourselves, out of the two of us, like and unlike us, to compensate us for all our barrenness until now, a child is duty and care, a source of sadness and joy and concern, all of it real, tangible, instead of motiveless anxiety it brings us purpose and meaning.

A shipwrecked person whose feet desperately seek something solid to keep him afloat will grab at anything, anyone, the first available object, and if it buoys him up he won't let go, he'll swim with it, and after a time he'll see he has nothing else! just this? and the object will grimly concur, yes, just this, nothing else! and the implacable impulse of self-preservation, joined of course by rationalization and mystification, will have him believe that the object that drifted his way by chance was really his, it chose him and he chose it, and by the time the sheer force of unrelenting waves casts him onto the shore of mature adulthood, his faith and gratitude will have made him worship what was accidental and adore fortuity, but can his rescue from destruction be really accidental?

Built on shaky emotional ground, the edifices of my sexuality, assiduously maintained for ten years and thought to be sound, were about to crumble; it seemed as if in all my previous love affairs I had merely yielded to the all-powerful instinct of survival, falling back repeatedly and ungratifyingly on pleasures I could always coax out of my body in lieu of one real gesture that might not even be a gesture; I could not grasp the meaning of my exertions, which was why I always had to grab something with my hands and hover over the depths with it, but once the ground had slipped out from under me, I could not regain my footing; that's why I could never really be consoled by physical pleasure, hence the constant, agonizing search for and pursuit of other, restlessly searching human bodies! and I wasn't shocked that through the body of the man sitting next to me I desired Thea, or that in Thea he sought me out, and that in her I found my way back to him, so that both of us were bound to hover over her; we were all trying to establish a relationship for two, but any way we looked at it, there were three of us; and if there were three, there could have been four or five; no, this sort of entanglement was no more surprising than a familiar image ready to become memory except we cannot locate its time and place of origin within ourselves; what did surprise me was that behind our entanglement I seemed to discover, in pure form, the sensual, physical embodiment of the elemental desire squirming around within me, and instead of paying attention to the action onstage, I was concentrating on this! small, sheathed in a bluish membrane, throbbing moistly with a life of its own, quite apart from them and even from me; it was as if I were seeing the bodily home of the pure life force which, regardless of modern theories, is neither male nor female: it has no sex, for its sole function is to allow free communication between human beings.

That evening I was given back some of the old freedom I thought I had lost, freedom of the heart, freedom of feeling, though today I'd say, and not without bitterness, that it was in vain to have regained that freedom, in vain to have all that sensitive perception and observation, because it was in understanding and assessing them that I proved myself a complaisantly foolish child of my times: I had a vague, elusive, but appropriate notion of the state of affairs, but I believed it to be a true discovery and wanted immediately to make it actual, to establish an intellectual position with emotional means, and further, I wanted practical results, success, to influence, run, control things, as though I were a high official of some ministry of love, making decisions based on information provided by available data; the conditioning of ten years spent in sexual manipulation came back to haunt me: I'd trust only what was palpably real, disregard everything that could not be reified and therefore physically enjoyed; in the name of reason I'd shut out of the sphere of reality anything that could not be fully comprehended, distancing myself from everything that could be perceived and validated only by the senses, which made up my personal, subjective reality; yet the opposite was also true: for the sake of my personal reality, I had to deny the existence of a larger, impersonal reality; and though my guilty conscience and a sense of my own unreality tried to tell me I was making a fatal mistake, I did not believe them.

I felt it necessary to relate all this before resuming my narrative and returning to our afternoon walk so I'd have a chance to set the intellectual and mental context in which to see two people interact, two people each of whom was not above using the other as a means to achieve specific ends, though their walk bound them together: to be metaphorical about it, they were walking along the same path that others had taken before them.

What was the point of honorable intentions, of the pursuit of neutrality, if continually, with every step we took, we sank into each other's emotional mire, and if that could not be separated from the living substance of our bodies; we may have confined ourselves to speaking in allusions, with intimations—never touching, at most falling into long silences—but even our words developed meanings that referred only to the two of us, leading us where we wanted to go, drawing out of us precisely what we honestly and not unreasonably wanted to achieve.

That's more or less how things were then; such were the emotional conditions in which we were moving out there in nature, as she began walking in front of me on the well-worn path toward the distant woods, and I, still surprised and pleased, was mulling over her quiet, bitter, terse confession, believing that her real aim was not to remind me of the true purpose and nature of our friendship—just at the point where our relationship turned too intimate and threatened to be impossible for both of us—but to draw me closer to her, take me into the deepest, most secret sphere of her life.

I could barely contain myself; I would have liked to toss all complications aside and reach after her and, moved by gratitude and the need to reciprocate, to pull her slender, fragile body to mine; I sensed her yielding even as she was moving away, although a moment earlier she had said that her whole life was a stupid waste, but for all the stupid things she might do, there were two people in her life, her girl friend and her husband, that she could always go back to; this, in our mutually developed language, meant that we could do anything we wanted to! I shouldn't be afraid of her, she felt safe, she could even abandon them and still they'd be there for her.

Too honest confessions, those that touch what we believe to be the most meaningful centers of our emotional life, are also betrayals.

If, for example, someone tells us why he dislikes his homeland, his confession will inevitably be an expression of his love for it and his desire to act on this love, while earnest, passionate affirmation of loyalty to one's country usually betrays loathing, suggesting that this country has caused one much pain, worry, despair, deep doubts, and paralyzing helplessness, and the crippled desire for action must retreat into enthusiastic expressions of loyalty.

Her restraint, laconic responses, and ambiguous yet well-formulated words made me realize that I wasn't wrong, Frau Kühnert was: Thea had changed during the past few weeks, and she was standing on a borderline; her confession to me was possible only because the bond that was the one certainty of her life had become burdensome and intolerable for her, and she shared this with me because she wanted me to thrust her across that border, so that she would break that bond—she did want to break it.

The most obvious means to do this, using my hands, perhaps my body, to give her that push, was out of the question, it would have been too much and inappropriate.

Just as on that memorable Sunday afternoon, when Melchior's heart-rending, animal-like sobs had taught me that the body alone would not suffice as consolation, he at the time wanted more, he was asking for my body's future, something I'd have control over only if I were to yield to him completely, unconditionally, and perhaps it was cowardice, but I did not have that kind of control and so I did not give him my body.

And I felt that my body was both insufficient and inappropriate for the task, though with the darkest, most instinctive knowledge that can be extracted from this same body, I sensed the possibilities in Melchior's and Thea's bodies, possibilities where my body could serve only as mediator; all I wanted was to serve them.

In the cause of achieving a distant goal, I offered myself as a neutral means of mediation, and they, obeying the rules of selfishness, accepted and used me as such; what we did not take into account was that no moral interest or romantic self-denial can neutralize the sex of any human body; all I had left was my own self-control, but this gave me the pleasurably turbulent excitement of a criminal before his act, so that the desire to help was no longer motivated by love but by the urge to murder love and banish the lovers from my heart.

But in that case it wasn't I who was walking along that trail but two legs, themselves strangers, carrying the hollow form of a servile intention, which is what it had turned into, without the joy of the moment of fulfillment: a leaden weight to be dragged along for the sake of a distant future that might restore one's life, or at least one's honor.

The dark green of the pine needles, like a single massive wave of the sea, tossed and tumbled above the reddish tree trunks.

The trail disappeared under a soft carpet of fallen pine needles once it reached the woods; under the trees it was almost completely dark.

Thea must have sensed that I wasn't too keen on following her there, because she stopped at the first trees and, without pulling her hands from the deep pockets of her red coat, leaned against a tree trunk, looked back as if to size up the distance already covered, and, sliding slowly down the trunk, lowered herself to a crouch, without sitting down.

We did not look at each other.

She was looking out at the soft undulations of a peaceful landscape growing dark under huge, swirling, rippling clouds now obscuring now revealing the light still playing in the sky, and I was looking into dimming woods filled with the pungent smell of decaying leaves, with ephemeral flashes of stray lights still cutting through the dimness, keeping it in constant motion.

After a while Thea rummaged in a pocket, pulled out a long cigarette, matches, and struggling with the wind lit up.

While still busy with the cigarette she said she was doing something she shouldn't.

Yes, I said solemnly, I've often wanted to do more of those things myself.

She blinked up at me, as if to understand the hidden meaning of my transparent witticism, but I did not return her look; I went on standing among the trees without any support.

I was always making these faces, she told me somewhat louder, as if I were smelling something rotten; then, more quietly and cautiously, she asked me if she had offended me in any way.

I looked past her shoulder, but still saw her face, the coy and provocative tilt of her head; what would happen, I suddenly thought, amused by the idea, if I took this soft red furball, knocked her over, and trampled her into the ground right here under this tree? in my jaw and teeth I felt my feet trampling the ground.

The sensation of violence made me nauseous; in the silence I imagined myself after the murder returning to the flat on Steffelbauerstrasse, throwing my things into a suitcase, getting on a plane, and from the air still seeing this place, shrunken to a dot, the telltale red of her coat still visible under the green carpet of treetops.

Just a woman struggling with her impending old age, I thought, but why was their youth so important to them? my annoyance and disgust was directed not at aging but at that special attraction I felt for declining forms, for I found her eroding features beautiful, like her struggle against her decline, which made her open up to me so shamelessly, giving away more of herself than she would have if she was still young and her features still smooth.

Actually, she said, she was sorry she wasn't in love with me.

But she is, I thought to myself.

For example, she imagined to herself, she continued after a pause—either misinterpreting the excited flutter of my eyes made her bold or the excitement triggered by her insincere candor had not yet abated—how I must look naked.

Judging by my face and hands and everything else that's visible, she'd guess I was a little soft and flabby, and if I wasn't careful I'd soon look as disgusting as Langerhans.

Everything about me was so ingratiating and obliging, so damn kind and decent and low-keyed, so self-consciously attentive, one might think I had no muscles in my body, and not many bones either, only aesthetic, smooth, hairless surfaces, yes, that must be me, and she wouldn't be surprised if I had absolutely no smell either.

I stepped closer and crouched down facing her; in that case, I said, taking the cigarette from her hand, would she mind telling me just what position she imagined seeing me in, I'd be most curious to know.

She followed the cigarette with her eyes, as if afraid I'd take too long a drag, but also thrilled that in this indirect way at least her lips would touch mine, then quickly took it back; though we were both careful, our hands touched, our fingers exchanging our anxious reserve as if fearing a catastrophe might befall us any moment.

Yes, she said in a deep and husky voice, appearances are deceptive sometimes; it was just possible, she said, that I was all skin and bones, as dry and cruel as I seemed.

Why don't you answer my question? I asked.

She didn't want to hurt me, she said before taking another puff.

You can't hurt me.

Though life is full of contradictions, she said, because when I opened my mouth she had the impression she was sticking her finger into dough, which wasn't necessarily a bad thing either.

Let's not kid each other, I said, it wasn't me she imagined, for her I was more like some necessary supplement, a little extra workout to keep her bones from getting rusty.

Brazenly she laughed in my face; in our crouching position our faces were only inches apart; then she pushed herself away from the trunk and, still crouching, began to sway, letting her face get even closer, then pulling farther apart, she kept playing with the space between us.

No, no, I was wrong, she said, offering the cigarette again; she did imagine me also for herself.

Also, I said.

We are greedy, aren't we, she said.

We were splashing about in the joy of boldness, crude openness, in the way we traded imagined nakedness for shamelessness; the wrinkles around her eyes disappeared; and yet there was something very uncomfortable in all this, as if we were exchanging our cheapest, most superficial aspects.

She even imagined, she said, or at least tried to imagine, what on earth we two could possibly do with each other.

Her face was beaming.

By now the cigarette, having gone back and forth, had only one good puff left; I carefully handed it back to her, and she took it from me just as carefully; as she took the last drag, a long one, as if in the time it took before the cigarette burned her finger, everything had to be decided, she blinked and buried her embarrassment in that blink.

And whatever it was we did together, why wasn't it happening to her, my mean and cynical self thought to itself.

However, the question struck me as a possible answer to a far larger question: why did we consider direct bodily contact, the pleasure deriving from one body penetrating another, more complete and more intense than any kind of mental pleasure, why was that the ultimate in human contact? and even farther afield, almost at the very edge of thought, loomed the question of whether war itself wasn't just such a necessary and deceptive pleasure in the contact between different peoples, for we know all too well that in most cases physical union is nothing more than the manipulation of biological drives, more like a quick, always conjurable, easy, and false consolation for unfulfillable spiritual needs than a true fulfillment.

In principle she had no objection, Thea said, and did not lean back against the tree.

The earlier brightness had gone from her face; pensively she stubbed out the cigarette and pressed it carefully into the ground, under the thick layer of pine needles.

Well, maybe a tiny one, she continued after a brief pause, and that's something every woman must feel when something is taken away from her, something that should be hers to give, but because in this case she was that woman, she involuntarily, almost instinctively, approved.

Oddly enough, she wasn't jealous of us, she said; yes, that first time, at the opera, when she finally figured out what was going on, she might have been, but only because it caught her by surprise, and did it ever occur to me that she was the one who had brought us together?

The next day when the two of us showed up at her house, and she saw what an effort it took for us not to let on that something had happened between us in the meantime, and how charmingly solemn and serious we became from all that effort, by then she wasn't jealous, but rather glad, well, maybe not glad, that would be going a little too far.

And did I ever notice, she asked, that women were much more tolerant of male homosexuals than men were?

All right, women would say, it's terrible, unnatural, disgusting, but still, I could be his mother.

She stopped talking, didn't look at me, kept patting and smoothing the ground over the buried cigarette, absently contemplating her fingers' fire-prevention activities.

I had a feeling she was going to say it—it was hard for her, but she would say it—and perhaps that's why I didn't want to interrupt, for this was about her and me, the two of us.

But in the present situation, which was very demeaning for her, she went on, she might have been very difficult and she might torment me and say ugly and stupid things to me, but she was really grateful to me, because just by being there I kept her from doing something that could turn into a tragedy—or a farce.

She fell silent again, still unable to say it.

Then she looked at me.

I'm an old woman, she said.

Her statement, her look, the slight quiver of her voice had not the slightest trace of self-pity and self-indulgence, not even as much as might seem natural and understandable; she looked at me so openly with her beautiful brown eyes that the physical image of her face blotted out the meaning of her sentence.

The inner strength she mustered to utter that sentence, the strength she hurled into my eyes, now did something to her: she was no longer a woman, or old, or beautiful, or anything, but a single human being struggling with the heroic task of self-definition in a universe still enthralling in its infinite possibilities—and that was beautiful.

She certainly could not have done it inside a room; there all this would have turned into sentimental soul-searching or lovemaking; between four walls I would have found her statement comical, too true or too false, either way it was the same, and would have protested vehemently or made light of it; but here, with nothing to echo these meaningful sounds, they left her mouth, came up against my face, I took some into myself, and the rest dissipated, vanished into the landscape, found their proper, final place.

And in that moment I realized that the source of her beauty was always her raw anguish; I had met a human being who did not want to eliminate her own suffering or exploit it either, but simply wanted to retain her capacity for pain, and that was the quality that might explain my attraction to her: she wasn't interested in enlisting sympathy, which was why she objected so strenuously to living-the-part or getting-lost-in-the-part method acting; she had nothing to conceal, since what she showed of herself was something she extracted from me—something I always tried to keep hidden.

And in exchange I was giving her my own pain, so similar to hers and forever obscured by clouds of self-pity and self-deception.

It wasn't her age that made her old, she added quickly, as if wanting to destroy any illusion that her self-pity was meant to elicit my sympathy, or her own; no, counting only her years she could still consider herself young, it was her soul that was old, but that was silly, too, she didn't have a soul, she said, she didn't know what it was, then, something in her or about her.

It was strange that lately she had to play all these lovesick women, vamps and all sorts of seductive females, and she was always good at it, but when she had to fall into the arms of strange men and kiss strange mouths, she found she wasn't there anymore, it was as if someone else were doing it for her, someone else was playing at being in love.

Love and desire in her—and she begged my pardon if she was about to say something stupid—became something no longer directed at another living human being but at everyone, anyone, yes, silly as it may sound, aimed at anything and everything that was humanly impossible to reach, and she was no longer interested in reaching, but feeling this way made her very pitiful in her own eyes.

If she really didn't want to reach it, she wouldn't be able to act, I said quietly, and since she did want to act, she had to reach what she no longer wanted.

Her eyelashes quivered hesitantly; she either didn't understand what I said or didn't want to; she chose to ignore it.

She said she'd be lying if she claimed this was the first fiasco of her life, it wasn't, not by a long shot, she was never beautiful enough or ingratiating enough to rise above a constant state of failure, she got used to it.

But she wouldn't talk about this anymore, she said, interrupting herself abruptly; she found it ridiculous and in bad taste to be discussing this with me, of all people, but then who should she discuss it with?

I didn't want to distract her with questions or friendly, consoling words; anything coming from me would have stifled her; I knew she wanted to talk, but would have understood if she hadn't said another word.

In the fragrant puffs of her voice bouncing off my face I felt she wasn't talking to me, she was sending words to the surface of my body, whose mediating reverberation turned them into the purest form of address directed at her self.

She had to stand up, but she did it as though her body had been filled with a single thought of anger that wouldn't let her straighten out her knees, making her look stooped and ugly.

The skin on her chin grew taut.

No, she said, this wasn't true either.

She said this and then bit off the rest of her words, also squelching the meaning of the unsaid words.

And this may have hurt me more than it hurt her; at least she had the courage to say what she wanted to.

But she wasn't interested in any kind of truth, in anybody's truth.

Sometimes she could make herself believe there was no such thing as humiliation.

There was a time, soon after they got to know each other, when she thought she could throw everything to the winds for him, but fortunately, she was more sensible now.

And for him she could have killed her husband, Arno, who snored away all their nights.

And yes, she admitted, it was she who kept calling Melchior at night.

And she came up with this stupidity about being old because her body was going to pieces in this humiliation which had been going on for months, and her mind could concentrate on nothing else, no matter how much she told herself she was over it; she was becoming like an addle-brained teenager who can only think about how ugly she is.

These stupid feelings would never leave her, and then, on top of it all, she had to look at our disgustingly happy faces.

And then I would have liked to tell her that the happiness she saw was indeed real but that I had never felt a more persistent suffering than this happiness; but of course I couldn't tell her any of this.

She wasn't jealous of me, she said; it was disgust she felt, rather than jealousy, the kind of disgust that makes men scrawl on toilet walls things like Castrate the fags, she said more softly, placatingly; of course she knew it wasn't the the same thing, she said, as a matter of fact she felt a certain approval regarding our relationship, and despite all her swearing and rage, she couldn't be jealous of me as she would be of another woman, she took it almost as if I were her substitute, but that was humiliating, because she didn't want to come between us, yet she just had to keep calling him on the phone, she couldn't help it.

Now that she said it, maybe she wouldn't be calling anymore.

And if in the midst of this constant state of turmoil she could retain a modicum of sanity, then she could feel that maybe she had chosen this impossible predicament because she didn't really want him anymore, she wanted something else, equally impossible; and that really put her at a loss, for that couldn't possibly be happening to her, she really was too old for that kind of perfect impossibility.

She didn't want anything anymore.

Not even to die.

Why did her life fall apart and why couldn't she put it back together, or rather, why did all the pieces she still had left add up to nothing.

Even as she was talking she felt her talking was nothing, her words were nothing, it was only habit that made her say these nothings out loud.

And now she was going to stop altogether, we should really get going.

And I should get up, too.

She wasn't talking loudly, and I can't even say there was passion or excitement caused by suppressed tension in her voice, yet she wiped away invisible drops of perspiration above her lips.

And in that gesture there was something an old person would do, which younger people wouldn't be caught doing, for they wouldn't find it aesthetic.

I stood up, our faces were again very close, she smiled.

Well, I had never seen her in an open-air performance before, she said, and tilted her head to the side.

This last, awkward attempt at ending things and distancing herself sobered me up, perhaps because it was so awkward and self-conscious, because she seemed to have bitten into herself and, though painful, that prevented her from revealing a far greater pain; once again I was aware of the coolness of the air, the pungent autumn fragrance of the pine trees, the reassuring smallness of our bodies that only moments earlier seemed magnified in the vastness of the flat landscape.

And I felt an increasingly impatient urge to leave the place, get back to her car, lock ourselves in its safe, confining space; at the same time, from so close, her gestures and words suggested unmistakably that I was treading on very dangerous ground if I gave her the impression I was trying to hold her back, since, in reality, with my sheer presence I was hoping to thrust her toward something; the wish to murder her that had flashed through my mind moments earlier was more than an innocent play of my imagination; consciously repressed sexual desires produce such violent impulses; but even if I did reach my goal and manage to get the two of them together, what would I have done with such an impulse— save using it to kill myself.

Or maybe it was the other way around, I thought, inverting cause and effect with a casual shrug of my shoulders: the reason I wanted them to get together, wanted to get away from them and get closer to a woman, any woman, felt a man's body to be insufficient, too little or too much, was that I wanted to kill my love for Melchior; and the reason I couldn't make anything last was that deep in my soul I feared the punishment which others, in their great anxiety about their own sexuality, scrawled as warnings on bathroom walls.

But I couldn't run away, or escape, not yet; there were still words hanging on her lips that she would dare formulate only after turning from the intimate proximity she had created between us to the petty world of practicality full of cold calculations, only after this alluring and circum-spect introduction.

I waited, and she could see in my eyes how this waiting was wearing me down; she had the upper hand, she could ask anything, say anything; she was vulnerable only while talking, but what she told me made me the more vulnerable of the two of us.

This mutual vulnerability began to affect us: the emotions emerging from a consciously controlled desire, my defenselessness, and my secret wish to reach her through the very man she loved drove me to the edge of helplessness and ridiculousness, to the verge of tears—yes, my futile exertion sent tears to my eyes, and she, pressing her advantage, stroked my face, kindly and with restrained excitement, as if making herself believe that it was her story that had moved me so, and didn't or wouldn't see that the tears had just as much to do with helpless, frustrated desire; still, her fingers trembled on my skin, I felt it and so did she, and we both knew that we were entering the time of catastrophe we had dreaded only moments earlier; this meant a renewed fear, or rather a cause for recoiling.

But she managed to grab my arm, as if holding on to her own advantage.

If the ethics of love were not stronger than love's desire, I wouldn't have left time for this move, I would have reciprocated the trembling of her fingers with a kiss on her lips; and if that had happened, she would not have demurred, I'm sure, but would have dissolved her own helplessness on my mouth, but since this didn't happen, her lips quivered for the lack of contact, for the shame of this lack.

Again we had to retreat, because the ethics of love do not tolerate the presence of the slightest foreign element, everything must be directed exclusively at one's partner, and only through one's partner can a third person have any relevance; this retreat again turned me into a means: she held on to me only insofar as she needed to get closer to Melchior, and we once again found ourselves in a rather dark territory where I also had to stick to my objective of reaching her through Melchior.

So, this meant, I stammered, that she didn't love me; in her language this could be expressed by using a more mundane, less emotionally charged word, as if I were to say in Hungarian that she didn't care for me all that much.

But she did love me, she did.

The last syllable was uttered on my neck, blown onto my skin from a kiss of parting and quickly closing lips.

Of course all the feelings we had had until then ceased in the wake of that kiss.

However, we were holding each other, filling up with many little details of ever-intensifying sensations, standing there, our arms entwined, a little lost, stunned by the newness of the other's body, not sure our minds could or even cared to name or analyze this new situation so deprived of logic; and it all turned out as if two coats were embracing, a little too theatrical, a little too rigid; what should have dissolved did not, for no matter how tightly we clung to each other, there was not enough passion in our bodies meant just for the other, or not enough details in the passion each of us had hoped would be exclusively ours, as if no power could dispel or neutralize the sensation that we were just two coats.

In such or similar situations our love experience can rush to our aid; with tiny, slow, cautious, and barely touching kisses I could have opened her lips resting bashfully on my neck; four little kisses like that could have opened her lips, and if at the same time I eased her body away from mine, broke the closeness, then she would again kiss my neck so that the rapid little kisses buried in our necks would rouse our desire for closeness, which could be quenched only by the closeness of lips, and so on, until we reached the state of no-closeness-is-close-enough.

It wouldn't have taken much to find the way to our bodies' biological urges, and without resorting to anything false or vulgar, for we did love each other, after all, and neither the coats nor our own clumsiness hindered us; but if that had happened, we would have transgressed against the ethics of love.

She had to stand on tiptoe to reach me, which I found especially endearing; her lips rested on my neck for a little while longer, waiting, as if wondering whether I would do what experience dictated now; and my mouth was on her neck, waiting for the possibility of a mutual response that would make a third partner vanish; at the same time I felt the wind's gentle little thrusts on my body.

Yet she couldn't have wished my mouth to make any of the experienced moves; she was the first to yield to Melchior's intrusive presence, and this was natural, since she wasn't as close to him as I was, and only if you're sure of possessing someone can you afford to stray; she pushed me away a little, but we did not break our embrace; she looked into my face with all of hers, she was so close that my eyes, trying to focus, ached a little, but the dull pain felt good, because at this close range the other's face can be superimposed on your own and the blurry sight is absorbed into your own uncertain vision.

Her senses had never deceived her, she said in a choked, agitated voice, her saliva's scent, mixed with nicotine but still sweet, pleasantly surprising my nose so unaccustomed to a woman's scent, what she said referred to both of us, as well as to the one who stood between us.

But the attraction of her scent was not strong enough to overcome a sudden revulsion, an urge to get away from this voice, from this face! for the face was not only distorted, like mine, it wasn't merely responding to my bewilderment with her own; hers seemed maniacal and possessed, and it occurred to me, not for the first time, that she might be insane.

Everything she said and did, every ounce of her strength, every wish, every aspect of her curiosity sprang from a tiny, sensitive, painful, and balm-seeking point of her being, and everything penetrating her from the outside world in the form of strength, desire, and curiosity was channeled back to the same point; if by some miracle I could have freed us of our clothes, and my body could have begged hers for mercy, and kissing and clinging to her I could have sunk into her wetness, I still wouldn't have reached her.

At the moment I saw her as someone willing to oblige but not to reciprocate.

In a way it was ludicrous to discover this about her in that situation, but she frightened me; I was alarmed that she might indeed be crazy, and then I must be crazy, too.

And against my better judgment I had to admit that Frau Kühnert, though she may have been driven by jealousy, was probably right: for Thea, people and feelings were only tools, means to some end; but since at that moment I myself was this tool, exposed and at the mercy of her sensitive touch, the fragrance rising from her neck and lips, I found this state of affairs tragic rather than amusing.

How did I ever get myself into this?

Whoever she picked out, she whispered hoarsely into my mouth, had to be one who had also picked her, she could be wrong about anything else, and also crazy and ugly and old.

No, no, she must be deranged or crazy, I thought, for thinking it made it less scary.

She might be vulgar and a fool, but she was never wrong about these things, and I must tell her—she was speaking right into my mouth and only a very abrupt, rough movement could have freed me from this position—because sometimes she felt, actually she felt for the first time, that she might have been deceiving herself in this case, so I must tell her whether Melchior had ever loved a woman.

Only madness could make somebody expend such an inordinate amount of physical and mental energy on so witless a question.

I pushed her away gently, but not so gently as to make it not seem cruel, for I had no intention of sparing her this cruelty.

Our arms fell helplessly to our sides, our bodies tilted back to their respective, balanced postures; as she looked at me, her face was so naked, as mine must have been looking at her, that it was as if we were seeing not each other's skin but the flesh, the bones, the rushing blood, the dividing cells, everything in the body that is selfish and self-serving and has nothing to do with another person; and at this point I should have said, It's over, let's quit, we're playing an impossible game, she's playing with me, at the expense of a third one, though we pretended to be playing for his sake.

I wanted to say all this but didn't.

It even seemed that the rudeness of my movement was useful in hiding a more calculating, more far-reaching act of kindness with which I could budge the moment of impasse into the next moment, delay and put off things and still leave her with a ray of hope.

Her hopelessness hurt me more than it hurt her, for she at least, by expressing it, could relieve herself of its pressure, and indeed, a faint glow of forced satisfaction did appear on her face, an almost audacious, sad smile that harked back not only to the question of Melchior's relation to women but also to the more provocative one about what Melchior and I could possibly do with each other that was so different from what she could be doing with me or with him, or could these things be completely identical? but this very common, pedestrian question only reinforced in me the feeling of hopelessness from which I wanted to save Melchior.

I was wrong, I thought, almost out loud, one could want another person only through that person's sex, except this was not to be, since everyone was more than his or her own sex, or maybe one never really wanted that other person; I was either wrong or crazy.

Of course, there was nothing to stop me from answering her, from explaining in simple terms what she wanted to know; but then I would have had to describe this relationship, unique and involving my whole being, in purely sexual terms, and that would have been a lie, an act of self-deception, a betrayal.

Let's go, I said out loud.

She said it was still early; she wanted to walk some more.

I could think of nothing except that I was wrong, and in the end things were very simple and she was the one who was right, because she felt the simplicity of things with her body, which I apparently couldn't feel; if she wanted to make soup she'd buy vegetables, meat, and seasonings, she'd put water in a pot which she'd set on the stove, light the stove, yes, that's how obvious it all must have been to everyone else but me; but then I must be wrong or insane.

And because I couldn't tell her any of this, I simply turned around, ready to walk back.

I would have started back, but like one just waking up and not knowing where he is, I found no path under my feet, because I had reached the end of a notion, or delusion; it was as though I had no idea what all this was, how and why we had ended up here, who this woman was, or perhaps we weren't at the place I thought we were, because the space around me had shifted and I found myself in an unfamiliar corner of an unfamiliar world, or more precisely, I did not find myself, I was nowhere, I did not exist; and then I must not have been waking from but sinking into an even deeper region of unreality.

Drained of color, the landscape was exhaling a gentle gray mist; only the edges of the massing clouds were still reflecting the windy red of dusk; down here there were no more curves, edges, or borders, and time itself had run out, though its infinitely divisible content remained inside me, but now it was formless, and what my eyes saw was also a similar formlessness.

I was making my way through chaos, moving neither forward nor backward, and certainly not along the trail, for a trail is only a concept we invent to help relieve us of our own bothersome physical mass; all right, no trail then, only the ground beaten flat by others before me, and no mist either, only water, and matter, everywhere and in everything only immovable matter.

Maybe the color of red light around the edges of vaporous clouds, but that, too, was only dust, sand, and smoke, the residue of the earth's matter; or perhaps it was light itself, which I can never see clearly.

I was quiet, because there was no landscape, only matter, weight and mass; I felt like screaming that I was deprived of beauty, there was no beauty and no form, for that, too, was but a notion with which I hoped to tear myself away from my own formlessness, but my mental exertion was laughable because, if there was still formless matter, if I could feel at least its weight, its chaotic state, then who was depriving me of anything?

When she opened the car door for me and I got in, I could see that she had calmed down, everything in her had gone silent, and from behind the silence she was listening to me, exclusively, attentively, rather as if she were tending someone very sick or a mental patient; before turning her attention to the always troublesome ignition she looked at me as if she understood something of what had just happened between us.

Where to, she asked.

She had never asked that before, I said, why now?

She released the handbrake and let the car roll down the hill.

All right, she'd take me home, then, she said.

No, I said, I was going to Melchior's place.

The engine coughed, shuddered, the whole contraption jerked violently, but the car started and we turned back onto the highway; the headlights cut a bright piece of the road out of the dusk which the accelerating wheels kept tucking away under them.

That's what we all do, we tuck the future under us in the front and let the past out in the rear, and we call that progress, but the division is arbitrary; the continuity of recurring elements in time can be checked only with the notion we call speed; and that is what history is, nothing more; that is my own story; I made a mistake, and I kept repeating my mistakes.

And yet with her silence, her tactful silence, she was now giving me a bit of hope; I felt that, too.

Later, I asked her if she knew that Melchior at one time had studied to be a violinist.

Yes, she knew, but let's not talk about him anymore.

What should we talk about, then? I asked.

Nothing, she said.

And did she know why he stopped playing the violin?

No, she didn't, but right now she didn't care to find out.

Imagine a seventeen-year-old boy, I said; the fact that I had to raise my voice over the tinny clatter of an ancient two-stroke engine, speaking so loudly, practically shouting into her ears things that would have real meaning only in the tranquillity of the soul, actually enhanced this last of my little performances; I decided to have one more try, really the last one, and by having to raise my voice I'd have my revenge, too, as if to say to her, You wanted to hear it, well, here it is, now you can hear it! and that helped me broach and sully a forbidden subject, and also overcome the shame of my betrayal.

So imagine a seventeen-year-old boy who, in a quaint old town, recently bombed to smithereens in the war, was admired as a prodigy—I was shouting in a strange voice to drown out the engine, and asked her if she had ever been in that town, because suddenly it seemed very important to me that she know the houses, the street, the air, the fragrant winter

536

apples on top of the cupboard, the wide moat around the old castle now overgrown with shrubs, and the spot on the ceiling over his bed.

And as I thought of this, I realized that my tone was wrong, wrong as all the others I had used; without the right tone and feelings the story itself could not be told.

No, unfortunately, she had never been there, but now she would really like me to talk about something else or, better yet, just keep quiet.

I should have told her about that evening, about the sticky, breezeless evening air as we stepped out of the house on Wörther Platz and just stood there on the street, because deciding on a route for our walk was always important, it had to match our emotional state and our plans for the future.

Could she imagine the condition, I shouted at her, in which an adolescent boy cannot yet distinguish between the beauty of the body and the power of its abilities?

Raising her head high to steady her awful glasses, she listened reluctantly, pretending to be interested only in the road ahead; I could just go on, my voice would mean nothing more than the clatter and drone of the engine.

That evening, or night rather, when Melchior told me the story, we must have been looking for open spaces, because we chose a shorter route, but then ended up taking the longer one to Weissensee, or White Lake.

On the terrace of the beer hall we took two iron chairs out of the stacked pile; they creaked uninvitingly in the dark; we settled down only long enough to have a smoke before moving on; it was cold.

It must have been around midnight, only an occasional call of wild ducks could be heard from the lake, otherwise everything was dark and still.

I was telling him about my little sister, about her death, about the institution my father had taken her to, where I had visited her only once, I hadn't the courage to go back again; I was telling him about that single visit during which, remembering our old game, she wedged herself between my knees, which was a call for me to squeeze her.

And I did squeeze her, and she laughed, and kept on laughing for an hour and a half, did nothing but laugh, which in her language meant she was anxious to please me, was telling me that if I took her away she'd reward me with her unending happiness, but it was also possible, I told Melchior, that it was the pain of my indifference that made me see it that way.

He put his elbow on the table, leaned his head on his hand, and looked down at me—I had pulled over two chairs and stretched out on them with my head in his lap.

Two years later, I told him, because I could never go back to that place again, I found a note on my desk: Your sister died, funeral at such and such time.

There was no light near us, we saw each other's face only in the glow of our cigarettes.

He listened patiently to the end, but not without a certain aversion.

Melchior shied away from everything that had to do with my past; whenever I talked about it he would listen, but in spite of his polite or seemingly polite interest, his muscles would grow tense as if to prevent my past from penetrating him; the present, the moment, my presence was more than enough for him.

I could also say that he was looking down at me with the reservation of a mature man energetically active in his present; he was slightly shocked but indulged this weakness in me, for he did love me; he clearly disapproved of my obsession with certain aspects of my past which normal adult men, done with their past once and for all, find improper to bring up.

But as he listened to me, a radically different process was also taking place in him: as usual, he kept correcting my grammatically faulty sentences, he did this almost unawares, it had become an unconscious habit between us; in fact, he was the one who shaped my sentences, gave them the proper structure, incorporated them into the neat order of his native language, I had to rely on his expropriated sentences to work my way through my linguistic rubble, had to use his sentences to tell my story, and didn't even notice that some of these jointly produced sentences were repeated two or three times, their place and value reshuffled, before reaching intelligible form.

It was as if I had to use my own past to coax the story of his past out of him. I didn't think of it then, but now I believe we needed these evening walks not just for the exercise but to relate to the world around us—which we both felt, though for different reasons, to be cheerless and alien—and to do it in a way that this same world would not be aware of what we were doing.

I also liked the way he smoked his cigarettes.

There was something solemn and ceremonious about the way he tapped the pack and pulled out a cigarette with his long fingers; the act of lighting it was special, too, as was each puff he took, inhaling voluptuously, long and deep, holding it down for a long time; and then he'd blow out slowly, curling the smoke with his lips; he truly enjoyed the sight of the smoke, reaching after it with his tongue, forming rings and sticking his finger carefully into them; and between puffs he held his cigarette in his hand as if to say, Look, everyone, here is a cigarette, and we now have the rare privilege of being able to smoke in peace; lighting up, for us, was not simply the act of common puffing on a common cigarette but the very essence of smoking pleasure.

This was neither the frugality of someone trying to deny himself all but the tiniest delights nor a sensualist's wallowing in pleasure; this was Melchior's tendency—doubtless the result of a puritan upbringing—to reflect on things very carefully, and continually to modify his goals as well as the means by which to achieve them; he wanted to be part of every occurrence, never to allow things just to happen to him, to be fully conscious of them, to give meaning and emphasis to his own existence every step of the way, to transcend the here and now with his reflections and ideas, to grasp and hold on to existence itself.

When I was with Thea, anything could happen, which also meant that nothing ever happened, though of course some things did, whereas with Melchior I had the feeling that whatever happened had to happen just that way, every occurrence was the right one, but it also seemed as though it had been decided beforehand what these occurrences might be.

I don't know what sentence or minor turning point in my story struck a chord in him, but his body, tense from uneasy attention, moved as if suddenly he had found my head resting on his lap uncomfortable; nothing changed, he did not loosen his muscles or reach out to touch me, he maintained his disciplined composure, but something intensely disquieting lay behind his restrained calm.

When telling someone about one's life, it's not at all unusual to find similar situations in the other's life, even if, in the intimacy of sharing, our story may appear unique; the reason we tell each other stories in the first place is that we are sure the same story is there, lying dormant in our listener.

And no matter how mature and content with his present a person may be, no matter how complete and foolproof his isolation from his own past may seem, upon hearing such an apparently unique story he cannot resist: his own similar stories will come to life and demand to be heard, as if he himself had exclaimed, gesticulating like a child, Hey, I've got one of those! and that joyful discovery of kinship is what makes two people in conversation keep cutting into each other's words.

If we view these stories, submerged in the events of our lives, from another, broader perspective, if we consider telling them as activities indispensable to maintaining our mental health, we could also say that in finding them to be common, even in just the telling of them, we measure the weight and validity of our experiences, and in the similarities appearing in these shared and jointly measured experiences we may find some regularity bordering on prescribed rules; so, telling stories, relating and exchanging events in our lives, any kind of storytelling—whether it's gossiping, reporting a crime, spinning a yarn while having a drink, or gabbing with neighbors on the front stoop—is nothing more than the most common method of ethical regulation of human behavior; to feel my kinship with others I must tell about my uniqueness, and conversely, in kinship and similarities I must find the differences that set me apart from everyone else.

There was a girl, he said, cutting me off with the kind of impoliteness that is mitigated by the relevance of the comment, I probably remember the house where his violin teacher lived, he pointed it out to me, well, this girl lived across the street; he no longer remembered how the thing had started, but after a while he noticed that the girl knew exactly when he would arrive for his lesson, because at just that moment she would appear in her window and stay until the lesson was over.

She watched him in an odd pose, or at least it seemed odd to him then, leaning against the window frame with her outturned palms and her tummy, and pulling her shoulders up she rocked back and forth very slowly; he always positioned himself so his teacher wouldn't notice their little game.

I had the feeling that a tremendous weight shifted in his body as he spoke, and when after a short pause he took a puff on his cigarette I could see in the brightening glow his self-conscious reticence giving way to a lighthearted tenderness, with which he was yielding to his memories.

And as he spoke, I also thought of his odd-sounding poems, not that in his poems he didn't show the ability for sudden shifts, soaring bravely then plunging to the depths; if anything, he must have been frightened by the force of these abrupt shifts, by the sharpness of his vision, because he'd hurl himself into a linguistic realm so burdened with abstract concepts that neither his past nor his present could appear there in plain, undisguised form; the weight or rarefied air of abstract thinking stifled the language that might have expressed anything simple or based on raw sensual experiences.

She was a beautiful girl, he went on after a pause, or at least he thought so at the time; since then she'd put on a lot of weight and had two awful children; anyway, she was about his height, which for a girl was pretty tall, and when he had a chance to take a closer look, he noticed that her hair, tied in a ponytail at the top of her head, began as blond fuzz around her forehead; and when he thought about her once in a great while, it was always this blond fuzz he saw; she had a strong, well-shaped forehead; her name was Marion.

He finished his cigarette, threw it on the ground, and to crush it with his shoe had to lift my head, but he lifted it as if it were a strange, troublesome object; I had to sit up.

I must excuse him for interrupting me, he said, he really didn't have anything more to say, it was cold, let's move on; and I should continue my own story, his wasn't important at all, he didn't even know why he'd thought of it.

On the way home not a word was said; we were listening to the sound of our footsteps.

Back in the apartment all the lights were on, just as we had left them.

It was very late, and we both pretended that by being busy, doing routine little things, we could bring to a close this useless day.

While he was undressing in the bedroom, I cleared off the remnants of our dinner; when I got to the kitchen with the dishes, he was standing naked by the sink, brushing his teeth.

In the yellow lamplight his body looked pale, colorless, his loins were like a curious bunch of curls, his shoulder blades an exaggerated protrusion; framed sharply by his bony pelvis, his stomach appeared sunken, and his long thighs were thinner than they should have been, that is to say, out of proportion to the rest of his body, at least when measured against some ideal male physique; he looked frail and forlorn next to my still clothed body, though he would have looked just as frail to me even if I, too, had had no clothes on, for he seemed so remote, standing there with his naked body as if he were not present at all, not even in his own body, and I seemed to be observing, from the sympathetic and neutral distance of brotherly feeling for human frailty and fallibility, a body I was otherwise crazy about.

As usual, the window was open; walls and rooftops seemed jammed together in the darkness of the night; from the lit-up stairwell anyone could have looked in, but this never bothered him.

Taking the toothbrush out of his mouth he glanced back at me, and with his mouth still foamy with toothpaste he said he'd sleep on the sofa.

Later, in the dead silence of the bedroom, I found I couldn't take this unexplained silence of his; tossing and turning I couldn't fall asleep; I went over to him and thought I'd lie down next to him if he was already sleeping.

In the dark I asked him if he was asleep.

No, he wasn't.

The drawn curtains let in no light.

The darkness was neither inviting nor forbidding; I found the edge of the sofa and sat down; he didn't move.

He didn't seem to be breathing.

I used my hands to take a look at his body; he was lying on his back, his arms comfortably folded on his chest.

I placed my hand on his folded arms, nothing more, just the weight of my hand.

Maybe you're right, he said in the dark.

I didn't understand, or rather didn't dare understand, and pushing my voice only to the edge of audibility I asked, Right about what?

Then he suddenly moved, pulled out his arm from under my hand, sat up, and switched on the reading lamp.

The wall lamp with its silk shade illuminated him from above, high-lighting the deep-toned, irregularly knotted Oriental rug that framed the sofa.

He thrust his back against the rug, the blanket slid down to his belly; he again folded his arms over his chest, and with his chin lowered he seemed to be looking up, although he was looking straight at me, our eyes at the same level.

The warm glow of the lamp shone through and whitened his unruly blond curls, stretched shadows across his face; the shadows drifted over his muscular chest, forming spots on his arms and on the white bedding.

He looked beautiful, as beautiful as a portrait of a pensive young man who for some mysterious reason has been stripped to the waist and who is contemplating himself rather than the world around him.

A portrait in which everything is balanced in the extreme: light is answered by lovely shadows, blond curls by dark chest hair, light skin by a dark background, the fiery colors of the background by the stark white and cool blue of the eyes, the gentle slope of the shoulder by the firm horizontals of the folded arms; it was beauty one can accept without understanding it.

We looked at each other the way an experienced doctor might look at a patient, with a deep, calm look, checking the face for possible signs of possible symptoms but betraying no emotion in the process.

I felt we were reaching a very deep and very dark point in our rambling exploration of each other's self; for weeks I had hovered over the most sensitive regions of his life, and now I had reached my goal; I had challenged him and he, against his better judgment, took up the challenge; but in this murky region he dug in his heels with such energy that it was as if he were plotting some terrible revenge, which is why it didn't bother me that I was sitting naked at the edge of the sofa, the awkwardness of my naked body and my defenselessness, I hoped, protecting me from a possible revenge.

This music teacher, he said after a few moments of silence, and his voice, rising out of the deep warmth that had been meant for me a short while before, became dry, cool, and detached, as if he intended to talk about someone other than himself; on his face there was no trace of the tender inwardness with which he'd started this story only an hour before, he wasn't talking to me or to himself, it was an image that was talking, someone who could handle himself the way a scientist handles a dead but preserved insect, sticking it on a pin and placing it in his collection, in its phylogenetically and morphologically proper location, but with the pin playing a greater role in the activity than the insect itself or its taxonomic place.

He was first violinist in the theater orchestra, just like his real, his French father, whom he knew nothing about at the time; the man was a mediocre musician and an even worse teacher, but in the local circumstances he was the best, and after the well-meaning and dignified Frau Gudrun, his previous teacher, a real relief; it was as if a magic door had opened for him and he had stepped from the den of a musical spinster into the hallowed halls of art; the teacher was a cultured, well-educated man, well-informed, sophisticated, well-traveled, almost a man of the world; he swam, played tennis, had valuable contacts which he knew how to cultivate without being at all pushy, making it seem that he was doing a favor to others, a confirmed bachelor and a famously gracious host, everyone who was anyone in town, or those who came to perform in town, considered it their pleasant duty to stop by his house, it became almost *de rigueur* to get a quick taste of his unselfish kindness, to bask in his bonhomie and in his sparkling wittiness, which was validated by genuine suffering; for above all, he was a good person, about the way Richard III would have been good if in those good old days of the interwar years he had decided not to be a villain but resolved instead to be infinitely, unbelievably good, for it was all the same, being good or evil; with his goodness he could tease a sweet melody out of the most horrid march.

And Melchior did not mean this as his afterthoughts; he was trying to recall exactly how he had felt at that time.

It was in those days that he first saw that play, most likely in a poor production; for him it seemed a monstrous, scarifying tale of evil, because they put a huge, pointy hump on Richard's back, two humps in fact, he seemed to be carrying two uneven mountain peaks under his coat; and he didn't just limp, his legs were twisted from the hip and he shoved and thrust them out in front of him, wincing with pain and yelping like a dog with every step he took; of course this was a slightly exaggerated directorial idea, for pain doesn't necessarily lead to evil, but it was effective all the same; in any case, his teacher always reminded him of that actor; his eyes seemed to play tricks on him, because he saw his teacher as a very handsome and attractive old man, though he was about forty-five at the time, slender, relatively tall, pleasant-smelling, with a dark complexion and bright dark eyes, but his long, mane-like hair, carefully swept back like an artist's, was almost completely white, the kind of white that children expect old men to have.

When he got carried away while holding forth on some of his theories, his hair would part in the middle and fall into his face, and then he'd smooth it back with artistic little gestures of his hand, for he could never get so carried away as to give up creating the impression that everything was just fine, and why wouldn't it be? these theoretical discussions, often lasting for hours, were fascinating, farsighted, passionate; the critical products of an analytical mind are always moving and inspiring, but when the time came for actual exercises, when something he knew had to be conveyed, when he actually had to show how to play something, to point out what was right or what was wrong, then, behind his magnanimous wisdom there appeared envy, an inexplicable animal selfishness, a fit of possessiveness, and even more than that: mockery, gloating, a miserly grin, as if he had possessed one of life's treasures so rare that its essence couldn't be penetrated; and he wouldn't part with it, he savored it, and he took pleasure in watching his pupil's frustration; moreover, he rationalized his behavior by stating flatly that there was no such thing as technique, he didn't have one, nobody did! and whoever said he did was no artist but merely a technician, so there was no point trying so hard; one had to teach oneself to develop one's own particular technique, though that, provided this self-education was successful, was no longer mere technique but a sense of existence wrested from and projected back into matter itself; it was the very essence of things, the utmost essence, the instinct of sheer self-preservation.

In his struggle with matter, the artist touched secret layers of his own being he didn't know existed; the revelation might be shameful, he'd much rather hide it from curious eyes; but if art was not an act of initiation into the most searing secrets, it wasn't worth a damn; he often yelled, almost going out of his mind, that he and his pupil were marking time in the antechamber of art, implying there was a certain place, like a great hall, they should eventually enter.

He couldn't say he liked this man, though he was attracted to him, yet for all his attraction he remained suspicious, at the same time reproaching himself for being suspicious; nevertheless he felt he saw something, knew something about him no one else did: he saw that the man was corrupt to the core, a liar, a cynic, an infinitely bitter man; yet he believed the man wished him well, and he not only did not dare reject this kindness but tried very hard to measure up to it, be worthy of it, while all along his ears kept telling him that all that talk about the antechamber and the halls of art was false, it had to be, if only because the man himself never gained admission, never got anywhere; he was full of longing, yes, and in this pathetic longing there was enough bitterness, and the credibility of sadness and despair, to make the things he said not complete nonsense, although Melchior also felt that this longing was not for music, not even for a career, the man had given up on that long ago, he didn't really know what he longed for, maybe just wanted to sound profound, mysterious, satanic, disturbing, and at the same time benevolent, decent, wise, and understanding, and in the end Melchior became the object of this longing, of this painful and pitiful struggle.

After each lesson he fled his teacher's house in complete defeat; during the four years he was his student, the demon of art, metaphorically speaking, inhabited his soul; he grew gaunt, he looked wasted, which didn't seem unusual, because in those years everybody was hungry and looked harried and worn-out.

He became humble and stubborn, he practiced compulsively and learned many things on his own for which he was grateful to his teacher, everything that was good had to originate with him; he was developing nicely, realizing his artistic potential, as people like to say, and his teacher acknowledged this, sometimes grudgingly, sometimes with furious emotional outbursts, which Melchior dreaded more than the annihilating criticism; now and then the teacher allowed him to perform in public, indeed organized some of the appearances himself, introduced Melchior to musical notables, had him perform before select audiences, and the result each time was overwhelming success; they simply loved him, they ate him up, he brought tears to their eyes, even though in those postwar years people were very reluctant to give way to tears.

But even at such moments, in the midst of the warmest ovation, his teacher let him know that while all this was well and good, we shall put it behind us, not dwell on it or let ourselves be carried away; and when they were left alone he proceeded to dissect the performance so mercilessly that Melchior was forced to concede that he couldn't make it, didn't know what heights he was supposed to reach but was sure he couldn't reach them, and his teacher was almost always right, about almost everything, and the only reason he was suspicious and ungrateful, the reason he could never be worthy of all that goodness, was that deep down he felt he didn't have the least bit of talent.

When alone with these feelings he was racked by anxiety attacks; for days he would huddle in a corner, stay home from school, and keep thinking that one day his complete lack of talent would be discovered; he thought he couldn't hide it anymore, everyone would see that he had no talent at all, and then his teacher would mercilessly give him the boot.

Sometimes he found himself hoping to see that day, though his mother would be very disappointed.

Maybe the reason he wasn't completely destroyed by all this, why he kept hoping his teacher might still be wrong, was that in the final analysis one is incapable of total self-annihilation, either mental or physical, not even after having taken cyanide, for even then it's the poison, or the rope, or the water, or the bullet that does the job; oh, how he would have loved to jump into the river, how he longed for the current swirling around the exposed pillars of that collapsed bridge! but then, even doing away with oneself came down to making an everyday decision: to pick the means to do the job for you; and mental suicide always left a little back door open: the sky is still blue, life can go on, and what is that if not hope?

The reason he thought of cyanide was that a few years later—he was already at the university—this poor man got hold of a dose large enough to kill a horse; it was summertime, no performances at the theater, no one looked for him in the evenings, a very hot summer it was, and then the neighbors were alarmed by this frightful, sickening smell coming from his apartment.

In any case, it was in such circumstances that he began to notice the girl in the window across the street; they were preparing for a very important competition; it was spring, he recalled, all the windows in the teacher's apartment were open; the stakes were high, the top three finalists would be automatically admitted to the conservatory; in his teacher's judgment the competition would be stiff, and he mentioned some of his colleagues and their capable students; but the difference between a talented and an untalented person, he went on, was that the talented one is inspired by his rivals, and since Melchior's rivals were very strong, his chances were very good.

He placed the music stand in front of the window so that each time he looked up, which he would make seem accidental, he could see the girl.

His teacher sat in a commodious armchair in the dark depths of the room, whence he issued his occasional instructions.

Interestingly enough, the tension thus created did not distract him from his work; it meant added pressure, of course, but the odd feeling that he was doing a balancing act with his violin on the borderline of two glances issuing from two very different, contrasting, and possibly even antagonistic individuals, that he was moving between a delicious secret and a dark betrayal, increased his concentration to an intensity he had never experienced before.

He wasn't trying to impress the girl or his teacher or himself; he was there, at once inside all three of them and outside the entire event; in a word, he was playing the violin.

Whenever it was raining or cold and the window had to be closed, the girl resorted to crazy stunts; with outstretched arms she'd lean so far out the window it really looked as if she might fall, or she would close the window and act very annoyed, pressing her nose, her mouth, and her tongue to the glass, making idiotic faces and mimicking him sawing away on his violin, or she would breathe on the glass and write letters in the mist, spelling out "I love you," would thumb her nose at him, tear at her blouse over her breast, implying that if she couldn't listen to that sweet music she'd go mad, stick out her tongue and blow tiny kisses from her palm; but if they ran into each other at school, they both pretended that none of that had meant anything, that none of that had ever even happened.

His teacher responded to the sudden qualitative improvement with pleasant self-satisfaction; he didn't praise him, but from the dim depths of the room he was radiating love, guiding his playing with angry, enthusiastic, and emotional interjections; and Melchior was overjoyed that after four years of hopeless suffering he had finally managed to deceive this seemingly wise and all-knowing man.

The game went on for about two weeks before the teacher got wise to them, though true to his cruel self he did not let on even then, slyly letting their story unfold and expand so that at the right moment he could pounce on them and wipe them away like so much snot; Melchior sensed this cruel anticipation, knew a catastrophe was imminent; but there was also the girl, who had no inkling of the impending disaster, who went on with her antics, swinging out the window, and he couldn't help watching and even laughing out loud at times, while keeping up his guard; he wanted both to protect himself and to annoy his teacher, and that—looking back now he was quite sure—made him even more seductive in the teacher's eye.

And in the meantime, he had to listen to long parables, colorfully told, spiced with exciting illustrations, all of them dripping with kindness, about the virtues of an ascetic way of life, about the psychological engine of aesthetics, the drawbacks of hedonism, the brakes, gears, and pistons of the human soul, and about those practical safety valves through which excess steam may and should be released from the body's power plant; the tales were filled with metaphors, figures, and verbal flourishes, yet when it became clear that these hints and allusions had no effect, Melchior had to pick himself up and with his music stand move deep into the room while his teacher took his place by the window.

The story might have ended there, because Melchior raised no objections: on the contrary, deep down he approved, he understood his teacher or thought he did, and considered the simple, physical regulation of human weaknesses to be the best, most helpful solution to the problem; he was innocent to the point of idiocy, an imbecile couldn't have been more innocent; not only did he have not the slightest notion of how babies were born, but he was also ignorant of the difference between the sexes, or more correctly, everything he was preoccupied with then moved in such a different dimension that even the things he did know he didn't truly grasp.

But the girl wouldn't give up so easily; she'd wait for him downstairs, and at that point all the clowning and mimicking came to an end, and a terrific struggle began among the three of them, a struggle in which Melchior could take part only with his senses—no, not even that, with his instincts—not realizing that it was a struggle, and that he was struggling for life.

And he could scarcely have had any idea of the agonies this man had to endure, the terrible struggle he had to wage with himself, yet he did know, for he was blackmailing the man all along.

He knew because on several occasions he overheard vague and embarrassed whispers about his teacher being a returnee from one of the concentration camps, Sachsenhausen perhaps, he didn't remember exactly, and about how in the camp his teacher wore not a yellow, not even a red, but a pink triangle, which meant he had to be queer; but as often happens, another story was also making the rounds, according to which he had to wear the pink triangle because of his liberal views—that charge was serious enough to have the accuser land in jail after the war—but what seemed to contradict this theory was the rumor that the teacher was in fact an outspoken member of the Nazi Party and had been active in the de-Judaization of German music; whatever the real story was, for Melchior it was all a bunch of empty words, they stuck in his mind, but he didn't connect them to anything, at most he concluded that for the grown-ups the war apparently hadn't been enough, they kept on squabbling even now, or that society had always viewed the artist as the carrier of some contagion, but sensible people paid no heed.

Nevertheless, his mother should have known better.

Melchior talked uninterruptedly until dawn, and this was the only moment when the cool, steady stream of his narrative was stemmed by an impassable emotional barrier.

His chest rose, and his gaze, still holding my eyes, turned inward and seemed to say, No, no more, the rest he couldn't let go.

His eyes filled with tears, he choked up, he seemed about to break into sobs or into loud accusations.

But laughing through his tears he yelled that I shouldn't take this seriously, nothing should be taken seriously.

Then, more quietly, almost finding his way back to his earlier tones, he said that every whore and every faggot had a mother and a soul-stirring story.

It was all sentimental junk, he said.

And several days later it was this story I continued telling Thea as we drove on that dark highway toward the city.

It's true, I did make a few unavoidable alterations: the mental state of a child prodigy was meant as a kind of introduction, a framework, and also, I tried to speak in impersonal tones, as if talking about a person neither of us knew.

But the impersonal tone and the attempted objective approach conjured up an abstract element in the story, one that allows us to weave the strands of personal causal relations into a larger and more general chronology which we tend to label—because of its impersonality and immutability—a historical process or the force of destiny, or even divine predestination; by insisting on this unalterable and impersonal viewpoint, which of course is an emotional rather than intellectual device, I tried to cover up my shameless betrayal of Melchior; I was retelling his story as if it were but a trivial episode in a larger history that, with its relentless flow of repetitions, kept extinguishing and giving birth to itself.

It was as if I had a bird's-eye view of a city; in it I could see an attractive young woman and a violin; I could see the cracks and empty spaces that history had cut out for itself and, using its own materials, would ultimately have to patch up and fill in; I could see a pretty little theater and inside the theater an orchestra pit and musicians in the pit, but at the same time I could also see a far-off pit, a trench somewhere near Stalingrad; in one pit I could see the vacant seat of the first violinist, and in the other pit a soldier wrapped in rags just about to freeze to death.

And looking down like this, from the bird's-eye view of impassive history, I would consider it a matter of little consequence that a few musicians disappeared from the orchestra pit and others vanished from the family bed and some people were hauled off to concentration camps and others to the front; details were beside the point, for history or fate or Providence ordered all this with one curt command: fill the empty space, music must be made in the orchestra pit, and in the trenches there must be shooting, and other pits and trenches were there for burials; someone has to fill in for the first violinist, no seat must remain empty, and the replacement must play the same music, wear the same historical disguise of white tie and tails, to make the changeable look permanent; and it must be made to appear negligible, barely worth mentioning, that French POWs from the neighboring camp have been ordered to occupy the chairs left vacant in the orchestra pit, and if, as a reward for ensuring unbreakable continuity, the guards should take these prisoners over to the Golden Horn Inn, this should not happen as if by accident, as if out of compassionate human concern dictated by fate or Providence or history, but for the sole reason that for a brief hour the new first violinist could slip into the innkeeper's second-floor apartment—the innkeeper himself was breathing his last on the snowy steppes of Stalingrad—and believe that it was for his sake that history skipped a beat.

But history or fate or Divine Providence never skips anything and filled the space the innkeeper left behind in his conjugal bed, and in this sense it again matters very little that in that bed an attractive young woman and an attractive young man experience something they rightfully call fateful love; they keep saying they would rather die than live without each other, and describe their feelings in such extreme terms because they are describing fate's own design.

Seen in this light, it's quite irrelevant to ask whether or not the quietly drinking guards noticed this impermissible breach of regulations, it's no problem for history temporarily to intoxicate a couple of slow-witted soldiers, or bribe them, or make them overlook a sudden burst of passion, so that it can use them later, once sobering light was shed on the terrible deed, to beat to death the French miscegenist, which would again create a vacancy in the historically important orchestra, but it's all right, history would fill that gap, too, later, when it would return somebody to the city, someone who had been banished on charges of sexual perversion.

So I don't think, I said to Thea, that the mother's blindness, viewed from this loftier perspective, could be faulted in any way, because whatever she had lost with her husband's disappearance she more than regained from her lover, and whatever she seemed to have lost when he was gone, too, she was compensated for, thank God, by the fruit of her womb, even though the gift thus received she would have to return one day.

Thea said quietly that she'd understand me just as well even if I didn't make a point of blaspheming in such a complicated, roundabout way.

And she continued to pretend that she wasn't really paying attention to what I was saying.

The day his teacher ordered him away from the window, Melchior went on with his story, the girl waited for him downstairs; for a while they just looked at each other, but then he didn't know what to do, for although he was glad to see that they had managed to deceive his teacher, he was also terribly embarrassed, he still doesn't know why, maybe because he was wearing short pants, anyway, he couldn't think of anything to say, so he started walking away, swinging his violin case, but then the girl yelled "Idiot!" and he turned around.

They were standing facing each other again, and then the girl asked him to come to her place because she'd like him to play once just for her.

He thought that was a terribly dumb thing to say; these things couldn't be mixed up in such a crude way, so all he said was "Idiot yourself."

The girl shrugged her shoulders and said, All right, then, in that case he could kiss her right there.

And from then on she waited for him every day, even though they decided each day that she wouldn't do it again; with arguments and intonations borrowed from his teacher he tried to explain that this competition was an awfully important thing in his life and they shouldn't be doing this now.

Actually, no; it happened just the other way around.

He recalled that on the first day, when they were both so excited they didn't know what to do with one another and talked instead to hide their excitement, they were standing in the old, dry moat, in the midst of garbage, bushes, debris of all kinds, it was all very smelly, and the girl was telling him how much she loved him and was willing to wait for him for the rest of her life, and since this competition was now more important than anything else, they should just break up and she would wait for him, and they both felt that this was a terribly beautiful sentiment, yet she was there every day, waiting for him.

And there was one more thing he had to confess.

Though at the moment he had no idea how to talk about it sensibly.

We were sitting motionless, but his gaze was running headlong inside me, and I was backing away and stumbling with my own blinking glances, trying to get away, jump out of the way of his words, as if we were blindfolded and chasing around an elusive object that slipped away just as one of us touched it.

The capacity of our modesty was at issue now, and the laws of spiritual modesty are far stricter than those of physical bashfulness, which is as it should be, since the body is perishable matter, but once it starts revealing itself as not matter, then suddenly its limited, finite nature becomes frighteningly infinite; in panic I fled from this boundless thing, not wanting to see the thing I myself had forced into existence.

His words remained sharp and deliberate, so many thrusts and parries, but no coherent sentence emerged, nothing more than so many powerful unfinished allusions, statements, exclamations, as well as their negations; questions and doubts that only I could understand, inasmuch as one can understand modestly fluttering scraps of words stirred by the repressed mental energies of another human being.

These confused, clipped, suppressed, and still meaningful words referred to the relationship between a long-buried memory now springing to life and another, prudently unspecified recent experience—that of meeting Thea, whose name he couldn't bring himself to say; there was, after all, a huge gap of ten years between the two experiences.

I was lucky enough to have heard two versions of how they got to know each other.

No more of that, he said.

Not even with me, he said.

He said that comparisons never made any sense.

And still, he said.

With her . . . the guilty silence now had to do with Thea; this whole unfortunate mess started with that.

He didn't want to be tactless or ridiculous, yet he couldn't be anything else.

He didn't want to hurt her, but that's exactly what he was doing.

He just didn't want those kinds of feelings anymore, it seemed.

This state of affairs lasted about a week, he said pensively, and I could tell by looking at him that he was referring to two different times at once, one ten years and the other only a few months earlier, more correctly, the events of ten years ago coming aglow in those of a few months ago.

There is no memory without the recurrence of emotions, or conversely, every moment of lived experience is also an allusion to a former experience—that is what memory is.

The two recollections converged on his face and settled down, one superimposed on the other, each fueling the other, and that made me feel such relief and satisfaction, as if at long last we had hit upon the true topic of our conversation, the one we had been blindly groping for until then.

Needless to say, this little digression I did not mention to Thea in the car.

But he did want to tell me the end of the story, because one day his teacher opened the door, and though he tried to look very solemn, his expression was so desperate that Melchior knew right away that the end he'd always feared was at hand.

He indicated that he should put the violin down, they wouldn't be needing it, and led him into another room.

The teacher sat down but let Melchior stand.

He then asked how Melchior had been spending his evenings.

For once he stood firm and wouldn't say anything, but then his teacher calmly enumerated the days of the week and told him precisely, to the minute, when he had come home each night.

He made no mention of the girl, not even a hint, simply ran down the list: Monday, 9:42; Tuesday, 10:28; and so on, like that, very slowly, without comment. Melchior, wearing his short pants, was standing in the middle of a rug, and when he heard the list he just passed out, right there, in the middle of the rug.

What made him faint was the sudden thought that this respectable, horrible, worshipped, old, handsome, gray-haired, unfortunate man had been following him—a mere child, an untalented nobody—sneaking after him, tailing him day after day, and he must have seen everything, everything.

It was probably just a dizzy spell, a blackout lasting no more than a few seconds.

He came to, smelling his teacher's familiar scent from very close up; he was kneeling over him, and his face remained an unforgettable image: a spider at the moment the longed-for green fly is caught in its web.

The teacher was hugging and kissing him, so distraught with fear that he almost cried, whispering, begging him, imploring him to trust him, for if he didn't he would surely die, he was already dead, they had killed him, and amid these frantic whispers he also blurted out that no one really knew who Melchior's real father was, so why not consider him his father and trust him like a father.

Melchior cried, protested, trembled; after he managed to calm down somewhat and his teacher thought it safe to let him go out on the street, he saw the girl waiting for him, but he ran off without a word.

Luckily, his mother came home very late that night.

By then he had managed to pull himself together; he told her that they should move somewhere else, anywhere, and look for another teacher, any teacher, because this one was no good; he didn't say anything else; he couldn't think of anything else except that his teacher was an evil man, but this he didn't dare say out loud, so in response to his mother's every question he kept repeating that he was a rotten teacher, as if they were talking about his musical education and not about his life.

His mother's lack of suspicion was the last straw, the final proof that no one was there to help him, not even his mother, and everything that really mattered in his life had to be kept secret.

He let himself be comforted, tucked in, and put to sleep; in spite of his misgivings, he let her go through the motions with which an uncomprehending mother can show her love in such a situation.

Having listened to all these minor details, Melchior said, I could no doubt guess what happened next.

Occasionally the girl appeared in the window, cautiously, timidly, because she meant to show him that she understood and was willing to wait for him, but the waiting caused so much pain it was best to block it out.

The day before the competition he and his teacher took the train to Dresden; he wasn't going to reveal what happened that night in the double bed of the hotel room, he'd say only this, that not before or since had he seen a man struggle so mightily with himself, and that his strength held out as long as it could.

It wasn't really a hotel but a quiet, old-fashioned boardinghouse somewhere outside the city, in a secluded valley, with somber little turrets and latticed balconies, like a quaint, forgotten, haunted castle.

They got there by streetcar from the railroad station; their room was large and pleasantly cool, and everything in it was white: the washbowl, the oval mirror, the marble washstand, the pitcher filled with water, the bedspread and the curtains, too; outside their window dense foliage rustled all night long.

He was speaking rather haltingly now, as if ready to break off at any moment, but he couldn't find his way back to silence, because after each word he thought would be the last, there was still another.

He asked me for a cigarette.

I found the pack, gave him a cigarette, and put the ashtray in his lap; I also looked for a position to support myself and something to cover up my bothersome nakedness and to warm my feet, numb with cold, so I moved to the other end of the sofa, leaned against the wall, pulled over the blanket, and slid my ice-cold feet under his thighs; he went on, still speaking haltingly, but compelled to carry on with the story.

Now I probably understood, he said, why he had asked his mother who his father was; his teacher's odd remark must have preyed on his mind.

It was also odd, he said, pausing long enough to take a puff, that three years later, when he was home from the university during a break, his mother still didn't seem to understand anything, and with stupefying innocence told him how his teacher had killed himself, talking about it as if it were a trivial piece of news.

He made no response; instead, he quite casually announced that in a few days they'd have a guest, he'd invited a classmate of his, and to avoid any misunderstanding, he pronounced the guest's name, Mario, very distinctly, in case she thought he said Marion.

And then, as if she finally understood, and this, too, happened while she was standing by the sink, the dish she was drying stopped in her hands.

It doesn't matter, darling, she said; this way you'll always be mine.

Once, long after that day, she repeated the same sentence to me.

Melchior's pauses grew longer, but he couldn't stop.

Some crazy delusion would have you believe that the events of the world happen just for you, he said, everything, including things that happen to other people; his experience, your experience are also mine, all mine.

The reason for this, he went on, may have to do with the fact that the first thing every living thing takes into its mouth is its mother's milk-filled breast; and that's why we want our father's red-veined cock in our mouth, too; everything alive, everything that can be stuffed or poured into it, whether it's sweet or salty, everything that assures life and is essential to it must be ours, we must possess it, make it our own.

I understood well why he couldn't stop; the more forgiving and understanding toward his mother and his teacher, the more he was tempted by a secret, unacknowledged desire to shift the moral burden of his experiences partly onto history, something conveniently intangible, and partly onto the two all-too-tangible people closest to him; but because his moral standards would not allow him simply to hate these two people—one absolved by death, the other his mother, after all—and also because he had no penchant for self-hatred, he had no choice but to see himself as a victim of history.

But a victim that talks is always a little embarrassing, his accusations comical, just because he is talking, whereas real victims of history, as we know, are always silent.

And that is why he could no longer abide this place, I understood that now; that's why he had to risk everything and try to get away, reject and sever all ties with his own history, or die for the hope of a new beginning, even letting himself be shot like a dog while crossing the border.

As we reached the city we both stopped talking, withdrawing into our own silences; side by side, there were two interconnected yet separate silences.

I felt a slight excitement in my stomach, in my bowels, as if my conscience had shifted its activities to those places; I was anxious to calm these rumblings and growlings, to ease the urge to pass wind, which was all the more difficult since Thea remained mysteriously and unpredictably closed and aloof—I couldn't tell what effect my response had had on her.

Her curious comment that she would understand even if I hadn't blasphemed in such an elaborate and roundabout way—if I related the story without making a moral judgment, that is—still stung a little.

Nevertheless, it made me realize that neither Melchior's story nor any other could be traced directly to historical circumstances or biological determinants; the moral onus cannot be shifted onto anybody or anything; to think so would imply a certain narrow-mindedness, a poverty of reason; in every story one ought to accept the power of an indivisible whole that pervades its every detail; this is by no means easy if one is used to focusing on details and one is not even a believer.

I had to look at her, almost as if to check the physical state of the person who put such a question to me.

But she seemed not to have heard the rumbling of my stomach, and appeared untouched by my searching look.

Her comment also struck me as curious because never before or after that day had I ever heard her utter God's name, either in prayer or as a curse.

I could interpret her silent features as impassive and indifferent, or as signs of being sympathetic and deeply touched by Melchior's story.

And the closer we got to Wörther Platz, the more impossible it seemed that this day was drawing to a close and something else was about to begin, something inconceivably different, and that she and I had to part until tomorrow, so terribly far away.

The feeling was not totally unfamiliar, though; when I was with either one of them, I was very much present, and the more I managed to be present in the in-between place, the better I could answer their needs, exactly as they wanted me to, and the harder it became to give up my place.

On such nights, for example, after getting out of Thea's car, I'd walk up to the fifth floor to see Melchior, annoyed by my lateness, open the door, and open it wide, and then not only his controlled, almost impersonal smile would seem strange to me but everything about him: his attractiveness, his smell, his skin, the stubble on his chin, his cool blue eyes peering out of his smile, and—I'd almost be ashamed to admit it—his sex, his maleness, though not his essential self.

It seemed I was always closest to the things and people I had just left and had to leave them to stay close; perhaps that was the source of all my errors, I thought, although it couldn't really be called an error, because it wasn't I but my experiences that went this way: in my stead, my own story was doing my thinking for me; I was alive yet continually kept saying goodbye to life, for at the end of every experience a death loomed; as a result, saying goodbye became more important than life itself.

Some such thoughts were going through my mind when we stopped in front of Melchior's building; with her head thrown back, Thea managed somehow to be looking down at me, then she took off her glasses and smiled.

This fast-spreading, expansive smile must have been lying dormant in the muscles of her mobile face, but she hadn't let it out before, held it back, out of tact perhaps, or guile, so as not to distract me, to be able to absorb the story as an undisturbed whole, the way I'd wanted to present it.

And I asked myself again, delving into the mystery of my cultural conditioning, why I was constantly inching away from the life of my most private self, why this readiness to conform to other people's image of me? was it because death lay in wait at the end of every memory? and wouldn't that be the most primitive historical experience rather than divinely inspired destiny?

Softly she put her hand on my knee, her fingers spread and wrapped around my kneecap, but she did not squeeze; in the darkness of the car I looked at her eyes.

Maybe she wasn't holding my knee at all; with that gesture she was holding together our bodies, our silences, and I could tell from her eyes that she wanted to say something, or rather, that she couldn't say anything because she was feeling precisely what she had to understand.

And to give voice to this feeling would be an exaggeration; certain things should not even be hinted at, life must not be interfered with, but still, if it hadn't been so dark in the car with only the light of streetlamps filtering in through the foliage, if we had been able to see each other's face clearly, if what we felt had not remained on the border of anticipation and consciousness, if it had turned into words, then, chances are, everything would have turned out differently among the three of us.

Later she did start talking, but by then that charged moment had passed.

Yes, she said, everyone had their life story to tell, and had I ever noticed they were all sad stories? and why was that? she wondered; yet it seemed to her that what I was telling her was the story of my own life, which she really knew nothing about, or perhaps the story of my personal hurts.

My hurts? I asked, because the word surprised me.

Without responding to the surprise in my voice, the smile on her face broke into a laugh, and out of that she shot a question at me: Did I know she was Jewish?

And then she began to laugh in earnest, probably because of the surprise and puzzled incredulity that must have been written all over my face.

All right, she said, still laughing, I should go now, she squeezed my knee and immediately withdrew her hand; that story she'd tell me some other time.

I said I didn't understand.

No matter, I was a smart boy, I should think about it; besides, one didn't have to understand everything, it was enough to feel it.

But what was there to feel here?

Never mind, I should just feel it.

She wouldn't get away with this, I said, this was a dirty trick.

I won't, eh? she said, laughing, and leaning across me, she pushed open the door on my side: time to get out.

But I didn't have the foggiest; what was she talking about?

She was no longer interested in what I was saying, what I did or did not understand; pressing her hands against my shoulders and chest, she was bent on squeezing or pushing me out of the car; hesitating slightly, I grabbed hold of her wrist; I hesitated because I felt I shouldn't respond violently to her violence since she was Jewish, she had just said it, hadn't she, she was a Jew; still, twisting it slightly I pried her hand off; we were both laughing at our awkwardness, and at the same time we both wanted to end it.

Don't, don't, she whined in a dull, artfully painful voice, at once the mature woman's crumbling defense and the erstwhile young girl's endearingly inept playacting: Let go, let go now, that's enough.

But perhaps it wasn't enough, not yet, because she jabbed me in the chest with her head; she wanted more, so I squeezed her hand harder, she winced, and for a moment her head rested on my chest, nice and cozy, as if she'd been looking for just that spot, and this tense meeting of our bodies meant that I was the broad-chested he-man and she the weak woman; she wasn't giving in, not yet, she'd push a little more and then she would yield.

I won't let go, I said out loud, expressing a feeling that was flattering because it conformed to the generally accepted sexual role-playing; and I gave voice to this feeling of male superiority eagerly, as if declaring that I had no intention of passing up the chance this feeling gave me.

I may have gone too far, however; insulted, she yanked her head back, accidentally knocking it against my chin, hurting us both a little.

Her offended withdrawal meant she was unwilling to concede the obvious difference between us, or at least was not about to make use of it, even if the pain thus caused was undeniably mutual.

What's wrong? I asked.

Wrong? she said brazenly, nothing, nothing.

But at the same time she was looking into my eyes so tenderly, imploringly, retreating into the role of the weak woman with girlishly sly and coy humility, illuminating the role with the mastery of a real professional; and this mockery, making our involuntarily assumed roles look ridiculous, was so much to my liking that slowly, gradually, I eased my hold on her wrist, though I didn't let go of it completely.

What was she trying to tell me? I asked, and the sound of my voice told me how reluctantly I was making my way from promising silent touches toward false and loud words.

But in fact I started to speak because I didn't want my mind to let go of my instincts; at the very least the mind should follow closely and understand what these instincts are after and why, and instincts and feelings should operate neither against nor instead of the mind; if there was something between us, if such a thing was possible, it shouldn't be some sort of supplement, a working off of other emotions, or a round of common sexual gymnastics; and she must have felt the same way.

Everything that had happened between us so far could still be seen as friendly banter, though it was hard to tell where good-natured rough-housing ended and the pleasure of amorous touching began; the borderline was carefully guarded by sober intelligence, even if the situation itself, precisely because of its delicious inherent possibilities, seemed irreversible; we'd either crossed the line already or simply didn't know where we were.

She'll tell me another time, she said dryly, now I should let her go.

No, I won't, I said, not until she explained what she meant, I don't like this kind of nonsense.

But reason could no longer help our feelings, because the words themselves were trying to decide about something startling and final, yet we no longer had any idea of what we were talking about—again an unmistakable characteristic of a lovers' quarrel.

Angry and impatient, she jerked her head sideways, hoping perhaps that a change of position would also change the situation.

Come on, let go, she said, almost spitefully, Arno had no idea where she might be, he was waiting for her, he'd get all crabby from so much waiting, it was very late.

As she jerked her head away, a ray of light fell on her face, the harsh light of a streetlamp; it was perhaps this light that defeated me.

Pretty funny that she should think of Arno right now, I said with a laugh.

Because in the harsh light from the street—and there is no other way I can put it—his face appeared on hers.

For a moment her face did seem to resemble Arno's long, dry, mournful face, yet it wasn't so much his features that showed through as a feeling, or the shadow of a feeling, just a trace of sadness belonging to that strange man to whom she felt she belonged, and whom, simply by pronouncing his name, and therefore not unwittingly, she now placed between us; he wasn't just the old husband she had to think about even at the moment she was unfaithful and whom she treated like a father or a son; no, it was this man's sadness to which she had to remain faithful, so she could remain faithful to the abiding, all-encompassing sadness that was the basis of their life together—could this be the reason she mentioned being Jewish?—a sadness that was not only his but hers as well, it would appear; was there something between them that was truly unbreakable? could their common bond be the fact that she was a Jew and he a German?

I should have overcome, wiped away, or at least banished temporarily this hitherto unfamiliar, never-before-seen sadness, except that Arno's sadness confounded me; it was the sadness of a man I didn't feel close to, a man I couldn't touch, and I couldn't pretend I didn't see that they shared this sadness—hence her victory, or theirs, over me.

And now I knew even less just where my place was in this somber situation, but the stark sadness that broke through all her possible masks and faces, now illuminated by the harsh streetlight, was like a sudden violent discharge, a clash of the most opposite forces.

All right, I'll let her go, I said, but first I will kiss her.

It seemed that by simply saying it, the act had become impossible, and then we could consider it done.

And then that famous whole that should pervade all details of a relationship must also include what in the ordinary sense does not take place yet is a reality.

She turned her face back toward me slowly and with a surprised look on it, as if she were amazed on behalf of that other person as well, I was faced with the astonished gaze of two people.

As she turned, the light vanished from her face, but I knew that the strange face would not leave her, and the half-open mouth said or rather moaned from behind that face, No, not now.

I let go of her; some time passed.

This moan issuing from their shared sadness did not mean what it seemed to mean, it had to be translated: in the language the two of us had in common it meant just the opposite, it meant that she felt as I did, and if not now, she did mean maybe later.

If it had meant next week or tomorrow perhaps, that would have meant not now and not later either; but that's not what she meant.

Our faces began to undulate between yes and no, between now, the next moment, and any time.

With my casual statement I seemed to have awakened our mouths, and now we had to look at them.

Yes, the features of our faces were undulating, wavering, the skin trembled as our faces relaxed and tensed again, and the next moment did arrive, but without turning into now or anytime, what remained was the uncertain later, yet what was vibrating on her lips was a definite yes—only its when was unknown.

But this began to be painful, because if it didn't happen now then the yes must have meant no, after all.

Like a pendulum, our faces swayed between the subtle pain of tentative rejection and the equally subtle joy of tentative consent; I might even say that our faces oscillated between self-defense and self-surrender; and because this was true oscillation—when pain flitted across one face, the other flickered with joy, and when one was suffused with joy, the other showed pain—even when the long-awaited decisive moment seemed at hand, yes and no could still not be separated.

So to avoid having to wait for the next moment, I cut through our shared time by making a move; and I did it simply because I was in pain, and while one escape route was closed to me, the car door behind me was open; the pain, unable to turn into joy, sought relief at any price.

But true to the movement of the pendulum, Thea was ready to swing forward as I was about to pull back; and she wouldn't allow her joy to turn into pain either—this was her yes moment—and with her hand she had to turn the anytime I created with my move into a now.

When we are awake and fully alert, our jaws are conditioned to keep the mouth closed, the upper teeth resting on the lower set, and the upper lip lying neatly on the lower one; at this point, however, the jaw relaxed and reverted to its original, preconditioned state, easing the alertness and discipline which, except in the hours of sleep, maintain tension in the facial muscles; regulating the extent and nature of this tension gives character to the face, which, in turn, causes the tongue inside, arching sensitively from the rim of the lower teeth, to hover, and the saliva collecting on the tip of the tongue and around the impeding row of teeth to trickle back into the hollow of the mouth.

Heads tilt sideways, if one to the left, the other definitely to the right, because when two human mouths seek each other out they must avoid the collision of noses protruding from the facial terrain.

Once the eyes measure the distance, from the features of the terrain estimate the angle of the tilt, and from the speed of the mutual approach can also determine the moment of contact, then the eyelids slowly and softly drop over the eyes—seeing at such close range becomes impossible and unnecessary, which of course should not lead to the conclusion that everything impossible is also unnecessary—but the eyes do not close completely, a narrow slit remains, so the long upper lashes need not descend and mix with the lower, shorter ones; in this way the eyes put themselves in a perfectly symmetrical position with the mouth; one is fully conscious now, but not quite aware; the amount of tension relinquished from consciousness equals the loss in awareness; whatever opens up here, but not completely, will shut down there, but not completely.

If one wished to say something specific about a kiss, the joining of two mouths, about the moment when the direct sensation of two sense organs turns into direct bodily sensation, it might be best to step into the open mouth, between the vertically grooved, tender skin of the barely touching lips.

If this were at all possible without the aid of a scalpel, the peculiarities of the living organism would force one to choose among several alternatives: should we follow the facial muscles rippling toward the interior of the mouth, or the intricate network of neurons, or the crisscrossing veins perhaps? in the first case we'd have to cut through the cluster of salivary glands in the lips and cheeks, traverse some connective tissue to reach the mucous membrane; in the second instance, it would be like being absorbed by the tiniest capillary roots of a tree and from there to reach the trunk and travel on to the nerve center of the crown; in the third case, depending on whether we took the red or the blue trail of blood vessels, we'd reach either the ventricle or the auricle of the heart.

Fortunately, it's only in fairy tales that out of three possible paths we have to choose the one that will lead us to safety; but since we don't need to be rescued and are merely yielding to simple, most likely superficial curiosity, we shall choose yet a fourth option and slip through the grooves of the barely touching lips; it won't be a smooth glide, though, because at this moment the surface is almost completely dry; the glands are producing saliva in abundance, but the insecurely hovering tongue is not wetting the surface; consequently, the longer it takes for the lips to meet, the more parched they become; sometimes they look like cracked soil in a protracted dry spell, even though in the hollow behind the lower teeth, under the tongue, a proper little lake of saliva has formed.

If we proceed along the craggy ridge of the lower teeth and, avoiding the little lake of saliva, clamber up the slippery back of the tongue to take a look at the distance covered, the sight greeting us there promises to be quite remarkable.

The undertaking is not without dangers: if we don't cling fast to the taste buds, we might easily slide down into the gullet, but it's all worth it, and where we are is actually a well-protected cave: over us stretches the palate's lovely arch, and looming before us, in the form of an obtuse-angled triangle, is the great orifice of the mouth itself; if we hadn't purposely invaded this spot to catch this breathtaking sight, we might cry out in astonishment, because from this vantage point the anatomical view of the orifice bears a striking resemblance to the conventional representation of the eye of God.

And while looking out through this opening, and seeing everything suddenly turn dark—for prompted by simultaneous pushing and pulling, yielding and receiving, another triangle clings not quite symmetrically but somewhat aslant to the triangular opening of our hiding place, in sum, a kiss is happening—we get the feeling that in the darkness of the two interlocking caverns, God's one eye is looking into the other eye of God.

We tend to dampen the joy of this discovery with pangs of doubt, asking even at this exalted moment whether the joining of two pairs of lips is really an event of such significance, during which God's single eye looks into God's other single eye?

When grappling with doubt, we try to dig up useful knowledge and experiences with which to deny or confirm our doubt, but to unearth evidence in this instance, we must first explore the body—anyway, we are in it already!—and take a look at those organs that play a role in one's love life.

A close inspection of these organs and their properties will lead us to the curious and for some people no doubt scandalous conclusion that sexual pleasure, though a prerequisite of our instinct for self-preservation, may be induced in any individual, male or female, through the manipulation of the sexual organs and, by means of self-stimulation, orgasm may be achieved without the presence of another individual.

Isolation and self-gratification, touching oneself while fantasizing about touching another, is something we all know from personal experience.

Neurotic, inhibited, or bashful individuals do not even have to touch their private parts to be aroused, it's enough if the palm of a hand grazes their naked thigh or belly or pelvic region; there the friction between the body and its own skin produces, accidentally as it were, the mutuality needed for sexual excitement; in the case of women we might include touching the breasts, the nipples, and the dark areolae, which may be followed, or accompanied, by stroke-like pressure applied to the mons veneris; without intending it, the stroking will grow more rhythmic, and that will increase the blood pressure, quicken the rate of breathing; this pressure corresponds, in the male, to the gentle groping men begin at the root of their thighs, and then transfer to the testicles and bulb of the penis; women can touch the tiny body of the clitoris, though not its supersensitive head, which at times can be painful; similarly, men can also take hold, with a slightly rougher grasp, of their hollowed member and, rhythmically pulling back the foreskin, free and then re-cover the bulb of the penis, the motion causing the excitement that releases the tiny valves through which arterial blood rushes in to fill the hollows of the shaft.

And since this is an individual activity to suit personal needs, and promises private satisfaction, the activity's form and the methods used may vary greatly.

The variety of ways used to induce physical pleasure cannot obscure the fact that, from a strictly somatological point of view, the same process takes place in every instance and in every individual; at most its intensity, efficacy, and, above all, results differ, for the process itself always creates a physically predetermined and closed organic unity, and it seems irrelevant whether the act takes place between two individuals of different sexes or the same sex, whether some external stimulus or mere fantasizing is at work, or if the same result is achieved by fantasy-induced self-stimulation.

Yet, however closed this unity created by the factors responsible for inducing, maintaining, and gratifying physical pleasure, certain effects appear even when the process seems entirely self-generated—in the case of masturbation or in nocturnal seminal emission—and these effects disrupt the apparently closed and from a physiological point of view perfectly self-sufficient system.

It is as if nature opposed a system that completely isolated the individual from others; during masturbation imagination steps in, and during nocturnal emission a dream is at work; imagination and dream connect the individual, and the ostensibly self-sufficient act, to another individual, or at the very least presuppose the presence of one.

This is the most, and also the least, that can be said of an individual's dependent relationships.

We might add, though, that an impulse is also at work in all of us that manages to create simultaneously feelings of isolation and self-absorption and of openness and dependence on others; isolation hampers while openness fosters the establishment of relationships, and the two feelings function in an inseparable tension that makes up the whole of the impulse.

If two individuals unite those of their organs which, though meant for another, can also function in isolation, if, in other words, two individuals wish to relieve or overcome their own isolation not by relying on imagination or dreams but in the possible openness of the other, then the resulting meeting is that of two closed units, each consisting of identical elements maintained in the tension of openness and closeness.

The tension, in this case, uses its openness to match itself to that peculiarity of the other's closeness, namely, that the closeness in the other is also open.

The meeting of two self-contained entities results, therefore, in a common openness that transcends their individual openness, creating a new, shared isolation; within this shared isolation they can step out of their individual isolation, and conversely, their individual openness is enclosed within the shared isolation they had opened up for one another.

If this is indeed what happens, it would mean that the meeting of two bodies signifies far more than the aggregate of two bodies; they are present in each other in a way that adds up to more than their individual selves.

We are all slaves to our own as well as to other people's bodies; we signify more than we actually are only to the extent that freedom signifies more than slavery, and the community of slaves signifies less than the community of free men opting for slavery.

And nothing proves this more strikingly than a kiss itself.

For the mouth is the same kind of physical window of the body as the imagination is the spiritual window of the mind, both connecting one to the universe.

Within the closed system of the body the mouth is a functionless, in and of itself neutral sexual organ, possessing no inherently usable properties; only by coming in direct contact with the body of another individual can it realize its potential for the most sensual stimulation, display its exceptional sensitivity and its very close and intimate relationship to all the other inherently excitable sexual organs; we might even say that it is the only sexually active organ that, within the closed system, is naturally open, physically and universally, since there is constant, if dormant, readiness in it to be open to others; in this sense the mouth is the physical counterpart of intangible imagination.

The mouth, then, is a bodily organ that, because of properties it lacks, differs from all other organs involved in the procreative act, whereas the imagination is that faculty which ensures the functioning of the sexual organs even in the absence of a sexual partner.

Because of its unique and in some way deficient character, the mouth differs so much from other sex organs that in a certain sense it cannot really be classified as one, if only because the meeting of two mouths is neither a prerequisite nor a precondition of two individuals' sexual union; mouths can even be excluded from the closed process of such union; yet it is no accident that two individuals, imagining the openness of the other's body, showing mutual readiness to unite the closed systems of their respective bodies, prove their readiness and wish by first uniting those organs that are not indispensable to the union but are open to begin with: their mouths.

Naturally, and luckily for me, I wasn't thinking about all this in the car when Thea put her arms around my neck to prevent me from getting out; I am thinking about it now, while filling this page which, considering how these reconstructions work, is a rather perverted form of thinking; but back then I couldn't have thought of anything like this, because around the age of thirty you have a pretty fair idea how these organs function, you know from experience that they work more or less the way you want them to work, though you are also past the stage when you still act blindly, without control, and you are past it even if you allow instinct and experience to take over; in reality you flounder among associations and comparisons floating about in your memory, which is also a kind of thinking—so I can't claim that I wasn't thinking at all.

Teetering on the border of sheer abandon and conscious control, I decided that this was what I wanted now.

Or rather, I yielded to the weight, to that curious heaviness, that at moments like this gets hold of one's head, pulling by the forehead and pushing at the back of the neck, toward the other person's head, as if you had voluntarily relinquished the mechanism that normally allows you to see, breathe, and think; you just want to fall into something, give yourself, entrust yourself to something, and above all not to ask why, though in most cases that would be the right thing to do.

There is a half-open mouth before you, which is the question the other's body is asking you, and your mouth is also open, that's where you'll get the other body's answer; and when the two mouths meet, on those other lips you will find your breathing again, yes, you can consider it an answer, and there you will also recover your lost sight as well; you draw your breath from the other mouth, from the breath you gauge the possibilities of the body that is now turning toward you, the inner landscape of that body is unfolding before you, and that is just what the other person offers you: a void, a hollow space that can and must be filled, and that puts an end to the falling sensation, because the lips, caught on the rim of the hollow space, touch fragrant, slick, warm, rough, cold, and soft live matter; touching so many different things at once and at once in so many different ways that our mind, conditioned as it is to act, is properly stimulated.

Rushing to act, with lips dry and rough, eager and wild, we fell on each other as if in that fraction of a moment we wanted to make up for all the meaningless wasted time that was now behind us, all the time we had not spent together; in great haste we had to get around all the blind alleys and detours of our mutual attraction and aversion, we had to prevent any separation again; at the same time it seemed that all our previous detours now gained meaning precisely from this dry and hasty eagerness, as if we had to keep avoiding each other so that now, with all the obligatory pretense and falseness behind us, passion could be real passion, and dryness could be the parched longing for each other, a desert in which the only drink would be the other's mouth; and when lips met lips the encounter should take a new turn, one of tenderness, of leisurely, melting softness; and though each tiny dry crack could still be felt, let the joy of discovery relieve the tension and allow the separate streams of the saliva of anticipation to flow into each other.

Our tongues delivered, and out of each other's mouth we drank the fluid our lips needed.

Our arms followed suit in a spontaneous move to squeeze and hold tight.

With both hands she gripped the back of my head as if she wanted to stuff it all into her mouth, swallow it whole—how she used to make fun of just such things!—while I slipped my arms under her open coat and drew her close; this move was still the trickery of self-conscious thinking; as if we were trying, with fitful groping and exaggerated squeezes and holds, to avoid experiencing how closed our bodies still were; as is often the case, the energy spent on avoidance made us sense all the stronger what it was that we ought to be avoiding.

The mouth itself, however, made no attempt to avoid the unpleasant feeling of the body's frustrating confinement; the lips' parched desire for one another was so intense as to preclude all but the mutual quenching of their thirst; for the mouths there was nothing to avoid with their craving, with their irresistible coming together when, in the joyful moment of finding each other, their saliva of anticipation mingled and lubricated the two surfaces, the better to slip into and slide over each other, thus foreshadowing the possibility of even greater pleasure ahead, and, ignoring the grips and holds of the hands, alluded to the climactic moment of mutual gratification that every tension-racked body strives for.

For a fraction of a second, even the tips of our tongues cleaved together, and the feeling beyond joy found in this firmness, like a foretaste of what was to come, flooded our bodies, obliterating all selfish designs and will-fulness; yielding to the heat that can relax the muscles and fill the blood vessels under the skin, both of us shuddering and enervated, we stepped across the protective layer of outer surfaces.

In the interior landscape opened up by a kiss everything is sharply visible yet suspended in a mutable state; nothing resembles the external landscape our eyes are used to.

It is a feeling of being in an empty space; of course, one tries invol-untarily to define one's place in it, and relative to one's position there is up and down, and background and foreground can also be distinguished; the background is generally dark or a blurred gray; there are no palpable landmarks, no forms familiar from dreams or reveries, only spots, flashes, and glimmers that, being in an empty space, appear to be flat rather than round, and they seem to follow a geometrical pattern as they separate from and then blend into the soft, probably infinite background of exis-tence.

It's as though every sensation had its geometrical equivalent, and in these forms and shapes, in these visual codes, I could recognize another person's emotions and sensory capacities, needs and peculiarities, for in this interior landscape the boundary between me and the Other is blurred, the two merge, yet the feeling remains that the Other is the empty space and I a single spot or shape or streak in it.

She is the space and I am a restlessly but not impatiently moving con-figuration in it, ready to adapt myself to her space.

I am the space and she is a restlessly but not impatiently moving con-figuration in it, ready to adapt herself to my space.

Her promise is my promise.

And this promise, made to each other's body, we did honor, quite recklessly, a few days later.

The Nights of
Our Secret Delight

I would have said no and no, and again no, if someone at that moment, in the words of the ancient philosopher, had called life a rushing river, insisting that nothing could ever be repeated, the water was always different, and you couldn't dip your hand in the same river twice; what was is already gone, and replacing the old was something new, itself becoming old instantly, and then new again.

If it were really so, if we could experience the irresistible rush of the new unaffected by anything else, if the old did not cast its shadow on the new, our life would be one ceaseless wonder; every moment between day and night, between birth and death, would be a thrilling miracle; we couldn't distinguish between pain and pleasure, hot and cold, sweet and sour; there would be no boundaries, no borderlines between our most extreme sensations, because there would be no in between, and thus we'd have no word for the moment, no division between day and night, and out of the wet warmth of our mother's womb we wouldn't come wailing into this cold, dry world; and in death we'd only crumble like stones scorched by the sun and lashed by icy rain, for there would be no slow decay, and no dread, and no language either, for words can name only recurring phenomena; in the absence of recurrence we wouldn't have what we like to call intelligent discourse, only the divine gift, the ineffable joy, of permanent impermanence.

And even if it were so, for as children we all felt the urge, in a darkening room, to catch time at its word, to really understand just when, at what precise point, day turned into night; in the invisible and vanishing dimness we did try to grasp and hold on to the apparently simple meaning of words, so even if we did make ourselves believe that there were no boundaries, no division between day and night, even then, after a time, yes, after a time, slipping off the hard wall of divinely permanent impermanence and running back to the softer realm of human thought, we'd have to concede that it is night, even though we couldn't tell just when it got dark; the eyes perceive the difference but never the dividing line, and maybe there is no such thing at all; yet it is night, because it is dark, it is night because it isn't day, just as it happened yesterday and the day before, and we fall asleep in the reassuring yet disappointing knowledge that soon it will be light again.

The sense of the permanent and the sense of the eternal may be part of our divine inheritance, yet I feel that it's just the other way around: our human senses and the emotions stemming from them are too crude not to feel the familiarly old in everything new, not to sense the future in the present, not to discover in every new physical experience a story already known to our body.

Although not in a divine manner, time does seem to stop at such moments; it's as if our foot did not step into a rushing river but trod desperately on some sinking, soft marsh, trying to stay on the surface of deadly boring repetitions, which nevertheless appear to be the single most acceptable proof of life, until our foot loses the battle and quite literally tramples itself to death.

But far be it from me to affect philosophical airs; the only reason I mention all this is to give some idea of an especially overwrought emotional state in which things appear startlingly new and at the same time stiflingly familiar; I found myself in just such a curious state at the end of my two-month stay in Heiligendamm, as I was standing by the handsome white desk in my room—no, it's no mistake, I had stood and sat in such a state before, in my robe, unshaven, unwashed, waiting for some fateful judgment; now, however, prompted by the coolly inquisitive and somewhat watery eyes of a police inspector, I began to read my fiancée's letter, and even if the situation were not so strikingly similar yet different, even if I hadn't felt those commanding eyes on me, eyes that could read a criminal's mind, her opening line would still have stunned me or, more precisely, would have deepened my astonishment in this wakeful state of bewilderment.

My darling, my dearest, my one and only, wrote my bride, using words she had never used before, the unusual address falling like fiery slaps on my face and, along with the sudden rush of awful memories, making me dizzy; it took all my self-control to keep my head straight on my neck; and as I scanned the rest of the letter, I felt hot perspiration inundating my whole body under the robe; with my hands trembling, I slipped the letter back into the envelope, and to steady myself I grasped the back of a tall armchair, though what I really wanted to do was to flee.

To escape, away from the chaos of my life! which was impossible, of course, if only because of the presence of my strange visitor, to say nothing of the fact that one can never satisfy the animal urge to escape, since from the chaos of one's soul there is no place to escape to.

The reason this worthy officer of the law was standing there by the terrace door, and the reason I so readily complied with his audacious request that I open the freshly arrived letter in his presence, was that that very morning the young manservant, Hans Baader, with a single stroke of a razor had slit the throat of the young Swedish gentleman to whom I had been introduced the day after my arrival, at the luncheon table, in highly unusual circumstances, almost at the very moment Count Stollberg's death was announced; with his throat slit, the young Swede was lying in his own blood on the floor of the neighboring suite; police officials who rode over from Bad Doberan located the murderer in the pitch-dark coal cellar, where, evidently unhinged by his own deed, he was huddling and screaming frantically; within half an hour these same officials shed light on the intimate relationship that had developed between Gyllenborg, myself, and Fräulein Stollberg, and on Gyllenborg's and my special attachment to the young manservant himself; with my courteous and obliging behavior, not completely devoid of a certain condescending haughtiness, I intended to dispel the suspicion that I could have had anything to do with this sordid affair that led to murder.

I thanked my good fortune and my stubbornness for not appearing in those ravishingly beautiful photographs, taken by poor Gyllenborg, that showed the young countess partially clad and the valet completely nude— photographs that might at any moment come into the hands of policemen who were just then rummaging through his belongings—even though my ill-fated friend had repeatedly asked me to pose, indeed beseeched me piteously, with tears in his eyes, saying that a triad was needed: next to the rough-hewn robustness of the valet's body, my own more delicate angularity, so that, as he put it, "these two extreme poles of health would flank what is so alluringly ill."

I was able to reject categorically all allegations, couched in polite, con-voluted legal phrases, according to which my relationship with the valet and Fräulein Stollberg was reprehensibly intimate and my knowledge of the motives behind the crime a virtual certainty; but there was not a shred of evidence that could be used against me; in point of fact, during the two months of our friendship, as if all along anticipating a possible dis-covery, I always used the terrace door to reach Gyllenborg's room, con-verted of late into a studio, just as Father, twenty years earlier, in pursuit of his nocturnal secret delights, used to slip into Fräulein Wohlgast's room; consequently, no one could have witnessed my afternoon or nighttime visits there; without making much of a fuss, or even being especially cautious, I characterized the allegations as slander, pure and simple, and with a nonchalant shrug of my shoulders assured the inspector that I had absolutely no idea whether the murdered gentleman carried on any inti-mate liaisons with the persons in question.

It is true, I added, that I wasn't a close enough friend of the victim to have knowledge of the more intimate aspects of his private life, but I knew him to be a man of taste and breeding for whom it would have been unthinkable—howsoever he may have been inclined to behave—to enter into such a dubious relationship with a mere servant; I played the innocent, almost to the point of idiocy, but I had to be sure to avoid the dreadful snare, for, the valet not being of age, I could have been charged not only with indulging in perverse sexual acts but also with corrupting a minor; to give my professed naïveté some psychological support, I low-ered my voice to a confidential whisper, shrugged my shoulders again, and asked the inspector whether he had had a chance to see Fräulein Stollberg's hands without gloves.

The inspector's unblinking eyes were staring at me steadfastly, and they were the strangest pair of eyes I have ever seen: light and transparent, cold and with almost no color, a curious transition between vaguely blue and hazily gray; the two eyeballs were large and, because of some weak-ness or chronic ailment perhaps, constantly swimming in a bowl of tears, and this made it appear as if all his ostensibly plainspoken, unassuming questions, as well as my supposedly innocent replies, had filled him with profound sadness, as if everything had pained him—the crime committed, the lies, even the hidden truths—and all the while his face, and the eye-balls themselves, remained totally impassive and cold.

Using only his eyes, the inspector now indicated that he did not un-derstand my remark and would be grateful for an explanation.

Naturally enough, I assumed that Fräulein Stollberg would not betray me, would hold her peace, perhaps even deny everything, although she herself was somewhat implicated by the photographs Gyllenborg had left behind.

The inspector's silent request prompted me to remain silent myself, and I proceeded to show on my own hand how Fräulein Stollberg's fingers were fused together; that is why she had to wear gloves all the time; like hooves they were, I finally said.

The inspector was a large, jovial man with an air of quiet, commanding professionalism; his powerful build must have been an asset in his line of work; he stood in the terrace doorway with his arms folded; we were both standing as we talked, which meant that this was not yet an inter-rogation, but no idle chitchat either; he broke into a smile, which his tearing eyes made look almost painful; and then lightly, as if tossing back my argument, he remarked that from his experience he knew that certain people, usually emotionally troubled or weak, not only did not find phys-ical malformations or deformities repulsive but, on the contrary, were often attracted by them.

I felt myself blushing all over and could tell from the teary glint in his eyes that the telltale change in my complexion did not escape his notice, though the sudden rush of emotion he unwittingly elicited in me affected him, too; the satisfaction he must have felt at having unmasked me for a moment caused such an abundant welling up of tears in his eyes that if he hadn't quickly pulled out a handkerchief from the pocket of his baggy trousers, with a movement that for him seemed almost too abrupt, the tears would have rolled down his plump, ruddy cheeks.

I must be one of those emotionally weak people, then, I thought to myself, suddenly recalling the moment in that compartment when in the silence punctuated only by the clatter of the train, under the light of the swaying ceiling lamp, she pulled off her gloves, slowly and merci-lessly, and, looking deep into my eyes, revealed the secret of her hands to me.

Frozen, without breathing, I stared at the weirdly inhuman sight: on both her hands—nature's cruelty in her was symmetrical!—she had only four fingers; the middle and ring fingers on each hand were fused together in a single, thick digit ending in flat, hard nails; yet I must admit that the peculiar deformity did not really come as a surprise, and the inspector was right: I wasn't repulsed; if anything, the sight gave an attractive if cruel explanation of her delicate and vulnerable beauty, which during the long journey I had kept scrutinizing, entranced and mesmerized, and whose secret I had been unable to puzzle out.

By revealing her defect, she seemed to be telling me that we carry all our physical qualities, abilities, gifts, faults, blemishes, and passions in the features of our face; modesty had but one duty: to cast a gentle veil over what was self-evident; her face, after all, was perfectly formed, exquisite, each of its fine lines and charming curves complemented other, equally fine and charming features, yet even before I saw those awful hands I felt as if all this perfection hung suspended over the chasm of its own uncertainty, at any moment the finely cut features could unravel and become deformed; it seems incredible, but I felt that a law of nature was being embodied right before my eyes, I thought I could almost see how beauty could mature into itself only by going through the malformed and the ugly, that perfection was but the degeneration of the imperfect, and that is why beauty was engaged in a constant game of hide-and-seek with ugliness and degeneration; her lips were full, sensuous, yet quivering with gentle, soft currents, as if she had to stop some terrible violence or pain with them; and her eyes were wide-open and round, penetrating but also haughty, as if with each glance she were challenging, and at the same time trying to forestall, some imminent disaster; on her face I saw the dread of, as well as the longing for, annihilation; it was madness in the guise of beauty that excited me, so the gesture itself, the slowness and cruel dignity of the gesture with which she exposed the secret of her hands and that of her whole body racked with desire and the dread of desire, moved me to respond with a very rash, extreme gesture of my own: I seized the strange hand and, finding the root of my desires in this no doubt repugnant sight, kissed it.

Not only did she tolerate my humble kiss but I could feel that for that brief moment she yielded her hand totally to it and then slowly, savoring the warm touch of my lips, she began to pull it away, yet I felt she did not really want to, she wanted something else, something more cruel, more extreme; in our clumsiness we let the gloves drop to the floor, but then she shoved her unspeakable, hoof-like fingers between my lips, and while we both remained silent, like thieves—with eyes not quite closed, her mother was sleeping right next to her and being bounced around by the moving train—she deliberately bruised my lips and my tongue with the sharp tips of her broad, flat nails, turning my quiet humility into my humiliation.

The smile on her face then was unforgettable, and it was this smile that later Gyllenborg captured in his equally unforgettable photograph.

The picture itself was dominated not by the two intimately familiar bodies but by a heavy, undulant drapery whose folds swept down diagonally from the upper edge of the picture toward its center, where it twisted around, concealing some kind of studio hassock or stool, swung down farther, less ruffled, until its graceful sweep finally vanished from view, giving the viewer the impression that he was looking not at a complete picture but at a random detail of a larger composition, and thus the models assuming their position against the background of the luxurious drapery also looked rather tentative; the young servant's unruly hair was adorned with a laurel wreath; his legs spread apart, his chest puffed out, he sat in the middle of the picture with his work-hardened hands resting on his knees, and though he didn't face the viewer, his body did; as if following the folds of the drapery, he was looking out of the picture, over the head of Fräulein Stollberg, who, down on one knee, positioned herself in front of the young valet in such a way that her slightly bowed head concealed his groin; at the same time her head and her face with a gracefully cruel and voluptuous smile were framed by his two enormous thighs and powerful legs.

But with all this I haven't said anything about the photograph itself, which, naturally, revealed much more about its creator than about the people used as models; following some wise old rule of aesthetics, Gyllenborg uncovered the man's body, keeping the genitalia invisible, while the woman's body, with the exception of one breast, he draped with a sheet, slinging it over her shoulder in a classical manner; however, the sheet he used must have been soaked in water or oil first, because it clung to her, wet and shiny, accentuating even more, almost to the point of disgusting immodesty, what it so modestly covered up.

The picture could have turned out disgusting, ludicrously precious, frighteningly contrived and tasteless, a textbook illustration of a strained, dilettantish performance that, in its attempt to achieve well-balanced proportions, obliterates just those human traits, thought to be imperfect, flawed, and unseemly, that are a natural and inalienable part of any example of human perfection; except that the young lady in the picture— and for this the artist deserves praise—folded her healthy fingers into her palm, and held those awful, hoof-like fused digits before her face, those unnatural, deformed fingers! and as if not even conscious of the warm closeness of the valet's open thighs—heavens, what fragrant warmth must have streamed from those thighs!—she was busy looking at the repulsive, malformed fingers, contemplating them with that cruel smile of hers, yes, a cruel smile that turned everything in the carefully arranged picture, every self-consciously aesthetic and voluptuous detail, into its own diabolical parody; nevertheless, it wasn't the two subjects that were mocked and laughed at but we, the peeping viewers, you and I, and everyone else who looked at the picture, even the person who made it, for what the picture was saying was that with a smile one can accept one's deformities, with a smile one had to accept the objective cruelty of things, that is what real innocence is, the rest is mere decoration, detail, convention, affectation, the smiling acknowledgment of the perverse turned the wreath on the valet's head into a devilish parody, the tense indifference with which he looked out of the drapery folds also had the effect of a parody, as did the raw sensuality which, in spite of their affected aloofness and pensive inwardness, still bound them together; in the final analysis, the gauchely displayed beauty of their bodies also became disillusioningly pathetic.

I might have blushed more deeply and longer had the inspector not had the tact, or calculated cleverness, to wipe his eyes for a long time, dabbing them carefully with the corner of his handkerchief wrapped around the tip of his little finger, making sure he removed every bit of the yellow discharge which prolonged tearing always leaves in the corners; but his delicate little activity was nothing but pretense; rather than exploiting my momentary embarrassment, he wanted me to regain my composure; there was no hurry, he seemed to be saying, we had plenty of time, if not now, then later, and if not later, then I would tell him now what I had to tell, it was all the same to him; but in truth, his apparent tactfulness was his somewhat cruel way of making me nervous.

And not without results, for at the moment, though still overjoyed at being able to suppress the outward signs of my inner turmoil, I did become unsettled, I felt I had lost my bearings, the ability to control the situation, and that he had gotten me to the point where he wanted me to be, more or less; so be it, I suddenly thought to myself, I shall tell him everything, if only to be done with it.

It seemed so simple to tell everything, for it was really nothing: four people had been engaged in erotic games, and one of them wanted out, but another began to blackmail him with scandalous photographs he took of the two of them; if I could have found the first, simple little word needed to tell this nothing of a story, to formulate the first all-meaningful sentence, I could have told him the whole thing.

Fortunately for me, a quiet knock on the door came just then; I know I gave a start, not because of the three soft raps, but because they brought me back to my senses.

Thinking clearly again turned out to have a jolting effect; something inside me was trying to expand, shout out, and at the same time it fell back into itself; the battle of conflicting impulses, like an intermittent fever, made me turn so pale and faint that, while through the haze of my helplessness I watched the hotelier approaching us—his portly figure especially obsequious now because of the murder case—the inspector was ready to grasp my arm and help me into a chair; summoning the last remnant of my strength, I declined, and as if completing the same gesture, I took the letter from the tray offered to me, because I saw immediately whom it was from.

I must have looked a pitiful wreck of a man, trying with every move to convince those present that I was in control of my actions, yet in this situation, in this room, nothing surprising enough could happen anymore that would justify such desperate behavior.

Strangely, it wasn't the situation itself but certain details that stunned me: the sharp shadow the inspector's figure cast on me seemed more important than the words spoken or suppressed; how close and how loud the sea sounded to me, even though the windows were closed; the cold winter light flooding through the windows, witness to the frenzied floundering of my soul.

Although I knew perfectly well what had happened, I did not comprehend why the hotel manager himself and not the valet brought me my letter, yes, the valet, Hans, whom I had just moments earlier banished publicly from my heart, no, from someplace deeper than that, from all my senses; and I didn't understand where he was, where he could be, if his absence hurt me so much; it was my betrayal of him that hurt.

And I didn't understand why this stranger standing before me, folding his arms across his chest again, was telling me to read the letter, and saying it as if somebody else in the room also had to read a letter; I didn't understand why he was saying out loud what at that moment was going through my mind; the servile cowardice with which I obeyed his command, put to me in the guise of a polite request, hurt me so much that in my pain I had the feeling it was a stranger acting the coward in my place, a stranger who nevertheless had to be me.

Even now, as I write these lines, so many years after the event, I don't quite understand what happened to me then; the magnitude of the danger alone cannot explain my behavior; to be more precise, I do understand but am deeply ashamed of those little scenes of falling to pieces, of insanity, buffoonery, betrayal, and cringing, in which I hoped to find refuge; my shame is like a stuck blood clot, and no justifiable motivation or elaborate explanation can be the pill to dissolve it; the painful clot has remained proof positive of my fall from grace.

It was a short letter, barely a page, conceived no doubt in a sudden paroxysm of happiness: My darling, my dearest, my one and only, it began, and this salutation, brimming with joy, caught my eyes immediately; I went over it twice, thrice, and again; I wanted my eyes to comprehend what they were seeing, because with this salutation, suddenly it was a ghost speaking to me from this letter, the ghost of a woman whom I've already mentioned on an earlier page of these recollections, a woman who even as a ghost is more alive in me than anyone living but about whom I mustn't talk, for I cannot; and it was her image, no, not her image but her smell, the smell of her mouth, of her secret parts, of her armpits, that wafted toward me from that opening line, a fragrance I could never quite reach, only she could write to me like this, only she loved me and called me tender names in this way, only she—even though I knew very well that I was reading Helene's letter.

It was during that fraction of a second, while longing for that evanescent fragrance, that I made up my mind: I can't stay with her, I must run away from Helene.

It was ten long years of my life which I had rejected and wished to forget that stared back at me from the salutation; Helene may have expropriated them, but they couldn't have been hers, I couldn't let her have them; thinking of this just then could not have been an accident, for I knew that the police had detailed and creditable data about my ten-year association with secret anarchist societies; if, therefore, I did not act with animal cunning, I'd have to pay for those ten years, and my attempts at finding refuge from the subversive, even murderous activities of those years in Helene's arms would have been in vain.

Death spoke to me from that letter, death multiplying itself and still unique, death lurking at every turn, in every corner, death desired and death dreaded, the death of that one special sweet-smelling woman, rising from the bloody corpse of my now publicly rejected and abandoned friend; but every other murder and death also called out from that letter: my mother's unspeakably slow and painful wasting away at my father's side, and Father's own ignominious death under the wheels of a speeding train between Görlitz and Lebau, at Signal Station 7, and the mutilated body of the girl he had violated, that hideous lye-soaked sack oozing sweat, piss, shit, and snot; all deaths of the body, and yet Helene's letter was in fact sending blissful waves toward me, the prospects of a wonderful life: "That achingly beautiful morning," she wrote, "when we had to part, has become a morning of consummation whose fruit I now carry under my heart"; we had to move up the date of our wedding, she said, and therefore I should hurry back to her without fail, and that was her parents' wish as well; this was followed only by her initial, the first letter of her Christian name.

If fate chose to stage a scene such as this, having me read this letter while a detective investigating a murder keeps his moist eyes on me, then everything but everything is but an illusion and a bunch of lies—so thought one half of my split self, while the other half of course couldn't help being dizzy with joy, thrilled at the mere thought of life's relentless continuation, and the more it felt that this, too, was but an illusion, a deception, a false hope, the more it let itself go in absurd jubilation.

She wanted to give a son to this body oozing with corruption, the body that hoped to find its freedom in blissfully dreaded death.

What monstrous demons can crawl out of one's thoughts.

I began to laugh, a loud, harsh, boisterous laugh; I was laughing so hard I had to hold on to the back of the armchair to keep myself from falling over.

I don't know at what point I slipped the letter back into the envelope, but I can still see my trembling hand fumbling with the paper.

First there was a little tussle between my hand, the letter, and the envelope, and it was after that hard-won victory that I had to grab the back of the chair to stop myself from bolting out the door, and perhaps it was the uncontrollable trembling that made me explode in laughter.

I was laughing insanely, I could say, but the sound of my laughter betrayed the fact that by laughing I was trying to drive myself insane.

From then on I was carried along by the demon of my own sound.

Nearly a decade later, in a huge tome by Baron Jakob Johann Uexküll, I came across this illuminating and endearing statement: "When a dog runs, it is the animal that moves its legs, but when a hedgehog runs, it is the legs that move the animal."

This subtle distinction helped me understand that it was a primitive animal's instinct to escape that had appeared in my laughter; it wasn't I who sought refuge in that loud laugh but the laugh that saved me from my plight.

At the moment of its explosion the laughter revealed my utter desperation, but in the very next moment it tripped over itself and changed direction, route, and above all intended meaning, so that it could pretend that it wasn't even a hearty laugh but a titter, and not even that, only the inane display of overwhelming joy, though nothing like total abandon even then, for the incongruity of the situation inhibited this sort of tittering; my ears registered every shift, modulation, and distortion as if I were hearing it with the inspector's ears; and then it was the joy of life, cleansed of everything and bathed in bliss, that was laughing along with me, until I managed to be moved by my own performance to the point of tears, which in turn made the sound tremulous and faltering, and I felt moved even more, until I finally regained control and, haltingly, could say something.

"Do forgive me," I stammered while wiping my eyes, and my demon, so very sure of itself, still holding my voice captive, clinging to it, guiding it, graciously allowed me to sound sincere, as if to claim that lies and deceptions could very nicely turn into truths, there was nothing to be ashamed of! they became more convincingly real this way, more authentic than purportedly simple and immaculate truths; anyway, we can never gauge the moral worth of our actions so it's useless to fret and agonize over them, we might as well push ahead, especially since my demon used my fiancée's very intimate letter to refute, and refute triumphantly and unequivocally, any suspicion about my own involvement in this affair: "Do forgive me," I repeated, "this outburst was totally inappropriate, I am deeply embarrassed; yet if I say that I must nevertheless decline responsibility for it—for without being requested to do so, I would not have dreamed of perusing such a letter in front of a stranger—then I am in effect begging the forgiveness of my dead friend lying in the next room"; I said all this in my demon's cool, measured, dignified voice, though also affecting the nonchalance of a man of the world; "However," I continued, "I would be as loath to offend you as I would my poor unfortunate friend; I can assure you, therefore, that the content of the letter is strictly private, and with an eye to dispelling any lingering doubt that it might have something to do with today's tragic occurrence, I am willing to dispense with proprieties and reveal, ah, hell and damnation, what could possibly keep me from saying it—what I received was very happy news, the kind of news one should be only too glad to share with anyone."

I took a deep breath and even, I remember, lowered my head, and the voice inside me turned gloomy, or unpleasant somehow, perhaps too bashful, as soon as I uttered those words.

I remained silent for so long that after a while I knew I had to lift my head.

And it was as if a rainbow-colored, shiny soap bubble had burst in the air.

His eyes were shining at me from behind the distorting curve of a teardrop, but as we looked long into each other's eyes, I had the impression that for the first time his face was showing genuine astonishment, even shock.

"On the contrary," he replied very quietly, and I watched with enormous satisfaction as his apoplectic complexion turned several shades darker, though clearly anger and not shame made him blush; "On the contrary," he repeated almost too cordially, "it is I who must apologize, if only because your comment is well taken; my request was needlessly intrusive, I clearly overstepped my authority; and if I reiterate—your evident and quite understandable wariness compels me to reiterate—that we are assuming nothing and accusing no one, the case may not be closed, of course, but we do have the culprit in our hands, if I stress all this once again, I really mean to apologize, above all for creating a false impression, and at the same time I beg you to consider my intrusion as excessive caution, which in such circumstances is almost inevitable, or, if you like, as the blunt, unseemly curiosity of a seasoned professional, think of it what you will, but I beg of you, do not think ill of me, and since what is done is done, allow me to be the first to express my warmest good wishes, and please remember, the man offering his most sincere congratulations is one who is daily confronted with the seamy side of life and very rarely has a chance to share in the happy events of life, especially those connected to nature."

The deep flush vanished from his face, he smiled kindly, even ruefully; instead of bowing we merely inclined our heads, and all this time and even afterward he did not move from his place but remained standing by the terrace door, his arms folded over his chest and, in a shaft of slanting winter light, casting his shadow over me.

"May I ask you one more thing?" he said after a moment's hesitation.

"I am at your service."

"I am a rather heavy smoker, and unfortunately I left my cigars in the car. May I help myself to one of yours?"

This sort of behavior—apologizing for an inappropriate, unwarranted, and obtrusive act, and then committing just such an act, and to exploit a tense situation flaunting one's hold over another—reminded me of someone or something, though I couldn't at that moment tell who or what, but the familiar, almost physical disgust I felt led me to believe that this man was of very lowly origin.

"Please do, by all means," I answered graciously, and now I was the one who did not make a move; I did not wish to open the cigar box for him, and I did not offer him a seat either.

There was someone who could make me just as helpless, and whom I hated just as much.

However, the inspector did not let himself be bothered; he strolled in a leisurely way over to the table behind me and took a cigar out of the box Gyllenborg had given me a few days earlier; and now this hit me so hard I didn't have the strength to turn around; I knew what he was up to: in the deceased's room an identical lacquered box lay on the table; so this was the missing link he was looking for.

It got so quiet I could hear him slip off the cigar band; and then, just as slowly, he walked back and stood before me.

"Would you happen to have a knife?" he asked with a friendly smile, and I simply pointed at my desk.

Ceremoniously he lit the cigar, and I had the impression he'd never smoked one before; he praised its aroma and smacked his lips; then he blew out the smoke silently, and I had to stand there and look at him.

But I felt that try hard as I might, I couldn't watch him finish that cigar.

"Is there anything else I can help you with?"

"Oh no," he said, cocking his head amiably, "I've taken up too much of your time already, and in any case we shall meet again tomorrow, shan't we?"

"If you feel that another meeting is absolutely necessary, I'd be glad to give you my card," I said. "By tomorrow evening I should be in Berlin."

He took the cigar out of his mouth, nodded assentingly, and blew out the smoke along with the words: "I'd be much obliged."

He placed my card carefully in his billfold, and there was nothing left for us to do but bow politely to each other; without a word, puffing on the cigar, he walked out of my room.

Drained and exhausted, I was left to myself, and like an ice floe cracked in two on the dark waters of a turbulent river, like two light spots in the night, the two halves of my self were drifting farther and farther apart; while one was singing a selfish little victory march, the other hummed a dirge of utter defeat, while one searched through its memories, wondering why this disagreeable character, whom he may have resembled, looked so familiar, and fretted over not finding the key to the puzzle, the other pondered the chances of escape, imagining in every detail the arrival in Berlin's Anhalter Terminal, the attempt to melt into the crowd and, having eluded possible pursuers, immediately getting on the train to Italy; I also have to say here that all the time a third self was present, who in a way held the other two together, showing me an image that also sprang from the suddenly opened storehouse of my memories but seemed completely unrelated to anything, an image from a childhood garden on a hot late-summer afternoon when, wandering among the trees, I noticed a green lizard drowning in the stone bowl of a little fountain; it could keep only the tip of its tiny head and its open mouth out of the water, its hollow ears and open eyes were below the surface; it couldn't move up or down, forward or backward, though its outspread little legs were treading wildly; this was my first, perhaps my oldest memory of the world; it was a dry summer, and I knew the lizard must have climbed into the fountain bowl for a drink and then slipped into the water; stunned, rooted to the spot, I stared and stared at it, and I was no eyewitness but God Himself, for it was up to me whether this creature would live or die, and the mere possibility of having to make that decision so horrified me, I thought I might as well let it drown; but then, placing both hands under its body, I fished it out of the water, and shuddering with disgust at the touch or at the finality of my act, I flung it on the grass, where it stayed motionless, though it was breathing, its heart beating through its whole beautiful body; and this image, the shimmering emerald-green grass and the motionless lizard, didn't just cross my mind but was there before me, sharp and vivid, in all its color, light, and supple form, as if I were seeing it for the first time; I was standing in that garden of yore and not in this room.

I was that green lizard for whom this sudden gift of life, this reprieve, this near-death, the renewed beating of its heart, breathing the air again, was as much a mystery as was the drowning—perhaps an even greater, more profound mystery.

And I also wasn't aware that for some time I had been sitting, my head submerged in that image; I was sitting somewhere, no longer standing, and tears were trickling through my fingers, pressed against my face.

My sobs sounded like the crying of that little boy, it was as if he were looking, alarmed and with tearless eyes, at everything that happened to him later and had but a single, foolishly repeated question: Why, why, who wanted this, who made it happen this way, why?

As if already then he was repeating this eternally inane question to himself, and even today that was all he could do.

It wasn't the beloved friend I mourned, not Gyllenborg, not the handsome, cheerful young man whom even in his death I admired and envied, for however his life may have ended, he had managed to tell us more in a single, outrageously beautiful photograph than I ever could in my frantic, agonizing, pathetic struggle to string some words together, yes, I did envy him! for needless to say, in those two months spent in a riot of sensuality I had not been able to put down a single passable sentence of my planned narrative, while he, forever suffering from rashes of mysterious origin, always feverish on account of a diseased lung, could create, and with the nonchalance of a condemned man and the incredibly simple elegance granted him by death's proximity, could toy with all those weighty questions I could only brood on in my dilettantish artificially whipped-up zeal; yes, I admired and envied him, because with fatal constancy he achieved and completed what his body had prepared for him; he did not confuse his ideas with the objects of his curiosity and attraction but on the contrary fused them together so well that his ideas barely showed through, while I only indulged in reveries and thinking because I was hoping to escape and to save myself with ideas forced out of my own words—perhaps this is what separates art from dilettantism: the object of observation is not to be confused with the means of treating it as a subject!—Gyllenborg never made that mistake, so in him, and by him, something was brought to completion, there was no need for me to feel sorry for him, and I wasn't mourning Hans either, not his innocent youthful vigor, now in the hands of fate; yet what heavenly pleasure it was with all the tenderness of my frailty to love his fiery red hair, the soft smoothness of his milk-white skin, his freckles, which at places swelled into birthmarks I could feel with my fingers, the silky richness of his pubic hair, and the hot spurting milk of his warm groin; no, I wasn't mourning my betrayed, forfeited pleasures, not that body which I made my own and understood so well down to the depths of its pores—oh, it's not a mere body that will slowly waste away within the walls of a cold jail cell!—and I wasn't mourning my own base treachery, or my mother, whom I missed so terribly in these moments that I dared not think about her, and through my mother I wasn't mourning Helene, whom I was now sure to abandon, and in my child yet to be born, whom I'd never see, I wasn't mourning myself, or my lost fatherhood, or the ultimately guiltless father in myself, and I wasn't mourning my father, or the little girl he so viciously murdered, whose dead body I had to look at, along with our maid Hilde, as part of the elaborately cruel process of identification that also took place on a dreadful, sunlit morning such as this one, the same Hilde who a few months later, in an effort to get even with her cruel fate, made herself my first woman and who since has died, no, I wasn't mourning any of these people, and I wasn't mourning myself either.

While my eyes showed me the rescued lizard, my brain was working like a needlessly overheated engine driven by a steam of emotions, with its gears, belts, pistons, and levers dredging up from the depth of the soul everything that was similar to the image in the eyes, everything that could hurt as only a deep childhood hurt can; it wasn't exhaustion that made me cry, and not the impending danger, but the sense of helplessness I felt in the face of so much human filth.

And at that moment I already knew who it was that looked back at me so familiarly in the figure of the inspector, and I also knew that with my loud, racking sobs I was mourning my one and only dead, my only love, the only person untouched by this filth; it was she I was mourning, it was she I was coughing up, the one woman I cannot talk about.

I felt hot, was soaked with tears, shivered in the misery of my cold body, my limbs seemed to be melting away, and then, without knowing why, I had to look up.

Who possesses the divine ability to distinguish the separate times within a single second; yet in who, if not in us humans, do these divine distinctions of time, reduced to the thinness of a hair, weave their gossamer thread?

Yes, it was she, the face of my one and only, whom I saw standing there in the doorway, silent and reproachful, all in black, veiled, one hand still on the door handle ready to shut the door behind her; I wondered why she was dressed in black, she was dead, she couldn't be mourning herself! though in the fraction of the next second I realized it wasn't she but Fräulein Stollberg in the doorway.

And how strange it was that in this immeasurable space of time the terrible pain yielded to an even more intense throb, a pain caused by a loss that was final and eternal, and the Fräulein could see only the twitch of my face that was not meant for her.

She lifted her veil, slipped her gloved hand back into her muff, and waited, hesitantly, not quite sure how one conducted oneself in this situation; her face was pale, like marble, smooth and untouchable; I suppose it was some shock that made her look like that, quite alien and distasteful to me, yet I could see my own pain reflected in her face, perhaps in the timid, exceptionally fragile smile that hovered around her lips and that I also felt around my own mouth.

I had last seen her a few hours earlier in that tumultuous scene when we all rushed out into the corridor, alarmed by the raving screams of a chambermaid, and she, along with the others, ran toward the wide-open door of our friend Gyllenborg's suite, though at that point not knowing, not understanding yet what had happened, she seemed to be enjoying the noisy confusion.

Now her tiny smile served to alleviate her pain, to make it less humiliating; I could see on her face that her cruel little games were over and done with, and a far greater act of cruelty was to follow; the smile was meant to offset this next act but only made it more painful, the shame of it did, the same shame I felt at having to smile, at realizing that I could still smile, and that a smile was perhaps longer lasting than death itself, which of course was still not my own death.

Carrying in her smile the shadows of her offended, proud, humble, and beautiful cruelty, she hurried toward me, and I received her with much the same smile; but in me the weight of that smile was such that I was unable to rise, whereupon she suddenly yanked her hands out of her muff and, letting the fine fur piece drop to the floor, sank both her gloved hands into my hair and face.

"My dear friend!"

The whisper issued from her throat like a choked sob, and shameful though it may be to admit, the touch of her hand gave me painful pleasure.

A sharp pang that finds joy in pain—maybe that is what must have made me spring up from my chair, the terrifying joy of my shame; my face slid along her lacy dress, then up, face touching face, her hard, cool lips grazing my tear-soaked skin; she was searching for something, hesitantly but irresistibly, and she had to find it quickly, and I was also looking for something on the untouchable smoothness of her face, clumsily, greedily, and the moment her lips found mine, in that fraction of a second when I felt the cool outline of her lips, that gentle fold of flesh, that alluring, curved shape, and she, too, found something similar; then, without parting her lips, she let her head sink to my shoulder; though the withdrawal was deliberate, she threw her arms around me and held me tight, so that we wouldn't feel what we both felt: the taste of the dead man's mouth on our lips; without him it was impossible for us to make contact.

We stood like this for a long time, with our arms pressing our bodies against each other's chest, loins, thighs, or at least it seemed like a very long time; and if just a moment earlier pain sought release in tender touches and tiny kisses, in our quickly flaring and immediately fading sensual energy, then this furious but insensate pressing and squeezing was a way of sharing a pain that found its way into our grief and our guilt, a pain that would not let us eject the dead man, we let him squeeze in between us.

It seems we needed just enough time for my body, feverish from sobbing, to warm up her cold one, because then, with her head still on my shoulder, in a very different, sly, conspiratorial, and rather inappropriate tone of voice, she whispered:

"I was a very good little girl," she said, almost laughing, "I lied."

I knew what she was talking about: the very thing I wanted to know more about, for knowledge of these unnamed but important facts meant time and a chance to get away, but I couldn't ask her about them without giving myself away.

But she, too, was in flight, and betraying me would have meant betraying herself as well; still, she would have liked me to be grateful.

I, however, wanted to vanish from my present life without leaving a trace, not even a telltale, breathless, inquisitive question from which those who remained behind could afterward surmise my real intentions; I wanted to leave nothing behind but a traceless void.

She understood all this, though she couldn't really know what she understood, and though I wasn't going to deny her my gratitude, I had to pull away a little to see all this on her face.

Yes, it was all there, but I was wrong about her laughing, in fact she was crying.

With my tongue I lapped up her large teardrops, and was glad I could show my gratitude in such a simple way, and when I drew her to me once more, the strange feeling of a moment ago, that we were not alone, simply melted away.

But this feeling made me realize what deadly silence reigned in the room, indeed in the entire hotel, and that the soundless light streaming through the window came from an infinite silence.

It occurred to me that the valet had already been taken away.

Later she whispered something about having come only to say goodbye, they were leaving.

I'm going home, too, I lied, but it wouldn't look right if we traveled together, I added.

No need to worry about that, she said, breathing hotly down my neck as if we were exchanging words of love; they'll go to Kühlungsbronn first, and will probably spend a few days there before returning to their estate in Saxony.

After so many years, with a very different sort of life behind me, a respectable life free of dangerous passion and excesses, what shame prevents me still from describing our farewell?

It was as if we had to part not from each other—that we wanted to do most anxiously, to get away, and the quicker and farther the better— but from him, we had to take gentle leave of the one who was staying behind.

She didn't give me away, she lied for me, something I'm not at all sure I would have done in her place, and for this reason, even in this situation, in this impossible parting, she had to be the stronger.

She pushed me away and stepped back; I could say we were looking at each other, but what we both did was to look at him in each other.

By drawing apart we left him too big a space between us, it made him loom too large.

Flustered and stammering, not knowing how we could get around him, get around someone who was growing larger and larger between us, not to mention his corpse still lying on the other side of the wall, I said that maybe I ought to go and say goodbye to her mother; I thought that if we left the room together, we could somehow shake off his lingering presence, but in response, something so sharply painful flashed in her eyes that one could justifiably call it hatred, hatred and reproach, reproach for using such a poor alibi to get away from the dead, but hatred, too, because at the same time I'd also be pushing her away, who was still alive; I had to stay.

But staying meant the hopeless intermingling of the living and the dead.

And then she smiled, the way a mature woman smiles at the blundering of her child.

After a little while she took off her hat, slowly pulled off her gloves, threw hat and gloves on the table, stepped closer to me, and with those fingers touched my face.

"Silly, how very silly you are!"

I said nothing.

"It's only natural," she said, and while instinctively responding to her advance, I felt on my hands that the face I was touching was not the face of the woman I loved and to whom I was about to make love; I was holding the woman that he, the dead man, had loved, and would keep on loving; even now he loved her through me, by reaching into me, into my hands and my body, just as this woman wasn't touching me directly.

No more words passed between us; what's more, we had no more moves and gestures of our own, everything was his.

With measured and dignified slowness we consummated his time for him, and for this long hour, whose every minute was sober and serene, even the specter of Hans the murderer had vanished.

As if responding to some inner upheaval, our pupils widened and narrowed; we were staring at death through the alluring veils of each other's eyes.

After she got dressed, pulled on her gloves, arranged her hair in front of the mirror, and put on her hat, she turned around once more to look at me, as if to say that if I wished, I could now say goodbye to her mother.

But after what we had done in that long hour, a polite goodbye would have made no sense; it was best to leave everything just the way it was.

I may have shaken my head, or she may have guessed my thought and agreed.

She lowered her veil over her face and walked out.

The following night, standing at the window of my speeding train, I was looking out to see—for I did want to see—my departure forever from the part of the earth that others, more fortunate or less fortunate than myself, called their homeland.

It was a dark, foggy winter night, and of course I couldn't see anything.

No More

I am a rational man, perhaps too rational. I am not inclined to any form of humility. Still, I would like to copy my friend's last sentence onto this empty page. Let it help me finish the job no one's commissioned me to do, which should make it the most personal undertaking of my life, the one closest to my heart.

It was a dark, foggy winter night, and of course I couldn't see anything.

I don't think he meant this to be his last sentence. There is every indication that the next day, as usual, he would have continued his life with a new sentence, one that could not be predicted or inferred from the notes he left behind. Because the novel of a life, once begun, always offers an invitation: Come on, lose yourselves in me, trust me, in the end I may be able to lead you out of my wilderness.

My role is merely that of a reporter.

I begin, then, my voice choking, with the fact that it must have been around three o'clock in the afternoon. That's when he usually stopped working. It was a bright, cloudless, summerlike late September afternoon. He got up from his desk. Outside, the old garden that had thinned out in the August heat was now slumbering peacefully. Now and then, through the sparsely grown tree branches and bushes, he could catch a glimpse of the shining dark river. The unusually narrow, vaulted windows of the house were framed by creeping vines, their yellow and red berries ripened by the sun at this time of the year. Lizards and the various insects that made their home in the clinging vines were now basking in the sun or cooling themselves under the shady leaves. He described something like this in the first chapter of his memoir, and he must have seen something like this on that day, too. Later, he had a bite to eat, exchanged some pleasantries with my aunts in the kitchen, then tucking the morning paper and the day's mail under his arm and throwing a thick towel over his shoulder, he went down to the Danube.

Two mangled legs, a crushed-in chest, and a cracked skull. That's all that was left of him, that's what they brought back.

So, without attaching any symbolic significance to it, the sentence quoted above was the last of an eight-hundred-page manuscript. It was left to me, though I am not his legal heir.

And now I would like to state most emphatically that by prefacing this report about my ill-fated friend's death with a few words about myself and my own circumstances, I do not wish in any way to push my own person to the foreground.

One reason for my doing this is that if I were to speak only of him, I'd get stuck too often, my voice would choke and falter.

My name is Krisztián Somi Tót; if not the last name, my first name should be familiar to those who have gotten as far as that last sentence of this long yet still incomplete life story. Because my poor friend, now through the distorting effects of romantic idealization, now that of romantic disappointment, did record for posterity a boy named Krisztián, the boy I once was but with whom today I feel I have little in common.

I could almost say he wrote it for me. Which does make me just a little proud. Maybe not proud. Rather a little surprised, childishly, awkwardly surprised, as when somebody suddenly shoves under your nose a secretly taken and therefore completely revealing photograph. In another sense, I'm embarrassed by the whole thing.

Having read the manuscript, I think that the more desperate the will to live, the larger the gaps memory must leap over. When activities aimed at survival are driven by sheer, ruthless will, the shame evoked later by memory is that much deeper. Nobody likes to be embarrassed, so we'd rather not remember morally deficient times. Repression makes us both winners and losers. In this sense my friend was right: I've also turned out to be a man with a divided soul, and in that I'm not so different from other people.

To clarify what I have in mind, let me confess that the events of that freezing day in March which were so fateful in his life, my memory simply tossed away. I was there, and I've no doubt it happened as he described it. The overwhelming joy and terrible fear evoked by the tyrant's death, our own long-lasting but uneven attraction to each other, and the deadly fear of being discovered and betrayed—all these were within me, too; I felt them more or less the same way, and I said so. But I never thought about them again. I must have felt that that kiss settled something between us.

And I did say, while urinating, that the old train robber finally croaked. Or some such silly thing. It gave me such pleasure, like the body's pleasure, to be able to say a sentence like that out loud. Afterward I was terrified he might report me. In those years we lived under the constant threat of being evicted from the capital. Of all the houses of our neighborhood right next to that notorious restricted zone, we were the last original residents. Every official-looking envelope made my mother tremble with fear. Maybe our house was too small or too run-down; to this day I don't know why we were spared.

My mother I loved with the tenderly domineering, overly solicitous, forgiving yet controlling love that only a fatherless son can have for a mother struggling with loneliness and terrible financial problems, a widow mourning her husband unto death. For her sake I was ready to make any concession, be open to the most humiliating compromises. That's why I hoped we could avoid that reporting business. And if it had already happened, I wanted to know what to expect. I am not inclined to humility, as I've said, but when it comes to compromises I'm willing to go to extremes, even today.

What should be understood from all this is that no event in my later life could induce me to think that that kiss was really a kiss and not simply the solution to an existential problem I had at the time. I couldn't allow myself to be caught in dangerous psychological predicaments, I had all I could do to ward off tangible external dangers. I came to appreciate the advantages of psychological self-concealment, and with the years I continued to avoid ambiguous situations and judgments that didn't square exactly with my wishes or interests.

Now that I'm aware of how he perceived me, and what a lasting impression I had made on him—which I never could have sensed—I feel rather sad. As if I had missed out on something I couldn't possibly have wished for. And that, of course, is flattering to me. He could allow himself the luxury of being hypersensitive. And that, of course, is something for which he is to be envied. At the same time, my sadness is free of any kind of reproach, accusation, self-accusation, free of any kind of guilt. I must have been more interesting, more attractive, and also more slippery, rougher, meaner, and altogether more sinister as a child than I am as an adult. It had to turn out like that. I had to push and cajole and continually twist arms just to secure the bare necessities of life, and in this unrelenting struggle, in this ruthlessly pragmatic personal cold war, I must have appeared more resourceful, more pliable, and more versatile than I did later on when, wearying of the struggle for basics, I could finally carve out what seemed like a secure niche for myself.

By the age of thirty he turned into a dangerously open person and I into a dangerously closed one, though we both became vulnerable. He found a love he hoped would fill a painful gap in his life, and this hope compelled him to tread on unfamiliar ground. I, on the other hand, recovering from the weariness of constant struggle, had to realize that in my hopelessness I had chosen the most common route to escape my miseries, and having run as far as I could, I was just short of turning into an alcoholic. He told me once, not long after our reunion, that men stuck in their assigned sexual roles were prone to grow fetid, both physically and spiritually.

Looking at the course of my life and career, I don't feel out of place in this country. If my friend was the exception, then I am the norm; together we make up the rule. And I make this distinction not to flaunt my own ordinariness, my limited perception, my poorly functioning memory, and in this way, somehow, still to place myself above him whom I've called exceptional; no, with my description I don't mean to label either one of us, to shift the blame for my insensitivity and obtuseness; all I want to do, in my own way, is to take a good look at our common life experiences.

I am an economist, and for the last few years I have been working in a research institute. My work in the main consists of gathering data, analyzing recurring and, on occasion, atypical patterns in one particular sphere of the national economy. I try to isolate the unique features of a specific set of phenomena. I'd like to do the same regarding this manuscript. Creative writing is not my forte. I never tried my hand at poetry. I played soccer, I rowed, I lifted weights. Ever since I stopped spending my evenings drinking, I run considerable distances every morning. The only kind of writing I do is occasional articles for professional journals. I suspect that as a consequence of my social origins and upbringing, my life, from earliest childhood, has been guided by a desire to examine given peculiarities most painstakingly, with the greatest degree of detachment.

Already as a young child I had to think carefully about the ways of thinking, or rather to be careful and not necessarily really think the things I said out loud. The reason I don't describe this intellectually demanding self-manipulation in terms that would suggest any kind of emotional involvement is that I am quite aware that concealed behind my perceptiveness and discernment—developed in circumstances I mentioned above—lie a good deal of resignation and self-discipline, all dictated by necessity.

When young, all living things are passionate, and their passionate hope of mastering the world is what makes them attractive. How passionate that hope is, how and to what extent it is realized, is what determines the distinction they make between what is ugly and what is beautiful, and how they call the good beautiful and the bad ugly. By now, however, nothing in me would make my view of things an aesthetic one. Whatever I see or experience, however intimate, I do not judge as beautiful or ugly, for I simply do not see them as such. At most I feel a quiet gratitude, reminiscent of warmth, for things I find favorable, but even that feeling cools very quickly.

I may have been filled with passion at one time, and it may be gone now. It's possible that something is already missing, gone from me forever. And it's also possible that this missing trait, or its excess, for all I know, is what made me appear cold and aloof even as a child. I can't claim that too many people love me, but most consider me a fair-minded person. Yet in view of my friend's poignant analysis, I am compelled by fair-mindedness to ask whether I may not appear to be fair-minded because I always manage to keep my distance from my own endeavors as well as from the people who love me, so that I can avoid having to identify with them while still retaining my control over them.

I am not fortunate enough to be the ideal embodiment of any one life principle. I might have become a most vicious cynic if not for the continually recurring absence or surfeit of emotions from which I suffer terribly.

A few days before my high school final exams, I decided to demolish the tile stove in my room, and I did manage to take it halfway apart. I got home from my girlfriend's house very early in the morning. I always had to sneak out of her place to make sure her unsuspecting parents would know nothing about my being there all night. I was alone in our house; my mother had gone to visit relatives in Debrecen. That stove had been bothering me for a long time. I felt it was in the wrong place, and I didn't really need it. At night it poured all its heat on my head, and I couldn't open my door all the way because of it. So I took a big hammer, and could have also used a chisel, but all I could find was a cramp iron, which served the same purpose. I began to take the thing apart. The broken tiles I threw out the window into the garden. But dismantling the stove's inside ducts proved to be more complicated than I had thought. And since I had made no preparations at all for this messy job, my room began to fill up with dust, debris, and soot. Soon everything was covered: the carpet, the upholstery, the books, my notebooks, and my carefully worked-out answers to previous finals that were lying on my desk. When I stopped for a while, coming out of the hypnotic pull of my feverish activity, and looked about, I couldn't see the mess around me as an inevitable natural by-product of this kind of work; I saw it as sheer, repulsive, unbearable filth, the boring filth of infinite emptiness. This feeling assailed me as suddenly as had the idea of dismantling the stove. I was staring into the sooty, stinking, mangled body of a once useful man-made structure. I must have been halfway through when I stopped. I thought I was sleepy and tired. I closed the window, threw off my clothes, and climbed into bed. But I couldn't fall asleep. I tossed and turned for a while, tried to curl up, but I couldn't roll or fold myself up, couldn't make myself as small as I would have liked to. I don't remember thinking about anything else. And I don't know if I'd call my awful wish about shrinking a thought. I had to get up, because it was impossible to lie there awake without being able to fulfill this wish. And without giving myself time to weigh the situation properly, I began to swallow, almost indiscriminately, the pills I found in my mother's medicine cabinet.

I needed a lot of sleeping pills and tranquillizers. After a while I could no longer swallow without water.

Today it seems that I may be the one remembering the incident, but not the one it happened to. First I drank the water from a vase, then from the little trays under the houseplants. Why I didn't just go into the kitchen is still beyond me. I was overcome by nausea. And dry retching. As if I had no more saliva in my mouth. I would have been afraid to throw up on my mother's furniture. I fell on my knee, and with my hands clasped on the back of my neck I laid my head on the edge of the sofa. I tried with all my strength to calm my heaving stomach. I don't remember anything else. If my mother, prompted by an odd premonition, had not returned a day earlier than planned, I wouldn't be here to talk about this. My stomach was pumped, the tile stove reassembled.

I had never before attempted anything so crazy, and certainly don't intend to ever again. Yet whatever else my actions may have led to—joy, grief, happy resolution, or indecision—the group of emotions usually referred to as angst has become a permanent part of my psychic makeup.

And this in spite of the fact that until then I had never had feelings even remotely resembling angst. But I don't wish to dwell on them, not only because I am not clear on their origins, but because otherwise I appear to be a well-adjusted man with a cheerful disposition, and to me this genuine appearance is more important.

When one is asked to define family origins, one begins by making selections among one's ancestors. When I am asked that question, I usually say I come from a military family. As if all my forebears were professional soldiers, whether generals or privates. Which may be an impressive notion but does not reflect reality. It's a little like saying one comes from an old family. Every family is equally old. It's true, though, that the sons and daughters of different peoples climbed down from the trees at different times. For instance, the Incas and the Hebrews did it much earlier than the Germans, and in all probability the Magyars did it somewhat later than the English or the French. But from this it does not follow that a family of serfs of a certain nation is not as old as a prince's family in the same nation. And just as a nation distinguishes between racially identical families on the basis of social status, so does an individual when he begins to choose among the motley group of his ancestors, based on the personal evaluation of his own interests, desires, and ambitions. This peculiar mode of selecting one's ancestors—tailor-made for the person doing the selecting—is something I noticed in my friend's manuscript, too.

The only way he can maintain the equilibrium of his personality, splintered by extreme contradictions, is by observing himself, by continually scrutinizing the origins and causes of the unconscious forces raging within him. But for this all-important psychological self-analysis he needs the kind of balanced and sober perspective that, because of his unbalanced state, he does not have. He is trapped in a vicious circle. He can break out of it only if, for the duration of his self-analysis at least, he adopts the perspective of a person or group of persons in his surroundings who have the stability he needs. This is the reason for the decisive role his maternal grandfather plays in his life story, this liberal bourgeois who, even in very dangerous conditions, remained a model of moderation and self-discipline. And it is also the reason he views with mixed irony and affection that tenacious, stoic, and uncompromisingly respectable bourgeois woman, his grandmother. Through them he would like to identify with something to which his real-life situation no longer entitles him. Still, this is how he selects his origins. He chooses to trace this one line back to his past, though in principle he could have chosen a number of others. While I was reading the manuscript, it struck me that his leaving out his other set of grandparents couldn't have been completely unintentional. I'm not suggesting he did this because he was ashamed of them or because they weren't as important in his life as his maternal grandparents.

On weekends or summer mornings sometimes we would ride out on a streetcar to visit them in their home in Káposztásmegyer.

After completing my university studies I began working for a foreign trade company. For about ten years I traveled to many parts of the world. Yet when I think of travel, what comes to mind first is that rickety yellow streetcar and the two of us bumping along on its open platform. Sometimes, on long plane rides, I'd be wrapped up in some technical reading, and this old image would suddenly flash before me. And I'd feel as though I wasn't even flying but riding across the globe in that yellow streetcar. Rattling along old Váci Road, interminably.

The old man was a disabled veteran of the First World War who managed to retain his robust physique, despite his handicap; he had a booming voice, and his pockmarked nose was a blazing red from steady drinking. Though he was nearly seventy, his hair was just beginning to turn gray, and he still worked as a night watchman at the waterworks, where he also lived with his roly-poly wife in a basement flat. This grandmother had a habit of sending telegrams to her grandson: I am making pancakes today. Come for strudel tomorrow. If I said it was these visits, this environment, that cemented and sustained our friendship, I wouldn't be far from the truth. If too long a time elapsed without anything happening, I'd ask him: Are we having apple fritters? To which he would respond: No, apple pie. Or he'd simply turn to me and say: Apricot dumplings. And all I had to ask was when. We developed a whole language of our own that no one else could understand. And it had to do with more than just delicious food.

In those days I got very excited about machines, things mechanical, anything moving, not to mention making things and setting them in motion, and nothing could satisfy these interests more than what I found at the waterworks. But my friend's enthusiasm was roused exclusively by my unquenchable curiosity. He must have known that with the promise of a visit he had an emotional hold over me and could even bribe me. All he'd have to say is nut roll, and I'd forget everything else and be off and running. The shop stewards, soberly dressed in shirt and tie, even their apprentices in their undershirts, were as inexhaustibly patient as I was infinitely curious. They showed and explained everything to us. It must have been tremendously gratifying for them to realize that in the final analysis most questions can actually be answered. The general overhauls were the most exciting times at the plant. On these occasions extra help was hired from the neighboring villages. Girls and women in rubber boots and hitched-up skirts got busy scrubbing and scraping the tiled walls of the emptied water tanks; greasy-faced men and pimply-faced shop boys cleaned and repaired the disassembled machines. There was a lot of laughter, horseplay, telling of coarse jokes, teasing, and pawing. As if they were all participants in some ancient ritual. They kept inflaming themselves and each other, men doing it to men, women to women, men to women, and women to men, as if this stimulation had as much to do with the work at hand as with something very different, something into which we, two young boys, had not yet been initiated. It was like some strange work song. To be able to do justice to their daytime labor, they had to sing out of themselves their nocturnal lyrics. But the two of us could wander about freely in the fascinating, outsize engine rooms built at the turn of the century, and in the pristine park planted around the giant wells, in the echoing halls of the storage tanks where everything was so spotless, so sparkling clean, we never dared do anything but stand and quietly watch the water level rise and fall, the surface remaining strangely motionless.

He has nothing to say in his manuscript about this very early, almost idyllic period of our friendship. I confess I first found this conspicuous omission so insulting I felt myself blushing every time I thought of it. For more than once we spent the night there, with the two of us sleeping in his grandparents' onion-smelling kitchen on a rather narrow cot. I once read in an ethnographic study that when in the cold of winter children of poor Gypsies cuddle up with each other on the straw-covered floor, their parents make sure that boys lie next to boys and girls next to girls. I don't think that this clinging brotherly warmth, which later my friend desperately pursued all his life, was something he intended to forget.

I remember that on hot summer days his grandfather would unlatch his wooden leg, and slapping the horrible stump staring out of his cotton shorts, he'd begin extolling the advantages of an artificial leg. For one thing, it doesn't stink. No bunions, ever. If it creaks, he oils it. Can't do that with a real one. And another thing: the leg will never be hit by gout, that's for sure. At worst, woodworms would get to it. There was only one thing he was sorry about. Booze made him feel nice and tingly all over. Including his asshole. Only the leg didn't join in with the rest of him.

As for me, I selected two dead soldiers out of all my ancestors, which included small-town tradesmen, humble peasants of the Great Hungarian Plain, headstrong Calvinist schoolteachers, newly rich mill owners, and sawyers turned industrial entrepreneurs. The two soldiers were my father and my maternal grandfather. And that's how we became a military family. Because soldiers were different. Besides those two, there were no other professional soldiers in our family. What is more, I couldn't have had any memory of either of them.

Of my father we had few photographs, of my grandfather quite a lot. One of my favorite activities as a child was to study these pictures.

Today, in the family stories that grew up around the figure of my grandfather, it would be all but impossible to separate the exaggerations from the real events that serve as the bases for them. But I believe that the special light radiating from him, intensified a thousandfold by a return glow, had to do not only with his outstanding abilities, his interrupted— and therefore considered to be very promising—career, but also, most probably, with his physical attractiveness. Slapping me affectionately on the thigh or kissing me on the cheek, my older relatives would tell me, a satisfied twinkle in their eyes, that I would never be quite as handsome as my grandfather. But my mother would always say, in a playfully captious though no less pride-filled voice, that at least in appearance I took after Grandfather; she was only sorry I wasn't quite as bright. But both statements were seductive enough for me to start believing that this resemblance was important; I had the feeling I was following in somebody's footsteps, and I also had the desire to measure up to this somebody. Somebody who in a sense was myself, although I had no way of judging whether or not my efforts in this direction were to my advantage.

We had a big magnifying glass in the house, the kind used by mapmakers. It had belonged to Grandfather and came to us after his death. With this magnifying glass I examined the various photographic likenesses dating from different periods of his life. It may be that I have no feel for aesthetics, but one thing is certain: I could almost never see as beautiful what others called beautiful. So it's no wonder that, as opposed to my friend's general outlook, a landscape, object, or person said to be beautiful might give me food for thought but in no way would excite me. The reason I spent so much time with my grandfather's portraits was that I realized that what others considered attractive in me evoked highly unpleasant thoughts. If two lines are parallel to each other, they meet in infinity. Two that are not parallel can meet here, right before my very nose. The person I resemble most I can meet only at some hypothetical point, but one who is different I can meet anywhere, anytime. Looking at my grandfather's face made me seek not the validity of the two complementary principles familiar to me but that of a third one. I found his face and his build almost repugnant, even though my instincts told me that we were very much alike. It was mostly his eyes that frightened me; his look made me shudder.

I haven't held the photographs of my grandfather in my hand for at least twenty-five years.

Was it true? Did introspection evoke such fear, horror, and revulsion in me, hurling me toward dangerous inner conflicts in which I could no longer control my will to serve my own interests? Or did I resemble him so much that the very resemblance made him repugnant? Could I have been thinking about the short distance separating the living and the dead, and about our hypothetical meeting? Was it, therefore, the faintheartedness with which I viewed myself that tormented me and kept me from appreciating beauty? I don't feel qualified to answer these questions. Or rather to answer them I'd have to think and talk about certain details of my life that wouldn't be to my liking.

The experiences of nearly forty years have convinced me that psychological reticence has its existential advantages. At the same time, ever since my friend's death I've been curious to see whether I could reach a self-knowledge similar to his, but without letting myself be destroyed in the process, as he was, and also without becoming dishonest.

I'm at the threshold of abstraction, and stretching my sense of modesty to its limit when I divulge, in the interest of shedding a brighter light on this whole question, that women who may otherwise rate me as a very good lover in every sense of the word sometimes, in the midst of lovemaking, driven by frenzied desire, try to violate my lips with theirs. And when I silently deny them this pleasure, they often urgently ask why. Why don't you let me? Because I don't want to. That's what I usually say. If I answer at all with words. I admit my conduct may seem arbitrary, but for me this silent denial is as deeply instinctive as it may be for someone else to resort to a kiss, silently, instead of words. I don't feel the need to reduce the gains of my personal and racial survival instincts at the expense of maintaining my personality's independence. With a kiss

I'd lose my control over myself and my lover. A less than conscious force would take over, one I could never fully trust.

And if I were to classify women's reaction to this singular foible, if I asked how seemingly very different people respond to having no gratification for a basic emotional need, which I personally find almost beside the point, then, based on my experience, I would differentiate among three types of behavior.

The first is the nervous, fragile, excitable, soulful, and sentimental adolescent type that is quick to take offense and is forever passionately in love; this type withdraws at once, indignantly, breaks down, starts hitting me with her fists and yelling that she knew it, she knew it, she knew I wanted only one thing from her, she calls me a liar and threatens to jump out of the window this minute. I should love her. But no one can love another if it means doing violence to himself. Still, calming women of this type or gratifying them tempestuously is not very difficult. If I can rape them at the height of their hysteria, if I choose the right moment to attack, then everything turns out all right between us. They are masochists waiting for the kind of sadistic animal that of course I am not. Their orgasm is brief, sharp, fitful, and they experience it not at the peak they strive for but on a far lower, rougher ground. These women I like the least. The second type is given to quiet submission. If they trust my body's tyranny, then their otherwise delay-prone pleasure tends to increase, slowly passing through ever higher peaks, until they reach a climax that shakes the very foundation of their being, and its effects last until the next climax. It's as if every inhibition overcome propels them toward new heights of pleasure, and though pleasure persists, inhibition pulls them back, so ultimately it isn't pleasure alone that dominates them. The process is more like pleasure having to run a stressful obstacle race. These are retiring, unpretentious girls, unhappy over their plain looks, carefully avoiding calling attention to themselves, and made somewhat wily by the charmingly merciless infighting so rampant among women. And even if they don't have faith in my masculine dominance, they pretend nothing is amiss. This is when they are most submissive and show complete devotion. And when it becomes clear that this won't help either, because I respond to their devotion not with gratitude, as they do, but with increased alertness and even more careful precision, then they display their tender humility even more openly. They have an ulterior motive for this: to offset my lack of devotion with their all-too-yielding lips, hoping to cajole mine to respond in kind.

By making their mouth my body's most humble slave. And as a consequence, these tedious little affairs end then and there. I feel the greatest pity for this type, but in practice I am most pitiless with them. It is the third type I feel closest to. These women are usually heftier, more solid. They are the large ones, cheerful, proud, passionate, stubborn, and fickle. Our preparations are sluggish. The way lumbering beasts circle and size each other up. Our meeting is devoid of emotional complication. Yet the boisterous crescendo of our pleasure is often checked by the frontal clash of two aggressive natures. At such moments, briefly, the din of battle ominously abates. These spacious and luminous plateaus of stopped time are very precious to me. And they keep occurring, capriciously, unpredictably, putting to the test all my sober attempts to control my impulses, creating the impression that we want not to reach a single peak but to scale a seemingly endless mountain range. It seems as if I've reached a plateau where the vegetation is sparse. And this is not merely a rest stop, a way station where one eats, drinks, gathers new strength. It is when reaching these plateaus that these women feel the lack of something. Or a thirst I cannot slake. Realizing in a flash what has happened, they try to save the day by concentrating their overwhelming and now recoiling passion on my mouth. For they have no intention of losing out just because I happen to have this odd quirk. Coming up against my cold intransigence, they seem to be saying: Oh no? Then here, take this! They want what's coming to them, and I can't say I blame them. And in this new situation I can afford to humble myself a little, if only because the game gives me some pleasure, too, and not merely because I know that now it's not their lips I have to touch, but also because, in a few moments, in the throes of their punishing, vindictive game, they will lose all self-control anyway, and with pleasure multiplied and shared, I can be myself again. And that is how their void is filled with my excess. Like me, they are realists, too. They know that the equilibrium needed for life is achieved not by reaching for an ideal but by using whatever comes to hand. In our resourcefulness we are accomplices, comrades. We thumb our noses at the world's ideals, and always feel sorry for those who are still trying for them. I am grateful to these women. And they are grateful to me for not having to conceal their blatant selfishness in front of me. I could do without them, of course, because experience tells me there is no irreplaceable need in this world, yet I'd say they keep me alive.

About matters such as these, and even more delicate ones, I should be talking only to myself. But man was not made to talk to himself. All such attempts are no more than foolish experiments that hark back to one's mental childhood.

Of course, I also loved my dead friend's maternal grandfather more than I did the other one. It wasn't really love, more like a flattering tribute to my ego. He treated me and communicated with me as if I were not, mentally and physically, still a gangly adolescent. What provided the opportunity for these conversations was his habit of taking long walks every afternoon in the neighborhood. He ambled along, thrusting his long, ivory-knobbed walking stick carefully before him, and if by chance we ran into each other, he would lean on his cane, tilt his gray head to one side, and listen to me with the attentiveness and empathy he believed was the due of every human being. His interjections, approving nods, pondering hums, and warning exclamations led me down a path I wanted to take only when complying with my innermost wishes. His empathy could be so disconcerting that sometimes I deliberately avoided him or, after a polite but hurried greeting, rushed past him.

In adolescence one tends to relate to intellectual urges in the same timidly willful way as one does to erotic ones. But he never forced the issue. There was nothing demanding or tempting about him. Yet the possibility of voluntary self-disclosure kept drawing me back to him.

Directly or in veiled, metaphoric terms, we discussed political issues, and he told me once that according to a very clear-minded philosopher, whom I would not be able to read since he wrote his works in English, what is important in human societies is not that the majority have as much right as the ruling minority. That's just how it is, and it's inevitable. But if this were the only social principle regulating societies, there would be only strife in the world. There would be no possibility of reaching any agreement between individuals or societies. But we know that this isn't so. And the reason for that is that there is also an infinite goodness in this world, and everyone without exception, rulers as well as subjects, would like to have an equal share. This goodness exists, he said, because our desire for equality, symmetry, and harmony is as strong as is our lust for power, our need for total victory over a foe. And we must understand that the lack of this symmetry and harmony in us is also evidence of the existence of this goodness.

I couldn't then have possibly remembered, let alone understood, this complex thought, but later, when I came upon the book of this very significant philosopher, I rediscovered it with a surprise that took my breath away.

And if now, after so many years, I take out these photographs and spread them before me, I am again reminded of this same, seemingly complex thought, and begin to suspect why I shied away from the symmetry that other people found so very attractive in my grandfather's features.

Grandfather's straight, almost rigid posture, which gave an unpleasant first impression, need not be taken as a peculiarity of his own. It has as much to do with the fashion of his day as with his profession, which made this kind of bearing almost compulsory. And there may have been another reason for the stiffness: in those days the long exposure time of cameras demanded that, with the help of all sorts of invisible supports, the subject be completely motionless. However, there are also two snapshots among the photos. One of them was taken at the Italian front in an improvised trench. They must have picked part of a ravine for the purpose, because you can see that two sides and the bottom of the trench are made of flat, layered blocks of limestone. Sandbags are piled on top of the stones, and you can tell the bags are loosely filled, they probably didn't have enough sand. Flanked by two fellow officers, my grandfather sits in the foreground of the picture. His long legs, elegant even in heavy boots, are crossed, his torso is bent forward, and his arms are supported on his elbows; with his mouth slightly open and his eyes wide, he is staring into the camera. The faces of the other two, lower-ranking officers are worn and haggard, their uniforms seem neglected, but the look in their eyes is fearlessly determined, if somewhat artificial. In this setting my grandfather looks like a self-indulgent playboy who can enjoy himself even in such circumstances because he has nothing to do with anything or anyone there. The other snapshot is one of the nicest pictures I have ever seen. It must have been taken at sunset, on top of a hill where only a single puny little tree stood. In between the sparse leaves, the sun shines right into our eyes, or rather into the lens of the long-gone amateur photographer. Grandfather is chasing two young girls in long dresses and straw hats; they are my aunts. One of the girls, my Aunt Ilma, has apparently gotten away; waving her ribboned hat, she is running, on her way out of the picture. Her triumphant grin is therefore very blurry. The other little girl, Aunt Ella, is in an odd pose, leaning out from behind the slender tree, and Grandfather catches her just as the photographer clicks his shutter. Grandfather is wearing a light summer suit, he either unbuttoned his jacket or it had opened by itself. He is coiling out from behind the tree while still clinging to it, like a well-groomed but momentarily disheveled satyr. In this picture, too, his mouth is half open and he is wide-eyed, but not only is there no sign of pleasure in his eyes, it almost appears as if he were carrying out some painful duty, although in the snatching, clutching movement of his hand there is something of the supple greed of a predator. In other photos, I can see only his harmoniously motionless face, photographed frontally, concealed by his rigid posture.

In old novels such faces are called ovoid. It's a full, well-proportioned, oval face, strongly, smoothly articulated, easing into a forehead framed by irrepressibly wavy locks of hair. His high-bridged nose has sensitive nostrils, his eyebrows are dense, his lashes long, his irises surprisingly light, almost luminous, against the generally dark tones of his features. His lips are almost vulgarly thick, and on his aggressively protruding chin there is the same hard-to-shave cleft I have on mine.

The face, like the brain or the whole body, has two hemispheres. The common peculiarity of these two hemispheres is that their symmetry is only approximate. The unevenness discernible in a person's body or face stems from the fact that impressions received by our more or less neutral sense organs are separated in two unevenly developed hemispheres of the brain, and which side of a person's body or face seems more striking to us depends on which side of the person's brain is more developed. The right hemisphere processes the emotional connotations of the impressions, while the left hemisphere deciphers the meaning of the same impressions, and only afterward, as a second step, does the brain establish a direct relationship between the intellectual and emotional aspects of the same impression. One perceives a phenomenon with one's eyes, ears, nose, and fingers as an unprocessed whole, then breaks it down to its components and, based on the relations between the different components, re-creates for oneself the whole that one first came to know through sensory perception. But, because of the uneven development of the brain's two hemispheres, the perceived whole can never be identical with the analyzed and assimilated whole, which in turn means that there is no such thing as a perfectly harmonious emotion or a perfectly harmonious way of thinking.

Anyone can observe this phenomenon in himself when talking to another person. People in conversation never stare directly into one another's eyes—only madmen do that—rather, they move their eyes from one hemisphere of the face to the other, back and forth. The glance oscillates between thought and feeling, and if it is fixed on any one point, it will inevitably be the left side of the face, the one expressing emotions. It is this side of the face that the neutral glance, taking in the whole of the impression, uses to check whether the words it comprehended mentally are identical with the emotions elicited by the interlocutor's words.

Language, in certain set phrases, also follows this functional peculiarity of the human body. If, for example, referring to a given phenomenon I say that I couldn't believe my eyes, what I'm admitting is that neither intellectually nor emotionally could I process the received impression as a whole, or more precisely, I tipped so far toward either a mental or an emotional evaluation that I could no longer establish a connection between the two poles. I saw something but could not reconcile it with my inner sense of order and balance; therefore, although I may have seen it as whole, I could not comprehend it whole, therefore could not assimilate it. The reverse phenomenon takes place when we say that we are trying to stare somebody down. In this case the searching glances of the speakers come to an absolute standstill. For two reasons. Either the glance finds harmony, perfect agreement between the emotional and intellectual spheres—and harmony always comes as an unexpected surprise, for it is a theoretical whole with, theoretically, no differentiated parts. Or, since the contradiction is irreconcilable between the emotional and intellectual aspects of the phenomenon, it intends to settle at the dead center of this unachievable harmony, fixed on the other person's neutral organ of perception, his eyes, trying to deprive itself of any further impressions and, with its impassivity, to force the other to decide in which direction it wishes to tip its own scale.

Of course, the state of I-couldn't-believe-my-eyes can last but a few seconds, just as you can't stare someone down for too long. The appearance of a harmony coming into being, or lacking totally, cannot be sustained for long, and not only because the relationship between emotion and intellect is disharmonious, even physiologically, but because the internal image we want to assimilate is not identical with the image our sense organs perceive in a neutral, unprocessed form. At the same time, the face as a whole reflects quite faithfully this complex triple relationship. We can confirm this phenomenon, too, by examining with the aid of a pocket mirror both our profiles, and then comparing them with the frontal view of our face.

The two profiles appear completely different. One of them expresses the emotional, the other the intellectual aspect of our character, and the greater the disparity, the smaller the likelihood that they will blend harmoniously in the frontal view. Yet blend they must, a natural necessity that excludes the possibility of the two being totally different from each other—just as they cannot be totally identical either.

Logically it should follow that we should consider a face in which emotion and intellect appear to be in radical imbalance just as beautiful as one in which the two are in perfect harmony. But this isn't so. Insofar as we can choose between two near-perfect forms, we always choose the near-perfectly-proportionate over the near-perfectly-disproportionate one.

If I were to take any of my grandfather's photographs showing him from the front, and with a pair of scissors cut it in two along the line between the cleft of his chin and the bridge of his nose, and then superimpose the pieces, one half of his face would cover the other near perfectly, like two geometric constructs. The reason for this unique trait must be that in individuals like him the two hemispheres of the brain developed evenly. Assessing the physical appearance of such people, one is tempted to conclude that neither emotion nor intellect predominates in them, pulling them in one direction or the other; and whoever looks at them cannot but be intrigued by the magical possibility of perfect symmetry.

If the brain's two hemispheres could indeed assimilate with a perfect blend of feeling and thought what the sense organs had already perceived as a neutral whole, if there were no differences between parts and the whole, if an individual's unique image were not formed in accordance with the brain's inevitable biases, if each individual could reproduce a perfect whole comprehensible to all, then it wouldn't even occur to us to differentiate between beautiful and ugly, good and bad, because there would be no difference between emotional and intellectual properties. This would be the ultimate symmetry we all strive for, which the man of ethics calls infinite goodness and the man of aesthetics calls beauty.

The only reason I've thought it necessary to explain all this is to demonstrate what an unbridgeable gap separates ethical thinking, which even in the absence of ultimate symmetries finds certainties, or aesthetic thinking, which cannot survive such an absence, from the kind of thinking I can also call my own. In my youth, because of my attractive physical appearance, people thought of me as exceptional and treated me accordingly. The advantages stemming from their admiration and devotion made up for the social disadvantages I had to endure on account of my family background. But in my thinking, perhaps for this very reason, I have remained the epitome of the average person. I did not become a believer like the ethical ones, or a doubter like many aesthetically sensitive people I know, because I never longed for the impossible but learned to make good use of the qualities I possess. Of course my own secret torments do enable me to empathize with the certainties of ethical believers and the uncertainties of skeptical aesthetes, with their happiness and tragedies, but my thinking is not directed at realizing hidden possibilities or at grasping metaphysical insights born of contemplating the impossible; my thinking deals only with real possibilities, things within reach of my two hands.

My activities don't touch on any systematic philosophy of life. I am guided by the conviction that whatever appears as debit on one side will show up as credit on the other. Despite my well-developed theoretical bent, I occupy myself only with the practical organization of my life. I draw on my credit, I make up my debit. And while doing so, I never forget that symmetries thus gained are valid only for the moment of their creation.

And if I said before that studying those photographs, whose allusion to ultimate symmetry filled me with such distaste, was one of my favorite pastimes as a child, then my statement is in need of further clarification.

As becomes evident from my friend's confessions, I wasn't a quiet, retiring child. As an adult, too, I am very active, although I'm tempted to consider my urge to keep busy, sometimes reaching the point of frenzy, to be one of my darker traits, even if others envy this seemingly inexhaustible supply of energy. What spurs me on is not a desire to win or to succeed but rather the indolence and inertia that thrust my immediate and not so immediate environment into a state of permanent defeat. And since there are so many more defeats than victories in one's life, I haven't had much opportunity to withdraw into a state of quiet contemplation. I don't like to use big words, but I'll say that our sorry national history, piling failure upon failure, defeat upon defeat, is partly to blame. For when confronted with seemingly impossible situations, tasks that are clearly beyond our resources, we don't even consider the possibility of regrouping our forces, but with a fool's defensive cautiousness we avoid the issues, put them off, pretend they don't exist, or with almost masochistic pleasure proceed to enumerate the reasons why rational solutions are simply not in the cards. This petty cunning irritates me no less than our fatalistic air of superiority. I believe that playing for time, lying low, waiting it out, is a justified tactic only in situations that hold out the prospect of solution; in the absence of such prospects the question of what can or cannot be done, and why, is futile, though it is as familiar to me as it is to the rest of my compatriots. When there is a solution, delay is superfluous, and when there isn't, talk is a sheer waste of time. But my annoyance and irritability seldom prove to be reliable counsel. In my feverish activity I myself pile error on error, stumble from defeat to defeat. And all the while, and not without a measure of arrogance, I keep telling myself that even a blind hen will find a seed if it keeps knocking around with its beak long enough.

But if between two erroneous decisions or two defeats I still manage to achieve some kind of breakthrough, then the feeling of surprise makes me retreat. At times like that I have to decide whether my success is the result of a correct decision or merely a stroke of luck. I observe, I weigh things, I distract myself and others, I become despondent and helpless and long for solitude. I look for something to read and, all of a sudden, softly lit corners in cozy, familiar rooms become very important.

In my childhood, during lulls in my fight for freedom, in my personal cold war, I studied photographs and military maps and browsed through dictionaries; as a young man I experienced in these periods, having grown timid with success, my casual conquests blossoming into tense love affairs, and I'd disappear for weeks and hole up in warm little nests with the unlikeliest girls; later, when I was a married man, the so-called periods of success got me started on quiet and carefully arranged but all the more persistent bouts of drinking.

My aversion to cowering and useless arguments, my propensity for acting recklessly, and my inability to handle success must all stem from my basic character makeup, which can balance feeling and thought so as to neutralize each other, but since I traveled a great deal and spent a lot of time in foreign countries, and therefore had a chance to realize that elsewhere I would probably have turned out differently, I feel that any attempt at discovering the character of a nation in something other than the particular traits of an individual is a very risky undertaking. We are all variants of the same thing. Variants determined by character, sex, family origin, religion, and upbringing. If someone, while still a child, wants to find his place in this community, he will select ancestors with the characteristics that seem most striking, but there is no personal characteristic that is not yet another version of the national character, and so, in reality, the child is selecting for himself only certain variants.

I chose two variants of the same dynamic character type: the hedonistic, social-climbing version in my grandfather and the ascetic-heroic variant in my father. They seemed as different as night and day. Their fates had one thing in common: they both died in wars that for their nation ended in defeat and had catastrophic consequences. My grandfather was thirty-seven, my father thirty-four when they lost their lives. They were united by their untimely passing, and this single connection between them made me decide that while death, most naturally, stands above all else, it doesn't have to mean the end of life. My mother grew up with one parent and was a widow when she raised me. Victory is probably a good thing, but one can also live with the misery of defeat. It was in line with this tradition that my own variant developed; and it is probably with this variant in mind that my son and daughter will choose their own.

I am thirty-seven years old. Exactly as old as my grandfather was when he lost his life in one of the bloodiest battles of the First World War. To lose one's life without losing life itself—a good trick, only how to do it?— that's what I'm thinking about now. My friend's been dead for three years. It's nighttime. I'm busy measuring different sorts and periods of time. It's drizzling outside, a fine spring rain. The pearly drops on the large windowpanes are illuminated by the friendly glow of my desk lamp, until they get too heavy and fall. I think of my children and wonder when I will have to let them go for good. As if I am somewhat surprised that I have had this much time with them and that I still have some left. Here I am, sitting in this book-lined, slightly disorderly—just the way I like it—quiet, nocturnal room. Moments ago some bad feeling or unpleasant dream must have startled my wife out of sleep, because she got up and came, or rather staggered, out of the bedroom. I followed her with my ear as she groped her way through the dark hallway, went into the kitchen, drank something, I heard the glass clink, and after taking a long look into the children's room, she went back to bed, her footsteps softer and steadier. When she opened the children's door, I followed her not with my ears but with my nose. I could smell the sweet fragrance of the children, and not even with my nose but with my flesh, my bones. No doubt my wife is even more powerfully aware of this sensation than I am. She doesn't look in on me. Although we haven't said a word about it, I know that ever since I started going over this manuscript she's been as restless again as she was when, sitting at the same table, I used to spend my time alone, drinking. She fears for our children.

We couldn't have been more than ten years old when my friend Prém and I decided we were going to be soldiers. My dead friend portrays Prém as subjectively as he does me, and sees some kind of erotic mystery in our relationship. True, he views Prém with petulant aversion rather than affection. I am not nearly as well versed in psychological analysis as he was, so I have no way of judging how accurate his conclusions are. But I certainly don't want to give the impression that I am biased in this regard and would therefore reject his particular interpretation of our relationship out of hand. If two human beings are of the same sex, their relationship will be defined by the fact that they are. And if they are of different sexes, then that will be the decisive factor. That's how I feel about it, and for all I know, I may be insensitive on this issue, too.

Prém and I have remained the best of friends to this day. He didn't become a soldier; he is an auto mechanic. And, like myself, a settled family man. If you're looking for faults, well, maybe his tax returns are not quite above reproach. A few years ago, exactly at the time my friend returned from Heiligendamm and I gave up my lucrative job as a commercial traveler, Prém opened his own shop. While the two of us went spiritually bankrupt, Prém got rich. When something is wrong with my car we fix it together, on Sunday afternoons. Prém is an absolute terror tracking down a malfunction. In the way we huddle in the greasy pit of his workshop, or rub against each other while sprawled under the car, making contact as we handle parts of a lifeless mechanism, in the way we curse and quarrel and fume or, in perfect agreement, we acknowledge the other's move to be perfect, just right—in short, in the way we enjoy each other's physical presence, there is undoubtedly something ritualistic that goes back to our childhood bonding, and it must reawaken in us the need for such bonding.

As children we made a pact and sealed it with our blood, though I no longer remember what prompted us to do it. With a dagger that belonged to my father we pricked our fingers, smeared the blood on each other's palm, and then licked it off. There was nothing solemn about this. Maybe because there was no real gushing of blood. We were embarrassed about our ineptness. Still, sealing our mutual aspirations with blood proved to be our deepest and strongest bond. What others used words for, we entrusted to the language of our bodies. And I am convinced the body has words that have nothing to do with eroticism. For the sake of an end to be achieved, we turned our body into a physical means. But our bodies had the goal in mind, not each other. And what reinforces this conviction is that it never occurred to us to consider each other a friend. To this day we call each other buddy, which to me—because I've been infected by intellectual self-consciousness—sounds a little phony, but which to him, precisely because of the differences in our background and social position, is a word that carries a most important distinction. He has other people for friends. But when it comes to straightening out his petty though by no means unprofitable financial indiscretions, he can always count on my professional guidance.

For us to become soldiers, we knew we had to outsmart the existing social order. Actually, neither of us could have picked a worse profession. I was the son of a captain on the general staff of the prewar Hungarian Army, and his father had been a fanatic fascist. My father fell on the Russian front. His father laid his hands on confiscated Jewish property, served a five-year sentence after the war, and then, six months after his release, was relocated to a camp for undesirables—much to his family's relief. The reigning spirit of the new age, in its shrewd cynicism, conveniently blurred the distinction between two lives that were predicated on ambitions and values that could not have been more different. We were both considered children of war criminals. Unless we wanted to appear stupid or insane, we had to keep our plan secret. And we didn't talk about it even to each other; after all, we didn't want to be soldiers of the Hungarian People's Army, just soldiers in general.

But all this needs some explanation.

Up until the mid-1950s, I could still hear members of my family voice the seemingly pragmatic and well-founded view that the English and the Americans would soon relieve our country of the Soviet Union's military presence. And the fact that in 1955 Soviet troops did withdraw from Austria kept these expectations alive, up until November 4, 1956. I considered my family's situation outrageously unjust, but with a child's unbiased sense of reality I also noticed that people around me did not really believe what they were telling each other. When my aunts and uncles discussed these matters, their fear and self-deception made their voices nervously thin and hushed. I had an aversion to these distraught and fretful tones. I must admit, therefore, that for lack of a real choice I would have wanted to become a soldier in the People's Army. Still, I had to realize my ambition without betraying my family. And in my morally dubious ambition, the example of my grandfather's life came to my aid.

As the fifth among a village schoolmaster's eight children, my grandfather had only two opportunities to utilize his exceptional mental abilities, already apparent in early childhood: a military career or the priesthood. As he was an irascible, unruly child, a priestly vocation was out of the question. His military ambitions were at first blocked by my great-grandfather's unshakably nationalist, anti-Austrian sentiments. In his stubborn opposition he went so far as to prevent Grandfather from joining the Hungarian Territorial Army, even though the language of command in that force was Hungarian, and according to the historic Compromise of 1867 with Austria, the Territorial Army could not cross the Hungarian frontier without Parliament's approval. It's still a joint army, he grumbled, and no son of his would rub elbows with traitors. Then, in the heat of an argument, my grandfather said to his father, If you won't let me join up, I'll run away and become a professional dancer. For that he got two huge slaps on his face, but the next day he also got the necessary paternal consent. He graduated with distinction from the Military Academy of Sopron.

In short, we were preparing to be good soldiers in any Hungarian army, and to that end we put ourselves through the most difficult tests possible. With knapsacks filled with rocks, we went on long marches in the most sweltering summer heat. In winter we'd crawl in ditches filled with icy water. We had to learn to climb any tree and jump off the tallest one. With no clothes on, we'd cut through thorny bushes, and we wouldn't go home to change even if our clothes got sopping wet or stiff with ice in the freezing cold. I am neither hungry nor thirsty, neither cold nor hot, I am not afraid, I feel no fatigue, disgust, or pain. These were our basic principles. We frequently sneaked out late at night, and without first designating a meeting place, we had to find each other. In doing that, the functioning of our instincts was truly remarkable. We slept in haystacks or stayed up all night, especially in the snow, experimenting with ways of avoiding fatal frostbite. And on the days following such exercises we'd show up in school as if nothing had happened. We challenged each other to see who could hold his breath longer. We repeated the experiment under water. We took care of each other, not with the warm attention of lovers but as two people guided by mutual interests. We learned to creep silently over dry leaves, to imitate birds. We built a snow bunker, packing it so hard we could light a fire inside. We lifted weights, climbed rocks, ran on the toughest terrain, dug trenches. We designated no-food or no-water days, or ate and drank the most outrageous things. Lapping up water from puddles, eating grass or raw eggs snatched from nests were not unusual assignments. Once, I made him eat a slug and he had me swallow an earthworm fried on a spit; these, too, were only tests, not acts of cruelty. Naturally, our bodies were always bruised and covered with scabs, our clothes were in tatters; Prém was often beaten at home, and I had to resort to all sorts of artful lies to comfort my worried mother.

I remember only one instance when I couldn't come up with a credible explanation. But even this experience, jolting as it was, did not break my will. The incident did expose me, yet I was not about to give myself away. I've been a practicing liar ever since, a prevaricator and concealer in matters small and great. I can't help it, but it is with considerable indulgence that I observe the transparent duplicity of my fellow humans in their search for unequivocal truths. But now I'd like to relate the incident.

From my readings about the art of war I knew that logistics units were just as important to the success of an operation as were armaments, preparedness, and the morale of the front-line troops. It's important that every soldier be equipped with the best available weapon and that he be convinced of the necessity of having to fight, but it's just as important that supplies follow each phase of the operation like clockwork. We had to gain experience in this area, too.

We spent unforgettable summer days at the Ferencváros railroad station and the Rákos switchyard. The trainmen tried to chase us away more than once, and they were rough about it, too, but we sneaked back every time. The railroad tracks, winding through the stations and branching off to different destinations, the switches, turntables, and signals, all parts of a coherent system almost like a living organism, are still vivid in my memory. The knowledge I picked up there had a lot to do with the tense social relationship between the railwaymen and the track repairmen. If we managed to attach ourselves to a maintenance crew, we had it made for the rest of the day. We drank their watered-down wine, ate their bread, their bacon, and enjoyed the shy, fatherly affection and interest shown us by these lonely, silent, middle-aged men who worked and lived far from their families. If supervisors or a group of engineers came by, they'd just grumble: Come on, men, you know better than to bring your children to the workplace. Only vagrants and professional criminals knew better than we how easy it was to move around in a freightyard. From their towers, controllers see only busy, purposefully scurrying ants. They never bother to check the number, color, or size of these ants. And you can easily leave the colony. Just make sure you avoid the switchmen's booths, the kind of loose-limbed way of walking that might suggest loafing, and running accidentally into any supervisors.

We also took rides now and then. Of all our activities there, the most exciting, and riskiest, was climbing into one of the cars of a freight train about to be assembled. Then we really had to pay attention to what was happening between the control tower and the assemblers. We could board only from the side away from the tower, but once we were inside, the commands issuing from the tower would tell us what would happen next. After the instruction from the tower—nothing but the car number followed by the destination number—we heard noises of jostling and jiggling around the buffers and connecting cables, all accompanied by colorful cursing, and then silence. That was the time to find something to hang on to good and tight. It was hard to tell when, but the jolt would come. Not a big one—yet. The truly great pleasure always makes you wait for it.

Two hard bodies clink, giving the car its initial momentum on the open track. It starts rolling slowly, sluggishly, and maybe it is held up a little by a switch thrown at the last minute. If the car comes to a complete halt, there's real trouble. Frustrated yelling from the tower, cursing from down below, because the entire train has to be moved to give the errant car one big push. More grousing and screaming and yanking, but once the train gets rolling, the pleasure is so great you can't even comprehend what's happening to you. The uniform acceleration due to the weight and direction of an inert body, slowed only by surface resistance, hurls you irresistibly and at staggering speed toward the next moment.

We loved the tremendous, thunderous impact, which was followed by smaller, gentler bumps. If it was no longer safe to jump off, we'd go for a ride. Generally, they would just shunt the newly assembled train off to a sidetrack, but it happened sometimes that it was sent immediately on a regular run. That morning the train we were on started out for Cegléd; it was picking up speed fairly rapidly, it was too late to jump off. It slowed down once in a while but didn't stop. We weren't too concerned—it wasn't the first time this had happened—maybe just a little more jittery than usual. At one point when the train was again slowing down, Prém gave the alert sign. I jumped first, he was right behind me. As I landed, one of my legs sank knee-deep into a pile of rubble, while Prém neatly tumbled down the side of the embankment. But the momentum of the jump was still propelling my body forward. To this day the memory of that moment is crystal clear. The bright sunshine, the sight of his freely rolling body, and the bone cracking in my trapped leg—whose sound couldn't be heard in the noise of the passing train yet which I did hear. Then fast-approaching rocks. The way I smack into them, face first. We were done for. All our secrets exposed. Even in my pain, descending like a terrifying gray curtain, I had only one thought, that my clumsiness was unforgivable. Prém dug me out and wanted to carry me on his back. Whimpering, I begged him not to touch me anywhere. As it turned out later, my left arm and two of my left ribs were only cracked, but the pain on that side was more intense than in the open fracture of my right leg. Blood was pouring from my head and face. And to make matters worse, we were in the middle of nowhere. Not a soul, not a vehicle or a house anywhere. Just flat, scorched grazing land, a cloudless sky. He had to go for help. My only consolation was that he didn't lose his head.

By the time I was being rolled toward the operating room, a dozen figures in white were running alongside us. That's when I said goodbye to him. I heard one of the medics say: You wait here for the police, son.

When I came to, I could peep out with only one eye from the thick bandage on my head. I was in a cast, and my whole body was wrapped in white. A nurse was sitting on my bed. Her face was like a huge, beating white heart. She was humming and mumbling, trying to sing to me; she made me drink, she was stroking me and wiping me with a wet cloth. She was working hard, fussing over me. I must have looked pitiful, in need of comforting, for she kept singing that everything was all right, everything was just fine, and soon everything will heal, get better, be good as new. Only I mustn't move around too much. I should just tell her if I was becoming nauseous or had to pee. She'll stay with me until my mother comes, no need to worry.

Until then I hadn't thought of my mother. But from that word, just as from the ether-soaked mask they had put on my face in the operating room, everything grew distant and feather-light, though I felt myself very heavy, and then everything went dark.

As if kicking my way to the surface of some terrible dream, I woke up to realize that my body was cooling off and if that kept up I would definitely die. I was wrapped in wet sheets. I heard the nurse's soft voice: It's all right, it's all right. My temperature had shot up, she was bringing it down. But it seemed that changing the sheets over my naked limbs didn't help much, the fever kept slipping back from under the cast and the bandages. After a while, however, the temperature did subside, and I still remember that when she covered me with a dry sheet, quite pleased with herself, I was sorry I couldn't show off my naked body to her anymore.

Judging by the lights and by the noises in the ward, it must have been early afternoon. Luckily, my mother hadn't come yet. Later I had another attack of high fever, and by the time she got it under control, it was evening. The nurse told me she had to leave, her shift had ended, someone else was taking over for her. I don't know why she was so touched, she couldn't have seen much of my face. Maybe it was a gesture I made. Or maybe she could sense, even through the thick bandages, that I had never entrusted myself so unconditionally to another human being. Hardly any time went by and she was back. As soon as she appeared in the doorway, I ventured to say that she was right to come back. Why, she asked, was there anything wrong? No, nothing, I said. And I really felt that I was regaining my strength and was seeing clearly with that one eye. Then why did I say it? Because I needed her, I said. We reached for each other's hand at the same time, and she blushed. I was twelve years old and she perhaps ten years older.

We don't need to imagine how people close to us will behave. Certain situations always bring with them the appropriate form of behavior. Until the end of our lives we keep repeating identical gestures, and this is very reassuring for those around us. With this in mind, I was preparing myself for my mother's arrival.

The ward was full of white mummies like myself, lying strapped to their beds. I somehow wanted to dissociate myself from them. They wheezed, moaned, snored, groaned, and they stank. I had my back propped up with big pillows. I asked the nurse to turn on the overhead reading lamp, to take the bedpan out from under me, and to bring me a newspaper. I watched her slipping in and out of the room. But I was in too much pain and couldn't read with my one good eye long enough for my mother to arrive while I was still in this position. I dozed off. When I opened my eyes again, to my great surprise, it wasn't my mother I saw at the door but a she-devil dressed in my mother's clothes. Just as she was barging into the room and heading straight for me. This I didn't expect. With her arms outstretched she flew into me, her handbag hit me in the face, she seized my shoulders, and if the nurse hadn't hurled herself between us, she would have given me a thrashing then and there. And she had never raised a finger to me before. Never. Now the two of them were scuffling right on top of me. While in a voice choked with rage the she-devil was screaming, What did you do? What did you do again? the guardian angel, her voice a falsetto, kept shrieking, What are you doing? Don't touch him! You're crazy! Help! It suddenly turned light, blindingly light in the ward, and in an instant everyone was up and yelling, but very quickly it was all over. The she-devil vanished, evaporated, and my mother broke down, sobbing, on my bed. The nurse let go of her. She then checked my cast, felt my healthy as well as my bandaged parts, made everyone go back to bed, giggled nervously, told them everything was all right, turned off the light, and, grinning at me one last time, left the ward.

In a situation like this, the most sensible thing a child can do is to explain to his parent what he has done and why. He must confess all his sins, reveal at least a third of his secrets, and with a show of contrition gain her forgiveness. Still, it didn't even occur to me to give us away. I was convinced that Prém would tell the police only what was absolutely necessary. Perhaps the reason for my decision was that for the first time in my life I was caught between two women. This stormy scene had made me realize that Mother was not just my mother but also a woman. I had never thought of this before. One woman was sobbing on my bed, the other giggling as she circled my bed. As if she were gloating over my being in the clutches of a madwoman.

Still sobbing, my mother kept repeating her questions, hovering around the most critical problem of my life. I had to make a decision about my own independence. Using my good hand and the arm in the cast, I turned her crying face toward me. I was angry with her, I wanted to steer her away from this sensitive area, but in a way that wouldn't hurt her too much.

She could have come sooner, I said.

But she just got home. A policeman was there, waiting for her. A policeman.

I've been lying here all day with not a bite to eat.

She raised her tearful eyes to me.

I said I wanted some sour-cherry compote.

Sour-cherry compote? she asked incredulously. Where would I get you sour-cherry compote?

In the meantime, though, her tear-filled eyes regained their old familiar look: compliant and somewhat frightened, a widow's look. I managed to change her back into my mother.

Today I know that it was I who killed the woman in her.

I need not emphasize that this life, our life, was different in every way from my friend's life. Although there was a brief, and for my development decisive, period in our youth when, like him and his girlfriend Maja, we also caught the fever of counter-espionage. Prém and I called it reconnaissance. We had to penetrate enemy territory, then clear out unnoticed. We invariably chose apartments and houses whose occupants we didn't know. We thought it more honest this way. Friends whose houses we may have entered we wouldn't have been able to face afterward. We'd reconnoiter the garden, pick out the deserted room, find the window accidentally left ajar or the shutter that could be forced open, the door that just had to be pushed in, and then select the object to be removed. One of us did the job while the other covered him.

We never kept anything. The objects we took as evidence of our ability were later slipped back. At worst, we'd throw them back, or place them by the door or on the windowsill. Documents, clocks, paperweights, pens, pillboxes, seals, cigarette cases, the oddest knickknacks went through our hands this way. I remember a lacquered Chinese music box and a very pornographic statuette with movable joints. There isn't a jealously guarded secret of my love life that I can recall more vividly than I can these objects. We violated the defenseless lives of strangers—and exposed, unsuspecting, silent apartments. This was the point at which our community of two passed the boundaries of the permissible. At the very thought of an operation our stomachs would tighten, our eyes glaze over, our hands and feet shake, our insides rumble shamelessly, and in our nervous agitation, not once, we moved our bowels in plain sight of each other.

I believe that the moral value of an act can be physically measured in one's body. Such measurements are taken by everyone and in every moment. And the unit of measurement is nothing but the peculiar ratio between urges and inhibitions. For action results not only from urges attributable to instincts but from the relationship of inhibitions, attributable to upbringing, to these urges. Character makeup, social attitude, inherited aptitude, and family origins all look for their proportional share in any action we take. To repeated denial of such proportional sharing, the body reacts with fear, perspiration, anxiety, in more serious cases with fainting, vomiting, or diarrhea, in the most serious cases with actual organic dysfunction.

Theoretically, society should hold as ideal the person who feels the urge to do only what is not forbidden. And as most dangerous the one who feels the urge to do only what is not permitted. But this seemingly logical principle, like that referring to the asymmetry of beauty and ugliness, does not really follow the laws of logic. There is no person in the world in whose action there would be no tension between urges and inhibitions, just as there is no one who wants to do only what is forbidden. The ideals of social harmony and a well-adjusted life are predicated on the masses of people who manage to keep this tension in themselves to a minimum, yet it wouldn't occur to anyone to call them wise, good, or perfect. They are not the monks, nuns, revolutionaries, inventors among us, and not the madmen, prophets, or criminals either. At best, they are useful in maintaining social tranquillity. But the greatest usefulness can measure itself only in an environment of the greatest uselessness.

If before, in thinking about beauty and ugliness, I contended that when made to choose between two near-perfect forms we invariably pick the near-perfectly-proportionate form over the near-perfectly-disproportionate one, then now, reflecting on good and evil, I must conclude that in setting the moral standards for our actions, we never choose what is necessarily good or beneficial, never the boringly average, but the disturbing, provocative exceptions, life's necessary evils. Which also implies that for our senses the highest degree of perfection is the standard, while for our consciousness the standard is always the highest degree of imperfection.

On one page of his manuscript my dead friend claims that I sometimes asked Prém to take off his clothes. I remember no such thing. But I don't wish to cast doubt on his claim. Perhaps I did ask Prém to do that. But if I did, I must have done it for reasons other than those my friend had assumed.

There's no doubt that boys are greatly interested in the size of their own and others' sexual organs. One of our favorite games was to compare them in either words or deeds. Most men don't get over the effects of such games even in adulthood. Their unalterable physical endowments forever remind them of psychic injuries sustained in childhood. Depending on whether their organs are small or large in these games of comparison, the injury may take two different forms. If it's large, they must feel privileged, even though this privileged status later provides no advantage in their love life. And if it is small, then they must suffer the psychic consequences of feeling inferior, even if in their sexual life no disadvantage results from it. In this matter, everyday experience and scientific evidence are at odds with cultural tradition. I don't know how other cultures deal with the disparities between emotional and mental experiences, but our own barbaric civilization, in awe of the act of creation, does not respect creation at all. I'm sure of this. A childhood hurt does not develop into an emotional scar because of physiological factors but because of the contradiction between individual and cultural perception: an individual, geared to procreation, perceives his endowments as natural and unique, but his culture, disrespectful of creation, uses a different set of criteria—disregarding the limits given and defined by nature—to evaluate individual endowments. And so the individual wants to squeeze more out of what is already a lot, or suffers because what he has, which is not little, cannot be more.

It is clear to everyone that the quality of one's sex life depends on happiness, however fragile that happiness may be. Although it's true that sexual happiness cannot be separated from the sex organs, it would be foolish to relate it to the size of these organs, if only because the vagina by its very nature is capable of expanding to the size required by the penis. Its expansion is governed exclusively by emotion, as is the erection of the penis. But the cultural tradition of an achievement-oriented consumer society obsessed with the accumulation, use, and distribution of wealth cares not one whit about this mundane, albeit scientifically verifiable sense experience. It suggests to both men and women that something is good only if it's bigger and there's more of it. If you have less than the next person, something's wrong with you. And something is also wrong if you can't squeeze more pleasure out of what you have plenty of. And if there's something really wrong with you, you can either accept it or try to change your whole life. You sow envy and reap pity. That is how a culture bent on self-definition and self-propagation is forced to acknowledge the limits set by creation. All clever revolutionaries eager to change the existing conditions of life are as foolish in practice as the dull conformist is wise in accepting life as it is. When dealing with this delicate question, which touches on all aspects of our lives, we act exactly like those primitive tribes who make no connection between conception and the function of their organs causing sexual pleasure. Our own supposedly highly developed civilization posits a direct relationship between sexual organs and sexual contentment that nature cannot confirm. A precondition of procreation is the regular functioning of the sexual organs, which may result in conception, but sexual happiness is merely a potential gift of nature. Hence the fragility of this happiness.

After expounding on these ideas, it would be risky for me to claim that I'm neither scarred nor warped in this respect. From my earliest childhood, circumstances have forced me to satisfy not my cultural longings but my natural inclinations. And for this reason I can honestly say that I find the culturally inspired masochism of resignation and the sadism of forced change equally abhorrent. Unlike my poor friend, who ventured into the realm of human desires and turned his body into the object of his emotional experiments, I turned my body into an instrument, a means to an end, and thus my desires have become only the stern supervisors of my natural inclinations. Because my origins were so problematic, I viewed with great hostility anyone who tried to convince me there was something wrong with me, or anyone who considered me exceptional because of my physical attributes. I couldn't accept these judgments. Life for me was not something to accept as inevitable or something that had to be changed; what I wanted was to find, in the only life that was mine, the possibilities congenial to my character. And in pursuing these possibilities I have been, if not passionate, definitely obsessive.

I have been coaxing out of myself during these lonely nocturnal hours, though I am temperamentally ill suited for it, reflections and confessions. Having desires does point to some sort of suitability, however, and this compels me to become active in an area where I should prove to be inept. But two complementary principles necessarily put into motion a third one.

Not being filled with longing, I am moved to reflect and to remember. What I want from myself is to eliminate everything that might embarrass me or make me biased. It is true, of course, that bias affected the way my memory obliterated my own image as recorded by my friend. But I've no reason to complain, because my memory neatly preserved another image.

A seemingly innocuous one. I don't know how often I may have recalled it over the years. Once in a great while, I suppose. It's like a pinprick. The sun is blinding. The grass is green. Prém is squatting in this raging light. From between his closed thighs his prick is dangling. And in thicker, longer, and harder sausages, shit is coming out of his ass. I have more of such images but none of them quite so distinct.

In the middle of our reconnaissance operation we'd suddenly feel the urge to relieve ourselves. We were not embarrassed in front of each other. Either I would have to go, or he, and sometimes both of us at the same time. And in the most impossible situations, too. We didn't have time to clean up, either, for whether we had reason to be afraid of getting caught or not, we always had a deeper shame to flee from. I believe that this more serious injury protected us from the other, much milder one.

Our compulsive shamelessness created a peculiar order of importance. What to others was a titillating sight, reaching into their sensuality and satisfying their curiosity, for us was only a trivial circumstance, though it still reminded us of our shamelessly affected shame. So if I indeed asked Prém to take off his clothes and show his nakedness, I did it not because I was suddenly seized by an uncontrollable desire to see his emblematically significant organ but, on the contrary, because I knew that in the other boys there still lived that inescapable attraction which our shame had already killed in me. This was the feeling I wanted to free myself from, or recapture the feeling of community with the others. That I could never succeed in this is a different matter. Perhaps this is the reason I don't easily tolerate being kissed.

I was toilet-trained by means of the most frightful prohibitions. I learned that I must perform one of my most basic life functions, relieving myself, in complete secrecy, alone, never in the company of others. The taboo was so strong I knew it could never be violated with impunity. Rules of sexual conduct seemed far more lenient in comparison. How profound and unavoidable the urge must have been for me to violate that prohibition. For I did violate it, we both did. For others there had to be a war, a state of emergency to do the same. Yet our conscience didn't trouble us, because it was not the cultural norms concerning toilet-training that we wanted to breach, just as nations don't go to war to squander the treasures of their moral sanctuaries. We lived in days of illusory peace, and we simply wanted to prepare ourselves for the day when we'd have enough experience and resolve to carry out the greatest reconnaissance mission. The ultimate proof of our preparedness would be the execution of an actual plan. If, for instance, we could penetrate the area near our house guarded by killer dogs, barriers, barbed-wire fences, and heavily armed men. If we could do it unnoticed, effortlessly, without getting hurt, like master spies. Unlike my friend and Maja Prihoda, we weren't trying to expose spies, we wanted to become spies ourselves. To spy out that quintessential enemy territory whose very existence and unfathomable character brought into question the validity of our own existence. But for this cold-war operation we didn't, couldn't possibly, have the necessary courage—just as my friend and Maja ultimately shrank from denouncing their own parents. For that we would have had to break the seven seals of the darkest secret and do something that the country itself, sunk in a stupor of peace, could not do. And this was the greatest shame we all shared.

But I couldn't give up the idea of doing something like that.

It was autumn when I wrote this last sentence. There are sentences I have to put down so I can cross them out later. The truth is, I'm not happy with that sentence. Still, I can't cross it out, strike it from my heart. It's spring now. Months go by. I do very little else. I've been trying to figure out why I couldn't give it up. If I knew, I wouldn't have to write it down, or I could just cross it out. What I've been really thinking about is why I still can't give it up. Why I'm ready for the most humiliating compromises just so I won't have to give it up. Wouldn't it be more dignified to bow to irrevocable facts than to wallow disgracefully in the filth of obstinacy? Why am I so afraid of my own filth when I know that it's not just mine, and at the same time why do I shudder to look into a mirror that reflects only my own image, after all?

If memory serves, we broke into ten or twelve apartments. That's quite a lot. And we had to take a crap on eight or ten occasions—enough to fix the experience indelibly in my mind. But what was the point of devising the most impossible tasks for ourselves, and piling one senseless crime on top of another, when we both knew very well that we were after something else? And we didn't need to talk about it either. Helpless and dejected, we hung around the fence of the restricted area. Trying to make friends with the guards. Did small favors for them, which they repaid with spent cartridges. We kept wondering how we might render the watchdogs harmless. We even asked the guards. There's no way, they said. But no amount of clever maneuvering could make us equal to the task, because what we were demanding of ourselves, in fact, was that our courage, strength, resourcefulness, and determination match the brute force that this untouched and untouchable restricted area had come to symbolize.

I remember well our last clandestine operation. I was trying to climb out through a small pantry window when a shelf laden with preserve jars gave way. It happened on Diana Road, in a villa surrounded by a high brick wall. Luckily, I was able to avoid falling on the bottles, which rained down with a terrific racket. I held on to the windowsill and took a look under me. The indescribable sight still haunts me. Green pickles plopping on and mixing with sticky jam, marinated yellow peppers sliding and rolling all over the tile floor. And more jars and bottles falling onto this soft, squishy mess, shattering one after the other.

My life does not abound in memorable turning points. Still, this moment of long ago I ought to consider as one. I felt I had to seek other, different means of action, and without ever again derailing any of my desires.

I was always an excellent student. Moreover, I was blessed with the diligence and perseverance of a teacher's pet. But my adaptability and pleasing appearance kept me from becoming thoroughly dislikable. I am one of those few who actually mastered Russian in school. My mother and I had visited all my father's fellow officers and soldiers who were returning from Russian POW camps. It was while listening to their stories that I decided to make a serious effort to learn Russian. In this I took after my mother, emulating her grim, obsessive ways. If she could learn the true story of my father's disappearance and death, she would get him back. This is what she must have felt, and this feeling took root in me. And since I was preparing to become a soldier, I hoped I'd be able to investigate the circumstances of his death exactly where it had happened. German I had to learn twice. The first time, it was acquiring a language nobody spoke anymore. Among the books we inherited from my grand-father was a two-volume leather-bound set with a mysteriously simple gold-embossed title on its spine: *On War*. The margins were filled with my grandfather's notes, in Hungarian, written in his tiny, crabbed, but quite legible hand; the book itself was printed in Gothic letters. I had to acquaint myself with this book, because I thought that from it I could also learn everything there was to know about war.

In December 1954, on the last day before winter break, as I recall, a sizable delegation of grim-looking men showed up at our school. They arrived in huge black automobiles. They all wore dark hats. From our classroom window we saw the hats disappear in the doorway downstairs. All teaching ceased. We had to sit in silence. Footsteps echoed in the corridors, never just one but several pairs of footsteps, and then silence again. Some people were being led somewhere. Not a peep out of anybody, hissed our most hated instructor, Klement, when somebody would stir to change position. The door opened. The janitor called out someone, barely whispering the name. Footfalls. Then the waiting: will he come back? After a short while the student would come back, looking pale, and sidle into his seat, followed by our curious stares, and the door would close again. Trembling lips and ears rubbed red told us that something must have happened. Something was going on. But the most unlikely people were taken out; I saw no pattern, so I could draw no conclusion.

Nevertheless, after a while I had the feeling we were being surrounded.

Klement had a huge bald head with tiny watery blue eyes. A stomach the size of a barrel. He weighed at least three hundred pounds. He carried a small cardboard valise. Now he was sucking candy, clicking his tongue, and smacking his lips in the silence. With deep moans and long wheezing sounds he kept himself busy with himself. He'd pull up his socks, which had slid down to his swollen feet. Or he'd open his sorry little valise, check his bunch of keys, then close the valise, but you could tell he was still thinking about it. He kept scratching his nose. Pinched something from it with his nail, examined the extract intently, then smeared it on his pants. After cracking his knuckles for a while, he kept sliding his rings over his pudgy fingers. Or he'd clasp his fingers over his stomach and twiddle them, with the thumbs always touching a little as they circled each other. He was like a living, breathing machine. He'd raise his bottom slightly, pull a handkerchief from his back pocket, unfold it, bring up phlegm and spit it into the hanky, and then, as if to guard some rare treasure, carefully refold the handkerchief. It wasn't excitement that deliberate cruelty evoked in him but the most voluptuous sense of self-satisfaction. So from his behavior we could only surmise that we were in trouble, worse trouble than ever before.

My mind was whirling like a windmill grinding grain. To all the questions they might have asked, I answered with a definite no. Looking straight into their eyes, I'd deny everything, even things that by their standards would be helpful to me. I would even deny knowing Prém. And deny poisoning the dogs, though we never went through with that. He wasn't being called yet, and neither was I. The only reason such a deathly silence could be maintained for so long was that this wasn't the first time. Nobody dared ask to go to the toilet. About two years earlier they had found a little poem on the wall of the third-floor boys' bathroom, written in the style of one of our classics: "Don't ask who said it, Lenin or Stalin, it's all the same. If you're up to your neck in shit, hold on to the rising standard of living. It might've been Rákosi who said it. So make him your guiding star." I didn't quote it in metric feet because the authorities weren't interested in poetics either. They could always find something if they wanted to. So how could anyone think of going to the bathroom at a time like this? Two years before, the investigation had lasted two whole days. They interrogated everyone, lined us up, took writing samples, photographs, searched through schoolbags, pockets, pen cases—we couldn't easily forget that.

I couldn't control my anxiety. Prém and I caught each other's eye, but he didn't have much to grin about either. I could go on vehemently denying everything, but it wouldn't help. I felt as if I were perfectly transparent. As if anybody could read my thoughts. As if I couldn't hide myself, not even behind myself. I don't want to bore anyone with an in-depth analysis of this state, but I would like to say something about the useful experience I gained while in this situation.

If someone has to be afraid of his own thoughts, because he must fear other people's thoughts, then he'll try to substitute his own evidently dangerous thoughts for those of others. But no one is capable of thinking with somebody else's brain, for the thoughts thus produced are merely his own brain's assumptions about how others may think about the very same thing. So not only must he eliminate the telltale signs of his own thought process and pretend to be second-guessing somebody else's thoughts on the subject, and then substitute these for his own, but he must also eliminate the uncertainty that this substitution is based on a mere assumption. And if one is forced to make one's brain play this game long enough, one will no doubt learn a great deal about the mechanism of thinking, but the real danger is that one can no longer distinguish between one's assertions and assumptions.

At least an hour and a half went by. When my name was called, I felt utterly unprepared. Still, I was glad I could spring up and at last go somewhere. Just then, Klement threw another piece of candy into his mouth. The janitor was standing in the doorway. But Klement, while shifting the candy with his tongue and smacking his lips, said to me, "You, Somi Tót, you can really count yourself out." I was crushed by his comment. It implied that I couldn't possibly have had anything to do with the terrible crime, of which he of course had full knowledge. Yet the pitying tone of his comment couldn't have implied that I was therefore off the hook. It couldn't have, even if there was something vaguely encouraging and even kind about it, an acknowledgment of my high standing in the class. He smashed to smithereens the system of assumptions I had constructed during the past hour and a half. I felt the way I had in the hospital when the nurse, out of sheer kindness, mentioned my mother. In the ruins of my system of assumptions and defenses, there was no other assumption to cling to. Besides, there was no time to go over all my calculations in the light of the new data provided by Klement. All things considered, my feet were carrying me rather steadily. Like those of a fleeing animal, through the only possible opening, straight into the trap.

We passed through the empty teachers' room, and when the office attendant threw open the door to the principal's office, nothing could have topped my astonishment. The razor-sharp blade of the guillotine had already chopped off my head. I died. But my eyes were still peeking out of the sawdust-filled basket, I could see that what was waiting for me on the other side was not horrible but rather bright, festive, and friendly. An alfresco breakfast. Picnic on the hillside. A stag party with the smell of fine Havanas.

The moment I entered I was addressed in Russian.

The door behind me closed, but all the doors of the principal's apartment, adjacent to his office, were wide open. Through these huge, elaborately ornamented, brown double doors you could see all four connecting rooms of the spacious flat with its heavy furniture and thick carpets. It was much later that I got to know the works of Hans Makart, a Viennese court painter, but his crowded interiors, filled with draperies, statues, plants in deep reds and browns, always reminded me of this improbable moment. We knew from Livia, the janitor's daughter, that the former principal, who had been summarily dismissed and later deported from the capital, had to leave all his possessions behind. In the farthest room two young girls, our current principal's daughters, were playing on the carpet. The rooms were brilliantly lit by the morning sunshine and its rays reflected from the snow outside. For a second I even caught a glimpse of the principal's graceful wife flitting across the flood of light. Somewhere a radio was playing, I heard very fine, very soft music.

A bright-faced young man sitting behind a large carved desk in the shadow of oversize philodendrons and potted palms asked me how I was. From his appearance and accent I could tell he was addressing me in his native tongue. The other gentlemen were sprawled out comfortably, in jolly disarray, in easy chairs and straight chairs that had been kicked away from their regular spots. The principal, as if indicating that he wasn't really part of this group, was leaning against the warm tile stove with a forced little smile on his face. Enveloped in the undulating cloud of smoke, they had wineglasses in their hands, some were munching on canapés or enjoying coffee and cigarettes. None of this would have suggested an official visit if it hadn't been for a few ominously strange-looking sheets of paper lying on the table, on shelves, and even on the floor near the chairs.

In answer to the question, a single Russian word came to my lips. I even remembered that I had come across this expression in one of Tolstoy's fables. I didn't just say, I'm fine, thank you. I said, Thank you, I feel splendid. This made some of them laugh.

What a smart lad you are, said the man who had first addressed me. Come closer, let's have a little chat.

A straight-backed upholstered chair was waiting for me in front of the desk. I had to sit down, which meant that now all the others in the room were behind me.

I didn't know what might happen. I had no idea what sort of examination this was. But while he was asking his questions and in my blissful ignorance I kept answering them without difficulty, I felt I was on the right track. Yes, the track was right, but where was it leading me? Suddenly it got quiet, a tense silence. Their satisfaction made it very tense.

I was already sitting when the bright-faced Russian asked me if it was snowing today.

I answered that it wasn't snowing today, the sun was out, but yesterday quite a bit of snow fell.

Then he asked me about my grades and acknowledged my reply with a satisfied nod. Then he asked what I would like to be when I grew up.

A soldier, I said without hesitation.

Splendid, the Russian shouted, kicked his chair out from under him, rounded his desk, and stopped in front of me. He is our man, he said to the others, and then holding my face between his two hands, he told me to laugh. He wanted to see if I could laugh.

I tried. But probably didn't do a great job, because he let me go and asked if somebody in the family spoke Russian, from whom I could have learned it so well.

I said my father had learned to speak it, but then I got stuck, because I shouldn't have said that.

Your father? He looked down at me inquiringly.

Yes, I said, but I never knew him. I learned from books.

He thought he didn't hear me right. What was that, I didn't know him? he asked, amazed.

All my resolve, my dissemblance, and my hope got caught in my throat. I was still trying to smile, at least that. He died, I said, and managed not to burst out crying.

And then, in the silence behind me I heard a slight stir, the rustling of paper; somebody was evidently turning the pages of a book or notebook; of course I didn't dare turn around, though the Russian was also looking in that direction.

The principal came over, holding our open grades book in his hand, and with his finger pointed to something he apparently had already shown to the others. In little black boxes next to our names our class origins were noted in red letters.

The Russian cast a fleeting glance at the rubric, returned to the desk, sat down, and with the desperation of a disappointed lover buried his face in his hands. What was he to do with me? he asked.

I didn't answer.

In a louder voice, almost rudely, he repeated the question in Hungarian.

I don't know, I said quietly.

Do you think you could be worthy enough to speak the Russian language, he asked, again in his mother tongue.

This made me think not all was lost. I was very anxious to win back his goodwill.

Yes, I groaned in Russian.

He said I could go.

Less than a half hour after they had left, word got around that those who had passed the test would get to go to Sochi, in the Crimea, on a winter vacation. I had never before begun a school holiday in such a foul mood. I squeezed that yes out of myself in Russian, yet I remembered my voice sounding rather decisive and soldierly. I would have liked to hear myself with their ears, because if I could be sure I did all right, then I could forget about my betrayal. I had no desire to go on any winter vacation, and anyway, as the days passed, the likelihood of that grew more and more remote. But I avoided Prém. I didn't want to play with him anymore.

On December 31, I was summoned to school. They sent Livia's father to get me. There were six of us waiting outside the teachers' room, three very pale girls and three eager-looking boys. We didn't say a word to one another. The principal again received us in the company of a strange man and proceeded to deliver a little speech. He tried to make his voice sound appropriately solemn and emotional. An extraordinary honor had been bestowed on our school, he said. On the occasion of the new year, and on behalf of the Young Pioneers and the entire school-age youth of Hungary, we were going to deliver greetings to our nation's leader and wise teacher, Comrade Mátyás Rákosi, in his home. The stranger talked to us about the details. He told us exactly what was going to happen, how to behave, and how to answer any questions we might be asked. The ground rule was, he cautioned, that we mustn't say anything that might cause sadness. Surely we were familiar with the teachings of Zoltán Kodály. While singing, one should keep smiling. That was the next basic rule. After the greetings we would be served hot cocoa with whipped cream and cake. And if Comrade Rákosi's wife should graciously ask us whether we would like some more cake, we must answer no, thank you, because the visit mustn't last longer than twenty minutes. Maja Prihoda would deliver the greeting in Hungarian and I in Russian. He gave us the text, which, he said, we had to memorize and know perfectly by the next morning. No one must know about our mission until afterward, and he would strongly advise us not to show the text to anyone. The bouquets of flowers and further instructions would be handed to us at the gate on Lóránt Street.

As soon as I left the others, the noiseless thunder of this last sentence propelled me to Prém. The gate would be raised, after all. He was playing cards with his older brother in their kitchen. Outside, we took only a few steps from the house and I told him right away that we could get in, after all. I made it sound as though we both would. He kept shifting his feet in the cold. The snow crunched under his shoes. And he kept blinking, looking confused, as if he thought I was making a bad joke. I was already pulling the piece of paper from my pocket. To show him the speech as proof. But he cut me off. He had a great hand, he said, he must finish the game, and anyway, I could kiss his ass.

I wasn't offended. In his place I would have said the same thing. Prém was a very poor student. Year after year he barely passed his finals. And his family was dirt-poor. Of course, we weren't rich either; we, too, ate mostly beans, peas, and rotten potatoes, but in a pinch my mother could sell a rug, an old piece of jewelry, or some silver. We were friends; the unbridgeable social gap between us was fully calculated into our friendship. In our war games I was always the officer and he the private. He wouldn't even be corporal or sergeant, for the in between rank would hurt his pride. So this unpleasant little interlude didn't stop us from restoring the old order a few days later. And his eagerness to hear more didn't seem to embarrass him. He had me recount the story of the visit several times a day. I obliged him, and even the first time I gave him a rather imaginative version of it, which I kept embellishing as time went on. It would have been unthinkable to admit that what we had treated as a profound mystery until now, a secret worthy of a reconnaissance mission, was in reality something infinitely boring, colorless, dreary, and mundane. I held the secret in my hand and did not believe my eyes. I couldn't have known then that no secret was drearier than the secret of despotism.

Everything did go just the way the strange man had told us it would. In this secret there is no room for contingency. At nine in the morning we had to show up, in our Pioneer uniforms, without hats, scarves, or coats, at the Lóránt Street gate. They stuck two bouquets of carnations in our hands. Maja got one, I got the other. It was a bright, snowy morning, at least ten below freezing. We must have looked pitiful, though, because our parents, quite correctly, wouldn't let us leave the house in white Pioneer shirts, as the instructions prescribed, and made sure we put on lots of warm underthings. We all looked stuffed and bulky, and after we'd moved around awhile, all sorts of things were sticking out from under our holiday outfits. Of course, this detail I didn't mention to Prém. Instead, I told him that on the other side of the gate was this well-concealed structure where they searched us. And to make it sound even more alluring, I added that the girls were stripped to their birthday suits. And that's where they gave us the bouquets, I told him, to prevent us from hiding poison or explosives in them. Actually, one of the guards brought the flowers from his booth. All right, children, who is giving the speech? I couldn't reconcile the terrifying thoroughness of the preparations with the sloppiness of the execution. So I embroidered my tale to fit my harrowing expectations. Our little troupe marched down the road that cut across the forbidden territory, where the snow hadn't been cleared away, just as it hadn't been in the rest of the streets of the city. Against my will, my eyes made the incomprehensible observation that there was no appreciable difference between the two places. But according to my report, the road was heated by a secret underground radiator, so not only was there no snow but the pavement remained bone-dry. On the left, among the trees and quite far apart, were two shabby villas. There was nothing on the right. Snowy woods. And then an ugly house in the woods. In my story, it was a white mansion and we drove up to it in a black limousine. Two armed men guarded the entrance, and we were led into a red-marble hall.

During the last days of October 1956, members of the newly formed national guard removed the barriers to the place. And the following day newspapers reported that the compound was no longer a restricted area. Yet Prém did not reproach me. I did lie to him, but he wouldn't have known what to do with the real facts either. I told him what he wanted to hear. Or rather, I said what our mind's eye had to see in order to understand what otherwise defied understanding.

If in what follows I should discreetly amend or correct some of the statements made by my deceased friend, I do so not out of a burning desire to establish the truth. What I'd like to do is examine our common life experiences from my own particular perspective and for my own sake. Whatever we may have shared can be approached via not only similarities but dissimilarities. In fact, I take the position of the most extreme moral relativists, making no qualitative distinction between truth and lies. I maintain that our lies prove as much about us as do our truths. Yet, when I concede that my friend was perfectly justified to speak of his life as he saw fit, I ask for the same consideration: that I be allowed to lie in my own way, to fantasize, to distort, to hold back, and, if it suits my purposes, even to tell the truth.

I read on pages 492 and 493 of his manuscript that after much struggle I finally got into a military academy, and that we happened to be in Kalocsa on fall maneuvers when news of the October uprising reached us, which resulted in our abrupt dismissal. And after I had related to him the adventures of my journey home, I took my leave, walking off into the twilight, and we never saw each other again.

I'd be no doubt more respectful of his memory if I left his version unchallenged. I can't do it. I can't accept his story as the only one, the exclusive one, because right next to it there's my own. The substance of our story was identical, but in it we moved in totally opposite directions. Thus, from my perspective, of his three seemingly innocuous statements I must judge the first as too simplistic, the second as totally erroneous, and the third as an emotional distortion that simply does not square with the facts.

My friend's father, if he was his father, I met very rarely. As a rule he ignored me. He barely returned my greeting. This much I can remember, but very little else. His face, his build, I can hardly recall. I was afraid of him. I couldn't say why. My fear wasn't unfounded, after all he was among the most ruthless men of the era, although I had no specific knowledge of that until after his suicide. And that late October afternoon I did take my hasty leave, for when I saw this much respected and feared man climbing over the fence, I knew I mustn't witness such an odd homecoming. If I'd stayed, I would have humiliated my friend, and I didn't want to do that either. I did say goodbye to him, but exactly eleven years later we met again.

Eleven years later, in late October 1967, I had to travel to Moscow. It wasn't my first visit there. I had accompanied my immediate supervisor twice during the previous year and three times that same year.

Each time we were put up at the Hotel Leningrad, near the Kazan railroad station, in a palatially spacious suite with a foyer, a reception room, and a bedroom complete with silk-draped four-poster beds. No ordinary mortal could possibly fill the dimensions of these rooms. My boss spoke Russian rather poorly, while I reveled in my knowledge of it. I seized every opportunity to use it and to improve my vocabulary. In my free time I roamed the streets, rode the metro, made friends, even had an affair. The pervasive, sugary, choking smell of gasoline was no longer a novelty for me; it drifted up to the thirteenth floor of our hotel, blew through the parks, filled the metro tunnels, got into your skin, your hair, your clothes, and made you smell like a Muscovite. I found myself a fast-talking blonde; returning to her for the third time was a real joy. She lived on the Pervomayskaya with her mother and sister and a niece who had recently moved there from the country. The powerful voices of these large women and their unbridled sentimentality just about burst the walls of their tiny flat. It became my secret home. I admit timidly that neither before nor since have I seen such delectably firm and enormous female thighs. In the summer they rented a dacha somewhere near Tula, and we made plans for me to visit them the following year. We'd swim, gather mushrooms, and pick blackberries to flavor our tea with, come winter. At that time my resolve to make it to the Uriv region one day, to Alekse-yevskaya, was still very much alive. We discussed this plan in great detail, too. In the end nothing came of it.

The series of negotiations in which I participated concerned the details of a long-term trade agreement involving the sale of chemical products. The contract itself that we, representatives of various trading companies, had drawn up had to be signed by the appropriate ministers in December. We were nearing the last round of talks, there wasn't much time left. Everyone was nervous, the prices hadn't been fixed, though this in itself was nothing unusual. Even after they'd been set, prices could still fluc-tuate.

In socialist business dealings, prices are arrived at in a manner that has precious little to do with pricing as we know it in conventional trade relations. It's as if someone was trying to catch a mouse and ended up trapping the cat instead. We usually refer to this as the double-trap prin-ciple. The process begins with a socialist commercial firm asking for a price quotation not from another socialist firm but from a capitalist one, for a product which it has no intention of buying but which in fact it wants to sell. The capitalist firm knows exactly what is going on, so it quotes not a realistic price but a blatantly unrealistic one that does not threaten its own real trading partners. However, the socialist firm takes this for the real world-market price of the product in question and makes its own offer to its socialist trading partner accordingly. The partner knows of course that the so-called real price is not real at all and, just as arbitrarily, makes a counter-offer, amounting to perhaps one-third of the quoted price. As a result, they wrangle over two totally unrealistic prices that, during the course of negotiations, acquire an air of reality. If two people who do not believe in ghosts begin to talk about ghosts in a dark room, sooner or later a ghost will appear, though they won't be able to touch it.

The process continues with the seller trying through further negotiations to narrow the gap between the two unrealistic prices, knowing well that the considerable difference can be made up only with the help of a state subsidy. But the buyer also knows that if the deal is important enough for commercial or industrial-policy reasons, he too can count on state funds, so he eases off, which in terms of the bargaining process is tantamount to driving up the price. If he misjudges the situation, and the seller is not swayed by insurmountable political considerations, then either there is no deal or some compromise is worked out. But regardless of whether or not a bargain is struck, neither party will ever be aware of the true relationship between the price finally arrived at and the real value of the commodity on the international market.

My superior, ingeniously combining the teaching techniques of the peripatetic Greek philosophers with the habits of French kings, used his morning toilet to lead me into the mysteries of these negotiations. He was of the opinion that the Russians were the world's most unpredictable business partners. They could be unexpectedly flexible on one occasion and equally stubborn and immovable on another. Whether you deal with Swedes, Italians, Armenian-Americans, or Chinese traders, what drives the negotiations is the logic of mutual interest. Differences arise from different assessments of a given situation. If you're dealing with Russians, however, you can give logic a rest.

Later, having gained a certain amount of experience myself, I came to regard my supervisor's conclusions as an enjoyable myth. It would take too long to expound my own view, which differs greatly from popularly held beliefs. To put it simply, I think Russians view the relationship between reality and unreality differently from the rest of us. Whatever we might consider an unreal phenomenon—because by violating realistic value relationships it brings our inner order to a halt—from their point of view is something incidental and negligible, for their inner order, independent of the outside world, remains functional.

On the first day of negotiations my boss fell ill during lunch. To make sure he didn't notice my forbidden nocturnal absences, and to make sure, too, that I could wake him up at six in the morning, as he requested, and while he splashed in his tepid bathwater I'd be ready to listen to his always instructive musings on economic concerns, I had to get up at the crack of dawn in that flat on Pervomayskaya, far from the center of town. Also, that morning, I was too sleepy to make much of his complaint that he wasn't feeling quite right. Anyway, he was a big, robust man.

We had trouble getting down to business that morning. It was hard to find the right tone. If I abandoned my sense of humor and accepted what they considered a realistic position, then I myself became unrealistic; and if I didn't accept it and made light of things, then my position in our relationship would become unrealistic. These are the times one really feels how much flexibility, imaginative insight, and infinite patience it takes to function as a son of a small nation. In my days as an apprentice negotiator I often felt it was best to get past the table-pounding stage quickly; I was frustrated because my boss, with the experience of four years in Russian captivity behind him, preferred holding back, delaying, putting things off, turning evasive—but even with these tactics we made no headway.

After the morning session we had lunch with two of our local commercial representatives in the hotel restaurant, a cavernous affair, more like a grand hall of columns than a restaurant. At one point my boss slowly put his knife and fork down on his plate and said it might be a good idea to open a window. Considering the size of the place, the suggestion didn't make much sense, so we more or less ignored it. There is no air, he said. I never saw anyone sit so still. A few moments later he spoke again: we should get his medicine from his pocket. At the same time he opened his mouth, letting his tongue hang out a little. Beads of perspiration were forming on his ashen face. He said nothing more, he didn't move, his eyes stared vacantly, but the way he was sticking out his tongue clearly indicated that he wanted the medication placed under his tongue. As soon as the tiny tablet dissolved, he felt much better, let go of his knife and fork, wiped his face, and color began to return to his cheeks. But again he complained that there was no air, and as if groping for air in the air, he got up restlessly and went in search of more air. We tried to support him, but he took such forceful steps he didn't seem to need us. We let go of him. When he got to the lobby he collapsed. He was taken to a hospital. In a deep coma, he lived for two more days.

The talks were broken off. I called the director of our company to tell him what had happened. Hopes for recovery were slim, and the patient could not be moved. I asked him to notify the family. Conversations with my boss had centered exclusively on professional matters, yet I imagined members of his family, whom I had never met, to be just like him: strong, agile, a little worn-out, but sturdy. My director's position was that the talks must resume without delay. He thought that all the wrangling had been mostly a show and therefore superfluous. The Russians' offer had to be accepted. He had given my boss—who always started fussing when there was no need—very specific instructions to that effect. He was authorizing me to lead the negotiations with these instructions in mind. He would telex his decision to the head of our trade office, who would then officially inform the Russians of the change in our delegation. If the whole thing weren't just a matter of formality he would send a replacement, but as things stood now, I could step right in. I should keep that well in mind, too. But it didn't happen that way at all. A senior member of our embassy's commercial section took over formally, but he let me handle the practical end of the negotiations, saying he hadn't been sufficiently briefed.

In the next two days I had a great many things to attend to. Feverish activity always generates more energy and the need for more activity, which is maybe why I couldn't stay put at night in my four-poster bed in the hotel, though I knew I should be there to receive a phone call. I went to sleep with a guilty conscience in the flat on the Pervomayskaya. In the embrace of a strong, calm female body I relived the death of my father, whom I now lost forever.

I had trouble falling asleep. Not even with making love could I get death out of myself. Hovering between sleep and wakefulness, I was drifting along a snow-covered highway. It was a scene deep inside me, often imagined, endlessly replayed.

More than two weeks after the enemy broke through the bridgehead at Uriv, on January 27, 1943, to be precise, my father set out by motorcar to make his report. That was the day their retreat began. They were not completely surrounded yet, but the Russians were closing in fast. There was a point in my drifting when I either fell asleep or had to start the scene over from the beginning. The only thing we knew for certain was that at 2030 hours the retreating battalion encountered the Russians and within half an hour suffered a defeat, losing 50 percent of its troops. But they did manage to break through the Russian lines. The car in which my father had left earlier that day was found about six hundred meters from the scene of the battle. It was riddled with bullets. Its doors were flung wide open. It was empty.

For years we waited for Father to come home; after all, the car was empty.

I've got a picture of him, sent from the front. An endless field of sunflowers under a perfectly clear sky. In the middle of the field a tiny figure waist-deep in flowers.

Quite early on the morning of the second day, when I took a taxi back to the hotel, I could hear the persistent ring of my telephone even before reaching my room. Such rings are unmistakable. There was really no need to pick up the receiver. But we are such fools. We pick it up to find out when exactly the thing we knew was going to happen did happen. An hour and a half later the talks were resumed. In a curious atmosphere. The Russians were emotional and quick to express their condolences, yet we all tried to sit down at the negotiating table as if nothing had happened. The slight hesitation over the agenda, the preoccupied air with which we shuffled and exchanged and leafed through our papers helped to preserve the semblance of normalcy. However, when it was my turn to speak, I couldn't keep myself from briefly eulogizing my colleague. And these men, all of them much older than I and for the most part hardened war veterans, listened in stunned silence as I spoke of our morning bathroom ritual.

For us Hungarians, death evokes stark terror. For Russians it is like the softening sign in their language: silent in itself, it cannot be voiced, but it softens the letter preceding it. My instincts perceived this difference during the two nights I spent on Pervomayskaya. My blond friend was the first and for a long time to come the only woman on whose lips my own mouth came alive. After the brief commemoration, I immediately got down to business. I don't think my motives were improper in any way, yet I didn't follow my director's instructions. There was nothing in me but this terror, and it made me stubborn. The session lasted all of ten minutes, and the Russians accepted every one of my proposals. We spent the rest of the day working out the details, even skipping the usual lunch break. The man from the embassy's commercial section did not dare reproach me, but he was fuming. Both parties were anxious to get the whole thing out of the way, if only because all this was taking place on November 6, the eve of their most important national holiday. Nobody felt like working anymore.

It was late afternoon when I got back to the hotel. I was tense, wound up from lack of sleep. In such an overtired state one always feels energetic somehow. I was dying to get rid of my necktie and that impossible black suit and head for Pervomayskaya. I couldn't really enjoy my little breakthrough at the talks, even though it was something of a coup. It came at too high a price. And it was really the dead man's coup, not mine, and the breakthrough was death's breakthrough, not mine. I was pretty sure my director wasn't going to give me a hard time. And even if he did, our commercial people had no choice but to back me up. One thing was certain, the way I handled the matter would evoke his fierce displeasure. I'd be considered some kind of liability for quite some time, which meant kissing promotion goodbye. That's the kind of mood I was in before stepping into the hotel elevator.

It was nearly full and the operator waited for me to get in. But I hesitated. Deliberately slowing my last two steps. I didn't feel like squeezing in. I also noticed that all the passengers were Hungarians. Which turned me off rather than attracting me. But standing among them in a long fur-collared coat was a dark-complexioned girl with curly hair who caught my eye. In response to a question they must have just asked, the disagreeable elevator operator was saying no, no, not allowed, room reserved for banquets. Hearing this, they began to laugh as if they had just heard a priceless joke. Banquet, banquet, they kept shouting. I had walked into an infantile cacophony, and I can't say I liked it. My compatriots tend to feel lost when they are abroad alone, but in groups they can act quite silly and rowdy. I had the feeling that they also sensed the compatriot in me and their reaction was the same as mine, so they finally quieted down. I positioned myself so that I could be close to the girl and watch her from the front. Her slightly old-fashioned coat, tapered at the waist, outlined a slender figure, and the face framed by the upturned silver-gray fur collar was ruddy from the cold. On her hair, eyebrows, and even her lashes half-melted snowflakes were glistening. The first snow of the year had fallen that day, and it hadn't let up since morning.

In my callous simplicity, I thought she was what I needed. And I could see in her eyes that she not only caught my glance but understood my meaning. She didn't think I was pushy, but she wasn't going to respond. She was noncommittal without turning me down, she was holding on to my offer without making one herself, she was impassive but not without a certain amount of curiosity. There was even a hint of impudence in her look, as if to say, Well, big boy, what else can you show me, real quick? We must have ridden about three floors like this, staring in each other's eyes.

We were caught up in each other, but she was playing to the others a little, too, not wanting them to notice just how caught up she was. What I also felt then was that someone standing next to me was staring into my face, with a persistent, unmoving look that suggested he knew full well what I was up to. I had to find out what that was all about, yet I hesitated, for if I turned my face it might appear that I couldn't take her stare, though in truth I couldn't take his.

It would be very hard to describe the feeling I experienced when, turning my head, I looked into the face of this obtrusive stranger. As adults, we always maintain a certain distance, which we determine, from the face of another adult, and the extent and nature of the closeness or distance is invariably regulated by our own interests and aims. But this adult face, suddenly cropping up from our long-gone childhood—no matter how much it may have changed—wound up intolerably close to mine. A melting tenderness came over me. As if I were seeing not a person but the passing of my own lifetime. Everything had changed, and yet nothing had changed. I sensed transience in myself and permanence in another man's features. At the same time I was so shocked to see the features of a child I'd known so intimately in the face of a man that a feeling of repugnance also began to stir in me. I didn't want this. Our glances scanned each other's features. He hadn't made up his mind either. And with that we irrevocably exposed ourselves in front of each other. There was no going back. Even though we both would have liked to avoid this meeting as much as we wished it to happen. There's nothing more humiliating than a chance encounter. But not giving in to it is even more humiliating.

I couldn't possibly benefit from this chance meeting. On the contrary, it could only work against me. I wanted to be already in my room, open the refrigerator, take a good long swig from the iced vodka bottle, and then leave this place as quickly as possible. Anyone seeking solace in alcohol knows what these moments are like. He reminded me of things I didn't want to deal with at all. And I was in such a state that my body would not tolerate delay. Still, I couldn't prevent what had to happen. I think our hands moved simultaneously, and in the gesture two very different weaknesses met. It couldn't turn into a real handshake, we were standing too close for that, it became more of a crude grasp. Hesitantly, eagerly, two hands seized and then immediately let go, almost thrust away, two hands. Just touching fingers was too little, but anything more would have been too much. And through it all, clumsy, stammering questions about what the other was doing here. Here of all places. As if "here" had some special meaning. I mumbled my own little story, and I blushed, which rarely happens to me, while he muttered something about a delegation of artists, and with a silly grin pointed to the others. We must have been on their checklist this year, he said. His tone was unfamiliar, alien.

But all this was surface; our tone, our blushes merely the appearance to provide some protection. Because what the moment was really all about was that our lives had turned out to be so very different, yet neither he nor I, neither before nor since, had ever loved another human being as we loved each other. Back then. Yes. This was our confession. And even now, when we are still so different, even now, although in a different way. And since then, too. This is an enduring part of our lives. It can't be helped. This love has no purpose, no meaning, or motive. Nothing can be done with it. I blushed because I wanted to forget it, and did. He was acting silly because he didn't forget, and probably couldn't.

His features seemed so indistinct and blurred that each line or curve or angle could mean three different things at once. And there was a danger that he might just ignore the glances of these strangers and mawkishly revert back to our lost time. In the end, however, it was his grim self-discipline that averted my always obliging though noncommittal bear hug. I saw brittle coldness in his face, dread in his eyes, though he was making lighthearted, cynical noises. Still, he, not I, was the one who stayed outside the situation. For if I cannot be guided by sober reason, if I cannot comprehend the meaning, direction, and purpose of a signal or a gesture, I freeze. I can yield to no person or situation. He, on the other hand, had it in him to act, to put his feelings on display. He burst into laughter. I wanted to shut my eyes. I showed up just in time, he said, as if we had last seen each other only yesterday. They had just come from a holiday reception. And now it was off to the Bolshoi for a gala performance. It promised to be quite an event. He sounded as if he were inviting me to his grandmother's for noodle pudding. Galina Vishnevskaya was singing. They had an extra ticket. Just for me. Box seats, too. Wouldn't I join them?

The maddening artificiality of his tone made it easier to decline the invitation. By then we were on the thirteenth floor, standing in the narrow hallway, in front of the *dezhurnaya*'s table laden with keys. The others passed us in silence on their way to their rooms. I told him I had no time, unfortunately. And looking over my shoulder, I involuntarily followed the brown-haired girl with my eyes. I'd already made plans for the evening. The girl opened her door slowly and disappeared without looking back. In the meantime, we kept laughing at the discovery that evidently the Russians always reserve the thirteenth floor for Hungarians. We should meet for breakfast, though. But no later than eight. They'd have to attend the parade on Red Square. We'd open a bottle of champagne.

I'd have to say that as soon as I closed the door of my palatial suite, I forgot this accidental meeting, as one might forget a fleeting unpleasantness. I didn't want a champagne breakfast. I didn't turn on the light. The strange rooms were glimmering faintly in the reflected light of the snow. I heard the soft murmur of the city below. Compared to the events of the past few days, what could these fleeting moments mean to me? Nothing. An embarrassment, at most an annoyance. Anyway, while I struggled here in vain, they were having fun. Still in my overcoat, I sank into an armchair. I had never before felt such a heavy, all-pervasive fatigue. It wasn't my bones or my muscles but my heart that seemed to give way. As if my blood had stopped flowing. I felt drained, empty. I didn't even want that drink of vodka anymore. Or I should say I did, but didn't have the strength to get up. That's not precise enough either. What I felt was that I must gather strength. But you need some strength to gather your strength, and I didn't have any.

No, I won't go on like this, I won't. That's what I kept saying to myself. I didn't know what the denial was referring to, or what it was I didn't want to go on with. I simply kept repeating the words. And let my head drop, my arms dangle. My legs were thrust out in front of me. Still, I couldn't let go completely, couldn't yield to my own exhaustion. A stern pair of eyes judged me self-indulgent, a show-off. As if I were playing in some cheap melodrama, with my limbs dangling, puppet-like. And I wasn't playing my role well and would have liked to get out of it. A fever was coming on, I was sweltering and shivering in the coolness of the enormous room. I fell into a deep sleep.

I was awakened by the horrible thought that I'd been left behind. As if they had yelled "Fire!" and run away. It wasn't even a thought or a cry but an image that I recalled, sharp and detailed, of that girl opening her door slowly and, contrary to my expectation, not looking back. For a moment I didn't know where I was. I jumped up and tried to figure how long I'd been asleep. Not too long, I decided. I can't get this woman out of my mind, I must see her. I'll run after them if I have to. Or sit and wait for her in front of her room. I wasn't thinking of my childhood, revisited just now in the features of my friend. Yet the feeling was definitely a childhood feeling. As when everybody went off to play but didn't tell me because they wanted to exclude me. If this is my room number, I figured, and the numbers keep going up, then hers must be such and such. While dialing the discovered, or inferred, room number, I looked at my watch. It was six-thirty. I'd slept for twenty minutes.

Hello.

There was just a hint of hesitation in that hello. As if she didn't know what language to use. But this one word made my heart leap with fright. It began to function. It was made of pure joy, in the shadow of an unknown fear. I heard her voice for the first time. From the moment I had gotten onto the elevator she'd said not a word to the others. I had no way of knowing what her voice was like. She had one of those female voices that have a very strong effect on me. It seemed to come from deep inside her body, a voice with a very strong, solid center, whose surface was nevertheless smooth and soft. It wasn't gentle, for that it was too proud and assertive. When I think of it, I see a dark, hard marble. A marble can fit snugly into the palm of your hand, a marble is something you can lift easily. But a marble is nearly impossible to penetrate. And if you do, it's no longer a marble.

I introduced myself, apologized, was very courteous, and very elaborately explained that I'd changed my mind and would like to join them. I rattled on. She listened patiently. She remained a silent island I lapped around with my words. I said I didn't know my friend's room number, that's why I called her. Though that wasn't the only reason. If she'd be kind enough to give me the number. I should hurry up, then, she said by way of reply. Yes, do hurry up. I used the familiar form of address, she stuck to the formal one. When I tried again, she pretended not to hear the more intimate form. She meted out her silences as reservedly as she did her glances in the elevator. She let me go on, but she was brushing me off.

I wouldn't attach importance to this brief conversation if what followed had been merely another one of my moderately gratifying adventures. But what followed was a bitter four-year struggle. I could also call it an agony, a series of hopeless quarrels, the low point of our lives, certainly my own darkest period up to that time. It would have been all that if it hadn't also been filled with the hope of newfound happiness. Yet the joy we found in each other only reached us unexpectedly, catching us by surprise, sometimes for weeks, at other times only for days, hours, or brief moments. We strove for it but could never really achieve it. What remained was the agony. The agony of missed happiness, or perhaps the joy of agony.

Yet we had no greater desire than to preserve for a lifetime the profound feeling of having found each other. Compelled by painful need, we set conditions for each other and failed to notice that we were breaking, crushing each other with them. She demanded absolute faithfulness from me, while I would have liked her to accept my infidelities as proof of my faithfulness. In vain I explained to her that I had never loved anybody as much as I loved her, but to counter these feelings of unfamiliar quality I needed at least the semblance of freedom. I could no longer live without her, but with her I turned into something like a faulty communicating vessel: if, with the greatest effort, I gave up my freedom and, complying with her condition, didn't even look at other women, my alcohol intake promptly shot up; if, however, I reduced my alcohol consumption by getting entangled in meaningless affairs, then the tension between us became simply unbearable. Our mutual degradation was greatest when she should have felt most secure, for that's when she used the most underhanded methods to spy on me, to probe and snoop, for which I beat her up. I did this twice, and it took a great deal of self-control not to do it more often. But her suspicions even at these times were not completely baseless. What made her jealous were not my occasional lapses but my enforced fidelity. Similarly, I didn't raise my hand to her because she got her girl friends to spy on me but because I couldn't comprehend why she didn't understand me. She sensed and felt everything. I couldn't make a move without her sensing its subtlest meaning. And she knew that the fidelity she forced on me caused intolerable tension, that it turned my behavior false and unnatural, because I wasn't used to giving up anything. But whenever her jealousy managed to drive both of us to distraction and I couldn't help seeking relief in some silly affair with no strings attached, then she wanted to break with me for good. She was capable of uttering not a single word except a morning hello, for weeks on end. Of letting all my questions go unanswered, pleas, threats, pledges, and promises. As if punishing me just for being alive. As if playing only to lose triumphantly, so that I'd have to play to win, though she'd never let me. Her real victory would be to push me out of her life completely, though she knew I could never push her out of mine.

The distorted values of my youth came back to haunt me with a vengeance. Because my actions were determined not by aesthetic or ethical principles but by sheer necessity, for me the line between freedom and license became forever blurred. Then, after four years like that, in the lull of one of our cease-fires, we quickly got married. Since then another six hopelessly difficult years have gone by.

One thing I know: that November evening, in a most curious way, I entered a very dark period in my adult years. The meeting turned me into an insecure, anxious adolescent, which I had never been. And the reason had obviously to do with my character and natural inclinations, but also with an accident of fate. A complete life must include lost or stolen time, but what one doesn't actually live through cannot be made up afterward, and there's no point blaming yourself or anyone else for it. Until the age of sixteen I wasn't all that interested in girls. I found their admiration as self-evident and natural as I did the uncritical adoration emanating from my mother. If for some reason I lost one girl's admiration, another one would take her place. And if necessary I could easily have a third or fourth. I accepted the aggressive signs of my biological maturity with the understanding that I'd neither resist nor make too much of them. It still seems odd that my brand-new manhood called attention to itself not in dreams or even in relations with girls but while riding on public transportation, on bumpy streetcars, and buses taking sharp and sudden turns. I wasn't ashamed of it, didn't even try to curb it, at most I'd put my briefcase in front of me. But at times the excitation came on so suddenly and was so acute that to prevent a minor accident, I'd have to get off in a hurry. And this was enough, because the physical tension, the body's excitement, wasn't directed at anyone in particular; it seemed independent even of me and had to do only with the bumpy ride.

In 1957 summer came on us suddenly. In the city quite a few houses still lay in ruins. Charging out of spring, this summer's hot explosion seemed to release energies of life the devastated city badly needed. When the school year had resumed, Mother and I had several hysterical fights, but in the end she won. She didn't let me go back to the military academy and enrolled me instead in a local high school in Zugló. One afternoon, after walking a new school friend home on Gyertyán Street, I got on a streetcar. When I think of this afternoon—it must have been the end of May—I see great big chestnut trees with their erect, candle-like white flowers reaching to the sky.

As always, I was riding on the open platform. The sliding doors were left open, the warm air rushed unhindered through the almost empty car. Across the platform stood a young man. His clenched fists were casually sunk in his pocket, his legs spread wide for support. On the other side of the open door was a young blond woman in a light, almost see-through summer dress. Bare, very shapely legs; on her feet white sandals. Holding on to the straps, she had nothing on her except the tram ticket. This, or perhaps something else, made it seem as if she had no clothes on or that her dress made little difference. First I watched the woman watching the man, but as soon as she noticed my curious glance and raised her bright, impudent blue eyes at me, I switched to the man or, more precisely, avoided her brazen look by turning in the man's direction, while he followed the woman's glance to register this developing interlude between the two of us. He was slender, ordinary-looking, of average height. The most conspicuous thing about him was the dark smoothness of his face and skin. A smooth, shiny forehead and, between his fists thrust into his pockets and his shirtsleeves rolled to the elbow, somewhat paler but still very smooth arms. The kind of smoothness that had to be, I felt, more than skin-deep. Having followed the woman's glance, he had to look at me. But then, prompted by an indescribable bashfulness, I had to look away. I returned to the woman, for I wanted to see what her eyes had to say about all this.

She was large, fair-skinned, on the verge of plumpness, but still at a point where her well-fed body was in harmony with a deeper vitality; however much food she might stuff into her pleasure-seeking body was sure to be worked off or burned up by other kinds of activity of the same body. Her firm, well-proportioned limbs did not simply fill out her dress but fairly burst out of it. The warm currents of air mussed up her hair and kept lifting her dress. We could see the strong, remarkably white insides of her knees. She'd sway now and then, springing up and down on her feet, relishing our eyes feasting on her. She couldn't have been more than twenty, but she was ripe, solid, everlasting, like a model poured into a heavy statue. By which all I mean to say is that she was at once available and unreachable.

After our glances met for the third time, she grinned into my face, showing her somewhat uneven teeth, and I, involuntarily accepting the grin, passed it on to the man. But I quickly realized I had first received a smoother, more discreet version of that grin from the young man. Now he took my grin and slipped it back to her. And then, simultaneously, we turned away, taking each other's grin with us.

Outside, the broad avenue, trees, and buildings were running after us. And then, again together, we turned back. It would be almost impossible to say where we trained our eyes. The grin we couldn't wipe off by turning away was now growing stronger, and it seemed as if something terribly important was lying on the greasy floor of the streetcar and our eyes had to find it. We were staring not at each other but at a point equidistant from all three of us, sending our grins to the geometric center of the imaginary triangle we formed. And somehow we had to stay together even when we threw back our heads to accommodate the laughter that burst out of us. But the laughter was not equally distributed among us. The woman giggled, tittered, let out little squeals and tiny bubbles of laughter, popping them and sucking them in again. The man was almost silent as he laughed, chuckling at short intervals, as if trying to form words. This stammering, almost talking laughter made me notice on his otherwise smooth face a deep, bitter crease around the mouth that wouldn't let the laugh fully erupt, even though he was shaking harder than the woman or me. Of course I could hear my own runaway horselaugh, too. With it I revealed all my innocence, but I didn't mind. The streetcar was crawling along, though to me it felt as though it was tearing up the tracks. Maybe the only time you feel free is when you don't bother about consequences, when you trust the moment and let yourself go.

The laughter was unstoppable, it terrified itself, its own brazenness made it falter; and we didn't just spur one another on with liberating little jabs; it seemed that we all had our own reserves of laughter, and their variety created such an enjoyable common sound that it would have been senseless to stifle it. Yes, let it come; no one has anything to be ashamed of. And it came, it grew, it hurt, it made us cry. This felt good, because all the while my sheepishness made me tremble; I felt my arms and legs shaking visibly. The streetcar was approaching the intersection of Thököly Road and György Dózsa Road, it slowed down. The young man thrust himself away from me, though he seemed to shove himself out of his laughter. He slipped his fist out of his pocket and raised a warning finger. A single finger held way above his head. We watched that single finger in the air, and in a flash all laughter stopped. The woman let go of the strap and just stood there with her ticket, her impudence gone from her blue eyes. Then slowly she stepped out onto the platform. It was perfectly clear what was happening, and I was trembling too hard to do anything about it. The young man bounced off the still-moving streetcar and looked back not at the woman stumbling after him but at me, taking in with one last sweeping glance my schoolbag, which I placed in front of me to cover my embarrassing state of arousal. There was still time to back out of the situation. For a moment we froze. A pair of huge liquid brown eyes in that smooth face. There was nothing to think over.

We probably needed that tiny delay. It made the mad race that followed that much more frantic. Our mouths were good only for catching our breath, but our feet could giggle and clatter away on the pavement. Dashing across streets and roads, weaving through crowds without bumping into anyone while your feet, your arms, your eyes became alert sensors, jumping on and off sidewalks. Feinting and dodging smoothly, the man was galloping ahead and sending us a message with his every move. Whatever he had been unable to tear from himself with laughter he was now pouring into his running. With his shoulders squeezing and thrusting, his neck craning, and his back straight, he not only controlled the situation but played it out for us. It looked as if at any moment he would cross the finish line; having pulled away from his rivals, he was already in the straightaway, unchallenged. That's how he kept playing with us. He'd change direction with lightning speed and career into a side street. Somewhat confused, we'd follow, but just then, without curbing his leaps, he'd disappear into an open door. The woman had a funny way of running; she wasn't clumsy, yet she seemed heavy and sluggish as she filled the trail cut for her by the man. Not until the next day did I check the name of the street.

It was cool in there. Dark. Smell of cats. We crashed against the flaking plaster. Watching one another's eyes and body. I could still beat a retreat, but I seemed to have run the trembling out of my limbs, and a quiet but sober voice told me to stay. If not now and not like this, it would happen some other time, some other way, so why not get it over with? We were panting. We were looking at one another as if we were at the end, and not at the beginning, of our story. Everything was calm. There was nothing to be afraid of. The woman sneezed into this panting silence. Which would have been cause for renewed laughter, but the man raised a finger to his lips and, as if to continue this warning gesture, started up the stairs.

Through the slats of lowered blinds, the hot afternoon sun streamed into the completely empty apartment. A slight breeze was also blowing in through the open windows and doors. In the long hallway and three large interconnecting rooms there was not a single piece of furniture. Except for a couple of mattresses thrown on the floor of the largest room, with pink and not altogether clean bedding: a turned-up blanket, wrinkled sheets, just as he must have left it in the morning. On picture hooks left on the wall hung a pair of pants, a shirt, and in a corner there was a pile of shoes. I knew we were beyond all rules and conventions. I was ignorant of what was to follow, yet I made the first move. I flung myself on the mattress, lay on my back, and closed my eyes. Showing them just how inexperienced I was—not that they could have had any doubt about that—whereas they seemed to be familiar with the ritual. During the time I spent in that apartment not a single word was spoken. But no explanations were needed. I knew I was in one of those flats whose occupants had left the country the previous December, or early January at the latest. And the man had to be a squatter. He couldn't have been a friend or relative of the former tenants, because then they would have left him something: a chair, a bed, a cabinet. He must have broken into the abandoned apartment, for if he had bribed the caretaker and got the key to the apartment, then he would have let us laugh freely in the stairway.

I have no way of figuring how long I may have stayed in that apartment. Perhaps an hour, maybe two. The three of us were sprawled out in three different positions on the mattress, two of us on our back, the woman on her stomach, when at one point I sensed that I was in the way. The feeling just came over me, even though neither of them gave a signal or made a move. Perhaps they began radiating a different sort of calm, and the energies passing so evenly between the three of us until then simply changed course. As if with their special calmness they were detaching themselves from me. They both seemed to want it this way, and I knew that with my more restless repose I could no longer find my place between them. Very gingerly I slipped my finger into the inside curve of her drawn-up knee. I was hoping she might be asleep. If she was not, she'd squeeze my finger by closing her knee. She stirred. First she turned her head toward the young man, and then she drew her knee up even higher so as to escape my finger. The man slowly opened his eyes and with his look said what the woman had told him with hers. There was no mistaking their message. It would have made no sense to experiment further. I should have felt very hurt, but what made the rejection bearable was that in the young man's eyes there lurked an almost paternal encouragement. I lay on the mattress, quite defenseless, yet my fiercely persistent erection could not have been offensive, as it was alluding to our joint endeavor up to that point. Nevertheless, standing in that state would have been awkward. I waited a little; I closed my eyes. But this way I sensed even more strongly what they had hinted at just before, that they wanted to be alone. I gathered up my scattered clothes, and while I was pulling on my shirt, my shorts, my pants, and buckling my sandals, they both fell asleep—I didn't think they were feigning.

They did nothing to offend me. Still, for the next two days I felt as if I had been cast out of paradise for having committed a mortal sin. It wasn't the expulsion itself that was so hard to bear. After all, I left of my own free will, doing what I felt was best for me. Still, I would have liked to hold on to my newfound bliss. The following noon I went back to the house on Szinva Street. The blinds of the second-story windows were still drawn. I was hoping the woman would open the door. I imagined her being alone in the flat. The little brass disk moved in the peephole, and the man could see my face. Slowly, very considerately, he let the disk swing back into place.

I dragged myself down the stairs, trying not to make any noise. I didn't understand what he could have meant by the encouraging look he'd given me before. Feeling cheated, I roamed the neighborhood for two days, waited, hung around the house. Had I given myself completely over to my pain, I suspect many things in my life would have turned out differently. Pain would have given me a chance to think through what had really happened in there. And if I had thought it through, I might have reached the frightening conclusion that I had learned to make love from the body of a man—not exclusively, but from the body of a man also—and this despite the fact that I have never, not then or at any other time, touched another man's body. And except for a bashful curiosity I have no desire to do so. Nevertheless, through the woman's body we did communicate. In trying to possess the woman, the other male body instinctively sought a common channel in which all our bodies could flow in a common rhythm. And that was the experience they deprived me of, but they also deprived themselves and each other of it. Something did happen, but what they took from me they could make use of only between themselves. Just as later, when I was with others, I made good use of what I'd learned from the two of them. The paternal encouragement in the young man's look referred to future times—it wasn't an invitation for me to come back.

Of course I didn't think all this through, I couldn't have. I found diversions, I avoided my pain. My urge to return to that place I sublimated in much more conventional ways. I formulated a code of behavior for myself. I never again indulged in pawing, grabbing, kissing, or running after girls; no courtship, no pining, no writing of love letters for me. Be smart, I said, with the encouraging paternal glance I had acquired from that stranger. I may not have been fully conscious of the origin of this high-handed, knowing glance, but I used it all the time. In some ways, I still do. And the girls, at least the ones I've wanted something to do with, have always proved to be smart.

I became part of an open world in which the laws of exclusive possession and appropriation do not apply, in which I enter into a mutual relationship not with a single chosen individual but with everybody. Or nobody, if you like. At the same time, my mother, ever since I can remember, all but forbade me to return her affection, which was, now that I think of it, a clever and instinctively cautious move on her part. In me she loved the man she had lost, but only through a tragic deception could my emotions have compensated her for that loss. She spared me from the pangs of love, and that is why it took me a very long time to understand that suffering is as much a part of a human relationship as pleasure is. I resisted tooth and nail every form of suffering. And it didn't occur to me that anyone expected me to reciprocate intense feelings; after all, my good looks earned me special privileges. Not that my looks could in any way make up for the indignities I had to endure on account of my family origins. But the tension between my social situation and my physical looks was enough to make me want to take root in a world that, whether it adored me or rejected me, did not lay claim to the whole of my life.

The devotion and admiration were meant for my physical attractiveness, the rejection for my social position. Unlike my friend, whose greatest ambition was to get to know, conquer, comprehend, bond another human being to himself and make that person his own, my own need to know and possess was fueled not by an overwhelming, self-effacing desire to understand, to identify totally with another being, but by the ambition to create order in my own affairs. We each lacked half of ourselves. I had a home, but not a homeland. He had a homeland, but not a home.

When it came to practical, expedient self-control, I was no less irrational than my friend. This self-control became my freedom. I used the natural affection of others as a means to an end, and to the same extent I curbed my own inclinations if they didn't fit a given situation and might hamper me in realizing my goals. So much for my moral justification. I never expected more from another person than I was willing to give of myself. I preferred to get less. I trained myself to be so sensible, so hard-nosed, that the very possibility of love was out of the question. My first adventure in physical pleasure most likely determined my subsequent experiences, but it was only part of a process. If one is forced to use oneself as an instrument, one remains an instrument in relation to another person as well. The quality of my first sexual adventure I consider to be identical with the quality of my ambitions. But I am neither so stupid nor so insensitive as to have let the need for love die in me completely. Except I couldn't have any experience in love—it would catch me unprepared—

because I acquired my experiences in affairs and relationships. And that's how things stand with me.

Actually, it was that visit to Rákosi's residence that gave me courage to apply for admission to the Ferenc Rákóczi II Military Academy. I didn't understand, and still don't, how they happened to pick me for that honor, but they did, and that meant that the impossible could happen. I didn't understand, because I knew that before summoning me to the principal's office they had to have clarified my family background. Or if for some reason they had neglected this, why did they disregard my principal's explicit warning? The reproachful gesture of his finger, the way he pointed to the little box next to my name in the class grades book and made sure everyone saw it, can never be forgotten. Cows are branded, not out of some conviction, but out of the practical necessity to distinguish one from the other.

Even as a child, with my still limited comprehension, I concluded that the system I lived under could not possibly regulate life by enforcing the inhumanly rigid and passionless rules it had devised. I sensed that only in the gaps and loopholes of this incomprehensible and absurdly rigid set of rules could I develop my own potential. True, I couldn't decide whether they fell into my trap or I into theirs, but I wasn't eager to know. I did know, however, that I wanted to get into that restricted zone. And the very people who created restricted zones were the ones to get me there. The condition of entry was my knowledge of Russian, yet it would never have occurred to me to study the language seriously if my father hadn't perished in a POW camp or maybe in that bullet-riddled automobile. The only way I could crawl through the tiny gap they offered me was by cunningly revealing something of my real intentions. If I could appear trustworthy enough to be able to go on being insincere. My knowledge of Russian and my pretty face got me in, and all they asked for was a trifle, that I pledge my faith. And why shouldn't I have considered myself worthy of speaking any foreign language? It's true of course that in the process I wound up rejecting my father and betraying my friend. But the system compensated me for my pledge of faith and for my services. It revealed its weakest side to me. Namely, that for all its professed ideals, it can make soup only from the vegetables that grow in its own garden.

If all this had happened a year earlier, or had the restricted zone really been significantly different from its surrounding area, if they had led us into a marble hall instead of a conventionally furnished living room, if the cocoa were not lukewarm and the disgusting skin on its surface hadn't reminded me of the milk we got in the school lunchroom, if the cream had been whipped properly and wasn't limp and slightly sour, or if I hadn't suddenly had the impression that the reason the much-feared and respected couple seemed in low spirits had nothing to do with lack of sleep but most likely with a simple domestic quarrel they had to suspend because of our arrival, if, in other words, the visit hadn't turned out the way it did, it would never even have occurred to me that the small gap I was offered could accommodate all of me. The system's forbidding sternness seemed to leave no room for the contingencies of human life. No wonder, then, that seeing so much ordinary action and mundane behavior in the restricted zone would make me all the bolder. In exchange for new and exciting opportunities, I was ready to give up my childish fantasy of someday becoming an officer in some army. I was in, inside the gap, I could feel its proportions and believed I could make decisions according to its rules. But all my calculations proved false. They rapped my knuckles very quickly.

The same day I submitted my application to the military academy, signed reluctantly by my mother, I was called into the principal's office. All the windows were open, though a fire was burning. When I walked in, the principal was rubbing his back against the tile stove. For a long time he didn't say anything, just kept shaking his head in disapproval.

Then he pushed himself away from the stove, walked across the room to his desk. He must have had some back problem; he bent over a little, favoring one side, sidling rather than walking, and it seemed that only by pressing his back to the warm stove could he straighten up properly. As he pulled out my application from a pile of papers and handed it to me, he quipped, Miracles don't happen twice. If you know what I mean.

Obligingly, I took the application from him. He was quite pleased with himself. Then he motioned for me to go. But I got stubborn and wouldn't budge. And that irritated him.

Anything else? he asked.

I stammered that I didn't understand.

That would disappoint him, he said, because I was not only the best pupil in his school but also a young man who was as clever as he was cunning. So why try to outsmart him? If he were to forward my application, he would get into trouble. His advice to me was to apply to a school where my background did not present a problem. Considering my scholastic record, he wasn't telling me to go to a vocational school, but a specialized technical high school was out of the question. And he wasn't •

recommending a parochial school either. The only thing he could do for me was to help me get into the science program of a regular public high school. I should just go home now. He was giving me permission to leave early. And I should fill out a new application.

My eyes filled with tears. I saw that he noticed. I knew this wouldn't move him, though it might have some effect. I felt he misunderstood: he thought these were tears of sadness and desperation, when in truth they were tears of anger. His long desk was between us. Nice and slow, I let the application drop on the desk. It wasn't real impudence, just a bit of cheek. As if to say: you can wipe your ass with it. No way was I going to take that application with me. Mumbling the usual parting words, I started backing out toward the door. Even in normal circumstances the required phrase was hard to utter with a straight face. According to the rules we were supposed to say, "Forward, Comrade Principal." The idea of calling a man who just wrecked my future a comrade! Saying forward while backing out of his office! Pointing to the form on the desk, he told me to pick it up and leave. But I left, pretending to be too confused to have heard his last words.

Getting out of school before noon, without your schoolbag, is in itself one of those semidelirious experiences. You are free. But your schoolbag, which you stuffed nervously in your desk drawer, still ties you to the scene of eternal bondage. You feel like a plaything of fickle fate. It seems to you that this early-afternoon life around you, proceeding at its own normal pace, could be yours as easily as anybody else's. The sense of liberation, so short-lived, was fading fast. I was in a daze, and also fuming. And then, at the Városkúti Road station of the old cable car, just as I was counting out change for the fare, I realized where I was heading. It would have made no sense to go home. I wasn't about to create new anxiety for my mother, who in those days worked as a typist for a foreign trade company. By the time my plan could have scared me, I was on the train.

I went to see my father's onetime friend and comrade Colonel Elemér Jámbor, at the Ministry of Defense. When I got downtown, I had no money left for a streetcar, so I rode without a ticket. We had been to his place only once, and he never visited us. Yet Mother was convinced that the allowance that arrived each month came from him. At Christmas, Easter, and on my birthday, he sent me presents, accompanied by a brief letter, which I had to acknowledge with an equally brief thank-you note. The navy-blue gold-buttoned overcoat my friend describes in such loving

656

detail was also one of his gifts. Mother believed that it was his quiet intervention that had saved us from being deported from the capital. Owing to the awful turn of events, we were able later on to repay his family some of his concern and kindness for us. He was arrested in late November 1956 and executed the following spring. His widow lost her job, and she had to raise two daughters, both of them about my age, on her own.

The guard at the gate said that the comrade colonel could not be reached at the moment. For about an hour and a half I roamed the neighborhood. In Miksa Falk Street there was a pet shop with cages and a fish tank in the window. I stared at the fish as they kept returning to the glass wall of the tank and with their mouths agape nipped at something invisible. A little farther on in the same street, I saw a girl with close-cropped hair charge out of a house, crying. She ran like crazy, as if being chased, but then stopped in her tracks and spun around. Her eyes fell on my curious glance, and that much sympathy was enough for her to burst into tearful sobs. I half expected her to throw herself into my arms. But she ran back and disappeared into the doorway. I waited for a while, thinking she might reappear. Later, I walked to the Parliament. The huge square was deserted. From a proper distance I watched the comings and goings at the side entrance on the right. Now and then a barge-like black limousine pulled up, a gate opened, someone got into the car. The glossy blackness, the gleaming chrome receded majestically in the midday sun. People were leaving but no one was going in. I figured enough time had passed, I'd try again. The guard was annoyed but agreed to ring the office. Cupping his hand over the receiver, he not only gave my name but added with a chuckle, It's a kid, and pretty pushy, too. I could tell he was talking to a woman. And I was let into the lobby, where I could sit in a comfortable chair. While waiting, I was troubled by a single unpleasant thought: What's going to happen to my schoolbag if I don't make it back to school in time.

It must have been four in the afternoon when I finally got to see my father's friend. The guard took me up to the fifth floor, and in the bright, spotless corridor I saw the colonel coming toward me. He put his large, heavy hand on my shoulder, as if to make sure it wasn't some tragedy that brought me here. He led me into a room where a military operation might have been discussed before. Rolled-up maps seemed to imply this, as well as heavy cigarette smoke hanging in the air, empty coffee cups and glasses and ashtrays still filled with cigarette butts on the glass-topped conference table. He offered me a seat, walked around the table, and on the other side made himself comfortable, too. He lit a cigarette. So far he hadn't said a word and I'd offered no explanation. He was a husky man, bald, with blond hairs on his powerful hands. I could see it wasn't just the cigarette smoke that made him blink and smile. He was sizing me up and was responding favorably to my appearance. He addressed me in the pleasantly solicitous and jocular tone of voice many adults used with me. He asked what mischief I was up to this time.

After I told him, he rapped his signet ring on the glass tabletop. He said the school would definitely forward my application. That much he could promise. Of course, that didn't mean I'd be accepted. While he respected my decision to apply, there was nothing optimistic he could say about the possible outcome. But whether I'd get accepted or not, from now on I'd have to fend for myself.

He put out his cigarette and got up. He rounded the table and, while I was getting up myself, again put his hand on my shoulder, and this time there was indeed nothing encouraging in this gesture. I should heed his advice not only because his own influence was very limited but also because anyone unable to make the best of his own opportunities could no longer understand his own situation. My own father would not think otherwise. He spoke quietly. With his hand still on my shoulder, he was steering me toward the exit.

A month later I was notified that my application had been rejected. No reason was given for the decision.

In all probability I must have responded with stubbornly laconic answers to my friend's persistent questions, and he must have gathered from this that there was some struggle about my going to a military academy. I know he was afraid of losing me. He hoped that my hopes would be dashed and then we might still wind up in the same high school. But frankly, that possibility got as big a rise out of me as my soldierly aspirations did out of him. In any case, there was no struggle at home. If anything, my mother was happy. Prém conceded defeat and decided to become an auto mechanic. I remained alone with my obsession. The anger I felt for my father's friend would not abate. I couldn't understand why he wouldn't help. I felt like a child who craves chocolate and can't understand why adults don't eat chocolate day and night—after all, they have the money to buy it. I did the very opposite of what he in his paternal wisdom advised me to do. Or more precisely, in my anger, I did exactly what he advised me not to do.

I wrote or rather tapped out a letter on a typewriter and sent it to

István Dobi, President of the Republic. I kept a copy of it for years and destroyed it only after I noticed that my wife had been rummaging through my papers. Shame keeps me from quoting the actual words used by that humbled, abject child. What I said more or less was that making the acquaintance of Comrade Rákosi—and of the new Soviet man, or rather woman, in the person of his wife—was a fundamental turning point in my life. I continued by mentioning that in our family the love of the Soviet people was a tradition; it was by following in my father's footsteps that I mastered the Russian language. That's how I got to somewhat safer ground. I acknowledged that my father was forced to fight in an unjust war against the Soviet people, but I asked that his steadfast anti-German attitude also be taken into consideration. Finally, I vowed that I'd dedicate my life to righting the wrongs committed by him. I wanted to lend credence to my words with documentary evidence. Nothing I have done in all my life fills me with greater shame. I appended four notebooks with checkerboard covers to the letter—they were my father's war diaries.

I know very little about opera and even less about ballet. I find people singing and dancing onstage both fascinating and repugnant. People comporting themselves in a way that normal, sober adults would never do in public. Still, I am amazed that these people are capable of such shamelessness. The voices, the bodies, the decor, the cloying splendor of opera architecture so repels me that it's a trying experience whenever I have to set foot in an opera house. It feels as if I were sitting inside a fancy powder box and somebody was stuffing cream puffs into my mouth. As soon as the curtain goes up I begin to feel queasy, I have to close my eyes, and before long, without noticing it, I doze off with all that music going on. And on that November evening we weren't sitting just anywhere but right next to the huge imperial box.

I've no idea how this particular opera is supposed to be staged, but behind the curtain that rose to the first strains of the overture, another curtain became visible. It was tacked together from shimmering silks, shreds of gold-spangled muslin, smoke-gray tulle, as well as pieces of coarse sackcloth and soiled rags. While the orchestra was busy playing, this multilayered patchwork, independent of the music, was slowly pulled, floated, flapped, and fluttered before our eyes. This went on until the set of Red Square appeared, where crowds of people with smoky torches, candles, and swaying lanterns were dancing. And at last you understood that the curtain was supposed to represent the slowly lifting morning fog.

Two huge black cars came to pick us up at the hotel. And although I managed to end up in the same car with the girl, I soon had second thoughts about joining them. Apart from the secret, largely unexpressed joy of seeing each other again, there was nothing much my friend and I could talk about. For one thing, I was tired, and also distracted by the girl. What's more, they were rather loud under the influence of something they'd had earlier, while I was still in need of a drink. And the strenuous effort to conceal from each other the joy of seeing each other created an unpleasant tension between us. As for the girl, I could only watch her, keep an eye on her, but could not really get any closer. She let me know that any advance on my part would be met by a refusal. One thoughtless move and she'd rebuff me so spectacularly, I'd have to give her up for good. Which also meant that she didn't want to give me up. She hadn't made up her mind yet. We kept avoiding each other's eyes, but we couldn't avoid the desire for each other's glances. The whole time we kept each other in a state of tension. The only thing I permitted myself to do was politely to take her fur-collared coat from her when she took it off. She thanked me with the same noncommittal politeness. The tension was mutual, because we both tried to hide from the others our mutual interest. We couldn't succeed completely, not only because the four people and the interpreter accompanying them had already had an afternoon of copious drinking behind them, but also because they shared the special intimacy that develops among people traveling together. I remained a stranger among them.

One member of the group, a bearded young man who appeared anxious to call attention to himself at every turn, was especially eager to show me up. It's possible the girl had sounded so cool on the telephone because she wasn't alone in the room. The bearded young man was watching me, and I was watching them. Later it turned out that my suspicions were not unfounded. My friend and the third man in the group were watching and waiting to see where all this was leading to. And the interpreter, an unfailingly kind and solicitous lady, kept a watchful, maternal eye on the entire group. Reminding them of my position as a guest, I politely let them go first, and took a rear seat deep inside the box, next to the lady interpreter. The girl sat in front of us, leaning forward on the railing. From time to time I had to look at her bare neck. Her unruly hair was gathered in a bun. And she sensed every time my glance lingered on her neck; she'd move imperceptibly. Or rather, she seemed to dictate to me when I should be looking at the stage and when at her bare neck.

When the last shreds of the fog's silks and rags had lifted, the ideological significance of the vanishing fog-curtain also became evident. The rags-and-riches motif was now repeated onstage: rich and poor folk were whirling about and mingling in apparent confusion, though in still identifiable clusters. Princesses like golden puppets, drunken boyars wrapped in furs, merchants and lascivious priests frolicking with courtesans in flimsy silks, half-naked beggars, contortionists in dirt-encrusted rags, wounded soldiers writhing in blood-soaked bandages, peddlers hawking their miserable wares, and here and there, among gaping loafers and street people, provincial grandees in gaudy folk costume, demure maidens and handsome lads. All this abundance made me sick to my stomach. I felt like leaving. I felt like going to Pervomayskaya. Where I was expected. Where I wouldn't feel so out of place. Where in the morning three women in large pink satin bras and even larger pink satin panties paraded around the house and I could scratch and mope to my heart's content. Searching for a deeper clue to my discomfort, it occurred to me that for a disciple to sit in a theater just one day after his master's demise was an unseemly thing to do.

The whirling and dancing were still in progress when the bearded man put his paw on the girl's hand resting on the railing. He leaned over and whispered something into her ear. I could see they were accustomed to such intimate whispering, though it immediately made their two companions curious. They craned their necks, wanted to be in on whatever was going on. The bearded man, without letting go of the girl's hand, began to explain something to them. And my friend, after catching only the first few words, quickly moved closer and over the bearded fellow's shoulder whispered something to the girl. They both laughed. But the girl tilted her head so that I could catch a glimpse of their merriment, and at the same time she pulled her hand out from under the bearded man's paw. And that gesture, too, was meant for me. She made up my mind for me: I couldn't leave now. But all this fidgeting and chuckling and carrying on made me extremely uncomfortable. I belonged to this group yet had nothing to do with it. I understood their game but wanted no part of it. Because from this point on, everything that happened onstage made them laugh. I couldn't completely ignore the solemn atmosphere in the theater, but from then on I was compelled to see the stage with their eyes.

No doubt it isn't a particularly brilliant artistic concept to use irreconcilable class struggle and the conflict of social classes as the basis for a ballet piece within an opera. It's also true that the opera's overture didn't quite work as ballet music. Yet the group's judgment of it rubbed me the wrong way. I was also afraid they might create a scene. And I was right. After a while the interpreter, startled out of her patriotic rapture, tried with alarmed and cautious touches of her fingers to make them come to their senses. But this only added fuel to the fire. The poor woman was like a kindhearted schoolmistress who is herself terrified that the principal might get wind of the rowdiness of her charges. They didn't dare look at one another, and probably didn't much look at the stage either. The interpreter didn't understand any of this, she kept hushing and admonishing them in her softly accented Hungarian. Their backs and shoulders were shaking with suppressed laughter. Now and then the laughter would pop, erupt, and be immediately stifled, but that only hastened and amplified the next explosion.

I don't know how many dancers were on the stage—a great many. It's rare to see so many dancers all at once. But when after the overture the victoriously entering soloists were followed by fresh throngs singing away jubilantly and carrying church banners and military insignias, creating an incredible mass of bodies, and when, to top it all off, to the accompaniment of booming church bells a red sun rose, pulled by wire, over the crenellated walls of the Kremlin, all hell broke loose in our box. They began punching one another, their laughter turning to snorting and belching. Trying to calm them, the frightened interpreter was also punching them. In neighboring boxes a counter-movement was brewing; general consternation now found expression in indignant hissing, muttering, and muffled cussing. I lost my head, sprang up, and fled.

This row of boxes did not give directly onto a corridor but onto a brightly lit lounge with red silk wall hangings. I was incensed, indignant, but also relieved to know that whatever happened to them, I was out of there. I got my coat. But just as I was putting it on, the silk-covered door of the box was flung open and, with a resounding bass aria serving as background, the four Hungarians, clinging to one another in their uncontrollable fit, literally fell out of the box. For a second I could see the interpreter desperately gesturing behind them, but then one of them slammed the door on her. The four continued laughing and pushing and shoving and stumbling into one another, in turn shrieking and whimpering, with tears in their eyes. Four unruly children sent out of the classroom. As far as I was concerned, I wanted to put an end to this impossible scene, the sooner the better. The girl and her bearded friend fell holding on to each other, against the wall. After the impact, the man sank to the floor. I would have made my getaway then if my friend, on purpose or by accident, hadn't let go of his partner in a way that had him fall against me. I had no choice but to catch him. For long seconds we stared into each other's eyes. I couldn't hold back the contempt and hatred that loomed out of the shadows of our remote childhood, as the joy of our reunion had only an hour earlier. I felt my own hand—or rather, I realized I was—grabbing his shoulder. I shook him. Clowns! I was yelling at him, bunch of buffoons, that's what you are! Miserable buffoons! His face relaxed at once, and he glared back at me with the same implacable hatred. And you are a lousy opportunist gone sour, he said. A shitty little Julien Sorel, that's what you were and that's what you still are. A filthy playboy. And he said something else, too. The hatred was still in his eyes, but his voice had a phony cynical ring I hadn't known before. It came hissing out of him. In the sudden silence the others could hear it, too. I couldn't have picked a better time to tell you, he hissed in that odd voice, but I was madly in love with you, you chickenshit.

The girl regarded my defenselessness with indulgent contempt. Well, well, she said, and as she headed for the exit, she gave my arm a pitying touch. She meant it as a coup de grâce. She even pursed her lips. Only the muffled sound of music could be heard. Four of us were standing in the lounge, facing in four different directions. And then she took the pins out of her bun, letting her long hair fall down. She shook her head and walked out the door.

What followed strikes me now as something phantasmal, out of a fairy tale. With slow, measured steps, she was going down the red-carpeted stairs. Her shapely, stockinged legs were going down, down. Silently, a bit dejectedly, we followed her, leaving the last strains of music behind us. On the second floor, the glass doors of the onetime imperial reception hall were wide-open. Under glittering crystal chandeliers, breathtakingly opulent tables were waiting for the guests at the gala performance. The U-shaped table followed the curve of the room. Except for us, not a soul was in sight. Without betraying the slightest sign of surprise or embarrassment, she sauntered into this room. Timidly the others followed. She walked around the table laden with cold meat, fruit, drinks, and sweets, decorated with garlands and flower baskets and gleaming with silver cutlery, crystal, and china. Then she picked up a plate, took a fork and napkin to go with it, and served herself. The others chuckled and, some-what flustered, followed suit. Within a few moments they were continuing where they had left off in the lounge. Except now it was all silent. They guzzled and stuffed themselves. I found a bottle of vodka, filled a glass, and gulped it down. Then I walked over to her and asked whether she'd like to come with me. Actually, she was the most vicious of them all, because she wasn't stuffing herself but, moving methodically from platter to platter, only sampling things, digging, poking into every dish, ruining everything. And all the while her face remained perfectly straight. When I spoke to her, she looked up. No, she said, staring at me steadily, she was having a good time right here.

The snow would not let up. The streets were full of lively, happy sounds, but the slackening traffic, muffled by the heavy snowfall, made it evident that the big holiday had already begun. There were staggering drunks on the streets, too. I walked back to my hotel, took the vodka out of the refrigerator, and put it next to the telephone. I drank and waited for her call. Later I called her, and kept calling her at ever shorter inter-vals. A few minutes after midnight she called me. By then she was alone.

And this is about as much as I am able, or prepared, to tell about myself.

After this accidental meeting in Moscow, I didn't see my friend for a long time. Now and then his name would crop up. Reading his pieces about alienated, anxious, and feckless young men was like eating sawdust. A little over five years had passed when a few days before Christmas I had to fly to Zurich. Since I'd be away for only two days, I left my car in the parking lot of Budapest's Ferihegy Airport. When I returned and walked out of the terminal, as usual I couldn't find my car keys. They weren't in my coat or in my pant pockets. I kept feeling for them all over. They must be in my bag, then. Or I had lost them; it wouldn't have been the first time. My possessions don't stick with me either. All I had was a small suitcase stuffed with shirts and papers, and a large shopping bag full of presents. Putting my things in a luggage cart, I began searching for the keys.

While rummaging in my suitcase, I noticed that somebody just an arm's length away from me was sitting on the concrete guardrail of the steps. I took a good look at him only after I'd found the keys in one of my socks. He sat so close I didn't even have to raise my voice.

Did you just arrive or are you leaving? I asked, as if this were the most natural thing to ask, even though I saw that something was wrong. Neither the season nor the place nor the hour was right for anybody to be sitting there. It was getting dark; in the fine, drizzling fog the streetlights had been turned on. It was unpleasantly cold and clammy. He looked up at me, but I wasn't sure he recognized me. Until he began to shake his head I had the feeling that I might have made a mistake.

Are you waiting for somebody? I asked.

He said no, he wasn't waiting for anybody.

Then what are you doing here? I asked, a little annoyed.

He again shook his head silently.

In the intervening five years he probably hadn't changed more than I. I was still surprised to see his face so narrow and dried out, his thinning and graying hair. He looked as though the last drop of moisture had been squeezed from him. He was dry and wrinkled.

I stepped closer, showed him my key, and told him I'd gladly take him into town.

He shook his head no.

What the hell did he want to do, then?

Nothing, he said.

He was sitting between two large, well-stuffed suitcases. On the handles I could make out the tags of Interflug, the East German airline. Which made it clear that he wasn't departing but had just arrived. I simply thrust my valise in his lap, grabbed his heavy suitcases, and without saying a word headed for the parking lot. By the time I found my car and put his luggage in the trunk, he was standing there with my bag. He was handing it to me while his face remained inert, frighteningly expressionless.

Yet, strangely enough, his face was more determined-looking than ever. For all its softness, almost forceful. Gone, too, was that odd ambivalence that had so surprised me at our previous meeting. A clean face, free of shadows. And yet it was as if he himself did not reside in his own face. As if he'd sent himself away on some vacation. He was dry. I can't find a better word to describe him.

My car is usually pretty messy. I had to make room, toss things on the back seat. I tried to be quick and decisive, because I had the impression that he might slip away any moment, leaving his luggage behind. Or I should say I had this impression because he remained totally impassive. He was standing there but wasn't really there.

We were already on the highway when I offered him a cigarette. He declined; I lit up.

I told him I'd take him home.

No, not there.

Where, then? I asked.

He didn't answer.

I couldn't say why, but I had to look at him. I wasn't waiting for an answer. I knew he couldn't answer because he had nothing to say. He had no place to go. And anyone without a place cannot talk about that. At regular intervals we passed under bright arc lights, and therefore after a while I had to turn again to make sure I saw what I thought I saw. He was crying. I'd never seen a crying man look like that. His face remained dry and impassive, as before. Still, drops of water were coming out of his eyes and trickling down along his nose.

I told him to come to our house. It's Christmas tomorrow. He'll spend it with us.

Oh no.

I wanted to say something simple and comforting. We might just have a white Christmas. Which sounded pretty inane, so after that I kept quiet for a long time.

I never before had the feeling, except with my children, that someone was so completely dependent on me. It was a feeling I probably wouldn't have experienced even if I had to save him from drowning or cut a noose off his neck. But he gave no indication that he intended to part with his life. The empty shell of his body was still alive. There was no need for heroic gestures. I couldn't have known what had happened to him and wasn't eager to find out. I didn't have to save him. Besides, one can sense when it's all right to ask questions and when it isn't. He was only entrusted to my care for now, and it didn't seem such an unpleasant burden. Many of his passions had burned out in him, and the void made it possible for my simple, pragmatic abilities to come to the fore.

We reached the city. I always have to cast a glance at the huge building of the Ludovika Military Academy, where my father had spent so much of his life. Then came the Polyclinic on Üllői Road, where, in a second-floor ward, my mother had died two years earlier. And right there, while driving between those two buildings, I felt an urgent need to decide just where we were going. I didn't look at him.

I said I had another idea. But for that I had to know whether he insisted on staying in the city.

No, he didn't insist on anything. But really, I shouldn't worry about it.

I should just drop him off somewhere. Anywhere. On the boulevard. He'll get on a streetcar there.

I said I wouldn't hear of it. That streetcar idea sounded rather fishy to me, anyway. But if he didn't mind staying with me for a little while longer, we could go for a ride.

He couldn't answer.

Later, however, I had the impression that something vaguely resembling a feeling drifted back into that empty shell. It got very warm in the car. Maybe it was this heat that deceived me; still, I felt my solution was wonderful, if only because it couldn't have been simpler.

My paternal grandfather was a very wealthy man. He was a mill owner, a grain merchant, and he also dabbled in real estate. The brief period of unparalleled growth and prosperity around the turn of the century seems to us almost too fabulous to be true. It was a time when great fortunes could be made almost overnight. It's all the more incredible since the economic history of Hungary, starting from the last days of the Middle Ages, has been the history of crises, depressions, and emergencies of one sort or another. Yet, we know that there was such a period because most of the schools where we study, the edifices where decisions affecting our lives are made, the hospitals we go to to be cured, and even the sewers where we empty our waste were all built around that time. Maybe not too many people like the ponderous style of these structures, but everybody appreciates their made-to-last sturdiness. During this period, not too long after the turn of the century, my grandfather had two houses built for himself: a fully winterized summer home on Swabian Hill, where Mother and I had lived until her death, and a spacious and romantic-looking two-story hunting lodge. He liked to hunt small game and chose a spot not too far from the city where he could indulge his passion. In a flat region along the Danube he could shoot ducks and coots in the tideland willows, and pheasants and rabbits in the open fields.

I can't divulge the name of the village itself. It will presently become clear why not. Actually, I should adopt the ingenious method used by authors of the great Russian novels and note places with asterisks. The human settlements they identified this way had unique, unmistakable characteristics and could therefore be found on the map, although they could also be anywhere in that vast land. It is the painful consequences of possible recognition that prevent me from naming the place. If I wanted to be coy about it, I could say that starting at the zero marking of the main highway and traveling at a good clip, one could reach the place where we were heading that late afternoon in about sixty minutes.

I should also add here that in January 1945 my mother's two sisters, Aunt Ella and Aunt Ilma, were bombed out of their apartment in Damjanich Street. The house remained in ruins for a long time. Even in the 1950s I remember seeing piles of the uncleared rubble on the street. As soon as the war was over, my two aunts moved into this country house. None too soon, as it turned out. The house had been broken into and vandalized, though strangely enough, few things were taken. Garden tools from the shed and two huge handwoven tapestries that used to hang in the trophy room. Years later, my aunts came upon some pieces of these wall hangings—many of their neighbors insulated their doghouses with them. Neither the Germans nor the Russians ever occupied this village; they only passed through it. The vandals were most likely local people, and the reason they had no time for a more thorough job was that about the time of my aunts' arrival the village was going through some terrible days.

A few days before they arrived, three Russian soldiers, separated from their unit, had rowed across the icy river. They helped themselves to some wine, brandy, a couple of ducks and chickens. They also discovered that in one of the houses there lived three marriageable daughters with their widowed mother. Neither the girls nor their mother minded throwing a wild party and enjoying the commandeered booty. They baked and cooked, they feasted and danced, had such a good time they even fired shots in the air. The house stood at the edge of the village in a waterlogged hollow at the foot of cemetery hill. To this day villagers talk about the incident with the utmost circumspection. The way they tell it, the party went on for two days and two nights, and the women didn't even bother to close the curtains over their windows. Through it all, the village played possum. No one ventured outside. Nevertheless, on the second night, bullets were fired through the windows. The bullets, fired from a pistol and a hunting rifle, came from the top of cemetery hill. The first rounds wounded one of the girls and hit one of the Russians in the stomach, who then bled to death. The other two returned the fire. Bullet marks can still be seen on some of the old gravestones. But the battle was uneven, because in their earlier merrymaking the soldiers had almost emptied their submachine guns. The few rounds they had left they used to cover each other as they retreated to the riverbank. The mother immediately hanged herself in the attic of her house. She got the message, it seemed. The next day, a large contingent of Russian military police arrived. The wounded girl was taken away. My two aunts walked into the village that afternoon. All the interrogations, lineups, and house searches, even the hauling away of some people, failed to produce any results. There were few clues to follow, and they found no weapon. In a small village like this everybody is somehow related. The Russians had to press a few men into service to bury the mother. To this day the village does not want to know who fired those shots. One thing is certain: if my grandfather's house had stayed vacant, nothing would have saved it from destruction. Not to mention the fact that only because of my aunts' foresight and cunning has the house remained in my family's possession.

Two old warhorses—that is how the more outspoken members of my family refer to my aunts. Not a very flattering description. But they are indeed exceptional creatures. Whenever I read some agonizing essay about our nation's slow demise, I immediately think of them. Because it's hard to decide what sustains them: their infinite adaptability or their uncompromising resourcefulness. They eat little, talk a lot, and their hands and feet never stop moving. In recent years, having aged visibly, they keep saying that constant activity wears you out, and if the body is worn out it's easier to die. The year and a half age difference between them doesn't show. They are so much alike they could be twins. Both of them are tall and large-framed; they cut each other's hair, which they keep very short. They may have been attractive in their youth, the way a plowhorse can be said to be attractive. They must wear size 12 shoes; when they walk, everything shakes and rattles around them. If they were not moved to tears so easily by compassion, or if they didn't show an almost exaggerated understanding of the most varied and peculiar ways of the world, one could say there was nothing feminine about them. But their gentleness is so refined, so discreet, so very caring, they surely meet all the spiritual requirements of the most traditional female ideal.

At the age of eighteen, my Aunt Ilma had a child out of wedlock. For the family this was no less an outrage than Grandfather's threat to become a dancer if he wasn't allowed to join the army. Ella very decisively defused the impending scandal by having her sister move away from home. The baby died when it was only a few days old. The two of them have been living together ever since. They must have made some final arrangement among themselves. No man has entered their lives since then. Or at least it appears that way. And that's when time must also have stopped for them. They do not subscribe to newspapers, do not listen to the radio;

only a few weeks ago did they buy their first television set. They are believers, but do not attach much importance to either church attendance or prayer. They talk about God in the same tone of voice as about the expected yield of their plentiful vegetable garden. As far as they are concerned, battling evil requires no greater passion than does the struggle with, say, plant lice or potato bugs. They sprinkle wood ashes on the former and hunt for the latter, on all fours, in the flowering potato plants, squashing the bugs with their fingers.

They start the day in the garden. From late May to mid-September they go swimming in the Danube every day, come rain, come shine. They put on their ridiculous, tight-in-the-bust-stretched-out-in-the-buttocks bathing suits made of rubberized cotton whose onetime wildflower patterns have completely faded. They put on white bathing caps and white rubber shoes. That's how they go trekking up the shore, squelching in the silt or crunching on the gravel. Ella leads, Ilma follows. Then comes a charmingly girlish interlude. They wade in waist-deep and with skittish delight let their skin get used to the cold; before long they are squealing and splashing each other. Then suddenly they stretch out in the water, abandoning themselves to the current. On their buttocks, the bathing suits balloon up like rubber tires.

The two-acre property, a park in which every cultivated plant ever planted as well as weeds of all kinds bloom and perish at will, is separated from the village by a high brick wall, and on the shore another high red retaining wall protects it from flooding. This is how far they swim with the current, then march up the steep, moss-covered stone steps, put on their bathing robes, and go back to the house. It was along this stretch, right by the stone wall, where my friend was killed. It had been a dry summer, and by autumn the river receded to where it was normally the deepest; its water turned a dark brown.

In the evening, while one of them was busy sewing and mending or perhaps knitting a sweater for me, or crocheting one of her endless lace runners, the other would read out loud. Their friend Vince Fitos, the Protestant minister, lends them books of inspirational literature. They both assume an appropriately serious and solemn expression, but that wouldn't stop them from sniggering at a particularly inane passage.

I don't know what signals they use to make their judgments, but their ability to see through things is as unerring as if they were the most well-informed people in the world. They pump me regularly about exchange rates on the international financial markets, and from the boys in the village they find out the latest soccer results. Their personal needs are very modest. When I bring them a present, they look around, bewildered: where will they put it, they don't really need it. If, therefore, they want or do not want something, their action will be motivated not by personal interest but by family need or moral consideration. That is how they acted when we were notified of my father's death. We all expected him to return, of course, but they insisted that Mother sign the house over to them. We shouldn't own two houses. In other families such a questionable proposition might open old wounds and sow suspicion and discord. But Mother was cut from the same cloth as her two sisters. She welcomed their suggestion. As a first step, they rented their own house to the village council. Ella is a licensed kindergarten teacher, Ilma an experienced schoolmistress. And the village had neither a suitable building nor a properly trained staff to start a pre-school program, though the need was clearly there. And that's how the two of them opened a nursery school right in their own home. Along with the richly paneled trophy room, they lost the use of all the other rooms on the main floor, but now they had a regular income, received a nominal rent for the premises, the four upstairs rooms remained theirs, and maintenance of the building was also taken over by the village. In the early 1960s, when the threat of nationalization no longer hung over their heads, they began their quiet little scheming. Ostensibly, they were cutting off the branch they were standing on. But in the end the health authorities ruled that the old house was unfit to be used as a school, and when a few years later a new schoolhouse was completed, my aunts announced their retirement. The enemy surrendered unconditionally and left the battlefield with the pleasant feeling of victory.

After all this, I need not say too much about my two hardy aunts' feeling about me. To them I am perfection incarnate. In my student days I had to give them detailed reports of my progress, and now they are just as interested in my job and the advancement of my career. They are so delighted with my successes, they accept blindly all my decisions as correct. They never voice approval or criticism openly but follow me with glances that tell me that in a similar situation they would have acted exactly the same way. To be sure, I usually regale them with stories I know will please them. Ever since my mother passed away, their doting fondness has become almost too much to bear. I don't have to announce my visits in advance, because in my reckless youth, when I never knew where I would spend the night and therefore roamed the world with a toothbrush in my pocket, they got used to my showing up at the oddest hours, and not always alone. Later on, when I was married, they learned to accept that it wasn't always the wife and the children I brought along to their house. This was the only sensitive area in our otherwise cloudless relationship. They let it be known that they did have reservations about my love life—on moral grounds. For example, they'd always find old girlfriends more charming than the current one. Or they'd list the physical attributes and personality traits of my casual companions and, with an innocent air, present me with their devastating conclusions. It was their way of telling me that, though somewhat proud of my numerous conquests, they didn't think this was right, that more was not necessarily better.

They still occupy only the upstairs rooms. Except for the kitchen, the ground floor is unused and in the winter unheated. I can come almost unnoticed, I don't have to bother them. In fact, I can stay in the house without letting them know I'm there. We keep a key in the back porch, on a beam under the eaves. And in a small room downstairs the strike of a match can kindle a cozy fire in the tile stove.

For three years he lived with them in this house. In this room. And if in these reminiscences I've been referring to him as my friend, it is not because of our shared boyhood but because during these three years we became very close. Even if we spoke mostly in allusions. Whether we talked of our past or our present, we both cautiously avoided total candor. I learned nothing about his life I hadn't already known, or was forced to witness. And I didn't show him a new or different side of myself. But after twenty years we did return to that mutual attraction which had once transcended our dissimilarities and which we didn't know what to make of as children. This reversion may have had to do with the fact that slowly but surely my successes were turning into failures, and that he never again wanted to be united with anyone on any level. Not with me, either. He remained attentive, sensitive, but shut up in himself. Turned cold. If I wasn't familiar with the painful reverse side of this coldness, I'd be tempted to say that he became an accurate, intelligently responding, precisely calibrated machine.

My experiences in human relations have made me see everything in this world as temporary and ephemeral. What I perceive today as love or friendship can turn out tomorrow to be nothing but the need to gratify a physical urge, or a move prompted by crass or sly self-interest. I acknowledge this with the greatest of equanimity. I have never lied to myself, because I know all about the necessary fluctuations of purposeful action. In the foregoing pages I have already prepared my balance sheet. No loves, no friends. When down in the dumps, I feel the world is nothing but a pile of disappointments. If I could be disappointed, in myself, in something or somebody else, then I could yield to this feeling of disappointment. But in me the absence of this feeling has remained so vivid that it is all I can feel. Which simply means that I haven't yet sunk into total apathy. And that is probably the reason why during those three years it became a vital necessity to have the attentiveness and sensitivity of someone whom I didn't need to, wasn't allowed to, touch. And he himself no longer had such desires. Still, he was closer to me than anyone whose body I could possess.

My aunts did not communicate their astonishment with so much as a flash of their eyes. Maybe a stiffening in their backs hinted that they didn't quite understand. They were more talkative than usual. For long moments they kept moving and fussing about us as if my friend were not there at all. They completely ignored his two suitcases. They were upset. They both talked at once. Not cutting into each other's words, just rattling on, dwelling on different details of the same story. The day before, two boys from the village had hanged themselves. I knew them, too. To help my memory, they went into detailed physical descriptions. Luckily, they were discovered in time to be cut off the rope. They both survived, they were in the hospital. They did it with a single rope. Tied a sliding loop at both ends and threw the rope over a crossbeam of the barn. They stood on apple crates and kicked them away at the same time. Supposedly they were in love with the same girl, who told each of them she was in love with the other. Now if the neighbor's hens didn't lay their eggs all over the place. If she wasn't looking for eggs just then. If she didn't manage to shove the crates back under their feet. It wasn't easy to put a stop to all this. Quite abruptly I told them we were hungry. They quickly improvised a supper for us.

Ella holds the power, Ilma is more sentimental. I followed Ilma into the pantry, where she went to get some pickles. While she was poking around in a huge jar, I briefed her on the situation in a few whispered words. For a certain amount of time, I don't know how long, they must keep him here. This one's soft, she said, and threw back a pickle. They must nurse him as they would nurse me if I were sick. She nodded nervously. Why are these pickles so soft this year, she wondered aloud. The two sisters must have a secret system of communication. Because from that point they weren't alone for a second, couldn't exchange a single word in private, yet Ella went ahead and lit the fire in the tile stove. By the time we sat down to eat, they had both gotten over their nervousness, they were relaxed and back to their amiable, good-natured selves. They tried to draw my friend into conversation and did not once mention the two suicidal boys. In the end they had to see the situation for what it was, though my friend kept smiling throughout. The conversation and the continued smiling took so much out of him that when dinner was over I had to put him to bed, literally. Pull off his clothes and shake him into his pajamas. He protested feebly. He couldn't possibly stay here. Felt awful about it. Being a burden to strangers. I should take him back. I covered him up well, because the room was still freezing cold. I said I'd be back to shut the stove when the fire died down.

The details of his recovery I learned from my aunts. There is a sofa in that room, and in front of the unusually narrow, vaulted windows there's also a walnut table, worn marble-smooth with age, and some old arm-chairs. Opposite the entrance is a big chest of drawers with a simple mirror above it. The white walls are bare, the beams of the ceiling heavy and dark. He slept for two days. Then he got up, put on his clothes, but for another few days left his room only at mealtimes. On the second day of Christmas, and again shortly after New Year's, I drove out to see him. On both occasions I pretended to be visiting my aunts and exchanged only a few words with him. He lay on his bed. He sat at the empty table. He stared out the window. That's what he did all day. It was quiet. I sat on the bed while he was staring out the window. He was silent for so long that my mind began to wander and I was startled when he finally did speak. He would love to have the mirror covered. Nobody's died here, I said. It seemed we couldn't find the right words. There was a copper candlestick on the table and he kept pushing it back and forth, giving it all his attention. When there are many objects in a given space, he said, our attention is taken up by the relationships among them and we lose sight of the space itself. If there are only a few objects, we look for the relationships among the objects and the space. But it's very difficult to find a permanent, final place for a single object. I can put it here or there. Compared to the whole of the space every possible place seems contingent. It was something like that he said, obviously talking about himself. As if the thinking machine were talking. He was talking about his own situation like that, and it made me laugh, which I did. It wasn't very kind of me to laugh at him, but it was also ridiculous the way he wrapped his confession in transparent abstractions. And then we looked at each other, trying to see where this mutual antagonism would lead. Our eyes were smiling. I was smiling at my own urge to laugh at him, and he at his self-conscious cerebrations.

In the morning he'd sit at the table. The afternoons he'd spend lying on the bed. At the end of the day he'd be at the table again, staring out the window. His daily routine for the next three years grew out of the rhythm of these three compulsively assumed positions. The recovery itself didn't take very long. At the end of the second week he ventured into the trophy room, where my aunts had put back my grandfather's more or less intact thousand-volume library. It may be an exaggeration to call it a library, as it consisted of turn-of-the-century literary dross, collected with unerring bad taste. He began to work. Papers appeared on the table, finally determining the place of the candlestick.

Within a few weeks it became clear that my idea of bringing him here wasn't half bad. It proved to be such a good move, in fact, that my aunts were ready to take over for me. On my next visit Ella drew me aside and said she was sure I would have no objection to my friend staying with them for a longer time. It was so restful for him here. And good for them, too. Because, frankly, there were days when they were afraid. She couldn't really say why, but they were scared, and not just at night but during the day, too. They'd never brought it up before, because they didn't want to trouble anyone. They were familiar with every noise in the house; they checked the doors and made sure the gas was turned off. Still, it was as though danger was lurking about, a fire perhaps, or somebody eaves-dropping or prowling, and not an animal, either. She laughed, because my friend wasn't exactly a strong lad who could protect them. If anything, he was a weakling; just the same, since his arrival their fears had vanished. But if I needed the house for my own entertainment or if I felt like a little vacation with the family, there were plenty of extra rooms, down-stairs or upstairs. Everything here belonged to me, I must know that. That's why they'd like to have my consent.

She said something about certain financial advantages. That was laugh-able, because I knew that my friend's financial situation was worse than hopeless. The rent he offered to pay for the room should be considered symbolic. They didn't even mention food. Anyway, what they ate they grew in the garden. At worst, they'd give my family a little less of their surplus. In short, they grew fond of him and were trying hard to find a material framework and financial assurances for their affection. The unconditional admiration they had for me they now transferred to him. What is more, his conduct fit their ideals better than mine ever did. In three whole years he had no more than five entirely harmless visitors. While they kept busy around the house or in the vegetable garden, he worked silently in his room. Between eight in the morning and three in the afternoon not a sound was heard from that room. He ate little and went to bed early. But a new taste in the kitchen, a winter sunset, a late-blooming plant that defied the season—such little things could make him happy. He helped with the more difficult household chores. He chopped wood, carried manure, could work the chain saw, repaired broken objects. And what was most important, he listened to them, and not just patiently but with genuine interest in what they had to say.

His stay, assumed by all to be temporary, aroused a mixture of suspicion and curiosity in the village. My aunt reported that some of the villagers asked for permission to peek into his room, through the window, when he was out. What they really wanted to see was what anybody could be doing alone within the four walls of a room. He knew nothing of this specific request, but he felt his situation to be precarious. He was afraid, he once said to me, that my aunts might look at his manuscript one day. If they did, he'd surely lose their trust. He was also afraid, he said another time, that when he got up from the table at three in the afternoon everybody knew what he'd been up to, because he felt he was walking stark naked among them. He was afraid, he said with a laugh, that one day they'd club him to death like a mad dog. And it was true that the villagers didn't know what to make of his long, solitary walks. A few times a ranger followed him from a safe distance, but of course my friend noticed him. The Protestant minister was the first man in the village whom he befriended. The old women called the minister the man with a smile.

The police investigation concluded that three motorcyclists were the likely perpetrators. Because of good visibility that day and unmistakable track marks, the possibility that the death was accidental was all but ruled out. A body lay on the gravelly shore closer to the water than to the retaining wall. When the water recedes as far as it did that autumn, one can see the layout of the riverbed. There is a wide strip of sand, closest to the central channel, above that a narrower band of silt strewn with larger pebbles, and the area nearer the shoreline is covered with fine pebbles. He was lying on his back, on a towel. His head reached the strip of silt. He'd probably fallen asleep. Before that he may have gone for a swim, or at least a dip, because his swimming trunks were still wet. The three cyclists, riding side by side, were approaching at about forty kilo-meters an hour on the slightly sloping, pebbly, dried-out shore. In prin-ciple, it's not possible to ride any faster on such terrain. They were coming upriver. At the same time, from the opposite direction, a tugboat towing barges was heading to the nearby pier. Otherwise the riverfront was in all probability deserted. Vacationers are gone by this time of the year. And the villagers come to the river only to scrub down their horses or to fetch a wayward goose. There was no one at the boat station either. When they were about sixty meters from my friend, two of the cyclists accelerated, though the experts could not agree on the rate of acceleration. The third cyclist followed suit only when he was about forty meters away; perhaps he hesitated, or maybe he was the last one to spot the fallen figure. In any case, he rode over the legs. The middle one rode over the chest, then tipped over. After a long skid upward, he slid into the hardened strip of silt. The third hit a stone, leaped in the air, and then landed on the victim's head. The one who fell over got back on his bike, made a loop around the body, presumably to have a look, and only then did he follow his friends. About ten minutes later death completed the job they had started. While waiting for the third to catch up, the other two apparently kept looking back; for about a thirty-meter stretch the two sets of tire marks showed them circling, weaving in and out. Then the lines became straight again and in parallel formation led to the pier. Here they formed a single file and got on the paved road. And that's when the tugboat reached the pier. From the deck, one of the ship's engineers saw the three cyclists. Although he couldn't give anything approaching a detailed description, he thought they were young men, possibly teenagers. Later, he also saw a man lying on the shore, but thought nothing of it.

By the time I made it to the village, alerted by my aunt's telephone call, the police had already finished taking pictures and examining the evidence. It was almost dark. His body was brought up from the shore on a makeshift stretcher. I walked alongside him, accompanied him. Once, just once, I cast a glance at what remained. One of his hands hung down and flapped about. The outspread fingers now and then grazed the ground. I would have liked to catch that hand, hold it, put it back in its place. But I didn't dare.

When the water level was low, local boys often rode their motorcycles along the shore, emulating cross-country competitions. Now each and every motorcycle in the area was thoroughly examined. Nothing substan-tial turned up, no lead, nothing to build a case on. At the hour in question, the men in the village who owned motorcycles or knew how to ride them had not yet returned from work. One man, a baker, left for work two hours after the murder, but because of other circumstances he had to be considered above suspicion. This late in the season the campground at the edge of the village was no longer open, but some rowing enthusiasts always pitched their tents there. They hadn't seen any cyclists either. The investigation was never officially closed, but with three years gone, nothing is likely to turn up. From the very beginning the inspector in charge thought they should be looking for drunken rowdies who were also quite young. He seemed to be the right man for the job. I don't think anyone in the village knew more about the taverns and pubs of the area than this officer. He was looking for three young men who were clearly drunk when they left one of these taverns. He was looking for three motorbikes parked in front of a pub. Until the day of the funeral I, too, was inclined to believe his theory.

Vince Fitos, the pastor, eulogized my friend in the village cemetery. While he spoke, dried leaves kept falling from the trees, spinning slowly to the ground. It was a pleasantly mild, breezy autumn day with a faint smell of smoke in the air, and an unusually large number of people came to the funeral. The old peasant women sang psalms at the open grave. I kept looking at the faces around me. At the minister, crushed by the event, struggling hard with his tears. And at the infamous house at the foot of cemetery hill where, to meet the demands of the recent increase in tourist traffic, an inn had opened. The memory of its former inhabitants will live forever, because among themselves the local people insist on calling it the Three-Cunt Inn. We could hear the clatter of dishes and even got whiffs of the heavy kitchen smell.

And then I thought of something. It was no more than a hunch, but I seized on it eagerly. If it was done by some drunks, it had to have been an accident—a shameful, terrifying accident. And then there would be no explanation for it.

It couldn't even be called a suspicion. It was too vague a thought to jell into any sort of lead. Besides, I had no desire to play the sleuth. When staring death in the face, one looks for explanations.

On the other side of the grave, wearing a dark, ill-fitting suit, a young man was standing, his face deathly pale. I knew him well. My aunts had been buying their milk from his folks for years. Now and then his body would tremble, as if shuddering in his fight to hold back his tears. Each time this happened, he would sing a little louder. He was one of the boys who had tried to commit suicide. The other would-be suicide, who wasn't at the funeral, had to undergo a laryngectomy and as a result lost his speech forever. This boy I knew only by sight, as a kind of local celebrity. He was born out of wedlock, his mother was barely four feet tall, a midget. No one knew who his father was. Ever since I can remember, the woman has worked in the same tavern, washing glasses behind the bar, standing on a kitchen chair to reach the sink. Rumor had it that she'd kept experimenting with drunken men in the shed behind the tavern until she got herself pregnant. She had everything going against her, yet her condition, and the fact that she went through with the pregnancy, did not bring down the wrath of the village. To this day people like to tell appreciative anecdotes—well sprinkled with spicy details—about her deft manipulations in that shed. She gave birth to a healthy boy and has been a model mother ever since. And the boy grew into such a big, powerful, attractive young man that, the circumstances of his conception notwithstanding, people have admired him as living proof of the unpredictable forces and wonder of nature. Consequently, no one found it objectionable when he became friends with the son of one of the village's wealthier farmers. They were inseparable. Leaders and trendsetters among the village young. They remained close even when the midget's son began working as a butcher's apprentice while the other boy went on to high school. It was almost as though they decided on a suicide pact, too, just so they wouldn't have to fight each other for the love of the same woman. Two male animals in whom natural love proved weaker than the need for friendship.

In those years I could gauge the social changes taking place in the village by the changing behavior of my aunts. Until then they had been bent on scrimping and saving. They would rather do without than part with anything that constituted family property. But now, with almost girlish ease, they succumbed to the enticements of the new mercantile spirit. Perhaps they grew tired. Perhaps they feared old age and wanted to keep up with the times.

The village, isolated as it was from its environs, was fast losing its people. In direct ratio to this loss, the number of abandoned farms around the village began to increase. Part of the working population moved away, and others, as if preparing for the same step, began to commute to the city. Lovely vineyards and orchards, as well as much of the farmland, were sold to city dwellers in the market for vacation property. For them this was the only means of converting ill-gotten cash, dubious windfalls, or modest inherited capital—earning next to nothing in state banks—into sound real estate. With their unused capital, city folks bought up the unused land of country folks. Jumping on the bandwagon, my aunts began to sell, too. I tried to convince them that when there is too much money floating around and real estate is the only sensible investment, the thing to do is buy, not sell. First they unloaded a vineyard for a pittance, and later, when my friend was already staying with them, they sold a big slice of the park around the house, in the face of my strenuous objections, of course. They gave me the money and told me to buy a new car. That's how they tried to rationalize an irrational move, but in fact what they were saying was Let everything go, let's lose everything that can still be lost. The new owners weren't much different. They mercilessly uprooted everything. Shrubs, rose gardens, orchards, hundred-year-old lindens and chestnut trees. They wanted to wipe the slate clean; they wanted something of their own. They found great pleasure, after so many years, in doing as they pleased with whatever was their own—even if what they did went against all reason. The long-lasting repudiation of private ownership wreaked havoc not only on state property but on newly repossessed private property as well. Sorry-looking, shoddily built vacation homes sprang up. A large field was turned into a modern campground. The temporary boom prompted people to hold down three different jobs and to break with all forms of traditional activity. The incidence of heart attacks among middle-aged men increased dramatically. And the pastor had to contend with a flock that stayed away from church even on holidays.

After recovering from their shared suicide attempt, the two friends turned into deadly enemies. The young man in the dark suit who would fight back his tears while singing psalms at the gravesite began to pay visits to the minister. First he went there just to chat, but then stayed for Bible class, where he met my friend, and after a time was attending services every Sunday. A group of village youths followed his example. A small circle formed this way, relentlessly hostile to another group, led by the now mute former friend and partner in suicide. This latter group was made up only of motorcyclists, all of them boys. Not exactly a gentle bunch. They drank heavily and got into fights, chased after girls in the campground, blasted their radios, harassed vacationers, broke into vacant summer cottages for wild parties. My friend, for the first time in his life, received holy communion from the minister.

I know very little of the circumstances of his religious conversion. But it was around this time that he befriended the meeker suicidal boy, who, after graduating from high school, was studying to be a mechanic. The two met every afternoon. The young man accompanied my friend on his long walks. If the latter's solitary walks had seemed odd to the villagers, the two of them strolling together in rain or in winter snow was even more baffling. The following year the young man applied to divinity school.

After the funeral I stayed on for almost two weeks. My aunts asked me to. I wasn't conducting an investigation, but I did talk to a number of people. I had no difficulty getting them to open up. After all, they've known me since I was a child. I couldn't be privy to their innermost thoughts, yet my hunch can't be far off the mark. I say this because the young man, who was very modest and shy, and who weighed his words carefully, maintained that, regarding the two of them, my friend had done nothing that would render him impure before God. However, I also found out something the young man had not told me. On one of their winter walks, on the riverbank, the motorcycle gang surprised them from behind. They rode around the two, but as the mute leader roared by, he grabbed my friend by the sleeve and just as quickly let go of him. My friend fell on the stones and bruised his face. As I recall, it must have been shortly after this incident that he said he was afraid one day he might be clubbed to death like a mad dog.

After his death, it took me a year and a half to muster up enough strength to sit down at his table. I found the individual chapters of his life story in separate folders. Most of my time was taken up with the careful study of his notes. From the general outline covering the entire manuscript I could determine the sequence of the chapters, but even after a thorough review of his notes, I haven't been able to decide in what direction he intended to steer his plot. However, I did find one additional, sketchy chapter, a fragment really, that I could not place anywhere. It doesn't appear in any of the repeatedly revised tables of contents. Yet he may have meant it to be the keystone of the whole story.

My work is done. The only thing left for me to do is to append to the text this last fragment.

Escape

Opening night at last.

Snow begins to fall in the afternoon, a soft, thick, slow snow, with only an occasional gust of wind buffeting and stirring up the big moist flakes.

It stuck to the rooftops, covered the grass in the parks, on the roadways and sidewalks.

Hurrying feet and rushing tires soon soiled it with black trails and tracks.

This white snow came much too early; true, our poplar had lost the last dry leaves of its crown, but the foliage of the plane trees on Wörther Platz was still green.

While outside this early snow keeps nicely coming down, in the den one is lying on the narrow sofa, the other is systematically decimating his extensive record collection; squatting in front of the cabinet, he takes every record out of its jacket and, according to some unknown criteria, breaks over his knee the ones he doesn't like.

He didn't answer any of my questions, and I didn't answer any of his.

And even later there was no screaming, cursing, and crying from which to escape with a quick, dramatic, tearfully tender embrace; what there was was irritable bickering, fitful mutterings, quiet indignation, all those closely watched opportunities for bloodless scrapes and bruises, as if by causing each other some deceptively minor pain, they could avoid the greater ones.

So many excuses and pretexts, and not a single word about the things that truly irritated and troubled us both, and made us feel this was too much, more than enough, the very limit.

A few hours later, when they finally left for the theater, it was clear the snow had won: the city had turned all white; snow sat on the bare branches, slowly covered up all the dirty tracks and trails, and put a glistening white cap on the green domes of the plane trees now glowing in the light of streetlamps; all sounds were muffled in the white softness.

That's how blood, pulsing quietly through the eardrum, reports good news.

I thought I was lying to him; I still didn't know then that he was also lying to me.

It wasn't even deliberate lying but rather a way of mutually and systematically keeping quiet about certain things, which is something that can grow, spread, and stifle any intelligent exchange.

He was busy, he said, he was waiting for a telephone call, he'd see the play another time, but I should go, he said, he wanted to be alone at last.

The phone call was true, he was waiting for somebody to call, but I didn't understand what it was he had to be so secretive about.

Everyone is familiar with the kind of reconciliation that, instead of bringing peace, prolongs hostilities; that's how they are walking, sometime later, in the snow, side by side in their warm coats, with their collars turned up, their hands deep in their coat pockets, just walking, seemingly at ease, stepping softly in the wet snow sloshing under their feet.

This semblance of smiling calm is forced on them by their own self-esteem, but their strenuous, defensive self-control is making them very tense, and this tension is the only thing they have in common now, it's their only bond, and it cannot be broken, if only because neither of them is willing to name the real cause of his unease.

They are waiting for the underground at the Senefelderplatz station, and there something very strange happens.

About ten days were left before I was supposed to leave for home, and we never again mentioned my plans to come back here.

The station was empty, and one should also know that these echoing, drafty, bleak stations, built around the turn of the century and therefore having a role in the imagined story as well, were very economically lit, which is to say, they were almost completely dark.

A good distance from them, on the opposite side of the platform, one other passenger was waiting, a lean, shivering figure.

A grubby-looking, self-absorbed boy, attracting attention only because the way he held his shadow-thin yet sharply outlined body showed how cold he was; he hunched up his shoulders, pulled in his neck, pressed his arms to his trunk, and tried to warm his hands by holding them flat against his thighs; he seemed to be standing on tiptoe to keep his feet from touching the cold stone floor; a burning cigarette was dangling from his lips, its occasional red glow the only reassuring sign in all that dimness.

The unlighted, vanishing subway tunnel remained silent and empty for a long time; no train, not even a rumble to hint at its coming, and for me every minute counted; if I wanted to describe this performance, including the details of the entire production process, I couldn't very well miss those very moments in which all that preparation was to culminate.

And then the boy with the cigarette dangling from his mouth started walking toward us.

Or, I should say, heading straight for Melchior.

First I thought they must know each other, though considering the boy's appearance, that was not very likely.

I felt uneasy.

His feet made no sound; he moved with a soft bounce, thrusting his body up in the air with each step, as if in moving forward he also had to move upward as well, and the unpleasant impression he created may have had something to do with the way he wouldn't let the weight of his body drop all the way to his heels; he wore a pair of tattered, slipperlike shoes and no socks; the white of his ankles flashed with each bouncing step.

Socially conscious empathy is invariably bundled up in a nice warm coat.

His pants were tight, rather short, well-worn, and ripped around the knees; his synthetic red jacket was stiff, came barely down to his waist, and made rattling noises, as if frozen, with his every move.

Until now he had been standing with his back to the boy; he reacted to this cold rattling sound, amplified in the vast space of the station.

With a single, elegantly indifferent movement of his shoulders he turns toward the boy; but as he is turning, the boy stops and, with an inexplicably hostile and deranged look, seems ready to pounce on him.

This may be the place to say something about city parks at night; about the shadows under the trees where it's blacker than black, and where strangers signal their hunger for a lustful touch with the intermittent red glow of their cigarettes.

In becoming an animal you cannot sink deeper into yourself than that.

It was hard to decide what he was looking at, maybe at Melchior's neck.

He wasn't drunk.

It seemed as if a tiny goatee blackened his chin, but a closer look revealed that this black spot wasn't facial hair at all but the chin itself, and that some horrible skin disease or blemish covered that entire area; or perhaps it was a black-and-blue mark, the traces of a well-aimed punch or a sudden fall.

Melchior didn't turn pale.

His features, reflecting a total lack of interest in the world around him, merely quivered as he shifted into an entirely different state of mind, yet I did see this as a sudden paleness.

And this subtle shift in his expression told me he didn't know the boy, yet he seemed to discover something very important in him, something so important that realizing it, and the long-dormant joy that came with the realization, terrified him; it was like an irresistible inducement, an idea that could save him; but he didn't want to betray his excitement, and so he remained very controlled.

How can you get deep enough into your memories so that you won't need to remember anything anymore?

But then he did betray himself, because he gave me a quick, cold, withering look that said I was out of my depth, as if I had committed some grave offense, as if I had offended him personally; in a quiet and deep voice, hardly moving his lips, trying in fact to conceal with his mouth the meaning of his words from the boy's wide-eyed stare, he said, Get lost.

Which in his language sounds even harsher.

And I thought: This is how he's getting back at me.

What did you say? I asked sheepishly.

Get lost, get lost, he spat the words at me from behind his clenched teeth, from his throat, his face turning red; then he quickly pulled a cigarette from his pocket, stuck it into his mouth, and started toward the boy.

The boy is waiting for him, on tiptoe, motionless, ready to fight, bending forward.

I didn't understand anything; this new turn of events was already past any kind of surprise, but I was sure there would be a fight, and soon; we were still the only people on the platform, a wind smelling of dank cellars whipped through the empty station.

He walked up very close, almost bending over the boy's burning cigarette, and said something to him that made the boy not only lower himself back on his heels but also take a few awkward steps backward.

But Melchior goes after him, is all over him, and now I feel it's the boy and not Melchior who needs to be protected; but I couldn't see anything except Melchior's back.

Like two madmen facing each other, one more insane than the other; when Melchior says something to him again, the boy leans aside hesitantly, quickly and obligingly snatches the cigarette from his mouth, and with a trembling hand offers its burning end to Melchior.

But during the shaky contact of the cigarettes the burning tobacco must have been dislodged, it fell out and scattered on the concrete platform.

Disregarding this little accident, the boy starts talking, rapidly, feverishly, going on and on; I couldn't make out what he said, something about being cold, he repeated the word "cold" again and again in the echoing darkness.

From the tunnel we heard the rumble of the approaching train.

And if until then there was something uncontrollable and maniacal about Melchior, it now suddenly snapped, got deflated.

It was over, all over.

He fumbles in his pocket, drops a few coins into the boy's open palm, then turns around, disappointed and weary, and starts back toward me.

Now he is tossing his cigarette away, crushing it angrily with his next step.

In the few seconds this unexpected confrontation had taken, he did turn pale, was humiliated, grew angry and desperate—and he came back to me in that state.

And I kept staring at the boy, staring as if the sight itself would provide the explanation; with one hand holding the coins he'd just wheedled out of Melchior, with the other crumbling the cigarette that had gone out, the boy again raised himself on his toes and looked at me accusingly and insistently, disconsolately and reproachfully, as if this whole incident were my fault, yes, mine, and he was ready to rush me, knock me down, and kill me.

And for a fraction of the next second it looked as if he'd really do it.

That's right, look at me, go ahead, keep on looking at me, he screamed at the top of his lungs, managing to overcome the noise of the train roaring into the station.

You think you can buy me off, don't you, he screamed.

In public, like that, he screamed, buy me off in public.

There was no time to think.

Between two screams, in a flash, Melchior tore open the door of the nearest car, shoved me in, jumped after me, and we continued to move away from the raving boy, though still staring at him, mesmerized.

You think there's forgiveness.

We were moving farther inside as the razor-sharp voice of madness penetrated the car with its quietly huddling passengers.

You can't buy forgiveness for a few lousy pennies.

A face marred by huge red pussy pimples; damp, sticky, blond, fuzzy hair of a child, and sensitive blue eyes untouched by his own rage.

A strange god was screaming out of him, a god he had to carry with him wherever he went.

While we kept backing away, seeking protection among passengers who were now raising their heads, the conductress, slovenly and looking bored, emerged from the next car, her hands resting on the leather bag that hung from her neck; she walked in a leisurely way down the platform, past the cars, remaining perfectly calm and unresponsive to this awful screaming; All aboard, she intoned apathetically, though besides the boy there was nobody on the platform, all aboard; how is one to explain the infinite sobriety and shameful orderliness of things?

She shoved the screaming boy out of her way.

He lost his footing and reeled back; but to chalk up a tiny victory, not much, just a modicum of satisfaction, something that even in his profound humiliation could comfort him, for a brief moment at least he rushed to the train, and just before the doors closed he threw into our face—no, not the money—the crumbled, cold cigarette butt; but he missed, and now the refuse of this little scene was lying at our feet.

When people in the speeding car finally calmed down and were no longer watching us with a reproachful curiosity that did not hide their eagerness for a scandal, when they stopped trying to figure out what we must have done to the unfortunate child, I asked him what that was all about.

He didn't answer.

He stood there motionless, upset, pale; with his hand on the strap he was hiding his eyes from me; he refused to look at me.

Nobody is so sane as not to be touched by the words of a madman.

Holding the strap next to him, I felt as if the senseless mechanical clatter of the train was also jostling me to the verge of madness.

Wheels, tracks.

I'd get off at the next station, without a word, and end it all, leaving everything but everything behind me on those tracks.

Fat chance; I couldn't even bring myself to swallow the pills.

This was not madness, not even close.

In those years the sense of any kind of perspective was missing from me; it was only inside or on the surface of other human bodies that all my words, movements, secret desires, goals, ambitions, and intentions sought fulfillment, gratification, and even redemption.

Yes, I lacked these perspectives, like the awesome, magnificent perspective of madness manifest in a strange deity, because everything I perceived as madness or sinfulness in myself spoke not of the great chaos of nature but only of the ridiculous snags of my upbringing, of the sensual chaos of my youth.

Or maybe it wasn't like that; maybe it was the perspective of the merciful, punishing, and redeeming deity, the one and only, that was missing in me, because what I saw as a touch of grace in me was not part of a grand, divine order but the work of my own petty machinations, spitefulness, and trickery.

I believed that the sense of uncertainty could be eliminated from my life; I was a coward, the sucker of my age, an opportunist feeding on my own life; I believed that anxiety, fear, and the feeling of being an outcast could be assuaged or, by certain acts of the body, even be evaded.

But how can one be familiar with the nearby affairs of men without a perspective on the remote affairs of the gods?

Shit never reaches to the sky; it merely collects and dries up.

Leaning close to his ears I kept repeating the question: What was that all about? was this what he'd been waiting for? was it? I wanted an answer, though I should have held my tongue and been patient.

He'd had enough of the whispering and answered rather loudly: I could see for myself, he asked for a light, a light, it was that simple, except he didn't realize that he'd picked a raving lunatic.

What I felt then inside me was my little sister, the one I'd never see again; I felt her heavy body in mine.

I am like a house with all its doors and windows wide-open; anyone can look in, walk in; anyone can pass through, from anywhere to any-where else.

I can't take your lies anymore.

He didn't answer.

If he won't answer, I said, I'll get off at the next stop and he'll never see me again.

He swung the arm that was raised to hold the strap and with his elbow struck my face.

From the open window one could look out on a spring afternoon.

And then, opening night, at last; snow began to fall in the afternoon, a soft, thick, slow snow, with only an occasional gust of wind buffeting and stirring up the big moist flakes.

It stuck to the rooftops, covered the grass in the parks, on the roadways and sidewalks.

Hurrying feet and rushing tires soon soiled it with black trails and tracks.

We were on our way to the premiere.

This white snow came much too early; true, our poplar had lost the last dry leaves of its crown, but the foliage of the plane trees on Wörther Platz was still green; a few hours later it was clear the snow had won: the city had turned all white; snow sat on the bare branches, slowly cov-ered up all the dirty tracks and trails, and put a glistening white cap on the green domes of the plane trees now glowing in the light of streetlamps.

She was the only survivor, so I went to see Mária Stein; I wanted to know which one of the two men I should remember as my father, though it didn't really make that much difference.

Last year's weeds grew waist-high; sitting on the embankment, men stripped to the waist were enjoying the breeze in the hot afternoon sun.

The river flowed lazily, forming tiny funnels under their feet; over on the shipyard's island the willows now showed yellow as the branches seemed to be drifting in their own reflections.

It couldn't have been a Sunday, because across the river everything was clattering, hissing, creaking, a giant crane was turning slowly.

First I took the well-trodden trail along the railroad tracks all the way to the Filatori Dam stationhouse; I knew that my father's body was brought here, and he was laid out on the waiting-room bench until the ambulance arrived.

Now the waiting room was cool and empty, they must have used saw-dust dampened with oil to clean the floor; a cat scurried by my feet on its way out the door; the long bench stood against the wall.

The curtain moved behind the bars of the ticket window and a woman looked out.

No, thank you, I said, I'm not buying a ticket.

Then what was I doing here?

She must have seen the corpse, I was sure, or at least heard about it.

This is not a lounge but a waiting room reserved for passengers, and if I didn't intend to take a train, I'd better clear out.

In the end I didn't have the courage to ask Mária Stein which one of the two I should consider my father, and later I tried in vain to compare features, to scrutinize my body parts before a mirror.

In Heiligendamm, too, in the hotel room mirror, I was trying to es-tablish my physical origin and intellectual identity; my own nakedness was like an ill-fitting suit; but the policemen weren't knocking on my door because they were interested in the circumstances of Melchior's dis-appearance; it was the hotel clerk who had found me suspicious, after seeing me come in at an unusual hour and with my face all banged up, and he decided to call the police.

By daybreak the wind had died down.

The only thing I kept thinking about was that I had to deny ever having known Melchior.

They asked to see my papers; I demanded to know the reason for their investigation; they in turn ordered me to pack my things and then took me to the police station in Bad Doberan.

I heard the raging of the sea, although outside there was hardly a breeze.

While huddling in my cold prison cell I decided to face all the con-sequences of my action, and afterward I'd have the valet kill my friend.

After they returned my passport, apologized for the inconvenience, and requested that I leave their country as soon as possible, I toyed rather wickedly with the idea that in parting I'd tell them all about Melchior's escape; and to make them even happier, I'd tell them that in the valet they'd put an innocent man to death, because I was the mur-derer.

In the meantime, the sea had calmed down and was gently lapping the shoreline; I was all set and waited for my train.

There was nothing much to see from that bench, so I left the cool waiting room for the warm spring sun outside.

I knew I'd find Mária Stein at home; she was still too scared to leave her apartment, her neighbors did her shopping for her.

She opened the door; the blue sweat suit she was wearing was stretched at the elbows and knees; she was holding a cigarette in her hand.

She didn't recognize me.

The last time she had seen me was at my mother's funeral.

Five years had passed, yes, and I saw her again at Mother's funeral; she'd been let out of prison earlier, but she didn't come to see us.

Or maybe she pretended not to recognize me so she wouldn't have to talk to me.

She led me into the room where they had tormented each other all night long; the bed was still unmade, and from the window you could see the train station.

My father, or the man whose name I carry, said to her, All right, Mária, I understand, I understand everything, and you are right; Mária, all I ask of you is to look out the window.

I'm not asking this for myself, it's for you; I want you to be sure that I'm really leaving.

Will you do it? the man asked.

The woman nodded, though she didn't quite understand.

The man got dressed, the woman put on her robe in the bathroom; without a word the man walked out of the apartment and the woman walked to the window.

But not before taking a look in the mirror; she touched her hair and face with her finger; her hair was gray and looked strange to her, but the skin on her face seemed smooth and tight, and she realized she'd better put on her glasses.

She found them under the bed; now she could see the man better.

As if an empty overcoat were making its way through the waist-high rubble-strewn weeds, on the trail still frozen hard; someone was leaving, was gone, in that cold dawn in the light of a streetlamp.

The first snow that year fell in January.

The woman was happy to see it, was grateful for it, for she kept telling herself all night long in her messed-up bed that it was no use, no use; with every little scream and sigh, with every choked breath, she tried to silence this dreadful inner protest: no, no, no, she couldn't be the wife of a murderer, she just couldn't do it, she didn't want to.

I'll still be your mistress, like before, that I can't deny myself, but nothing more.

I have to raise two children, and I am a madman, he said.

No, nothing more; we'll just make love like animals.

That we don't need, the man said at the very moment he penetrated her, and not for the first time that night.

The word was on her lips all night, but she couldn't say it; instead she said, I couldn't care less about your children.

You're the only one I can say this to, child, she said to me; I didn't tell him that I couldn't be the wife of a murderer.

And she turned her body so the man had no choice but to penetrate her even deeper.

Besides, it wasn't you, it was never you I was in love with, him, always him, and I'm still in love with him, him and nobody else.

János Hamar, with whom Mária Stein was so much in love, left a few months later to take up his post as chargé d'affaires in the Montevideo embassy; he left his light summer suit in our house.

In love, in love, the woman groaned with his every move inside her; all my life I've been in love, and still am, even in prison, that's why I survived, because I never stopped being in love, with him, only with him, I never even thought about you, it was always him, you I only used.

Well, use me.

I always have.

It's also possible that all this didn't happen quite this way.

But one thing is certain: early on the morning of Christmas Day, 1956, the man walked down that dark, rubble-strewn trail and reached the well-lit railroad tracks at the point where the commuter train makes a sharp turn just before entering the Filatori Dam station.

The woman waiting in the window was about to turn her eyes away, there was nothing more to see, when she saw him turn around, pull something from his pocket, and look up, probably trying to find her window.

This became his last wish, that she should see it.

He shot himself through the mouth.

She called me child, but talked to me as if I were not a child, and neither man's son.

From the hints she dropped I could more or less figure out what must have happened between them, though it was much later that I deciphered the meaning of her words; but my childhood experiences did give me some understanding of what is meant by hopeless love.

You're the only one I can say this to, child, she said to me; I didn't tell him that I couldn't be the wife of a murderer.

I couldn't become your stepmother.

If there is some sort of god somewhere, he'll forgive me; honor must be important to him, too.

He knew it two days in advance; he had plenty of time to warn me.

I wouldn't have run away; if they had asked me to, I probably would have turned myself in on my own, because I've always done everything for them; but not like that.

No, not at that price.

My mother earned her living with her body, you know; she was pretty and she was a whore, but she was also a miserable consumptive, a poor man's whore; if she had to, she sold herself for pennies, yet she taught me that you must have your honor.

And if no one ever taught you that, I'll teach it to you right now.

They broke down my door, dragged me out of bed, slashed all the upholstery with knives, though they knew better than anyone they wouldn't find anything, and if they did, it would be something they had planted there themselves, because I gave everything, my whole miserable life, to the cause.

And yet I didn't give them anything; they exist only if there is some sort of god, and there isn't.

If I gave anything, it was to myself; so whatever happened to me, I brought it on myself.

They handcuffed me, woke up the whole building on purpose, wanted everybody to see that even a member of State Security had something to be afraid of; they blindfolded me and got me downstairs from the fifth floor by kicking me all the way, making sure I hit the wall at every landing.

They took him away on Easter morning, in 1949.

The day before, I talked to your mother on the telephone; she told me the forsythia in your garden was in bloom, wasn't it wonderful? we were both ecstatic, spring was here, we chattered away on the phone, even though she also knew.

She knew what was waiting for me in the next three days; I knew it, too, yet it was more than I could imagine.

But I will tell you all about it, child, everything, step by step.

I've never told anyone, and I still can't, I'm still in their clutches; but now I will tell you, I don't care what happens.

I was never a big fish.

She was in charge of the day-to-day maintenance of secret locations used by State Security; she had to make sure that the furnishings and special equipment were in proper order, and that the houses were cleaned, well heated, and the staff well fed.

My rank was much higher than my actual position; the only reason they hauled me in was that they wanted at least one defendant who was involved with the practical end of the operation; I was needed to complete the picture.

She was still sorry she didn't just mow them all down, shoot all the bastards when they came for her.

I had time to reach for my pistol, but I still thought it was all a mistake, a misunderstanding that could easily be cleared up.

They couldn't trick me again, that's for sure.

They watch my every move, you know; I'm on all their lists.

They won't take me back, but I can't leave for good either.

Where would I go, anyway?

The only thing my neighbors know is that I did some time.

But they could start spreading the word anytime that I was still one of them.

She raised a finger to her mouth, stood up, and motioned me to follow her.

We went into the bathroom, which was filthy; she flushed the toilet and turned on all the faucets; there were piles of dirty laundry everywhere.

Giggling, she whispered into my ear that she wouldn't buy their poison from them.

Her lips tickled my ear, her glasses felt cold against my temple.

Luckily, her neighbor knows the score, goes to a different food store every day, she'd never bring milk from the same place twice.

Milk is the easiest to put the stuff in.

When they let her out, they gave her this apartment because it was bugged already.

She turned off the faucets and we went back to the living room.

All right, now listen, all of you, hear the things you all did to me.

I will tell this child everything.

I was like a fly caught by a huge warm hand.

For once you'll hear me out, hear what you've all done to me.

From that moment on she wasn't talking to me, and I also felt as if the two of us were not the only people in the room.

They took her away in a car, the ride was long.

Afterward, judging by the sound, they lifted the grating off a sewer or some other trapdoor and on steep iron stairs led her down what may have been a large water tank.

It couldn't have been any of the houses under her care; this was special treatment, then, to make sure she didn't know where she was.

They waded through knee-deep water, climbed a few stairs, and then they locked her up behind a steel door.

She could hear no sound; she tore off the blindfold with her handcuffed hands and hoped her eyes would get used to the dark.

A few hours must have passed; wherever she reached she touched wet cement; the space she was in felt enormous and every little move produced an echo.

She tried to determine at least the height of the ceiling, so she started yelling.

Later, the steel door opened, people came in, but it remained as dark as before; she tried to get out of their way, but they followed her; there were two of them, they were closing in, she heard the swish of truncheons; she managed to avoid the blows for quite a while.

She came to on a silk-covered sofa.

She thought she was dreaming and in her dream she was in a baroque mansion; she didn't know where she was.

Her instincts told her to pretend she was still asleep; gradually she remembered what had happened to her.

The handcuffs were gone, and this confused her; she sat up.

They must have been keeping an eye on her from somewhere, because the moment she did, the door opened and a woman came in carrying a cup.

It seemed to her that it was late afternoon.

The tea was lukewarm.

She was grateful to the woman for bringing the tea; but as she sipped it, she noticed an odd look on the woman's face, and the tea tasted strange.

The woman smiled, but her look remained cold; she seemed to be very intent, as if waiting for some reaction.

She knew they tried out all sorts of drugs on people here; this she still remembered, but as she tried with her tongue to locate the strange taste in the tea, her mind went blank.

The first thing she remembers after that was a feeling of being very ill; everything was huge and bloated; as soon as she looked at something it began to swell, and from this she concluded that she must be running a high fever.

And all sorts of loud sentences were screaming inside her head.

It seemed to her that she was talking but that she screamed her words, and every word hurt so much she had to open her eyes.

She saw three men standing before her.

One of them held a camera; the moment she budged he started clicking, and after that he wouldn't stop.

She screamed at them, she demanded to know who they were and what they wanted from her, and where was she, and why was she sick; she wanted to see a doctor, wanted to jump out of bed, which was some kind of low couch next to the wall in a large sunlit room full of mirrors; but the three men didn't say a word, they kept out of her way, and the one with the camera took pictures all the time she was having this fit of anger.

First she lost the feeling in her legs, she collapsed, but managed to hold on to a chair; she wanted to grab the camera, but the man photographed that, too.

Then the other two fell on her, punching and kicking, while the third one kept clicking away.

This happened on the second day.

On the third day they pulled her up from the water tank on a rope; she was blindfolded again, and she kept knocking against the iron stairs, but she was glad, because at least she knew where she was, she knew for sure, she heard them slam the steel door.

A long journey followed; they gave her no food or drink, they didn't let her go to urinate; she was so weak she made in her pants.

First she heard the crunch of gravel under the tires, then an iron gate creaked open and they pulled into a closed space, presumably a garage, where the car quickly filled up with the smell of gasoline and exhaust fumes; then with a huge bang they slammed the door shut.

She was overjoyed.

Because if they were going to take her down a winding staircase now, and then along a narrow corridor, where linoleum covered the stone floor to muffle footsteps, and if they were going to shove her into a cell that was like a woodshed, then she knew exactly where she was.

Then they must have brought her back.

Then she was in the house in Eötvös Street, the house she herself had picked out and where she'd supervised every alteration; and then everything was all right, and soon she'd be surrounded by familiar faces.

There was a winding staircase, but no linoleum; there was a woodshed, she could smell the freshly chopped wood and the sulphur smell of coke briquettes, but what her bound hands touched was a damp brick wall.

She was lying on something soft; she kept falling asleep and waking up.

Her lips got so puffy from thirst she couldn't close her mouth; she had no more saliva left, her tongue was sticking to raw, swollen sores.

She tried to relieve the hot throbbing pain by pressing her face against the damp bricks, but there wasn't enough moisture there for her dry tongue.

After a while she managed to work the blindfold loose.

No, it wasn't that house, after all—and then there was no hope.

Very high up she noticed a windowlike opening covered with a plain piece of cardboard; around its edges some light and air seeped through, which meant there was no glass.

In the wall she discovered the sharp edge of a rusty hook; on that she rubbed and scraped the rope used to tie her hands together until she managed to undo it.

Now she had a piece of rope, but it wasn't long enough for a loop and a knot; and besides, there was no place to fasten it.

In her sleep she heard soft music, soothing, lovely music; she was sorry to wake up, but the music continued; it wasn't as lovely as before, more like regular dance music.

She must be hallucinating; she knew that thirst could drive a person mad; she'd lost her mind, then, but not completely, if she was aware of it.

All right, then, she'd gone mad, she just couldn't figure out when it happened.

She even knew she was going to have another fit of anger, she felt it coming on; she was fully aware and felt that she was throwing herself against the wall, and although she had no strength left, she went on slamming herself against the wall.

The music was coming from outside; it got much cooler in the cellar, and no light at all filtered in from anywhere.

It had to be evening.

But she couldn't decide anymore when she was sleeping and when she was hallucinating and seeing images that weren't really there, because the music turned into a little stream in the wall, the trickle became a flow, a flood—a burst pipe, she thought—turning into a roaring, rumbling waterfall; she almost drowned.

The next moment, or a half hour, or two days later—she wasn't sure anymore—she woke up thinking that everything was all right; with her finger she was trying to scoop out wet plaster from the spaces between the bricks.

She even managed to clamber up all the way to the window, but just at that moment the music started playing again and that made her fall back.

But she didn't give up; she tried once more, and with the tip of her finger, with her nail, she reached the edge of the cardboard over the opening.

The cardboard was fastened to the wall, but she kept jabbing and prodding it until she moved it, and then it simply fell down.

She looked out on a terrace lit by colorful Chinese lanterns; people dressed for the evening were dancing to this same music, and on a staircase leading to a dark garden two men were talking in a foreign language with a beautiful young woman.

She wore a colorful print dress, her expression seemed serious.

If after a short while they hadn't come for her and walked her up the same staircase, and if the two men and the young woman hadn't let them pass as casually as they did, and if she hadn't been led across the dance floor on the way to another part of the same house, then she would still be convinced that this garden party with the Chinese lanterns was one of her hallucinations.

From the smells, the overheard foreign words, the look and shape of ordinary objects, she surmised that they had taken her across the border, and they were somewhere near Bratislava.

First they showed me your father's signature; I had to read his official testimony, and then a statement by János Hamar confirming the accuracy of that testimony.

Two men sat facing me in comfortable armchairs.

I told them this wasn't true.

They acted surprised; why wouldn't it be true, they said, and chuckled, and interrupting each other, they kept making pointed and vulgar references to my relationship with both men.

Either they are lying or you tortured them, too, or they've gone mad; there's no other possibility, and that is all I have to say about this.

There was a glass of water on the table in front of them.

One of them said, We've prepared a statement, if you sign it, you may drink the water.

I told them there was no interrogation, no statement, how could I sign anything?

The other man gave a signal and I was dragged out through a side door.

As soon as the door closed behind us, they started beating me; they shoved me into a bathtub, poured hot water on me, struck me with the shower head, called me a spy, a traitor, and said, Now you can drink all you want, you slut.

When I came to, I was in the cellar, but they soon dragged me upstairs again.

Not much time could have passed, because my clothes were still sopping wet and I could still hear the music.

This time they didn't lead me across the terrace but up the spiral staircase, through the garage, and into the garden; we probably used the main entrance this time.

They brought me to a very small room with only a large desk and a chair in it.

A blond young man was sitting behind the desk, by the cozy light of a lamp; even from here the music could be heard.

As soon as I walked in, he jumped up and seemed quite happy to see me, as if he had been waiting for me for a long time; but he greeted me in French, asked me to sit down in French, and expressed his indignation in French that contrary to his strict instructions I'd been treated this way.

From that moment on everything would be different, that he could promise me.

I asked him why we had to speak in French.

The odd thing was that he sounded pretty sincere, and I let myself be a bit hopeful, that maybe I was in good hands, after all.

He spread his arm apologetically and said that French was the only language we had in common and it was very important that we understood each other well.

I insisted on knowing how he knew I spoke French.

Come on, Comrade Stein, we know everything about you.

When your friend was released from jail, in May 1935, and he confessed to you that the secret police got him to work for them, you neglected to report this very significant fact, didn't you? the two of you left for Paris and returned only after the German occupation, with false passports, on Party instructions, if I'm not mistaken.

That's almost how it happened, except my friend was not recruited by any kind of secret police, and he didn't confess anything to me, consequently I had nothing to report, and we went to Paris because we were out of work, we had nothing to eat.

Let's not waste time on meaningless quibbles, he said, let's get to the point.

It was his solemn duty to convey a request, and it was only a request, nothing more, made by Comrade Stalin himself and addressed directly to Comrade Stein.

It consisted of only six words:

Do not be stubborn, Comrade Stein.

She had to think a long time, because on this third day nothing could happen that would still strike her as improbable; and as she kept looking at the face of this blond young man, she realized that this was the request she'd been waiting for all her life.

If this is truly how things stand, she said, then Mária Stein would like Comrade Stalin to know that in the given circumstances his request cannot be granted.

And the blond young man was not at all surprised by her reply.

He leaned all the way across the table, kept nodding and staring at her for a long time, and then, in a very quiet, very threatening voice, asked if Mária Stein really believed they could find anyone crazy enough to deliver such an impertinent message.

Stars shone brightly in the spring sky; it was getting chilly.

I knew I just had to get up sometime; she also stood up but didn't stop talking; later, I walked across her room, and she came after me and continued talking.

I walked into the hallway; I already opened the door for you, she said; I looked back at her, and she was still talking and didn't even lower her voice.

I closed the door and began running toward the staircase, still hearing her voice; I ran down the stairs and out of the building, and on the trail continued to run toward the railroad tracks, where just then a well-lit but empty train was screeching terribly as it made its turn.

It was getting late.

The yellowish light of streetlamps cast a soft, festive shine on all that whiteness.

The snow's reflected light made the sky look lighter, yellower, and wider, the softness of the glow toning down every sound; on high, from behind the thinning edges of the dark slow-moving clouds every now and then the moon showed its cold face.

It must have been around midnight when I got back to the flat on Wörther Platz.

In the lobby I shook the snow off my shoes; I didn't turn on the light in the stairwell.

As though anyone, at any time, even at a late hour like this, could demand to know what I was doing here.

First feeling and moving aside the tongue-like lid over the opening, I carefully slipped my key into the lock.

Not to wake him, should he already be asleep.

The door lock snapped back in the dark, that was all the noise I made.

Careful not to make the floor creak, I reached the coatrack almost without a sound, when he called out from the bedroom that he wasn't asleep.

I sensed that he had left the bedroom door open because he wanted to see me.

Yet he didn't want to pretend to be asleep, either; he himself would have been offended by such a pretense.

I hung up my coat and walked in.

It was a pleasant feeling to be bringing in the chill of the snow and the smell of winter.

The bed creaked as he made a move; I could see nothing in the dark, but assumed he was making room for me. I sat down at the edge of his bed.

We were silent, but it was a bad silence, the kind one should never get into, even if the conversation replacing it is forced or trivial.

He finally broke the silence and in a hollow voice said he wanted to apologize for hitting me; he was truly ashamed, and he'd like to explain.

I didn't want his explanation, or, I should say, I didn't feel I was ready for it; I asked him instead what he had thought of the performance.

He couldn't say that he liked it or that he didn't; it just didn't do anything for him, he said.

And Thea?

She wasn't bad, he said vaguely; she was probably the best of the lot, but he couldn't feel sorry for her, or hate her, or admire her; nothing.

I asked him why he had run away.

He didn't run away, he just wanted to come home.

But why did he leave me there, why didn't he wait for me?

He could see we needed each other, she and I; he didn't want to disturb us with his presence.

I couldn't leave her there, I said; Arno had moved out, for good this time, and he didn't leave anything in the apartment, not a pencil, not a handkerchief; but it had nothing to do with me.

He lay silently on his bed, and I sat just as silently in the dark.

And then, as if he had heard nothing of what I told him, or found nothing new in the little that he did hear, an episode in a life that no longer concerned him, he continued where I had interrupted him before; he would like to tell me something, he said, a simple thing, really, but also difficult, he couldn't tell me here, could we go for a walk?

Now, I asked, go for a walk now? in the cold? for I really wanted to skip the explanations.

Yes, now, he said.

The night wasn't even that cold.

We took our time; with slow, leisurely steps we walked all the way to Senefelderplatz and crossed the silent Schönhauserallee, and where Fehrbellinerstrasse touches Zionskircheplatz, we turned and went along Anklammerstrasse and then followed Ackerstrasse, until the street came to an end.

On our nocturnal walks we never chose this route, because we'd find ourselves facing the Wall.

While we were walking, I looked at the streets, stores, and houses with the eyes of a professional, as if all this were only the locale of my invented story and not a place where my own life was unfolding.

I plundered my own time, and wasn't displeased with the looted treasures of an imagined past, for it stopped me from being overwhelmed by the present.

Along this stretch of the street the Wall was also the brick wall of an old cemetery, and beyond it, in a mined, floodlit no-man's-land, stood the burned-out skeleton of a church destroyed during the war, the Versöh-nungskirche, the Church of Reconciliation.

It was beautiful how the moon shone through the bare ribs of the bell tower, penetrated the hollow nave, and made some broken pieces of stained glass glimmer in the rose window.

Yes, it was very beautiful.

The two friends were standing next to each other and watched both the church and the moon.

A little farther away, a border guard's footsteps sloshed softly in the wet snow.

They saw the guard; he took four steps in front of his booth, then four steps back; and he noticed them, too.

The whole scene was so strange, I almost forgot Melchior might have something bad to tell me.

Very gently he lowered his arm onto my shoulder; his face was lit by three different lights: the moon, the yellow streetlamp, and the floodlight, but they cast no shadows, for all three sources of light were also reflected by the snow; and still, it wasn't light around us, there was only the glim-mering of a many-colored darkness.

So I'm leaving, he said quietly, it's all arranged; two-thirds of the cost, twelve thousand marks, has already been paid; for ten days he'd been waiting for the confirming message.

He was waiting for a phone call, after which he'd have to go for a walk; he'll be followed, will meet a man smoking a cigarette who will be heading straight for him; he'll have to ask the man for a light, and the man will say he doesn't have his lighter on him, but he'll gladly help.

It was a good thing he left the theater in such a hurry; as soon as he got home he received the phone call and he did what he was supposed to do.

That's why he'd asked that crazy boy for a light, he thought he had botched something along the way; there was no phone call yet, it was only the tension that made him do it, I must understand; what with all that waiting, he had a hard time controlling himself, that's how it happened, I shouldn't be angry with him, that's why he hit me.

I don't know when he lifted his arm off my shoulder.

But why do we have to do this here? I whispered; let's get away from here; why here?

The guard didn't come closer, but after every four steps he stopped and looked at us.

I'm still at home, he said in his familiar old voice.

Yes, at home, I repeated.

It wasn't that he was afraid to tell me any of it; he wouldn't want to do it as originally planned.

He wouldn't want to leave without a word of explanation.

He won't say goodbye to anyone else, won't remove anything from his apartment; he's written out a will, but they'll confiscate all his things, anyway, let them! so it was a kind of symbolic will, and he wants me to take it, but only after he's left.

Maybe he'd go to see his mother one more time, but he won't tell her either; it would be nice if I went with him—but not if it's too hard for me—because with me there it would be easier to keep quiet about all this.

He's supposed to get his last instructions three days from now, and by then he won't have time for anything.

That's why he was telling me these things now.

I don't quite know when we turned away from each other and looked only at the moon; I said he didn't need to be concerned about me.

In the next three days I would do whatever he wanted me to, whatever was for the best.

I shouldn't have said this, because it may have sounded like a quiet reproach.

We fell silent again.

Then I said, the quotation may not be exact, but according to Tacitus, Germanic people have this belief that fateful enterprises should be embarked upon under a full moon.

Those barbarians, he said, and we both laughed.

And then a tentative, quickly and mutually checked movement of ours made me understand why he had to tell me this here, at the Wall, in this light, within sight and earshot of the guard: we couldn't touch each other anymore.

I said I'd better go back to Schöneweide now.

He thought it was a good idea; he'd call me, he said.

By the following morning most of the snow had disappeared; dry, windy days followed, at night the mercury dropped below freezing.

I was sitting in the Kühnerts' apartment, on the second floor of the house on Steffelbauerstrasse; I left every door open and was mulling over all sorts of crazy plans.

The last hours of the third night we spent together; we sat up in his flat as in some waiting room.

We did not turn on the lamp or light a candle; now and again he said something from his armchair, now and then I did from mine.

At three-thirty in the morning the telephone rang three times; before the fourth ring he was to pick up the receiver but not say anything; according to the prearranged plan the person at the other end had to hang up first.

Exactly five minutes later there was a single ring and that meant that everything was all right.

We got up, put on our coats, he locked the flat.

In the lobby downstairs he picked up the trash-can lid and casually dropped in his keys.

He was still playing with the fear that gripped us both.

In the glass-enclosed Alexanderplatz station we took the city line that went out to Königswusterhausen.

When we got to Schöneweide I touched his elbow and got off; I didn't look back at the disappearing train.

He had to stay on till Eichenwalde.

They were waiting for him at the Liebermann Strasse cemetery, and from there he was taken, on Route E8, to the Helmstedt–Marienborn crossing, where, in a sealed casket, with documents certifying that the casket contained a disinterred body, he was shipped across the border.

It was raining.

In the evenings I'd walk to the theater; on the soppy carpet of fallen leaves the soles of my patent-leather shoes would soak through a little.

In the abandoned apartment the refrigerator kept humming quietly; when I opened its door, the bulb lit up helpfully as if nothing had happened.

The telegram contained only three words, which in my language is a single word.

Arrived.

The next day I left for Heiligendamm.

I did not take the police warning seriously; I waited until my visa expired, until the very last day.

Two years later, in a picture postcard filled with tiny letters, he informed me that he was married, his grandparents had died, unfortunately; their little girl was a month and a half old.

The postcard showed the Atlantic Ocean and nothing else, only angry waves reaching all the way to a blank horizon; but according to the printed inscription the picture was taken at Arcachon.

He hadn't written a poem in a long time and was less given to deep thoughts; he was a wine supplier, dealing exclusively in red wine; he was happy, though he didn't smile as much anymore.

And the other one was standing, still in a strange house, with this news in his hand, looking now at the written side of the card, now at the picture.

So it was that simple.

That's what he was thinking, that it was that simple.

That simple, yes, everything was that simple.